Guy of Gisborne
Book 3: Broken Arrow

L. J. Hutton

Copyright

The moral right of L. J. Hutton to be identified as the author of this work has been asserted by her in accordance with the Copyright, Designs and Patents Act 1988.

All characters in this book are fictitious, and any resemblance to actual persons living or dead is purely coincidental.

All rights reserved. No part of this publication may be reproduced, stored in a retrieval system or transmitted in any form, or by any means, without the prior permission in writing of the author, nor to be otherwise circulated in any form or binding or cover other than in which it is published without a similar condition, including this condition, being imposed upon the subsequent purchaser.

Acknowledgements

I am again grateful for those members of staff who, back during my time at Birmingham University, gave me such a sound grounding in the lives of medieval peasants. So much is written of the lives of the 'great and the good' in medieval fiction – and never more so than about Richard the Lionheart – but the lives of the ordinary people can be just as fascinating, you just have to dig an bit harder to find them. Where I have got it right they must take their share of the credit, while any mistakes are mine alone.

I need to thank Jennifer Garrington and the ladies at Healing Waters, who helped me through a personally tough time while I was writing this book. Ladies, the chance to take a step out of the stress was appreciated more than you know. And again, Mary Ward was willing to have someone wittering about medieval history to her while completing her PhD. It's great to have someone who shares your enthusiasm for the past! I should also mention Dr John Young, who has been curate at some of the villages mentioned in these stories, and who assures me I've got the locations correct – it always helps to have a local perspective!

And last but by no means least thanks are due to my husband for coping with me being in another century so often, and to my lovely lurchers who keep me company and (relatively) sane during the writing process.

Dedicated to Blue – the best of lurchers and deeply missed friend.

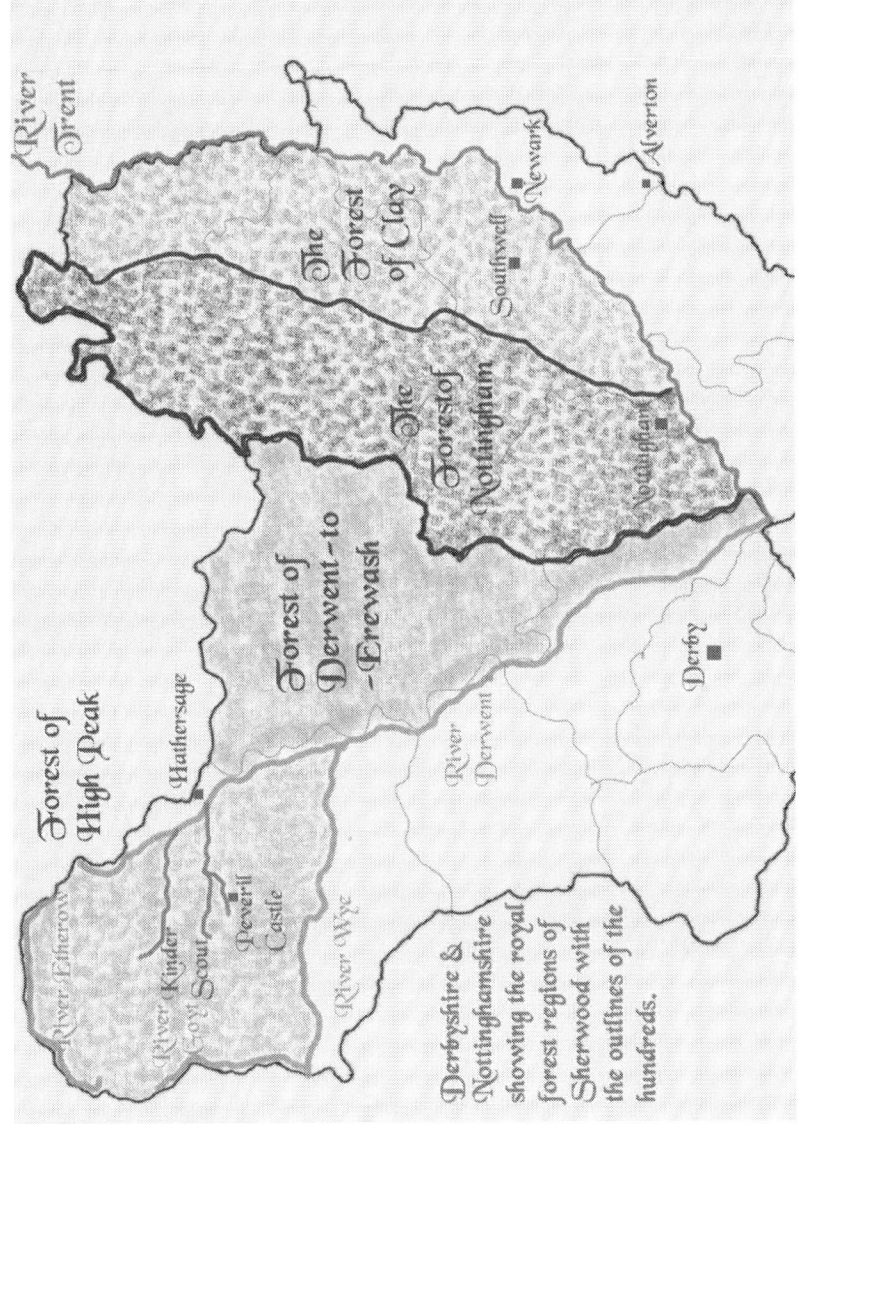

Nottinghamshire villages

Derbyshire villages

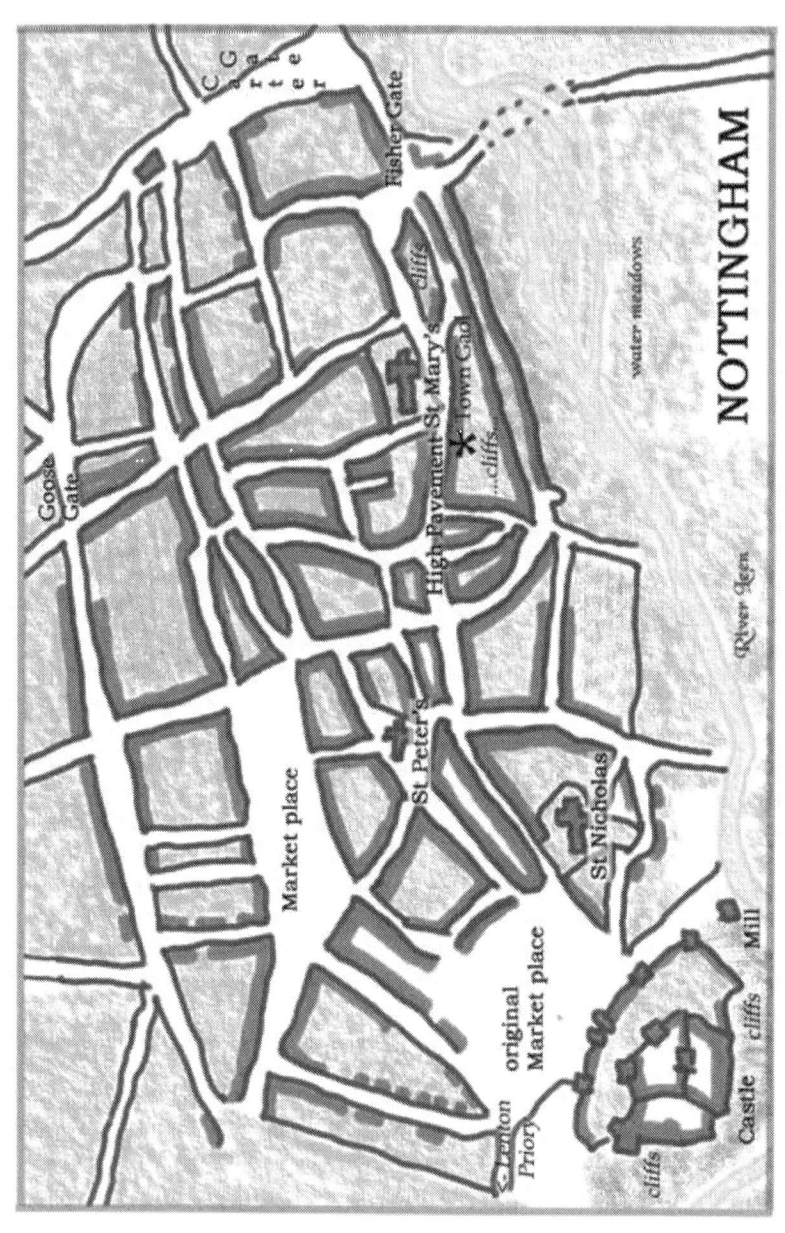

Nottingham in the 12th Century

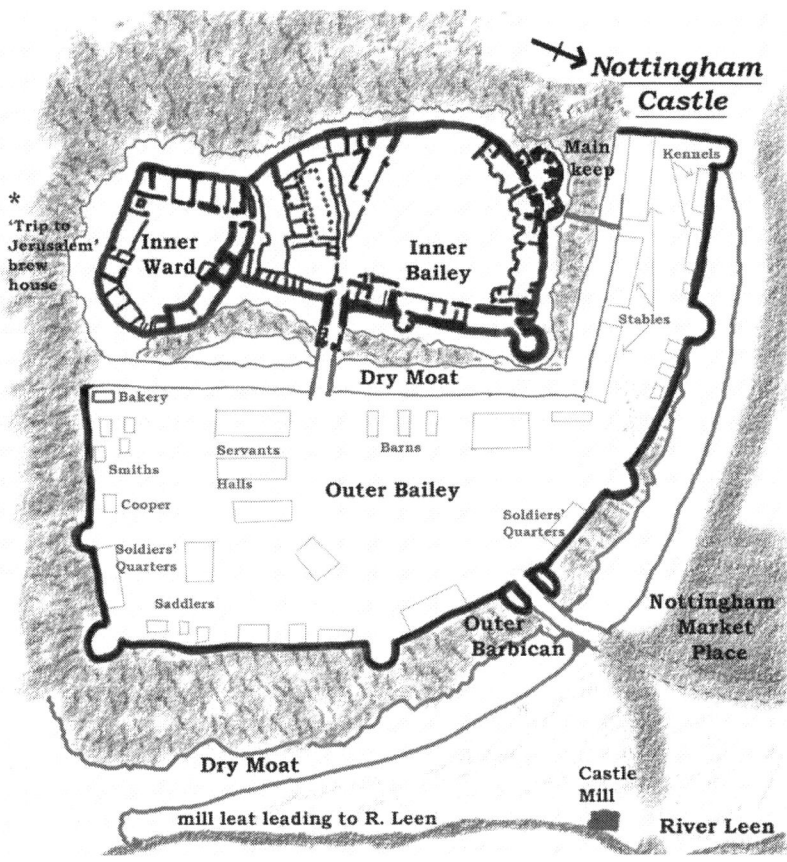

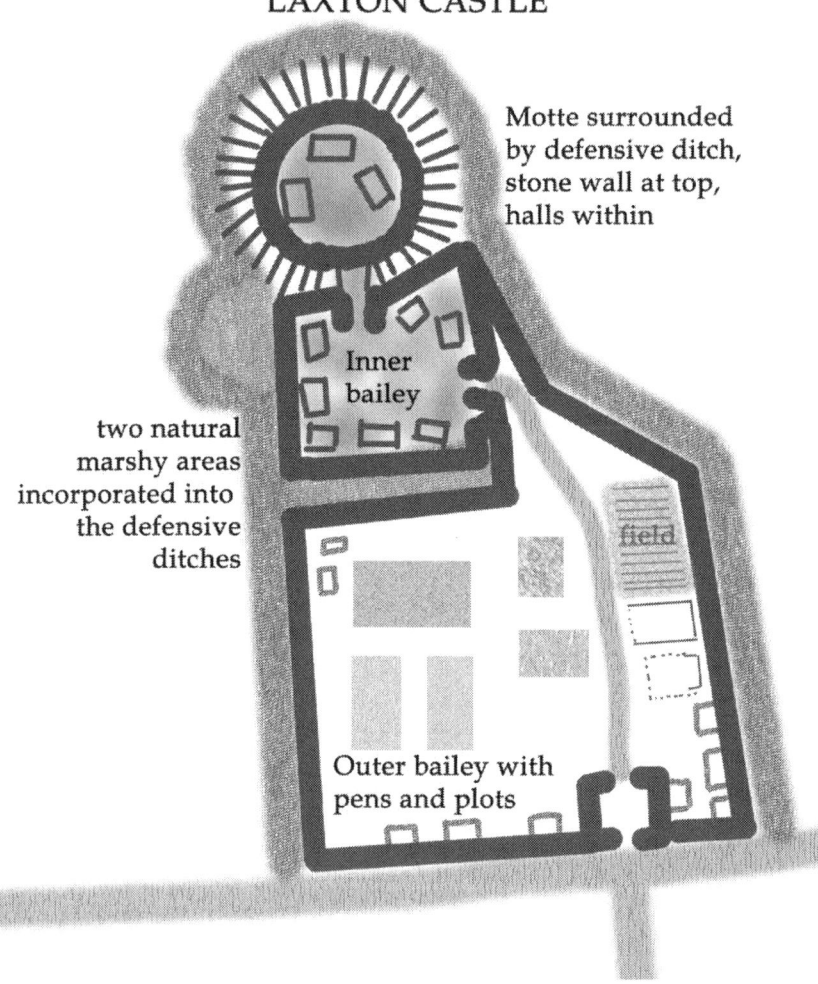

Cast list & preface

At this stage it seemed reasonable to give my readers a cast list to recap on who is now with the outlaw gang. And so we have, of course, Guy of Gisborne and Robin Hood (Guy's cousin Baldwin, now known to all as Robin). With them are their two other cousins, John and Allan who now start to assume their legendary names of Little John and Allan o' the Dales; their long-time friends Brother Tuck, Much the Miller's son, Marianne and her fellow Hospitaller sister Mariota, Hugh of Barnby, Allan's friend Roger, the three Welsh brothers, Thomas, Piers and Bilan Cosham; and the former crusaders who arrived with Robin who are Will Scathlock (Will Scarlet), Siward of Thorpe, Malik the former turcopole (who were the native Christian soldiers who served with the crusaders), and Gilbert the Irishman. Recently arrived are: Gilbert's fellow Irishman, Colm; Ed the carpenter from Durham; Martin and Simon who are both from the village of Walesby; and up at the camp at Loxley are Aneirin ap Gwilliam the master bowyer and his friend Rhys ap Morgan, the fletcher.

It is also briefly worth saying, that it is impossible to extract Christianity from the lives of ordinary people in the late twelfth century. It informed so much of their daily lives and the Church owned nearly one third of England by this time, making them the direct landlords of an awful lot of people in a very secular sense. Therefore I am not trying to evangelise when the characters express strong Christian views (personally I'm not), but rather, I'm trying to show the century as true to what it was like as possible.

Confiteor

Good morning to you Gervase. Did I sleep well? No, I am afraid I did not, and I probably will not until I have told you the whole story of my life, for this dredging up of the past brings so many memories with it. Some of them are happy, I will grant you. The memories of good friends and people whom I loved dearly, but there is much sorrow in those memories too, and when I wake I am sad to realise that many whom I would love to talk to again I will not see until God calls me into His presence. And although I give thanks to you and your brother infirmarer for bringing me back from death's door, during those first waking moments it weighs heavily on my soul that I am one of the last left of those times, even though I was not the youngest.

So, where had we got to last night? Ah, yes! The departure of the illustrious King Richard from the shire of Nottingham. As I said to you yesterday evening, while I had to applaud his efforts in the Holy Land, as any good Christian would, having met the man I could not like him. There was a single-mindedness about him which I found chilling. Whatever he set his mind upon, he would pursue that cause or person to an extreme few other men could match, and for me what was repellent was the way he scarcely saw those whom he trampled underfoot in the process. He may have had extraordinary high ideals, Brother, but to my eye he was callous and downright cruel in his pursuit of them. And so you will find me having no regrets that he was never to set foot in England again as I take you through the rest of his reign today.

And then there was Robin. Oh yes, I know you are desperate to hear more of what happened to Robin, given that the last you heard he was riding off in the king's wake and had already left Nottinghamshire. Do not worry, he will reappear again soon, but the aftermath of the siege of Nottingham Castle was far from straightforward, and it impacted on so many people's lives – including my own – that I cannot skip over it to bring you faster to the excitement again. Indeed, if I did so you would miss some vital information, for the next sheriff to arrive was one who would very much be the making of the legend. So far our sheriffs have come and gone in a relatively short period of time, but there were two who held office for several years and who were ˜Robin Hood's˜ greatest adversaries. The latter one we shall not come to until well into King John's reign, and he was to be the last sheriff whom we fought against so bitterly, but William Briwere's arrival in the summer of 1194 was to signal a terrible shift for the worse in all of our lives.

With Briwere in the castle my life became far more difficult, but you should be grateful to his miserable soul, Brother, for his heavy-handedness, his cruelty, and his open thieving of that which even as sheriff he had no right to take, made sure that whatever differences I had with my cousin, I would never think of not passing on whatever information might help him. Nor during his evil tenure did I ever have doubts that I was doing the right thing. Even some of the more hard-hearted of the knights who came to the castle would be expressing worries over Briwere before too long, for it was not just the poor who suffered but many of the nobility too.

He had risen through the ranks in the latter days of King Henry's reign, and like so many of those men, he did not come from the upper tiers of the nobility. Like Geoffrey fitz Peter, the royal head forester whom King Henry had appointed and who was still in that role, Briwere was a man who desperately needed the king's patronage to rise to the heights of being a justiciar and sheriff. Therefore his greatest fear was to be reminded of where he had come from, and where he might fall back to! And to meet someone who had known him as the young and striving lowly nobleman he had been was, for him, not merely embarrassing, but a flail lashing his soul. So as a consequence, while he would ingratiate himself with those great nobles, such as William Ferrers, earl of Derby, he hated with a passion those lesser knights of the same station as his own family. And if you think I am already straying too far from Robin in telling you this, Gervase, Robin's view of some of those knights whom I worked with would cause conflict between us.

Yet this will become more apparent as we go on. Let me have some more of your restorative wine and a few bites more of this excellent honey-bread, and we shall begin again. What was that? No dreams for you to hear this morning? Oh I dreamt, have no doubt about that, but the last one which I can remember was all of a muddle. But you still want to hear it? Very well, but I warn you, I shall not tell you what was past, what future and what was definitely to come about, rather than my conscience plaguing me! You must wait until I have told the story somewhat more calmly to find that out.

Again I was up on that knoll south of Nottingham, with Will Scarlet, Brother Tuck, Malik, Hugh of Barnby, and Gilbert of the White Hand – my dear friends – and down below us were the king's party and our two former sheriffs with them. And all over again I saw in my dream Hugh issuing his challenge to the king, and then Robin heeling his horse forward to taunt de Wendenal, and Siward of Thorpe's desperate attempts to silence Robin. Even in my dream state I could feel a repeat of the wrenching in my gut as Robin all but betrayed me to the assembled nobles and soldiers, and in the way that one sometimes does in a dream, even as I was dreaming I wondered if I would wake and find that I had soiled myself for real.

And as I felt the sweat of fear on me in both present dream and past body, my mind flipped and again I saw in a flash another instance when Robin would put my life in danger. I saw the other outlaws calling warnings, in truth meant for me, but being misheard by the sheriff and his men as warnings for Robin. This was a different time and place, but every bit as perilous. There was danger, and we were trying to save a life by taking a life. I was trapped both physically and mentally. I saw both sides of the crisis – something my cousin could never do, and for both of us it was our weaknesses and our strengths, something that made us cross swords more than once.

Will and I fought up there on that white-stone ridge; Siward and I fought; and then Robin and I fought, and that was to prove the most treacherous fight of all. He near killed me, but I cannot tell you more now, for without knowing what came before you will think me solely to blame, and I was not. Some of it had been carefully planned, but fate, or God – as you would no doubt wish me to concede – took a hand in things and our plans went awry.

And then my dream turned again, and I was standing below looking up at Robin. A big Welsh bow appeared in my hands, my fumbling hands found an arrow and I took aim at him, but then the blackness came again. I awoke sobbing, as I always do when this dream strikes, for it cannot be extricated from tragedy, and it haunts me for hours after I have woken. That is why I am not cheerful on this sunny morning, Gervase. I know what is to come – you do not – but do not fear, you will hear much of Robin Hood today.

Did I kill him? And you thought Robin Hood fought on for years? Well you will have to come with me through my confession to find that out. So let us begin again... mea culpa, mea culpa, mea maxima culpa.

Chapter 1

So now we shall begin in earnest, Brother. As you will recall, although Robin was travelling south in the king's retinue, with Siward supposedly with him, but secretly there to drag him back to us when the right moment arose, the rest of the outlaws had returned to Sherwood. Will had declared that he wished to get Aneirin, the master bowyer, up to the main camp at Loxley as fast as possible, and with him had gone Rhys, Aneirin's fletcher; but also Ed the carpenter, and Simon the smith's son with Martin, both of whom came from Walesby. Keeping Will company were Much and Roger, and Marianne and Mariota – the younger lads because we all felt they needed some relief from the tensions of the last week or two, and the two women because Marianne was still not recovered from the way Robin had walked away from her.

Will had had a conference with Hugh, Gilbert, Malik and Thomas and Piers, and together they had agreed that the production of more weapons was now a priority, and so the sooner they could get their own small armoury up and working in Loxley the better. Arrows in particular were going to be needed in abundance if the dreadful news I had brought of what our new sheriff was like turned out to be accurate. But spare bows would also be an asset, and Aneirin had been most clear that preparing the wood for such great wyche-elm bows as he made could not be hurried. The wood for such bows needed to be matured for three years before even the basic shaping could be done, and although Thomas and Piers had already amassed a stock pile of seasoning timber, it would not do to be complacent that every piece would be usable. Therefore the sooner they started the better.

We had half contemplated the rest of the outlaws going north for a while too, leaving just a couple of men at a time in the Inkersall camp for when Siward returned. You may think it strange, Brother, but we had no doubts that Siward would come back to us – unless to do so would put him in danger of losing his life – to escape the king's army. We were in no way certain that Robin would be with him. Therefore two men would have been enough to bring Siward to the others, in theory.

However, Gilbert, Thomas and Piers in particular had real fears that Siward might be pursued; for a knight – albeit a very humble one raised up in Jerusalem – was supposed to set a better example. We were all realistic enough to presume that there would be many knights who would buy their way out of fighting in Normandy once the king's ire had subsided. They were no doubt waiting until his overweening pride had been soothed by the second coronation we had heard would be taking place, and then when he was awash with good wine and good humour, they would pledge every penny they could raise to get out of getting caught in the meat-grinder which spat out corpses that Normandy had become. Unfortunately Siward would have no such option. He could only flee, which would be seen as him breaking his vows of fealty and make him a hunted man. Therefore we feared for him.

So all but Will of the real fighters of the gang – Malik, Gilbert, Hugh, Thomas and Piers – stayed, and with them remained Bilan, who did not want to be separated from his brothers again so soon (and anyway was fast becoming as expert an archer as they were); and also Tuck, John and Allan, all of whom were there in case Robin came too. What state he would be in under those circumstances we could not even begin to guess. He might be angry, contrite, bitter, or even suicidal; for Tuck had grave concerns about how he would take the destruction of his own myth that King Richard would be another man like King Baldwin of Jerusalem, and Tuck was determined to be on hand to administer what spiritual help he could in that event.

As for me, I had to return to the castle. This was becoming ever harder for me, Gervase, I have to confess. The vows I had taken to serve both king and sheriff were the least of my worries, although you will no doubt chastise me for saying so. I knew that, come what may, I had to stick to my guise as the loyal forest knight at least until I had word back from Scotland that those friends I had sent north had arrived, and had settled in at the manor I had been granted by David, earl of Huntingdon and brother of the Scottish king. After that, if life became too unbearable, I could at least move those precious fugitives who lived at Gisborne manor northwards, and then leave myself. It was not much of a bolt-hole, but at least it was in the hands of someone less fickle than our own king, and the having of it was a serious balm to my shattered soul in those days of the late spring and early summer of 1194.

Therefore I went back into that terrible place and helped my fellow knights pick up the pieces there. And in truth, the three knights who were permanently based at Nottingham Castle were fast becoming good friends. Sirs Hugh of Woodham, Robert of Packringham and Richard of Burscot were all mature men whose only flaw was an inability to see things from the point of view of those below them – and in that they were as any noble man of our times. I am well aware, Gervase, that I would have been just like them had my life taken an alternative path.

It was being thrown out of our comfortable little manor on the east side of the Trent which had set me on such a different course. Having to find my way in the world, without the ability to call upon those rights a knight's son ought to have had, had been a salutary lesson. One which had been a nasty shock from which I had never fully recovered, for living down with the ordinary men of a castle, and at the mercy of such a brutal and callous sheriff as William de Braose had been, had permanently warped my view. Never again would I be able to play the noble Norman except as an outward show, and beneath that show, knowing that wherever possible I would then do as much as any man could to set things right afterwards.

But enough of this philosophy! I can see you already squirming on your stool, Gervase! Sharpen your quill and let us commence with today's confession, although you do not seem to be approaching it in quite the manner of the sober priest, if I may say so. You have become very eager for the gory details, Brother! Yet I will tease you no longer. April had blown in with its usual mixture of bright sunshine, squally showers, the occasional frost, and the promise of better days to come – everywhere except Nottingham Castle. Therefore, mea culpa, mea culpa, mea maxima culpa...

Nottingham Castle
April, the Year of our Lord, 1194

Guy walked to the edge of the oldest tower in the castle and stared bleakly out at the burgeoning countryside. It was over two weeks since he had stood with Hugh and the others watching Robin ride away, and for all that he was still seething over Robin's stupidity, there was a part of him which could not stop worrying over the fate of his cousin. A small, gnawing, fretting bit inside of him that was doing nothing for his health and temper, either, because the rest of him was angry at it for being there. After all that Robin had done of late, there was no reason why Guy should still care, and his logical side said he could not and did not, but somehow his heart wasn't quite ready to give up yet.

He leaned his arms and head on the cold stone of the battlement, hoping for some kind of respite. Just at the moment he could have sobbed his heart out, and the only thing stopping him from letting go and giving his feelings vent was the fear that once he started he wasn't sure when he would stop. Already he had had to concoct an excuse to get him out of the great hall for a while. Sirs Hugh, Robert and Richard were doing their utmost to restore some kind of sanity to the castle with the help of the two senior forest knights, Walter and Martin, but everyone was struggling, and each of them at various times had had to walk away from the task for an hour or two. No-one was censured, though. They all recognised that every last man left in the castle was at the end of his tether, and better someone walk away than snap at another equally fraught and start a fight.

There had been some fights down amongst those few men-at-arms left to watch over the castle. Stupid scraps over nothing which were soon smoothed over, but they were a clear sign of what it had cost them all to have the vengeful king in their midst. But it was wearing having to deal with others' distress, and somehow Guy had ended up being the one to do much of this kind of sorting out, simply because he was the one who knew the ordinary soldiers the best and whom they would listen to most.

Things had eased a fraction once they were sure that the king had got through Leicestershire and into Northamptonshire. At that stage they felt there was so little chance of him coming back that they could at least take down the bodies of the luckless sergeants whom he had had hung post-siege, and give them all a Christian burial. The makeshift gibbets had then been willingly broken up and fed into the fires to keep the ordinary folk of the castle warm during the chilly spring nights.

Much work still had to be done to repair the wooden servants' halls and other buildings which had been wrecked in the outer bailey, and Guy and the other five knights had tried to balance out the work needed on the grand buildings, which would hardly ever be used, against the desperate need to get the workers properly housed again.

"We'll have to wait until we get some money in to make good most of this stuff anyway," Sir Hugh had sighed, rolling weary eyes at the great hall's interior where they were currently assessing the damage. "All the windows in here are shattered and that alone is going to cost an arm and a leg."

The uppermost storey of the building in which the great hall was located, and which contained a few small chambers originally intended for Prince John's personal use, was in an even worse state. The roof was full of holes, and a few of the missiles that had come over the walls from the king's mangonels had also gone down into the great hall below, and a few even down again into the cellars beneath.

What King Henry would have thought of the magnificent suite of rooms he had had built in preparation of his youngest son coming to live there, Guy couldn't imagine. They were a right mess! But then King Henry had probably never anticipated that his two remaining sons would come to such a state where one would besiege the castle of the other here in England. In Normandy, maybe, but not in this Midland shire.

"Getting the postern gate repaired has to be a priority," Sir Richard said gloomily. "It's all very well the bloody king barging his way into here like that, but just at the moment, given the way he skinned us of soldiers, too, we couldn't fight off a bunch of travelling mummers, let alone a real attack from outlaws or any other opportunist who likes the look of us. We've got more holes in the walls than that bloody awful blue goats' cheese that Arnold of Warwick sells at the fairs!"

Sir Martin nodded sagely. "Yes, and the motte around the great tower! God helps us, we have to get that shored up again or the whole thrice-be-damned tower might come down on us."

"Surely it's not that precarious," Sir Ralph objected, but Guy was already seeing what Sir Martin meant.

"No, not now it isn't," he agreed with Ralph, "but what Sir Martin's thinking of is that now there are deep holes in the side of the motte from the mangonels' work, if we get a few good torrential downpours, the water can get right into the heart of those packed stones and earth, and if that happens..." He left his words hanging, but the others were already filling in in their minds' eyes what would happen if they got serious water erosion beneath the huge tower.

"The motte." Sir Richard declared firmly. "That we don't need much money for, and we have enough ordinary workers from the town to make a start on that. Let's do that first. All of this stuff," and he waved a disgusted hand at the shattered decorations on the hammer-beams of the hall roof, "can wait until someone comes up with the money. Whatever courts we have to hold here will have to take place in the old halls."

It had been that mention of courts which had sent Guy running for the roof and space to breathe, not faking it when he said he suddenly felt sick. Soon the eyre would be coming round. Only a few months ago he had been praying it would come soon and relieve the congestion in the town's gaol and in the overspill in the castle's dungeons. Now he feared it would become as bad as the king's siege – a means to beat more money out of all and sundry in the two shires, let alone what cruel punishments might be handed out to those who could not pay.

For himself it was bad enough. He knew that a fine would be coming because he had been in the castle, and he shuddered to think how much it would cost him, but if all else failed, he knew that he could ask the outlaws for something to help towards the cost. But it was the thought of having to sit in and listen while others were driven into penury which he was already dreading. And it would be a point at which they would get some indication of just how bad their new sheriff would be.

William Briwere was very much a favourite of King Richard's, that they all knew, but would he turn out to be as awful as they feared? Technically William de Ferrers, earl of Derby, was the sheriff for now, but they knew that it was only so that Briwere could take part in the coming eyre in order that he could visit this shire and sit in judgement, which he could not have done as its sheriff. That Briwere was even doing such a thing, and with the king's blessing, did not bode well.

Guy believed he could be the worst sheriff yet. Briwere had been crafty enough to take the Cross when Richard had been crowned, so that although he had been appointed one of the king's justiciars, at that point he had been well out of the way when Longchamp had been chancellor. And Guy had a nasty suspicion that he might be hand-in-glove with the royal chief forester, Geoffrey fitz Peter. The two of them had gone out of England with the king, but had equally reappeared rather sooner than expected.

Had Briwere even got as far as the Holy Land? Guy thought not. Somewhere along the line there had been a need for someone to come back with a message direct from the king, and Briwere had no doubt volunteered, thereby getting all the benefits of taking the Cross without ever having to endure the hardship of actually fighting in the Holy Land. But if Briwere was close to fitz Peter, or worse, was trying to impress fitz Peter, then Briwere's impositions of the forest laws could become truly appalling.

That thought was now plaguing Guy terribly, and his mind would not give him peace from running through the names of the men currently awaiting trial for crimes against the royal forest, and worrying what fate might befall them. He stood up and looked north-eastwards to where he could see the spread of farmland that had been brought under forest law. The great sausage-shaped tract of dense forest which ran up the middle of Nottinghamshire, known as the old Forest of Nottingham, had long been in royal hands, but King Henry's bringing of all of the rest of the shire west of the Trent into the forest legal system had already caused great hardship to those simple farmers.

Now more than ever we shall need a Robin Hood, Guy thought miserably as a sudden hail shower began to batter him with its icy shards. *Why couldn't Robin have listened to me? Why did he have to be such a bloody dreamer and so ...so....!* Even in his thoughts the words failed

Guy. Maybe it really would be better if someone else took up the mantle as 'Robin Hood'? Hugh or Siward could still play the part when an appearance was necessary, as the ones about the same height, build, and colouring as Robin was, but having the band led by someone a bit calmer might be a boon to all of them.

Yet who would want to step into his cousin's shoes so soon? Could Hugh command the loyalty of Will, Malik, Gilbert and Siward when they had fought with Robin in the Holy Land and Hugh had not? And Will was a wonderful soldier and a smith of the kind Guy had never encountered before, but he was too headstrong and driven by his emotions to be a good leader; yet he could also badly undermine anyone who didn't have his full support.

Guy sighed wretchedly and found the tears coming despite his best efforts to suppress them. His younger cousin could be so charismatic, so inspiring when he got the mood on him. That was what had got everyone believing they could do this damned thing, after all. Yet Guy felt that having all that charm and fire was worth nothing – was to all intents and purposes wasting such God-given gifts – if Robin could not apply them. To be so devout and so focused on the next world that he was no earthly use in this one seemed, to Guy, to be almost sinful, let alone to be so careless of the repercussions to others.

Why had Robin not thought about what would happen to all those ordinary people while he was away fighting beside his king? Or how they would cope if they called on him for help and neither he nor any of the gang were around? Or had he always presumed that someone who was one of the gang would be staying, and would be acting in his name? That almost seemed more arrogant to Guy, and yet again he wondered where the kind and caring lad his cousin had been had disappeared to? If such a transformation was as a result of fighting for the Holy Land, then Guy for one thought that the price had been too high.

Sighing and cuffing away the tears with the melted hail, Guy resigned himself to going back downstairs and finding the others. They all seemed to be doing it – this disappearing for a while when it all got too much, but then coming back because they couldn't in all conscience leave the remaining five to do this miserable work. When he found the others, they were clustered around the fire in the small chamber at the base of the old tower which had become their unofficial office. Nobody wanted to use the rooms which the sheriff would soon have. It had never been said in so many words, but there was a fear of what might happen if this new sheriff thought someone had been so presumptuous as to use his chambers before him.

They were all standing looking gloomy, and as he walked in Sir Martin told him, "We've had a letter. It seems that the king is going to have his second coronation on the seventeenth of April in Winchester – so that's this coming Sunday. After that the various justices will be coming out on eyre. We've been told here to expect Briwere sometime in the third week in May."

"The feast of St Dunstan of Canterbury – the nineteenth," the fearful scribe who had read the letter to the others supplied.

"Oh well, at least not on my birthday," Guy said wryly.

"Really?" Sir Walter was surprised. "You know the day of your birth?"

Guy shrugged. "My mother was an educated woman. She told me I was born on the feast of St Helena, the twenty-first."

The scribe looked impressed. "The mother of Constantine, who made the Roman Empire Christian, and in her own right the finder of the remains of the True Cross. You have an auspicious birth date, Sir Guy."

The others clearly hadn't a clue about this but were prepared to take the scribe's word for it.

Guy just smiled at him with what little enthusiasm he could summon, but then asked the others, "So should we be expecting the earl of Derby to hand over to him? It might be helpful if he's here. At least he can tell our new lord and master how much progress we've made in getting the place cleared up."

They all looked to the scribe, who hurriedly re-read the letter and then shook his head. "Nothing about my lord Ferrers, I'm afraid."

Hugh of Woodham grunted. "No doubt he'll be required to attend this fiasco of a new coronation. I suppose it all then depends on whether he's to cross to Normandy with the king in order to keep what land and titles he has." He sniffed disparagingly. "Seems to me that if you want to keep what's rightfully yours you have to do an awful lot of bowing and scraping to this king. His father was by far the better man. He was a hard bastard but you knew where you stood with King Henry."

Guy sighed in sympathy along with the others, but added, "And I fear we'll be having to do an awful lot of bowing and scraping to this damned sheriff too. My lord Ferrers had a word with me before he left. He said that Briwere is very touchy about his ...well let's put it this way, he's not from the top layers of the nobility! Someone had better warn Mahel about making any claims of being on the same level as Briwere. I don't think that will go down well!"

The collective groans were enough to indicate the dread which was seeping into all of them. De Wendenal had been a brute, but a rather stupid one, and Ralph Murdac had been one of the old sheriffs of King Henry's reign who had got the job because of his ability to do it, not because of ingratiating himself at court. But if this new sheriff was going to be crafty and overly sensitive, then their lives were about to get a lot worse.

"Can I suggest something?" Guy said tentatively. They all looked at him. "We've got to survive this sheriff somehow. All of us! And I have a nasty suspicion that he's going to be the sort who will see his way of keeping control of the castle being one of setting us against one another. All my instincts are saying that he'll think that if we're fighting one another then we won't be fighting him.

"Well I don't know about you, but I think that way lies disaster. If the left hand never knows what the right hand is doing, there are so many ways we could end up tripping each other up it doesn't bear thinking about. So how do you feel about the six of us meeting up once a week to compare stories? I think it needs to stay just between the six of us. If we get more folk involved then the danger is that someone will let it slip to Briwere, and we'll all be in the shit then! But if the three of us from the forest knights, and you three from the castle get together, we can sort out where Briwere is trying to lay down the poison.

"We trust one another, don't we? So if we've been told, for instance, that the knights coming to do service at the castle are calling us foresters every name under the sun, then before that escalates into a fight, if Hugh, Richard and Robert can reassure us that nothing of the sort has happened, we can calm things down. And the same if something happens the other way – if one of the visiting knights gets accused of poaching, for instance."

The others had started looking increasingly worried as Guy spoke, and now they were all exchanging glances which spoke volumes.

"By Our Lady, Guy!" Hugh said swallowing hard. "That's a worrying thought. And I fear that we may be coming to you more than you to us – the potential to throw accusations around of breaking the forest laws are far greater than any misdemeanour in the castle. Yes, I for one say that's a very good idea! We need to have some way of at least knowing who is throwing accusations around, and that they aren't coming from our own kind. And if the words are coming out of someone else's mouth, we've a chance of working out who is trying to ingratiate themselves with the new sheriff."

The others were quick to agree.

"Right, then," Guy said wearily, seeing how they all now looked to him. "If this sheriff is coming on the nineteenth, what day is that?"

"A Thursday," the scribe answered, and now Guy was glad that it was Brother Oswald whom he had used before who was here, because he could be persuaded to say nothing of this to anyone else.

"Thursday. Very well, then let us agree right here and now that if we don't have any other chance to confer, that we'll meet up after witnessing Mass on the second Sunday after Briwere's arrival. That will have given him ten days to get his feet under the table and start showing us his true colours. Even he can't order us to do much on a Sunday, so let's meet outside of the castle walls at the *Trip* if we can, or if he has the gates closed, in the castle chapel. Men going for a quiet beer, or to pray on a Sunday, is pretty innocent enough. When we meet up then, we can arrange our next meeting somewhere else. If it's moved around we're less likely to arouse suspicion."

They all willingly agreed, but Guy thought the real test would be seeing how many of them turned up. He was already feeling the loss of his friends from High Peak Castle amongst the ordinary men-at-arms, and although he still had his friend Harry down in the stables, Harry wasn't someone who could help much when it came to military matters. So Guy really wanted some other men on his side here in the castle – he was just hoping that these were the right ones.

That evening he decided that he would go down to the *Trip* for one of the current brews of malty beer. *The Trip to Jerusalem* was officially the castle's brew-house, but the current brewer did such a good job that his ales were popular with the townsfolk too, and the way he was turning a nice profit meant that even under a new sheriff he was likely to be able to keep selling his ales as a sideline. But Guy thought Alfkell the brewer deserved a warning to at least halve what he declared as profit when the new sheriff came. Alfkell's son Hama was learning the trade, and Guy wanted him to be taking over when Alfkell felt his time had come to take things a little easier, but that meant keeping the family on the right side of the sheriff but also in business.

When he'd had a quiet word with Alfkell, Guy went and found a stool in one of the back rooms carved into the rock on which the castle stood, and leaned back against the rock as he took much needed swigs of the beer. He could feel the malty brew taking its effect on him, and for the first time in a week – indeed, since the last time he had come down here – he felt able to relax just a little. It was now that he realised just how exhausted he was. Surely there had to be a way to get out of the castle, even if it was just for a day? He longed to get out into the quiet of Sherwood, and simply take the time to see the new growth coming on the trees and to hear nothing more stressful than the mating calls of the birds.

He had not said much to the others, but he feared what fines they would be facing soon, and he really wished he could get to Gisborne and find out how things stood there. The fact that he, like the others, had had very little choice but to be in the castle once the siege had started would no doubt count for nothing. Could he plead for help from the earl of Derby or the earl of Chester? Both men knew that he had made no active decision to be on Count John's side. But probably not, he decided after very little thought. Those two had followed the king's orders, yet they too must be worried what the king might come up with to wring more money out of them.

William de Ferrers had said something about the vast sum he had been called upon to produce as part of the king's ransom, and that he still owed a goodly portion of it. Undoubtedly he would be dreading the king demanding that the rest be paid up, and smartly too. He was going to be in no position to help a lowly knight who wasn't even one of his tenants. And much the same would go for

Ranulph of Chester, for although Guy's manor of Gisborne lay within his lands, it would be unwise to remind him too much of that in case he asked for extra money to help him pay whatever he still owed for the ransom.

Sighing deeply, Guy went and got another ale from the taproom, acknowledging that the likelihood of him getting to his manor any time in the near future was remote. But as he went back to his stool away from the crush around the bar, he decided that he had to come up with some reason to get out into the forest for a day and see if the outlaws had had any news. One day of freedom before Briwere arrived was surely not too much to hope for?

His excuse finally came the week after the coronation took place in Winchester. It seemed that after the celebrations the king had dealt with the prisoners taken after the siege, but a list had been sent back to Nottingham of men who would have to appear before the justiciars and account for why they had been in the castle.

"They have to appear before Briwere," Sir Hugh declared despairingly, "but that's not the worst of it, even though we're on the list too and will have to answer for that ourselves. Apparently the Archbishop is determined that this eyre will be conducted properly. Four knights are to be selected each from Derbyshire and Nottinghamshire. Those four will then elect two knights from each hundred or wapentake, and they will then have to form juries – well that's going to be interesting!"

"Isn't it just!" Sir Robert agreed, speaking for all of them. "It might be alright in the more inhabited parts of the shires, but High Peak wapentake? How many knights have there ever been up there on those bleak moors?"

"Oh and it gets worse," Hugh said grimly, having been the one to whom the letter was read. "Those two elected knights then have to find *ten* more *knights* or 'law-worthy men' to sit with them as the jury for the eyre! That's some order! By St Thomas, between the ones carted off in chains by the king and the ones who had little choice but to go and fight with him, we're rather thin on the ground for knights these days! Where are we going to find these men from?"

Guy grunted in disgust with the others but had a thought. "How are the first four decided? If we have to do the picking we might just be able to work things so that we choose village headmen for the juries. That would at least ensure a bit of common sense gets into the process."

However Hugh of Woodham was already shaking his head. "Sorry, Guy, the bloody archbishop and Briwere have clearly got their heads together down in Winchester. They've nominated the four already."

"Who?" Guy asked, feeling his stomach starting to churn stressfully yet again.

Sir Ralph gestured to Brother Oswald to read the names out, and the young monk tremulously recited,

"From Nottinghamshire, our nominated knights are Sirs Roger de Buron, Ralph Musard, William de Stuteville and Hubert fitz Ralph. From Derbyshire we call upon knights William Albini, Oliver de Aincourt, Richard Vernon and Hugo Bassett to form our juries."

"Christ on the Cross!" Guy swore softly. "De Buron we can hope to sway into a bit of sense, but William de Stuteville's always been a man of the court, as have Albini and de Aincourt. As for Musard, fitz Ralph and Vernon, they're worse than a bunch of dogs smelling a bitch in heat for having their noses wedged up the arses of men in power! They'll follow Briwere's lead even if it leads them to the very gates of Hell! In Derbyshire, Bassett's the only one who might have a clue as to what's actually reasonable or fair."

"That's what we were just saying when you came in," agreed Sir Richard. "Briwere's picked the most highly born of the shire knights he can in the hope of ingratiating himself with them."

"And to be fair," his friend Sir Robert added, "since most of them are down in Winchester, they may well have been ingratiating themselves with him, the chancellor, or even the king. Let's face it, they've already been forced to dig deep for the king's ransom. In their place, who could blame them for wanting to make sure they start off on the right footing with a sheriff known to have the king's ear?"

"So what happens next?" Guy asked.

"Well at least we won't be called for this duty," Sir Richard said with some relief. "I never thought there would be such a benefit to being a third son, but they're hardly likely to call me back from here to the family manors on Oxfordshire – I haven't been there in years, so I could hardly testify what the state of them is! And the same goes for Hugh and Robert, but what about you Martin? Walter? I know Guy's in the same position as us in that he holds no lands in these shires."

Sir Walter looked gloomy. "I'm probably one of the few knights who remain who could be called upon for Broxtow Wapentake. Lots of men who could be on the jury, of course, when you take into account the guildsmen and free-men of Mansfield, Kirkby-in-Ashfield and Nottingham itself. But I'd be amazed if I wasn't called as one of the two knights to get those men together this time – especially seeing as I've been serving the sheriff directly regarding the forest."

Sir Martin looked equally as wretched. "Same goes for me but for different reasons. My family are up in Oswaldbeck Wapentake. Sod all but trees and farms up there for the most part! We're hardly awash with knights at the best of times, and I've not got a single town of a decent size I could hope to round up some guildsmen from."

"Will they allow guildsmen, though?" Guy wondered. "I mean, if they want to know about crimes in the towns, that's fair enough, but how many of those have we got awaiting trial? Not many. Most are from out in the countryside. I can think of several pleas regarding manor boundaries and inheritance which need sorting, but overwhelmingly it's the cases we've brought in regarding the forest which are backed up, even aside from those cases which fall under forest law. How could a guildsman testify to the state of affairs there? I fear we forest knights will all be called on to serve on the juries this time – and probably in more than one hundred!"

Sir Walter shuddered. "Six hundreds in Derbyshire – all of them needing knights and juries! ...And Nottinghamshire is going to be even worse! Because aside from the five within the royal forest, there are Newark and Bingham and Rushcliffe Hundreds on the other side of the Trent, and they'll all get a visit too! That's another eight hundreds who all need to find knights, may Christ in His mercy help us."

"Could we foist off some of this onto the bishop, do you think?" Guy asked hopefully. "For pity's sake, the Newark court is bound to be held in his castle there, and quite possibly the Bingham one too. What do you say to me riding over to Newark Castle and telling the constable there that he'll need to prepare for the courts? And in the process warn him that he needs to have some suggestions for knights to serve on the three lots of juries from his side of the river, because we'll be so court-bound ourselves we won't be able to help him. At least then things will be under way when the bishop gets back, and it'll be all the harder for him to wriggle out of doing his share."

"Brilliant idea!" Sir Robert declared, brightening instantly. "Brother Oswald? Get some parchment, we're going to write to Newark! Go and get yourself a horse, Guy, you can ride out today!"

And that, dear Brother is how I managed to be out in Sherwood when your hero returned! Yes, he came back. Have mercy, Gervase! I am coming to it now! But you had to understand that I did not expect to be there. I was riding out with a desperate need for news of my friends, and I thought all would have been settled one way or the other long before I found them. I was sad for Robin, I was even worried for him, but at the front of my mind was the need to warn my friends of this coming scourge in the form of the eyre and courts, and all that that would entail. And also that although I wanted them to stay well clear of the procession of knights and hangers on which would trail through our shires, that there might be desperate need of ˜Robin Hood's˜ help in their aftermath. I did not remotely imagine that I would be sitting in the camp when he reappeared.

Chapter 2

I took off from the castle like a scalded cat, I can tell you, although I maintained a collected canter while I was within view of the castle.

I did not want anyone wondering why I was in quite that much of a hurry! After all, we still had a few days left yet before we could expect anyone to appear regarding the courts, and there was no reason why I should work a good horse that hard by galloping all the way to Newark. Luckily, I knew the way like the back of my hand by now, and therefore the shortcuts I could make through woods and across country to save time.

I made Newark by nightfall, and gave my unwelcome news to the harassed constable of the castle. Like those of us at Nottingham, he was less than pleased at the imminent arrival of Briwere, in his case because he feared that such a sheriff would be quick to exploit the bishop's frequent absences on ecclesiastical business to interfere in the running of another castle within his shire. I told him that I suspected his fears were all too likely, and soon had him on our side in believing that we had to do what we could to prepare for this eyre before it landed in our laps and began running riot.

Therefore I was able to leave at the crack of dawn the next day, having been able to plead for a second, fresh, horse to make the ride to the Inkersall camp without arousing suspicion. The constable was so grateful for the warning I doubt he thought twice about what I was doing next. And so I rode with all haste into the green refuge of Sherwood and breathed what felt like the first truly fresh air in weeks.

No, I am not delaying you unnecessarily, Brother! Patience! I skirted the small villages to remain unseen and revelled in the peace and quiet. After the chaos which had torn through the shire in March, everyone in it seemed to be taking the opportunity to stay close to home and recover. For once, I saw no signs of the casual poaching of hares, or of people coming into the forest foraging, even though the forest had only just come out of being closed for the winter on St Felix and St George's Day. Normally I would have expected to see a flurry of activity, but the rough passage of so many armed men in a place unused to such sights seemed to have crushed the life out of folk. In such unaccustomed quiet, movements I would not normally have heard were magnified greatly, and that, dear Brother, is most relevant to our tale!

Sherwood Forest
April, the Year of our Lord 1194

Guy and his friends met up well before he got to the Inkersall camp. He was just north of Kirklington and heading to skirt Bilsthorpe on its south side when he heard the soft bird call. Nothing odd about that, except that reed warblers did not frequent these parts! He reigned in his horse and looked about him, seeing nothing until Bilan appeared from around a large oak waving furiously at him.

"The others are just behind me," the lad panted, running up to Guy with a broad grin of welcome on his face. "I could run the fastest, so they sent me to intercept you. We saw you when you crossed that track a few hundred yards back."

Guy dismounted and, looping the reins of both horses over his arm, draped a friendly arm over Bilan's shoulders and hugged him to him. "By St Thomas, I'm glad to have found you! It'll be good to see some friends again."

"Has it gone that bad in the castle already?" Bilan asked worriedly.

"Not yet," Guy told him wryly, "but it's bloody-well going to be soon!" He gestured to where he could hear the others running even if he couldn't see them. "I'll tell you when they get here."

However he was the recipient of news first.

"We've still not seen Siward," Gilbert told him anxiously as soon as they reached him. "That's why we're out and about. We all agreed we need to patrol the edges of Sherwood in case he's coming in a hunted man."

Hugh embraced Guy and then added, "Actually we've been a good deal further than the edges of Sherwood. We got right down to the Trent, and we've even begun to wonder whether we shouldn't go across it and start searching."

"No!" Guy gulped. "Don't do that!" and he told them of the impending arrival of Briwere and whatever party he chose to bring with him. "For the love of God, don't go too far from your hideouts for the next couple of months!" he pleaded. "I have no way of warning you which hundred he will visit first. He could go south, he could go north, he might even do Derbyshire first – I don't know. And the worst of it is that the less well-populated of our subdivisions might actually suffer more, because the village senior men may have to act as jurors if there aren't enough knights to serve."

"How will that be such a bad thing?" Bilan asked. "I mean, they're used to attending the Hundred Courts for the hundred – or wapentake as they seem to insist on still calling them in some places round here. *Tsk*, we never had 'wapentakes' in Wales! They know what their neighbours can pay, and who is likely to have really done something wrong. If they testify as they normally do, how can that be wrong?"

Yet Guy shook his head sadly as he explained. "It's not them but Briwere I'm worried about, Bilan. I have this dreadful churning in my belly that says this is a sheriff who won't want to hear that a man has done less than he's being accused of. Those jurors could be telling the God's honest truth, but if it's not what he wants to hear, then he may well accuse them of lying to him, and then they could end up with at best a large fine, or at worst being brought before him as accused themselves. And don't forget, the knights in charge will effectively be able to over-ride their decisions anyway, which will make it seem as though they are even more in the wrong – and I fear those knights will, because they too must be sweating blood over what will happen under Briwere's tenure as sheriff."

He rubbed a hand across his weary brow. "By St Issui, I was hoping that Siward would be back by now, because I fear that 'Robin Hood' may soon have an awful lot of work to do helping the poor of these shires! The fact that he isn't yet may force you down a route you don't want to go. You may have to choose between waiting for Siward outside of Nottinghamshire – in Leicestershire or Northamptonshire – until the eyre is gone, or hoping that he'll just catch up with you somehow and you all can focus on helping the villagers. But I tell you, if 'Robin Hood' doesn't appear when he's desperately needed, then the people may very quickly lose faith in their saviour, and then it will be far harder to regain their trust."

Thomas gave Hugh a sad smile. "I think you'd better have your green hood to hand! ...I think we all should, come to that, but you're the one left who looks as the people expect Robin Hood to be."

To Guy's surprise and relief, Hugh didn't object to that in the way he expected. He'd thought the former soldier would instantly protest that he wasn't the one to lead them, but instead Hugh's only comment was, "So soon! I'd really hoped that with the king gone it would be a while longer before this happened."

That none of the others even looked as though they were going to object also surprised Guy. Maybe they had been getting more fed up with Robin's imperious ways than he'd thought? As they set off once more for the camp, Tuck came up alongside Guy and confirmed his suspicions by saying softly,

"May God forgive me for this, but it's been so much easier without Robin these last couple of weeks. Everything has been talked over between us, and if we haven't all necessarily agreed with every step we've taken, at least we've had a chance to have our say, and it's been listened to."

"Who's been having the final say?" Guy couldn't help but ask.

"Well without Will here, it's tended to be Malik, surprisingly enough, although I can't think of a single instance where he and Hugh haven't agreed. Malik brings the greater experience of war, and Hugh brings the local knowledge. You won't be surprised to hear that the main arguers have been Gilbert and Piers, but even that's been more because of their natures than any real dissent. I think John and Allan are more worried about Robin than they're letting on."

Guy had noticed that his two cousins had not arrived with the others, and now Tuck explained, "They decided to remain at the camp today. There was some serious food preparation needing doing, and they told me they wanted to have a chance to talk to one another alone. I think they're trying to sort out how they feel about Robin's leaving, if I'm honest."

Guy gave his old friend a wry smile. "I've been doing a lot of that myself. I know how they feel! Because of the way he left there's a part of me that wants to crack his jaw with a good punch if he shows his face around here again. But the part of me that remembers our young cousin Baldwin just wants him back safe and sound. And in truth, Tuck, it varies from day to day which side of me is winning!"

At the camp, Guy's reunion with John and Allan was emotional. In the aftermath of the siege there had been no time for fond farewells, but now they hung onto one another as if their lives depended on it.

"What are we going to do about him?" John finally said to Guy, as they bedded down on the bracken-filled hollows in the camp, the three of them choosing to sleep side by side that night.

"I don't know, John," Guy confessed. "I'm not even sure there is anything we can do. If he can't see how the king is treating him – if Siward can't make him see that when they're right under the king's nose – then what can we do? We can hardly march into the king's camp and drag him out!

"And there's also the not exactly small matter of how quickly King Richard will go across to Normandy. Even if we set out tomorrow morning – and if I took my chances of never going back to the castle, but moved Ianto, Maelgwn and Elias up to the new manor in Scotland – we could still get to the south coast and find that the king had sailed weeks before. And what then? We could never hope to make the crossing and find him in the chaos over there. We'd be more likely to be taken for men on the run from their lord and get hauled into some lord's army."

"Guy's right," Allan's voice said sadly from Guy's other side to John, and his arm went around Guy's middle as he rolled over and hugged him tightly. "Robin has to come back to us of his own accord or not at all. I'm so sorry, John, but I had to make that choice and now so does he. He has to want to come back to us, we can't force him, even if we know it's for his own good."

In the morning there was no objection from the others to John's request that they go as far as possible back to Nottingham with Guy, all of them knowing that Guy needed this show of friendship, as well as the cousins needing to spend whatever time they could grab together. They all trooped along through the soft, bright new grass, no words being needed, and all of them taking silent comfort from those walking alongside them. Tuck had already told Guy over breakfast that they now all agreed that of all of them, he was the one they feared most for because of his isolation in the castle. Their concern touched Guy, and in a strange way he now felt better about returning because he knew with certainty that the risks he was taking were not being taken for granted. That meant that he also knew that should he decide that he could no longer go on, that they would support him in that decision – with Robin leading he had never been quite so sure.

So it was with some shock that he realised that suddenly he could hear the sound of two men running their way, and the familiar voice of Siward saying to someone,

"Get up, God damn you, get up! Keep running!"

In an instant the others had melted off the track, and Guy saw them stringing their longbows, and pulling arrows out of their quivers in readiness. He himself had a simple choice – to pull the horses into the undergrowth quickly and try to hide them while staying out of any fight, or to mount up and play the sheriff's forester and provide a distraction for those fleeing. To his inner discomfort it was the desire to distract the hunt from Siward which was most urgent for him, but it got him mounted up on his own horse, and straightening his jerkin and forester's lanyard and horn.

When Siward plunged through the tangle of hazel, hawthorn and burgeoning bracken onto the track, Guy was already heeling his horse towards the noises. Siward's expression flickered from outright terror as he suddenly saw the mounted figure, to astonishment as he registered just who it was, but Guy was already gesturing him to keep going and behind him. That Siward was all but dragging a staggering other figure vaguely impinged on Guy's consciousness, but he was too alert to the pursuers to bother looking twice. It might have been Robin but it might not in its bedraggled state. What mattered more was deflecting these coming men.

In short order, four men, all mounted, all wearing chain-mail birnies and well-armed, came plunging through the undergrowth too.

"Who are you?" the leader snarled belligerently at Guy, who assumed his most frosty stare and demanded back,

"And who are you to hunt in the king's forest without license?"

That made them blink and Guy forced his advantage. "I am Sir Guy of Gisborne, forester to the sheriff of Nottingham. I have every right to be here since I am on the king's business inspecting the forest, I do not think you have such permission!"

His steely gaze and air of authority did the trick, and the leader paused, albeit with grinding teeth. "God's hooks, man, we're not hunting the fucking deer! We're chasing two traitors! Men who've absconded from the king's camp in the south, and thieving valuables from noble men as they did so. They must have come past you, for Christ's sake! Which way did they go?"

Guy merely quirked an eyebrow. "No-one has passed me, soldier. If you heard anything above the crashing and racket you were making, it was probably the stag which you startled and which just went by me before you appeared."

"But we heard voices, I'm sure we did!" another soldier exclaimed indignantly.

Guy inclined his head frostily, "Indeed, so did I ...but further over to your right, maybe heading towards Eakring or Winkburn. I do believe I passed a carter arguing with his lad back that way on the wider track. How many men were you tracking anyway? You didn't say. Was it four of them? Because there were four ragamuffins heading for Bilsthorpe when I passed through Kirklington earlier. They said they were hoping for sanctuary overnight at Rufford Abbey, although I seriously doubt whether the abbot would welcome such rough travellers in his precinct."

By now the soldiers looked fit to scream at his prevaricating. "No, not four, *two*!" the leader all but screamed, but Guy's assumption of the wrong numbers convinced them that he had not seen their quarry, and they wrench their unfortunate horses around and spurred them into retracing their tracks.

Waiting until he could hear that they had fully returned the way they had come and were unlikely to come back, Guy then called softly, "All clear! You can come out now."

He swung down from the saddle as the outlaws melted out of the undergrowth and converged on Siward and the figure huddled on the ground at his feet.

"Nice one, Guy!" Allan declared, even as he and John hurried towards the figure who had still not moved.

"Sweet Jesu, that was some bluff!" Gilbert agreed approvingly, coming to clap Guy on the back.

The two of them joined Malik with the Coshams converging on Siward, hearing Malik say with more emotion than they had ever heard from him before, "My friend I feared you were lost!"

"Not quite yet," Siward said with a shaky laugh, "but I've never been so glad to see anyone as you lot." Then his gaze caught Guy and he reached out and pulled them together. "You saved our lives there, Guy. They'd have strung us up from the nearest tree if they'd caught us!"

"*Duw*! Why?" Thomas demanded, outraged. "What gave them such a right?"

"The king's fucking justiciars!" Siward spat. "That's who! The bastards have sent out riders to every shire. We've been barely one step ahead of them all the way from bloody Winchester!"

"No," Guy immediately contradicted him. "I'm sorry Siward, but those messages were about the coming eyre. I was in the castle right up until yesterday. We've had nothing at all about fugitives. No messages at all. If these men have been chasing you, then they've had a much more personal message." He suddenly had a chilling thought. "Please God, tell me Robin hasn't been alone with the king, or at least not fully alone but rather out of your hearing and sight."

Siward's expression told Guy enough. "Oh *Dewi Sant* and all the saints! Then I think your troubles might have come from Robin telling the king that he was Robin Hood, and then someone like Ralph Murdac telling King Richard just what a thorn in the sheriff's side Robin Hood has been."

Siward turned a horrified gaze towards the man he had no doubt been half-carrying across England, and Robin stared balefully back at him. But it was a Robin who was a pale shadow of his former self, a man Guy had had to take a second glance at to recognise as his cousin.

"I thought he would listen," Robin was saying in a cracked voice. "I thought he would understand. I tried to tell him."

"Tell him what?" Guy's voice was like ice, unable to credit that his cousin had been so irredeemably stupid.

"That he can't keep asking this much of the people of England," Robin said as if he had made the most obvious of statements, and now Guy belatedly realised that Robin's voice was so hoarse because, going by his red eyes, he must have been sobbing his heart out all the way from Winchester too.

Yet Guy's sympathy was all with Siward. "You bloody fool, Baldwin, what did you expect him to say?" he heard himself saying as if from a distance, even as he turned to look at Siward.

"I thought he'd understand!" Robin all but howled.

"Hush, you fool!" Gilbert snapped. "For God's sake, Robin, we've only just got rid of those soldiers. If you make that kind of racket they'll be back!"

"Let's get to the camp," Tuck said firmly, as he and John hoisted Robin to his feet between them, and then threw him over one of Guy's horses as the easiest way to keep him moving.

With Thomas and Piers leading the way with drawn bows, they set off. Allan and Bilan walked closely behind Tuck and John and the led horse, but Malik, Gilbert and Guy hung back a little and clustered around Siward, whom Guy insisted ride the other horse.

"You've obviously had the journey from Hell," Guy sympathised with him, as he walked on one side, while Malik and Gilbert walked closely by Siward on the other. "By Our Lady, Siward, did the idiot really try to tell King Richard what to do?"

Siward just hung his head, shaking it dejectedly. "I don't know, truly I don't. I was so tired I'd lain down in the stable we were billeted in with dozens of other poor knights. I fell asleep without even meaning to. The next thing I know, one of the lads is shaking me awake and telling me I'd better get over to the great hall at Winchester, because my 'mate' was stirring up a right hornets' nest. I ran as fast as I could, but by the time I got there, Robin was already being thrown out of the king's presence by four of the biggest men-at-arms I've ever seen. And I mean thrown! They had an arm or leg each, and they swung him and then let him go!"

With a shudder Siward continued, "For a horrible moment I thought they might have killed him, because he hit the side of a cart head first. It was one hell of a crunch! I ran to him and he was out cold, so I hoisted him over my shoulder and got out of there as fast as I could. Something in my gut told me not to go back to the stable. Even before he woke up and told me what he'd said, I had the feeling that Robin had just burned all our bridges for us.

"I got right to the edge of the camp and then went and stole what bits of food I could find. I don't know why, but when I ran out of the stable I'd instinctively grabbed my sword, and my knives were still on my belt, so at least I wasn't without weapons. Robin didn't have a thing, of course, because he'd had to disarm before they'd let him into the king's presence. I don't think anyone is taking any chances given that the Holy Roman emperor hasn't had all of his ransom yet – they must be worried that a knife in the dark will dispose of King Richard and leave the throne in the hands of Count John."

He shuddered again. "It took a couple of days before Robin could talk and make much sense. Thank God I found a merchant with a wagon full of heavy cloth and tapestries heading away from Winchester – I didn't care where to at that point. I just bundled us in amongst the bolts late on the first night and then let the merchant take us where he would."

"Probably not a bad thing," Guy told him soothingly. "Wherever that merchant was ultimately bound for would have been so random that no-one could anticipate it when thinking of you two."

Siward gave a weak smile. "Well it was certainly that, because by the time I had to get Robin out of the wagon because he was starting to groan too much, we were in Surrey! Not exactly on the way to Nottinghamshire."

"Probably saved your lives, though, like Guy says," Gilbert agreed. "If they spoke to the men who'd been around you, and knew you were from around here, they would never have thought you'd be heading towards London."

Siward gave a grudging nod. "It was certainly only when we got to the northern part of Leicestershire that they found our trail again."

"But did Robin ever tell you what he said to the king?" Malik asked, a worried frown creasing his forehead.

"Not really," Siward admitted, but then looking down at Guy, added, "But I think once we're at the camp he's going to have to!"

However, when they got to the camp Robin was immediately taken off to one side by Tuck and John, and the others could hear Tuck's voice rising and falling in Latin, hinting that he was trying to soothe Robin's shattered soul.

"Do you think it would help if I left the camp?" Guy asked Siward as they sat and shared another bowl of the stew left over from the previous night. "I daren't stay longer than dawn tomorrow anyway or it'll arouse suspicion at the castle. Would it be better if I left now?"

Yet Siward immediately put a restraining hand on Guy's arm. "No, stay! You need to hear something he told me on the way to Winchester, and I want him to tell you himself – although if he baulks at it, I'll tell you myself in front of him!"

If Siward hadn't had such an awful time getting back to them, Guy would have pressed him harder to tell him anyway, but as things stood he hardly thought it fair.

It took a couple of hours, but then Robin returned with Tuck and John and sat down in the circle surrounding the camp fire.

"I owe you all an apology," he said contritely. "I truly thought that if I could get to speak to the king in person that he would want to hear what was going on behind his back. King Baldwin always did!" That last sounded very plaintive and the disappointment was hanging about Robin like a thundercloud wrapped around a hill.

Guy was gritting his teeth not to say 'what did you expect?' So he was relieved when Gilbert with his normal forthrightness said,

"So have you finally got over that by-Our-Lady stupid idea? Because I have to tell you, Robin, you were really starting to piss me off being so blind to what was glaringly obvious to the rest of us!"

Coming from one of those whose loyalty he had taken so much for granted, that stopped Robin in his tracks. For a moment he sat open-mouthed looking at Gilbert, then went very red and asked,

"Did you think it so very obvious?"

Gilbert gave a snort of incredulity. "What? That a fucking arrogant Norman was hardly going to listen to one of us? Judas' balls, yes! Blindingly fucking obvious! Holy Mother of God, Robin, how could you not work out that someone like Longchamp got away with doing what he did, precisely because he knew that the king wouldn't give a rat's left swinging bollock what happened, just so as long as Longchamp kept the money pouring out of England – and Wales and Ireland!" He rolled his eyes in exasperation. "And if you'd ever listened properly to what Hugh's been telling us about what it was like fighting in Normandy – listened properly, instead of hearing half of it and then making assumptions as you tried to make it fit with your cock-eyed view of the world – that would have filled in a lot of the gaps for you too."

Robin was aghast, and it brought it home to Guy that he had genuinely had no idea of how his actions and behaviour had been seen by the others.

"Oh. ...So is that why you refused to come with us to fight with the king?"

Gilbert threw his hands up in despair. "God's hooks! Of course it fucking is! Christ on the Cross, Robin, it wasn't just to spite you! Or did you have the gall to think I'd lost my courage?"

Guy swallowed hard. If Robin said yes to that last, then one almighty fight was going to break out, because that was the one thing Gilbert would never tolerate. They'd be pulling Gilbert off him and sitting on him for the rest of the night while they got Robin far away, or there would be blood spilled. Mercifully Robin simply said,

"I don't think I thought either of those. I just couldn't understand why you couldn't see what was so clear to me."

Gilbert snorted in disgust, but some of the anger went out of him and all he said was, "Well I hope hitting that cart with your head knocked some bloody sense into it!"

"You were the *only* one who thought like that," John said with considerable firmness, staring hard at Robin. "The rest of us only went along with it out of loyalty to you. But don't *ever* ask us to do that again!"

Such a tough stance from the cousin who had been most on his side clearly rattled Robin even further, but he was sitting going pale and more than a little shaky by the time John had finished saying,

"And you owe us more than just an apology! If you want to come back – let alone lead us again – you have some serious making up to do to a lot of us. I followed you into that bloody camp, and not once did you ever come and look for me once we got separated. I could have disappeared for good in that mêlée if it hadn't been for Allan and Roger! By the time you'd have woken up and come looking for me I could have been in Normandy.

"But that's as nothing to the callous way you treated Much. I can just about work out that in your daft head you thought that Thomas and Piers would look after Bilan, but what by all the saints did you think Much's fate would have been? Did you care? Did you stop to think even once about how an innocent lad who's never been far from home would cope with being shoved around by some hardened army cooks?"

"He damned near got dragged off on the second night by some roughs who wanted to enlarge his arse," Bilan added bitterly. "It was only me threatening to cut their balls off and feed them to them for breakfast that stopped them. I was cursing your name with every breath for leaving me to care for him on my own!"

"No!" Robin croaked in horror. "No! Is he all right?" He cast about the group as if suddenly aware that Much wasn't there.

"Much isn't here because we sent him up to Loxley with Roger to look after him," John said bluntly, "And it's a pity you didn't think to look for him a lot earlier. Yes, he is safe, but it's no thanks to you! You're no hero to him anymore!"

Robin buried his head in his hands, but John seemed unable to stop now that he'd started. "As for Marianne, I think you can forget ever getting back together with her. She'd rather be handfast to a spavined bull with hoof-rot than you after the way you walked away from her! You'll be lucky if she doesn't claw your face and scratch you to shreds ...*if* you get to see her again, and we won't be in a hurry to pull her off, either. You'll deserve what you get there!"

Robin's tear-streaked face looked up and did the circuit of everyone, getting more and more distraught as he saw no sign of sympathy in any of them.

"Will's most likely to punch your lights out," Allan added dryly. "To say he's not impressed with how you've behaved is an understatement. But the person you owe the biggest apology to of all of us is Guy. You damned near cost him his life. I'm amazed that he's still sitting here, because had that been me, I'm not sure I would."

For the first time Robin's gaze actually met Guy's and immediately he flinched away. "Yes ...Guy." He paused and took several very deep breaths. "Siward ...Siward told me... I understand now that I did something very stupid when we were riding from Nottingham. I never thought ...I never meant ...I..."

"You just thought you could rub de Wendenal's nose in the dirt," Guy supplied coldly. "That's it, isn't it? You were so full of yourself for having ...well what did you think you'd achieved, Robin? Do tell me. Because I'm not sure whether I'm more disgusted if you thought that you had somehow single-handedly been responsible for bringing down a sheriff, or if you thought that I needed bringing down a peg or two. Or was it just your overwhelming pride which needed puffing up a bit more like some pig's-bladder football? You tell me, what was it?"

"If you don't tell him right now, I will," Siward's icy voice fell into the tense quiet which followed Guy's words. "Tell him what you said to me on the road."

The tears began streaming down Robin's face and he couldn't manage to even look at Guy, let alone meet his eye. "I was so angry when you took my place as Robin Hood up on that hillside. I thought you'd finally taken what you'd wanted for so long. That you were glad to see the back of me so that you could be leader. I was angry that you couldn't even wait until I came back to hear what concessions I'd got from the king. That you'd prefer to carry on fighting some petty war rather than give me credit for ending it once and for all."

He took a deep, ragged breath. "I was so angry. I just wanted to get some acknowledgement of what *I'd* done. *That's* why I started taunting de Wendenal. I wanted you to hear. I wanted you to stop messing up my plans! I wanted bloody 'Robin Hood' to disappear for a bit so that I could negotiate with the king. And then you got Thomas to make that shot for you. The one that killed de Wendenal. That was cheating! I practised and practised so that Robin Hood would be the superb shot, and then not only did you take my place, but you got someone else to go through the motions for you too!

"It was only when all those soldiers went running up the hill after you that I realised that maybe I'd put all your lives in danger." He took a final deep breath. "And then when Siward grabbed me and shook me and said that de Wendenal had been about to call out your name, and that's why one of you had to kill him, that's when I wished I hadn't taunted him. I'm sorry, I never expected them to go after you. I didn't think I was actually risking your life."

"You fool! You bloody fool!" was all Guy could say, stunned by how wrong Robin had been on all counts.

However Tuck had no such reservations, and now the big Welsh monk finally gave vent to his own disgust. "And now you listen to me, *brawd*! Because I have done my best for you this afternoon, but now you need to pin back your ears and listen, and if you don't, I may be giving you that thump long before Will gets the chance!"

Robin turned to him in open horror, and Guy thought that maybe this was the first time he'd had Tuck speak to him in such a way, not in sympathy.

"Your vanity is your overweening fault!" Tuck declared sternly, giving him a sharp shake of the arm so that Robin's wavering gaze once again met his. "By *Dewi Sant*, Guy never did any of those things you've just accused him of, do you understand? It was Hugh who acted being Robin Hood that day, and he did it because the rest of us *asked* him to. Guy was the one standing back who shot the warning arrow up into the air."

"It was," Hugh said firmly. "I issued the challenge. We'd actually agreed it *couldn't* be Guy in case the sheriff recognised his voice. We were desperate to make sure that Guy wouldn't be unmasked as the one who'd been the traitor in their midst. But you undid all of that!"

Malik cleared his throat. "And it was I who made the shot which killed the sheriff. Guy had no part in that."

"And if you'd bloody-well bothered to look around, you selfish English bastard," Piers snapped, "you would have known that it couldn't be Thomas, because we were still bloody stuck behind you! We'd only just got out of that mess ourselves and were taking Much to safety. *Duw*! You can be a pompous prick!"

Tuck gave him another brisk shake. "So you listen up and hear this too! In the weeks since you've been gone, Guy has been back in that cursed castle risking his neck for us yet again. Not once has he ever tried to be our leader, not even with you gone. All this nonsense is in *your* head, Robin, nowhere else! And it's got to stop, do you hear me? It stops now! If you ever endanger his life like that again, it will be you who gets an arrow through his throat, because your stupidity nearly cost not only Guy his life from being revealed to all and sundry, but the lives of Malik, Gilbert, Will, Hugh and myself by drawing down those soldiers on us. All we wanted was to issue a challenge, and God knows why, but we wanted to give you a chance to go off and be the bloody knight you keep on rattling on about being. We decided that if everyone in that damned procession saw Robin Hood up on that hillside, then they would never look twice at you amongst them."

There was a chorus of "that's right"s and "he's telling the truth"s from around the circle but what Guy heard most clearly was Siward saying,

"You see? I told you that was Hugh's voice, but you wouldn't have it would you?"

So Robin had been so full of wounded pride that he hadn't even been able to get past it for long enough to recognise his own cousin's voice, and suddenly Guy felt he could not sit there a moment longer.

"I really need to get back to the castle," he said, having no trouble in sounding dog-tired. "There'll be an almighty fuss if I don't."

Robin rose shakily to his feet to stand alongside Guy. "I'm sorry. I'm so very sorry," was all he kept saying, and although Guy could tell it was from the heart, somehow it just didn't feel like enough. Indeed he couldn't think of anything he could say back which wouldn't sound either childishly spiteful or churlish. So doing nothing more than giving Robin a nod of acknowledgement, he went and embraced John and Allan, and then Tuck.

"Making a tactful withdrawal?" his Welsh friend said softly in his ear. "Tactful of you, Guy, and probably wise. But I promise you this, my friend, when the shock has worn off a bit more, I shall be insisting that he make a full apology to you for this."

"I doubt you'll get it," Guy said with more sadness than he'd intended to seep out.

"Oh I will!" Tuck insisted with some asperity. "And not just for your sake! This arrogance ...this misguided spite towards you, will weigh heavily against his soul when his time comes to meet his Maker! And as his confessor I shall be making that very clear to him."

And did it work, you ask, Gervase? Sadly not as well as you and Tuck might have hoped, I am sorry to say. Oh I got my formal apology a few weeks later on, in that instance Tuck was not to be argued with, and at

the time I have no doubt it came from the heart. But in the long-term it changed very little except to make things worse between us, as you will eventually hear.

Initially I do believe that Robin was appalled at how wrong he had been in his assumptions, and certainly he would never talk again about King Richard in such glowing or fanciful terms. That misguided faith in the crusader king was crushed forever after Winchester, and in true Robin fashion, soon he was questioning King Richard's motives in everything, including why he had gone to fight for Jerusalem in the first place. As I have said to you before, in Robin's world things were either good or bad, black or white – there were no shades of grey. And having fallen from the high pedestal on which Robin had set him, the king had now made a plummeting decent to the depths of iniquity and was condemned as evil in all respects, and even his achievements in the Holy Land now became tainted in Robin's eyes.

As for myself, for a while I was once again restored to his good books. Yet as time went on, I believe that he looked back to that night when he increasingly felt he had been humiliated in front of the company and, unable to cope with the reality, found it easier to blame me. He could not bear to see that it had been his actions alone which had shaken the band's faith in him. Can you understand that it made him question whether he lived up to that ideal of the ultimate knight? And it was to such an extent that I believe, looking back now, that he either had to do as he did and shift the burden onto someone else, or else he would have completely broken down and maybe never been the same man again.

What did I wish for? Oh Gervase, sometimes I wish that his mind had snapped. No, do not look so horrified! I mean that if he had fallen apart, then I could have sent him to the peace and quiet of my newly acquired manor in the north and given him the time and space to truly heal. Maybe then the Baldwin of my youth would have returned in spirit at least, rather than the vengeful Robin who turned so many who loved him against him. Yes, he did win the others of the gang back this time, you need not fear for your hero yet, Brother, but I would look back to that time myself over the years and wonder whether that terrible blow to the head had maybe knocked something further adrift in his mind. Something which as time went on got steadily worse, and did that because it never had chance to heal.

I do not now know whether it was a blessing or not that the early stages of Robin's ...well let us call it a change of state, was so focused on me that it was less evident to the others for a while. Some days I think that it was no bad thing that I was the object of his ire, given that I was mostly far away and not in his presence daily. He kept many of his thoughts hidden at first because I was not there to dredge them to the surface. It certainly saved our friends from much prolonged distress, and maybe even saved the band from splitting up, allowing ~Robin Hood~ to help many more people. On other days, though, I wish that it had been more apparent earlier, because then maybe the high cost could have been averted better.

No, I am not going to say more on that, Gervase! It will come out at its proper time, and not before. For now we must return to Nottingham Castle with me, for portentous events were about to take place, and I would be in the middle of them. You may not be delighted to have to follow my life rather more than your hero's, but you will soon see that the things which at first affected me soon gave me the means to help Robin and the others even more. Does that satisfy you? Good.

Chapter 3

So, dear Brother, we come to the aftermath of the siege in the form of the dreaded eyre. And I shall tell you of this not to string out your impatience to hear of Robin's next exploit, but to introduce you to William Briwere exactly as we were to meet him, in all his cunning and venom! Indeed much was to happen in the remainder of that terrible year of 1194 which was to have great impact upon our lives for years to come. So bear with me, Brother, because today you shall be hearing about the forging of the legend of Robin Hood.

Good, now that you have brightened considerably and I have your full attention, let us begin. And what will no doubt please you as well is when I say that although I had managed to win the favour of William de Ferrers, earl of Derby at the siege, and to also increase my standing with the man from whom I held my Gisborne manor, Ranulph de Blundeville, earl of Chester, I would not see anything more of them for many years. Those men of power, despite thinking kindly of me, would not even be in England, let alone on hand for me to appeal to when trouble threatened. Nor was David, earl of Huntingdon, brother to the Scottish king, and the man from whom I held my new manor in Scotland, any closer. These great lords were walking on eggshells themselves when it came to King Richard's capricious favours, and they were dancing in attendance on him to ensure their own positions remained in their hands. They had no time to be looking to a humble knight like myself. Therefore I was alone at the castle except for those few knights I could trust with some (but not all) of my secrets, and my friend Harry down in the stables with his lads.

We had staggered through April, and with the approach of May the next one in our yearly round of woodmotes was looming on the fourth of that month. Oh come, Brother! What do you mean, how do I know the date? What falls on that day, pray tell me? You who are so immersed in all things holy! That momentary look of panic before you said the Feast of the Veneration of the Thorn does not bode well for you when it comes to your time to confess all as I am doing now. And I shall give you a prod and remind you that it is also the Feast of St James the Less, for our secular year was as governed by the saints' days as yours are. Just because I so often appealed for intercession to the Welsh saints *my dear friend Tuck introduced me to, it does not mean that I am ignorant of the others by which we measured our year. And so it was that I rode out on St Edmund's Day, the twenty-ninth of April, to check on the state of some oaks which I would have to give evidence over, and to bring news to my friends in the forest.*

Sherwood
April & May, the Year of Our Lord 1194

"Thank God I've found you!" Guy exclaimed, vaulting from his horse to greet the outlaws as they streamed towards him.

"More trouble?" John asked, coming to hug him in a way which Guy would never have expected a month ago.

"You wouldn't believe how much," Guy replied, doing a quick inventory of who was there.

Catching him doing it, Siward said, "Robin's not here, nor is Tuck." His face broke into a wry smile. "I think there's some very muscular spiritual guidance going on up at Loxley at the moment!"

That, at least, made Guy wring out a smile of his own. So Tuck was holding Robin to account for his actions, was he? Thank St Issui and all of the other Welsh saints for that! Going by the way John looked more relaxed than he had in over a year, Guy reckoned it wasn't before time either. Marianne and Mariota were both here, so clearly they were waiting to see what transpired before spending much time alone with Robin, but interestingly Malik was missing.

"Where's Malik?" Guy asked worriedly. For a horrible moment he feared that the turcopole had had enough and gone to try and find James with the Jews who had left England for Spain.

"Oh, don't worry," Siward said coming to clap Guy on the arm in friendly fashion. "He decided to stay with Tuck after we got Robin up to the camp. Although I have a feeling Tuck may have asked him to stay. You know how Malik's always been a calming influence, and with Will already at Loxley trying to get our own armoury set up, I think Tuck didn't want Robin getting the chance to exert too much influence on our newest recruits just yet. Or for Will to lose what little patience he has and thump Robin, given some of his dafter statements and that Tuck's not sure yet just how much damage that head-first dive into the wagon side has done – Malik and Will have always been close, so it helps there too."

"But we had a feeling that you might be wanting to talk to us sooner rather than later," Allan added, coming to hug his cousin as well. "So what news, couz'? You've got a face like a salt cod on you, so it can't be good!"

This time Guy's laugh was genuinely in pleasure. Allan had a way of lifting the tension like no other.

"Can we go and sit down?" he asked. "I'm not in a desperate hurry and there's a lot to tell!"

As Siward gestured for him to carry on into the hidden Inkersall camp, Allan added,

"But don't expect one of Tuck's stews, we've been taking our lives in our spoons eating Marianne's cooking," then yelped as the sound of a slap came from behind him, and Marianne's voice saying,

"Cheeky beggar!" but with amusement, making Guy think that Allan had been working hard on distracting her from brooding too hard about Robin.

When they had all settled and Guy had had a chance to eat, and was trying out some of the new brew of beer which had been brought back from Loxley, he finally got to his news.

"I'm afraid this is going to cause all manner of problems," he told them regretfully. "There's going to be an eyre.

"That's because of the sheriffs who'll be coming, right?" Much ventured. "You said that it would be dangerous when they showed up."

Guy had already warned them that Sirs Roger de Buron, Ralph Musard, William de Stuteville and Hubert fitz Ralph would be riding around the shire accompanied by their guards even as they were speaking, rounding up the ten knights in each of the five hundreds which fell within Sherwood's Nottinghamshire boundaries.

Guy sighed. "Yes, that's very true, but what bothers me every bit as much is the fact that it's just come to light that it's only going to be the regular eyre. The forest eyre isn't going to come, and we've had no hint of when that might happen."

"What, not at all?" Hugh exclaimed. "So what of those who are waiting for trial on forest matters? When does their day come?"

"Exactly!" said Guy, glad that someone else had already grasped the significance of what he was saying. "I don't think it's going to be any time soon."

Siward was stroking his chin thoughtfully as he wondered, "Is that because the bail money is so lucrative, do you think?"

"But the fines and bail monies aren't that great," Allan protested. "You've said before, Guy, that what gets asked for is a burden on the poor who mostly get caught out by the laws, but that of themselves they don't make up huge amounts of money."

"So I did, and no they don't. But what you have to remember is this: they can keep on asking for those payments over and over again, year upon year, and who is going to stop the sheriff? The sons of guildsmen, who go out hunting when they shouldn't, will have no trouble keeping the bail money coming, nor will any other high ranking men. So although they'll be an inconvenience to them, they aren't so big that anyone with any real influence will get up and start protesting loudly."

He looked around at his friends glumly. "I think someone, and possibly the head forester of England, fitz Peter, has told the king what a neat hole in the ordinary laws this is, and what can be milked because of it. I fear that fitz Peter has used this as a means of making sure that the king sees him as indispensible, and to Hell with the laws' victims."

"I fink it's a good job we broke into Nottingham gaol when we did," Roger said into the shocked silence. "At least we knows that nobody's been stuck in there for years."

Guy agreed. "Yes, thank St Issui you did! My conscience had been pricking me over that, making me wonder if we haven't made things worse for anybody who gets put into the gaol from now onwards. But since hearing this news I've come to your way of thinking, Roger, that whatever happens at least we're starting with a clean slate regarding who is in those cells."

John heaved a sigh. "Good job Robin isn't here in his old state of mind then, isn't it? I can already imagine him fuming and railing at this news, and planning a raid on the gaol again."

Guy found it terribly sad that John who had been Robin's staunchest supporter should now be grateful for his absence, but had to agree with him. "I'm afraid I thought that too. In fact, that's what I wanted to say to you all. Please don't do anything like that again – or at least not yet. Give me time to get to know this new sheriff's weaknesses, I beg you. I came hoping to appeal to you all to stop Robin if he looked like going off on a crusade against the sheriff, so I'm beyond relieved that he isn't here and not likely to be for a while."

Now Thomas cleared his throat pointedly, and when they all looked at him he said cautiously, "I don't know how you'll all think about this, but I've been wondering..."

"Go on, tell them!" his brother Piers prodded. "You know Bilan and I are with you."

Thomas puffed his cheeks. "Well it's like this, see? We've been thinking that it would be no bad thing if 'Robin Hood' did something now, while Robin is back, but before he gets well enough again to think that he might be our leader again. Make him see that he's wanted, but that he needs to keep it clear in his head just who he really is. That he's a man who sometimes plays the people's hero, but that he's not ...oh it's hard to explain! The best I can say is that 'Robin Hood' should be something he puts on, like a hood, not be going around as if he's walking inside 'Robin Hood's skin like it was his own."

He paused and looked worriedly around, only to be surprised to see the others all nodding or smiling.

"I think that's a great idea!" John praised, making Thomas' jaw drop in shock that Robin's own cousin should agree. "I've been worried about how we can take some of the strain off him. I think ...no, I *know* that he's been feeling the responsibility of being 'Robin Hood' getting heavier and heavier."

The big man hung his head and shook it. "I'm thoroughly ashamed to say that all I did was kept telling him that he was up to the job. I didn't see how it was warping him. Well now we have a chance to do something to prove to him that we never expected him to take on the running of a whole crusade by himself. Never did, never will!"

With Thomas too amazed to continue, it was Bilan who took up for the Coshams. "We were thinking of you too, Guy. We thought that while the ordinary people need to have some kind of sign that Robin Hood hasn't forsaken them with this new sheriff coming, for your sake it needs to be something a bit more controlled and thought out. Something we plan carefully and stick to the plan! No rushing off in wild, random directions like an arrow with warped flights. That way you won't have the strain of worrying what's going to happen and can watch the sheriff properly."

Guy's relief must have shown on his face, because the Coshams now looked very pleased with themselves, yet Hugh and Siward were also nodding enthusiastically, as were Allan and Roger.

Only Marianne looked miserable, but explained, "I feel such a wretch! Just seeing your face when Bilan said you were always worried about what might happen, brought it home to me how little Robin thought about any impact on you." She brushed away a tear which instantly brought her a hug from Mariota. "If Robin thought about you at all, it was just about making sure we didn't skewer you on an arrow or something. He's never given a moment's thought about how you *feel* about any of this."

Mariota gave her friend another squeeze as she added, "I'm as guilty. I know I don't know you as well as Marianne, but it should have occurred to me that you must have been worried sick every time you went to a woodmote that you might end up fighting us. That wasn't fair, not when you've helped us so much. We should have at least tried to get a message to you about where we might strike next."

Guy knew he had to be gracious about this, even though he was screaming inside, 'and you only just thought of this?' "Well at least my shock was convincing to anyone watching me," he managed with a weak smile, but saw that Hugh, Siward and Allan were giving him sympathetic looks as if they could guess what he was thinking.

"So what would you like us to do, Guy," Roger asked outright. "What's goin' to make a splash wiv'out causin' you terrible trouble?"

Given that his greatest fear had been to find Robin once more in charge but still barely sane, the question took Guy by surprise. "By Our Lady, now there's a question! Well straight away I would say don't even think of making any grand gestures against the castle. We're still in the middle of repairs – I left just as the king's two representatives had come to assess the damage – and what I fear is that if you show up and highlight where it's vulnerable, then as work is going on anyway, the castle may be made really impregnable by just adding in more stone, or whatever."

"*Dewi Sant*, that's something we didn't think far enough ahead about!" Thomas gulped. "But you're right, Guy, by St Thomas you are! One day we might really *need* to get into the castle – maybe to get one of us out. We'd be kicking ourselves something terrible if we then realised we were the very ones who'd made it impossible for ourselves."

"I agree," Siward said emphatically. "As one who's been through a different kind of siege to what Guy experienced, but also having seen this king working his way into Nottingham, I think we need a few escape routes far more than we do the grand gesture against the castle." He looked around him. "No one here disagrees with this, do they?" No-one did. "And I think I can say that on this matter that Malik, Will and Gilbert will think the same as me, so we can tell Robin, if he should question us, that we are all in agreement over this: we do nothing which might panic the new sheriff into extra works on the castle which might come back to bite us later. ...So, Guy, what else?"

"Hmmm, I'd say avoid any attacks on the sheriff himself. That's a bit of a tricky one, I'll agree, because it means no attack on the eyre when it comes – and it's going to be soon, make no mistake about that. I know it might be tempting to think it's worth bloodying this sheriff's nose as fast as possible, but I'd advocate caution.

"You see Briwere is no novice sheriff as Wendenal and fitz John were. He's got years of experience behind him, so he'll have the day to day stuff down to a fine art, and I'd bet he'll bring someone he can delegate things to. Some glorified clerk, probably, but that will mean he'll be giving his full attention to our two shires, and consequently that means that I'll need to watch him very carefully to see how he'll react.

"Don't forget that he's a favourite of King Richard's, so that means he must be pretty adept at wringing money out of his shires. But it's how he does it that I need to see. Is he going to be a brute? Will he have the soldiers marching into villages and taking his dues by force? If he's going to beat stuff out of the villagers, we're going to have to be mightily careful that we don't bring terrible retribution down on the very folk we're trying to protect. You see, I fear that after this siege the king will see us as the treacherous shires, and not care how ham-fisted his sheriff is. May God help us, but Briwere may get away with murder in ways he never would have before, not even a year or two ago.

"And on that subject, don't forget that at the eyre he won't be alone. Even if the two other justices out on eyre in these shires with him sit independently at separate courts, they're likely to be stopping at Nottingham Castle before they move on elsewhere. So any move which humiliates them too, could rebound on us by having them coming back to the shires with their own men-at-arms and knights to add to Briwere's, and looking for revenge."

Hugh spoke for all of them, saying, "These are all things we hadn't thought hard enough about. I'm glad you're telling us this stuff, Guy. There's just one thing I'd like to ask, and it's what about the prisoners brought before the eyre? 'Robin Hood' won't look much of a hero if men whom the villagers know are innocent are swung up from gibbets in the market square without anyone lifting a hand to help them."

However Guy had no trouble grinning this time as he replied, "Oh at that stage I think you can act! When I said the eyre I meant the actual courts. And I don't think that the visiting sheriffs who are acting as justices will have the time to linger and watch the punishments being handed out. Not this time at least. The king wants all the fines brought in as fast as possible, so they have to get around the circuits pretty fast – and especially as these shires have been without an eyre for so long that this will take a lot of time.

"In two or three years when they come back again it might be a wholly different story, but we'll worry about that when it happens. For now I'd say that any hangings in the market square or any village centre can be considered a target, providing that there aren't too many soldiers about – don't show yourselves to be too strong or that might provoke a man hunt. But then I'm guessing that the punishments will be carried out in the leading towns of each of the hundreds, not in the outer bailey of the castle."

"That's a relief," John declared, "and it's something which Robin might want to get involved in if we decide he's up to it later on."

"But what about sooner? What can we do in the next week or so?" Bilan asked.

"I'd go for the woodmotes," Guy said with growing certainty. "You've a proven record at striking at the verderers. Pick a court run by one of the two newer verderers, Adam de Everingham or Roger de Lovetot, or even the new viper in the nest, Griffin Presbiter – he's the cousin of Ralph of Woodborough whom I told you about. Yes, Presbiter's court at Calverton would be a nice one! Let's give this little shit a baptism of fire! He deserves it after the way he treated Ralph's widow. And you can do it soon because he'll be sitting in just about a week's time. What's more, I've no business at that court, so you won't incriminate me, but it's right by Nottingham and the sheriff."

Later on Guy managed to speak alone with Allan about Robin. "I think it's a good thing if I'm not any way involved in this next raid," he told his youngest cousin. "Then even in his warped head Robin can't think I'm replacing him as leader. I know Tuck said that has to stop, but for once he might find that harder to make happen than to say."

"I'd thought that," Allan agreed sadly. "I think you're right to do something very explicit like standing back from the raid."

"Will he recover, do you think?" Guy wondered. "Head wounds can be funny things."

Allan shrugged. "I think if prayers will work then he'll come round, because Tuck's certainly said enough of them."

"Then will you ask him to say a few for me," Guy said with such misery in his voice that Allan started.

"Guy? What's wrong?" His tone must have alerted the others, because suddenly the other conversations around the campfire stopped, and once again Guy was the focus of their attention.

"It's another complication. I've been called upon to sit on a couple of the juries," he said glumly. "I can't get out of it. Oh, not here in Nottinghamshire, I'm going to be up in Derbyshire in The Peak. I'm one of the two knights who have to round up the jury of ten other men. I got the job, ironically enough, because Hugo Bassett and Oliver de Aincourt remembered that I've spent some time at High Peak.

"They're having a terrible time rounding up enough men of standing because of the number of knights who went with the king. Until that happened, and half the ruling families belatedly remembered that they needed to keep the king sweet, there were enough younger sons sculling about who could have been given the job. But at the moment they're all playing puppies gambolling at the king's heels in Normandy. So because I know the state of things up there with the added complication of the miners, I got the job."

He shook his head wearily. "Robin will never understand this, I know. That's why I wanted to make sure you were sorted with any retaliation you were likely to make in Nottinghamshire. I won't be around in the castle for a while should anything go wrong."

"By Our Lady, Guy!" Allan gasped, "I can see why you were worried about what Robin might think!"

Mariota, though, asked, "Why is this so bad? I'm sorry but I don't know enough of your English systems to understand what you're talking about."

"Actually, I've been gone so long I was wondering the same," confessed Siward.

Guy sighed. "Well you can be forgiven for not knowing. The reality is that the last few eyres of King Henry's reign came after so many years of stability that the actual trials were a bit of a formality. You see at each eyre in each hundred there needs to be twelve men who know the state of the land there. So you'd be talking about the lesser knights mostly. The men with small manors who were in contact with the ordinary people and would know who the disreputable characters were, who was likely to be a trouble-maker – probably who had been in trouble in the past in a lesser way – and where the field boundaries lie. There are – God help us – one hundred and forty-three questions which need to be asked of the state of the area covered by each eyre, all regarding the keeping of laws and who has broken them, which of course is why it takes so bloody long. Please don't ask me to list them, because I've never sat in on an eyre, so I don't know yet how this works in detail.

"However, when a man gets brought before the eyre accused by his neighbour of stealing off another man's land, for instance, those twelve men will testify as to whom the land actually belonged to in the past, and the character of the men involved. Or if it's murder, then they'll be telling the visiting sheriff if there's been some long-standing family feud, or whether the man was seriously provoked, or potentially even to have been defending himself as the innocent party until the fatal blow was struck. They'll be dealing with crown pleas – which are your murders and the like – and civil pleas, which are things like merchants suing one another for loss of trade or theft of goods. But the third set of cases are the ones which I'm dreading, because they'll be hearing cases of offences against the king's property, which are also called crown pleas, and with so much land round here being royal forest I'm sure you're already seeing how dangerous that could get!

"Now back in King Henry's reign these jurors would have been the same men who had helped run the Hundred Courts, so petty local matters would have been dealt with long before they got serious enough to get to the eyre. And to be honest, sometimes it didn't take the full twelve men to give evidence against, or for, a man for the case to be decided, again because they were familiar with the people around them. But in King Richard's reign we've had the upsets of the changes of sheriffs, not to mention most of the noble families suddenly feeling their positions becoming very precarious! So the Hundred Courts haven't been as regular or as consistent as they used to be, yet now we have to find men to act as those twelve jurors again, and the consequences could be terrible if we put the wrong men in."

The others looked at him pityingly as Hugh added, "So that's why you feel you have to do this, quite aside from not being able to get out of it. But it means you have to sit in judgement on people. Blessed St Thomas, that's rough, especially up in the Peak where you know so many people personally."

Guy nodded. "It is. But I'm hoping against hope that if I, a knight, stand up and say that I don't believe a man is guilty, then it will lend credence to the other local men saying he isn't. Because what I've never liked about the eyres, is the fact that despite all of this swearing as to the state of things by local men good and true, if the judge takes a dislike to the man before him, then his word overrides everyone else's, and the man can still hang! Therefore, I can't be seen to be too soft on people, because otherwise the sheriff who is judging them will simply disregard what I say. I'm going to be walking a very fine line, and I'm not looking forward to it one bit!"

Then John shocked him to the core by saying, "Then I think we need to help you too. If Robin needs a lesson, then we can certainly go and disrupt the woodmote of this Griffin Presbiter. But I think maybe even more of one would be if we disrupt the eyre courts Guy's at. Which hundreds are you going to, Guy?"

"The ones covered by the forest laws, of course – Blackwell, because that's pretty much the Forest of the Peak; and Scarsdale next door to it, which covers all those villages around Bolsover Castle which had never previously been under forest law. That's the one I'm dreading most, to be frank."

"Really?" John was surprised. "I thought you'd be more worried about the one where some of your friends are?"

Yet Guy shook his head. "No, because the villages where our friends are, right up in the Peak, are so few and are such a small proportion of the hundred that I'd be shocked beyond belief if one of them was brought in. Let's face it, John, if anyone in Hathersage or Kinder or Castleton had been murdered or was in trouble, we'd have heard about it by now. They'd have found a way to get a message to you somehow. Now, there's only a thin strip of that hundred which runs on the east side of the Derwent, and is therefore now counted as being in Sherwood. The vast majority of the villages are on the west side of the Derwent and between the two forests. So I'm expecting the usual array of complaints and accusations from them, and if it's not going to be a happy event, at least I know what to expect.

"But Scarsdale Hundred has villages like Stainsby and Bramley, who I've been involved with back when those priors decided to have their illegal hunt. And Williamthorpe – I know the people there too! Not to mention some of the charcoal burners and miner up in the north of the hundred, like Coal Aston. Robin Hood might not have visited them very often, but *I've* turned a blind eye to their goings on more than once. And I've then covered it up when others have gone there by saying that I took the payments previously; or knew that the charcoal kiln was there because it was an old one, not one set up when the forest was closed. They're the people I dread seeing, because they'll look to me to save them, and I can't!"

"So where will they hold the court?" Allan asked. "Which village?"

But Guy was already shaking his head. "I don't think it'll be a village. With Bolsover Castle sitting right in the middle of a cluster of villages, I'm sure that they'll hold the eyre there. Blackwell's eyre will be held at Tideswell, of that I'm also sure, not High Peak Castle.

So it's rotten luck that the one where I'm *not* likely to need your help is the one which you'd have far more chance of getting into."

However Allan wasn't to be so easily quashed. "No, just hold on a moment! You said earlier that we shouldn't seem too powerful. Not enough to draw any retribution down on us. Well I think you're right but for another reason as well. If we just disrupt things – and I really do mean disrupt and nothing more than that – while the visiting sheriffs are here, then it'll make our new sheriff seem all the more incompetent when he can't capture us, won't it?"

The way Guy's expression brightened told Allan that he was on the right track. "So I think we need to just disrupt this court, not go barging in waving our swords and taking on the guards and knights. ...So what do you think to fire arrows? Even if we set fire to just a few tapestries it will cause chaos."

Guy was now grinning. "Oh yes! I like that! And I'm much happier with that idea than you trying to get into the castle and then not be able to get out. Brilliant idea, especially as Bolsover's a wooden castle!"

"Oh, and there's more," Allan declared, just a touch smugly. "You see, we'll need our best archers for that. So that means our three Coshams here, and Malik and of course Robin!"

Now Guy was actually laughing out loud. "You crafty devil! Oh yes, that's very clever, Allan! You have every reason to ask Robin to do what he does exceedingly well, but as part of the team, not the leader. But it'll make him feel wanted without putting any expectation on him of leading. Thank you! By *Dewi Sant*, thank you! I shall go to the courts feeling so much better now!"

You are disappointed, Gerevase? Robin no longer the leader? Ah, but you must bear with my story. All will become clear in a moment.

In the meantime I will simply say that I was genuine in my dread of taking up this role of juror at the eyre. It is a wicked thing to have to sit in judgement on your fellow man. No, I am not confusing you deliberately, Brother. Indeed the sheriffs who ran those courts did have the final say in what happened to an accused man, regardless of what the jurors might say. But I saw too often how some men would use their roles in these courts to exact petty revenges on their neighbours. They should have given their evidence truthfully, for they swore an oath to God that they would do so, but men are weak, and the chance to have some gain in this world often outweighed the fate of their souls in the next. You may accuse me of many things, Brother, but I can say truthfully that I have never dragged another man down just to raise myself up a degree, or to have some small vengeance on one for a slight to my name which meant little to others. In that respect Sir Guy of Gisborne is not the villain of legend at all.

Chapter 4

So we came to the woodmotes, and while I had a peaceful enough court up at Edwinstowe, giving evidence as to the state of the forest in that very hundred of Scarsdale that I would return to shortly, ˜Robin Hood˜ gave Griffin Presbiter a rough ride in his first court. I was told by Allan with great glee of how Hugh, Siward, the three Coshams, Much, Marianne and Mariota, along with John, Roger and himself, brought chaos to that court. And if you wonder why I list them so, Brother, it is to highlight to you that they did this with only half of the experienced fighters. Only Siward of the former crusaders was there, because Will, Malik and Gilbert were at Loxley with Robin and Tuck. Ah, now you see it! Robin would have thought it impossible, I know, and would never have planned it like that, but they proved how wrong he was in that. So how did they do it, then?

What they did was play to their strengths. Marianne and Mariota went into the back of the hall, mingling in with the ordinary folk. In those days, the woodmote gatherings inevitably brought in somebody who was not known to the immediate locals, primarily because of folk coming from within the wider boundaries of the royal forest, so no-one remarked on two strange women being there. They then waited until Presbiter was really getting into his stride as verderer before signalling to the others that the time was ripe for them to appear. With glee, Allan related how the Coshams had positioned themselves so that when the double doors of the hall were flung open by the two women, they could shoot arrows straight in to the far end where Presbiter sat. I recall him saying to me, ˜By Our Lady, Guy! What a difference it made to take the time to scout the place properly!˜

You see, they had gone straight from speaking to me to Calverton, and three nights before the woodmote, in the small hours of the night when everyone in the village was fast asleep, they had opened the hall doors, lit a couple of torches within, and made several practice shots. And when I say hall, Brother, I really mean a place little more than a barn, not some vast ornate building – indeed many village halls doubled as temporary barns when needed, hence the double doors which a wagon could be taken through, and which my friends made such good use of. As Thomas would say to me later on, after doing that, he and his brothers could have pretty much guaranteed to hit any target in that hall, because they knew just where to stand for the best angles. They had also craftily rolled some empty barrels into places where they could quickly wheel them to the right spots to stand on, thus giving them the ability to aim over the heads of the crowd. I was deeply gratified at this, Brother. Not in a smug, self-congratulatory way, but simply glad that each member of the outlaw gang was now able to use their skills in the way they knew best.

It had been Siward and Hugh who had led the actual assault into the hall, with Siward acting as ˜Robin Hood˜ this time, with our John very much in his new role as Little John and close companion of the chief outlaw. John was happier, too, because he went in armed with just a hefty quarterstaff and was only ever expecting to knock a few heads. And I know this because he likewise told me this later on, saying that knowing that the archers would be there to cover their retreat if any soldiers showed signs of trying to be heroes, relieved him of the worry of having to do any killing just to get out of the hall. And for him that was a huge relief. To kill when there was absolutely no other choice he could accept, but not the way he felt with Robin, when he had been forced into the miserable choice of killing some poor soul who was in the wrong place at the wrong time because things had not been thought out, or risk being killed himself.

Yet the real crux was, I felt, that they had all agreed beforehand that if Presbiter turned up with more soldiers than they felt that they could handle, that they would abandon the mission and find another target. This, Allan said most vehemently, had <u>never</u> happened on any mission Robin led. Once the target was chosen there had been no going back, no matter what then happened to change their plans.

Of course the reality was that with so many soldiers having been swept up by the king, this time there had only been two men-at-arms there to guard the fines money from any pilfering attempts by the ordinary folk, and consequently – being the residue – they were neither the brightest nor the sharpest from our garrison. Therefore when Siward had bounded in, sword drawn, and put its point to Presbiter's scrawny throat, the guards had frozen like lambs before a hungry fox, and Allan had seized the chest with the fines before they realised what was happening. To cap it all, he also had the presence of mind to take the scribe's parchments, so that all records of what was to pay disappeared as well.

With Much and Roger then barricading the door to the hall with a cart as soon as their friends had run out, they were all able to make a fast escape into the countryside and nearby woods before anyone could follow. And Allan had mischievously written another missive from ˜Robin Hood˜, which Bilan pinned to the side of the hall with a long shot just as the first of the soldiers stuck his head over the cart, which a few old men and women on the outside were trying to shift. It had been rammed so hard against the hall wall that the wheel bosses were digging deeper into the wood with every turn and those within were truly stuck, you see. The raid was therefore a complete success with everyone escaping without injury to anyone, except Presbiter's pride, and with the money to give back to those who had been fleeced. And I must give Allan credit for that, for he had realised that if he took the records, then the money could be given back to precisely the right people against the time when they might be asked for it again.

I tell you, Gervase, I had not seen any of them quite so happy before at being the dreaded outlaws, and it did much to make me feel better about the role I had to play. And before you ask how I could know this, they made themselves briefly visible to me as I rode back to Nottingham with the proceeds of the Edwinstowe woodmote. So from a distance I saw the cheerful waves and smiles even though they kept themselves hidden from my accompanying guards. Then Allan and Roger met me a few nights later at the ˜Trip˜ to tell me of their success, and to say that they would be running with all speed north to meet the others, who would even now be telling those at Loxley of the plan to disrupt the eyre.

For me the only doubt in my mind was whether Robin would go along with this plan. Was he so disturbed in his mind that any challenge to what he saw as his very personal role would cause him to rail against any sort of cooperation? I never doubted that the others would now turn up at the Bolsover court, but I confess to you now, Brother, that since Robin had nearly unmasked me on that knoll only months before, his destructive behaviour towards me was a raw scar which was far from healed, and I feared his presence.

As you will recall from what I said to you, all he had to do was call out my name and I would be marked as a fugitive for life. And you have to acknowledge that that event was still far too recent for me to behave calmly in the face of a threat of a repeat performance. Consequently, I very much feared him turning up, even as at the same time as I devoutly prayed for the others to help me. Moreover, if that sounds *contradictory, it was, but I am being utterly honest with you, my confessor, and I will not tidy things up for the sake of it.*

Therefore we will commence with the arrival of Sheriff Briwere, but I must briefly tell you one more thing before that, for I know if I do not, that you will berate me later for not forewarning you, and it is this: I have never seen such avarice as I saw amongst those men who were sent to dispense justice. Truly brother, their greed and grasping knew no bounds, and the churchmen amongst them were far worse than their lay counterparts. I know you do not wish to hear that, and would rather that your fellow men of God were shining lights of justice, but if I am to tell you the truth in my confession, then I cannot omit or change what I saw and knew to be the truth. But we shall start with Briwere's first appearance, for it will explain much of my subsequent apprehension about the eyres.

Nottinghamshire
Summer, the Year of Our Lord 1194

William Briwere came in through the still shattered gates of Nottingham Castle like some demon belched up from Hell. His horse was all of a lather, and its eyes were rolling in fear as he sawed on the reins to make it halt.

"St Thomas watch over us and save us," Harry intoned from the heart as he stood beside Guy, watching the retinue stream in. "That horse has been cruelly used or I'm no stableman, and that doesn't bode well for us."

"No it doesn't," Guy sighed mournfully. "As soon as I get chance, I'll come down to you and help you brew up a stock of poultices and lotions. I fear greatly that you'll have urgent need of them, and soon, because looking at the rest of those beasts you'll have in your care, too many of Briwere's hangers-on are trying to ingratiate themselves with their master by mimicking his behaviour. That arrogant squire on the grey, for instance. Poor beast looks as though there are sweat sores under that saddle, and he hasn't spared the whip on her either."

"Fucking Normans!" Harry hissed and spat in the dirt. "I'm off to the stables now. I can't paint a smile on my face, and I certainly can't grovel to men like that! I'm best off keeping out of their way."

"I wish I could join you, but somehow I think my absence will be noted – if not right away, then when Briwere gets to know who lives at the castle and thinks back on who he first met."

"Holy Mary, save us!" Harry suddenly gasped as he was turning to go. "What in God's name are *they*?"

Behind the riders and wagons had come a kennelman with a dozen sleek hounds, all bounding along and with happy tails wagging, but in their wake came two servants whom Guy guessed to be the kennelman's assistants, each holding on for grim death to a huge hound. Instead of a leash, the beasts had sturdy wooden poles linked by a very short chain to their collars, which allowed their keepers to remain at a goodly distance and away from their jaws – not that there was much danger just at the moment because they were tightly muzzled.

"Oh you bastard!" Guy seethed under his breath. "How could you do that to wolfhounds?"

"You know what they are?" Harry gasped.

"Oh yes! And a more beautiful animal you couldn't wish to see usually," Guy sighed, feeling his throat tighten in grief at the cruel way these two had been treated. "St Melangell and St Cadoc help me! Harry, I need you to keep that stall free that you use for birthing mares!"

"Sweet Jesu! You're not thinking of bringing those monsters in with my horses, are you? They'll tear them to shreds!"

"No they won't. And that's why I asked for that stall, not the open stable. I need somewhere secure to put those two while I heal them."

Harry patted Guy on the arm. "My friend, you're all heart with your animals, but I don't think even you will get close to them without getting savaged. And if you want them that secure, why don't you put them in the old bread oven?"

The baker's large brick-built oven in the outer bailey had taken a stone from a manganel straight through the top of its domed roof during the siege, and the baker had declared that the only way to ensure that the first time it got fired up it wouldn't collapse and crush the bread was to demolish it and start again. So far, a new oven was up and running since the castle couldn't afford to be without bread, but nobody had had the time to pull the old one down yet.

"Harry, you're a wonder! Actually, the old oven is far better. That way no-one will be able to see what I'm doing with them. So can you get one of your lads to shovel some straw in there now, before they get busy grooming all these horses?"

Harry shook his head resignedly. "For you..." he sighed and hurried away.

Turning back to the performance going on at the head of the procession, Guy saw that Briwere had finally dismounted and was speaking to the three castle knights and Sirs Martin and Walter. Down on the ground Briwere turned out to be quite a short man, and he was having to look up slightly to all five of the knight. No doubt to compensate for this, he had developed an habitual sneer which allowed him to seem as though he was looking down his nose at the world and everyone in it, rather than struggling to look up. A mischievous urge welled up in Guy to go and loom over Briwere, because if he was struggling to look Sir Hugh and Sir Robert in the eye, he was going to find it damned near impossible with Guy, who was half a head taller. However, caution prevailed, and Guy made sure that he stood several feet back from Briwere as Sir Richard turned and made the introduction.

"We're lucky to have Sir Guy working with us in the forest," Sir Martin said with as much firmness as he dared. "He worked as a forester to Sheriff de Braose and is our best tracker by far. He can match the walking foresters in skill and then some."

"Do you have experience with hounds, then?" Briwere demanded, making it sound as though Guy was little better than a kennelman if so.

However, Guy was not going to take that as the insult it was intended to be. "Indeed, my lord, I have a great deal of experience of working dogs both to hunt deer and boar, and to track those who hunt illegally. I see you have a fine pack of hounds. If you wish to hunt then I hope to be able to take you to where they can show off their skills to the best advantage." *There, you cruel bastard*, Guy thought. *Take that how you will, but I'll have the better of you yet!*

Briwere blinked slightly at being foiled in his first attempt to crush Guy, but hardly missed a beat before saying, "Well let's see how good you are at handling those two at the back. You're a big brute yourself, so you should be able to fight them off better than those two pathetic weeds my hound master has helping him. I shall expect you to make sure that they don't savage any of my precious ones."

There was no mistaking the implication. If the wolfhounds got into the main kennel and went on a killing spree, then Guy would be held to blame.

"Oh never fear, my lord," Guy replied smoothly and with an icy smile. "We have just the place for them – the ruined bread oven. They won't get out of there in a hurry. I already have one of the grooms putting some straw in there."

Briewere's responding smile was distinctly sickly. "How very ...prompt of you, Sir Guy."

Guy knew he'd not made the best first impression, but then he suspected that even if he had, that it wouldn't have lasted more than a day with this man. All his instincts said that Briwere was someone very easily prickled and quick to take offence. So there was little to be lost by asking the question he most wanted answering.

"How did you come by them, my lord? You clearly have no love for them, so I would dare to presume that you did not purchase them with the intention of adding them to your hunt?"

Briwere couldn't have looked more affronted if Guy had asked him to take his pick from the local brothel. "Christ on the Cross, no! They were a gift to me from de Lacy, if you must know."

"On the Marches? Sir Walter?" Guy hadn't meant to cross examine, but the memory of his exploit with Prince John to which the then young Walter de Lacy had been witness, sprang up unbidden.

Briwere gave a sniff of disdain, as if associating with a mere Marcher lord was way beneath him. "*Hugh* de Lacy!" he corrected Guy, as if it were blindingly obvious. And it was, Guy realised, not because Lord Hugh was head of the senior branch of the de Lacys, but because who but the second Hugh de Lacy to rule over Meath in Ireland would have sent such hounds?

He'd not been so wildly adrift in his memories, mind you, because it had been the elder Hugh de Lacy to whom Prince John had been going when the escapade on the border had happened that resulted in him being here at Nottingham. No doubt the current Lord of Meath had been given these dogs by some local chieftain, and had passed them on to Briwere, but it wouldn't have been done as quite the compliment he thought it was, if Guy was any judge. He was already mentally imagining the de Lacy lord of Meath's lack of appreciation for the rough-coated hounds, and his regarding of them as being as coarse as his tenants. So him handing them on to Briwere was as good as calling him a peasant within the subtle system of compliments and insults at court.

That Briwere hadn't quite grasped that gave Guy a moment of silent mirth which he would savour later. For now, he merely inclined his head as if standing rebuked, and the conversation flowed onto other matters. As Briwere was brought swiftly up to date on the repairs being done to the castle, it became clear that this was nothing more than a flying visit to establish Briwere's authority as sheriff and bring his household here. He would be gone within two days to return to London, and the eyre would not be coming round until the autumn. For everyone at the castle there was therefore a sense of a stay of execution, even if they would be run ragged in the interim trying to affect the repairs that Briwere wanted done before he came and took up residence. The only bright spot was that he wasn't so irredeemably foolish as to expect the impossible, and he was leaving a hefty purse in the care of Sir Hugh to fund the work.

The first night was excruciatingly tense as all of the knights, and those whose presence was required of the senior servants, gathered in the old hall for the evening meal. Everyone seemed as though they were treading on eggshells around the new sheriff, with no-one knowing quite what to say to make conversation. Luckily Briwere liked the sound of his own voice, and he kept up a running commentary to which everyone else was merely required to nod or make some appropriate sound, whether good or bad.

As they all gratefully fled to the safety of their own shared rooms, Sir Richard tapped Guy on the arm and asked,

"What on earth are you going to do with two savage beasts? He's sodding off and leaving them here, you know! The hounds are one thing, but those two..." and he shuddered.

However, Guy grinned and clapped him on the back. "And I was never so glad as to hear that he's going and leaving them. That gives me hopefully a couple of months to work on them before he terrorises them any more."

Sir Richard looked at him askance. "Him terrorise them? Haven't you got it the wrong way round?"

"No." Guy shook his head sadly. "They could be beautiful dogs given half a chance, and I'm going to give it them."

The others looked at him as if he was mad, but Guy was hopeful.

Hurrying down to the stables while his companions went to their beds, Guy got Harry to bring out the poppy infusion they had kept in amongst the other remedies. Taking a loaf of the dog bread, which the baker had automatically started adding to his bake once he'd been told that there would likely be dogs coming to the castle again, Guy absolutely soaked it in the poppy syrup.

"Won't you kill them with that much?" Harry asked dubiously. "We don't use that much on a wounded horse."

"I need to totally knock them out," Guy explained. "I'll be back just before dawn and then comes the dangerous bit."

Harry sniffed. "I'd say it's all bloody dangerous! Why this bit?"

"Because I've got to take those muzzles off so that they can eat the bread."

"Huh! Rather you than me!"

Several hours later, as the first glimmer of light was appearing on the eastern horizon, Guy clumped down to the stable again, dressed in his thick gambeson and his mail shirt over it.

"Bloody hell, you like you're going to war!" Harry gasped, taking in that Guy even had his mail headgear on and his mail-backed gloves tucked in his belt.

"Oh I'm expecting to get bitten this time," Guy admitted, "so I'm just trying to minimise the damage. And maybe if it hurts their teeth biting me now, they might think twice before doing it again. Now follow me. I need you to slam the door shut behind me, and then on my call throw in the two halves of that loaf, preferably one on either side of the oven so that they don't fight one another in their hunger."

"You think they're that hungry?"

"I think they're starving! I can't imagine those lads taking the muzzles off while they were on the road, so I bet those dogs haven't eaten much in days. They'll barely have been able to lap water."

At the oven, Guy gave Harry a leg up to scramble up the side and hang a lantern from a pole across the hole in the roof. Already there were snarls and growls coming from inside, making Harry ask,

"Are you sure about this? Wouldn't you just rather put them out of their misery with your bow?" but Guy was resolute.

As Harry opened the door a crack he dived in, and then as Harry slammed it shut there was an almighty thump from inside as Guy was hurled back against it by the two hounds. There were thumping and grunts, and then a proper deep bark as the first hound's muzzle came off. His admiration for Guy rose dramatically as he heard Guy's voice calmly saying,

"It's alright ...you're going to fine now ...steady now ...steady. ...No, no! ...Easy, boy ...there you go," all the while accompanied by the sounds of being attacked. "Harry, quick! The bread!" came as he was so mesmerised by the sounds that he jumped in shock, but flipping the latch he tossed one loaf in to his right, and then as Guy dived out at his feet, threw the other in to the left and slammed the door shut again.

When Guy staggered to his feet, Harry was appalled to see that even through the ring-mail the heavy gambeson had been torn from where a hound had grabbed a jaw-full of mail and shirt and yanked hard.

"Did they get you? Are you bleeding?"

"No, but I'm going to have some wonderful bruises in a day or so."

"So what now?"

"Well I'm going to go and get out of this, and then when the poppy has done its trick and they're fast asleep, we're going to go in and see what the damage is."

Harry wasn't so sure he liked the sound of the 'we' bit, especially when Guy pulled the mail coat off and Harry saw the lumps of wool flocking dropping off the gambeson where the one hound had tried to rip Guy's back open while he released the second one's jaws. Yet when Guy opened the door again and let the morning light flood in on the two comatose hounds, he screwed up his courage and went in. What he saw there made him gasp in horror. Guy was trying to undo the enormous thick leather collar around one of the dog's throats, but it was so tight that there was no slack to be able to pull the tongue of the buckle back enough to release it.

"We're going to have to cut it off," Guy sighed. "I feared it would be so. God knows what we'll find underneath. Hold his head for me," and Guy produced his heaviest knife which he'd sharpened to a razor edge. Even so, he had to saw away at the thick leather, and stop to clear the blade of the fur from either side which kept clogging it. He couldn't avoid nicking the dog every now and then, but suddenly the collar parted. Yet if Harry had expected it to drop off, he was horrified to see that it still clung to the hound's skin. With great care, Guy now took a much finer blade and began teasing the collar off. When it was finally clear, Harry was distraught to see a great weeping, festering mess beneath, raw and painful.

"Blessed St Thomas!" he gasped. "Oh the poor beast! No wonder he's been biting everyone."

Guy's eyes were glittering with anger as he said tightly, "That's what happens when the collar's been on so long that the dog grows around it. I feared this was what I'd find. Quick, let's get the poultices on it and get it wrapped up. This needs to be properly cleaned or it'll turn septic."

Together they worked to clear the necrotic tissue away, salve the raw skin, and dress it with some linen gauze before Guy wrapped a cloth around it to prevent the hound from scratching himself. With Harry now as committed to helping the hounds as Guy was, they worked swiftly on the second dog and repeated the bandaging process.

"Jesu!" Guy sighed as he peeled back a furry lip. "Looking at these teeth they're only pups!"

"Pups? How big do they get?"

"Well not much taller, but they should be much heavier. Look!" and Guy parted the matted fur so that Harry could see the dog's side, where every rib showed so prominently that Guy's fingers disappeared into the hollows between the bones.

With both dogs still sleeping soundly, Guy now began shaving off the matted, filthy fur.

"I'm not even going to try to comb this mess out," he explained to the growing audience of Harry's lads who were now watching in awe through the oven doorway. "Can someone get some more straw so that we can clean out what needs removing?" Guy knew his prediction of them being short of food was right going by the small stinking puddles laced with blood littering the straw, but that at least would improve with a better diet.

Two of the lads hurried off and came back with a rake and shovel and some armfuls of fresh straw. Meanwhile, Guy had handed Harry his spare knife and they were working like demons to strip off the stinking mess of hairs while the dogs still slept, throwing handfuls at a time into a heap by the door.

"Someone gather that up and go and throw it on a fire," Guy instructed, and again the grooms eagerly helped.

The next step was some warm water, and with help, the dogs were temporarily lifted out of the oven and sluiced down, before being taken back inside, rubbed with some herb infused lotions, and bedded down on a soft bed. Guy's final act was to prepare some meat and bread and leave it, along with a very large pail of fresh water, in the oven for the dogs when they woke. They would need small but regular meals until their stomachs got used to proper amounts of food again.

"I've never seen such cruelty towards a beast," a young lad called Walter said despairingly as they all headed into the servants' hall to get their breakfast porridge. "Why would someone do such a thing, Sir Guy?"

Guy shrugged. "I have no idea. I find it incomprehensible. But take it as a warning, lads, because what Briwere did to those dogs he'll one day do to a person, and maybe soon."

He gratefully took his breakfast in the companionable atmosphere of the servants' hall, but afterwards forced himself to go back to his rooms, change into something rather less stained and disreputable, and go and present himself in the hall where Briwere was just starting the business of the day. However, to everyone's relief it transpired that Briwere would be leaving the following morning. Already he was grating on everyone's nerves, but in Guy's case he was glad that this dreadful taster of what was to come had only reinforced everything he had said before. Now they would have the chance to put things into place to help themselves against the time when Briwer became a permanent resident, and Guy knew by the way his fellow conspirator knights kept glancing at him that they were now already committed to the covert meetings he had suggested. In that respect, at least, they were going into this better prepared than when the dreadful fitz John had become sheriff.

By the time two weeks had gone past, Guy was able to get in with the two wolfhounds without them trying to shred him, and they had been moved to a newly built kennel between the kennels proper and the stables. And when Guy then had to ride out on his duties, at least two of the lads were able to feed the dogs and change their water in his place without taking their lives in their hands. One dog turned out to be a lovely dark silver-grey once his coat was revealed in its true colours, but the other was a beautiful wheaten cream, which Guy was able to tell the awed grooms and kennel lads was a very prized colour indeed.

"What are you going to call them?" Harry had asked Guy after a couple of days' peace, and when Briwere's kennelman had confessed that he had no idea of their names and he thought neither did the sheriff. "If you're going to train them they'll need to know their own names."

Guy had given it some serious thought, not least because he wanted something which Briwere would find distasteful enough not to use. The last thing he wanted was for the sheriff to look at the dogs once Guy had done all the hard work on them and decide that he did want them after all. If he wouldn't bring himself to call them by name that was another way of keeping a barrier between him and them. That meant no emperor's names or kingly ones for a start, and he had already crossed a few saints' names off too. And so he had asked Tuck and Gilbert's advice when he'd seen them next, and a month on from when the wolfhounds had arrived he was pretty certain that he had the right names.

He didn't want to use anything like the current royal families of Ireland in case anyone started wondering how he would know such a thing, given that he hardly moved in such circles as to have met any of them. However, Gilbert had told him that Máel effectively translated as 'Baldy', and given the grey dog's lack of coat at the moment, that seemed fitting. It was short, too, which was always useful when training a dog. The wheaten coloured dog, though, needed a more distastefully Irish name since he was the one who would draw admiring glances, and Guy decided he would be Domnall.

"That wretched savage we have for a lord has no idea of the value of what he was given," Guy told the grooms bitterly. "In Ireland or Scotland or Wales a lord would pay a fortune for a dog of this quality. But here, just because they're shaggy and not sleek like greyhounds, they're thought coarse and ugly. Bloody fools! Well I'm going to show Briwere what he's thrown away, and he won't get it back easily."

"Steady, Guy," Harry warned. "He won't forgive you if you cross him."

Guy snorted in disgust. "And if he thinks these two will forgive him he's sadly mistaken! We'll have to make some sort of harness I can attach a lead to, because I reckon they'll go for him at every opportunity, and I can't see us ever getting a collar back on them."

Already the hounds had nearly savaged Briwere's kennelman, which confirmed Guy's suspicion that he had beaten the dogs more than once. In his case, though, it was just because he was an ignorant fool, and he certainly looked after the greyhounds well enough not to incur Guy's wrath over that. However the ruin around the wolfhounds' necks had only just stopped weeping, and Guy reckoned it would be several months before the fur grew back, but it might never lie normally with that much scar tissue beneath. What was blindingly clear to everyone was the fact that Máel and Domnall now adored Guy, and by the time the summer ended they had taken to following him around the castle, much to the disconcertion of everyone else.

"God help anyone who decides to try and waylay you when you go into the town," Sir Martin said with feeling one night, as the two hounds lay before the fire in the old hall the foresters used, grinding their way through an ox bone Guy had found for them. "Looking at the way those jaws are working, I wouldn't want to be on the receiving end of a bite!"

"I think you've got your own bodyguard," Sir Mahel declared as he carefully edged around them to get another tankard of beer.

"Well I'm not taking them out into the forest just yet," Guy told them all. "They need a lot more training before I'll risk losing them if they see a deer. They can stay here while we deal with the eyre."

You think I digress in telling you of the dogs, Brother? Oh no, that was no pointless reminiscence. I told you that tale because it shows so clearly what sort of man Briwere was. On the one hand, he was callous and cruel to a level that his predecessors could never have achieved, but on the other, he rarely got his hands dirty. He would never have done as de Wendenal did, for instance, and personally held up someone at sword-point and without back up. The only times I ever saw Briwere with a sword drawn was when he was surrounded by his own men-at-arms who would have skewered his victim long before they had the chance to fight back and do him any harm. And in that, you might say that Briwere was a coward – I certainly came to see him as one – but like many cowards he was very dangerous because he was determined to keep his failing hidden at all costs.

Yes, and you are right in saying that I relished having canine companions again, not least because this time the sheriff could not take them away from me, since officially they were his and not mine. By the time he did come back into the castle, they had filled out nicely, and it was then that I realised that Briwere was frightened of dogs, because gorgeous as the two now were, he would not go near them. Oh, he revelled in having those sleek greyhounds as a status symbol. No lord above a certain rank would want to admit that he lacked such a thing.

But Briwere did not gain real enjoyment from them in the way that someone like the Earl of Huntingdon would have. I never saw the Earl's hounds, but on the few occasions when we met, he spoke of them with great affection and of the pleasure he got in letting them run. Briwere was not like that. Even the greyhounds were only allowed in the great hall when someone important came to visit, but I will tell you this as a small sweetener for you for having listened to this: even the greyhounds did not like their master! They edged around him and would not go anywhere near him any more than he wanted to pet them. They might not be able to speak, but when you know dogs as I do, their behaviour made it blindingly clear. Dogs know when someone is unpredictable and dangerous, Brother.

Therefore, when the sheriff wanted to show off his prize hounds he had no alternative but to let me be the one who brought them in. It galled him mightily, of course, but that was better than having to confess that only his kennelman could handle them aside from me, or with the wolfhounds that he had to have a lowly knight present or they would have torn him limb from limb. To have someone as coarse as a kennelman at table would have been unthinkable, and so Briwere had to swallow his bile and let me bring the hounds in, whereupon I got hear of all manner of things I would otherwise never have known about, and all thanks to the dogs.

Chapter 5

So now we shall move on to that first eyre. If it came later in the year than we expected, I could not say in truth that that made us any the happier. It felt, rather, as though we were like men who desperately needed a rotten tooth taking out – we might dread the event, but we wanted it to be over and done with too, so that the pain would go away. What I will tell you, Gervase, is that your hero is about to reappear, although you may not like what I have to say of him.

Derbyshire
October, the Year of Our Lord 1194

Guy reined in his horse on the outskirts of Bolsover village and watched the grand procession approaching him. He had been here off and on with Sir Richard of Lea ever since they had finished the forest courts in July, desperately trying to scrape together the twelve jurors they needed for the eyre, and a long a wearying task it had been. It hadn't been helped by Guy needing to go across to Blackwell hundred and help Walter le Ragged, the chief walking forester of the area, round up men there too. Yet Blackwell had been easier by far, because Walter had been able to call upon his own brother, Robert, and three of his fellow foresters, Adam Eyre, Oliver Woodrofe and Rad Barley, before they even had to start searching further afield. Whereas this hundred of Scarsdale had been far harder to find men for, and Guy was hoping that Sir Richard had the two most unwilling men safely trapped within the castle bailey and unable to flee.

It had only been after the swanimotes in the middle of September on Holy Rood Day, and then the round of hectic business that always came with Michaelmas Day and the collection of rents, that the message had come that Briwere and his fellow judges were at last on their way, and finally the proceedings could begin. Since then Guy hadn't been back to Nottingham Castle, and all he knew of events was from messages brought with William Albini, Richard Vernon, Hugo Bassett and Oliver de Aincourt as they had come back to Derbyshire to begin the selection process for jurors. Yet going by the way these four seemed relieved beyond measure that Guy and Sir Richard had begun to get things set in motion, Guy got the impression that they had rapidly revised any thoughts they might have had of ingratiating themselves with Briwere – and that had to mean that he was either so capricious as to be untrustworthy, or outright dangerous in their eyes. That, Guy thought, was telling, because if even men like them were treading carefully, then Briwere was without doubt a total menace. Now those four were gone again, quick to get away from Bolsover and on to another hundred before the justices arrived.

Guy turned and looked back at Bolsover Castle. For all of its high status, compared to Nottingham it was a very insignificant castle indeed. The palisade around the bailey was nothing more than huge oak timbers, and even the castle itself was little more than a fortified wooden tower up on a motte. Yet its political significance was substantial because of being at the heart of the Honour of Bolsover, and that, more than anything, was what had drawn the dreaded William Briwere to come in person and sit in judgement here. That, of course, and the need to establish his authority in what he, as an ardent support of the king, would see as a rebellious shire.

It was Briwere's banner which flew at the head of the group of riders wending their way ever closer, but Guy could also see the banner of William de Sainte-Mère-Eglise as a very close second, and then further behind was a second churchman whom Guy knew to be Ralph Foliot, archdeacon of Hereford. Besides his role as the king's justice, Foliot was no doubt here to protect family interests, given that a relative, Robert Foliot, held Wellow Castle, which lay within Sherwood Forest between Edwinstowe and Laxton. Guy had not been pleased to hear of his coming, especially when Tuck had sent word that he knew of him from his own time in the Welsh

Borders as another imperious and avaricious Norman churchman like his uncle Robert, the previous bishop of Hereford, and one who had been known to promote his own family at every opportunity. Foliot would no doubt be making sure that his family's tenants were sent strong warnings against having any rebellious thoughts.

As for William de Sainte-Mère-Eglise, all Guy knew of him was that he was also currently charged with overseeing Jewish affairs in England alongside William of Chimillé, and that he was a canon of Lincoln cathedral. He couldn't spend much time at Lincoln or have any local knowledge, Guy thought, because he seemed to have a finger in every administrative pie at the royal court, as well as being the dean of St Martin le Grand in London. Moreover, there had been further letters sent north from the court at Winchester when Richard had been there, of the king's (and undoubtedly Hubert Walter's) thoughts on the Jews. Because it had been made clear that another aspect of these coming courts would be the official recording of all debts to the Jews under pain of confiscation if deceit were discovered, and if Sainte-Mère-Eglise was controlling that then he was a very powerful man indeed. Clearly the man was ambitious and that made him another dangerous man who would need watching.

"St Issui, please let me get through these next few weeks in one piece and without having my neck stretched above Nottingham's walls," Guy prayed under his breath, then heeled his horse forward to greet the king's men. "Welcome to Bolsover, my lords," he said in English, then belatedly wondered whether he should have spoken in Norman French instead. For one blissful second he hoped that at least one of them would ask him what he'd said, for a justice who needed everything translating for him would be a man much more easily duped. Unfortunately all three had clearly understood him.

"Is this it?" Sainte-Mère-Eglise, asked incredulously in heavily accented English. "Is this the famous castle of Bolsover?"

"I'm afraid so, my lord," Guy responded, feeling his heart sinking even further. Some of the locals were going to have a terrible time understanding what this one said, and the potential for deliberate misunderstanding on Sainte-Mère-Eglise's part would be considerable.

"*Cher Dieu!*" Sainte-Mère-Eglise snorted, "We must stay in this hovel, *eh*?" and he tutted as he urged his horse past Guy's with his haughty nose in the air.

William Briwere, however, was sitting in front of Guy and clearly not intending to move. "And who are you?" he demanded.

Guy resisted the urge to bite back and tell the new sheriff exactly where to put his trials and leave, yet managed to grind out civilly, "I am Sir Guy of Gisborne, my lord, you met me back when you first came to Nottingham. I'm one of your forest knights at Nottingham Castle, but I have some knowledge of this area and so I was asked, with Sir Richard of Lea, to assemble the jurors here ahead of the arrival of your four chosen knights. Hugo Bassett and William Albini were very satisfied with the selections we presented them with."

There, chew on that, Guy thought bitterly. *Your chosen minions have declared they could have done no better, so I hope you don't start picking flies in the choice of jurors. And what sort of man are you, that you can't even be bothered to remember who works for you?* Evidently, he hadn't made that much of an impression on his new master the first time, and that might be a small mercy, although whether that would continue once the sheriff saw his dogs again remained to be seen. Yet oddly there was someone else who did know who he was.

"Oh you're Gisborne, are you?" Ralph Foliot chipped in. "I've heard of you from my family over here." He turned to Briwere. "They say he's a useful man, knows the forest well. Ralph fitz Stephen speaks very highly of him."

The dropping of the name of the hereditary keeper of the old Forest of Nottingham, now within the greater royal forest of Sherwood, seemed to have its effect. Presumably Briwere and the others knew fitz Stephen from back when he had been a leading light in King Henry's court, and therefore his word was accepted where others' wouldn't have been. Thinking back to his helping of the keeper when he'd had terrible back pain, Guy was never as grateful as now for the liniment he used on his dogs – it had eased the keeper's pain, and now, albeit unconsciously, the keeper was returning the favour.

"We have given your lordships the upper rooms in the castle," Guy explained as Briwere allowed him to pass to lead the way. "The rest of us are camped out in the bailey. Since the king took most of the men-at-arms who were here, there's room enough, but I'm afraid some of your retinue may have to join us – the castle isn't that spacious."

In truth it was not that different to Grosmont and Skenfrith which Guy had known and lived in for years over on the Welsh borders, and Guy recalled only too well how Prince John (as he'd been before being made Count of Mortain) had looked down his regal nose at those. So he'd warned Sir Richard that they would need to give every inch of space over to the visiting lords. In another time and place, with different visitors, it would have been perfectly acceptable for everyone to squeeze in together, but Guy wanted these lords to be in the best mood possible for the coming courts. Please God that the nights remained relatively mild for the time they were here, because if the October nights turned frosty, the ordinary men amongst them were in for a miserable time sleeping under canvas, particularly if the process dragged on into November and the closing of the forest limited their ability to get decent fires lit.

Guy had already gone and hunted down plenty of meat for the lords to eat, taking down a couple of hinds who had been trailing behind the herd of fallow deer in the park at Nottingham. Both had looked as though they wouldn't make it through the next winter and their carcasses had been hanging in the undercroft at Bolsover for three weeks now and had tenderised nicely. The first would be sent to the lords' table tonight, and Guy would gauge what their reaction was before telling the terrified cook what to prepare for the following nights. Too many probing questions could be asked where the meat had come from. And so the secret hoard Guy had in reserve would remain there and get shared out amongst the villagers later, for he would not serve up red deer unless he was sure he could get away with it.

The rougher cuts of those deer which could not be so easily identified, like the leg bones, had already gone into the cook's pot to render down and become the base of hearty vegetable stews for the ordinary men, which at least helped spin rations out there. The prime cuts, though, were hanging in sacks high in the branches of a huge old oak, safe from predators and the sheriff's eyes. The wild boars he had brought down he knew he could excuse under the pretext of them causing terrible damage to crops and fences – something boars were notorious for, even if this pair hadn't been guilty of such attacks – so they too were on the castle's menu.

Briwere appeared at the evening meal swathed in a rich velvet robe and bonnet, which to Guy's eye was totally ridiculous for such a humble place. Why Briwere had bothered to lug such a wardrobe of finery with him could only be explained by a desire to overawe and impress, and that did not bode well. The two clerics in contrast wore sombre black robes, but Guy wasn't fooled. Their garments might be plain, but they were made of the finest Lincoln wool and were in *graine* – the insanely expensive dye made from tiny shellfish which had to be brought from the other end of the Mediterranean – and which was the only way to get a proper colourfast black dye, as opposed to the quick-to-fade vegetable dyes most folk used. Wearing Lincoln *graine* was an ostentatious statement of wealth. Anyone who mistakenly thought these men were humble clerics was in for a nasty shock, because to anybody who mattered they were proclaiming their status loud and clear.

"May God preserve us," Sir Richard sighed softly to Guy as they went to take their places on the table below where the three senior men were going to sit to eat. "This is going to be torture."

Luckily, the three were hungry enough to eat the first dishes without too much inspection, but as soon as the venison arrived, Briwere snarled,

"This is venison! Who has dared to poach the king's deer?"

"Blessed St Thomas," Sir Richard groaned from Guy's side and buried his head in his hands as Guy stood up and said as deferentially as he could manage,

"Nobody has been poaching, my lord. These two were from the park beside Nottingham Castle. One broke her leg trying to jump the park fence and the other got tangled with her and went lame. They were brought from there by me specifically to feed this gathering."

"*Hmph!*" Briwere snorted, tearing a lump of meat off and trying it. "Not bad meat. Could do with a decent sauce, though."

"I do find venison rather overrated," Sainte-Mère-Eglise declared. "I much prefer duck or goose myself."

"Has my lord had any of the red deer meat we've sent south in the past for the king's courts?" Guy asked the cleric, as if making polite conversation, but desperate to know if these men could taste the difference as he could. "It has a stronger flavour."

Sainte-Mère-Eglise, wrinkled his upper lip, "Almost certainly, but it did not impress me."

"Oh, I'm rather fond of proper deer," Foliot said with a smirk, making Guy suddenly aware of the competition between these two.

"And when would you have eaten the *king's* deer, Foliot?" Sainte-Mère-Eglise snapped back.

Urgently wanting to prevent these two winding themselves up into the kind of state where they might try to outdo one another over who could deliver the harshest punishment tomorrow, Guy hastily said,

"I'm sure my lord archdeacon has had red deer at William de Braose's table in Herefordshire. When I was huntsman over there, King Henry was gracious enough to allow my lord de Braose to hunt in the royal Forest of Dean there, and of course not all of the forests on the Marches are royal ones for which he would have needed such assent."

The reference to his neighbouring sheriff caught Foliot off balance, while for the other two the name of William de Braose was well enough known not to provoke further questioning.

"Huntsman to de Braose, eh?" Briwere slyly questioned. "So is it really *Sir* Guy of Gisborne? Or are you barely a knight at all?"

"Oh I am the son of a knight," Guy confirmed coldly, but doing his best not to show anything that would give Briwere further desire to bait him. "My father served the de Hodenet family until the Welsh made our position untenable. I took the job of huntsman to de Braose because I needed to provide for myself, but my own knighting came directly from King Henry himself."

That made Briwere open his eyes. "King Henry? How very ...singular!"

He was fishing for details that much was obvious, but Guy decided he'd given him enough of those for one evening.

"It was a personal matter, my lord, and one I am not at liberty to discuss."

"Oh come now," Briwere snorted, "the old king's long dead and we're all men of the court – it's not as if you're revealing secrets to servants!"

Guy glanced down the table and saw how the men-at-arms who had ridden in with the justices were doing their best not to look their way, but were hanging on every word. Briwere was either a fool or believed he had these men very cowed if he could be so tactless.

"King Henry may be dead," Guy replied carefully, "but the matter concerned one of his sons who is most definitely still alive, and I'm sure *he* would not appreciate his actions being held up for scrutiny by the likes of us."

There, he thought, *ponder on that! You don't know if I mean Richard or John, and neither is a man you want to antagonise, especially after what's just gone on at Nottingham.*

Mercifully, his words had their intended effect. Briwere closed his mouth with a snap but spent the rest of the evening giving Guy very strange looks, as if trying to work out just how closely attached to the king or his brother he might be. Foliot had a sneaky look about him, and Guy reckoned he had heard rumours if not details of how years ago Prince John had had to be rescued from his ill-fated hunt in the Marches. Clearly, the archdeacon was saving that knowledge up for a time when it would serve him, though, rather than throwing it away to score a minor point over Briwere and Sainte-Mère-Eglise now. And that other cleric was regarding Guy curiously too, but Guy had had very little to do with Lincoln in general let alone the canons, and so he was enough of an unknown quantity for Sainte-Mère-Eglise to be treating him with caution now that the royal household had been mentioned in such an ambiguous manner. Should Guy unexpectedly turn out to have the royal ear, clearly Sainte-Mère-Eglise did not want to shit his nest.

Late that night, however, Guy and Sir Richard went for a stroll beyond the bailey to confer.

"Dear God," Sir Richard sighed, "it's even worse than I expected! Those three all know one another and yet are all trying to find ways to outdo one another. They're like overgrown and spiteful children! By Our Lady, but I wish at least two of their chosen knights were here to deal with them instead of us, but then this is probably precisely why they aren't."

Guy put a consoling hand on Sir Richard's shoulder. "And as long as you keep that in mind but defer to them at every turn, with any luck we'll come out of this in one piece. Sadly, I doubt the same will be said for the poor unfortunates who come before them in the coming days. I was hoping to speak up for a few of them, but I see now that I'll have to be most circumspect if I do, or not speak at all."

"If it's your skin or theirs you have precious little choice," Sir Richard sympathised. "May the Lord watch over us, because this new sheriff seems like the Devil incarnate."

When the court convened in the main hall of the castle the following morning, Guy was relieved to see that word had already gone round that maybe this wasn't the spectacle to come and watch after all. The ordinary people who might normally have crowded into the back of the hall out of nothing more than curiosity were thankfully missing, and only those who had no other choice were present. What was even better in Guy's eyes was that the first cases which would be heard today were all of men for whom there was little doubt that they were guilty, and of serious crimes at that. Derbyshire was hardly a hotbed of murder and mayhem – except for when the king came calling – but it had been so long since an eyre had come that the backlog of cases was substantial, and amongst them were several murderers.

The first man dragged in by the soldiers from what passed for a dungeon at Bolsover, had been caught in the act of plunging his knife repeatedly into his wife. That he had been experimenting with trying to make his cider even stronger that winter by letting it freeze so that the water could be removed leaving only potent liquor behind did much to explain, but not excuse, his behaviour. And the balance of his mind had clearly been permanently disturbed, because throughout he mumbled and occasionally ranted, oblivious of where he was.

Nor were the others much better. One was a notorious cutpurse who had gone one step too far when his merchant victim had fought back, and he had bludgeoned the poor man, leaving him to die beside the roadside. The two clerics' outrage at leaving a man to die unshriven was something Guy was wholly in sympathy with, and so when he was called upon as the leading man of the jury to testify as to the state of the road and the chances of the victim having been found in time to save him, he had no qualms about asking for the man to be hung. It meant that two of the three judges at least saw him as a man after their own hearts. Had they known Guy's other feelings, which were that men like that only made life all the more dangerous for his outlaw friends when they drew manhunts into the forest, they might not have been so impressed.

By the end of the day, eight men were to swing and the three judges were feeling satisfied and appeased.

"A good day's work!" Briwere chortled as he led them off to their rooms so that the courtly set up could be rearranged to allow those staying at the castle to sit at tables while they ate that night.

Once he was sure they had gone beyond hearing him, Sir Richard exhaled with relief and led Guy out to enjoy a welcome breath of late autumn sunshine and some much-needed fresh air.

"Well that could have been worse," he said softly to Guy, as they stood on the shooting platform of the bailey palisade, looking out over the countryside beneath the steep escarpment.

Guy nodded thoughtfully but cautioned him, "We can but hope that that's set them in a decent mood for the rest of this week. As time goes on we'll be finding it harder and harder to moderate them, you know. Not everyone will be so deserving of their fates as that lot, and we're going to have to work hard at getting sentences down to a flogging or a week in the stocks. I think we need to have a word with the clerks they brought with them. We need to intersperse the poor – who they can do with as they like – with the merchants and their sons whom they can merely fine. They mustn't get carried away with handling out bloody punishment after bloody punishment.

"The fines handed out will no doubt be crippling, but there's someone who will help them out with those." He didn't say 'Robin Hood' aloud, but Sir Richard knew whom he meant. "But he can't revive the dead or give a man back his hand, or even help a family if their man is crippled under the lash and can't work the fields anymore."

Guy had been saving up the wild boars' meat for the third evening of the trials, and by the time they got there he was glad he could offer the three some good bloody meat to assuage their blood lust. Twice he and Sir Richard had had to approach them at their bench and remind them that they were about to exceed the legal limit of punishment for the crime in question, which were known and well established from King Henry's days, and from handing them out to men who were not without influence.

"My lord, the lad's father is a wealthy wool merchant with a brother in London in the same trade," Guy had to mutter to them, as they were about to order a young poacher's death. "I know he's a repeat offender against the forest laws, and this time he went too far in killing the abbot's horse by mistake – which is why we're trying him here and not in the forest eyre – but if you make him swing, you may find your standing amongst the London merchants severely damaged."

"Merchants are not above the king's law," Briwere sneered.

"No my lord, they're not," Guy agreed, "but King Richard wants his money, does he not? And that will get all the harder to claim if these men manage to take their wool out of England before they sell it. There's a lot of coast between here and London where small boats may put in, and it's not such a long trip over to Ghent or Bruges. This year's fleeces may have been sold, but it's not so many months now until they'll be shearing again in the spring, and the death of a son or nephew will take longer than that to get over."

"He has a point," Ralph Foliot admitted soothingly. "Let us fine him the maximum and order his father to hand over six sacks of his best clippings next spring."

"Oh very well," Briwere tutted, rolling his eyes in disgust, "the fine and the wool." But it was as Guy was stepping back to his place that he heard Foliot hiss in French,

"Yes, Briwere, I know! The clippings are no good to the king! But Christ have mercy, man, wake up! We may take two of those sacks each to be woven into whatever finery you wish and at no cost to ourselves. We're due something for enduring this misery of trials, surely? From what I have heard of this shire and its twin, you may be glad to get your next robes for free, because you'll be sending every penny you have to Winchester to keep the king off your back."

Briwere audibly snorted, replying back in French under the misconception that no-one would understand him when he said,

"Oh I don't think so, archdeacon! I intend to rule these shires with a rod of iron. They won't get the better of me the way they did with that fool de Wendenal. I'll soon sort them, you just watch!"

That was news Guy desperately wanted to share with his friends, and so as soon as he had again placated Briwere with a gruesome tale of gored villagers and ruined crops to account for the roast boar, he ate swiftly and left the hall under the pretext of trying to arrange to hunt some duck to appease Sainte-Mère-Eglise. With that in mind he rode out quite brazenly into the dusk, armed with his hunting bow, proclaiming that he might get lucky as the birds came to roost for the night.

He hadn't gone far when he heard a whistle off to the side, and turning down a track under the eaves of some wide-branching old oaks, he was greeted by the sight of his friends melting out of the shadows. Dismounting he let himself be hugged by John and Alan, then saw that Robin was with them.

"Cousin," he said calmly, although his heart sank. Robin had better not make this any worse than it was going to get.

"How is it?" Tuck's familiar Welsh voice came from behind him, followed by a friendly pat on the back which nonetheless came close to winding him with its force.

"Bloody awful," Guy told them morosely, and proceeded to tell them about the courts. "But don't worry about the first eight they're going to bring out to hang on Saturday," he said firmly. "Five have killed family in cold blood, one of the others is a cold killer who I'm not sure is even remotely sane, and the other two are without conscience or remorse."

He looked Robin straight in the eye. "I know eight men seems like a lot, but hold onto the thought that if the eyre had come as it ought to have done, it would barely be one man a year. It's the king's fault that they're all coming to trial at one go. None of them are any loss to their friends or families."

"Remember what we agreed, Robin?" Malik's calm voice reminded him. "Until we know what evil this new sheriff might bring down on the villages, we are just here to disrupt."

Guy was quick to seize on that. "Once those three bloody awful judges have gone, I have no problem with you releasing men from the stocks, giving villagers the money to pay the damned fines with, or anything else you feel needs to be done. All I'm asking is for you to not do it under their noses *this time*."

"Don't worry, Guy, we know what's at stake, we'll stick to the plan," Hugh reassured him, and Guy was pleased to hear Tuck saying softly to Robin,

"Remember what we talked about? Of what Guy risks for us all, and that it's not just about you two?"

Guy was less convinced, though, by Robin's response of, "Yes, my pride and my immortal soul, Tuck. Yes I know." It sounded worryingly like the child he had known when he'd been told to do something he didn't want to, and was only going through the motions because he had no other choice.

He was therefore more than pleasantly surprised when Saturday came around, the court did not sit and the first men were brought out into the bailey to be hung, and nothing happened. Maybe the others had finally got through to Robin?

Sunday was a day of rest in which Guy had enlisted the Coshams help in hunting some wild fowl for the judges' table, and the court would not sit again until late on Monday morning. It gave Guy a reprieve from the pressure he'd felt building, and he enjoyed the day out with his three friends who were joined by Malik. They were hunting on their own behalf as well, but it was a convivial day and Guy went back with his horse draped with feathered bodies, which also pleased the castle cook. The poor man had been wearing an increasingly harried expression as he fretted over what he would offer two senior clerics for a suitable Sunday feast, terrified that he might break some edict he knew nothing of concerning what foods were suitable. The fishponds had provided trout for Friday, and Saturday had been a stew of all the leftovers, making Guy's replenishment with something easily cooked anew a source of great relief to him, even though there was still a deer and a boar left to cook.

Guy was even able to enjoy the meal himself, because now he knew that the planned disruption would be coming early on Tuesday. He had managed to convince his friends that late on Monday would not be such a good time.

"Too many innocent people in the hall by then," he'd explained. "Everyone we've called forward as witnesses will have been forced to linger and the hall will be crammed with folk. If the fire arrows catch a bit too well then we could end up with someone dying, if only from the smoke, and that's not what any of us want."

Therefore he got through Monday, glad that the novelty of so many juicy cases had worn off with the judges and that they were now trying to get through the remainder as fast as possible, even if what they were handing out was hardly justice. Tuesday dawned bright and fair but with the threat of a good storm later, going by the clouds building up away in the south-west and the heaviness in the air. That suited Guy, and he offered up thanks to all the Welsh saints he normally prayed to. Just in case the castle caught light more than expected, a good deluge could save the day nicely.

Therefore Briwere was just announcing, "Forty lashes and a fine," to a frantic miller accused of repeatedly doctoring his milled wheat with chalk and other unsavoury ingredients, and then selling what he had skimmed off to fill his own purse instead of that of the monks of Dale Abbey from whose monastic grange it had come, when the first arrow appeared. Arcing gracefully through a high and narrow lancet window, it came like some fiery vengeance from above and landed on the rushes. It was the shot of a master archer at the peak of his craft, as even getting an arrow through the tight space was far beyond anything an ordinary soldier could have done.

"What in God's name?" Briwere spluttered in shock as the fresh rushes brought in only yesterday caught light.

Before anyone could do or say anything more, two more fire-arrows came in through the other lancet windows and joined their mate smouldering in increasingly large billows of smoke.

"Everyone out!" Guy bellowed. "Quickly, while we can all still breathe! Out!"

The ordinary folk needed no encouragement and neither did the common soldiers, especially as three more arrows followed. They had come expecting a boring time and were unprepared for a fight even if there had been something to fight. These swirling billows of thick smoke were quite beyond them. How could they fight those?

"Someone throw water on those bloody things before they really catch light!" Guy was yelling, but even as he dashed forward and began stamping on the sparks at the edge of the smoky mass, the great door of the hall being flung open by the panicked crowd to the gusting breeze coming in advance of the storm did its worst.

Suddenly the sparks were being fanned, and to Guy's horror what should have been mere smoke began glowing a dull red as the tinder-dry rushes caught easily.

"Get a chain with buckets going!" he ordered, but he and Sir Richard found themselves pushing and shoving the dazed soldiers into a line and everyone acting far too slowly. Now Guy didn't have to act the part, he was genuinely trying to save the castle.

To his amazement, he heard Briwere screeching to his servants, "Get my robes from up there! If they get as much as a singeing I'll have all of you flogged, do you hear me? Flogged!"

Were robes really that valuable that they were worth a servant's life?

Then he was treated to the sight of the two clerics scurrying past him, gowns hoisted up to reveal scrawny white ankles, and their arms also filled with their prized robes. It would have been hilarious had he not been so desperate to stop the fire getting a proper hold. Only when they had doused and stamped out every spark, and shovelled up the affected rushes into buckets and dumped them outside, did Guy realise how well done the attack had been. His friends must have calculated very carefully how much fuel they had attached to the arrows, because there had been just the right quantity to get a smoky fire going once the air hit it, but not sufficient to burn hot enough and long enough to start a truly bad fire.

"Who would dare to do such a thing?" Briwere screamed across the bailey to everyone in general as he realised that the fire was out and his precious robes were safe. "Who *dares*?"

"Robin Hood dares, sheriff!" a voice called from the palisade platform, carrying above the heads of the subdued and frightened crowd.

Guy turned with the rest of those congregated outside, and saw a figure clad in the familiar green hood and jerkin he had been shown in the outlaw camp. But who was under it? Hugh or Siward? And if them, why? What would they hope to achieve by exposing themselves to danger? Or, God forbid, was it even Robin? That could mean things were about to plummet into mayhem any moment.

"Shoot him!" Briwere was screaming, almost apoplectic with rage, and belatedly a few of the men-at-arms he'd brought with him began frantically winding their crossbows.

Knowing he had to appear to do something, Guy ran to the stables and grabbed his hunting bow from his saddle. While the first crossbow bolts rattled ineffectively off the oak trunks of the palisade, yards away from their target, Guy pulled back and took careful aim. He had no intention of hitting whoever that was, but he had to make a shot. Loosing the arrow he was pleased to see it embed itself in the planking at the figure's feet.

"Who was that? Who nearly got him?" cheered Sainte-Mère-Eglise, and was amazed to find some of the soldiers pointing at

Guy, who was already taking aim for a second time. "Kill him!" screamed Sainte-Mère-Eglise, and Guy let fly.

The second arrow this time embedded itself right in the parapet beside the figure, and Guy was beyond relieved to see it turn and leap over the edge away from them. Undoubtedly whoever it was had a sound grasp on a rope, given the nearly sheer cliff beneath that stretch of walls, but the effect from inside the castle was dramatic. Robin Hood just vanished.

Leading the race for the walls, Guy got there in time to lean over and see five figures in green disappearing into the undergrowth of the woods below the escarpment, and found a rope tied around a pair of the great timbers. Now making a show as much for the benefit of the sheriff below as anyone, Guy shot two more arrows in quick succession, then made a great show of throwing his bow onto the platform in disgust at having missed.

Back down within the bailey he let his frustration at the act of defiance show, knowing that it would be completely misread by Briwere and the others. Foliot commiserated with him, saying,

"Well at least you nearly got him," while Briwere marched up and down the line of his hapless escort, batting at them with his smoke-blackened velvet bonnet as he shrieked,

"Useless, lack-witted, toad's spawn! Incompetent cur's whelps! Men-at-arms? I've seen turds with more spine than you! You couldn't hit a barn door from ten paces with flung *shit!*"

He turned and spied Guy. "Gisborne! Since against the odds you seem to be the only real man here, I'm putting you in charge of this bunch of goat-fucking worm-brains, and when we get to Nottingham, I want you to do whatever you deem necessary to turn them into something I wouldn't be embarrassed to lead a saint's day's parade at the front of. I won't say battle yet, because Christ and all his saints would be hard pressed to work that much of a miracle any time this side of Christmas, but I *will not* be embarrassed by you pitiful excuses for soldiers again, do you understand me, you sons of rat-bait whores?"

The men were all looking pale and shuffling uncomfortably, giving Guy darting glance of little short of pure terror, and immediately Guy saw the problem. They were all so damned scared of doing the wrong thing for this volatile sheriff that they ended up doing nothing, or doing it badly in their fear. This could either be a gift from God for him, or his worst nightmare – and the nightmare would actually be that he came to like these men and had his loyalties torn between them and his friends, because he was under no illusions that he would ever be able to trust them with his secret as he had his old soldier friends who had recently left the castle.

Oh it was a problem all right, Brother, but you want to hear about Robin, I can see, and that was uppermost in my mind at that point as well. So you should know that since the trial had to be postponed for a day while the servants scrubbed the soot from the hall and made it presentable for our judges again, I was able to ride out under the pretext of tracking where this outlaw had gone to. I was able to avoid taking the men-at-arms with me by bluntly stating that they would do nothing but get in the way, and being believed. Briwere's opinion of them could hardly have got any lower at that point, and so I rode out alone looking armed and dangerous.

It took no great skill on my part to head off into the right direction, given that I had seen my friends escaping, but as soon as I was out of sight of the castle, I clapped my heels to my horse's sides and took her as fast as I dared after them, for I hoped that they were already a goodly way away. If they were lingering, I dreaded why that might be. Unfortunately, I was to catch up with them much sooner than I had hoped, and when I did so what they told me did not sit easily with me.

˜What we you thinking?˜ I demanded as soon as I saw them. ˜You nearly had me dying of shock seeing Robin up there! Who was it? Which one of you?˜

It turned out it was Siward who had appeared on the walls, but only because it was the only way to stop Robin from doing it himself. Apparently Robin felt that it was important that ˜Robin Hood˜ should make himself known to this new sheriff, and had convinced the others of the rightness of that. Truly, Brother, I did not know whether to weep or scream at that point, for as I pointed out to them, they had put me in the terrible position of having to act the true forester knight, and that had never been in the original plan.

My two cousins looked aghast, as did everyone except Robin, whom I was no longer thinking of as being the same person as my once dearly loved cousin Baldwin, and therein I saw the problem. When he was filled with that bright desire to do good, Robin was utterly convincing as you stood before him. It was only when you got away from him and thought back over what he had said that you saw the flaws and the gaping holes in his reasoning. And of course that was why I was always seeing what the others did not, because I constantly had that distance.

Now Siward apologised to me, and said that he had decided to take the role of Robin Hood, because it required someone fit enough to slide down the rope from the wall, and Robin was nowhere near well enough yet to do that. He said that the intention was only ever to issue the challenge and escape, but admitted that the strength of the response had come as a bit of a shock, even though he had spotted straightaway that it was only me who was shooting arrows close enough that they might harm him. But what chilled me to the bone as we talked, was Robin turning away from me with a sniff of disgust and saying to Tuck,

˜And who has the pride now, Brother? I who stepped aside so that Siward might act as Robin Hood, or my cousin who demands that we consider him above all others, even men condemned to die?˜

Chapter 6

Truly, Brother, I was so shocked at Robin's statement that I was unable to answer. Was that really how he saw me? As this man with such an overweening sense of his own importance as to put himself above all others?

Yet I think Robin's reaction shocked several of the others too, especially Siward, and you should take notice of this, Gervase, because that was the last time that Siward would be so taken in by Robin. He had dragged him halfway across England to save him, and I know because he told me so, that he had believed that after all of Tuck's ministrations that Robin had turned a corner. He honestly thought that all of Tuck's praying and talking had made a difference to how Robin saw the world around him, and that this request for Robin Hood to appear was being done in the right spirit. And so Siward had gone to the ramparts by taking the dangerous step of entering the bailey amongst the crowd of ordinary people coming for the court, his forest green covered by a dirty old cloak, and Allan had gone with him but separately, carrying the rope.

However both had been of clear intent that this would be nothing more than the briefest of shows, a display to simply prod the new sheriff. What they both said to me later was that afterwards, they came to see the whole incident in a very different light. Robin had been chipping away at them all ever since the idea had been mooted, and yet his suggestions were such that it was never blatantly obvious that he was aching to step back into the role of the hero. Tuck only had to sigh or look his way, I was told, for Robin to hold up his hands and say that it did not have to be him that did this thing, and because my friends were good people, they believed him. But once Tuck had said most firmly that Robin was simply not well enough to make such a climb, I am sure in my own mind that he had decided that he would use this episode against me. If the others had not foreseen that I might have to shoot at Siward, he most certainly had, and to this day I am not sure whether he thought me so treacherous that I would actually aim to hit him believing it to be himself, and not Siward, under that hood.

Why did he still insist on doing it, you ask? I fear, Gervase, that in his warped mind he felt he would win whatever happened. You see if I had hit this ˜Robin Hood˜, then Robin could have smeared my name to the others as being so against my own cousin that I would try to kill him; maybe in his head reasoned as some kind of revenge upon him for nearly getting me killed, if he even acknowledged that he had done so. Or he may simply have seen it as spite on my part, with himself as the wholly innocent party.

On the other hand, he knew that if I did not hit ˜Robin Hood˜, then I would come after them to find out why they had not stuck to the plan, and then he could say exactly what he did to make me look bad. And that comment, Brother, was off too pat, too well thought out, for it to have been a spur of the moment thing, given how disjointed his conversations were generally at that time. He wanted to put himself in the right by making me look bad.

I am sorry if that offends you. I know that in your eyes Robin should remain the pure and righteous hero, but no man is <u>that</u> good, Brother, and my cousin was rapidly losing his mind. Yet we have a way to go before you need worry about him not appearing in this story, and what is more we are not done with that first eyre yet, for Robin would do something else which even I had to admit put him back in my good graces, albeit far more temporarily than with the others.

Derbyshire
October, the Year of Our Lord 1194

With the cases at Bolsover moving to the more mundane, Guy didn't know whether to be relieved or worried when the three judges said that they would be splitting up. The court at Bolsover had already dragged on for far longer than Guy had ever expected. Those men who had most offended King Richard were the wealthier men of the shire towns whose lands, such as they were, were primarily in Morleystone and the neighbouring Litchurch hundreds. For those men, the three judges would again join forces, although Guy suspected it was so that Briwere could not be accused of being partisan, rather than there being any need for three such men to debate the cases. Yet that still left Wirksworth, Appletree and Walecross hundreds' courts to be dealt with, as well as Blackwell up in the Peaks; and what was nerve-wracking in the extreme was the discovery that with one hundred and forty-three legal questions needing to be answered at every eyre, it was going to take so long that there would be a break for Christmas and then continue in January.

"What in Jesu's name do they need to ask all of those for?" Sir Richard had asked Guy in despair when he heard the news. "Is the king so worried he might miss a few pence?"

The four knights sent with the archbishop's authority to get the courts under way, Sirs William Albini, Richard Vernon, Hugo Bassett and Oliver de Aincourt, had already split up and were ahead of the justices, rounding up jurors as if their very lives depended on it – which with King Richard was an understandable belief to have. And so while Briwere now left to sort out the smaller and less populated Walecross hundred's cases, and then deal with the minor ones close to Derby, Foliot would ride with an escort led by Sir Richard to Appletree, while Guy took Sainte-Mère-Eglise up to Blackwell to hear the cases at Tideswell. That at least was something of a relief in Guy's eyes, because if Robin was fixed on the sheriff then he would be a long way away from himself, and whatever Robin did would fall on his own head. There would be no implicating Guy if it went wrong.

"I do not wish this to take months!" Sainte-Mère-Eglise declared forcefully to Guy as they set out. "I have important business to attend to back in London by the winter, and I must go to Lincoln before then. I want these courts dealt with swiftly, so I hope you have competent jurors waiting for me?"

Blessing Walter le Ragged for his foresight in using his foresters for the north and west of the hundred, and for finding some suitably senior merchants from Bakewell and other towns in the southern part of the hundred, Guy was able to reassure Sainte-Mère-Eglise that they had. And with any luck they would be sufficiently eager to get back to their own businesses that they would give concise information and not ramble on. Minor knights could be a pain in the neck, he knew from past experience in the verderers' courts, especially if they had no other office but their own manors to attend to. Courts could make men like that puff up with their newfound importance and have them wittering on for hours, and this time Guy was desperate for that not to happen. The sooner they got rid of Sainte-Mère-Eglise the better.

Yet disastrously, once at Tideswell where Hugo Bassett was already waiting for them, Sainte-Mère-Eglise took one look at the lodgings available to him and declined to stay in any of them.

"Pig sties, all of them!" he declared.

"Unfortunately, my lord this is all there is around here," Guy said in what he hoped was a soothing tone, and not the irritation he felt. What had this grand man of the church expected of rural England? Tideswell wasn't Lincoln, much less London, and even in Lincoln stone-built houses were few and far between. Those men of influence who lived round here were out at their manors, not here in the village, and the manors round here weren't exactly great either.

"Then we shall move the court," Sainte-Mère-Eglise snapped. "But I will not live in this ...this hovel ...while we go through days of complaints and counter suing. There has to be somewhere more suited to my station in this desolate corner of nowhere."

Hugo and Walter looked at Guy, and all of them knew with sinking hearts that the only place they could take him was High Peak Castle. Hugo was anxious because of the aggravation of packing everyone up and moving them up to the castle, but for Guy this move was like a knife to the heart. To go back to the castle he loved was bad enough, but he didn't know what he was going to do if anyone greeted him with what Sainte-Mère-Eglise would see as improper familiarity.

"I knew seeing sun-dogs back in June was a bad omen," Bassett muttered darkly, as Sainte-Mère-Eglise turned his back on them and stood there waiting for something to happen. The phenomenon where mirror images of the sun appeared on either side of it had been widely seen back at the time of the St Edmund's Day swanimote, and people had seen it as a warning of more bad times to come, but Guy wouldn't have expected someone of Sir Hugo's standing to believe in such things. But then these last few months had had everyone jumping at shadows, let alone three 'suns' in the sky.

"Can you get things packed up and bring him with you?" Guy pleaded. "I really need to ride ahead and get the castle prepared. We can't just turn up for something like this unannounced."

Bassett looked balefully at Guy, but knew that he'd had it easy so far compared to Guy. He was also shrewd enough to realise that he and Guy would need to work together to get through this, and being the one to ride off now would do nothing to endear him to Guy.

"I served for a short while as constable of High Peak," Guy reminded him. "I'll be able to get the people up there moving far quicker than you might. Sir Richard, the current constable, is away attending to the eyre closer to his manor, so a message to him won't help us."

That sealed it for Bassett and he waved Guy towards his horse. "Go! Go get the place ready for this querulous churchman. He'll have to put up with what we have for tonight, but it's not a long ride so I'll have him with you by tomorrow evening – you'd best work fast!"

Guy needed no further encouragement, vaulting onto his horse and heading off at a brisk canter before Sainte-Mère-Eglise had even realised he was going.

He arrived at High Peak long after nightfall and gaining access to the castle was his first challenge. The few guards left there point blank refused to open the gates to a stranger after nightfall, and Guy found himself riding back the short way into Castleton and the inn. There, at least, they greeted him like the returning prodigal son, which soothed his frayed and harassed soul somewhat. Between the sheriff and his cousin, it was good to come to somewhere without complications where folk appreciated his efforts.

Earnwine the beremaster appeared out of the night, having been summoned from his cottage, and Guy outlined to the leading miner what was about to descend on them.

"Ralph Murdac was hard but fair," Guy reminded him, recalling the time when the sheriff he had first served over here in the Midlands had come collecting the Saladin Tithe. "And de Wendenal was a brute but as thick as two planks. This sheriff is cunning and sly, and he's been at the job long enough to have a shrewd eye for anything he might be able to cream off for his own benefit. May St Michael and all the angels protect us in these coming weeks, because although Sheriff Briwere isn't coming himself this time, he seems to have some kind of pact with his fellow judges where he splits the profits from this eyre with them. So this cursed churchman will be looking for anything he can add to the fines or punishments which will line his and Briwere's purses."

Earnwine gave a grunt of disgust. "I hear you, Sir Guy. We're back to making everything look that bit shabbier than it is – not that we ever really stopped, but at least once de Wendenal became sheriff he wasn't around here that much, and Sir Richard is a good man who doesn't ask too many awkward questions of us." Then he gave a grin. "But thanks to you we have a goodly store of lead ore hidden away up in an old worked out mine nowadays. Not a full year's quota by any means, of course, but enough that we can pay whatever fines and extra taxes come our way and still afford to eat."

Guy's heart warmed at that. It felt good to know that he'd done some real good in his short tenure as constable of High Peak. Yet he then saddened at the linked memory of what it had been like when he'd first been reunited with Robin and met the others up here. It was only five years ago, and yet somehow it felt like a lifetime when so much had changed since then.

Forcing himself to focus on the present, he asked, "Is there anyone up at the castle who knows me from my time there? Anyone who might give the game away that I'm not wholly who the sheriff thinks I am?"

"No, you're safe there," Earnwine reassured him. "De Wendenal brought his own folk in, as you know. Then when Sir Richard of Lea took over, he just kept those folk on, and so did the other Sir Richard for the short time he was here while it was all chaos. If they have kindly thought towards anyone it's him, not you."

Guy sighed. "Poor Sir Richard of Lea is escorting Archdeacon Foliot to another court, for his pains, although I'm glad it's turned out that he's not come back here – God knows who Briwere will put in as the man on the spot here now it's under his control, since he can hardly do it himself and be sheriff. But at least that saves us from one potential disaster. And mercifully Sir Hugo Bassett will be coming with all the jurors who thought they would be giving evidence at Tideswell, so you won't have to round up anyone from here to serve.

"If I were you, I'd get all of the men you can out of the way and into the farthest mine you have to work, and get the women and children out foraging in the woods. I can say you are legitimately gathering in what nuts, hips and berries you can now, before the forest gets closed to you in a week or so. I doubt we'll have finished the court by then, but if this damned cleric wants to go back to London or Winchester for the Christmas court, and go via Lincoln on the way, I doubt he'll leave it much beyond a week after we close the forest to ride away. What we'll do when he comes back after all the celebrations, I don't know. But by then the days will be so short and dark, he'll hopefully not be able to see anything which might excite his curiosity."

In the morning, Earnwine escorted Guy up to the castle gates, and once the guards realised who it was he was welcomed in. The reason for their caution turned out to be because there were only half a dozen guards left in the place, the rest having long gone. What was worse from Guy's point of view was that there was only the same number of servants. Sir Richard had always lived simply, but it seemed that one of the families de Wendenal had brought to the place to serve him had up and run when they'd heard of his death. Maybe they had been left to spy on Sir Richard and his successor, and feared retribution now their paymaster was gone; but Guy was less worried about that than by the more mundane aspect that a couple, and their two daughters old enough to work, had suddenly vanished from the castle's staff.

"Earnwine, for the love of God, can you get some of the women from the village to come up and sweep the place out just for today?" Guy pleaded. "Those here will simply have to cope the best they can once everyone arrives, but at least if the place smells and looks clean, bloody Sainte-Mère-Eglise shouldn't complain too hard."

By the time a harassed Hugo Bassett led the procession up the long slope to the castle's stables in the lowering sun of the late afternoon, the main hall had been swept, mopped and fresh rushes laid. The one good bed had had its mattress dragged close to a goodly fire and had been aired as best it could, along with its blankets; and the braziers Guy had had set about the place had warmed it up to a reasonable level. He knew he'd been rather extravagant with the stock of logs, and had told the local men to get out and gather a replacement stock as fast as possible, starting on the next day, so that it would be gathered in before the Winter Haining began on the eleventh. However, the reminder that he himself would be needed for the final swanimote of the year the day before then, gave Guy some hope of cutting the eyre short.

"I fear I shall have to leave you, my lords," he told Bassett and Sainte-Mère-Eglise at dinner that night. "I must be at the forest courts on the tenth, so I will not be able to act as leading juror for you with Walter le Ragged. And of course, he and three of the jurors will also have to do their regular jobs at those courts too."

The head forester of the area had not reached the castle that night, but was following on with those who would have to walk or be transported in the farm wagon Walter had commandeered to help.

Sainte-Mère-Eglise swore vigorously in French, then gave the sigh of a man who felt he was suffering greatly. "So that means I must come once more to this wretched part of the country, I suppose. *Merde*! I had hoped to fulfil my duties and be done with it before leaving."

"I'm sorry," Guy apologised, but with little sincerity, "but it cannot be helped, my lord. The king took so many nobles with him this time that we have struggled to find suitable men to serve the eyre. We are all doing more than one job." *There, you villainous crow!* Guy thought. *Think you're the only one suffering, do you?* Then added for good measure, "And the forest courts do bring in regular revenue for the king, so they cannot be disregarded."

At the mention of the king's name, Sainte-Mère-Eglise's mouth turned down in a sickly smile.

Yes, you're caught in the same trap as the rest of us, Guy thought gleefully. *You daren't antagonise him, dare you? I wonder how much you've had to pay to him already to keep what you thought was yours?*

However, that did not make Sainte-Mère-Eglise any easier to work with. In fact, Guy would have sworn by the end of the first day that it had the reverse effect of making him less tolerant, and gave him a perverse appetite to make others suffer even more than he believed he himself had. What was worse, he had an unhealthy relish for watching his sentences being carried out, and he handed out lashes more often than a spell in the stocks, and physical punishments instead of fines. That seemed perverse to Guy, given that the king was supposed to need all the coin he could get, but when he finally could stand no more and challenged Sainte-Mère-Eglise on the matter, he was told,

"But when will they pay? We could wait years before the full amount can be paid. And what deterrent is that, eh? Knowing that you've got away with your crimes for so many years that they might even get forgotten about, or more likely, give the miscreant time to flee the hundred he's been sentenced in and set up a new life elsewhere under another name? No, they must pay *now*, and if they haven't the coin then they must suffer the alternative."

Guy had looked at Sir Hugo and seen the dismay in his eyes too. A shire filled with cripples was not what anyone needed, and Sir Hugo had the wit to see that even if he wasn't filled with Guy's sympathy for the poor.

On the Sunday following the first full week of crown pleas, while Sir Hugo made the pretence of putting the garrison through its paces as a reason to get out of the castle, where Sainte-Mère-Eglise was putting on a remarkable display of false piety in the chapel, Guy took his horse plus a spare and rode like the wind for Loxley. At the camp he was greeted warmly by Will and the newer members of the gang, but to his hidden horror, also by Robin and Tuck.

"What brings you here?" Robin demanded with enough asperity to have Tuck glancing sideways at him in surprise.

However, Guy was prepared to let that one go and instead told them all,

"I think we may have need of your services up at High Peak in the next few days. We have a problem!"

"We? Or you?" Robin challenged him.

Tuck's "Robin!" made him duck his head and keep quiet, but Guy knew his cousin's reactions well enough to know that he was seething inside at being publicly chastised. That would be another mark against him, he knew, because Robin would see Guy as deliberately having baited him.

However, Guy replied, "We," very firmly, adding, "We have reprobate priest on our hands again, Tuck!"

"*Dewi Sant*, help us!" Tuck intoned, "Another bloody Norman, no doubt?"

"And not just an English bred one this time. He's proper Norman – William de Sainte-Mère-Eglise."

Tuck tutted. "And there was me thinking that it would be Foliot who would be giving you the most trouble. Go on then ...what's the bastard been up to?"

"Well not much yet besides handing out the severest punishments he can for every crime, but it's his attitude which is worrying me the most."

Will's brow creased. "Why? What's worse than normal?"

"Oh Lord, Will, it's like he's swallowed a wasps nest. You'd almost say he was in mortal pain, but I don't think it his body that's being eaten away at. Everything seems to rub him up the wrong way, and it's getting worse. He takes a strange pleasure in watching the punishments being carried out, I can tell you that. While we had the three of them together I didn't see it, because he was – I suspect – torn between keeping up appearances with Briwere and Foliot, and leaving them to go outside and watch, and his fellow judges won. But now he's on his own, he's insisting that we don't start carrying out the punishments until he can come from the court to watch. You see, he ordered sixty lashes for Walter, the miner from Eadale, because of an accusation of him withholding payment to the king..."

"Sixty!" Much interrupted, appalled.

Guy nodded. "You're already beginning to see it. No way does that fit with any punishment laid down by law, but these are poor folk. Who are they going to complain to? The sheriff? Even the guildsmen who have come from the north of the hundred to act as jurors are positively poverty-stricken compared to their London counterparts, and that makes Sainte-Mère-Eglise disregard them.

"You've all heard me complaining over how a judge can overrule jurors, but I don't think any of these men have ever seen the like. Not even the most senior and elderly who remember serving on eyres in King Henry's day. And what they're seeing now is scaring them stiff. I can't blame them for that, because in their places I'd be worried about what might fall on me and my family if I crossed this powerful madman – and don't look at me like that Robin! They all know he has the ear of the king. The same king who only months ago ravaged his way across these northern shires like the Conqueror come again."

Ed, the carpenter from Durham, sighed, "No, you can't blame them at all. Since King Henry's been gone, things have gone from bad to worse up here."

"They're not soldiers, Robin," Guy added firmly, seeing his cousin's look of disgust at what was no doubt his perception of cowardice on the guildsmen's part. "But what's brought me here is this: I managed to get poor Walter only ten lashes by virtue of starting the punishments going as soon as they were handed out. So I told Sainte-Mère-Eglise that Walter had already had fifty when he came out. Earnwine had got me a bladder of pig's blood I'd asked for, and we'd slopped some over Walter just in time, so it looked like the poor bastard was dripping blood.

"What scared the crap out of me, though, was the way that lunatic dean's eyes lit up at the sight. Truly, he was practically salivating! But within a heartbeat it changed to fury. He screamed at me like some fiend from hell for having started without him. And he's made it very clear that that must not happen again. The men-at-arms are petrified of him. Up until then I think they just saw him as another de Wendenal, heavy-handed and brutal, so what I asked them to do to help save ordinary men like themselves, well, that was one thing. Asking them to fly in the face of Sainte-Mère-Eglise now they've seen the full extent of his malice ...that's a whole different thing.

"Even so, I think if they thought he would go and never come back, they might help as long as they weren't pushed too hard into rebellion. But they've all heard him bemoaning the fact that he'll have to come back after Christmas to get through the backlog of cases, and they're terrified that he might see someone who was supposed to be crippled for life walking about the village. Even if he was due to come back in a few years with a whole new eyre, it might be different, because nobody expects a lord like him to remember a peasant's face after a year or two, but this will be mere weeks."

"So you need someone to take a tougher stance than you or the guards can?" Will guessed.

Guy sighed. "Not just a stance, Will. I think once we resume the cases on Monday there's a very real danger that he'll order a hanging." He turned to Robin. "I know you were angry with me when I said not to interrupt the hangings at Bolsover, but those men truly were murderers. They were cold-blooded killers. But anyone handed out that sentence here will be equally as certainly innocent of *any* crime which would require a hanging sentence. I don't care what you think of my motives, Robin, but for the love of God, believe me when I ask you to come and disrupt this court before some poor soul loses their life."

Will drew a deep breath. "You know that most of our experienced men are still in Nottinghamshire?"

"Oh I'm horribly aware of that," Guy sighed, "and because of that I'm not asking for you to make a fight of it. But you do have enough of you who can pull a bow to make a nuisance of yourselves."

Gilbert had come to stand just behind Guy and he now declared, "Oh I think we can do better than that! You're right, we can't get into anything like a pitched battle, but Will, Robin, Tuck and I can probably get into the bailey and set fire to the gallows, and the like."

"And we can do fire arrows!" Much declared enthusiastically. He turned to Robin with just a hint of defiance. "I may not be able to make a shot like you did through the windows of Bolsover, but I can send an arrow over the walls of High Peak with the best of you."

"And we've been practising," Martin of Walesby declared, gesturing to his friend Simon as he spoke.

Gilbert nodded at Guy, knowing that he would want some reassurance that these newcomers weren't overestimating their abilities just to impress Robin. Guy was under no illusions when it came to Robin's ability to fire up these innocents to mayhem and slaughter with a false expectation of what a bloody fight would truly be like, but Gilbert's judgement he trusted rather more.

"Very good," he said, keeping his voice more even than his feelings. "Then if you can travel with me tonight I'll point out where the weak points are in the castle."

"I think we know those well enough," Robin said smugly, "after all we did live there with you."

Before he could stop himself, Guy bit back with, "Oh, so you've been watching the castle enough to know of the reinforcements de Wendenal made, do you? How wonderfully prescient of you, couz'! Because despite my many official visits here since we lived there, *I* didn't know about the extra trap he put in over the gate from the stables. That'll have you skewered on the spikes he had put on the rocky slopes below, after you've skidded off the walkway or bridge when you trip the twine trap that dumps oil all over it. Oil doesn't have to be boiling to do horrible damage, you know!"

With great effort, Guy managed to stop himself from saying more. It served no-one for him to get into a slanging match in front of the new recruits. "Please ...come with me, and let me show you what's *new*," he managed to grind out before walking back to where his horses were, enjoying grazing grass which hadn't seen a horse for ages.

"That was controlled," Gilbert complimented him softly as he fell into step with Guy. "Given what's gone on between you two, I'm not sure I'd have been as restrained in your boots."

"Having regrets about staying?" Guy gulped, dreading that Gilbert might say 'yes'. If he went, then Colm, the new Irishman to join them, would undoubtedly go too, but more worrying was what it might do to the remained of the company who had come home from the crusades. If Gilbert went, would Will, Malik and Siward stay?

To his relief, Gilbert gave a bitter sniff but declared, "There's nowhere else to go. From what Colm's said, I'd be as welcome as a boil on a knight's arse back in Ireland. The bloody Normans are making their mark on my homeland too. At least here I'm with other fools who want to fight back. I don't know who I'd go to elsewhere."

"Well I'm bloody glad you're staying! If nothing else, you lot who came out of the East with my cousin know that he doesn't walk on water."

Gilbert hooted. "And I'm glad we've a cynical bastard like you around! Robin gets stars in his eyes all too often. I trust your assessments far more. At least I'm prepared I might meet my Maker when you tell me it's going to be bad."

Guy couldn't help but grin back. "Jesu, you must keep Tuck busy with all those last confessions." Then coughed as Gilbert hooted with laughter again and slapped him hard on the back.

No, Brother, I was not intentionally trying to outrage you by denigrating the last confession. I was simply trying to show you that by this time the outlaws were not following Robin blindly. They had their own convictions about the rightness of what they were doing. Those beliefs might have been a lot more earthly than you would like them to have been, but the cohesion was much stronger than it would have been with nothing but blind faith in Robin.

And for myself, I was genuine in wanting the outlaws' help. I had woken from terrible dreams on several nights running, in which I had no choice but to stand by and watch men I knew swing from a gibbet for crimes they had never committed. Sainte-Mère-Eglise had hinted that someone might swing, but my belief that it would happen was way out of proportion to what had been openly said. I knew in my bones that if I could not get Robin to act on my warnings, then someone would die.

Now we must move smartly onwards, for you will relish what is to come next, Gervase.

Chapter 7

Truly, Brother, events are about to gallop up on us, but I will tell you now, that Archbishop Hubert Walter can surely never have intended for the eyre to slide into the kind of chaos as I witnessed up in Derbyshire. The worst kind of interrogation officially allowed was ordeal by water, and that had to be in the presence of a priest who was supposed to bless the water so that the result would be God's will. And maybe Sainte-Mère-Eglise was just enough of a churchman to not risk calling for God's blessing on his corruptions to go that far. However, I do not think Archbishop Walter ever anticipated such a priest as Sainte-Mère-Eglise – someone who would twist the proceedings so out of fashion, or warp the letter of the law in its application, especially when it came to punishments.

...No, in truth I personally never saw him actually torture anyone, Gervase, which is no doubt why you are so sceptical of my accusations, but physical torture is not the only way to subvert justice and he did everything *but* that. Instead of an ordeal by water, he simply overrode any information, or appeal to good sense, which did not suit his purpose, no matter how contrary to legal practice that may have been. And I wish I could say that it would be the worst I would see in my life, but instead it became a bad omen of things to come.

However, the other piece of significant news which reached us in the north around that time – and one you will relish – was that back in August the king had decreed that tournaments could once again be held in England. His father, of increasingly blessed memory, had had the good sense to ban them, seeing them as badly disguised excuses for young men to arm themselves within the kingdom. Unfortunately King Richard was too blinded by his love of these displays of what he believed was chivalry to see that.

And yes, Gervase, I do disagree with what he called chivalry. The king thought it something only those born of noble blood were capable of, and before you sigh at me again, I will tell you this: that it was the very fact that Robin aspired to being, and to behave as, a chivalrous knight which annoyed so many fine knights. Ah, so now you see it? Yes, dear Brother, a mere minor knight's son should never have been able to do what Robin did and challenge those above him, let alone get the better of them. Maybe in the wild mêlée of war, King Richard would allow that a group of ruffians might get the better of a knight trained from childhood, but not in the tourney – never in the tourney!

And soon we will come to that famous one where Robin proved what an exceptional archer he was. Oh yes, I thought that would make your eyes sparkle! You want more of the heroic deeds, I know you do. But do not chivvy me, because before that tournament he will make another superb shot which you will relish hearing about, and that is directly connected to that dreadful eyre and Sainte-Mère-Eglise.

Derbyshire and Nottinghamshire
Late Autumn, the Year of Our Lord 1194

Guy got back to High Peak without causing comment on his absence, but found Hugo Bassett looking pale.

"What's happened? Please don't tell me Sainte-Mère-Eglise has done something awful on the Sabbath?" Guy asked, dreading the reply.

However Hugo was already shaking his head. "No, not him. This time it's about me. You know I was visiting the castle just before the time of the siege? Well I'm worried I'm going to be fined for it. Blessed St Thomas, Sir Guy, my payment for my land in Baslow has gone up to one hundred shillings, and that's after I've had to pay ten pounds right now to keep my Heddon manor, so I shall be on my knees to all the saints for divine intervention if I get a fine on top of that. You should hear what some of the fines have been! Sanson de Strelley has been handed a bill for *forty-six* shillings *on top* of what else he owes, may God have mercy on him."

Guy normally had little sympathy for Verderer Strelley, but he could see what Hugo was getting at. What was worse was that he could also see what would happen if the lesser nobility of the two shires were reduced to poverty by the king's avarice – it would rebound onto the poor folk of their manors, because where else would these knights get the money from? So he had no trouble in sounding sympathetic when he replied,

"May Our Lady intercede for you all! That's grim indeed. I'm glad my paltry manor isn't in these shires, but on the other side of the Pennines. At least there they aren't stripped of everything by the forest laws, and with me being attached by the late king to the castle, I can carry some faint hope that I will be seen as having had no choice but to be there."

"Cling to that if you will," Hugo replied mournfully, "but don't count on it. I think this king of ours means to make us pay and pay, regardless of who actually was at fault. So much for him being the epitome of chivalry! Where's his charity and mercy in all of this, eh?"

Hugo's bitterness made Guy wonder whether he would be someone who in time he could bring round to being an ally. Maybe not a full confident over Robin Hood, but at least someone he might ask to turn a blind eye to something. However, with the coming of Monday morning, Sainte-Mère-Eglise was champing at the bit to get on with the eyre, and Guy's morning prayers were of the kind that would summon Robin Hood regardless of how annoyed his cousin was with himself.

They staggered through the morning session with questions going back and forth over the matter of stolen ore from a mine, and as to who would have had the motive and means to do so, in the process leaving the mine in such a state as to cause a miner to be crippled for life when he was the first man back there. The miner had been lucky not to be killed, although when the shadow of a man was brought in to testify, Guy wondered whether it wouldn't have been more of a blessing if he had. Every movement seemed to cause him pain, and his memory of the time had completely gone. Yet Sainte-Mère-Eglise was more worried about the value of the missing ore.

"This would have been part of the king's revenue," he kept on repeating, even though Earnwine the beremaster also repeatedly refuted the amount of money Sainte-Mère-Eglise thought it represented.

"It was raw ore, my lord," Earnwine said yet again, as they broke to take some refreshments after someone had reminded them that it was well past noon. "Raw ore would not fetch that much."

And then it happened, just what Guy had feared. Earnwine had contradicted Sainte-Mère-Eglise once too often for the haughty lord's liking, a mere miner (at least in his eyes) having the gall to correct his infinitely better.

"Why are you so determined to devalue this?" Sainte-Mère-Eglise flung back at Earnwine. "I believe you have a stake in all of this! ...Oh yes, I can see it clearly now! As the beremaster they must have come to you to sell the stolen ore, and you've had your cut of it, haven't you?"

It was such a preposterous accusation that both Earnwine and Guy were lost for words, but unfortunately, Earnwine's failure to instantly protest his innocence was taken as proof of guilt by the lordly priest.

"Ha! I have you! I have the thief!" Sainte-Mère-Eglise crowed triumphantly. "Soldiers! Go search this man's dwelling, whichever hovel down there it is. Find me lead! Find me proof!"

"My lord!" Guy managed to wring out. "That's unf..." He choked on the word 'fair'. This man wouldn't recognise fairness if it bit his over-privileged behind. "...unreasonable," he managed to hurriedly substitute. "Of course there will be ore at Earnwine's home – he's the beremaster and it's his responsibility to deal with the *refined* lead ore."

He'd put every ounce of emphasis on to the 'refined', but it slid off Sainte-Mère-Eglise's indifference like water off the crags surrounding them. Dare he himself correct this madman, and point out yet again that what had gone missing was the raw ore? Then he realised it would do no good, the soldiers had already gone out, too afraid of Sainte-Mère-Eglise themselves to dare risk not being seen to do his bidding, and they wouldn't know refined lumps from raw chunks any more than the archdeacon did. Earnwine was in serious trouble.

Leaving Sainte-Mère-Eglise smirking by the great hall's doorway, Guy spun back to the petrified Earnwine, who was too stunned to realise that Guy was trying to catch his eye. Hoping that the damned priest wouldn't turn round and see him doing this, Guy strode to Earnwine and hissed in his ear, "Robin Hood!"

It had the desired effect. Earnwine blinked and then looked properly at Guy as he gestured he was going out, grabbed his cloak, and mouthed, "I'll fetch him!"

Guy heard Sainte-Mère-Eglise throw some words after him as he passed him in the doorway which sounded like, "No stomach for a hanging?" and then he was out of the hall and hurrying across the bailey.

He didn't head for the stables – that would have been too much of a signal that he was up to something – but instead went to the gate which took the steep slope down to the village nestled at the castle's feet. Already he could see four guardsmen tramping up the main street of Castleton with four more about to follow them, and the horrified faces of the villagers at their doorways watching them. He could do nothing to stop this search. These soldiers had come with the sheriff, not from the meagre garrison which normally held High Peak and who perforce had to have some kind of relationship with the villagers. These men could be as brutal as their natures let them be, safe in the knowledge that nobody in authority here could protest, and that they would never have to count on these villagers for food rations in winter, or any other kindness.

What Guy did was hurry to the inn. He had begged a longbow off his friends back at the camp and hidden it under the eaves of the inn's lean-to stable, and he had chosen this spot for one very good reason – the inn usually had a fire going in the kitchen all day, if not for food, then to heat water for brewing or washing, and right now Guy needed a spark. He reached up and grabbed the bow, glad that his height meant that he could reach places easily which none of the miners could, which in turn had guaranteed that the bow would remain undisturbed. Rubbing the wood to warm it in his gloved hand, he bent it far enough to pull the string to the horn nocks, and then grabbed an arrow.

The kitchen was deserted when he went in, the innkeeper's wife and her helper too busy watching the nightmare unfold in the main street, and he thrust the fire-arrow into the glowing embers. This one was far better prepared than the ones he had had to hurriedly cobble together in the past, and it lit within moments, so that by the time Guy had hurried outside again it was firmly alight. Drawing back on the string, Guy aimed almost straight upwards, gave it an extra pull for good measure and then let go.

The arrow sailed high into the air, pointing slightly towards the head of the valley, for Guy guessed that his friends would not have waited in the woods on the northern slopes almost a mile away opposite the castle, but would be closer. Either in one of the great caves formed by worked out mines along the valley, he guessed, or more likely in the deep gulch behind the castle which wound its way up onto high ground to the south, before dropping down again to Oxlow. To his relief the arrow burned brightly even as it reached its limit and turned to fall earthwards, and it shone all the brighter for it being a dull grey day with a sky full of slate-coloured clouds, against which it stood out like a candle in the dark.

He didn't expect any replying signal. That would have been far too foolish. It would signal the outlaws' position as surely as he had just signalled his, and so his main concern now was to get away from here as fast as possible.

Grabbing from its hiding place the quiver containing two more fire-arrows and a stock of regular ones, Guy ran like a hare along the back of the humble houses, glad that he had got a whole lot better at running again just lately from taking the two wolfhounds out. So he was at the end of the run of buildings before the soldiers had even realised that anything was wrong, and got across the street unseen, to creep back along behind the other side of the village until he was close to where the path came down from the castle. He had already found a hollow right by the castle wall to hide the bow and arrows anew, and now dumped them into it and shoved some winter-dead bracken over them, safe in the knowledge that he could get to them easily if he needed to. Then he loitered by the castle path, as if merely waiting for the soldiers to bring the condemning evidence back with them.

"Did you see that?" he heard Hugo Bassett calling from above and behind him.

Turning with what he hoped was a convincing expression of innocence, Guy called back to Hugo,

"See what? What do you mean?"

"The arrow!" Bassett exclaimed. "Someone loosed a fire arrow above the castle."

"I was facing the other way," Guy declared, coming part of the way up the path to meet Hugo as he hurried downwards. "I was looking east, towards Earnwine's house."

"So you saw nothing?"

"No."

Hugo and Guy stood at one of the turns in the path which gave them a good view above the roofs of the village. "I don't like this, Sir Guy, I really don't. Who was that meant for? Who sent it?"

Guy decided to risk a small snippet of the truth. "To be honest, Sir Hugo, I'm surprised we haven't had more protests before this. The people up here are honest and they don't like being called thieves. If Sainte-Mère-Eglise had done a proper job, investigating things as they should have been done – the way they would have been done in the king's father's day – then I suspect things would be very different. But this insane throwing of accusations is bound to turn folks against us."

"You think this beremaster is innocent?"

Guy sighed and gave Hugo a weary look. "It was Earnwine who helped to sort things out back when Ralph Murdac was sheriff, and the old keeper of High Peak who preceded me was feathering his own nest. Earnwine is as honest as the day is long, and accusing him like this has turned the whole valley against this eyre and Sainte-Mère-Eglise in particular. They might have gritted their teeth and born the excessive punishments, but not this."

"Why?" Hugo Bassett was genuinely perplexed, and Guy found himself forced to explain.

"I'm guessing you've not had much to do with miners? No, I thought not. Well their payments of things like tithes are based on whether you are talking about raw lead ore, or the refined metal. The beremaster has the scales which weigh both. Therefore it has to be someone they trust, because anyone tipping the balance by using falsely weighted pans can make the difference between them making enough to survive on, or starvation over the winter.

"The old castellan, Ivo of Quettehou, was a thieving old bastard, as Ralph Murdac discovered. He filched enough to make himself a very rich man, had he lived, but left the villagers round here completely unable to pay the Saladin Tithe. That's what Earnwine and I sorted out. Murdac got the Saladin Tithe and nobody got hurt," although that was something of a lie remembering the fight up the valley, "and that's why the villagers won't stand for him being accused like this."

Hugo puffed his cheeks in dismay. "Oh dear, that really doesn't bode well, does it?"

"No, especially as we're up here with just a handful of Sheriff Briwere's tame ruffians. The miners are a tough lot, you know, they have to be to survive. If they decided to take matters into their own hands – and there are enough of them to do that – and then blame a bunch of outlaws for our deaths, who would know otherwise?"

"By Our Lady, Sir Guy, you paint a grim picture!"

"Maybe, but better that you realise what the worst could be. I hope it doesn't come to that, but I can't imagine a madman like Sainte-Mère-Eglise listening to reason and backing off a little. I fear he's of a mind to have a hanging, Sir Hugo, and that could be catastrophic."

"A hanging? Oh, Blessed St Thomas, surely not? There would be no justification for such a punishment."

"No there wouldn't, but we're alone up here in a remote part of Derbyshire, and who of us has the authority to gainsay him? And that terrified clerk we have with us will record what he's told to, not necessarily the truth, so there'll be no comeback when the records reach London – anyway, that would be far too late to save Earnwine from whatever fate Sainte-Mère-Eglise has in mind for him."

And Guy's prediction came true all too quickly. After a soldier had trudged back up the hill to the castle to inform Sainte-Mère-Eglise that there was a quantity of lead at the back of Earnwine's house, the man swept down to the village in person in his fine, flowing black robes like some ghastly carrion crow come to gorge itself on Earnwine's corpse.

"You will hang!" Sainte-Mère-Eglise declared loudly, then became exasperated when the sergeant timidly said,

"But we haven't a gallows here, sire."

"God's hooks, man, there's a bloody great oak tree at the end of the village! Throw a rope over the low branch of that!" the priest snarled, turning the Guy and Hugo and fuming, "Do I have to do everything around here? Organise it you pair of fools!"

"I'll do it," Guy said coldly, then adding softly just to Hugo, "They're less likely to start stoning me than you."

Hugo blanched at that and began urging all but the lone and terrified soldier who went with Guy, lugging the rope Sainte-Mère-Eglise had had him bring from the castle in readiness, to form a guard around himself and Sainte-Mère-Eglise. Meanwhile Guy strode forwards, shoving the poor soldier in front of him so that he wouldn't see Guy making placating gestures to the villagers who were starting to cluster around them with threatening rumblings. Every so often Guy would see someone he knew slightly better and would mouth silently, "Robin Hood," although he was far from confident that Robin would turn up.

There was a perverse element to his cousin these days where he himself was concerned, and inside he was praying that if his cousin wouldn't appear, that at least Malik would come. The former turcopole had got to know the people of this valley as well as any of them, and of those left with Robin at the camp, Malik was the one other capable of making an accurate long shot. Will and Gilbert could charge in and make so many meat cutlets of these soldiers, but Guy wanted this to be as bloodless as possible. A massacre of the soldiers guarding a judge on eyre or, God forbid, the judge himself, was the fastest way to have the archbishop sending soldiers back to these shires in force, and that was something to be avoided at all costs.

With trembling hands the soldier made the knots in the stout length of rope to make the noose, and then threw the other end over the almost-horizontal massive branch of the oak. It hung low enough that a handcart was enough to raise Earnwine up enough to get the noose around his neck when he was brought down from the castle, to boos, jeers and catcalls to the soldiers from the increasingly hostile crowd. And that was something else which horrified Guy – there wasn't enough height to make this a clean drop with a snap of Earnwine's neck, if the worst came to the worst, but a slow choking instead, and nobody but himself had noticed that. The villagers seeing Earnwine struggling and throttling in torment would turn this into a bloody riot, and that was another reason why it had to be stopped, because Guy could guess who would be ordered to pull on his feet to hasten his end, and he could never do that to a friend.

The soldiers formed an arc around the tree facing outwards, and so it fell to Guy to get up onto the cart with Earnwine to put his head into the noose.

"I'm going to have to pull this tight," he whispered in Earnwine's ear, "but not to hang you! If Robin's going to part it with an arrow it's going to have to be taut. If necessary I'll turn coat and cut you down myself, but I'm hoping our hero will do the trick."

"Thank you," Earnwine replied, but his voice was shaking and Guy knew that he was still expecting to meet his Maker today.

Jumping down, Guy made the rope secure against the cart, then made as if he was preparing to push it to make Earnwine drop.

"Come on Robin," he found himself muttering softly. "For God's sake, don't muck about making a performance of this."

Meanwhile Sainte-Mère-Eglise was making quite the performance of his part in this, proclaiming Earnwine's faults in the eyes of God for defying his divinely appointed king and his chosen judge here on earth. That the man couldn't feel the rising tension in the crowd made him worse than a fool in Guy's eyes, and he could see that Hugo Bassett was none too impressed either and was nervously fingering the hilt of his sword. Hugo kept making glances back to the castle bailey, and Guy could tell that he was at a loss as to why Sainte-Mère-Eglise had chosen to do this here, rather than within the security of the castle's walls. It was pure ego, nothing more. A belief that he was above all repercussions and that he was making more of a statement by doing this down here.

"You are condemned in the sight of God," Sainte-Mère-Eglise pontificated. "You will receive no unction, but will die with your sins hanging about your soul like so many rotten grapes. Take note of this, all of you, for this is what happens to men who thieve from the king! ...Sir Guy, you may push the cart away," and then when Guy hesitated, screamed in fury, "Now! Do it now!"

Then as Guy bent over to pull the sharp knife from where he'd slipped it into the top of his boot, preparing to finally reveal himself as the traitor he was, another voice rang out. A voice used to being heard over a noisy crowd not a hushed group of obedient canons.

"You shameful excuse for a priest!" Tuck's big voice rang out, as always at times like this more pronouncedly Welsh in his anger. "How dare you! By *Dewi Sant*! God sees all, he sees you and he knows the truth, he knows! You ...*you* will be the one whom God condemns, not this innocent man. I call on all the saints to witness this calumny and your mendacity *chi offeiriad cenhedloedd gwaedlyd* ...you ...you bloody heathen priest!" Tuck spluttered, returning to his native tongue in his fury and then realising that Sainte-Mère-Eglise wouldn't have a clue what he'd said. *"Galwaf damnedigaeth ar chi, chi ddyn annuwiol!* I call damnation on you, you Godless man!"

Where Tuck was Guy couldn't tell, but he was hardly in a position to look about him as the arrows began flying. A somewhat random cluster landed close to the soldiers, scattering them, and probably fired by Much and the new lads, Guy guessed. Then by sheer luck Guy spotted an arrow coming straight at him and dived out of the way. Christ, was that Robin? But then he realised another arrow had come almost on its flights which sheared the hanging rope, and as he lay flat on his back, realised that the first had been a very close call but unlikely to actually hit. That probably meant that it had been Malik's, possibly a warning shot to get him to duck out of the way for Robin's. A good ranging shot by Malik, and one only a first rate archer could have made, but what had followed it was something else entirely.

Robin's arrow had been a superb shot, coming from way back amongst the riverside trees and hitting the rope square on to the gasps of amazement from the crowd, parting it like so much dressmaker's thread. The head must have been razor sharp, and Guy mentally applauded whoever had made that, but even so it would not have been enough on its own to snap the rope in two if it had struck anywhere else but the centre and with considerable power. Earnwine had been lifted off his feet by the force of the arrow striking the thick rope, and was now sprawled in the bottom of the cart, coughing and spluttering but definitely still in the land of the living.

Sainte-Mère-Eglise on the other hand was not faring so well. He had pulled one of the soldiers in front of him just in time for the man to take the arrow meant for him, and the archer's big Welsh bow had punched the yard-long arrow through the mail surcoat the soldier was wearing. Shoving the howling man aside, Sainte-Mère-Eglise grabbed another soldier and he too took an arrow through the arm. Someone was aiming at him with real ferocity, and judging by the slight change in angle from the one which had parted the hanging rope, it was Robin who had swiftly changed target and had loosed these other arrows at a stunning speed. Where Robin himself was, though, was another matter, but it certainly wasn't within sight, and possibly even up one of the trees to allow him to get his sights on the targets. If that was so then to make such shots, even from the stable footing of a massive oak branch, was all the more incredible, but there was more at stake here than just proof of Robin's skills.

"No!" Guy yelled, staggering to his feet and starting towards the judge. "No, not him!"

Later on he would realise that this had sounded convincingly as though he had been trying to save Sainte-Mère-Eglise, but at the time he was more worried about the repercussions of a judge dying on eyre. He couldn't spot Robin in the clump of ancient oaks and elms, especially as the arrows aimed at Sainte-Mère-Eglise temporarily paused, and Guy could only yell and hope Robin would hear. And unfortunately the lack of any visible archer only made those arrows seem all the more miraculous to the crowd, who had even gone so far as to cheer. Please God that adulation would not egg Robin on to something even more reckless! Moreover, Guy's frantic casting about only served to unnerve the soldiers even more, since to them Guy was by far the more experienced knight.

Then suddenly Will and Gilbert were there, menacing the soldiers with drawn swords and the dangerous glint of experienced fighters in their eyes. Together they hauled Earnwine off the cart, and then Will shoved him back to the road leading out of the village. Whether Tuck had got Robin under control or he had come to his senses on his own Guy didn't know, or whether it was the lads following some proper plan now, but the next cluster of arrows were focused on preventing anyone from following Will. However, Gilbert danced forward, winked at Guy, and then clipped him on the cheek-bone with a punch of his mailed fist. It came hard and spilt the skin, but it wasn't enough to knock Guy out, just bowl him over, and he realised that Gilbert had given him his excuse not to follow as the one closest to the rescuers. So he stayed lying on the floor pretending to be more dazed than he was, and watching the escape.

"How dare you hang my people?" Robin's voice suddenly rang out clearly as Will, Gilbert and Earnwine jumped off the road into undergrowth on the other side of the bridge over the Peakshole Water. "You tell the sheriff this: that Robin Hood will have his vengeance if anyone here is harmed in retribution. Defy me if you are fool enough, but the next time, you foul crow of a priest, you won't be so lucky. Where is your mercy as a man raised to be a knight long before you were a priest? Where is your charity? You shame your family and you shame God! You are a marked man, and one day *you* will go to *your* Maker with your sins hanging about you. I am Robin Hood, remember that! I am the Hooded Man and the forest is mine!"

Oh yes, Gervase, he used those word, and that attack upon his knightly birth stung Sainte-Mère-Eglise more than Tuck's words, I fear. Those words about knightly virtues would travel back to London with him weighing heavier than his baggage. Such a proud Norman valued his earthly heritage more than what was being set up for him in Heaven, unfortunately. And what was almost worst, he had felt real fear for the first time in what I suspect was a very long time, if ever.

The villagers scattered like chaff in the wind as soon as the outlaws were gone, and in the blink of an eye all that was left was the official party clustered around the oak tree. I staggered to my feet, letting the blood from where Gilbert's mail-backed glove had cut me run down my face for better effect. It was not much, in truth, but I was using it for all it was worth to excuse my not having chased after Earnwine. I confess I even added in a stagger or two for good effect, yet it was worth it because that damned priest merely sniffed at me but lashed out at poor Sir Hugo for not having been more of a man of action.

Quite what he expected from a northern landowner of middling rank, I do not know, for Sir Hugo was not of a generation to have ever had experience of fighting in the lists, and had fulfilled his obligations of service to the king by handing over the money to pay for soldiers, not going to fight himself. The chances of him being able to tackle a man like Will or Gilbert were negligible, and although I admit I knew just how dangerous those two could be and had never expected him to challenge them, even to a stranger, the way they held their weapons and behaved positively reeked of professional soldiers.

Sainte-Mère-Eglise retreated to the castle in a fine temper, then before the afternoon was out, declared that he was returning to London, and would be making his report of our lawless shire when he got there.

When he had stormed off to the bedchamber, I took Sir Hugo to one side and spoke to him firmly. I knew that we had to get our version of events in with Sheriff Briwere before our lunatic judge had chance to tell anyone his. We had to make as much as we could of him warping the eyre, but even more of his folly in taking the retribution out of the castle and into the village, for that would be what would get Briwere on our side.

˜And you must be the main speaker,˜ I told Sir Hugo. ˜The sheriff took an instant dislike to me, so although he will have little choice but to hear my words, he will not attach any weight to them. Whereas if you tell him, and I merely stand beside you and confirm your version of events, then he may just send word of his own to the archbishop.˜

Did that happen? Yes, Brother, it did. We rode with speed to Nottingham, having once seen Sainte-Mère-Eglise on his way with his escort of soldiers, and reached there just as Briwere himself was returning for a brief respite from his own courts. It went very much as I expected, with Briwere at first spluttering and blaming us, but at least by that stage my surface injury had developed into a spectacular black eye with every shade of purple and green in it, so I looked convincingly the injured warrior. Mercifully Briwere was appalled at the tale of going out of the castle to hand out punishments, and he called Sainte-Mère-Eglise all the fools in Christendom. A letter was penned and sent by messenger to Archbishop Walter, and for my part I breathed a little easier, as did Sir Hugo, and I knew I had found an ally there.

However, Robin Hood's pronouncements as relayed by Sir Hugo nearly threw Briwere into an apoplexy. This challenge to his authority was something a man like him would never take lying down. Therefore right from the start of his tenure, this sheriff was an enemy of Robin Hood's, and their enmity rapidly escalated into something close to a personal feud.

Chapter 8

What you need to realise here, Brother, is that the aftermath of that awful eyre had another effect, and one which was possibly even more vital to our story. That arrow of Robin's was even more of a masterly shot than even I had realised, you see. There had been a stiff breeze blowing – something which I, being down in the village, had been less aware of – and that made it all the harder to hit such a thin target successfully. Yet Robin had done that. He had made, at the first attempt, what Malik had been warning him was an almost impossible shot, and one which might take two or three arrows loosed in rapid succession to fully complete, if the first only nicked the rope. That had been why he had those next two arrows to hand and ready to loose and to redirect at our hellish judge. Yet he had told his companions that God would steady his hand and help him bring justice to Castleton, and therefore when he succeeded first time, you can hardly blame them for having felt he was just a little touched by the Divine hand.

Oh no, Brother, I do not mean that in any sacrilegious way. I simply mean that they saw it as a sign of the Lord's blessing of Robin in what he did. And you must remember that aside from Malik, the really experienced archers were not there with them. Instead, the company who had remained in the camp with Robin, aside from Tuck and Malik, were Much (who still, despite the siege, was always easily drawn in by Robin) and the newcomers – Irish Colm, Ed the carpenter, and Martin and Simon from Walesby – none of whom had seen any sort of action up until then. To them, Robin's actions were the stuff dreams and miracles were made of, not those of a man who practiced obsessively for just such an eventuality. So I did not blame them for being totally swept along by his charisma, or for embroidering the event when the others rejoined them at the camp.

When Siward, Roger and Allan next got to Nottingham to see me over the midwinter festivities, I would witness Siward's rolled eyes over the way the newest recruits now hero-worshipped Robin. And for once I was less than pleased that even Tuck said the Almighty had had a hand in Robin making that rope around Earnwine's throat part, because Robin and many others took his words in totally the wrong way. What Tuck had meant was that it was more of the Lord and less of Robin, but too late he realised that he had been taken to mean that God was acting directly <u>through</u> Robin, and just how misguidedly that had considerably elevated Robin's status. Allan would tell me that he thought it was not good for Robin to so quickly have been reinstated as the gang's leader, but that also, there was little they could do about it. All three were quick to say that although they had serious doubts on that score, that all of the original gang had decided to stay, if only to put the brakes on the more far-fetched of Robin's schemes.

And were there such schemes? Oh yes, Brother! With his new adoring recruits, apparently Robin now even considered the taking of High Peak Castle for his own – another resurrection of his boyhood desire to have his own fortress, where he would protect his friends and family, although these days I was sure I did not count amongst them. Luckily my allies within the camp soon talked some sense into him over that, pointing out that the chances of the sheriff, let alone the king, allowing any castle to be wrested from the crown would be nil, and that Robin would be bringing another event such as had happened so recently at Nottingham down upon the poor folk of the Peak. I was told that Will and Gilbert refused outright to have anything to do with such a scheme, and that although Siward, Hugh and Malik were less confrontational in their approach, they nonetheless made it blindingly clear that they would not participate. And even Robin in the state he was in by this stage, was not so blinded that he thought he could take the castle without his key experienced men, especially when the Coshams were backing them up at every sentence.

I do think that in some corner of Robin's mind that he may have blamed me for that response, believing that I had somehow staked some claim of my own to High Peak which the others were not willing to override. Utter nonsense, of course. I could no more have hoped to be given High Peak in those dark days than the keys to the White Tower in London. And what I was almost more grateful for was that they also talked him out of striking at the next courts in Derbyshire, telling him, quite correctly, that it would only serve to bring the sheriff's wrath upon the very people we were trying to protect, if one place seemed to be the heart of an outlaw rebellion against him.

A more scattered approach was needed, they convinced him. One that would have the sheriff wondering which rabbit warren his enemies were going to pop out of next, and making him run around in circles searching. John and Tuck had managed to get the last word in on that one, pointing out to Robin that even a sheriff like Briwere could not search all of the two shires all of the time, and that that was actually to their advantage. Making him run around here, there and everywhere was far more disruptive than wresting one place from his grasp temporarily.

However – and here we come to more of what you long for, Gervase – in the opposing camp, the sheriff was not so easily talked out of acting. Such a blatant disregard for his authority, and so early in his tenure as sheriff as to come before he had even come fully to his castle, was simply not to be born. It slighted him in the eyes of the all-powerful archbishop Walter, which was never a good position to be in, and played upon his fears.

What fears, you ask? ...Ah, Brother, you must remember that Briwere was the sheriff of many shires over the long years of his service, precisely because he was seen as the right sort of man to wring them dry for the king – both Richard and John. So until 1194 he had been the sheriff of the similarly paired, but far more lucrative, Berkshire and Oxfordshire, or at least more lucrative in the sense of normal taxes, though he must have dreamed of bleeding his new shires white with the forest laws too. A man like that could not afford to be seen to fail in any way, and I will drop you a small treat with regard to this: Briwere would never again hold a shire for as long as he was to be sheriff of ours.

Oh he would continue to be used over and over as a caretaker sheriff by King John, but the men of Devon and Cornwall would pay the king handsomely to have him removed when he moved on to them from us, and his future tenures would never again last into years – that is the harm Robin Hood did to his reputation. However, that is getting ahead of ourselves, and in the troubled times we are talking of now, we had no idea how long he might stay with us, and neither did he. For all he knew, if word of this defiant outlaw reached the king, then fickle King Richard could just as easily remove him and give him nothing at all in return.

Therefore the events at High Peak preyed upon Briwere's mind mightily, and then when he received requests for a tournament to be held at the newly designated ground not far outside of Blyth (and under the supervision of the Honour of Tickhill which lay across the border in Yorkshire, even though Blyth was firmly in Nottinghamshire), he saw a way to kill several birds with one stone. Firstly there was the money, for a tournament was not the elegant and romantic affair you might think, Brother, with fair damsels conferring their favours on their chosen champions. It was like a real battle, and the losers were taken hostage in name if not actually removed from their homes, and were forced to pay a very real ransom. You can therefore see what the attraction was for many of the hard-pressed knights of the shire, who hoped against hope to win back some of the money they had lost to the king.

From Briwere's point of view, if he could field several competent knights who might do very well against the sons of local knights, who in their turn had not been good enough fighters for the king to have wanted to take them with him, then that would similarly line his personal pocket nicely. It would also give him a chance to watch the mêlée and then take into his castle those local men who were useful fighters, for we were hard pressed for ordinary men at that point as I mentioned before. Our men of ordinary rank desperately needed new recruits, and this was a good way to pick men who would not fall over their own feet the first time they picked up a spear.

These alone would have good enough reasons, of course, but to then have a means of luring this infernal outlaw with the arrogant attitude out of his hideaway, was the final push Briwere needed to sign the parchment on the first tournament at Blyth. And why was he so sure Robin Hood would attend? Ah, there we come to the tale once more, Brother!

Nottingham & Sherwood
Early Spring, the Year of our Lord 1195

"An archery contest," William Briwere declared with a smirk. "We shall have an archery contest."

"When were you thinking of, my lord?" Sir Martin asked warily. Everyone had learned to tread lightly around Briwere. It was worth cultivating an ability to at least seem to be ingratiating, even if the truth was quite the opposite. "The forest will be closed for quite a while yet, so were you thinking of after St Felix and St George's day?"

However Briwere gave his slyest grin and declared, "Goodness me, Sir Martin, you have no idea of how to cultivate a shire, do you? No, of course I'm not going to wait until April, where would be the benefit in that? *Tsk*! Should our local ragtag excuses for knights get their blood up in the tournament, then they may feel the need to satiate their urges further with some illegal hunting, do you see? Ha-ha!"

Guy saw Sir Martin bite his lip to stop himself from protesting. This was entrapment, pure and simple. The sheriff was going to tempt them and then punish them when they took the bait. None of the other forest knights looked any happier, all of them realising that it would be they who did the dirtiest work in this scheme. The sheriff was not about to ride out and be the one who confronted those knights when armed with boar-spears or hunting bows.

Even the three knights of the castle were looking grim, and Guy knew there would be much to talk about when they met up again for their covert meeting in the chantry chapel of St Nicholas' church on Sunday. Those meetings had got them through the first three months without any disasters, but all of them had seen only too clearly that things could have gone very wrong had they not conferred with one another, for Briwere was proving to be the master of pitting one man against another.

"What sort of archery contest were you thinking of, my lord?" Guy asked, hoping to steer the conversation onto slightly safer ground, and also towards the information he very much wanted to hear.

Briwere looked at him as though he was a complete fool. "An *archery* contest, Sir Guy," he said with withering sarcasm. "You know, the sort with bows and arrows."

Guy swallowed his pride and clarified, "I meant how many categories and over what sort of distances? Are you going to offer any reward for novices? In fact, what sort of rewards were you thinking of?"

Briwere wrinkled his forehead in a frown, already suspecting that he was making something of a fool of himself, but unable to wriggle out of it now. "What do you mean, categories? Blessed St Thomas, they can either aim a bow and shoot straight or they can't!" and he gazed around the room with the expression they had all come to realise meant that he thought he'd been particularly witty and should be receiving laughs of appreciation. Unfortunately this time he was met by blank incomprehension.

Feeling somewhat emboldened because the four main greyhounds had been brought into the main hall on this evening to be inspected by the sheriff, and they were currently all curled up around Guy's feet, seemingly asleep but would be alert the moment any real threat presented itself, Guy risked a further attempt at getting the sheriff to see what he was putting into motion.

"Well are you going to have a group for hunting bows and one for crossbows?" he asked innocently. "Only if you put them all in together, the hunting bows are going to walk all over the crossbow archers in terms of range. And are you expecting the archers to make one shot, or three or four? Because in any contest to do with speed, again the crossbows are going to lose spectacularly, regardless of how accurate they are."

William Briwere had been nibbling at delicacies made out of ground almonds and honey, artistically shaped like grapes, but now spluttered and dropped the one in his hand as if it had stung him.

Sir Humphrey, sat at Guy's right, ducked his head down as he bent to ruffle one of the greyhound's ears, but saying with much amusement now he could not be heard or his lips read,

"Oh nicely played, Sir Guy! Well done! You got the bastard!"

On his other side, Sir Thorsten was also covering his amusement with a coughing fit, but the twinkle in his eyes told Guy that he too was enjoying this. Feeling a touch rash tonight, Guy added,

"And what of a reward? These men are unlikely to take part in the general mêlée, so if you want any contestants at all, there will have to be something as a separate prize for the overall winner at least. For the different groups it will be enough to offer a coin or two, but not the winner – not if you want anyone to enter, anyway."

He knew he was baiting Briwere, but he got what he had been angling for when the sheriff spluttered,

"Anyone to enter? God's hooks, I want that rogue Robin Hood to show up so that I can arrest him! He dares threaten a king's justice with his arrows – that makes him arrogant and tempt-able. Well I'm going to tempt him! I'm going to tempt his vanity. I'm not going to have some rogue peasant archer rampaging around my shire. And going on what has gone on in the past he seems to like coin well enough, so there shall be a purse for the winner."

Guy picked up on the fact that Briwere thought Robin was a mere peasant. That could work in their favour. But then the visitor amongst them, the man Briwere had wanted to impress with his greyhounds, spoke. The abbot of Newstead, the same Eustace de Tuke Guy had encountered hunting when he shouldn't, and who seemed to have completely missed the comments about illegal hunting in his drunken haze, slurped at his wine and declared with a hiccup,

"We have a finger bone of St Sebastian encased in a silver arrow at Newstead, you know."

Briwere turned in surprise. "What, the one who was pierced with arrows, you mean?"

De Tuke sniffed witheringly, still able to be sarcastic when plastered. "Well there isn't another one! *Hic-hic-hic.*" The hiccups were followed by a loud belch. "He's the patron saint of soldiers and those who desire a saintly death. *Hic-hic.*"

"Maybe you should bring it to the tournament, my lord," Guy suggested loudly. "Such an important relic ought to be celebrated, and what better way for the saint of soldiers than for him to be present at a tournament and give it his blessing? I'm sure my lord sheriff could see his way to making the entrance payments of the archery contest a donation to your abbey."

Briwere looked as though he might have an apoplexy and die on the spot. Unfortunately the saints were not so kindly disposed as to remove him today, but he remained a strange puce colour as de Tuke declared,

"That would be a generous act, my lord sheriff, *hic-hic*, and one which would guarantee you were kept to the fore in our prayers."

However, once de Tuke had been escorted on wobbly legs to his room for the night, and most of the men had left the hall, Briwere rounded on Guy.

"What in the name of Heaven were you thinking, you cretin? I want to make money out of this, not hand it out!"

Stepping a little closer so that he loomed over the sheriff, Guy gave his iciest smile while a soft growl came from two of the greyhounds by his side. It made Briwere swallow hard and back away a little to Guy's silent amusement, but Guy also answered him.

"Offering a few clipped silver pennies won't draw much in the way of contestants," he said softly, showing the sheriff that he had read his parsimony in that respect all too well. "If you want the knightly classes to show up, you're going to have to offer something worthwhile. On the other hand, if you want them to come to Blyth rather than one of the other four tournament grounds King Richard licensed – and you can be sure the sheriffs in those shires will have had similar thoughts to you – then you need to offer them something more.

"What better, then, than to show their skills off to the patron saint of soldiers? To compete on a field overlooked by one of that saint's very own relics? And the entrance to the archery competition need be little more than a penny per man. There's no point in setting it much higher because archers aren't the best paid men in the army, but it also means that the largest income will come from the jousts, which you'll keep."

Briwere was already smiling evilly. "And what I hand to de Tuke will be a purse full of small change."

"Large in quantity but low in value," Guy completed for him, and saw that he had the sheriff trapped.

"By Our Lady, Sir Guy, you can be a cunning one."

That sort of praise from Briwere was not what Guy wanted, so he demurred with, "Not really, my lord. I just know the common soldiers and what will draw them. They know they would get little chance to spend a large purse, but they can be a surprisingly devout lot when it comes to the saints. And de Tuke is a priest who has more pride than a man of God ought to have, so playing his vanity against himself when it serves us seemed the obvious way to go."

Briwere departed for his bed snorting with satisfaction at the prospect of swindling the abbot, and Guy went to take the greyhounds back to their kennels. It was an excellent excuse for him to get out of the main castle, but also to have time to think away from everyone else. These days he shared a cramped turret room with Sir Thorsten, and if over time their relationship had warmed a little, he still wasn't the kind of friend Guy would want to talk anything over with. Handing out some treats of dried off-cuts of fallow deer to the greyhounds, Guy sat down on the warm straw they had as bedding and though out loud.

"Now why did I do that?" he asked Argent, the big silver-grey dog of the four. "Have I just been a real idiot? Because Robin will definitely be lured by that relic!" The big hound gave Guy a slurping lick on his hand and then subsided to rest his noble head on Guy's knee with a satisfied grunt.

"Briwere thinks the money will draw Robin, so that will be well guarded ...but the relic ...he won't expect that to be the target, will he? If Robin can steal that from under the sheriff's nose it will be more of a blow, because it will make him look a fool in the eyes of the abbot." Then Guy gave a chuckle. "And if it pisses off that arrogant bastard de Tuke, then that's even better! The money value of the reliquary will be less than the moral effect."

Argent huffed contentedly as if in agreement, and one of the bitches came and flopped down on Guy's other side – something Guy took as a possible sign from one of the Welsh saints who so loved animals that he was on the right track.

"But have I just lured my cousin into danger?" he pondered, "Or have I given him something he can use and prevented him from an arrogant show of power in the wrong place?"

Because Guy knew somewhere deep inside, that Robin would want to demonstrate his amazing archery skills in public sooner or later. The adulation which had come from the newest members of the gang would have fed that part of him which needed to feel the love and admiration of others for him in a very personal way. Just knowing that he had done good didn't fully satisfy Robin these days, and Guy realised that since he had met with Siward and the others, he had been increasingly worried that all of Tuck's warnings were fading fast.

The date of the tournament was set the following morning.

"We shall hold it over three days commencing the twenty-third of March," Briwere declared triumphantly to the assembled knights. "Three days of martial skills culminating on the first day of the new year – what better way to celebrate it? And with the last day being Lady Day they can pay their rents too, since I will be there. I shall not be expected at court to answer for the *ferm* of the shire at the close of year this time around, being so new to my office, so I will be able to preside over the proceedings myself."

"And then the victors may offer up their thanks the following day at the Palm Sunday services," de Tuke said with an oily smile, clearly anticipating some hefty donations from the prize monies.

Briwere's return smile was every bit as villainous, his thoughts equally dwelling on how he was going to get the abbot's support for what would amount to very little.

Rather more at the fore in Guy's mind at that point, however, was his return to High Peak in the company of the dreadful William de Sainte-Mère-Eglise for the conclusion of the eyre. He almost wept with relief when Briwere then announced at the same time that the pestilent priest had other commitments which would not allow him to return, and so he would himself be presiding over the remaining cases. It wasn't that Guy particularly wanted this bullish sheriff rampaging all over the Peak, and it was definitely irregular for Briwere to sit in his own shires, but at least he knew that Briwere had so much on his hands that he would get through everything as fast as possible. And also, having got the sheriff sized up as a man very concerned with keeping his skin intact, Guy knew that there would be no repetition of the disaster down in Castleton village.

What was less welcome was the appearance of a man named John Buche, who was clearly well known to Briwere.

"My man Buche will hence forth be holding High Peak Castle in my name, and acting as beremaster for the mines up there," Briwere told him as Buche rode out with them for Derbyshire.

Looking at Buche, Guy reckoned he would be a hard man, but probably not that imaginative. He would follow orders to the letter, so the villagers would need warning over that, but he hardly looked the sort to go out and about exploring, and sticking his nose into old mines. Therefore the miners would, with luck, continue to be able to hoard ore against the time when they might urgently need it.

On reaching High Peak, Briwere fulfilled Guy's expectations by ripping through the remaining cases at high speed, often dismissing certain of the multitude of questions as irrelevant – which in this area they were. It opened Guy's eyes to Briwere's abilities, though, and he felt a sinking in his gut as he realised that this might be the worst sheriff they had had to contend with so far. Briwere knew every rule and regulation off by heart. He didn't need his scribe to remind him, nor of the appropriate fines or punishments. In each case he handed out the maximum penalty, whether it was deserved or not, but equally, he never exceeded it either.

"May I go and do my normal patrol of the forest?" Guy requested of him, as they thankfully finished the last of the residue of cases.

"Of course," Briwere beamed, in a thoroughly good mood given how much money he'd extracted out of the defendants, although he'd shown a rather worrying delight in taking the hands of thieves, to Guy's mind. That was something else he needed to pass on to Robin and the others. Briwere was well able to assess a man and decide whether he would ever be able to pay a fine, or equally, whether he was likely to flee the shire before he paid up. In those cases Briwere was chillingly ruthless, and Guy could tell that if an outlaw came before him, then he would take a hand without hesitation, or if he could do so legitimately, hang someone.

It was therefore with great relief that Guy sat on his horse, and watched Briwere and his small entourage wend their way down the valley towards the Derwent, and thence to the roads back to Nottingham. After a brief word with the miners out of sight of the castle and John Buche, he rode for the Loxley hideout, at least relieved to hear that Earnwine was in hiding up at one of the mines, but still able to help his older two sons to work for the family quota. They had lost the prestige of being the beremaster's family, but Earnwine's experience of working the scales would be invaluable when it came to making sure that this new man did not fleece anyone. They were already talking in terms of making sure they submitted raw ore, where they could mix contaminates in with each load, rather than the refined lead, which could not be disguised. And Guy had suggested using the Forest laws to their own advantage for the winter half year, by claiming that they had not been able to cut sufficient wood for the necessary fires to process the ore.

He arrived at the camp by the fall of the early winter evening, and was soon telling them of what had passed.

"This eyre has been harsh, but nothing like what we saw before Christmas," he confided in them. "Some of those folk may need help with fines. Alfred the charcoal burner, for instance. His son was a fool to get into that drunken scrap with Edwin and then brain him with a shovel. He's guilty, no doubt about that, but we know that it'll be his father who shoulders the burden of that fine to get his son out of gaol in Derby town ...and no, Robin, breaking open the gaol is not the answer this time!"

Guy had seen the light appear in his cousin's eyes and knew he had to squash that one before it got any further. Struggling to keep his tone moderate, he tried to explain,

"This eyre is significant beyond these shires – it's a sign of the king re-establishing order on the kingdom. Anything which is seen as challenging these judges – and especially a judge who is also a sheriff – will without a doubt bring horrible repercussions down on everyone. What happened with Earnwine was overlooked because Sainte-Mère-Eglise himself acted illegally. I knew that would be the case when I called for your help, and Briwere knew it when I reported a different version of events to him back at Nottingham. That's why you didn't end up with a man hunt on your hands.

"Oh Briwere is furious that you challenged his authority, don't doubt that for an instant. In fact he's close to spitting nails through the bailey gate over it! But he won't do anything rash, let alone illegal. Indeed he already has a plan to trap you."

Tuck's chuckle diffused the tension as he said, "Does he now? Well you have to give him credit for trying."

"What is it?" Allan asked.

"A lure," Guy informed them. "He's not coming after you. He wants to tempt you to come to him. He's organising a tournament with an archery contest."

At this time of year when it was cold and dark, all of the outlaws had come back to Loxley to take advantage of the solid shelters they had there and the reserves of dried food. So Guy was glad that there were obvious contestants in the form of the Coshams and Malik, as well as Robin himself. All of them had perked up at the prospect, and so now Guy told them of the arrow reliquary of St Sebastian.

"Briwere wants you, Robin," he repeated after he'd told them of how de Tuke had been tricked. "I don't think the bloody man has ever seen a longbow in action. He had to have the difference between crossbows and hunting bows like the one I used at Bolsover explained to him, and I think he's still thinking that his crossbow men will win the day. He's totally in ignorance of how lethal a big bow could be in the hands of men like Thomas and Piers.

"What's more, he thinks you'll go for the money, that you're motivated by nothing more than greed. But that purse will be all pennies, not worth you thinking about taking, not even as additional salt to his wound – especially as he's already resigned to it going to de Tuke. The relic, though, that's a different matter altogether. Quite aside from its obvious importance, if it gets taken under the sheriff's very nose, de Tuke will be calling him every name under the sun, and broadcasting it far and wide to whichever of his fellow churchmen will listen."

Guy was already feeling a touch sick over having to denigrate his own efforts at Bolsover just to keep Robin sweet, but what he had to say now positively made his bile rise, yet it had to be done.

"You want to make a grand gesture, Robin? Then this is it! Briwere has had me putting his men through their paces alongside Sirs Hugh, Richard and Robert, but because I've been working with those three I haven't even got started on the men's archery skills.

"And I'm not just saying this to set you up for an easy win. What I'm telling you is that if all of you enter, even a lad like Much will put the fear of God into those soldiers. They've never seen the like. It will terrify them into freezing rather than acting when the time comes for them to face you. By the time you've won everything in sight, you lot will only have to turn a longbow their way and it will be all they can do not to start digging a hole to dive into like so many demented hares, they certainly won't fight back! So that means that all you have to worry about is the knights there for the grander events, and you'll have the advantage of range over them."

"How many knights do you think will come?" Hugh asked thoughtfully.

"A good many fewer than Briwere hopes for," Guy replied without hesitation. "Who is there to come? The king has taken any man who was worth taking. So you can be sure that any younger man at the tourney will be there because he has two left feet when it comes to fighting on the ground, and probably falls out of the saddle at regular intervals if he has to do anything more than sit on his horse to chase a fox. The ones you'll need to watch are those who have obvious war wounds, because they'll be the few there who've ever seen real fighting."

Now for the real hook. Sweet Jesu, had it really come to this?

"I shall have to compete," Guy declared with resignation. "Briwere saw me use a bow to good effect, so he won't let me get away with not entering on his behalf. But he's only ever seen me use a hunting bow, not a wyche-elm bow the way fitz John did, and I'm not letting on that I have one. So you have to beat me using a lesser bow – shouldn't be hard for you lot."

There were laughs from most of the outlaws, but Guy saw Hugh and Siward exchanging pained looks, while Allan looked as though he was holding back tears with effort. Those three had instantly grasped what he had done – he'd fed Robin just what he wanted to hear to get him to move in the right direction at his own expense. And now Guy caught Malik whispering in Will's ear and Will suddenly whipping round to give Guy a look of deep sympathy even as Robin crowed,

"Oh, I'm sure that we can all give you a sound trouncing in the archery, couz'!"

Why did de Tuke make such a foolish comment in front of the sheriff? Oh, Brother, you have seen the sheriff as we saw him from the outset, but you must remember that to men like de Tuke, isolated in their own small worlds, Sheriff Briwere was just another Norman lord to be cultivated in case he could be useful to them. They never saw the danger to themselves until it was far too late.

And Briwere had no time for men like de Tuke. He saw them for what they were – men who could not quite make enough of a mark to hold such an office in the more prestigious monastic establishments in Normandy and France; men who were distinctly of the second tier, in terms of importance within their own orders and the Church. And as for de Tuke himself, maybe St Sebastian was in his mind because they were about to celebrate his feast-day when he returned to Newstead?

Oh dear, Gervase, that momentary blank look gave you away, did it not? I foresee you doing some penance in the future if you do not remember the proper observances of the saints, Brother, or is it that you depend too much on the others of your order to remind you? Either way, you should have known this! The feast of St Sebastian is on the twentieth of January, my friend, and we were entertaining the abbot at the end of the Yule festivities, so it was not that far away and if it does not stick in your mind, it surely did in his as another opportunity to fleece the faithful – and yes, I am cynical about his motives, Churchman or not.

And you are confused over what I just said about Robin?

Surely his motives were only good?

Oh, Gervase, I wish they had been, I truly do, but where I was concerned, my cousin fell far from the ideal image you have of him. The now legendary animosity between Sir Guy of Gisborne and Robin Hood had become closer to reality than I would ever have dreamed possible only a few years before. I forgive him now, Brother, for I know he was no longer in his right mind already at that stage, but at the time it was so much harder to be tolerant of his actions, much less forgiving when it was my neck which could have ended up being stretched. However, what I can say is that his motivation where the silver arrow of St Sebastian was concerned was only of the highest. He thought it appalling that such a sacred relic should be in the hands of one so mercenary as de Tuke, and to some extent I agreed with him on that.

Why only to some extent? No, Gervase, I am not so fallen from grace as to doubt the power of faith, only questioning why the Church appoints such avaricious men to its highest positions where they have control over the most precious of artefacts, which they then use for their own gain in contravention of everything which those relics represent? There will be another churchman who will come into this tale soon for whom I had the highest regard, for he was a truly good man, but that was something which even the most charitable could never have said about de Tuke. That is why I set de Tuke up to fall from grace.

It was not arrogance on my part, but rather a clear-sighted realisation that a relic of the saint who intercedes for men who make the ultimate sacrifice, was in the hands of a man who was avaricious, deceitful, and above all a bullying coward. He was not worthy, Gervase! Not in any way or form, and I was not setting myself up in God's place to judge him on anything except as the man he had already proven himself to be.

As for my cousin, a part of me was heartbroken that he took the bait of the tournament so readily, and in the form which I offered it to him. I had been praying that something of the old Bladwin would have surfaced for long enough that, when not under stress or pressure, he would recognise what I had suggested, and would at least make light of the fact that he was about to give me a public drubbing. If you ask me what I really wanted, it was that Robin would have at least been a touch rueful. Maybe admitting that he liked to win, that he liked the adulation, or at the very least, that he recognised that I would be making a pretty public sacrifice to allow him his success. None of that happened, and I am sorely afraid, Gervase, that that was another nail in the coffin of my affection for him; for I was forced to realise that not then, or even later as they worked out the details of how they would do this thing at the tournament, did he ever think of what might happen to me as a result.

The Coshams did, and so did Malik, Hugh and Siward as well as my other cousins. The Coshams quite quickly agreed between themselves that there was a limit to how far I could be seen to be easily defeated by some common archer. But then they had already had the experience of being Welsh archers on the run, and fearing what would happen to them if they got taken captive. Consequently they were more than willing to defeat the locals, but then make poor shots to fall behind me, so that nobody questioned where these expert marksmen had come from.

How is this different from Robin, you ask? Were they not acting out of personal motivation? Yes they were, Gervase, but it was in equal measure with regard for me. They did not want to sacrifice me on the altar of their personal gain. Indeed I was told by Gilbert and Colm that my three Welsh friends had a quiet talk on the side within the camp, and decided that someone – and preferably more than one – of the gang had to lose to me long before they discussed the dangers of winning, and it being discovered that they were Welsh archers.

They recognised, you see, that they could melt into Sherwood and lead any pursuers a merry dance in a way that I never could from such a public event. That, perversely, made me far more inclined to do something rash to distract people so that they could escape than the way I felt towards Robin. I am deeply saddened, Brother, at the memory of how my only thoughts for him had become ones where my only concern was that he did not lead the others into needless danger from which they could not escape. For that I am genuinely sorry. I should have cared more, but it was no longer possible for me to do so. So for that, mea culpa, mea culpa, mea maxima culpa.

Chapter 9

And so we come to that most significant of tournaments in late March of 1195. I have to confess, Gervase, that I thought it a singularly bizarre way to mark the start of a new year which came with the Annunciation to the Virgin, on March the twenty-fifth. The conception of Our Lord was hardly something which should have been celebrated with men being beaten black and blue, much less losing an eye or a limb. But then as I just said to you, I could never fathom the reasoning of the senior churchmen when it seemed to be in such direct opposition to the messages the Church gave out to ordinary folk. That has much to do with my preference for Tuck's Welsh saints, Brother. The Celtic Church seemed to preach a much kinder and more gentle version of what a Christian should do than those haughty Norman prelates, and it was one I found a lot easier to reconcile myself to. You do not agree, I know, but I kept faith as best I could in those years, and even you must acknowledge that I was sorely beset for much of that time.

Moreover, I should confess to you that I found it a lot easier to think of the turning of the season into a new year at the time many of the ordinary folk celebrated it, which was in the dark of the year at Yule. Everything in nature seemed to scream at me that this was when things changed, when we moved from decay into new growth, from reaping into sowing once more, and my year was very much one governed by what went on out in the natural world, in particularly the world of the forest. And it did not help that Tuck even went so far as to express doubts as to how the Church could possibly know <u>exactly</u> when Christ had made his appearance on this earth, for who amongst the Romans would have known, or cared, to record such an event for a child who had yet to show his true greatness?

Yes, I so know of the wise magi, Brother, I am not such a heathen as to not know that, and of the other signs and portents which occurred, and I have never doubted that such things happened. All I am saying is that the Church seems surprisingly certain of the <u>dates</u> of things which could not have been revealed in their full significance at the time. As ever, my doubts have been of what earthly men made of things, not of the actions of God, Christ and his saints and angels.

And with that in mind I shall begin with the arrival of the relic of St Sebastian at the tournament ground, for I had had nothing to do with the setting up of the tourney, being too busy with the woodmotes in the previous days, and therefore can tell you nothing of that. I arrived at the point when we needed to prepare for the arrival of the sheriff and to set up the collection of entry fees, and so I was there when St Sebastian arrived at Blyth after the short journey from Newstead.

I had had quiet words with my friends amongst the outlaws over discouraging the seizure of the relic before it made its way to the tournament ground. Sadly, I did not trust Robin not to try to capture the relic first to get that out of the way, and then make some other daft gesture at the tourney itself. That, I assure the others, would be dangerous, because it would make Briwere issue some counter challenge, which might mean that the outlaws could find themselves fighting their way out of the ground against many armed knights.

Yes, Gervase, I did say that those knights would be the least able of their sort, but a man on a horse and armed with a mace or a morningstar might do terrible damage to men on foot in no armour, without him ever having to be anything like competent. And that was a fate I did not wish for gentle souls like Much or the two lads from Walesby. It was not arrogance on my part, some belief that I could plan a better attack than my cousin. It was purely down to me knowing how this sheriff would react, nothing more, and I did not want my cousin poking this hornet's nest any harder than we could hope to cope with.

However, my fervent prayers to Saints Issui, Cadoc and Melangell must have been heard, because for once Robin did not go plunging wildly off the set track on his own crazed crusade, but kept to the plan. Something I was devoutly grateful for, even if the end results made the less experienced members of the gang adore him even more.

L. J. Hutton

The Tourney Field at Blyth
March, the Year of Our Lord 1195

Guy was standing under the canvas awning the sheriff would be using, when the procession from Newstead Abbey appeared on the high common land, bordered by marshes, where the tournament was due to take place. The greater area was open to all, for there was little point in trying to charge admission to the peasants. They would probably turn up to watch the mêlée, in which some of the local lads would no doubt be showing off their skills, but few would have much of an appetite for watching the events on the tilting yard – it was too much of a reminder of the brute force which could be turned on them at the whim of some touchy Norman lord. Moreover, all the wattle hurdles available were needed to fence off the actual arena, the butts and the tilting yard, and there were none left for the wider circuit. Therefore de Tuke and his sub-prior, a bumptious Norman by the name of Odard fitz Ruald, rode in on their supposedly symbolic white palfreys – although neither man resembled purity in any way to Guy's eyes – and were followed by a dozen of their canons and lay brothers, of whom the centre four were carrying a litter draped with a fine cloth and on which sat a gleaming silver reliquary in the shape of an arrow.

Sir Martin looked up from the list of entrants they had been scrutinising, saw where Guy was looking, and shook his head. "I wouldn't have traipsed the thick end of twenty-five miles through Sherwood with that thing carried so openly."

He stood up and massaged his back. Sir Martin and Sir Richard had been here at Blyth for the best part of two weeks, camping out in more than chilly conditions. It had not been helped by Roger de Pauliaco, the prior of nearby Blyth Priory and a man known to stand on his dignity at the best of times, taking exception to Eustace de Tuke stealing a march on him and having the confounded gall to parade his relic on Blyth's turf. As far as de Pauliaco was concerned, the gates of Blyth Priory would remain closed to everyone involved with the tournament unless the king himself showed up – him or Archbishop Walter. From what Sir Richard told Guy, de Pauliaco was particularly irked with the sheriff for not having come to him if he wanted an important relic at the tourney, because Blyth had a few of their own and de Pauliaco always had an eye for making more money. That the relics of their saints had nothing whatsoever to do with soldiers, as St Sebastian did, was neither here nor there in de Pauliaco's eyes.

"If de Tuke's hoping to store it safely at Blyth, he's got a nasty shock coming," Sir Richard mused.

"Oh he won't have expected that," Guy said with certainty. "Don't forget de Tuke's a Black Canon, a follower of the Augustinian order, while de Pauliaco is a Black Monk, a Benedictine. The ordinary brothers' habits might look similar from a distance, but never confuse the two – they're in deadly opposition!"

He half wanted to say that the sheriff had been a fool if he thought that this infringement of de Pauliaco's perceived rights would go unchallenged, but as he was the one responsible for involving de Tuke in the first place, and as a result for Sirs Richard's and Martin's discomfort, it was best not to say anything of the sort. Instead he clarified,

"Those doing the lugging of the relic are just the lay brothers. The canons are the better clad ones at the front and back."

Sir Richard scratched his growing beard, an enforced growth given that there was no hot water for shaving, and pulled a face. "I'd have expected this Robin Hood character to have a go at stealing that much silver. He's fond enough of coin normally. You don't think he's put off by it being a relic, do you? It doesn't sound right for a rascal of an outlaw to be thinking of his eternal soul."

Guy found himself chuckling at the irony of that statement, then knew he had to explain himself as the other two turned surprised eyes on him. He could hardly say the truth about Robin. "A devout outlaw, that would be a novel thing," he declared hurriedly, and was glad to see them then smiling with him. Blessed St Issui, that had been a near thing! He must watch himself closer over these coming days.

He turned back to the rough model of the tourney ground they had set up using mugs and bits of sticks, as one of their sergeants ran up to de Tuke and began gesturing to an ornate tent set up close to the tourney ground. "No, I'm sorry, Sir Martin, but the butts will have to be further away from the lists. God alone knows what quality of archer we'll have turning up, but we can't risk wild arrows from hunting bows whistling around the ears of the knights as they ride at one another. That way lies chaos! I think we need to allow four hundred yards length for the butts, because I'd rather the bosses had a bit more clearance behind them when at the far end."

Sir Richard scoffed. "Oh come now, Guy, you can't really think that anyone is going to hit anything at that distance. Unless the crossbows are aimed upwards they aren't going to reach anything much beyond about a hundred and fifty."

However Guy was already shaking his head. "No, I'm sorry, that's not quite true. Yes, their most effective distance is about a hundred and fifty yards, but they can still maim at three hundred – not through armour, you understand, but few people watching will be in armour, not even in gambesons, which would at least give some protection. Can you imagine the mayhem if one of the canons got winged by a crossbow bolt?"

The other two knights immediately shuddered.

"And you're forgetting the hunting bows again," Guy reminded them, doing his best not to sound as irritated as he felt. Why did these knights keep forgetting the hunting bows? He could forgive them their ignorance of great wyche-elm Welsh bows, but knew he had to remind them, "Don't forget, we could even have a Welsh bow or two appearing amongst the hunting bows." Adding in a softer tone, "You know ...like the one I used during the siege."

The two men blinked and then swallowed hard. They had been aghast at the carnage Guy had wrought using the great bow which had been hidden away in the tower until Sheriff Murdac had given Guy permission to use it.

"Who would have one of those here?" Sir Martin hissed back, giving a quick glance over his shoulder to make sure that none of the arriving knights were close enough to hear.

Guy shrugged. "I don't know, but it would be beyond foolhardy not to allow for something with that kind of range, because if they come, they'll be the ones we have to keep moving the bosses further and further back for. On the plus side, they are far less likely to be the ones flinging arrows wide of the mark, so let's work on needing a good wide space closer to, for the poorer archers with hunting bows and the crossbow men, and a good bit of length for the experts.

"...Oh and by the way, do you think we could keep quiet about the fact that I can use a Welsh bow? I'm in enough trouble with the sheriff as it is for winning his dogs over. If he thinks I can pin an arrow through an oak door at several hundred yards, he'll either have me in the dungeon or out on my ear."

Given how useful Guy was to both of them, the two were instantly nodding their assent to that.

"Will you compete, Guy?" Sir Martin asked.

"Oh, I don't think I can avoid doing that after what happened at Bolsover," Guy sighed, "but it will be with my normal hunting bow. I know Briwere would like nothing more than for me to walk off with the prize, so that he can take the money back off me the moment we're back inside the castle, but I think that's more than a little mean. There are ordinary men who are not knights who are still excellent archers, and who would put even a few pennies to good use, so I'm really hoping that someone will beat me hands down."

They agreed on an area for the butts, and Guy went off to chivvy the harassed men who were doing the rough work into moving the willow hurdles further along the common, and at right angles to where they had been. As he supervised them, however, there was a part of him that dearly wished he could compete anonymously – some way that he could go up against Robin without his cousin knowing who it was, and give him a real challenge. Guy knew he couldn't win against Robin. He didn't get chance to practice enough. But for his own self-respect, he would like not to get thrown out of the competition at the first round just because he was using the smaller bow.

The thought persisted throughout the rest of the day as he was helping to take the names of those knights who had turned up, sending them to where they could pitch their tents, and trying to sort out a first round in the lists which would not see all but the top few knocked out immediately. Briwere arrived as dusk was falling and had to be pandered to, not least because he had assumed that he would be sleeping at the priory and was not best pleased to be shown to a tent, albeit one suitably luxuriously appointed.

"That one's sorted thanks to you, Guy," Sir Martin said, as the three of them wrapped themselves in what furs they had on their dried bracken beds. "At least he and that thrice-be-damned prior are camped in luxury tonight. God knows what we'd have done if you hadn't loaded that wagon up at Nottingham with bedding, furs and chairs. He seems to have thought of nothing for himself."

"I suspect he does that deliberately," Guy said around a massive yawn. "He likes to have something to complain about, and even more so if he can berate some poor sod in public for something they didn't even know they were supposed to be doing."

"You really don't like him, do you?" Sir Richard said from the other side of the cramped tent. "I thought he'd got under our skin, but it's worse with you."

"Máel and Domnall," was Guy's simple reply, which got a sympathetic "Aaah!" from the other two. "Any man who can do that to an animal is less than human in my eyes," Guy added. "You didn't see them when Harry and I got those collars off and razored off those stinking, matted coats. Those festering wounds would have killed them sooner rather than later. Well a man who can do that is capable of doing it to a person, you mark my words, and the more he gets away with it, the worse he'll get. I'm just hoping that this tournament is suitably bloody, so that he gets his fill of gore for another month or so."

The next morning Guy was glad to be out of the sheriff's way, for Briwere was in a foul mood and de Tuke wasn't much better, demanding that an armed guard was posted at his tent to watch over the arrow. There was something to be said for being the one to oversee the archery, since it removed Guy off to the butts, while Briwere and de Tuke continued to harangue Sirs Martin and Richard as they attempted to get the jousting underway. The tilt for the jousting had blown down in the wind overnight, and men were frantically re-erecting the line of gaily coloured flags and posts down the centre of the designated area along which the entrants would canter with their lances.

Thank God the March gales had subsided this morning, Guy thought as he strode off to the butts, or the archery would be in danger of descending into a right fiasco as well. In the gusting winds they'd had these last two days, the arrows would have been snatched off course from even the most experienced archers. This first tournament wasn't turning out to be quite the dazzling event Briwere had wanted.

A line of rag-tag men were waiting patiently for him when he got there, and he was glad that he had paced out the yard markers with the two soldiers from the castle who would be helping him, since that meant that they could start straight away. What he was less pleased about was that Briwere heard the *thunk* of arrows hitting the straw bosses, and decided to come and see what was going on while the first group of knights got their armour on, and their horses caparisoned in their drapery of respective colours and heraldic symbols.

"Well you seem to have got things organised, Gisborne," Briwere said snidely as he came to stand beside him, then looked Guy up and down, only to quickly look away again. Guy had dressed in his best tunic today, one of leather tanned so darkly that it was as good as black, and decorated with studs. Teamed with his heaviest and darkest woollen trousers, thick woollen jacket beneath the tunic, and his decent pair of equally dark boots, Guy was bulkier and taller by far than the sheriff and presented quite the menacing, black-clad figure.

It hadn't only been done for show, although Guy was more than glad of the effect it was having on Briwere. These were the warmest clothes he possessed, and he'd known he would need them if he was standing around on the open land of the common for hours. But now he put on his iciest smile, and drew himself up to his full height to look down on the sheriff as Briwere declared,

"Oh, good shooting!" as one of the men-at-arms from the castle hit the bull.

No doubt hoping to catch Guy out, Briwere then asked, "Why all the land behind? Rather a waste of hurdles, eh?"

Looking down his nose at the sheriff who barely came up to his shoulder, Guy replied coolly, "Oh this is just the crossbows. They're starting at a hundred yards. To be honest most aren't reaching that, although they should. If we get anyone even close to being good enough we might go back as far as two hundred today."

Briwere sniffed, clearly not happy at having his hopes for a crack crossbow company so dismissed, but he wasn't about to give up on chipping away at Guy to see how soon he would crack. "But you still have double that length out there, don't you, Gisborne, or could your men not count?"

Guy gave another frozen smile, "Ah, but that's for the hunting bows, sheriff. We'll start them off the same, and in truth I wouldn't try to bring a deer down at anything beyond a hundred yards, but we have a stationary target here and good shooting conditions. Depending on the size of bows we get entering tomorrow, we could end up going further back than we will with the crossbows."

Briwere mouthed a silent 'oh', and was clearly mulling that information over, then asked, "And how many contestants do we have here today?"

"Three dozen. We've got men from Bolsover, Tickhill and Conisborough castles, as well as Nottingham and High Peak. There are even a couple from the Forester's castle at Laxton. But these men were always going to be in the minority, because they'll only come from the castles. Crossbows cost too much for villagers to have. But when it comes to hunting bows, any halfway decent bowyer can make a single-wood bow good enough to hunt the odd predatory fox taking down their lambs, and most villages will have lads who can make a respectable attempt at hitting the target." *There,* Guy thought, *I've given you a good reason why these lads would have a bow,* but still Briwere couldn't resist adding,

"And maybe for some illegal poaching, eh, Gisborne? Need to keep an eye on a few of them perhaps?"

"I don't think the competent poachers will be daft enough to show their skills here," Guy responded witheringly before he could stop himself, then hurriedly added in more conciliatory tones, "But I shall make a note of those whom I think are a little too good, you can be sure of that."

Mercifully a clashing of metal and a roar from the direction of the lists announced that the jousting had got under way, and the sheriff hurried away.

Taking the chance to walk away to calm down and see what ranges the scribes had written down for each soldier, Guy was unaware of Allan sidling up to him until he turned to walk away and nearly fell over his cousin.

"Out of the way, peasant," he said haughtily, but with a wink and a flick of the eyes towards the lean-to canvas where the spare bosses were being kept in case of sudden squally showers, which might drench the straw and make the painted targets run. Allan took the hint and scampered away to disappear behind the canvas, while Guy strolled over to it and made much of inspecting the supplies.

"What news?" he asked Allan, now that they were unlikely to be overheard.

"We're all here and Robin is behaving," Allan replied. "That was a big sigh of relief. Did you think he wouldn't?" Then hurriedly added, "Not that I blame you for that. He hasn't given you much reason to trust of late."

"No, he hasn't," Guy sighed sadly, "and I wish I could believe that he will change towards me, but I don't think even all of Tuck's prayers are going to achieve that now. That's a miracle his saints are going to have to perform for us, if they are willing." Then he gave himself a mental shake and asked, "So everyone is ready? Are you going to use Welsh bows from the start?"

"We thought we'd save those for the second round." Allan's voice was full of mischief and it made Guy smile. "Don't want to worry anyone too early on, and this is about the archer not the bow, isn't it?"

"It is. As long as you can all hit the bull with hunting bows in the first round you'll go through, and to be honest I can't imagine even Much missing at that range having practiced with a bigger bow over further. Is Much entering?"

"Much, and Colm, Ed, Martin and Simon. Even Roger's having a go. The only ones not here are Aneirin and Rhys, because they're too valuable to risk, and neither is capable of doing the running we'll need to do to make the getaway once we take the arrow."

"Marianne and Mariota?"

"They're here. They're charged with scouting out the relic. We all thought that two women gawping at a nice bit of silver would be less obvious than a bunch of men staring at it."

"Clever."

"Hugh's idea. Robin wasn't keen. He muttered something about them not knowing what to look for tactically, but we all squashed him over that one and pretty fast too. We're going to decide our escape route when we all get back to camp tonight. There are so many men with bows camping rough round here we hardly stand out, and we've made sure we're back in the woods by Hodsock, not in the first clusters around here."

"Good thinking."

"We've got three wood bows that we're going to share between us, so we'll be coming forwards in threes – just so that you know. I think Robin was about to ask Aneirin to make us all a wood bow, but Will and Malik made it clear that he has better things to be doing, and anyway why would we lug two bows each? If necessary, Marianne and Mariota can scoop the smaller bows up and bring them away, and if we lose them it's hardly the end of the world."

"Thank you. I'm glad I know all of that."

"Means you're not trying to look through the back of your head all the time," Allan chuckled. "I know, Guy. I was listening to you and the bloody sheriff. God's hooks, he's a pain in the arse, isn't he! I'd never know where his mind was going to skip off to next."

With a heavy sigh, Guy agreed. "And the only way I'm staying one step ahead of him is because of all the practice I had with de Braose years ago. I've worked up to this bastard – the other poor sods in the castle are finding it all too much after what happened last year. We've never seemed to've had a chance to catch our breath from one thing before another disaster has landed in our laps. If this goes off to plan it will be the first thing that's worked for me since I can't remember when."

"Then for your sake we'll make it work," Allan said firmly. "I'll try and catch up with you later on or early tomorrow."

Guy sauntered back over to the butts with studied arrogance, positively daring the two men-at-arms to ask him what he'd been doing, but they and the clerk were too busy sorting out the next round to see or care.

"The three dozen are down to just nine, Sir Guy," one of the soldiers told him. "They were the only ones to hit the bull even once. The rest had bolts all over the place. Some didn't even hit the target but fell short. This is going to be a very short contest if the wood bows aren't any better tomorrow."

With the target moved back to one hundred and fifty yards, the final was swiftly decided, with one of the Keeper's men coming first, a man from Nottingham castle coming second, and one from Tickhill just about struggling in to third place. They had no idea how their collective incompetence warmed Guy's heart. Only the Keeper's man had any chance of hitting a moving target, and Guy felt sure that he would be back the following day with a hunting bow. If this was the best that the sheriff could call upon, the outlaws were safe from the crossbows at least.

However, as he had predicted, the following day the standard was a lot higher. Nobody was missing the boss at the hundred yard range, and there were enough men who were comfortably hitting the bull at least once for there to be a respectable thirty-nine going through to the second round. Guy had enjoyed taking his place amongst them and taking his allocated three shots, but he had also added the name of Drogo of Castleton to the list, under which name he hoped to enter a second time anonymously.

It had been a spur of the moment thing. Something he had done as he'd watched a figure who could only be Robin, almost swaggering onto the field to take his part in the first round. And Robin had made it look so ridiculously easy, making a tight cluster of three arrows right in the centre of the bull. But it was a foolish thing to do, as well, Guy thought. He'd immediately made himself the subject of chatter in the crowd watching, and that could well mean that any of the sheriff's spies would already know that there was a superb archer in the contest.

As himself, Guy had then felt he had to make his best shots when his turn came to make Robin's seem less singular, and was gratified to hear some 'ooh's and 'aah's from the audience. At one of the next butts he then saw that Malik had made a neat cluster of arrows on his target, and the audience was suddenly all eyes for what was turning out to be an unexpectedly fierce contest. The three Coshams also made good shots without resorting to the kind of showing off that Robin had done, while Allan, Roger, Much, Tuck and John all got through to the next round alongside Hugh, Siward, Gilbert and Will, and also Tuck, who hid his tonsure under a heavy woollen cap and for once dressed like all the others, not in his habit – although Guy could tell that he must be wearing a pair of John's long trews, as the only ones to go round his girth, by the way they were rolled up around the tops of his boots. Only the new lads of the gang fell by the wayside, and their shooting had been far from the worst. And to cap it, Guy made his appearance as Drogo in the last but one group, laying a neat cluster of arrows at the bull as well, his finery covered by a scruffy old cape and his height disguised by a hunched over walk. He was through to the next round twice over.

There was a pause while everyone went off and had something to eat while the bosses were moved back another twenty-five yards, and then the contest began in earnest. To Guy's delight, Allan found him and whispered,

"We're going to use the hunting bows for the next round, as well. Thomas, Piers and Malik reckon that, as it's a still day, we'll have no trouble hitting the targets at that range, so we're saving the Welsh bows for tomorrow. It'll be a surprise then!"

And so the afternoon wore on and the target got moved back another twenty-five yards to a hundred and fifty yards for a third round, because all the contestants had hit the target so well that it had been impossible to weed any but two out at the third round's distance. The locals were putting on a good show, Guy was delighted to see, and the Keeper's man was still in the game – which was a good thing, and showed that Guy wasn't the only man on the side of the law who could hit something at that distance.

But in the fourth round at one hundred and seventy-five yards, the extra yards with the smaller bows winnowed the field down. Roger and Much went out as Guy had expected, and Allan only remained by the skin of his teeth and a lucky last shot. Tomorrow, though, with the bigger bows they would all be heading for the final!

Taking a late night walk under the pretext of making sure that the guards on the arrow were still awake, Guy wandered off and found Allan, John and Hugh waiting for him by a big old oak which cast a dense shade even at night. When Guy told them he'd entered as Drogo and asked if he could borrow a Welsh bow tomorrow, he was touched by the way they all caught on as to why he'd done it.

"As Sir Guy you can only use a hunting bow, can't you," Hugh said sympathetically. "And even if you're not there to see it, you know that Robin is going to gloat over it when you go out."

"I do," Guy said sadly. "The only thing I've been able to do is make sure that I'm not in his actual group when it comes to taking the shots. And I did that, because I feared he'd do something really stupid like splitting his first arrow with his second just to rub it in with me, but without thinking how that would look if the sheriff comes to watch."

John put a hand on Guy's shoulder and squeezed it comfortingly. "Don't worry, we all told him to stop showing off after that first round – well all of us who've known him a long time, that is. I'm getting less and less happy about the way those two young men from Walesby dog his every step, looking up to him as though he's about to walk on water at any moment. Tuck's trying to mediate there, but us three and Siward, Will and Malik have all said that we have a nasty feeling that tragedy is going to strike there if we're not careful, because those lads would follow him into anything, even an obvious trap."

"Then can you make sure that they are on their way out of the tourney ground before you seize the arrow?" Guy asked.

"Already ahead of you, couz'," Allan reassured him. "Even Gilbert thought it would be a good idea, given that they're already out of the contest, if they joined Marianne and Mariota in doing some crowd watching for us, and the lasses have agreed to get the lads moving as soon as the first whiff of trouble starts."

"*Dewi Sant!*" Guy breathed in relief.

"And I'll let you use my bow," Hugh said. "John's will be too strong for you, and I'm not a good enough shot to be in the final, whereas you might make it. Once I'm out of the competition, I'll hardly be wandering around with my bow until we get to the point where we grab the arrow, so 'Drogo' can hand it back to me and vanish so that Sir Guy can reappear."

"Bless you," was Guy's heartfelt response, but Hugh immediately came back with,

"No, you deserve this! Why shouldn't you have a chance to show what you can do? By St Thomas, Guy, you risk more than all of us. You at least can have this."

"Well I have news for you all," Guy added. "Because the winners of each section of the tournament will have their chance to come up and touch the holy relic tomorrow, the guard will go from being just that pair of elderly men-at-arms you've seen so far, to two knights. And the sheriff is going to call forward the two who get closest to winning and are still on their feet. I say on their feet because we have the final of the joust to open with tomorrow, and then there's the mêlée – and in that, even the best of those we have here could end up being carried off! So those two knights who are standing either side of the arrow at the end will be the toughest two who withstood the mêlée. Not the best or most skilled, but the biggest brutes of the lot! So be careful!"

"Thanks for the warning," Hugh said, "We'll pass it on to the others."

"...And make sure Robin understands!" Allan added emphatically, knowing that that was what Guy needed to hear.

Was I that jealous of my cousin? No, Brother, I was not, not jealous. I had no desire to be the man he was or to walk in his place. But allow me some toleration for being merely human, please! Remember that we were only a year on from the time when Robin had come very close to making me a hunted man and labelled as a traitor to the king, and in the intervening months he had done very little to convince me that his feelings towards me were of Christian love. I went to Blyth as sure as any man could be that if the chance came to ruin me, then Robin would take that chance and revel in it.

No, Brother, that is not what you expected of him, but it is the truth as I perceived it, for I was the one person whom he could not sway – or at least he thought I was. The reality was that the more mature members of the outlaws were increasingly seeing him in a different light, but because he never behaved in the same way towards them as he did to me, Robin did not see them or their doubts as clearly as he might have. And if you ask did he take advantage of their loyalty and compassion, then I would have to answer, yes he did.

As for myself, I speak no word of a lie when I tell you that all I wanted to do was to pit my skills against Robin's in an equal contest. For the sake of the others, I was not going to do it openly as Sir Guy of Gisborne, because had anything happened to any one of my friends as a result of me poking Robin's prickly pride, then I would never have forgiven myself. I genuinely cared for their safety above all. But this was a rare opportunity for me to measure myself against him, not in the heat of a raid where the position of one or the other of us might be very different, but as equals under the same conditions.

If I lost, if he beat me by a goodly measure, then I knew that I would have to reconsider his opinions when he gave them as to whether or not a shot could be taken, or an action won by archers, in the future. I am, and was not, so full of pride as not to have given him that credit. But there was a part of me that wanted to prove to myself that my own assessments truly were as competent as his; and that in situations such as had taken place at Bolsover, that I was equally proficient to make the decisions as to whut was feasible and what was not.

That was it, Brother, nothing more. But I will delay our tale not longer...

Chapter 10

So I will not keep you in suspense, Brother. We will return immediately to the tournament and that moment you have been waiting for.

The Tourney Field at Blyth
March, the Year of our Lord 1195

Knowing that his friends were forewarned meant that Guy got some sleep that night, and when the competition began again the next morning he was almost looking forward to it.

They started the day at two hundred yards, because Guy could hardly whisk the bosses farther back than that, and therefore beyond the reach of most hunting bows, when nobody else knew that the big bows were going to appear. However, when Piers and Allan took their places in the first group to shoot, with the longbows which were as tall as they were, the collective gasps and hoots from the crowd rivalled those coming from the joust, and Guy knew that the sheriff would be sending someone over to see what was happening. For a moment he feared the other archers were about to start protesting, but with his usual quick wit and charm, Allan was moving amongst them and whatever he was saying was turning the scowls to grins.

Then bows were flexed, strings were pulled taut, and the first arrows of the day took flight. Six men were shooting at a time, and Guy was pleased that two of those four still using hunting bows nonetheless got through. Then the next six came up to shoot with Hugh and Thomas amongst them, and this time it was Hugh who was having quiet words with the other archers. So by the third group, when Guy and the Keeper's man were in with Malik and Gilbert, it was hard for anyone else to protest at the unfairness of going up against the big bows, and the fact that Sir Guy himself was willing to take a drubbing did much to ease the tensions. Robin, Tuck and John came in the fourth group, and then in the final six were Will, Siward and Bilan with 'Drogo' and another two men. The covert winks Guy got in that final shoot from his three friends reassured him that they all thought this was great fun, and were enjoying his moment immensely, as he pulled back on Hugh's Welsh bow and loosed an arrow straight at the boss.

Since only one man had gone out in five of the six groups, the targets went back another twenty-five yards, and this was when the limits of the smaller hunting bows became apparent. Even Guy with his own bow couldn't get more than one arrow onto the boss, despite his greater strength than the ordinary peasant farmers, who made up all of the other hunting bowmen aside from the Keeper's man, and all of them went out. Against the odds there were even murmurs of sympathy for Guy as he left the field and someone called out, "Bad luck, Sir Guy," in tones which implied that they actually meant it.

Mercifully he had restrained himself and managed not to grin, because when he got back to where the scribes were arranging the next groups, de Tuke was there, glowering.

"Like being popular with the peasants, do you?" he asked waspishly.

Guy looked back at him coldly. "Just because they are poor does not mean that they don't understand what is fair and what is not, what is right and what is wrong. And if they don't, then surely it is you men of the cloth who have not provided them with the right guidance, Prior?"

De Tuke looked like he'd swallowed a maybug – so unused to anyone answering him back that he was lost for words to riposte with.

"Now then, scribe, who do we have for the next round?" Guy demanded, giving the prior no time to engage in more spiteful banter.

"Drogo of Castleton, John of Hathersage, Will of ...of wherever that place is, Sir Guy?"

"It's a place in the Holy Land," Guy supplied. "The man is obviously a soldier returned from the crusades." And it was clever of Will to have given that name, Guy thought, because it meant he had every reason to be a good shot. The other former crusaders had also chosen places along the crusading routes to add to their first names, and it meant that word had gone around the crowd that these were the kind of men who had fought for Jerusalem, which softened the blow of them knocking out the local lads even more.

So now it was down to a contest between the outlaws and Guy, although only they knew it and with the bosses back at two hundred and fifty yards, although everyone hit the target, Allan, Hugh, Tuck and John couldn't make good enough shots to stay in the contest. The nine of them remaining were split into groups of five and four, with Guy making sure that as Drogo he went into the first group so that he had time to get back and arrange the final. Yet this was very much a contest of equals and every one of them hit the target, to gasps of amazement from the crowd.

Guy got back to the scribe's desk just in time for the sheriff to appear as Will was taking his first shot. For Guy had decided to give the crowd a treat, and although the men still stood in a group, they were now shooting in turn at a single boss rather than having two bosses working at the same time – with Guy's excuse, which he had called out across the field, being that at this range every man needed to be able to concentrate.

"Christ and St Thomas! What by the Devil and all his little demons are those things?" Briwere demanded in horror as he looked at Will's huge bow, and the way the smith's bare forearms were showing his massive muscles flexing as he pulled back on the string.

"That's a Welsh bow, sheriff," Guy answered calmly. "The man is a former crusader. Don't think he's local, but then we didn't exclude those just passing through, did we? He and his mates are probably on the way up to one of the Templar granges on the East coast."

Another yard-long arrow streaked down the butts to land with an audible thud into the packed roundel of straw with a by now very tattered target cloth on it. The bull was marked more by the gaping hole in the cloth than the red colour which had once been painted on it, and as Will's third arrow joined its companions in the centre,

Guy heard Briwere swallow reflexively. Clearly the sheriff was having no trouble imagining what that could do to a man.

"They can pierce armour easily," Guy said casually, as if throwing out information of no great surprise. "I saw the Welsh archers doing that a lot over on the Borders."

Briwere turned shocked eyes up to Guy, for once so stunned by what he'd heard that for possibly the first time Guy was getting a genuine reaction from the man.

"Pierce armour? What ...like a knight's armour, you mean?"

"Oh yes," Guy said, leaning back and folding his arms casually. "They put one straight through the oak door at Abergavenny Castle, you know? De Braose left it there so that he could brag about his revenge on the families of those men, but even he knew when to back off from the Welsh when they brought those big bows into a fight." His smile had something of the curled lip of disdain in it. "Did you not realise that was why the king wanted Welsh archers in the Holy Land, sheriff?"

"Crossbows," Briwere said weakly. "I thought they were just good with crossbows."

Guy gave a little snort. "Fuck all use they'd be against the Saracens' Scythian bows! I've heard about them, too, from men who were out there. Smaller but with more flexibility, they're every bit as deadly, especially as they can be used from on horseback. But don't worry, sheriff, you won't see them over here. They're made with sinew glued in layers, and the animal glue they use doesn't stand up to our wet climate – the bows fall apart."

Briwere swallowed hard again. "Really ...how fortunate. No Sc... What did you call them?"

"Scythian bows, sheriff." Guy was damned if he was going to 'my lord' Briwere when there was only the two of them and the scribe (who looked as if he wanted to melt into his stool out of sight at the exchange going on quite literally over his head). "Scythia – it's a place in the East."

"Fascinating. ...What range are you at now?"

"Two hundred and fifty."

"Two hun...! God in Heaven!"

"And if you'll excuse me, sheriff, now that everyone's finished we're going to take the bosses back to three hundred for the final, because with men of this quality and those bows there's no point in having an interim round. ...You soldiers, fetch two new bosses and bring those others up here!"

As the soldiers hurriedly ran down the field with a handcart and loaded the first boss onto it, Guy gestured for the sheriff to step out with him, and as the boss came past them, paused the two men dragging the cart and made a show of inspecting the boss so that Briwere could see how the arrows had gone in so deeply that the heads were poking out of the back.

"*Hmmm*, good shots, all of them," Guy declared with professional detachment, but with one eye on the sheriff's face, which for some reason had gone rather pale.

As the final was about to get underway, Guy made the excuse of leaving the sheriff to go and make sure that nobody was cheating by using barbed arrows which might stick and snag on the target without properly going in. They wouldn't, of course. For a barbed arrow to do what it was meant to do it had to penetrate like any other, but Briwere didn't know that, and Guy wasn't going to enlighten him.

Gilbert went first, and made three creditable shots although none hit the bull. 'Drogo' went next, and Guy was well pleased that he got one of his arrows on the bull, although the other two were distinctly out on the edge of the target. But that was no more than he expected at that range. Siward, Bilan and Piers managed the same, while all three of Will's arrows hit but like Gilbert's did not get near the boss. Then Thomas stepped up, and following Will using the second fresh boss, gave a glorious demonstration to the crowd by dropping all three of his arrows in the bull where they sat vibrating in clear view of all.

A roar of approval went up, and Briwere visibly winced, which Guy saw since by now he was back by the sheriff's side.

"Welsh," Guy said knowingly. "Has to be with that kind of skill. Probably hasn't been home in years given that he's given us a grange out in the East as his home, but that kind of skill only comes with years of practice. This is what de Braose is up against, sheriff. No wonder nobody else wants Herefordshire, eh?"

Briwere was looking distinctly sick and clearly making rapid revisions to his career options.

Then Malik came up and the crowd audibly gasped and seemed to hold its collective breath, because Heaven alone knew how he'd managed to construct it and keep it dry enough to use now, but for this final Malik was using a Scythian bow!

"*Dewi Sant!*" Guy gasped involuntarily. "He must have made that especially for this contest! ...*That*, sheriff, is a Scythian bow! That's what they were up against at Hattin and Acre!"

The lighter, springier bow made less of a deep thrumming noise when loosed than the big bows, but instead seemed to sing a higher note. Yet there was no mistaking the way the arrow flew down the field and lodged neatly in the bull alongside Thomas'. The next arrow flew with equal accuracy, but on the final shot the bow gave way just as Malik loosed. It wasn't enough to drop the arrow short, but the weakness had robbed his shot of some of its accuracy and the arrow hit the bottom of the target, but then drooped down having not gone in with any depth.

The crowd was so caught up in the spectacle that the groans of sympathy at Malik's misfortune were genuine. And his response of a small bow to them with his hand over his heart resulted in him being enthusiastically clapped off the field. The folk of northern Nottinghamshire hadn't seen the like of this in living memory! And it was about to get better, because last on to compete was Robin.

Making it look insanely easy, he dropped his first two arrows right in the centre of the bull, and then, turning for just a heartbeat to look back at the sheriff standing open-mouthed, he nocked his final arrow and loosed. It flew down the field and split his second arrow, which had been in the perfect centre of the boss, straight down the middle.

The crowd went wild! And if Briwere had had any thoughts of doing anything to this man who had done something so terrifyingly and dangerously improbable, one look around at the number of people there and he knew he'd be taking his life in his hands. The time to hammer this people's hero would be when surrounded by well-armed knights, not out here with only a rogue knight like Sir Guy at hand.

"Looks like you have a clear winner, sheriff," Guy declared, and watched Briwere's expressions flash between appalled, scared stiff and angry several times over. No doubt the sheriff had dreamt of handing over the prize to one of his own men-at-arms, but with a display of archery such as he had just seen, there was no earthly point in bringing back the crossbow winner to pitch against this man, either over distance or for accuracy. The man with the big Welsh bow had won hands down.

Turning on his heels, Briwere stormed off, not even waiting to do the expected thing of congratulating the winner. Instead, Guy was left to stand in front of the crowd as his cousin came up to him to be officially announced the winner. It wasn't hard for Guy to not seem overjoyed, although only the select few knew of his reasons, because Robin positively bounded up to him, handsome face wreathed in smiles as the crowd cheered enthusiastically.

Gritting his teeth, Guy gestured for Robin to turn and face the crowd and announced, "And the winner is ...Robin of Loxley!"

It had been insanity for Robin to use that name, Guy had known right from the moment he saw it on the scribe's sheet. Only Briwere's unfamiliarity with the fact that Robin Hood claimed to hail from the deserted village of Loxley over the border in Yorkshire had saved him from being instantly spotted, but Robin had given his name to the clerk before Guy got to him. That was something that was going to have to be dealt with back at the camp, because Robin had taken a stupid risk which could have killed their plans stone dead before they even started.

Luckily most of the crowd were cheering so wildly they didn't hear the name, and of the few that did only a handful stopped cheering for a moment as the name sank in, then looked at their neighbours and cheered even more vigorously. Those of the gang within earshot, though, visibly jumped at Guy's announcement, and then looked at him as though he was mad. That was going to cause some trouble if he didn't stamp on it fast, too!

"You will approach the sheriff this afternoon to receive your reward," Guy announced loudly, although few were listening, "And you may kiss the relic of St Sebastian, brought here by the grace of the prior of Newstead. Make sure you are not tardy in coming to the lists where the winners will be rewarded. The sheriff will not dally for the likes of you." Then Guy was able to escape and leave Robin soaking up the adulation as the crowd cheered themselves hoarse.

Behind the same awning where he had met Allan, Guy ran into a group of the outlaws.

"What the fuck were you playing at?" Will immediately demanded angrily. "You could have got him killed!"

"Why do you think I kept calling forward everyone by their Christian names?" Guy riposted, and as Will drew breath to launch another scathing attack it was only Malik's calm intervention with,

"Wait, Will! Let him speak," which saved the day.

However, it was Allan who got in first with,

"Oh, no! Don't tell me he enrolled under that name?"

That stopped all of them in their tracks, their expressions turning from anger to disbelief as Guy nodded.

"There was nothing I could do," Guy told them. "He made sure he was right at the front of the queue yesterday morning, and the clerk had already put his name down as I got there. If I'd been a bit quicker, I might have been able to publicly challenge him on something like the fact that Loxley doesn't exist anymore. But in truth, I'd been trying to avoid a confrontation with him of any kind, and so I hung back a bit thinking I was doing the right thing. Since then, I told the scribe that, as several of you had used foreign sounding names, the crowd would be less hostile if we just kept it to first names except for those three Richards we had amongst the other men, and the other Hugh who joined in."

"He registered *himself* as Robin of Loxley?" Tuck had to ask again to believe what he was hearing. "*Dewi Sant* preserved us today, then!"

Will came and clapped Guy on the arm, apologising, "By Our Lady, Guy, I'm sorry. I ought to have known you wouldn't do something so thoughtless. You always think things through. There's only one of us who plunges in so bloody recklessly."

Back a way in the group Guy heard Bilan saying, "I told you, Piers! I told you it wouldn't be Guy's fault!" and that warmed his heart, especially as he heard Roger joining in in agreement.

However, Guy could not linger, for it would be fatal for anyone to see him fraternising with the archers for too long. This much he could excuse as trying to recruit these men for the castle guard, and failing, but not much more, and so he made his excuses to go although not without begging them,

"Please don't argue with him about this now! Wait until you are back in camp. I don't want him thinking he's got to prove anything to you lot as well. And given what he's done, for the love of God don't tell him what I did as Drogo, either! That really will set him off like a bolting horse, and he might even think he has to try to do something crazy like kill the sheriff. That would be a bloody catastrophe! The king's army would descend on the shire like demon warriors from Hell, and we'd have more villagers dead than alive by the time they left."

That no-one argued with him at least reassured him that those here were with him, although he knew that the newer men and Much would see things only through Robin's eyes. Much's memory of how he'd been abandoned seemed to fail when confronted with Robin in the flesh, and the young man was as much Robin's devotee as ever.

At the main arena the mêlée was coming to a close. Most of the contestants were on the floor, with only a few hardy souls still battering one another off to one side. Totally uninterested in this bloody mess, Guy went around the back of the more luxurious seating which had been put up on a well-secured flat-bed wagon for the sheriff and the prior plus a couple of guests, which included de Tuke's fellow Augustinian, Prior William of Worksop, and the new constables of Tickhill and Bolsover. Normally Guy would have been very interested in learning what he could of these men, but today he had neither the energy nor the inclination. Instead, he wanted to see that arrow close to, and so he eased his way up to the two men-at-arms, who were far more interested in the fighting than watching the relic, and scrutinised the reliquary.

It had to be solid silver, of that he was sure just from the weight of it, for it had sunk deeply into the silken cushion it rested upon, and no arrow that bulky or short would ever take flight in reality. But that meant that the silver alone was worth a fortune, because unless St Sebastian had the build of an ox, even one of his middle fingers or a thumb would occupy only a tiny fraction of the space within. With a tentative finger of his own, Guy reached out and ever so gently touched the finely tooled surface, wondering if he would immediately feel the sanctity of the relic. He was so engrossed that he nearly jumped out of his skin when Prior William asked him in heavily accented English,

"Are you a man of faith, Sir Guy?"

Looking up and seeing the prior looking down at him from his place at the end of the wagon, Guy had no trouble in answering,

"Oh yes, my lord prior!"

"It is a rare opportunity for ordinary men to be able to get so close to something so precious, is it not?"

"Yes, my lord, it is."

The prior gave a smile which never quite reached his eyes. "Such an honour, then, for those who are here. I hope everyone will be suitably generous, eh?"

Pasting a sickly smile of his own on, Guy agreed, "Indeed, my lord, a great honour. We will be mindful of the grace," that was a word which stuck in his throat, "which has been bestowed upon us."

"Quite right, quite right," the prior intoned and turned his attention back to the mêlée, where a team of three battered and bloody men had finally overcome all other opponents, and were staggering back to their tents to the half-hearted cheers of the small crowd of the shires' nobility who were watching. Most of them, Guy realised, were wondering how much money they were going to be paying their neighbours as the scribes frantically worked out who could be deemed to have taken whom captive. In the meantime, the stretcher bearers that Guy had forewarned Sirs Martin and Richard they would need, were hurrying onto the field to take away those who could not walk off unaided, and there were a considerable number of those. If Briwere had thought that any of the local young bloods would be doing much hunting in the next week or so, the sight of so many of them now barely able to keep to their own feet must have seriously disabused him of that idea, and Guy realised that that was something else which would not help the sheriff's mood.

He was glad to see that his two knight friends from the castle were not armed in any way, and blessed the fact that he had no sword on him, while his bow was back at the butts. That meant that none of the three of them could get drawn into any serious fighting when the outlaws came for the arrow, and that would be soon. But his gaze was drawn back to that reliquary, because despite Prior William distracting him, he was nonetheless quietly amazed that he had felt nothing when he touched it. Not that Guy had expected lightning blasts from the heavens or anything, but he had thought he would feel *something* from such a holy object. Maybe a slight tingling in the finger, or the sense of some form of disembodied presence, but to be aware of nothing but a large quantity of cold metal disconcerted him more than he would like to admit.

However, he was not left to brood for too long. The knights who had won at the joust and the sword fighting event were discovered to be intact and capable of coming to receive their rewards, and so was the leader of the winners of the mêlée. And so with a growing crowd of ordinary people surging in to witness the ceremony, Briwere got the proceedings underway by getting the men-at-arms to bring the reliquary of St Sebastian forward to in front of his makeshift dais.

Far from looking happy, the sheriff looked for all the world as though he'd been slapped in the face with a particularly slimy and smelly trout from the priory fishpond. No knights guarded the relic, because most of them could barely stand up, much less guard anything, and Briwere had one eye almost permanently on the bulging purses on the scribes' desk beside the arrow. They were what he feared would be taken, Guy knew, but his mood wasn't helped by the fact that none of his wagers had won either.

Indeed the knight who had carried the day at the joust came from Conisborough Castle over in Yorkshire, so that was several shillings the sheriff would never see again, not even in taxes. Then the knight who had won with his sword was one of the sheriff of Lincoln's knights – more prize money going out of the shire – and only the bloodied lesser knights from the mêlée turned out to be anything like local. But they were three ex-crusaders who were in the pay of the bishop of Newark, whom the sheriff loathed even more than he did Guy. Briwere hadn't had a good day, and worse was yet to come.

As each of these men came and received their winnings and then reverently kissed the reliquary, Guy could see Robin and the outlaws edging their way further forward. Robin, of course, had to come pretty much to the centre of the field as a winner, but Guy noted that the others were well distributed and had picked their places very carefully, so that they had almost all of those men who were remotely capable of fighting back covered by their arrows.

"And finally," the sheriff declared in wearied tones, "the overall winner of the archery contest is," he looked down to the scribe who hissed a name at him, "Robin of Loxley. Come forward good man and receive your shilling. You may touch the reliquary."

It was a paltry reward compared to the others, and neither was it lost on the crowd that whereas the other contestants had been allowed to kiss the reliquary, their favoured winner would only be allowed to touch it. As a result there was a hum of disgruntled voices from the crowd as Robin bounded up to the scribe, but at the same time the penny dropped with Briwere,

"Just a...! Robin of Loxley? ...Isn't that the name that Robin Hood uses?" he asked of no-one and everyone, but nobody was answering because they were too busy looking at the man with the huge Welsh bow who was now clad in forest green wool, and had thrown back his hood to reveal his face.

The years back in England had removed the deep tan Robin had had when he first came back from the Holy Land, but there was still something of the exotic about him. While most of the Norman and English knights were either clean shaven or had full beards, Robin wore a small, neat moustache and a closely clipped beard just on his chin. Nor did he favour the Norman fashion of hair cut straight around from the base of the skull at the back – which always looked to Guy as though they'd been attacked with shears while wearing a pudding basin on their heads – but it was no peasant's shaggy locks either, despite its waves being neatly cut at shoulder length. Tall and broad-shouldered with dark, smouldering good-looks, this was Robin at his most charismatic, and he certainly had an effect on the crowd, most of whom simply stood and gaped at him.

"You called my name, sheriff?" Robin demanded insolently. "Yes, I am Robin Hood. Not quite the peasant you thought I was, I am? ...No! Don't you dare!" was aimed at the men-at-arms who had belatedly begun reaching for their swords.

In a trice, Will and Malik were there at the front of the crowd too, arrows nocked, bow strings pulled back tight on the big Welsh bows, and with the deadly arrow heads swinging back and forth covering those who might be foolish enough to act. The gasps from the rest of the crowd told of the others of the gang doing similarly.

"We were forged in the fires of Jerusalem!" he snarled, easily heard over the unnatural hush which had fallen over the tourney field. "We saw our friends fall and dies like flies to try and save the Holy Land. I touched the hand of King Baldwin himself, the Leper King, and received his blessings! So don't think I don't know who is deserving and who is not, sheriff. And you and these bloated prelates are not fit to hold this relic of the saint who protects soldiers!" and he snatched up the silver arrow to hold it in a clenched fist above his head.

"Does God strike me down for this?" he asked, looking to the slate grey skies which remained clear of any bolts from the heavens. "No? ...I think you have your answer, de Tuke! You have misused this saint, keeping his relic hoarded away for only a few to touch when he blesses so many who are ordinary men striving to do good, giving their lives to take back the holy places of the world. Shame on you, prior! Shame on you!"

The canons and priors were struck dumb in the face of this articulate and impassioned tirade, but Briwere wasn't so easily quashed.

"And what will you do with it, ...boy?" he meant it as an insult but wasn't prepared for Robin's instant riposte.

"Knight! That's what I am, Briwere, not a boy. A knight. Your equal! And all the more so for having been knighted at Jerusalem. Can you claim to have been knighted in the holiest place on earth? Ha! I thought not! ...And as for what I will do with this, the answer is that I will find a more fitting home for it amongst truly godly men. Men who will ensure that pilgrims get every chance to be blessed by the saint, not just a few fat canons who sit in their wealthy chapels, resting on the wealth that is brought in by lay brothers who are little more than slaves, toiling at lands given to the order by rich men who were trying to *buy* their way into heaven."

At that Robin thrust the arrow inside his jerkin, and drew his sword in one fluid motion with the other hand. As its point snaked back and forth at the men in front of him, a way parted for him, and despite Briwere's hysterical screams of, "Kill him! Kill him!" there were too few armed men close enough to present any challenge to Robin's escape. A couple of valiant souls tried to dive in to attack him, but hefty punches from Will and Gilbert soon put them on the ground, and then Robin was standing in front of Guy.

Guy knew that he had to make it seem like he was going to try and stop Robin, and so he dropped into the half crouch of a man about to make a tackle, even though he was unarmed and was having to weave to avoid that sword point. What he did not expect was for Robin to suddenly dart in and brutally smack him on the head with the sword's pommel.

Going down in an ungainly heap and seeing stars, Guy was faintly aware of Will calling, "Robin, no! Leave him!"

And then Briwere screeching, "Chase them, you imbeciles! Chase them!"

What happened then? Well when I came to and had been horribly sick, I was helped up by Sir Martin and there was no sight of the outlaws. Briwere was throwing the worst tantrum I had ever seen a grown man do until then, but his tirade was achieving nothing. Most of the men who could have fought were flat on their backs after the mêlée, and could not have got up if the end of the world had been announced; and even the ones who did try to give chase were already worn out, and unable to keep up with those who had done nothing more strenuous than loose a few arrows that day. Where Marianne and Mariota had got to with the younger lads I did not know at the time, but later on I learned that they were already well on the way to the major hideout they had not far from Worksop, hidden in the thick woods of Manor Hills, cheekily close to Welbeck Abbey but not close enough to ever get discovered by the lay brothers. And the rest of the outlaws had melted into the countryside as if they had never been there.

What did surprise me as I staggered along on Sir Martin's arm, was hearing him and Sir Richard bemoaning the fact that the ordinary people had milled around like sheep, getting in the way of those trying to follow Robin. They just saw it as peasant stupidity, but I knew the local folk better than that. They had a very understandable fear of armed men, and if they had got in the way of any of them then it had been done quite deliberately. The ordinary people had collectively aided Robin Hood's escape!

Oh, you like that, do you, Gervase? Yes, a handsome knight from Jerusalem had come into their midst and been revealed to them as the folk hero who had come to the aid of so many of them. Men of power always seemed to disregard or not understand how fast word gets passed by folk. They think that villagers live in isolation in their little groups, cut off from the rest of the shire, let alone the wider world. But news travels. It gets shared at markets and when the poor gather outside the churches to bear witness to a priest saying mass. I have known word of something be across from south on the Newark side of the Trent to high into the Derbyshire moorlands in under a week, and yet with not a man able to ride any distance or write any of it down. So the fact that pretty much every ordinary man and woman who was there on that day knew the name of Robin Hood and what he stood for, did not surprise me – that they would act on it did!

And I truly believe that it was that revelation that he had fought for Christ in the East which changed things, because in that moment he moved from just being a man who would fight for their bodies, to someone who had fought for their eternal souls too. In that he had outshone de Tuke and all the other churchmen there, as well as the sheriff, knights and men-at-arms, and there was something so very fitting about the fact that this paragon had won, not with any lordly weapon, but with something they themselves used – albeit in a much more dramatic way. For him to then claim a relic which only seemed to enhance that power ...well, Brother, in their minds it can have hardly seemed less than an endorsement from the heavens, and please do not scowl at that, because I do not believe for a moment that a single one of them thought of it in a blasphemous way. Rather, in their simple faith they thought that if God so objected to Robin carting St Sebastian off like that, then he would have done something about it, for were there not enough of his representatives on earth witness to it in the form of the canons and priors?

...Yes, you see it now, do you not? You cannot fill people's minds with the ideas that God will strike them down for their misdeeds as a means to control them, and then be surprised when that very belief turns around and bites you back! Robin Hood had seemingly been endorsed by God, and undoing that belief was going to take more than the irate ranting of a few churchmen and a sheriff frothing at the mouth. The people's hero had truly arrived.

Chapter 11

Yet the consequences of that tourney are not done with yet, Brother. To start with there was the matter of Robin having used the Robin of Loxley name so openly. I could not go back to the camp with them for obvious reasons – the sheriff was hardly going to let me disappear immediately after such a disaster, but also I was genuinely unable to do much of anything. Robin had hit me high on my left cheekbone close to my temple, and within the hour my eye was closing and my face swelling up like a pig's-bladder ball. Moreover, for once I did not have to fake the dizziness I felt whenever I tried to stand up, for I reeled like a drunk at a feast day, unless I had someone to hang onto in those periods when I regained consciousness and before the darkness took me again.

That, if nothing else, saved me from the worst of the sheriff's ire, and once he had drawn breath enough to realise that of all the knights present, Sirs Martin and Richard had been the only ones without weapons to hand, he backed off from blaming them. The other knights of the shire were not so lucky. They got screamed and shouted at for the rest of the day, with many of them packing hurriedly and departing for their manors as fast as they could go.

I am sure many of them thought that once the sheriff calmed down he would see that they could not have done much to save the silver arrow. In that they were soon shown to be horribly wrong, for of course Briwere had their names, and from that he could work out where their manors and families were. Those lucky enough to be across the shire borders were soon counting their blessings, while our local noble families found themselves with written demands for money from the sheriff, for what he saw as the money they owed him to help him recompense de Tuke at least for the value of the reliquary.

And what of de Tuke? Oh, Brother, he was in a fine state! Incensed beyond words at the loss of one of his finest relics, he left straight away, declaring that he would not spend another moment in a place where such sacrilege had taken place, but would rest the night in the sanctity of his brother prior's monastery at Worksop. Meanwhile, I am told that you could hear de Pauliaco laughing like a crazed mule even from outside of the monastery at Blyth, and over the following weeks, word *filtered through to us of him using words such as 'overweening pride' and 'arrogance' regarding de Tuke's misfortune, and that he believed the Augustinian prior had invoked God's displeasure for so invading the space of another holy place – in other words, his own. Evidently de Pauliaco was not prone to regarding his own reflection in the priory's fishponds to see how everything he said against de Tuke could so easily have been said of himself; but this episode ensured that for the rest of their lives these two men of God remained implacable enemies, for de Tuke never passed up an opportunity to do de Pauliaco a disservice, and of course that inevitably invited retaliation. Yes, Brother you may look aghast at this. Do you see why I had such little reverence for these men now?*

But they will flitter in and out of our story like moths, and I know you want to return to Robin.

The outlaws all returned safely to the camp beyond Worksop, you will be gladdened to hear, but once there, the older members surrounded Robin and demanded an explanation for his actions. I was relieved beyond measure when Allan told me that Hugh was the first to speak, and demanded with commendable calm why, by all that was holy, he had entered under the name of Robin of Loxley? Because Robin did not see the criticism coming he therefore did not deny that he had done such a thing, and there was no need for the others to resort to telling him that they had already challenged me over the matter. It may sound cowardly to you that I was so relieved, but in truth, Gervase, I was so weary of always being the one to make him account for his actions, and I also wanted the others to see how he would react when he could not place the blame for his ire straight onto me.

This time there was no bad cousin to shift things onto, and when he had it pointed out to him in no uncertain terms that he had come very close to jeopardising the whole mission, Allan said that it seemed to come as a complete surprise to him. It had never crossed his mind that after all the raids on forest courts, and against wealthy merchants and members of the nobility in Sherwood, that people would have caught on that ˜Robin of Loxley˜ was ˜Robin Hood˜. To have every last one of the more experienced men bluntly telling him that he had been a fool to do such a thing was something he had never expected to happen, and I believe that at that point he realised that while this had been an outstanding success, it also sank in that he could not have done it without those same men who were now demanding he account for his actions.

Therefore this achieved what no amount of haranguing on my part could have done – he actually conceded the point that he needed to listen to the others and talk through his plans more. At last he saw that he did not always see crucial consequences which others did. There was a tactful avoidance of any mention of the fact that the idea for the mission had in the first place been mine, which would have achieved nothing.

And I confess to you that I did not know quite what to make of it when Allan told me that Robin had agreed that future missions had to be talked through by everyone. But apparently Siward and Hugh had, with some equally calm interventions by Malik and John, strongly pointed out that none of them had ever expected Robin to actually be this heroic figure they had helped to create. Nobody was expecting him to be able to see all eventualities, they told him. One man alone could not shoulder such a burden. Nor, they said, should one person take all the blame when things went wrong if they had all agreed upon an action. But that if one person kept plans all to himself, and which he then acted on without forewarning the others, then when the inevitable happened, he would shoulder that blame alone.

That was a crafty move, I thought, for even as a boy Robin had always hated to be proven wrong. Back then we had all put it down to him having much older half-brothers who had eternally been disparaging of his childish efforts, but in a grown man it was harder to be quite so tolerant of this quirk of his, especially when it drew others into danger. So I confess to you, Gervase, and ask for absolution for my cynicism, that although I told Allan that I was glad that at last they had reached a sensible agreement with Robin, in my heart of hearts I was far from convinced that this would have any lasting effect.

Did it last? Both yes and no, Brother. Where I was concerned the answer was ~no~ almost straight away, but with the outlaws it lasted for much longer than I would have credited, only gradually sliding back into chaos – but that has its place later on. For now we must go back to that silver arrow, for you should know of its fate before we go any further.

Nottinghamshire
Spring, the Year of Our Lord 1195

Guy was still incapable of riding far two days later when the tourney ground had been cleared, and Sirs Martin and Richard decided that there was nothing for it but to leave him somewhere not far away. However, Blyth Priory's gates were closed to them, while nearby Wallingwells Priory just four miles to the south-west was a Benedictine nunnery, with no means to care for a soldier, and anyway likely to be following Blyth's lead. Prior William's monastery at Worksop was barely the same distance beyond Wallingwells again, but was also likely to be hostile to a sheriff's man given that Prior William had witnessed his fellow Augustinian Black Canon, de Tuke's, embarrassment. However, in the other direction, heading east and a little north, there was the small establishment of Mattersea Priory held by Gilbertine Canons.

"I don't know what they're like Guy," Sir Martin told him apologetically. "They were only founded ten years ago, and I'm told they scandalously have both nuns and canons in the same place, but at least they're likely to be a bit more kindly disposed towards you."

Yet when a local farmer had been persuaded to send a lad there to enquire, it seemed that they also felt they could not help. Blyth, it seemed, cast a long shadow in this part of the shire, and a small order could not afford to anger its powerful neighbour.

"Then it's going to have to be Welbeck Abbey down between Worksop and Cuckney," Sir Richard decided. Guy's groan of despair at returning to Cuckney, site of so many encounters already, was misinterpreted by Sir Richard as despair over the ten mile ride. "I'm so sorry, Guy. We'll make a litter for you if you like, and we'll take it slowly, but there's nothing else for it unless you want to attempt the whole ride back to Nottingham, or risk leaving you in some farm byre here. I've heard that Abbot Michael there is a good man if a little eccentric."

Guy managed a baleful stare with his one open eye. "I think you'll have already buried me by the roadside before Nottingham. And I'd rather ride than be swayed around in a litter. I know you're trying to help, but if I go in one of those with my head like this, I'll be puking myself inside out every step of the way. Welbeck it is, then."

They took it particularly slowly, starting very early so that they could make frequent stops for Guy. The fact that they had to pass through the dense woodlands of Manor Hills, where the outlaws' hideout was, was not lost on Guy. Of anywhere that ought to have been somewhere he could have sought refuge, but the twin problems of his knightly companions and his doubts over whether Robin would finish off what he'd tried to do, made Guy grit his teeth, hang on to the saddle pommel, and ride onwards.

By the time they reached the abbey gates he was slumped in his saddle and barely able to take much notice of anything. Vaguely he realised that he was being helped from his horse and carried inside, then there was the bliss of a cold cloth being placed on his pounding brow as his head rested on a proper pillow for the first time in weeks, and that was the last Guy knew for the next two days. When he came to, he thought he really had lost his mind from the blow because there, sat at the foot of his bed, was Tuck.

"Am I dead or dreaming?" he asked around a mouth so dry he feared his tongue might stick permanently to the roof of his mouth.

Tuck looked up from his contemplation and the wide smile which followed as he saw that Guy was awake said everything of his relief. "Blessed Saints Issui, Melangell and Caradoc, you're awake! Here, let me help you have a drink!" and Tuck's big hand gently lifted Guy's head so that he could sip fresh water from the wooden mug Tuck held to his lips with the other hand.

"Why are you here?" Guy asked in confusion.

"The arrow," Tuck said with one of his meaningful looks. "We had a big discussion about what to do with it. Will wanted to melt the casket down and use the silver, which near gave Robin an apoplexy. ...Yes, I thought that would make you smile! Robin does have some strange ideas of sanctity! The relic was one thing, but it took some time to convince him that the silver wasn't as equally blessed. The rest of us threw ideas back and forth, but what became clear was that none of us wanted to give it to one of the big monasteries with links to Normandy.

"That cut our options right down, but even so, Hugh and Siward were wary of coming here because of its links with the

Cuckney family we've had so many run-ins with, but I could at least tell them that each of these Premonstratensian abbeys or priories are autonomous – they choose whether they lead a contemplative life, or go out into the world preaching and seeing to the pastoral care of those in their neighbourhood. So everyone agreed that I should come here and see what the abbot is like. I think you're going to like Abbot Michael, Guy. He's quite the rebel!"

"Is he, now? That makes a refreshing change. And if you think he's a rebel I assume that he meets your Welsh standards for that?"

Tuck gave a guffaw. "Oh, *brawd*, you know me so well! Yes, Abbot Michael does meet my standards. I tell you, it has been such a relief to come here and join with them at mass. I am still committed to keeping the others on the path of the righteous, but sometimes I need a little salve for my own soul too, and I have found that here."

"I'm glad," Guy said, managing a weak smile for his old friend. "So are the others here?"

"Oh yes, we arrived the day after you – even Marianne and Mariota, although they're sleeping in the guesthouse outside of the inner precinct, as is fitting. But once we told Abbot Michael of their credentials as Hospitaller sisters, and their expertise in treating wounds, he let them come in and see to you. They're currently helping with the delivery of a difficult child whose mother lives locally, that's why they're not here, but I can tell you that Robin got a right tongue-lashing off both of them when they saw you."

"They know what happened?"

Tuck quirked an eyebrow. "Are you joking? We all saw Robin hit you! We just thought you went down so hard to act the part, like when you got hit at Bolsover. Finding that you had been as badly hurt as this was a nasty shock. He must have put some force behind that blow."

"He used his right arm," Guy replied, knowing that Tuck would not need it explaining that that was the one which had such terrible power, being the one which pulled the string back on the enormous bow that Robin used. Endless practice with a bow for a right-handed man made the bones of the left shoulder massive because of the compression from the power of the bow, but built incredible muscle in the right arm which pulled and aimed it. "He held nothing back."

"*Dduw drugarhau arnom!*" Tuck said fervently, 'God have mercy on us', and Guy guessed that he was thinking that they should maybe have thought a little more on how Robin behaved towards Guy before making the assumption that Guy was alright. "I shall tell the others. *Tsk*! Another thing we must have a word with Robin about!"

"There's no point," Guy sighed. "You won't change how he behaves to me. Just tell the others, but don't argue with him on my account, not here at least. ...So tell, me, what of the arrow? Is it here?"

"Ah!" Tuck said with a wink. "Well it turns out that our Abbot Michael is a well-travelled man, and he's heard of a lot of St Sebastian's relics – so much so that the poor saint must have been an octopus at least, if you follow my drift."

"Fake relics?"

"Even with a bad head you're quick, Guy. Yes, they can't all be real, there are just too many of them. So Abbot Michael suggested that we open the reliquary up by the high altar with due ceremony. Well we said mass over it, and then we opened it in the presence of all of his canons and ourselves."

"And?"

"Unless St Sebastian was an extraordinarily hirsute man, what was inside is the finger of a monkey – a Barbary ape, Abbot Michael and Malik are inclined to think."

Guy felt an uncontrollable giggle welling up inside, and despite the way it made his head ache, soon had tears of mirth running down his cheeks. "Oh, dear Lord! That's priceless!"

"I knew you'd appreciate the irony! ...De Tuke lugs the damned thing halfway across the shire, just so the nobility from all around can reverently kiss the finger of an ape while the sheriff and prior look on."

"So does Will get his wish?"

"He does! In fact he's already started. In his opinion the chasing on the reliquary wasn't very well done anyway. On the other hand, Abbot Michael has a genuine relic of St Wolfieus here that would benefit from a proper reliquary."

"St Wolfieus?"

"An Anglo-Saxon hermit who lived in Norfolk in the eleventh century. With Abbot Michael's order of White Canons being focused on the east and north of England, it's hardly surprising that he should know and revere a local saint. The abbey here has a whole hand – so this is definitely human! – and Will is in the process of making a lidded box out of steel with a glass window beneath the lid, so that the lid may be taken off for pilgrims to view. Not like that arrow, which had to be cut open with Will's toughest blade – they weren't risking anyone looking at that! Will and Malik think that with the help of the best scribe here, they can chase a suitable pattern onto the layer of silver Will's going to cover the box with. But that still leaves a substantial amount of high quality silver for Abbot Michael to sell so that he can do more to help the poor souls who come into his care."

"So everyone wins, that's nice," Guy said with a contented sigh, but then gave Tuck a quirked eyebrow with his good eye as he asked, "Even Robin? He's fine with this?"

Tuck's grin was reassurance all by itself. "Oh yes! He's rather taken to Abbot Michael as well, praise the Lord! It's done him the world of good meeting a genuinely good man of the cloth." Tuck gave Guy a wry smile, though, as he added, "It's also been good for him to have a different man as his confessor for once. I'm too close to you all. I know when he's behaved badly, even when he thinks he hasn't, because I see it for myself. With Abbot Michael he can just say what he feels and get the absolution he craves without too many questions."

Guy sighed. "If that makes him feel better, and in turn it means that he behaves better, then I'm not going to disabuse Abbot Michael by saying too much." It didn't feel fair to Guy that Robin should get such absolution, but if it meant that he didn't put the others in danger then he would bite his tongue and fume in private. But he did say, "I envy him having such recourse to confession. I dare not go to any priest in Nottingham. If I tell the truth they might betray me to the sheriff, because I don't hold their piety in great esteem, for truth, yet I wouldn't dishonor the sanctity of the confession by telling lies."

Tuck's jaw fell. "Oh, my dear friend! I had no idea that you suffered so!"

"Don't berate yourself, Tuck. When I'm with you it's hardly ever for long enough for you to be able to do anything for me."

"Yes, I know, but that doesn't mean that I shouldn't have thought of that. I will have a private word with Abbot Michael, if you like, and see if we can make some arrangement that you can call in here when you are passing as part of your duties. That way Robin will never know who you see, and he won't feel in competition with you, but you will get some relief too." He didn't add that it would do no harm for Abbot Michael to hear both sides of a story sometimes – he didn't want the abbot to become so swayed by Robin's charisma that he wouldn't see the damaged man beneath.

However, Much then poked his head around the infirmary door, and after that Guy had a steady stream of visitors, all wanting to tell him how worried they had been for him, until Tuck had to put a stop to it because Guy was quite worn out by all their affection. What couldn't be hidden was that Robin was the one person who didn't come. It didn't surprise Guy. He guessed that his cousin would certainly not want to lie about any regret for hitting Guy as hard as he had done while they were both under the abbey's roof, and therefore on sacred ground.

Yet to tell the truth – which was that he'd meant to do it – would be to invite a storm of criticism from the others, so Robin avoided the dilemma by avoiding Guy. It saddened Guy, though, because it confirmed in his own mind that Robin no longer carried any of the fond memories of their shared childhood with him in the way that Guy, John and Allan did. To all intents and purposes the Baldwin they had known was as good as dead, and this stranger, Robin, now inhabited his body.

What Guy also quickly realized was that for once he had a good excuse to be absent from the castle for a while, and he determined to make it drag out for as long as he could. And while he lingered, so did the outlaws, most of them making much of the pretext of going hunting to bring in a goodly store of deer and boar, which the monastic kitchens could cure to last both them and their constant stream of poor and ailing a goodly while, yet really wanting to spend time with Guy while they could. Only Robin avoided him during the days, and in the evenings sat at the other end of the group to wherever Guy was. As a result, it was why they were all there when visitors of a disastrously familiar kind arrived.

It was lay brother Alaric who alerted them first, dashing around the church to where most of the outlaws were hoisting a great roof beam into place on the new shelter for the sick they were helping the brothers to build.

"Father! Father!" he gasped at Abbot Michael. "Riders! Nine of them! Armed! They're coming towards the gate!"

The long timber settled with a satisfying *thunk* into its assigned cradles within the crooks, and the outlaws and various brothers cautiously let go of the great wooden arches they had been supporting. This was the moment of truth. The point when they discovered whether the beams would all interlock and hold one another in place as their carpenter had planned. They did.

"Praise the Lord!" Abbot Michael shouted joyfully, lifting his arms heavenwards and getting a chorus of "Amen," in response.

The more important issue in his eyes now being resolved, he turned to Alaric. "And why the concern, my son? All are welcome here. You know that."

Alaric turned pleading eyes toward the outlaws. He had been a soldier before coming here to spend his old age in peace and he knew what he'd seen. Abbot Michael was a good man, but sometimes far too trusting.

"Would you like us to come and take a look?" Tuck asked sympathetically.

"Please, Brother!"

Alaric's relief at them taking the hint made them all that bit edgier, for he was far from being a panicker normally.

They all trooped around to the south side of the church to where the main gates into the palisaded area around the buildings lay. The gates stood wide open as they did every day until nightfall, but the three remaining of today's rotation of groups of four brothers who undertook tasks near to the gate, in order to be close by to receive the needy, were now nervously clutching the edges of the gates in preparation of closing them.

"Bless me! Templars!" Tuck gasped as Robin surged forwards, a wide smile appearing on his face.

They were a travel-stained group, white surcoats badly begrimed, but what had Will and the other crusaders exchanging worried glances with one another over, and with Guy, was the fact that these men were wearing their mail hauberks, even if the ring-mail coifs were pushed back from their heads.

"There's no need for them to go around like that," Gilbert declared with a sniff. "This is bloody England, not Normandy or Cyprus! No outlaws other than us would take on a band like that."

Guy managed to catch Abbot Michael's flowing sleeve as he went to hurry past him. "Wait a moment, Father, please! Let Robin and the others make the first greeting. These men may be battle-fatigued and not wholly in their right minds. We know about such things. We had a disastrous meeting with some former crusaders a few years ago who turned out to be out of their heads. Let the others get them to leave their arms at the gate before you let them in further. You don't want them to lash out at your other guests when they think they've seen something that isn't there."

Michael turned and blinked at him in surprise, and Allan, whose shoulder Guy had been leaning on, added quickly,

"It can happen, Father. Ask Siward how he was when they first came back. It was only Guy finding them refuge where they had time to heal that saved them from doing something they would have regretted later on – if they'd ever regained their sanity."

Michael blinked again and gave Guy an odd look. That probably meant that he'd heard a different version of the time at High Peak from Robin, but Guy didn't care about that just at the moment. The main thing was to get those well-worn swords away from hands that might well cut down every soul within these gates.

"Greetings, Frères!" they heard Robin calling out, and saw the riders pulling up.

Allan sighed softly beneath Guy's arm. "Now is that because they're relieved at being called by their proper title, or is it that they didn't expect to have a big man like Robin coming pounding out to them?" his cousin mused worriedly.

"I don't like the look o' them much," Roger declared from Allan's other side.

"No, me neither," Guy agreed. "We don't want a repeat of what you went through at York here."

A conversation of sorts was going on between Robin and the leading Templar, but it was Robin doing most of the talking. By now Will, Siward, Malik and Gilbert had joined them, and those back by the gate could see the startled glances the other riders were now giving them too. Yet whatever was said had the required effect. The riders dismounted and now led their horses into the monastic compound.

"You must join us in the new building for the evening meal," Tuck said, bustling over to greet them.

That was a cunning move, Guy thought. Making out that the normal guest hall was too full to accommodate them, and he hissed to Allan,

"You and Roger get Much and the new lads and move all of everyone's stuff over there *now*! Make it look like you lot have always been over there away from the rest, but go round the back of the buildings so that you don't get seen. It looks like Tuck's trying to get them into the church, so you'll have a brief time to get it done. Go!"

Pulling himself together, Guy did his best to stride purposely towards the visitors.

"Who is this?" the leading Templar asked, giving Guy an appraising up and down look, and deciding that he wasn't what he'd expected to find here either.

"I'm Sir Guy of Gisborne." Guy pointed to his spectacularly bruised face, which by now was a riot of purple, green and dark blue. "Got hit at the tournament up at Blyth! I've been seeing stars for the last week. Abbot Michael's brothers have been caring for me until I can ride home."

"What was the other man like?" one of the Templars asked snidely, and Guy fed him the response he clearly wanted,

"Oh, he walked away without a scratch."

Robin blinked in surprise at Guy's rueful good humour but said nothing, although that might have had something to do with the furtive dig in the ribs he got from Gilbert. Better that these men thought that there was nobody here who posed much of a threat to them for more than one reason – if they were traumatized they didn't deserve to be troubled, and if they were a danger it was better they underestimate the outlaws.

Luckily they were already being shepherded on towards the church, with Tuck telling all who would listen about the services he had conducted for 'some other former crusaders', and how that had helped them.

In the cool shadows of the church the three leading Templars went up to the altar and immediately went down on their knees to pray, Tuck and Abbot Michael joining them and initiating a familiar pattern of prayers and responses which drew four more of the men to them. Two, however, hung back.

"Do you not wish to join in?" Malik asked them softly.

"Do you, brother?" one of them responded with a sad smile. "I think you are one of us."

Robin, Gilbert and Siward were too far forward to hear their words, along with John, Hugh and Colm, while the Coshams had stayed outside with Marianne and Mariota as if they were nothing to do with Robin's group. With any luck, if these strangers got nasty they would get a surprise, because the Coshams had made sure that the only time they'd been spotted they'd been sitting down, which hid their distinctive broad-shouldered archer's build. That left just Guy, Will and Malik back with the two men.

"You're turcopoles?" Will asked in surprise.

"We are. I am Janah al-Qalānisi and this is Khalīl al-Sinjil, the brother of my sister's husband."

"I am Malik," their own turcopole said warmly, grasping their hands, but carefully avoiding giving his family name. It wouldn't do to tell them that he was of Balian of Ibelin's family, albeit from the wrong side of the blanket, just in case there was more going on with these two than was clear at the moment as well. "You are very welcome here!"

"*Shukran jazīlan,*" Janah thanked him with a wan smile. "I confess it is something of a relief to find us in the company of men who understand what we are."

"Oh we've been told all about those of you who are native Christians in the Holy Land, and who were in our armies out there," Guy said comfortingly. "Which church did you belong to?"

"The Byzantine one," Khalīl said with some trepidation, but was reassured by the way Will immediately nodded knowingly and said,

"Ah! A very different set of services, then! Don't worry, Abbot Michael is no zealot – he won't take offence if you can't follow his prayers."

"That is a comfort to know," Khalīl sighed in relief. He gave a darting glance towards the others knelt at the altar and then said softly, "We have not been treated with such understanding at other places we have stopped at, and our commander is a peculiarly devout man."

For a moment Guy thought that the man had use the word 'peculiarly' in mistake for 'particularly'. It would be an understandable error for someone for whom English was not his first language. Then he saw the way both turcopoles were watching him and knew they were trying to tell him something else.

"Will, let's take these men to the refectory and get them something to drink," he said, before the smith could disrupt the fragile test they were being given. "I'm sure nobody could object to that. These aren't the prayers of one of the offices, after all. We have a while to go yet before the Vespers bell."

As Malik led the way, chatting cheerfully in Arabic to the two, Guy pulled Will back a bit and said very softly,

"I think they just tried to warn us that their knights aren't quite the sort of men we might think they are. By Our Lady, I hope they aren't extreme in their faith."

Will patted him gently on the back. "Don't worry, Guy, I picked up on that too. Let's see if they'll give anything more up while Robin's wearing his knees out with the others."

At the refectory they got Khalīl and Janah sat down on the end of one of the long benches, and brought them some of the weak ale most folk slacked their thirst with.

"I regret it's fermented," Guy apologized. "They don't have any water boiling at the moment, but when we come to eat properly there'll be the herb tisane that gets made for Malik and some of the rest of us."

Both men looked startled again.

"We've educated him in the ways of the East," Will said with a chuckle. "Sadly we can't get much of what we drank out there, but we do our best to make something like the tisanes when we're in our own camp. Tuck, the big monk who met you, has got some of the flavours as close as we're ever likely to get here, though, and he's been trying to instruct the brothers here."

"Do you have any news of our homeland?" Malik asked with such longing that Guy felt bad for not thinking that his friend must sometimes get very homesick.

"All is fire and chaos," Janah said mournfully. "The Franj lords," giving them the name the Franks were known by in the East, "do nothing but squabble like children in the few ports they still hold. Your King Richard was the one who gave them unity. Without him Jerusalem will never be taken again."

"But what of the people? Of our people?" Malik asked anxiously.

"They fare well enough," Khalīl replied. "Salah al-Din was a fair overlord. His fight was always with the knights and now they're gone, but then when he died coming up two years ago, all fell into chaos again. His sons fight one another, and all we can do is pray that his brother one day regains some kind of control. Al-Adil is as great a man as his brother was." There was a weary shake of his head. "But for now our home is a dangerous place to be for men like us. Our families are better off without us around to remind anyone of whose side we fought on. Men like Salah al-Din's sons and their followers think we followed the wrong lords, given that we are locals, and they're not prone to be charitable towards men they see as fighters who might come at them behind their backs – especially when the loyalties of their own men are broken and divided amongst themselves, not united as they were with their father."

Will kept his tone neutral as he said, "You'd think the Frankish lords would see that as a God-given opportunity to make another strike to take Jerusalem? Their enemies fighting amongst themselves, I mean."

However both men shook their heads, Janah saying, "For what purpose? Any force which retook the Holy City would have to be united or it would just lose again." He looked warily towards the door, then, seeming to be satisfied that none of his travelling companions were coming, said, "It was always destined to failure, you know – the retaking of the Holy Land for Christians. The Franj lords whose families had been in the East for generations distrusted the crusaders, thought they were trying to take what was theirs..."

"...and the crusaders thought they had gone native," Will finished for him. "We were out there, my friends. We know all about the infighting!" He looked across to Guy. "Malik, Gilbert and I have said much the same to one another of late. Too many lords all wanting a slice of the pie, and too worried about what the men they were supposed to be allied to would do next, to ever see the reality clearly, and that was that we were never there in big enough numbers to really hold Jerusalem."

"Do not say that to Frère Bornhold, though!" Janah warned them urgently. "For him it is like a slight to his personal honour that non-Christians worship within Jerusalem's walls."

"Him and Frère Conan and Godfrey!" Khalīl agreed.

But Will was already making pacifying noises. "Don't worry, our own leader is more than a little touchy on the subject too. We won't say anything, don't you worry."

They got little more out of them about the soldiers, instead allowing Malik the time to get more specific news of the towns and villages he had once known so well, and it wasn't long before the other men got brought in for much needed drinks and food.

Robin came in first, walking alongside a man Janah whispered was Frère Bornhold, who was saying,

"And is this Brother Tuck of yours truly a priest?"

"Most definitely!" Robin assured him.

"So this mass he is offering to say for us...?"

Siward stepped up to the other side of Bornhold, "...was a great comfort to all of us who had lost friends at Jerusalem, Frère. I don't think any of us realised how much it had weighed on us that no prayers had been said specifically for them."

Robin was nodding. "It's a hard thing to leave friends you have prayed beside unburied on the battlefield as carrion."

Frère Odilard was in the room then, saying, "You're the first men we've met who have understood that!"

"Aye," one of the ordinary Templar men-at-arms agreed. He gave a strange look Bornhold's way as he said with carefully chosen words, "While there's no greater honour than to die defending Christ's home, that has been all that most people we've encountered on the way home have perceived."

"No greater honour!" Bornhold declared emphatically. Indeed so harshly that Guy immediately wondered whether it was more for his own benefit than anyone else's. Was that the only way this man was hanging on to his sanity? Repeating over and over that all that they had been through was to the glory of God, and something all of them would receive eternal blessings for? If so, then he could be very dangerous if he was challenged at all on the matter, and Guy eased himself up off the bench, whispering in Will's ear,

"I think I'd better have a word with Tuck."

He found Tuck still in the nave of the church having a deep discussion with Abbot Michael about the psalms he had used in the mass he had said for Robin and the others at High Peak.

Tuck spotted him coming towards them as Guy's boots rang out on the flagstones. "Guy?"

"A word of warning, my friend."

"Really? Over what?" Abbot Michael asked naively.

Tuck patted the slighter man on the shoulder. "Guy has a very acute nose for trouble, Father – even more so than Robin most of the time – and he thinks things through a lot more. What's up, Guy?"

Guy sighed. "It's more of a caution really. The two who stood back are turcopoles like Malik. They belong to the Eastern Christian Church, Father, so they won't be familiar with our masses and offices."

Abbot Michael nodded thoughtfully. "Brother Tuck has been telling me about them. Would they be willing to come into our fold?"

Guy sighed. "With all due respect, Father, that's something for the future. I certainly wouldn't be raising that question yet! This is the first place they've come to where anyone has had the faintest idea of who or what they are, and that's been a huge relief. Even more than the others they've been living on their nerves, because they get mistaken for Saracens. Let's give them some breathing space, eh?" He looked pleadingly at Tuck and got a minute nod, assuring him that Tuck would get Abbot Michael to see the light on this matter.

Bracing himself, he went on, "But of more immediate importance is this: I think Bornhold at least, and maybe others amongst these men, are only holding on to what restraint – what beliefs they have – by telling themselves that the terrible losses they suffered out in the Holy Land were all validated by it being in a holy cause."

He held up a hand to halt Abbot Michael's immediate response. "I'm not saying that we shouldn't have tried to retake Jerusalem, Father. What I'm trying to say is that these men, and Bornhold in particular, need this mass to be phrased in such a way that you reassure them that the men they left in the desert, for the desert foxes and carrion birds to strip to the bone, are living in glory now."

He turned to Tuck. "What we did before was a remembrance of lost friends. Very little of what you used related specifically to the defence of the holiest place in Christendom..."

"...But for these men it needs to," Tuck caught on. "And if we don't...?"

"...I think we may break what little control they have left, and things could turn very bloody and violent."

Abbot Michael gasped in dismay, making Guy reach out and take his arm.

"It won't be a malicious act, Father. They're not sitting in your refectory planning to slaughter your lambs you have under your roof. I'm just trying to get you to see that these are men who have spent years and years living on a knife edge, and they are cut to shreds in their souls."

As Abbot Michael made a soundless 'oh!', Tuck smiled at him and said,

"I told you Guy was perceptive! Thank you, Guy. We'll make sure that we incorporate lots of 'in the service of God' and 'taken to the Lord's table' in what we say. Indeed I was just saying to the Father how effective it was to say the Latin and then put it into English for our friends. So given what you've just said, I think it's all the more important that we do it again this time, so that the words they want to hear are fully brought home to them."

Guy's deep sigh of relief told Tuck that he'd hit the mark.

"Tuck, did they say where they're heading for?" Guy suddenly thought to ask. "Yorkshire? We've no preceptories in our two shires."

"Actually they're heading for Willoughton in Lincolnshire. It was Bornhold's home preceptory a very long time ago, but he's been out of England for so long he's rather lost his bearings."

"What of the others?"

Tuck scrubbed his tonsure, grimacing. "Hmm, harder to tell what's going on there. Funnily enough, the two other knights..."

"...Frère Odilard and Frère Conan," Guy supplied,

"...Well they've come to the end of doing active service. They're much older, and I think they're just grateful to come home and take up a place in a grange somewhere. What you said about them hanging on to their faith like drowning men clinging to reeds fits very well with what I made of them." He turned to Abbot Michael.

"I think those two will become a lot less tense when we've done this mass. They'll go out to their grange and take refuge in prayer as they go about their daily duties, but I don't think it will be obsessive. The two older men-at-arms are, I think, going with them and are of much the same turn of mind."

"And what of the other two?" Guy asked, getting a nasty sinking feeling about this.

Tuck snorted. "It seems that Bornhold and those two have come from the Templar's head place in France with a message for the Temple in London, and that's now being passed on up here. Part of the deal seems to be that Odilard and Conan get to stay here as there's no room in preceptories in France with so many returning from the East, but Bornhold and his pair of men will be going back to London with any luck. He thinks England a godless land, Guy!"

Guy flinched. "Then we must convince him otherwise, or he's likely to start thinking that the reason the Templars and other crusaders got massacred was our fault for bringing God's wrath down on everyone."

"Blessed St Wolfieus!" Abbot Michael gasped. "Really? They'd think that?"

Tuck clapped a meaty paw on the abbot's shoulder, momentarily forgetting who he was talking to. "Sadly, my son, they might …they just might! We walk a precarious path with them."

Yes, I came here, to this very abbey! Did you not realise that the reason why I dragged myself to your door, even ailing as I was, was because I already knew this place? Not to this infirmary, though, for this place is new since I last visited. Yet some of the more elderly brothers recognised me, and they have been here to see me when you are not here. Yes, they have. That has surprised you, has it not? But I am surprised that you did not know more of Abbot Michael already, for he was in charge for many long years and was dearly loved hereabouts. How long have you been here?

˜Do not become distracted from your confession,˜ you say. Ah, I take your point, Brother, for we are in mid tale, but you have piqued my curiosity. At some point I shall find out more. Yet for now we must focus on this new twist in the tangled web of the Templars.

And what was the significance of this, you ask with such exasperation, Gervase? For truth, Brother, have a little more faith in me! You are about to meet some new members of that outlaws because of this – does that satisfy you? I thought it might. And for once Robin acted with great honour, in spite of my presence, as this incident played out, and I saw him as the others must have seen him more often. So shall we continue with your hero? Good, then I shall tell you one more thing – Abbot Michael, and St Wolfieus, will reappear many times in the following years, so the first time we met him is not to be swept aside as a passing comment. There, does that satisfy you?

Chapter 12

So we shall press on Gervase, since you prod me for what you see as digressions. I do not ramble in my old age, and no, this is not just a repeat of the incident back at York with the dreadful Eudo and Waldein, so do not roll your eyes so! What is more, we are coming to some of your badly behaved clerics again, so I would not be too disparaging of the Templars if I was you.

Sherwood
Late Spring, the Year of our Lord 1195

The first night the Templars were at the abbey went much as Guy expected. All of the newcomers woke them at some point during the night in the throes of terrible nightmares, and for once even Robin was glad that Guy had volunteered to come and sleep with them within the wooden skeleton of the new building, with just some oiled canvases thrown over the roof beams to keep the worst of the light rain and dew off them. He and Malik tended to Janah and Khalīl with some help from Roger, while the others – with the exception of the Coshams, who were still in reserve – did what they could for the rest. The two older Templar men-at-arms who would be staying in Lincolnshire, Hamon and Ilger, accepted what was offered in the spirit it was given, as did Odilard and Conan. Bornhold, however, seemed mortified that he had woken anyone and stormed off into the night, followed some distance away by Gilbert and Will – not because they thought he would come around, but to make sure that nobody else suffered for what he saw as his embarrassment.

"Leave him to it," his sergeant, a tough man of middle years called Godfrey, told them firmly. "You won't get any thanks from him."

However Godfrey and his fellow sergeant, Balak, did open up more to Robin and Siward during the night, and in the morning while the newcomers broke their fast rather later than most in the refectory, the outlaws gathered in the skeletal hall for a conference.

"So what's it all about?" Will asked for all of them.

Siward let Robin answer first.

"Well it seems that Geoffrey Plantagenet is set to remain in Normandy for the foreseeable future," Robin said with some disgust. "Apparently his duties as Archbishop of York are of less importance to him than ingratiating himself with his kingly half-brother."

"No surprise there," Gilbert sniffed, and rolled his eyes with his fellow Irishman, Colm. Neither of them had much time for the English nobility.

"Maybe not," Siward agreed, "but what we hadn't picked up on is that the sheriff of Yorkshire has taken control of the archbishop's lands in his absence."

"Has he now!" Tuck gasped. "Church land under a sheriff's fist? That's not going to sit well with a great many people."

"Especially not the Temple in London," Robin said with a flash of the wry humour Guy remembered he'd been so full of once upon a time. "Pretty understandably, the Templars feel that if anyone's earned the right to have a chunk of that pie, it's them."

"Can they do anything about it?" Hugh asked in amazement. "I mean, this has to have been approved by the king, surely?"

There was another of Robin's crooked smiles which so tore at Guy's heart as he said, "Ah, the king of *England* may have approved, but you forget that the king of France is liege lord where the Templars' headquarters are, and King Philip wants all the allies he can get at the moment. So encouraging the Templars to wade in to act as guardians of the Church's interests in the north of England, instead of a wholly secular sheriff, is his way of saying 'look at what a good Christian king I am,' to the Pope."

"*Dewi Sant!*" Thomas swore, the Coshams and the two women having slipped in to join them for now. "That's conniving!"

"It is," Siward agreed, "and from what Balak and Godfrey told us last night, the leading Templars have swallowed the bait wholesale – or at least some of them have."

Gilbert scratched the rust-coloured stubble on his chin, wearing an expression of distaste as he confirmed, "That fits with what we got out of Hamon and Ilger last night, as well. What's really creeping up Bornhold's arse, though, is that once they reached London they found out that there's sod all they can do about what Sheriff Haket does in Yorkshire – he's got too much power there. Whoever is in charge at the London Temple pretty much said 'you must be joking' to the Grand Master's request – and their supreme leader was cunning enough to phrase it as a request, not an outright order, to the English Grand Master. He clearly saw it for the trap it is, and is trying to appease the French king while not getting into hot water with King Richard!

"Anyway, all they can do is deny Sheriff Haket the archbishop's lands in the neighbouring shires, where he has no authority as sheriff; and Lincolnshire is the one where there's still a goodly chunk of land under the archbishop's lordship, and to be honest, they're going to struggle even to do that. But it doesn't sit well with a man like Bornhold. He can't bear that what he sees as holy property is being milked for political gain, instead of being sent to help those in the East. I think someone slipped up by sending him north with that message for the preceptories up here. They should have left it to Conan and Odilard, who would have known when to just let the matter drop."

"So that's why they're going to Willoughton!" John said with a disgusted snort. He'd never really got over the way the Templars over there had treated him and Allan, and for once Robin actually took notice.

"Steady, John," he said soothingly, coming to wrap his larger cousin in a hug. "These men are just acting out their orders."

"Maybe so," John said scathingly, "but can't you see that there's a danger of something little short of war happening in the next shire if this isn't nipped in the bud? Do you really see the sheriff of Lincolnshire letting a bunch of armed crusaders deny his neighbouring sheriff his rights and dues?"

"He has a point, Robin," Siward agreed. "The sheriffs might hate one another's guts as man to man, but they'll close ranks against any outsiders trying to deprive them of what they see as their rights. Simon de Kyme's position is precarious enough as it is as sheriff of Lincolnshire, given that he's had to go out of the shire on eyre and leave Peter de Trehanton in charge. He won't risk being dismissed from his office by such a capricious king as Richard for not stamping on something like this – even if he wasn't even in the shire at the time – or for supporting the wrong side in such an argument, surely? This has the potential to become very nasty very quickly!"

Tuck looked Guy's way and saw him mouth 'wool clip', and smiled. He knew Guy couldn't make the suggestion without Robin shying away from it, so said for him,

"Maybe we could offer to help?"

Robin turned to him in surprise. "How? What could we do?"

Tuck smiled beatifically. "Well we could remove the financial part, so to speak, if not the land. What makes those lands in Lincolnshire so valuable for the archbishopric?"

"The wool!" Allan answered immediately. "That's where the value of the land lies, in wool from the sheep. The finest in Europe!"

Now John was grinning too, having seen what Guy had mouthed to Tuck. "And what's just happened? The wool clip! Just about now all the fleeces from the farms will have been gathered into the archbishop's tithe barns, just waiting to go off to be spun or even be shipped straight to somewhere like Bruges or Antwerp."

Suddenly Robin was positively beaming. "So if, for the sake of the ordinary people, we can't let these Templars wrest the lands themselves from the sheriff, we can at least deny him the money! I think that's something we can most definitely help them with, don't you?"

Now Guy could join in. "And don't forget that here in Nottinghamshire, both Southwell and Cropwell Bishop are lands of the archbishop. This has come too late for you to be able to seize the rents due at Easter, but whatever they have in the way of wool clips will be at the tithe barns at Southwell Minster by now, and that's very accessible from here."

"I think we need to offer our service to our fellow crusaders," Robin said, wearing a huge smile, and for once Guy wasn't going to say a word against that. "If we take the fleeces then the sheriff has been robbed by outlaws, not the Templars. But we can give it to the Temple as if it was legitimately seized to placate their Grand Master – he'll never know the difference, will he?"

However, first they had to get through the mass Tuck and Abbot Michael had been preparing.

For this Malik had encouraged Janah and Khalīl to join in, telling them,

"I found it more of a comfort than I could ever have imagined when Tuck did this for us," and so all of the newcomers trooped into the church after the canons had celebrated the office of Sext at noon.

There had been some debate as to whether the abbey's canons should remain for the mass. On the one hand this was supposed to be for the crusaders. On the other, if this was to be a glorification of their sacrifice in God's name, Guy had argued, then having the devout canons there who would make the responses in innocent oblivion of what the cost had been in real terms might save the day.

Both he and Tuck knew that their own friends might struggle to make heartfelt responses in some places with the emphases altered this time around, so having the extra men there who would simply follow Abbot Michael and Tuck's lead was probably a good idea. They had also belatedly recalled that not only had Ed, Martin, Simon and Colm never been actively involved in any kind of formal mass in a proper church, rather than Tuck's services (since the nearest working lads like them ever came to such a thing, was being called up on to witness their local priest taking mass on high days, and that from a safe distance outside of their local church); but also that Allan, Roger and Much hadn't been in High Peak with them back then, and therefore none of them were prepared for how strongly these men might react.

"Let's have as many as we can in the church!" Tuck told Abbot Michael firmly. "If nothing else, they can sit on a man who might be in danger of harming himself!"

They had also debated just how much of Tuck's original day of prayer they would repeat today, but felt that even though Lauds (which was performed in the early hours of dawn) allowed for a service for the dead, that it was not fair to inflict this on the others sheltering in the abbey and its infirmary before they had een risen, when none of them knew how badly the crusaders might react. Remembering some of their friends' heart-rending cries, Tuck and Guy warned Abbot Michael that it might get noisy, and scaring the sick and the already frightened poor folk half to death was not what they wanted to do either. Nor was Prime, said barely two hours later, going to be much better. Much better to wait until everyone else was up and about and could be distracted.

"The Templars sometimes say mass after Sext anyway," Tuck assured Abbot Michael, "so they'll think nothing too odd if we do it then. And if we think they need any more relief, then we've still left ourselves the option of doing the Vespers for the dead in the late afternoon."

They could see that Abbot Michael was still dubious about the whole thing, but somewhere along the way Tuck had deeply impressed him as a man of faith, and Guy had the feeling that it was because of this that he was going along with them.

Therefore at noon everyone attending filed into the church, with the canons taking up their usual places in their stalls, and the crusaders making a front row before the altar with the outlaws behind them. Mercifully no-one had batted an eyelid at the request to leave all weapons at the door, but Guy still feared this might get messy.

As Abbot Michael assumed his place before them all and began with the familiar Psalm 42, Tuck began his translations.

"*Tu enim Deus fortitudo mea quare proiecisti me quare tristis incedo adfligente inimico,*" Abbot Michael intoned, and Tuck's resonant Welsh voice rang out with,

"For you are God, my strength. Why have you cast me off? Why do I mourn because of enemy afflictions?" at which point those at the back with Guy saw even Abbot Michael flinch, while some of the canons gasped out loud. Such a thing had never been done before, and few of them were good enough scholars to have translated the words for themselves.

"Do you think they've ever really known what they're praying?" Allan whispered softly in Guy's ear from where they and Roger stood behind Malik, who in turn was behind Janah and Khalīl.

"Possibly not," Guy admitted. "Not the precise words anyway."

And there was another of those barely concealed winces when Tuck translated one of the calls which came after the psalm as,

"For you are my strength, God. Why have you forsaken me? And why must I go in sadness while enemies harass me?"

Clearly the abbot had never thought too closely about how pleading those words were, but they were not lost on the crusaders kneeling at his feet, and the first of the sobs came from, of all people, the tough Conan. Guy saw Will lean forward and put a consoling hand on Conan's shoulder and softly say something reassuring in his ear. The elderly knight's shoulders were quivering, and Guy knew that the tears he so desperately needed to shed had begun.

Yet the other crusaders began to visibly relax again as the balm of familiar repetition took over, and they moved through to the Kyrie without incident. Tuck had wondered when or whether to include the Templars' psalm, which was Psalm 79, and at this point Guy began to wish that he had used it after the opening psalm, because it might have shaken a few things loose. There was still far too much restraint here for his liking.

Abbot Michael was now blessing the host and the wine, but the crusaders stiffened again as Abbot Michael intoned,

"*Orate fratres, et meum ac vestrum sacrificium acceptabile fiat apud Deum Patrem omnipotentem,*" and Tuck translated,

"Pray, my brethren, that my sacrifice and yours may be acceptable to God the Father Almighty."

"Here we go!" John whispered across to Guy from where he stood behind Hamon, and Guy took a deep breath. This would be when the depths of the damage done to these men would start to show. And it was only a short sequence of calls and responses before they got to the point where Tuck translated,

"Remember also, Lord, Your servants and handmaids who have gone before us with the sign of faith and rest in the sleep of peace. For these, Lord, and to all who rest in Christ, we beg You to grant in Your goodness a place of comfort, light, and peace. Through Christ our Lord. Amen." Then said, "This is the point I told you about. Here in this sacred place, name those you held dear who are no longer with us. Those whom you want remembered and to be called to the Lord, if they have not been so already because of where and when they died."

He paused and looked expectantly at them, but there was silence.

Looking along the line of men, all wide-eyed and rigid, Robin stepped forward and went down on his knees and said,

"King Baldwin of Jerusalem..." followed by Malik saying,

"Abraham of Acre, and Saul, Asahel, Joab, Nabal, Telem and Caleb all also of Acre," and then Will adding,

"Eadgar the smith, Robert the smith, Guillaume the smith, Oswald and Tancred."

Suddenly Hamon, Ilgar, Conan and the two turcopoles were stumbling over a list of names, practically tripping over their tongues to get them all out. For a moment the other four were silent, Bornhold looking down the line in disapproval from where Tuck had cunningly placed him at the far end, so that he could sway as few as possible to silence. Yet when Odilard next to him began saying names, albeit much more slowly and with more consideration, as if his memory was being jogged of people he had known long ago, even Bornhold found it in him to recall a few names. However he, Godfrey and Odilard finished long before the others, the seemingly stony Balak actually starting later than any, but soon slumping forwards so that his hands and head rested on the stone step before him, a constant stream of almost intelligible names pouring out of him. At one point Janah and Khalīl paused and looked worriedly to Tuck, but the big Welsh monk just smiled and said,

"Keep going if you need to. We will wait. This takes as long as it takes, there's no hurry," giving a pointed look over the men's heads to the canons, some of whom were showing signs of becoming restless.

Yet as the list of names went on and on, Guy's furtive glances their way saw the increasing shock on these cloistered men's faces. This was the reality of the crusades, not the neat and tidy reports which filtered through to them from the Church. And he was gladdened when a couple of the brothers who helped out in the infirmary slid out of their benches and moved silently up to beside Will with Conan, and to Siward who was already kneeling beside the human wreck that was Balak – if anyone knew how Balak was feeling just now it was him, but he gladly accepted the presence of the brother coming to kneel on Balak's other side.

As for Abbot Michael, his expressions went through surprise, to dismay, to distress. Whatever he had expected it was not this outpouring of spiritual suffering resulting from something he had believed was such a righteous cause. It was certainly having a profound effect, because when there had been enough of a silence for Tuck to believe that the men had come to the end, he looked at the Abbot only to find that he could not now continue.

Taking a deep breath, Tuck took over the service, and when it came to the point where the canons would sing the Agnus Dei while he prepared the communion, the singing from the canons' stalls was very ragged indeed, making Roger lean into Guy and whisper,

"I 'fink that was the biggest shock some 'o them 'ave ever had! Even wiv' the pilgrims 'n poor they don't 'alf live a sheltered life 'ere."

Guy looped an arm over the smaller man's shoulders and gave him a squeeze. "Siward was like Balak when we did this for them, you know. That's why I got so angry when Robin tried to take him back into an army. He'd have died in the first big battle, Roger. Siward couldn't have taken it."

Roger turned his face up to Guy's, eyes huge with shock. "Siward?" He looked at the prostrate Balak, who was being helped up enough so that he could take the bread and wine Tuck was offering him. His opinion of Siward's courage had clearly taken a massive leap upwards for bringing Robin back to them, and for a moment Guy felt guilty that he'd probably eroded even more of Roger's faith in Robin. His guilt didn't last long, though, they all needed to be aware of the cost of war. Robin was too good at emphasising the glory and not the pain.

For himself he was profoundly glad that Tuck was offering the host and the wine to these men. It was probably the first time any of them had even been offered it. Normally only the priest would have partaken, and Abbot Michael was now openly staring at Tuck in awe, for it had clearly never occurred to him to break with tradition this much. And then instead of ending by reciting the traditional Epistle of St John in Latin, Tuck said it in English and immediately followed it with the Templar's psalm, again in English.

"O God, the heathen have come into your inheritance; they have defiled your holy temple; they have laid Jerusalem on heaps," he began. "The dead bodies of your servants they have given to be meat to the fowls of heaven, the flesh of your saints to the beasts of the earth. Their blood they have shed like water about Jerusalem; and there were none to bury them."

And Bornhold broke.

With a scream that seemed to come from the soles of his boots, he flung himself upwards and began tearing at his shirt, wailing incoherently in his distress. Robin pounced on him, as did Thomas, their archers' strength only just being enough to stop Bornhold from clawing at his own eyes as the ghosts of the past rose up before him.

Hearing worried scuffles behind him, Guy turned and stepped up to the canons and lay brothers.

"*This* is what war does to men," he said sternly, as Tuck brought the service to a close. "*This* is the price of fighting for Jerusalem!"

"What demons have the infidels forced on him?" asked a young canon who, going by his speech, had come from a good family and had already been wondering what he had let himself in for in joining Abbot Michael's monastery even before today.

"No demons, brother," Guy told him sadly. "What ails him is the vision of all those he left as bloody corpses strewn across the Holy Land. This is not possession, it's a terrible wound of the soul which needed cauterizing before it killed them."

He looked at all of them until he was sure that they were all looking at him. "Those men up there – Robin Hood and four others – they were like this when I first met them. What you have done here today, brothers, is give these Templars a chance to heal just as they have done. Pray you never have to deal with others so afflicted, but if you do, remember this and treat them with as much kindness as you can summon, because they'll need it."

He turned back and saw that all but Bornhold were being helped out of the church, the infirmarer now finally understanding what Tuck had told him would be needed afterwards, and ushering them towards his domain. The canons also gratefully escaped whispering amongst one another in shocked tones. However, Abbot Michael stayed standing near the altar, watching Tuck like a hawk as the big Welshman joined Robin and Thomas in holding Bornhold, but praying with the intensity of one summoning every one of his beloved Welsh saints to his aid. The Abbot had clearly never seen the like, and Guy felt he should perhaps offer the man some solace of his own.

Sidling up to the altar steps he held out his hand to the abbot.

"Come on, Father," he said gently. "Let's leave this to Tuck. The Lord knows he's had enough practice. If anyone can sort Bornhold out, it's him."

Abbot Michael was white-faced, and gratefully accepted Guy's steadying arm as he led him away. At the church porch, however, he stopped and subsided on the stone seat which normally the weakest of his congregation resorted to to rest upon on their way in.

"May God forgive me, I had no idea!" he said shakily.

Guy plunked himself down beside him, realizing that he had to give some reassurance here. "Neither did we originally, Father. In truth, Tuck and I did what we did for Robin and the others out of nothing more than a burning desire to help. We had no idea what a storm we were going to unleash. How could we know? I've never been in a big battle. I've never even been out of England! The worst I've ever seen was a year ago at Nottingham Castle, and terrible though that was, I'm only too aware that that was nothing in comparison to the siege of Jerusalem my friends went through.

"It's only been afterwards that I've begun to question whether the crusade was worth the cost the ordinary men paid for their lords' and masters' arrogance. Maybe the reason we failed to take the Holy Land back was because so many of those leading the crusade did so for all the wrong reasons? Where there should have been humility and devotion, there was only greed and conceit, and some of the worst – from what my friends have told me – was amongst the leading Templars.

"Not the ordinary knights and men-at-arms like these, mind you. They could only follow orders and die like flies just as the other soldiers did. But just as you feel compelled to help the ordinary people here who suffer at their lords' hands, it means that we cannot ignore men like these. Not now. Not when we've come to realize what they've been through."

"What will become of them?" Abbot Michael asked worriedly.

Guy sighed. "It depends. Robin's anchor seems to have been his faith, but there are times when I still think he's horribly haunted by the past. I fear Conan and Balak will be like that. Others, like Malik and Will, seem to be able to heal. For them, the service got rid of all the ghosts that were following them. I think most of the others will be like them, and by the sounds of it, Odilard and

Godfrey never went through the hell of the Holy Land. They maybe never fought any further east than somewhere like Cyprus. Poor Bornhold, though… I don't know about him. I know Tuck would say that he had been keeping things too bottled up for too long. That his apparent callousness was the way he chose to keep from feeling anything anymore, because the moment he let himself feel *anything* at all, there was the danger that everything else would come boiling up to the surface."

"Have we done him more harm than good?"

Shrugging, Guy could only say, "I don't know. What I do know is that sooner rather than later he would have wanted to meet his death, and there was a real danger that he might have led unsuspecting others down that road. We may not have done him anything you could call 'good', but we've almost certainly saved some lives, and some of them were likely to be the folk of our shires here. If he'd gone to Lincolnshire and started a fight with the sheriff, who knows how many ordinary people would have got crushed in the process?"

Abbot Michael nodded slowly, his colour gradually returning to normal.

"Brother Tuck is a most remarkable man," he said thoughtfully, which made Guy chuckle.

"That he is, Father! I won't argue with you over that!"

"And quite the scholar. What a loss to the Church given the way he knows his Latin. I could not have done what he did, Sir Guy. I could not have put the mass into English as fluently as he did."

Guy patted him on the back. "Ah, but Tuck has had a lot of practice, Father. And long winter nights in Sherwood have given him a lot of time to think on the best choice of words. I've known Tuck for …Blessed St. Thomas, it must be twelve or thirteen years now! And he was already a rebel then, telling his flock what the bible actually said, not just what the bishops and abbots decided they should know. You've a way to go before you catch him up!"

That brought a smile to Abbot Michael's face, and together they got up and went and joined the others.

There was nothing they could do for the rest of the day, but when Tuck came and found Guy after he'd joined the canons at Compline, and after which the canons and lay brethren had gone to their beds with more gratitude than normal, he declared,

"There was a good deal more praying from the heart tonight, Guy. I doubt they have ever thought so hard before about what they are saying."

"You opened their eyes, my friend. Even Abbot Michael's."

But Tuck shook his head. "Not me, *brawd*, God! He was with us today, or at least his saints were. I don't know whether Bornhold will ever be the same again, but we have surely saved him from the danger of taking lives needlessly, and that is a *good* thing."

However two mornings on the first surprise came. Janah and Khalīl came to Robin and the others with Malik.

"We do not wish to go to the preceptor," Khalīl said fervently. "It was one thing to fight and kill for a... a..." he looked pleadingly at Malik as he groped for the English word.

"For a righteous cause," Malik supplied with an encouraging smile.

"Yes!" said Khalīl. "A *true* cause. But we do not want to become entangled in these games for power between kings."

Janah looked directly to Robin. "We wish to join you if you will have us. Malik has told us of what you try to do for the ordinary people here. If we cannot go back to our own homes, then what you do seems to be a more fitting use of our skills."

Robin's smile positively lit up his face, again reminding Guy of what his cousin could be like, and how appealing that smile could be.

"We would be honoured to have you," Robin declared.

"*Insha'Allah!*" Janah breathed in relief, 'God wills it.'

Then from behind them another voice said, "And me too, please, if you'll let me."

They all turned to see a pale and shaky Balak leaning against one of the timber posts. "I can't go through it, either. Odilard, Conan, Hamon and Ilgar were always going to retire up here, and Godfrey's too old to be sent back to fight even though he's said he'll go back to the Temple in London as planned. But me? If I go back they'll send me on to France. They'll say they need men like me with experience to train others, but you can bet that the next time there's a fight brewing I'll be in the front line, and I can't face being bawled at by some nobleman's son who's been sent to the Order to gain favour, and who's never seen a real bloodbath. I'll fight with you, don't worry – I'm not going to be a burden – but it has to be for a good reason, not just to beat some poor peasant witless because someone far away decided he doesn't say his prayers the right way, or salute the right lord."

"I think we can find you something more useful to do," Will said with a grin, coming to grasp the other man by the arms. "We've some young lads here who need to learn an awful lot before they face a proper man-at-arms or sergeant, and the rest of us have more than enough to do without being tied up in camp to train them."

The relief which spread across Balak's face had Guy softly blessing Will. That had been a good call.

"What are you going to do now?" Janah asked carefully.

"Well for a start," Robin said, with a grin, "we're going to get something for your friend Godfrey to take back with him – the archbishop's wool clip! That should keep the Temple happy, teach Sheriff Haket a lesson, and save the folk of Lincolnshire from any dirty fighting across their farmlands."

And what of Bornhold? We let the other two knights take him on to Willoughton as planned. He was not a man we could in all conscience leave with such innocents as Abbot Michael and his brothers, even though they offered to care for him. He was better off in the infirmary of his own brethren, and I believe he lived a goodly while in their care, finding comfort in the familiar offices in their chapel.

As for Khalīl and Janah, they were not just welcome for their own sakes. It warmed my heart to see how much it cheered Malik to have men around him whom he could talk to in his mother tongue, and about their shared homeland. It allowed me to hope that he would stay for a long time with us, for I had often wondered if he had come to regret his decision to remain after James left. I am sure their words of how they, too, could not return because of the political chaos at home also helped to settle his mind that he was better off with us, and for that I was grateful.

Robin needed stable men like Malik around him to keep his feet on the ground, for without them I was always worried that his schemes would become ever more ambitious and unrealistic. Will was also becoming one of those stalwarts of the gang, but I had fretted over whether he would linger long if Malik left, for I could foresee that if those two left then more of the strain would fall on Siward and Hugh, and also on Tuck and my two other cousins. Robin was a weight which was easier to bear when spread out amongst many – and that is not jealousy or pique at being overshadowed by him speaking, Brother! Rather it was a realization that his charm and charisma meant that if some of those cooler heads got taken in by him, then others would still keep a hold on the realities of life, and in truth it varied from plan to plan, and fight to fight, who was swept along by him and who was not. At this point in our story, your hero could still sway men with his words, Gervase!

Yet we are not done with this part of our tale quite yet, and we must press on.

Chapter 13

We set off from Welbeck in quite the cavalcade, for we borrowed several horses from Abbot Michael for two reasons. The first was speed. Bornhold's party had taken far longer getting to our shires than expected, and we wanted to be at this matter before anyone thought to send further prompts from London. Nobody knew who was in charge at Willoughton these days, for we had to concede that it had been many years since John had had any dealings with them, and men of more extreme views might have taken charge by now – not that John thought his former landlords had been overly filled with tolerance and charity!

But the second was the realization that we might need more horses than could be found locally to move the fleeces. The big bundles of wool were quite a weight, Gervase, and while we stood a good chance of finding wagons at the tithe barns – indeed we were hoping and praying that some of the fleeces might even have been left on some – the horses to pull them would not be so easily found. Yet this also meant that we could all ride in turns, for the stocky carthorses could carry two of the lighter men each without strain, and so with nobody having to walk all the way, we could set a brisk pace.

For now Bornhold also travelled with us, because there was little point in splitting our party just yet. And so we moved across Nottinghamshire, grateful of the fact that we could travel through the depths of Sherwood to disguise our movements, and taking some relief in being able to enjoy seeing the forest bursting into life as the oaks and other trees were decked in fresh green leaves, and nothing more threatening than the birds called at our passing.

Oh stop tutting, Brother! I am not waxing poetic to distract you! I was about to tell you that England in all its spring glory was a revelation for Khalīl and Janah, who had never seen the like, and even Bornhold stirred enough from his shattered state to say that he had forgotten how lovely his homeland could be. And that, Gervase, gladdened all of us, for we hoped that this man who had sacrificed so much for God might eventually be healed by the sight of what he had once held dear. Even the outlaws took time to breathe deeply, and take some soothing from an uneventful journey through the quiet of the *forest*; and as I seem to have to keep reminding you, we all needed that when it was scarcely a year since the shire had been so trampled by our king, and had spent the following months dealing with the resulting chaos.

For Robin and myself, it was a chance to ride in company without having anything to disagree about, and for the first time in far too long we recalled the happier times of our childhoods, when the cares of the world has sat less heavily on us. I for one look back on that journey with fondness, for it was the last time Robin and I would come together in something resembling our old friendship. I know you sometimes struggle to believe this, Brother, but I would have given anything for us to go back to our old closeness, and that is the truth, so help me God. And I did try to reconcile us, honestly I did. For all that Robin could infuriate and anger me, right up until his last breath there was still a place in my heart where I loved him. In the sanctity of this confession I swear I do not lie over that.

However, I will press on with our tale, but I wanted you to know about this moment so that you will not judge me too harshly with what is to come between Robin and me.

Where is Willoughton, you ask? Ah, you did not take notice when it was just John and Allan there, but now you know Robin is involved you wish to know. And was Southwell on the way there? No, Brother. Willoughton is five or six miles south of Kirton-in-Lindsey, which is itself a short day's ride south of the River Humber. Had we gone north from the abbey and crossed into Yorkshire at Doncaster, and then gone east, we would have had a shorter journey, but that would have taken us perilously close to the Yorkshire preceptories up on that great river. Remember, Brother, that we were trying our best to avoid creating any links with them which might be traced by their sheriff and cause conflict.

I would also remind you that while the Templars held no lands in Nottinghamshire, the Hospitallers had preceptories at Ossington and Winkburn; and that therefore we had had no dealings with them in general because of Marianne and Mariota, not wishing to bring them to anyone's attention as sisters of that order a long way from where they ought to have been. But on this journey we equally needed to avoid them for the sake of our Templars, for the last thing we needed was for some officious *frère* of that order to start wondering what Templars were doing in the shire, and send a message to Sheriff Briwere asking what they were doing here. No, Gervase, the two orders were not *friendly with one another despite having been in such close proximity in Jerusalem. Do not forget that they observed very different kinds of religious rules, but also were, in effect, in competition with one another for what patronage there was going in these straitened times in places like England and France.*

So we made the journey southwards to the camp near Inkersall, and then went on to the one close by Epperstone, swearing the Templars to secrecy over their locations. But the Epperstone camp was a good place to set out from to launch our raid on the tithe barn at Southwell, and it is there that I shall continue our tale.

Southwell & Lincolnshire
May, the Year of Our Lord 1195

Resting up during the day, the outlaws and Templars set off in the last glimmers of dusk from the Epperstone camp to travel the handful of miles to Southwell.

"With luck we can cross the Trent at Newark," Robin told those not familiar with the area.

"The bishop's still away at court," Guy confirmed, "so there'll be a minimal number of men at the castle – just enough to hold it against any lawless attempt at an attack, because there's no threat from anything stronger around here." He gave Balak a reassuring grin. "They're more likely to barricade the gates and just let us go past without a word. I know the soldiers there. They're not the stuff heroes are made of. With the bishop away they'll be taking life as easy as possible."

He saw his words relax not only Balak but the other Templars too, and hoped that Robin would give those joining the gang time to adjust before throwing them into a major fight. At least the plan as it stood meant that they would relieve the monks at Southwell of their wool and continue away from the hiding place, so no imprints of heavily laden horses would need disguising when he came back this way. It was the little details like that which Robin too easily forgot with his grand, sweeping gestures, and this fragile peace between them meant that Guy didn't want to remind him just now.

With Compline out of the way by the time they arrived by Southwell Minster, they had several hours clear until the monks there rose in the small hours for Matins, and with luck, that deep into the night they would be half asleep. At least there was no missing the great minster church, which towered above all the buildings around it, and from there it wasn't hard to find the huge tithe barn. Come harvest time this would be filled to capacity with grain, but at this point in the year there was little in the way of food stuff in there. So when John and Tuck heaved the bar off the double doors, and swung them open to reveal a barn full of large sacks, there was only one thing it could be.

"Right, let's find some carts," Allan said to the slighter built men, and they vanished into the darkness with the horses, as the others began heaving the bales out into the open. It was heavy work, and soon they had all stripped off their jerkins and were working in just their shirts despite the night chill.

Yet although Guy started off helping with the bales, he was soon called away by Allan to help with sorting harnesses out. Janah and Khalīl turned out to have the same knack with horses that Malik had, and so soon it was those three with Guy who were getting the horses teamed up to pull what would be some very heavy wagons.

"Do they not know these things?" Janah asked Guy, with a nod towards the younger outlaws.

"Not how to team horses up like this," Guy replied, adjusting a plough collar on one of the hefty beasts they'd brought with them. "Most villages use oxen to pull ploughs with. That's why this collar is such a bad fit. We'll have to make sure it doesn't start rubbing. This big cart we have here would also be pulled by oxen at harvest time, so the lads don't know how many horses it will take to pull it once it's laden."

Together they backed the pair of horses they'd been harnessing up to a pair already in place. "I hope these chains hold," Guy said thoughtfully, giving the length a tug which he'd attached from the hay-wain's side to a collar. "They're going to have to take some strain."

One thick length of timber was connected by an iron loop and pin to the centre of the cart, and the normal harnesses connected to that. But this only allowed for one pair of beasts, and this time they needed more, so Guy had rigged the extra chains to come up the side of the wagon from the front axle to the front pair, in the hope that it would spread the load and not pull the metal ring out of its socket in the cart. They would also be taking these carts at a far greater speed than the oxen usually pulled them at, and the last thing they wanted to happen was for the carts to fall to bits on them.

As they took their cart up to the barn, they saw that Malik had done something similar with ropes on the other high-sided hay-wain he and Khalīl had been harnessing. These two would take the greatest weight, as the other wagons being pressed into service were smaller and could cope with just two horses, and Guy was pleased to see that Allan already had two smaller carts lined up, which moved away fully laden as he brought his up to the barn.

What was more of a problem was that this was taking far longer than anyone had thought. It was no easy matter to stack the bales of wool so that they got as many as possible onto the wagons but remaining stable, for they had used all the rope for the extra harnesses and there was none spare to lash bales down with. All too soon they heard the bell for Matins, which forced them to hurry the carts away to the far side of the barn, and close its doors until they heard the monks beginning their chanting in the church. Luckily there was little more that they could load up after that, and so once the monks had tottered back to their beds to grab three more hours of blessed sleep before they had to rise again for Lauds, the wagons could set off.

"By Our Lady, it's a good thing the road from here to Newark is a good one," Thomas puffed as he and Piers helped shove one of the smaller wagon's wheel out of a particularly deep pothole. "I never thought thieving would be such hard work!"

"The penance of a life of crime, *brawd*!" Tuck joked, giving him a pat on the back and then wincing as he realized he, too, had splinters from the cart in his hands.

Half a dozen miles got them to the bridges at Newark as the first glimmers of dawn reached the eastern horizon, but they had travelled at less than the outlaws normal walking pace, making Gilbert fret,

"Are we going to get over that bridge by the castle without being seen?"

However Guy reassured him, "They're going to be expecting to see the wool being moved any time now anyway. The Church doesn't sit on its assets for long if they can convert them to cash. If anyone challenges you, just say that you're taking these loads over to the Wash to meet a barge. From all I've heard, the wool gets moved by sea when it's being done legitimately, so nobody will think that odd."

Even so, they all found themselves watching the ramparts of Newark Castle like hawks, and peering at the arrow slits in case they suddenly found themselves being shot at.

"Jesu, are these English all bloody deaf?" Guy heard Colm asking Gilbert in his broad Irish accent, and Gilbert's wry comment back of,

"They'd never get away with a raid over in Ireland, that's for sure."

That piqued Much's curiosity. "What sort of raids are those, Gilbert?"

Both the Irishmen laughed softly, with Colm replying, "Cattle raids, young Much, cattle raids! 'Tis a great sport in our country to go lifting cattle from your family's enemies."

"That it is," Gilbert agreed with a chuckle that hinted at memories of his youth. "It's not unknown for some to change hands three or four times over before they get to slaughter."

"But doesn't that cause terrible hardship to the ones who've lost their cows?" Much asked innocently.

"Jesu, no!" Colm scoffed. "They just go and take some from someone else!"

Guy couldn't help teasing Gilbert with, "So that's why you've taken to the outlaw life so readily. I didn't know you'd had practice!"

The big red-haired Irishman snorted jovially, "You have no idea, Guy, none at all! There's nothing quite so inspiring to making you run than tearing through the bracken with O'Neill's wolfhounds snapping at your arse!"

Martin and Simon of Walesby at the back of Allan's cart were hanging on every word, and Martin asked, "Are they worse than any other dog, then?"

It reminded Guy that these lads had never known Fletch and Spike, the dogs he'd had when he'd met John and Allan again for the first time, nor Motte and Bailey. "No, just bigger. I must bring Domnall and Máel out to meet you," he told them, and gave Roger a grin in the growing light, "they're even bigger than my deerhound crosses!"

Roger had adored Guy's big dogs once he'd got over his initial fright, and his face split into a happy smile, while Colm's eyes lit up too.

"Oh, I would dearly love to see proper wolfhounds again!" he declared, and obviously meant it.

"Then I shall have to find a pretext to bring them out now that they are fully fit," Guy promised. He was already thinking that when word of this theft reached Nottingham the sheriff would order a hunt, and it was just such a manhunt that Briwere would think the wolfhounds ideal for, especially as he was far from convinced of Guy's control over them, and so had not gone close to them since they arrived. Not that he would have seen a difference, Guy knew, because the dogs only had to scent Briwere for their lips to curl and their teeth to be bared.

However, they had passed Newark by now, and the rest of their journey was uneventful too, but not so their arrival at Willoughton. It was only Allan's chance remark of,

"The last time I was at a preceptory I got hauled out across Guy's saddle," which reminded the older members of the outlaws that both of them and John were in danger of being recognised. With Guy and John being well above average height they were the kind of big men the Templars were unlikely to forget in a hurry, and although it had been some years ago, nonetheless it wasn't a chance they wanted to take. As for Allan, he'd been such a thorn in their sides it would be a miracle if none of the frères remembered his face.

"Maybe you should go in alone," Guy suggested to Odilard and Conan, and for once Robin didn't argue but instead said,

"All you Templars should go, and have Martin, Simon, Much and Roger go with you. Tell the Master that you need to unload to fleeces so that these lads can take the wagons back."

"I'll go with them as a farmer whose cart they've borrowed," Will volunteered.

"And me," Bilan added. "We've got six carts, they'll expect at least one lad each."

"We'll come with you, too," Mariota volunteered. "Dressed like this we could be just young lads who haven't grown beards yet." Both women were wearing trews, baggy jackets, and had their hair covered by floppy hats, but even so Robin immediately looked dubious.

"It'll have to be them," John urged him. "The rest of us look far too threatening to fool experienced soldiers, and I know not all of the brothers at Willoughton were fighters, but there were enough who were for that to be a danger. They'd spot Thomas and Piers for archers straight away."

Reluctantly, Robin conceded that John was right, and so Odilard and Conan led the way, with Hamon and Ilger walking beside the first hay-wain, and Godfrey taking over the driving of the first small wagon with the still dazed Bornhold sitting up beside him.

The big gate to the preceptory precinct opened up and the first of the wagons disappeared inside, but then everything seemed to grind to a halt, with three of the wagons still outside.

"I don't like the look of this," Siward said softly to Guy.

"Me neither."

Then Bilan came loping back to them, taking care to stay hidden from anyone in the preceptories' view behind the bulk of the last wagon, which was one of the great hay-wains.

"We've got a problem," he gasped as soon as he could speak without shouting and announcing the others' presence to the men inside. "The Master won't accept the wool! He's furious that Conan even suggested that he take it and send it onwards. He says it will bring all sorts of trouble down on him. I think the only thing stopping him from ripping into Conan and Odilard, and putting them on whatever punishment the Templars do to knights, is because Odilard quickly told him that it was Bornhold who was under orders to do it, and then told the Master that Bornhold got taken ill after they'd taken the wool."

"Blessed St Thomas," Guy gasped, "they haven't said where the wool came from, have they?" He could foresee all manner of problems if the Master ordered them to take the wool back to Southwell, not least because he sounded like the kind of man who might send someone on in a few days to make sure that it had been returned.

However Bilan was shaking his head. "No, it's a good thing that Will was there, because he spoke up and said he was from Selby and had come to take the wagons back, so the Master thinks it's come from Yorkshire."

"I should have gone in," Robin growled and made as if to march in.

Siward grabbed his sleeve. "And what would that achieve? What could you say to that man that would make him change his mind?"

Robin looked back at Siward in surprise. "That the money this wool will make for the order will go a long way towards winning back the Holy Land, of course! Especially when we get the rest."

Hugh was now standing in Robin's way. "No, Robin, I don't think that's going to sway this Master."

"Why not?"

Gilbert gave a big sigh and came and took Robin's other arm gently but firmly, and said, "Because he no doubt sees what many others of us do: that the Holy Land cannot be won, never could have been."

Robin stared at him aghast. "What do you mean?"

Now Malik joined in, speaking very calmly but firmly. "We were always too few. Can you not see that Robin? A few hundred knights to Salah al-Din's thousands! And if the knights were outnumbered ten to one, we turcopoles and the men-at-arms were by ten times that many again. Nor we were ever one united force. If we had been it might have made a bit of a difference." Then cleverly playing to Robin's weak spot, added, "Maybe if King Baldwin had been healthy and lived it would have been different, too. He was the one man who ever seemed to be capable of forcing the various princely leaders to behave and bury their quarrels for the greater cause."

They saw his words start to sink in, and Tuck pressed them in by saying, "But God chose to take Baldwin. You've said yourself that he was too good for this earth, and maybe God was trying to tell us something by taking him back."

"I think this Master here sees it that way, that the Holy Land is lost forever," Hugh now prompted. "So the argument of funding another crusade would never sway him. And in the meantime, he has to live with the decision King Richard's man here in England,

Archbishop Walter, has made that the sheriff can administer his northern rival's lands. Would you want to get on the wrong side of Hubert Walter in the Master's shoes?" He turned to John. "You always described him as pragmatic. Who do you think he sees as the bigger problem: his Grand Master in France, or the archbishop of Canterbury who could expel his order from England in the name of the king if he chose?"

This was something Hugh, Siward and Guy had talked about in private during Guy's respite at the abbey, with Will, Malik and Gilbert also drifting in and out of the conversations at various times, and all had agreed that the Templars up here might feel caught between a rock and a hard place. It had been Robin who had insisted on the fleeces being taken to Willoughton first – Robin along with Odilard and Godfrey, the ones who had seen less of the fighting and were more used to the political wrangling in France which their order got caught up in.

"Archbishop Walter," John answered without hesitation.

"Then what are we doing this for?" a confused Colm asked, getting him a look of approval from Robin, whose jaw was setting in that sign of grim determination which boded trouble.

"We're doing it," Guy intervened, "for the same reasons we said we were back at the abbey, and that's to avoid a prickly conflict between the Templars and the sheriffs that might end up trampling the ordinary folk in the process. We're just going to have to do it the other way we considered. We're going to have to take this to a port ourselves – Boston would probably be good – and find someone to take it to London for us. Once it's there Godfrey can tell them what he likes, whatever will placate the English Grand Master."

"Or better," Siward interjected, making the suggestion that he, Guy and Hugh had worked out beforehand but knew Guy could not be the one to say, "take it straight to a French port. If there's a chance the English Grand Master is going to be just as difficult, then let's bypass him altogether. If the supreme Grand Master in France is the one prepared to dance on King Philip's whims, then let's give him the wool and keep the peace. God's wounds, he can hardly know what the worth of the archbishop's lands up here is! He probably doesn't even know where York is. It could be in Scotland for all he knows! And this load of fleeces alone represents a small fortune at market."

Robin's face relaxed into a smile, and the three conspirators inwardly breathed sighs of relief.

"That's good thinking, Siward," he praised, and even managed a genuine smile for Guy, which took him by surprise. "Yes, if the Master here will not see the greater picture, then we must act alone."

"In some ways that might help us," Guy risked adding. "I won't be able to help you in this because I really do need to get back to the castle, but if this is something you don't need the local preceptories to endorse, then there's nothing to stop you from liberating more bales from this shire too. I'd take a look at Bardney Abbey near Lincoln, because you might as well use the old Roman road as much as you can.

"But the place I'd really look hard at is Kyme Priory. It was founded by the sheriff of Lincoln's family, and so if there's anything of the archbishop's in the area, my money would be on it being stored in a tithe barn close to there on the basis that nobody's going to rob the sheriff. And I'd take a look at Billinghay and Billingborough. I know they're the archbishop's manors and there are bound to be tithe barns there. You can look at all of them on the way to Boston, and then when you've been able to unload these carts somewhere, you could go back to those others without trekking for miles."

"Not rob the sheriff, eh? Well there's only one thing for that," Robin said firmly. "We'll have to make a show of taking these wagons on the road back north and they'll have to be taken by Robin Hood! It's about time we showed we're not just lawless men hiding in the forest, but a force to be reckoned with."

Clearly Guy saying he couldn't be part of this was enough for Robin to overlook his redirection of the mission. Not that Guy would have put that to the test too often. This was probably because they had been on such relaxed terms for the past few days, but that couldn't continue indefinitely when Robin was so easily offended. Sooner or later Guy was bound to put a foot wrong however carefully he trod around his cousin.

For now, though, the main task was getting the horses to back up enough to let the wagons within the preceptories bailey come back out. Yet to everyone's surprise, Odilard and Ilgar came out as well.

"I do not think I could live under the rule of one who so disregards the Grand Master's orders," Odilard declared with some vehemence. "Conan says he will stay for now. He does not know what he will do eventually, but he has said he will see Bornhold settled."

Robin looked to Ilgar. "What about you?"

"I am prepared to travel with Godfrey," the older man-at-arms declared. "I will see what happens after that before I decide where I will retire to."

"You might be happier over at the Garway preceptory on the Welsh border," Guy suggested. "You won't have the fighting you would have seen in France and elsewhere, but they still form a vital defence against Welsh raids, and they tend to get a bit forgotten out there. When I lived over there I don't recall the frères getting anything like as entangled in secular politics as this."

Ilgar smiled. "Then I may well request that the Master sends me there. Thank you, Guy, that's a welcome alternative."

"Just don't mention my name!" Guy hurriedly reminded him. "I'm supposed to be on the sheriffs' side, not yours!"

"Do not worry," Odilard reassured him. "We will not forget your kindness towards us – not any of you. If you need help close to any preceptory we end up at, we will do our best to sway whoever is in charge to give that help."

Robin's face was falling into a frown at that, clearly thinking that this was something of a lukewarm kind of thanks, when Hugh saved the day by quickly responding with,

"We'd be very grateful for that, and we understand that you can't make promises you might not be able to keep. It's one thing you being personally grateful, and quite another to hope that you might be able to force a superior who sees us in a different light to give aid when they don't want to."

As soon as Hugh had said about promises which might be broken Robin was all smiles again, making Guy sigh inwardly. His cousin was too quick to judge, and he knew that Robin would have been outraged later on if he felt he'd been so let down, yet hadn't thought ahead in the way Odilard had.

In the meantime they were adjusting the loads, and the ways a couple of the horses were teamed up, so that Guy could take one of the horses to ride back with.

"I daren't linger longer," he told his friends regretfully. "As it is, I shall have to cover my absence by saying that I heard of Robin Hood stealing from Southwell as I came south, and tried to track you. Don't worry, I'll lead the hunt a merry dance around Sherwood while you get down to Boston. But could some of you then come back and lay a couple of false trails for me? It'll take me about the same time to get back to Nottingham as it will you to get this load down to the port, so by the time I've got men out to Southwell, a few of you travelling fast and light won't be too far behind me. If you seem to have me running around all over the shire, it will only add to the Robin Hood legend."

That had been said for Robin's benefit, of course, but Guy was surprised when Malik spoke up, saying,

"Janah, Khalīl and I will come with you and do that. We cannot help much with negotiating for a ship, and our presence will be more likely to arouse comment." He gave his most disarming smile to Robin. "If only those of you from these shores are seen in this port nobody will think anything of it, but Janah and Khalīl are still too sunburned to be mistaken for Englishmen, and in their presence I, too, would be taken for a Saracen."

"A good point," Will said hurriedly, before Robin could find something to object about with that.

However Robin showed no signs of arguing this time, and even suggested that they take Balak with them.

"Did that second mass for the dead help Robin so much?" Tuck asked Guy quietly on one side as he prepared to leave. "Had I known that I might have done it sooner."

Guy patted his friend on the hand. "Bless you, Tuck, but I think half of it was being in that big abbey – you know, with a proper altar and candles lit, and it being a formally consecrated place. Sadly, I think such things matter to Robin far more than to the rest of us, perhaps more than they should if I'm being frank."

"Hmmm," Tuck intoned thoughtfully. "I see your point. It matters in the same way that it matters to him that you have your manor over at Gisborne, however, humble a place it might be, and yet he was knighted on the battlefield, in effect, and yet has no manor to call his own." Tuck sighed mournfully. "I worry for Robin's immortal soul, I really do. I wish he would think less of these worldly trappings as you do. How did three sisters produce three sons as different as you, Robin and Allan, eh?"

Guy couldn't answer that. "Maybe we should just pray to all our friendly Welsh saints that this good mood lingers for as long as possible?" he suggested. "A permanent change might be asking a bit much, even for them, and you know that I, at least, have a lot of faith in Saints Issui, Melangell and Cadoc."

"I'll be calling on *Dewi Sant* a lot in the coming days, too," Tuck admitted. "You take care, Guy – you risk so much for us already, don't stick your neck in a noose, will you?"

You think this was rather tame, Brother? No, no, far from it. For a start, as I travelled with the three former turcopoles – who I would remind you were the local Christian fighting force in the Holy Land – and let Balak ride on my horse since I could walk much faster than him, we had an important conversation. Malik, it seems, was most anxious to get these experienced fighters alone for a short while and to explain some of the problems we had had with Robin in the last year or so. On our last night together at the camp by Epperstone, he told me that it was one thing for men like Colm, Simon and Martin to be enthralled with Robin, but something far more dangerous if these three experienced fighters got carried away by his charisma.

Oh do not look so horrified, Gervase! He was not maligning Robin, not least because that would have bounced back on us badly since we needed these three to stay, but they were not so attached to everyone as yet for that to be taken for granted. Therefore as we walked and talked, Malik told them what had happened at Jerusalem, and how Robin was probably the worst affected of all of them. That, he said, sometimes clouded Robin's judgment, and it would also be why sometimes he and the other experienced men would seem to go against what Robin proposed. It was not disloyalty, he told them, but a kindness, for Robin would be distraught if he got one of his men killed. He also explained what I did for them, and for that I was most grateful, for he could be much more open whilst we were alone in praising me for the risks I took. ~Guy was like Robin's older brother when they were growing up,~ he told the trio, ~and as sometimes happens with brothers, it means that Robin takes Guy's loyalty and help for granted. The rest of us do not.~

And that, Gervase, was a balm to my soul. I fear I did not think that Robin even saw that much of what I did, or in that much of a kindly manner, but under the circumstances I was not about to modify what Malik was saying. With such a prompt already in their minds, these men would soon see the truth for themselves, of that I became increasingly sure as I got to know them. As a result I went back to Nottingham sure that these men would not betray me should we meet by coincidence, and such reassurances were much needed by me in that time.

As for the wool, Robin managed to charm a captain in Boston to take it and the three Templars across to Antwerp, but not before they had tripled their load with bales of fleece liberated from the archbishop of York's tithe barns in Lincolnshire. It was a long time before we heard how it had been received, but a year later Odilard and Ilgar would come through Sherwood on their way to a Templar grange in the north of Yorkshire and would leave us a message at the Inkersall hideout to say that we had averted disaster. The fleeces were sold and the money sent to the Templars' headquarters nicely in time for King Philip's demand for his share of the money. Crafty man that he was, he had guessed that if Geoffrey Plantagenet was living off the income from the archbishopric, then it must amount to a tidy penny, and with the Templar Order being based in France, as their overlord he could tax them on the basis of that income. However, I believe that he was cleverly played by the Grand Master, who protested enough to be convincing and prolonged the payment, so that the king remained in ignorance of the fact that the lands had not been seized.

By the following year Normandy was in such turmoil that the whole thing was happily forgotten about, but you will be pleased to learn that Robin Hood would remain in the Templars' good graces for many years to come because of that – something which would affect later incidents, but which pleased Robin immensely. As a man knighted in the chaos of Jerusalem, it mattered to him that an order which had also fought out there saw worth in him and recognized him as a man of honour, even if his own king did not. But this incident was also important because it marks the point when he began to be obsessed with the futility of that fight to regain the holy places. Always the dreamer, right up until that point Robin had believed that there would be another crusade which would successfully retake what had been lost, but when that bubble was burst, it took with it all of his certainties in everything else that had gone on out there, and that was damage to his mind that he could ill afford to take and would have implications for the rest of us in the future

Chapter 14

For many months after the taking of the wool clip, we lived in remarkably untroubled times. Of course, Robin and the outlaws continued to disrupt the forest courts as they had done, and remained a thorn in the side of the sheriff. I, meanwhile, led a hunt through the shire for the wool thieves, which was positively merry. True to his word, Malik and his three helpers laid trail after trail for me to follow, some so blatant that even the men-at-arms who were with me spotted them, and for two weeks solid, we tramped the length and breadth of eastern Nottinghamshire, through woods and stream and bogs, and all to no avail. The only thing to be said for it was that for a brief while I was in Briwere's good graces, since he was able to say to Sheriff Kyme when they happened to meet at Newark Castle, that I was the one who raised the alarm first and acted on it first. Kyme's men, it seems, had not been so alert, even going so far as to dismiss the first report that Robin Hood had stolen fleeces from a tithe barn. ~Who is this man?~ Kyme was heard to ask, ~that he should clothe himself and his followers in Lincoln wool? Will he be dying it in <u>graine</u> next?~

Yes, Brother, that was it, the start of the Lincoln green legend, but Robin and the others soon took advantage of it when they heard of Sheriff Kyme's words, and a few bales of fleece were acquired on their own behalf. In small batches it was woven and then made into the outlaws' over-jerkins, and dyed green, Robin sadly admitting that although it would have been a blow to the sheriffs to have them dyed black with the insanely expensive graine from the Mediterranean, it was hardly a practical colour for blending in amongst the foliage with. Of all of them, I was the one who could have worn black and did, albeit coloured with local dyes, but no way could I have worn something so richly and deeply coloured as a <u>graine</u> black and not arouse suspicion from everyone around me. I, sadly, could not even risk having any of the beautifully soft wool for my clothing, but I did not begrudge my friends having what they did.

And so we move on, Gervase. Little happened on the grander stage during the summer of 1195 to impact on us; the exception being Archbishop Hubert suddenly announcing that he was curtailing the movement of monks and nuns on pilgrimage. Apparently he believed that too many were escaping the constraints of their monasteries and going out into the world under the pretext of being pilgrims. Now they would have to prove, by writ from their abbot or prior, that they were on a legitimate pilgrimage, and had also been found on a reasonable course between the two places. This was a great blow for the outlaws because it restricted Tuck's ability to go scouting for them, and it was a blow for me, for my friend could now no longer just wander into Nottingham to meet me with some of the others. Only with borrowed clothes and a hat to hide his tonsure could he move freely, and Tuck was not a man to hide his proclaimed faith.

That autumn I heard other unwelcome news, when word came back with Briwere from the Michaelmas Court that the awful Roger fitz John – whom all who had known him as sheriff had prayed we would never hear of again – had unexpectedly inherited the de Lacy's manors around Pontefract. Seemingly there had been no other male heirs, and so the dreadful man now became known as Roger de Lacy, and would have a base right on our doorstep. That, we all thought, boded ill for the future.

The other development over the summer affected me but not the outlaws except to arouse Robin's ire, but that was almost inevitable. After all of the mayhem of the eyre back in the winter, it transpired that Archbishop Walter was proposing to create a new office, which was to be known as a coroner. Three knights, of which I now became one, and a clerk were elected (in the legal parlance) to keep the pleas of the Crown. Yes, it does sound very official, Gervase.

However the reality was something else. Our job was to view the bodies of those who had died by violent means, or in suspicious circumstances, and make what we could of it. We were then to speak to any witnesses to the event and get their testimonies written down by the clerk, those testimonies then going to the justices when they came on eyre. With those who had died by misadventure – for instance, by being savaged by a village sow – then the value of the animal was assessed when it went to slaughter, and that money given to the poor. Or at least that was the theory. With an avaricious sheriff like Briwere the reality was an altogether different matter.

Now the first of the coroners had been sworn in at the previous year's Michaelmas Court. But although we had been allocated a knight by the name of Reinbold to replace poor Sir Sewel, who had been hanged at the siege, and who had also been elected as one of our coroners, clearly Reinbold's family had enough influence to prevent him from being sent to our rebellious shire, with the attached danger of getting *caught up in some other princely petty quarrel. As a result, one year on and we still only had two knights. What was worse, the two who had been appointed were hopelessly out of their depths with the duties.*

I need to explain here, Brother, that this was an unpaid office, and I am not telling you that just so that you are not under the mistaken belief that I was growing rich on my duties, which I never did. I make the point because such duties were viewed with dismay and almost as a punishment, not a reward. Therefore the two knight who had become saddled with the office locally were Sewel fitz Henry, who got the job in effect as punishment for being in the castle when the king besieged it, and another fellow knight at the siege, Hugo Bassett of Heddon, whom you will remember me getting entangled with during the eyre; and it was Sir Hugo who convinced Briwere that they needed a man who had hunting skills for the job.

Nottingham & Sherwood
Late Summer, the Year of Our Lord 1195

"We need a man who knows the signs!" Sir Hugo pleaded with Briwere. "That body over at Cropwell Bishop we saw the other week – neither Sir Sewel nor I could tell if they were telling the truth that the lad got bashed on the head when he fell into the mill race or not. They could have brained him with a shovel for all we knew! But Sir Guy would have known the difference." He threw an apologetic glance Guy's way, but Guy had already guessed what was coming. "I know you don't like Sir Guy, and think he's not a proper knight, but in truth, sheriff, we're dealing with common folk, not the knighted men of the shire, and we need both someone who knows how to talk to them, and a man who might have a clue about what some of their injuries look like."

That bit about not liking Guy was perversely the thing which sealed Guy's fate. Sir Sewel had already complained today that it was an excessive punishment to be forced on him, when all he had done was turn up to the castle to do his regular service only to become trapped by the siege, and that concept of punishment had stuck with Briwere.

He turned to Guy with his habitual sneer. "Well," he drawled, "It seems you have your uses, Gisborne. Very well, come here and take your oath of office."

It didn't take long, and soon Guy was walking out with Hugo and Sewel.

"I'm sorry to have to do that to you, Guy," Hugo apologised, "But we really do need your expertise. And as I told Sewel, I'd rather work with you than some of the other possibilities."

Sewel was nodding. "I heard about how things turned ugly up at High Peak back at the eyre. I never want to be caught like that in a village! Especially as we'll be alone without soldiers."

He glanced over his shoulder to make sure that Briwere wasn't close enough to hear them, then said, "I know the sheriff sees this as another chance to wring money out of the people, but he's not the one sticking his neck out. *He* may go everywhere with an armed escort, so he would never concede such a thing, but if we get something hopelessly wrong, then I'm not such a fool as to not foresee that a mob of angry peasants could overwhelm us. I'd rather something closer to justice be done."

Guy turned to Sir Hugo. "Are you of the same mind? I ask because I warn you now, I will not accuse an innocent man just to bring the numbers of felons up, in order to make it look like Briwere has a strangle hold on the two shires."

Sir Sewel gave a slightly startled smile. "How very moral of you, Sir Guy. I didn't expect that of you."

Sir Sewel might have come to the castle often, but he had thus far mostly avoided Guy's company, more often sitting with those forest knights like Sir Mahel, whom he thought of as being of the same rank as himself. Undoubtedly whatever he had heard had not prepared him for what Guy was really like, since Mahel liked to give himself airs and graces, and thought himself somewhat above the others. What he was even less prepared for was to get out to the outer bailey, expecting to just collect his horse, and to have Guy greeted by the two huge wolfhounds. As Domnall put his massive paws on Guy's shoulders and slurped up his face with an affectionate lick, Guy distinctly heard a squeak of shock from Sir Sewel two paces behind me.

"Don't worry, Sewel," Sir Hugo said with a chuckle. "They're fine as long as Guy's here – just get well away from them if the sheriff appears, because they're likely to try and tear him to shreds!"

Sir Sewel gulped, "God's wounds! What are they? The hounds of Hell?"

Guy laughed. "No, my friend, just Irish wolfhounds. I was told by a learned friend of mine that the Romans prized them so much that they accepted them as royal gifts and paid handsomely for them. Sadly, these days they're thought coarse and unkempt by Norman lords, but you'd be hard pressed to find a more loyal and valiant hound than these."

"I'll take your word for it," Sir Sewel said faintly, but Sir Hugo knuckled him on the arm and said pointedly,

"If they scare you, think what they'll do to the villagers if Guy brings them with him. Who's going to attack us with this pair in tow, eh?"

Sir Sewel blinked and then looked again at the two huge hounds, who were leaning affectionately against Guy whilst having their ears rubbed. Guy was no small man but they came easily up to his waist even on all four paws; when on hind legs they towered over even Guy, and probably weighed every bit as much as him, if not more.

"Point taken," Sir Sewel breathed, and then stiffened again as Guy said,

"Come and make friends with them. If they know your scent they won't harm you. This one is Domnall," as the great wheaten coloured dog came and shoved his nose into Sir Sewel's crotch, making him utter a sound very close to a girlish squeal. Clearly he feared his family jewels were about to be taken from him. However, with an enormous snort, Domnall huffed for the last time at Sir Sewel's trews and then licked his hand. Máel was somewhat more decorous, nuzzling gently at Sir Sewel's other hand and then leaning affectionately on him when Sir Sewel summoned the courage to pat him on the head.

Staggering under Máel's weight, Sir Sewel looked at Guy with renewed respect.

"Is it true what Mahel said that you went into the old bread oven with these two when they first arrived and came out with your gambeson torn to shreds?"

Guy laughed. "Sort of. Firstly, my gambeson had a couple of torn patches, that's all, and you have to understand that they had terrible suppurating wounds which were driving them mad with the pain. Any animal will attack under those circumstances. Have you never seen a wounded stag charge its hunter in a final act of agony?"

Sir Sewel shook his head mutely.

"Have you *never* hunted red deer?" Guy asked in surprise.

"Er, only the spotted ones," Sir Sewel answered weakly.

"Oh those," Guy declared, with a dismissive wave of his hand in the direction of the nearby deer park. "They're positively tame. You wouldn't get much sport out of them. I shall have to take you on a real hunt if I can combine my forester duties with these new ones."

With a whistle he strode away, summoning the wolfhounds behind him as he went to find a horse on which he could accompany the other two knights, leaving Sir Sewel standing open-mouthed in his wake.

Sir Hugo leaned in and said softly, "Now do you see why I wanted Guy with us? I tell you, Sewel, he's a deadly shot with a hunting bow, and I've personally eaten wild boar he hunted alone for the lords who came on eyre. If anyone knows all the ins and outs of butchering a carcass it's Guy, and you mark my words, he'll spot wrong doings far quicker than ever we will."

"Good choice, Hugo," Sir Sewel said faintly, "good choice!"

"From what you said, you have a body you want me to look at," Guy said to Sir Hugo, once they were on the road.

There was a deep sigh and a pause before Sir Hugo answered, which alerted Guy to the fact that he wasn't going to like this. "Unfortunately it concerns Sir Oliver de Aincourt. He was heading back into the village of Tansley near Matlock, over in Derbyshire to collect some fines still due from the eyre. There was a lot of contention over these cases, Guy. They were ones Briwere himself presided over, and the villagers hotly argued that they were made up charges brought against the headman of Tansley, and also the smiths from Shuckstonefield by Crich and from Ogston, and in truth, I'm beginning to believe them. I've never known villagers stick to the same stories for so long and with such vehemence, but if that's the case then I fear that Sir Oliver himself may be the culprit."

"Good God!" Guy gasped. "What on earth happened?"

"A man known to be at loggerheads with Sir Oliver was found with his head smashed in, is the simple version," Sir Hugo elaborated. "Unfortunately the man was the local miller, and he had accused Sir Oliver of taking water from his mill leet in order to expand the moat around his manor house, and when you see the place you'll see that the man had a reasonable complaint – the mill race doesn't race anymore!"

"But surely the miller must have died long ago?" Guy protested, having a horrible fear that he was about to be asked to divine over a mouldering corpse as to the cause over death.

"Oh he did," Sir Hugo said with an airy wave of his hand. "We can do nothing about that one," for which Guy breathed a quiet sigh of relief. "The body we need you to look at is that of Sir Oliver's right-hand man, Wilfred. You see Sir Oliver had incurred the wrath of that notorious outlaw Robin Hood for his high-handed treatment of the villagers of Tansley and Ogston. Ogston got a visit first and ended up with several men under the lash by Wilfred, and all of their seed grain taken in payment. God alone knows how Robin Hood got wind of it so fast, but he was there waiting for Sir Oliver and Wilfred at Tansley."

Guy knew exactly how Robin would have known – the outlaws had one of their smaller hideaways on the knoll between the two villages! They'd probably heard the villagers' cries of distress for themselves if they'd already been there, and Guy knew that under those circumstances, even the more level-headed amongst them would have acted and thought afterwards if they believed people's lives were in danger.

"Well they denied Sir Oliver access to the village," Sir Hugo was continuing. "Bastards dropped a line of arrows right across his path! Those bloody Welsh bows are a menace!"

"Good job I've got one with me, then," Guy said with a furtive grin.

"Wha...*what?*" gulped Sir Sewel. He stared at Guy looking all over to try and see it.

Guy patted the long oil-cloth wrapped pole which sat under his right leg alongside one of his spears, the other two spears being on the other side. "It's not strung yet."

Leaning back behind him from the other side to Sir Sewel, Sir Hugo jabbed a finger to the long black bag slung from Guy's shoulder across his back, and mouthed "arrows" to Sir Sewel.

"Oh," Sir Sewel said faintly, and then with a morbid curiosity he couldn't contain, "What are the spears for?"

Guy was almost as surprised that he had to ask. What was the world coming to when a lord like Sir Sewel didn't know what you used to hunt boar with? "Someone's died, haven't they?" he began with. "So what if it's a beast not a man that's the killer?"

Sir Sewel still looked bemused, while Sir Hugo picked up where he'd left off with,

"So the bloody outlaws drove Sir Oliver and Walter, along with four other men of theirs out of the village, scattering them as they went. Nobody knows what happened next, but there was a crashing and screaming in the undergrowth. When the others got to them Wilfred had a two gaping wounds in his chest and was as dead as a door nail. The man who had run with him was out cold by an oak – looked like he'd been thrown head first into it. Even when we got there, the man was too addled to be able to tell us what had happened, but Sir Oliver is convinced that Robin Hood killed Wilfred with the villagers' connivance, and the sheriff is halfway to believing him." He shook his head worriedly. "Sir Oliver thinks Wilfred got shot with an arrow, but to me those wounds don't look like arrow wounds."

"But if they're not arrows we don't know what they are," Sir Sewel admitted.

However, Guy already had a shrewd idea. "Even without seeing this man, I think one possibility is that the two of them ran into deep undergrowth and straight into a wild boar's wallow with the boar in it." He turned to Sir Sewel and made the man look him in the eye. "As you'll see when I unpack this, the arrows loosed through a Welsh bow would have gone straight through Wilfred and stuck. Even if he was wearing ring-mail, the arrow would have lodged well inside him and not come loose without being cut out. Whatever caused Wilfred's death, I'm already doubting that it was any arrow, and if it was a spear, then that would have meant hand to hand combat, and what you've told of what went on that doesn't sound right either."

Sir Hugo gave a satisfied smile and said to Sir Sewel, "*This* is why I wanted Guy to be our third man!"

It was gratifying that Sir Hugo wasn't arguing with his initial assessment, but Guy was hoping that somewhere along the line he would get the chance for a few brief words with one of the outlaws. Them denying Sir Oliver the village sounded perfectly normal, but it would signal a drastic change in Robin's attitude to the local Norman lords if the death of Wilfred was in any way intentional; and if that had happened, with Robin for instance, then why had none of the others tried to prevent it?

They claimed a bed for the night at Walter Ingram's manor at Alfreton, or to be more exact, the two other knights slept in Ingram's house. Guy preferred to sleep in the stables with Máel and Domnall. He'd already had more contact with Ingram than he ever wanted with the forest courts, and as soon as the evening meal was over he slipped away, leaving Sirs Hugo and Sewel to be bored to death by Ingram grinding on and on about achievements that were more in his imagination than reality.

"You bastard!" Sir Hugo chastised Guy the following morning as they rode out of the manor's gates. "You bloody scampered off and left us to him! It was hours before we could get to our beds!"

"Hey!" Guy said, holding his hands up in protest, "Welcome to my world! I have him most swanimotes and what feels like every other woodmote, forgive me if I was taking a break from him this time. Mostly there's only me, and I've heard every one of his stories so many times I could tell them word for word!"

Both Sewel and Hugo laughed, Sir Sewel saying,

"In that case you're forgiven. Jesu, but the man has a high opinion of himself!"

"That he does," Guy agreed, "and the older he gets the worse he gets. St Thomas stay my hand if he gets to fifty, because he'll be beyond bearing!"

As a result the three rode into Tansley in good humour, much to the disconcertion of the monk from Felley Priory who had come to act as their clerk until a permanent one could be assigned to them.

"Right, let's see the body and then let this poor man receive a Christian burial," Guy declared. "It's far too warm a time of year to have him hanging around."

He wasn't surprised that the body had been put in an old smokehouse a short way from the village. Poor Wilfred was distinctly ripe by now. However there was no mistaking what had made the two gaping punctures in his chest.

"That's the work of a wild boar," Guy said with conviction. "Look at the width of the holes." He put his bag with his quiver of long arrows in it down on the ground and drew one of them out. "See?" The arrow disappeared into the wound without touching the sides. Not even the barbs on it would have lodged in a wound of that size.

"Can we get him outside into the light?" Guy asked, and with reluctance four men took hold of the corners of the sacking on which Wilfred lay and hauled him out into the daylight.

Clamping a gloved hand over his nose and mouth against the stench, Guy knelt down and bent over to look at the wounds more closely. When he straightened up it was to see Sir Sewel looking positively green and standing as far back as he could, while even Sir Hugo was a little pale.

"There are boar hairs lodged in the wounds," Guy told them, taking one of his knives from his boot-top and carefully lifting some out on the blade. Getting to his feet he took them across to Sir Hugo. "See? Those are bristles from a boar's muzzle. They're actually inside the wound, and there's only one way that happened."

"God's hooks, you've a stronger stomach than me," Sir Sewel declared, waving Guy and his knife away from him. "No, I don't even want to look! I'll take your word for it. If you need me to I'll swear to the sheriff that I saw them, but I'll skip that part here if you don't mind."

"Well that was easily settled," Sir Hugo said with relief, but Guy was already shaking his head.

He turned to the villagers who were hanging back in a horseshoe behind them. "Has this boar been a danger to you before?" he called out.

"Her's bin a nuisance," an older man declared, "breakin' down the hurdles in the fields and the like, but nothin' like this afore."

"We've taken a few of her piglets in seasons past," another told Guy, "and right tasty they were too!"

"Aye, but that Sir Oliver went and hunted *all* of 'em this spring," someone else volunteered. "That's when she turned nasty."

Guy groaned and rolled his eyes in disgust. No doubt Sir Oliver was bragging about what a fine hunter he was, bringing down a dozen wild boar, never mentioning that they had been only piglets. Any hunter worth the name would have killed the sow too, not left her in distress, and Guy knew she would have been grieving the loss of her little ones – pigs were far more intelligent than most people cared to acknowledge.

"Well I'm going to have to kill her now," he said sadly. "She's killed once and now she probably won't stop." He turned to the other two knights. "I'm sorry, but this falls within my duties as a forester. You can come hunting with me if you like, or return and deal with the sheriff."

"I think maybe we need to take the boar's head with us this time," Sir Hugo ventured. "Briwere's got the bit between his teeth over this, and Sir Oliver got his version in first. We'll need whatever proof we can get."

Guy nodded. That made sense. "Very well. Then I think you should accompany me on this hunt." He took in how Sir Sewel had gone pale again. God's hooks, the man was a worrier! "For your own safety, stay well back behind me," Guy cautioned, "and if the boar comes your way, clap your spurs in your horse and run for it! If you give your horse its head it will flee without you needing to do more, and you should out run the boar. I'll be coming up behind it anyway, so you won't have far to go."

As Guy unpacked his spears and then strung the big bow, Sir Sewel leaned in to Sir Hugo and whispered, "He's very confident, isn't he. Will he really bring it down in time?"

Sir Hugo's faint sigh hinted that he was already finding Sir Sewel's timidity wearing. "It's not confidence, Sewel, it's professionalism. Guy's probably done this more times than you and I have been to court. Do as he says and you'll be fine."

However, when they had followed Guy in single file as he tracked the boar, and then spotted her in a wallow in a shallow dip in the nearby woods, even Sir Hugo found his stomach fluttering.

She was enormous! And as the huge head swivelled their way her size made both men swallow convulsively.

Yet Guy surprised them both by saying, "No, she's not the killer. We'll leave her be."

"What?" Sir Sewel exclaimed.

"Look at her mouth," Guy said softly, shushing him with a gloved finger to his lips. "Yes, one of her big tusk-like teeth is broken off, but look at the other one. Even if she bit Wilfred, that's not big enough to have made wounds of that depth. I wanted to be sure that it wasn't her, because just occasionally you do get a sow with longer tusks than normal, but now I'm sure that we're possibly looking for a male, or even a red deer stag. Thinking about it now, although it was hard to tell with Wilfred in the condition he's in, those wounds were a bit close together for a boar. Let's get back to the village and see what they've seen hereabouts."

However, as they now took the shortest way back towards the village, Guy suddenly got a whiff of something familiar. Holding his hand up to halt them he declared, "There's a rotting body somewhere around here."

"He can tell?" Sir Sewel whispered to Sir Hugo and got a withering stare in response.

"Wait here for me," Guy instructed, and taking his horse at a slow walk he followed his nose until he suddenly called, "Over here!"

As the other two joined him he pointed to the ground behind a large clump of broom bushes. There on the ground lay a stag.

"Look at his side," Guy said, his voice filled with anger. "Some bastard tried to hunt this big old fellow and made a bloody mess of it! By the look of him he probably died the day after Wilfred. And look at the left-hand side of his rack. See? Two of the horns are covered in dried blood. You don't need me to paint you the picture of this poor beast staggering through the forest in pain and Wilfred running into him. I doubt he even gored them. Wilfred probably ran onto his antlers while he was on the ground, and the other man no doubt fell over him, or was shoved into the tree as he struggled to his feet to make his last run. Tragic!"

"Yes, what a tragic accident," Sir Hugo said sympathetically. "Two accidental deaths after all."

"And a murder!" Guy said tightly.

"Murder?" Sir Sewel was lost again.

"The stag!" Guy snapped. "As a forester I have to investigate his death too!"

"You're really bothered by this, aren't you?" Sir Hugo said in amazement. He'd heard of Guy's fondness for animals, but he'd never imagined it ran this deep.

"I'm bloody angry, that's what I am!" Guy snapped. "I used to think it was high-handed to deprive people the right to hunt in the forest, but the more I've seen of what happens when stupid lordlings and rich merchants' sons start fancying themselves as hunters, the more I think King Henry did the right thing – even if it was for the wrong reasons."

"But surely this is Robin Hood's doing?" Sir Sewel protested and then flinched as Guy's eyes turned on him. There was something deeply chilling about the way those green eyes managed to be both icy cold and flashing at the same time, and in that instant Sir Sewel grasped why he'd heard the rumour that Briwere was a bit afraid of Guy. This was a man you wouldn't want to cross!

"Robin Hood?" spat Guy, reaching over his shoulder to grab the big Welsh bow and brandish it at Sir Sewel. "Do you think he'd have made a mess like that with one of these? And he has Welsh archers with him! *Pfah*! If he'd hunted that stag, it would have died instantly and the carcass butchered and taken away without any evidence left."

"How do you know?" Sir Hugo asked, which doused Guy's anger like thrown water over him.

By Saint Cadoc, he'd nearly dropped himself in it there! And all because of his feelings for the animal. Think! He needed a fast explanation! "Because I have yet to ever find a carcass they've left behind," he dredged up. "Every time – and I do mean *every* – I've found slaughtered deer it's turned out to be a bunch of wealthy young men trying to prove they're something they're not. Blessed St Thomas, Sir Hugo! Robin Hood is living off the land! Do you really see him and his men leaving enough meat to feed them and their sympathisers for weeks just rotting on the ground? No, this was someone out purely for the hunt – someone who suddenly got worried that they might get caught by someone like me if they carried on chasing down this stag. Someone who hoped that it would do what it did – stagger off into the forest and died out of sight – but too stupid to think, or know, how long it takes for something this big to decompose to the point where it's an unrecognisable pile of bones."

He got off his horse and went to kneel by the stag. "Look, you can still just about see ...four arrows hit this poor thing, none of them deep enough to kill. They came from a small hunting bow, not a Welsh bow."

He took out his big knife and with great care cut off the rack of antlers. Fetching a large sack from his saddlebag, Guy wrapped the central plate with it and then carried it reverently over to the others. "See? Here's Wilfred's blood!" He then equally carefully wrapped the whole thing up and handed it to Sir Hugo. "Take this back to the sheriff. You have your proof. You don't need any more. Tell him that Wilfred and the other man were unlucky enough to fall on this stag."

"And what about you?" Sir Sewel asked.

"I need to arrange for the villagers to come out here and help me dispose of this body. It needs to be burned or it will attract rats and disease, not to mention the danger of one of the other foresters getting told that there's a poached deer carcass in the vicinity, and the danger of the poor folk of Tansley getting a huge fine for something they're innocent of. This is the other side of my duties, so you can tell the sheriff I'm still working. Whether we find the culprit is another matter."

Luckily both knights had had enough of bloody messes and were only too glad to ride back to Nottingham immediately, for which Guy breathed a sigh of relief. He wanted to question the villagers out of their hearing.

"Has anyone come round here hunting of late?" Guy asked them as he brought a group of the leading men back out to the spot. He saw their worried faces. "Don't worry," he reassured them, "I know the signs of rich boys 'playing', I know it was none of you."

He heard the sighs of relief.

"Sir Oliver came through only a couple of days before he came back to get those bloody fines," one man volunteered.

"We were worried," another said tentatively.

"Worried, why?" Guy asked gently. He had to get their trust to get to the bottom of this.

The men all looked to one another, then the leading man said, "Well after Tim died and Sir Oliver covered it up by saying he'd fallen into his own mill wheel..."

He paused and looked at Guy to see how he'd take this.

"Are you saying that Sir Oliver hit Timothy the miller over the head and then shoved him into the waterwheel to cover it up?" Guy asked carefully. The way nobody instantly denied it was confirmation enough. "Go on, I believe you," he encouraged them.

Somewhat apprehensively, the head man continued, "Well after that, and 'cause of the arguments that had gone on between Timothy and Sir Oliver, we knew Sir Oliver had it in for us – that's why he kept sayin' we had to pay up a second time. So when he rode through with some fine friends of his from the other side of the Derwent and said we'd have somethin' else to pay for soon, we err... we got in touch with someone for help."

Of course they had! That was why Robin and the others had been here – they hadn't just been conveniently nearby, they'd been sent for.

"Don't worry," Guy reassured the villagers. "You don't need to say any more. I can see how this has come about." He sighed heavily. "Sir Oliver brought about his own man's death."

Someone at the back snorted and said, "He ain't gonner be missed, that's for sure. I know you shouldn't speak ill o' the dead, but Wilfred was a vicious bastard – far too quick with that whip o' his!"

Guy crossed himself, offering a silent prayer to St Cadoc, who watched over the deer. It looked very much as though the saint's patience had been tried one time too many, and Wilfred had died on the antler of one of those he had persecuted, for Guy had the distinct impression that Wilfred would have been involved in Sir Oliver's illegal hunts too.

At the deer, Guy amazed the villagers by saying a prayer over the deer before the butchering began.

"Sir Guy?" the headman questioned in a hushed whisper as he finished.

Guy sat back on his heels and looked up at the men. "I learned my skills over on the Welsh borders. The Norman priests have less of a strangle-hold on the Church over there, and a good man who was a Welsh monk told me of a lot of Welsh saints the Pope in

Rome probably doesn't even know about, let alone recognises. St Cadoc is one. He watches over the deer and boar of the forest, and the old huntsmen over in the west knew to offer a prayer to him for the spirit of the deer before they took its meat. Gratitude for what's been given is no bad habit to form, and besides, I've often felt St Cadoc's presence when out in the forest. No doubt the sheriff and my fellow knight would think me daft for this, and I've never bothered telling them, but my monk friend would say that Wilfred angered St Cadoc and paid the price, so a prayer seemed particularly in order this time."

He was gratified to see all of the men cross themselves, and the cutting up of the carcass was done with rather more reverence than he expected. That might have been in part because there was more usable meat there than even he'd anticipated. With the stag having bled out for the most part, the upper cuts of the carcass were still usable, being no worse than if they'd been hung to tenderise. Only the flesh that had been close to the ground needed burning, and even a goodly number of the bones could be taken away for cooking up in stews or feeding the village dogs. St Cadoc had surely been watching over this site.

Yet with that done, Guy knew that his work was still not done. The legal part was complete, but justice needed to be meted out, and for that he needed the outlaws.

When he found them at the camp and told them what had happened, Tuck confirmed what he believed.

"Definitely St Cadoc," the big monk said with an approving nod. "Too much of a coincidence not to be!"

That pronouncement certainly helped when Guy came to ask for Robin's help.

"Justice needs to be done," he told his cousin. "Oliver de Aincourt has got away with murder, because I'm now quite convinced that the miller did not die accidentally. I know mills are dangerous places, but this time I really don't think he fell into the mill race – not least because it's an overshot wheel, and that would be so much harder to be trapped under, given that the water is flowing away from the wheel by the time it gets to a place where someone could be pulled in. Timothy came here from Cyprus, I believe, because his sister married a soldier on crusade, and they both came back here."

Will grunted in disgust. "And I bet his difference made him a prime target for someone like Sir Oliver. The villagers might not have cared that he wasn't English, but I bet his landlord did!"

Guy thought the same. "Teach Sir Oliver a lesson," he begged his friends. "Don't kill him – that will bring the wrath of the sheriff down on the villagers, and anyway, that's too quick a way out! But do whatever you think to make this damned man think twice before hounding his tenants that hard ever again!"

And did they? Oh yes, Brother, they most certainly did! I had taken the stag's skin with me, since that was the one part the villagers would not be easily able to use, and now gave it to my friends. Cleaned and dried out they could use it for all manner of things, but the first was to have Robin decked in it standing at the bottom of Sir Oliver's bed in the depths of night and scaring him half witless. He thought Herne the Hunter had come looking for retribution, and I confess I laughed mightily at that when I heard of it. Then three young boar piglets mysteriously got let loose in the prized garden of his manor and wrecked it, all three happily escaping through the hurdle fencing around it and back into the wild before they could be caught. When a sack such as would come with milled flour was left in his kitchen and then turned out to be full of rats, well, I think Sir Oliver began to get the message! Certainly, when I heard of him next it was as a man who had taken a sudden liking for going to church. He was never going to be a kind lord to his people, but his overbearing brutality had been quashed.

So you see, Gervase, Robin and I <u>could</u> work together under the right circumstances. On this occasion I had set the limit at not crippling or killing the target and Robin had listened. That was not my ego talking. Truly, Brother, it was that I knew just how far they could go before the sheriff would feel compelled to act towards the villagers, and when Robin stayed within those bounds I had no quarrel with what he did. It was when he got carried away with his schemes, blithely *forgetting the consequences to others, that we fell out badly. But at least we got to the end of that year without any deep rift, and for that I will remain grateful.*

Chapter 15

Now before we leave 1195 altogether, I must tell you of what happened in the November, for that is coming upon us now.

In his perverse wisdom, King Richard decided to raise a carucage. You will have heard of these more than we had then, Gervase, because they were only ever supposed to be levied in an emergency. At this moment most of us had only ever known of a couple during King Henry's long reign, so for our absent king to now levy it purely to get the remainder of the money for his ransom was a bitter pill for all of us to swallow – especially since we knew that Normandy, which he valued far above us, had hardly paid its share.

It did not help that word came that the amount to be paid was not assessed on the old value of twenty shillings for each ploughland, which would have been bad enough, but at the current value of what was on it. Four shillings each for a horse or ox was no small amount for villagers to find – yes, I remember the amounts well because they so shocked us at the time, Brother – and when even the pigs were valued at twelve pence each, it was a tax which threatened to cripple everyone in the land. Even the great monasteries got stung, for fine-woolled sheep were valued at ten pence each, and even coarse-woolled ones at six pence, which amounted to more than a tidy amount for some of the monasteries' huge flocks.

Already the value of grain had risen sharply during King Richard's short reign, which you may think helped since everyone would get a better price at market, but it did not. Seed for replanting consequently cost far more, and another result was that the price of flour also rose, making that of bread almost half as much again as it had when King Richard came to the throne. This was a very sharp rise in just a handful of years and something which affected us all, Brother, right up to the sheriff himself, and there was little anyone could do about it.

Where this new tax really bit hard for the sheriff was in the means of collection. Briwere had his own bailiff, as most sheriffs did if only to oversee their personal land-holdings, and he and this man had, shall we say, an understanding – he made sure Briwere turned a profit, and if he made a little on the side too, then Briwere did not argue. Now, though, a royal clerk was to appear in our midst to record what was brought in, and he was to be helped by a local knight. Worse, there were to be duplicate copies of what was assessed, so that there could be no quibbling either way for under- or over-charging. No doubt Briwere had hoped to use one of my dimmer fellow knights for this, someone it would be easy to hoodwink along with an easily bullied brother from one of the local monasteries. To his horror, though, the knight was appointed down at the royal court and would be coming to us in the company of the royal clerk, so those two would have already got to know one another before they ever met us.

For once I had some sympathy for Briwere over this. You see the knight was a man called Durand fitz Robert whom none of us knew, and once the carucage was over he would be staying with us to fill the place still left vacant from when poor Sir Payne had died at the siege – the king scraping together every knight who could sit on a horse and hold a lance for his Normandy campaign, had seriously diminished the local men we could recruit, you see. It was a cunning move by Hubert Walter, since the role of forester knight effectively made Durand a local when he had never been so before, but ensured that he would be far more likely to place his loyalty with the archbishop.

Also, if Durand was trusted enough to fill this role with a royal clerk, it amounted to us having a royal spy in our midst. For my part it did not matter. There was little I did that he could interfere with. But for Briwere it meant that there was a danger that the ways in which he bent the law in order to meet the demands of Archbishop Walter might be reported back to this man who ruled on the king's behalf, and none of us doubted that if Hubert Walter told Briwere he was not to do something, then he would have to comply.

So over the Christmas of 1195 we were all on edge, and me more than most. Why? Come, come, Gervase! What would be like bait to a trout where Robin was concerned? The sheriff becoming even more heavy-handed, of course. And yet for once Briwere would not wholly be to blame. He was a man I would never feel sorry for – his behaviour towards his dogs ensured that – but I was not so blind in my dislike as to not be able to see that he was caught in a cleft stick this time. Yet the fact that I could see such a thing was the very instrument of my major falling out with Robin again.

Nottinghamshire
Early Winter, the Year of Our Lord, 1195 – Spring, the Year of Our Lord 1196

A terrific gale had ripped across England, uprooting trees and causing chaos, and this had been Guy's excuse to get out into the forest for several days.

"I genuinely need to see what mature trees have fallen," Guy told the outlaws, as they welcomed him to the camp above the River Derwent between Burley and Wadshelf villages. "Nobody else was keen to travel this far afield so late in the year, so I hardly had to fight to come."

"There are several big oaks that have come down along this ridge," Siward told him, immediately grasping that this was what Guy was talking about. "You don't want any of the villagers being accused of illegally felling them, do you?"

Guy smiled, glad that someone had caught on so fast. "No! Absolutely not! And there'll be plenty of folk in need of timber to make repairs with. It's horribly bad timing that the gale should have come just as the forest got closed for the winter hunting. Luckily Sir Martin and Sir Walter argued alongside me with Briwere to say that for once we need to record the fallen trees, and then let folk use them rather than selling off the timber to the highest bidder – there's more than enough for everyone at the moment. Even then Briwere's so bloody distant from ordinary folk that he couldn't see why, until we pointed out that we've already heard of three mills being badly damaged, and Sir Richard bluntly told him that they wouldn't be able to pay their taxes if they weren't working. By Our Lady, Briwere is hard work!"

There were sympathetic murmurs from all of the outlaws over that, yet Guy knew he had to break the additional bad news.

"I'm afraid there's something else," he began. "When Briwere returned from the Michaelmas court he brought bad news with him," and he told them of the carucage.

"He cannot be allowed to get away with this!" Robin immediately declared, making Guy wince inside. This was the reaction he had feared.

"In fairness, Robin, it's not of his choosing," he said with all the calmness he could muster. "This is King Richard making the demands for the remains of the money he owes to the Holy Roman Emperor. He's passed on the demand to Archbishop Walter, and he's just passed it down to all of the sheriffs. Even Briwere's not happy about it! He may be vicious and petty, but he's worried about it because of this new knight and the royal clerk. They'll be watching him like hawks, you know, and if he doesn't collect exactly what's owed then it will go badly for him with Walter."

"Serve him right!" Robin snapped. "The sooner he goes the better!"

Guy's despair must have shown on his face, because Hugh immediately chipped in with,

"But the archbishop would just send another sheriff in that case, Robin. We've talked about this so many times before – with a king like Richard who's determined to wring every penny out of England, there's no way that any shire will be left without someone to do that."

"There'll always be another one," Gilbert backed him up with, "and who's to say that the next one wouldn't be even worse?"

"Exactly!" Guy seized on Gilbert's words. "God help us, but at least Briwere is experienced and he has a vague of grasp of what's not possible. If he goes, what if the king sends some Normandy lord in his place? Someone who's been crushing his tenants over there and getting in the king's graces at the same time? It could mean a man who comes with soldiers of his own and who cares little whether there's anything left in five years time, because he can go home to Normandy and leave our shires as wasteland for someone else to deal with. I'm sorry, Robin, but much as I'd love to see a return to somebody like Ralph Murdac, who was hard but fair, men like him who served the king's father don't have the money to be able to buy a sheriff's office at the prices King Richard sets."

Robin was looking at Guy with disgust. "So you're saying you want to stand back and let Briwere bleed the shire white?"

"Want? No, of course I don't *want* to do that!" Guy protested. "I was just saying that whatever way we come up with of dealing with this, getting rid of Briwere right now isn't it."

"Twelve pence a pig," Tuck said with a shake of his head, clearly hoping to deflect Robin's attention away from Guy. "That's a lot of families who will end up killing piglets early rather than paying for them, and that means that they'll go hungry later."

"I'd had a thought about that," Guy ventured, "but it would need you all to join in for it to work."

Robin's disparaging snort and sarcastic, "Might have known it! Guy has a plan!" was covered by Mariota asking loudly,

"What's that, then, Guy?" and she and Marianne sharing rolled eyes over Robin.

Giving them grateful glances, Guy said, "Well if you can get the villages to band together – I'm thinking of half a dozen of them per group – then if they set the young lads to keeping a watch for the collectors, the first one that gets visited could take their pigs over to the next village. Then as soon as they know where the collectors are going next, someone runs on and warns them, and they move their pigs on. It's a chancy game, but if each village only has to pay for one or two pigs they won't need to slaughter so many."

"That's not a bad idea," Will mused. "There are enough of us now that we can split into groups and cover most of the villages within the forest – because they're the ones who'll be hit hardest. The west side of Derbyshire will cope because they can hide their pigs in the woods and forests without risking being dragged before the forest courts, it's the folk round here and in Nottinghamshire who'll be hit the worst."

"And I have a favour to ask," Guy added tentatively. "Could you not attack any of the woodmotes in December and February, please?"

"Why ever not?" Robin demanded hotly.

"For goodness sake, Robin, let him speak!" Marianne protested. "Guy's never asked us to do that before, so there must be a reason."

"*Hmph!* Worming his way into the sheriff's favours, so that he doesn't have to pay up for being in the castle at the siege, no doubt."

"That's bloody unfair!" Guy protested.

"It is," Malik said firmly. "That's uncalled for, Robin. Guy's refused to let us help him with that, and you know it was because he said others would need our help more than him."

"Precisely," Robin riposted snidely. "So where's his money coming from, then?"

"Gisborne," Guy snapped back, "that's where it's coming from! It's taking everything Ianto and Maelgwn can scrape together, and they're having a lean time of it over there, but it's a tiny manor and therefore my fine isn't as bad as that of some of the others. So don't you throw that in my face, Cousin!"

He was even more dismayed to see the newcomers to the gang staring at them in open horror, this being the first time that many of them had witnessed Robin's hostility towards Guy.

"Look," Guy continued wearily, "I'm asking this because Briwere is going to be like a bear with a sore head for the next few months. It's going take next to nothing to snap his temper. And what I'm horribly afraid of is that if you poke him while this royal clerk is here, he'll feel the need to stamp down far harder than whatever it is warrants. If you attack the Edwinstowe woodmote, for instance, he may take every soldier he has and strip both it and the villages to the east of it of everything they have in his fury. He'll do it because he'll have to prove to the royal clerk that he can collect the forest fines *and* this bloody carucage! This is one time when he cannot come away with only part of the forest fines – not when the archbishop's cleric is riding at his heels!"

"What does he do normally, then?" Much asked innocently.

Guy managed a faint smile. "Falsifies the record that goes to the royal forester, of course. That's why this clerk from Canterbury, or wherever he turns out to be from, is such a burden. One of the monks from Lenton would do as he was told, because having an angry sheriff on your doorstep is not what his prior wants. And you know yourselves that Briwere has ingratiated himself with most of the important churchmen in the shires, so if they got called upon to provide a clerk, they'd get their brothers to do what he wants in return for the odd illegal hunt we're told to turn a blind eye to – that sort of thing. So what Briwere and the previous sheriffs have done, Much, is get in what money they have and then adjust the record on the parchment that's going to court accordingly.

"And I'm not saying that our previous sheriffs haven't been spitting feathers over the fact that you've robbed them of what are substantial amounts of money – they have! Certainly they knew that it was clear that they've not been returning the amounts of money the chief forester was probably expecting. And that's been doubly unwelcome because they were also aware that they looked like failures because of it, which they certainly didn't want when they'd paid out as much as someone like Briwere's had to do of his own money to get his hands on, what he thought, would be a lucrative pair of shires he could turn a tidy profit from. You've made him out of purse and out of reputation with every blow."

He could see the grins spreading across everyone's faces except Robin's. "But that's why I'm asking this now," he said with the best he could summon in the way of an answering smile. "At the moment Briwere still has some hope of coming away from his time as sheriff here with something for his pains. Strike at him now and you're as good as showing him that he's got nothing to lose – and any man backed into a corner like that is dangerous. When it's a man like Briwere it's inevitable that he'll lash out. You don't want the deaths of innocent villagers on your consciences, do you?"

"Blessed St Issui!" Tuck gasped. "No! Definitely not!" and Guy could see that he was speaking for the others too. "Would he not get into trouble for that?"

"Almost certainly," Guy agreed, "but by the time that happens it's too bloody late for the villagers, isn't it? Nothing the archbishop does is going to bring them back from the dead." A statement which had most of the experienced outlaws already shaking their heads even before Guy had finished speaking.

"So when's this clerk due?" Allan asked.

"That's the worst of it," Guy sighed, "I'm not sure. We were talking about this at the castle, and our combined opinion is that this clerk isn't going to traipse all the way up here for just a week or two at the start of December, and then travel all the way back for the Christmas observances at his monastery. If they learned nothing else from the eyres last year, it's how long it takes to get to shires like ours! We think he'll come in the first weeks of January – which is why I said please not to attack the woodmote that comes right at the start of February. He could still be here, but even if he isn't, Briwere will still be smarting from his presence and as likely to go up in flames over the tiniest slight."

"Roger and I will come to Nottingham just before Christmas," Allan volunteered. "By then you might know more."

It was something Guy was grateful for, not least because those two had a knack for passing unseen through crowds, and were by now expert at sidling up to him without causing suspicion. If Tuck couldn't come nowadays, then he was going to have to depend a lot on these two from now onwards.

He was far less happy when the news came to him in the castle that Robin Hood and his gang had attacked and robbed several travellers who were on the road during the festive season. Nobody got hurt, but tales of near-impossible shots with arrows which parted horses' reins, or fixed a guard's tunic to the side of a wagon, only raised the chatter in market places about the heroic archer in the forest, and those got back to Briwere far too fast. As a result he went through the whole festivities either getting roaring drunk, and ordering the whipping of several unfortunate servants who crossed his path at the wrong time, or plotting ways of finding out which villages were hiding this miscreant. That the outlaws might not be living in any of them was something Briwere refused to consider.

"In winter? Camping out in the forest?" he scoffed when Sir Hermer and Sir Philip came back from scouring the villages close to the castle and reported that, even under various dire threats, everyone was swearing that the outlaws had not stayed there. "Don't be ridiculous! Do you think they're living on wilted grass? Fools! They're getting bread from somewhere, unless there are ovens in the forest you toad-brained lack-wits haven't fallen over!"

Clearly the thought that the outlaws could be so organised as to have their own ovens cleverly concealed and over the shire border never crossed his mind, let alone stores and proper cover to hide in, and so the season passed in far from convivial spirits.

When Allan and Roger caught up with Guy at the Nottingham market on the Saturday after Twelfth Night, it was to immediately offer apologies.

"Those of us who knew our way through the forest had gone out taking your warnings of the carucage," Allan told him. "We thought Robin deciding at the last moment to stay in the camp on the shire borders by Teversall, instead, was him just sulking because it was your idea."

Roger sniffed dejectedly. "'E said 'e was goin' to give the new lads some archery lessons."

Allan nodded. "Aneirin and Rhys were happy enough to stay in Loxley – they haven't really wanted to go far afield since they got there, and Balak was happy to stay with them. But Simon and Martin were getting really irritated with being cooped up, so taking everyone else with us on what might be the last journey for a month or two seemed reasonable." He sighed and shook his head. "The same was happening with Colm and Ed to a lesser extent ...you know, the sense of being cooped up.

"Anyway... to cover the ground as fast as possible we split into six parties. We," he gestured to Roger and himself, "went with Thomas." He gave Guy an apologetic half-smile. "We *thought* everyone had agreed that there should be one good archer with each group who would stay back and cover the others going into the village, just in case someone came along. It sounded sensible when we were sending only two in alone."

Guy reached out and squeezed Allan's shoulder. "It sounds very sensible to me, too. I'm not about to blame you, Allan, I just want to know what the fuck happened," then winced mentally because he knew how angry those last words sounded, even though his ire wasn't directed at Allan and Roger.

His youngest cousin smiled wanly back. "Blessed St Thomas, you're always the reasonable one to deal with Guy! Many's the time I've wished you were our leader."

"And me," Roger added mournfully, clearly as unhappy as Guy at what had happened.

With a deep breath, Allan ploughed on. "Well Tuck went with Marianne and Janah – that worked out fine – as did sending Khalīl with Siward and Gilbert, strangely enough. Piers and John took Mariota with them, while Bilan and Will went together, and so did Hugh and Malik. We'd also thought, you see, that it would be better if at least one person who went in to talk to the villagers didn't have an accent they would think foreign, or at least odd. Robin should have gone with one of the groups according to what we worked out at Loxley, as should Much, which was why we ended up with two pairs instead of threesomes; but when we got to the other camp and Robin said he was staying, Much said he was staying with him."

Roger wiped his nose on his sleeve, muttering, "I dunno' why Robin has such a hold on Much. You'd 'a' thought after what happened after the siege he'd 'a' got more cautious o' him."

"It is odd," Allan agreed. "We thought after what happened back then that he would have been closer friends with Bilan, but instead he seems to have slid into Martin and Simon's company, and of course they still hero-worship Robin." He gave another grunt and a shake of his head. "That's where it all went so wrong, Guy. Robin took those three and Colm and Ed – they were the six who held people up. I can't bloody believe it, but he told them it was time for them to prove themselves as proper members of the company. What a load of shit!"

Guy was too stunned to say anything for a moment, finally struggling out with, "But what if something had gone wrong? Even Colm's not a fighter! What if there had been guards who were real fighters?"

"Exactly what the rest of us said to Robin when he and those with him got back to Teversall after the rest of us, crowing about their 'victories'," Allan said with a heavy sigh. "And do you know what he said? That God recognised the righteousness of what he had done and would have protected them!"

"I don't fink I ever see'd Tuck so angry!" Roger added. "'E was so cross he stamped off and we heard him whackin' away at a tree wiv' his quarterstaff for ages."

Guy could imagine it. Such arrogance would offend every one of Tuck's religious sensibilities, and by the sound of it he had been too angry to even speak. That didn't bode well for the future, because if Guy knew Tuck at all, this signalled the end of him trying to reason with Robin. Tuck would see Robin as a lost soul hereafter, and would focus on saving the others, leaving Robin to whatever fate came his way. How could a man who could be as charming as Robin, manage to drive those who cared for him away time after time?

"Will you tell Tuck I'm so sorry to hear of that after all he tried to do?" Guy asked Allan, and got his arm squeezed affectionately as the best they could do huddled into a corner of the *Trip to Jerusalem* with a bunch of tipsy castle soldiers around them.

"When's the next woodmote?" Allan asked.

"Three days after Candlemas, the fifth of February. It's a Monday," Guy told him worriedly.

"'Ven we tells him it's the Monday after!" Roger said decisively. "We, 'n' John 'n' Tuck agreed that afore we left to come 'ere. We ain't gonna' tell him the proper day, just in case, and we wasn't gonna' make it afore the right day, 'cause that would still give 'im chance to do sommat daft."

"Add on a day," Guy suggested, "the thirteenth. Tell him it's St Dyfnog's feast. Tuck will get the reference straight away, and he'll back you up that it's a proper saint's day like the others we hold courts on. It goes back to when it was just me and him against Sheriff de Braose in Herefordshire. He'll twig to what you're doing and back you up without you having to spell it out, because no Norman lord would arrange something on an obscure Welsh saint's day."

Nonetheless he felt positively sick when the first woodmote of the new season came around. Had Robin got wind of the fact that he'd been duped by Allan and Roger? Yet the courts passed without disaster and Guy dared to breathe again.

However with the royal clerk had come even more unwelcome news – King Richard was going to demand an inspection of all of his sheriffs. Something had given the suspicious monarch the idea that not all of his sheriffs were trustworthy.

"Not trustworthy?" Briwere had spluttered apoplectically. "How dare he? After all the loyal service I've given, how *dare* he!"

"There will be an inspection of all sheriffs in March," Brother Mellitus of Canterbury confirm with a rather unsavoury smirk. He and Briwere had loathed one another at first sight, to Guy's despair. The rather effete brother was prone to wearing far from simple clothes, his habit being of particularly fine wool and his boots of top quality leather, and his accent pronounced him to be a younger son from a very good family who had been forced into the church, rather than entering out of any true desire or faith. Worse, Mellitus positively revelled in winding Briwere up, and Guy found himself wishing that the priest's cowl would entwine about his neck and strangle him during the night. Briwere in a froth was what none of them needed.

"Two envoys from my lord bishop of Caen will come to you," Mellitus was declaring to the assembled company in the castle's great hall that evening. "My lord bishop of Caen has been appointed by our king to oversee this matter."

"A small blessing that it won't be Mellitus again," Sir Robert whispered in Guy's ear.

Guy gave an imperceptible nod and ducking his head slightly so that those on the top table wouldn't see, added, "As long as they aren't two more like him! God's wounds, but he's been enough of a trial!"

From his other side Sir Hugh grunted his agreement, and equally softly added, "Please God we should not be so unfortunate! One like him is enough!"

Somehow Mellitus had managed to rile every one of the knights in the castle, which given their disparate personalities and temperaments was no small achievement.

Briwere, meanwhile, was demanding, "And when do these two paragons of virtue arrive, pray tell? Later? Or do we have to suffer all three of you at the same time?"

For once even Guy was amused by Briwere's waspishness, and the sheriff seemed startled by the ripple of amusement that ran through the room, having got used to his attempts at humour usually falling flat.

Mellitus wasn't amused, though, and snapped back, "They will arrive on the eve of St Chad's Day."

Briwere wasn't about to let his rare advantage go, and riposted with, "And what day is that? St Chad's Day? Hardly a Roman saint is he?"

Mellitus bristled like a poked hedgehog. "He was a founding father of our Church here in England! How dare you malign him!"

Taking the chance to make his own stab at this pompous prick, Guy cut across him with, "But the day you're talking about is Saint David's Day, surely? Whom I was always told preceded the Anglo-Saxon bishop-saints by over a century? And didn't Saint David try to create an arch-episcopate to rival Canterbury over in Wales, Brother? Or was it one of his followers who nearly succeeded in that?" He gave his most vulpine smile, adding, "No doubt you'll correct me on the matter, being a learned churchman, whereas I only heard it from the monks at Abergavenny, but Canterbury almost lost that one."

Mellitus had gone a strange shade of puce and was spluttering, while Briwere was momentarily startled by Guy's sudden showing of learning, but soon leapt on the advantage he'd been given.

"Ah, you Canterbury monks have to acknowledge some authorities besides yourselves, eh?" he badgered Mellitus with waspish delight. "So our envoys are coming with the blessings of the pestilent Welsh, and their saint, are they? How appropriate given that they no doubt intend to raid our coffers in the process! You must forgive Gisborne, he had enough of Welsh raids when he lived on the borders, but it gives him a keener sense than most for such things."

Good grief, Guy thought, *he's actually complimenting me!* But Briwere was continuing with, "And might we hope that your fellow monks will depart on the feast of that other outlander Celtic saint, Saint Patrick?"

Mellitus' expression could hardly have got any sourer if he'd been sucking lemons. "They will depart on Palm Sunday at the latest in order to be back with us by Easter," he bit back, then realised he'd been baited and with great condescension added, "This year it happens that Palm Sunday falls on the fourteenth of April – plenty of time for even you to accumulate the necessary monies, surely?"

The fact that Mellitus didn't register Briwere's immediate scowl of anger at both what he had said, and the lack of any show of a respectful title, said much for the monk's lack of any sense of self-preservation.

"I see," drawled Briwere with icy venom. "So these monks will come and do their worst just in time to report back at the close of our annual accounts. How bloody convenient! And will I be accompanying them south to the court, since I, too, will be heading for the Easter courts? Or will they be lingering here after I'm gone? Rummaging through my records to see what they can find behind my back?"

Guy could understand Briwere's anger. The timing was awful! If the Feast of the Annunciation, when all monies had to be in for the half year, fell one day short of a month before Easter, that meant Briwere had no excuse not to travel back with the brothers to London or Winchester; and no excuse to not only to have both the normal collection of rents and court payments with him, but this extra money as well.

The fact that Hubert Walter would be more likely to hold it at London for its closeness to his Canterbury seat was only a minor mercy when it came to travelling so far in company the sheriff was bound to find disagreeable. Normally it was a five day journey to London, which meant by Guy's reckoning that it was something a little over one hundred and twenty miles; whereas the old Kingdom of Wessex's capital lay down on the south coast more like seven days of hard travelling away. The chances of Briwere not speaking his mind during those five days if sorely pressed were slim, and Guy feared that any comments might rebound on them badly if the brothers spoke to the archbishop, which could mean bad news all round.

Something had finally percolated through Mellitus' thick skin that Briwere was becoming increasingly dangerous with this provoking, and took himself off to his chamber, but Guy didn't dare do the same. He needed to know what Briwere was thinking and what he might do when backed up against such a wall. It didn't take long.

"I shall conduct my half yearly tour of the shires early," Briwere announced as soon as Mellitus was safely out of earshot. "We need to get what money we can before these parasites arrive and bleed us of what little is left in the shires. What date is it now?" and he looked around the room but particularly at Guy.

Mercifully having only just got back from the woodmote, Guy knew. "It's the fifteenth today, my lord. That means we have just a fortnight before we can expect those bloody monks." He hadn't meant to put quite so much disgust in the words 'bloody monks', and his reason for doing so wasn't what Briwere assumed, but a dread of what provoking Briwere into doing might in turn provoke Robin to do. It earned him another of Briwere's perennially acidic smiles, though.

"You know ...I'm beginning to see your uses, Gisborne," he said slyly, and Guy could see him thinking, which didn't bode well. However, Briwere now turned to the room at large. "Very well. Since I must be back here by the first of next month, I want all of you riding out in the morning. You are to assemble the Hundred courts commencing from the end of this week. I want all payments of the frankpledge penny paid up, and you can double the frankpledge fines for anyone who has any outstanding. We need a reserve for whatever these two decide we should have paid to them above and beyond what we've already sent, and we won't be able to do a thing with them poking their pious noses in every nook and cranny."

Guy looked in dismay at Sir Martin and Sir Walter. Frankpledge was the system by which the freemen in each tithing – the multiple groups of ten men within the hundred – acted as guarantors for the appearance of the men in their manors and villages at the local courts. Here in Nottinghamshire that included the forest courts, which accumulated fines at a far greater rate than the normal courts did. And while most of the folk Guy knew took a very dim view of anyone trying to leave the area to flee from a normal fine, which left them to pay up on the renegade's behalf, when it came to the poaching fines it was a different matter.

Many villages or larger manors, Guy knew, scraped the forest fines together from everyone anyway. It was hard to begrudge a neighbour taking a hare to feed his family, and the size of some of the hares in Sherwood meant that several households might benefit from one man's successful night in the forest, and the same went for roe deer. But the way that they got that past the court system was to pretend that the miscreant had temporarily fled the village, even though he was most likely just hiding in one of the barns, and therefore the tithing system had come into play in order to produce the fine. Now, though, that was about to rebound on them, and badly too.

Yet worse was what Briwere was intending to do, for the frankpledge system had fixed fees. For Briwere to arbitrarily double the fines was just unheard of, if not downright illegal, and that worried Guy stiff for two reasons. If the inspecting clerks got wind of it, it only proved what the king thought – that his sheriffs were all as bent as butcher's hooks – and secondly, why did Briwere feel the need to take this extra money now? Was he anticipating having to bribe the king in order to keep his sheriffdom? If that was so, and England's shires were going to come up for the highest bidder every couple of years, the potential chaos, not to mention the financial hardship which would rebound on the ordinary people, was so awful as to make him feel sick.

Waiting until everyone else was soundly asleep, Guy made a run for the ramparts to make the warning signal he had arranged with Allan and Roger. When Lenton Abbey's bell rang for Matins, someone would be on lookout duty from back in the wooded farmland around the town – something Guy was blessing Allan for suggesting when he'd seen how deeply worried Guy was about what might happen, and now Guy's fears had been proven correct. The fire arrows he'd been able to surreptitiously make and hide away in oiled cloth up on the top of the old tower were still there, and he strung the big Welsh bow he'd brought up with him from where he normally hid it between his bracken-filled mattress and the wall. A simple striker managed to produce a spark and the arrow lit first time.

As soon as it was burning nicely, Guy nocked it in the bow, pulled back, and aimed it as high into the air as he could. It flew up into the night like a beacon, burning so bright that for a moment Guy panicked. What if someone within the castle couldn't sleep and saw it? None of the windows looked outwards from the castle, rather facing inwards to the baileys for safety's sake, but it didn't mean that they wouldn't see the glow and wonder.

Mercifully nobody came out asking what was alight, and within a shorter time than it felt to him, Guy saw two figures running towards the castle across the field, with two larger figures hurrying in their wake who could only be Tuck and John. Already he was uncoiling the rope he also had hidden up there and was lowering it down. They had pre-agreed that Roger should climb up to Guy, Roger being the one member of the gang who was scrawny enough to pass for a scullion amongst the ordinary servants within the castle if he couldn't go back the way he'd come. It was far easier than Guy trying to get out to them.

Hauling the younger outlaw up to him, Guy felt a rush of affection for this lad whose London accent had never quite deserted him. Roger had, against the odds, always taken Guy's part and had never been quite as enchanted with Robin as some of the others. It meant that now Guy had no worries over whether Roger would believe what he was being told, and that would save precious time.

"The bloody king is at it again!" Guy told him in an urgent whisper, and as briefly as was possible, told Roger of the coming inspection and Briwere's reaction.

"Bleedin' 'Ell!" Roger gasped softly. "What a mess!"

"I know," Guy sighed. "Can you get the others to be prepared to get some funds out to the worst affected villages for the forest fines? They're going to need it, what with the damned carucage having hit them hard already."

"Robin's goin' to be hittin' the roof over this," Roger warned Guy with a sad shake of his head. "There ain't gonna' be any holdin' 'im back now."

"I know." Guy caught Roger's arm in his urgency. "But can you see if you can turn him? Can you tell the others that the real culprits are this by-Our-Lady monk we have with us at the moment – this Brother Mellitus – and the two who are coming? Tell Tuck, he's just some lordling shoved into the Church. He has no faith of his own! And he had no conscience or understanding of what he's unleashing. So if Robin needs to lash out at anyone, do it at Mellitus!

"And I doubt these two new clerics will be any better. They'll be the sorts who have their noses wedged up Archbishop Walter's arse, men who are more interested in the political advancement the Church can bring them than in any good deeds. Having them come into Nottingham stripped of their finery and in sackcloth and ashes would be quite a statement, and bizarrely would actually appease Briwere more than Robin ever needs to know."

"I'll see what I can do!" Roger promised with his cheeky grin, and shinned back down the rope with an ease Guy envied. There was something to be said for being undersized and light.

Beneath him he saw a hurried conference going on, and then he heard Tuck calling softly up to him, "We'll sort these priests, never fear!" before they melted away into the darkness again. He hoped they really could direct Robin, because with the carucage's collection being documented several times over, there was no way that even Robin Hood could save the people of the shires from paying up.

To his horror, though, Guy found out that he was to be the one to ride out with the sheriff when he arrived booted and wearing a sturdy jacket against the late winter chill the following morning, and expecting to be directed to a group of villages instead.

"Bring the hounds and ride with me, Gisborne!" Briwere declared, as someone brought his white palfrey round for him.

Guy didn't dare take the two wolfhounds – they would savage Briwere the moment he got off his horse out in the forest! Instead he hurried to the kennels and got the kennelman to have three lads couple-up two greyhounds each and meet them at the outer bailey's gate.

"Good luck," Sir Robert said, coming to stand beside Guy's stirrup.

"I think you need it even more than me," Guy sympathised with him. "You've still got Mellitus in the castle!"

And now, Brother, I must tell you what happened as I was told it, for I was not present when Robin struck. My cousin was far too literal in his interpretation of my warnings and pleas – something I was deeply angered by, for reasons you will come to see.

Barely were we, the sheriff's party, out of sight then Robin was moving. He had to have been nearby in the small hideout close to Hucknall in the Leen valley to have acted so fast, and that all by itself told me that he had pressed Allan and Roger not to tell me about his proximity. I did not like that, Brother. It reeked of him fearing that they were too friendly with me and him wanting to draw their loyalties tighter to himself, and they did not deserve to be so manipulated.

How is that different to what I did? Blessed St Issui, Gervase, I never asked or expected them to act only for me! I always understood that they had to live with Robin in the hideouts, and that meant that, as in any big household, compromise would be necessary. All I ever asked of them was that they would do their best, and that was the big difference between Robin and me – he wanted more than they could give at times, and never saw why not. I did! Over what I am about to tell you, for instance: I was never angry that Roger and Allan failed to sway Robin's actions. That they even tried was good enough for me – that I swear by all that I hold sacred, Brother – and if they did not succeed, I did not hold them accountable for a grown man's actions when he could have reasoned such things out for himself.

But to our tale... The castle emptied of knights as we all rode out on the onerous task of trying to summon the courts virtually overnight, and everyone was too preoccupied by their own thoughts to wonder who was left in the castle. Well to answer that for you, it was Sirs Richard, Robert and Hugh, and even they were riding out to local villages like Lenton, Radford and West Bridgeford. The only other knight remaining in the castle was the newcomer, Sir Durand fitz Robert, since he hardly even knew where Derby was in relation to Nottingham, let alone the villages, and this would prove to be a fateful introduction to northern life for him.

I know, because Allan and I talked of it later, that Allan already knew how many knights and men were in the castle, having visited so often, and he told me that made sure that he counted as many out as he could before giving Robin the demanded signal that there were few enough left to be taken on, because his one thought had been to minimise the dangers and potential loss of life. And in that I told him he had been right, despite what would happen later on because of Robin's easy entry into the castle on this occasion. So all twenty-one members of the outlaws swarmed into the outer bailey on Allan's signal, producing bows and arrows from under their cloaks – for even Marianne and Mariota were by now expert with the lighter hunting bows – or quarterstaffs in Tuck and John's case. And with hardly a soul there capable of fending them off even if they had not been taken so utterly by surprise, they were in, through, and across the bridge over the moat into the castle proper before anyone drew breath, much less sounded the alarm.

What they found were Mellitus and Durand with their feet up on the sheriff's table, so mocking of his authority as to have begun sampling his wine despite the early hour, and chivvying the two poor brothers who were currently acting as the castle scribes to hurry with the counting of the money already brought in for the carucage. The shout of ˜Hold, in the name of Robin Hood!˜ must have shocked them to the core. Even so they tried to make a fight of it, proving my suspicions that Mellitus had been brought up with a knight's training, for Allan told me that he fought with unexpected skill, and it took Gilbert to rescue Martin after the lad had rushed in too fast in Robin's wake and nearly got his head sliced off for his pains, as Mellitus used Martin's clumsily dropped sword to deadly effect. Having a hearty dislike for the Norman Church, Gilbert had no qualms about laying out a priest with the pommel of his sword, and soon both Mellitus and Durand were unconscious, stripped down to their braes, and trussed like chickens for the spit. I am told that Tuck kindly trussed up the two brothers from Lenton as well, while explaining that he was doing it so that they could not be blamed for not fighting back if they were also incapacitated, but he tied them far less tightly than our two spies from the archbishop.

Did nobody else fight them, you ask? Like who, Brother? The servants? What could they have done against armed men? No, they all suddenly found tasks which took them as far away from the hall through the castle as possible, and I did not blame them for that. Briwere had lashed them with his tongue incessantly since his arrival, and often physically too, so what loyalty could you expect them to have for him? As for the few men-at-arms left in the castle, these were no match for those who had fought for real in the Holy Land. I was only grateful that Janah and Khalīl followed Malik's lead and only subdued rather than killing. It could have been a blood-bath, Brother, and no thanks to Robin's leadership, I assure you!

Anyway, the money was distributed into pouches amongst the outlaws, for with so many of them it was easy for everyone to carry some of the load, and there was no need for horses, even though most of what had been collected was in large quantities of small value coins. By now Durand and Mellitus had come around and Robin told them bluntly, ~You tell King Richard that when he chooses to go back and fight for the Holy Land, he can have his money back to pay for that!~

What he was not expecting was for Mellitus to laugh in his face and say that the king would never do that because he knew it was a lost cause. ~Better late than never,~ Mellitus told Robin sarcastically, ~the king has come to understand that the fight for the Holy Land was lost before it was even begun. What a bunch of simpletons to go out and fight for that fool's quest!~ and Allan said that he laughed. He laughed right in Robin's face. He did not laugh for long!

I am sure now, looking back at things, that at that point something came adrift in Robin's mind. Allan said that he screamed, ~God's own land is not a lost cause!~ and Mellitus, who was too much of a fool to know when to shut up, replied that no king in his right mind would fight for something when there was no possible reward, no kingdom to take and gain the wealth from, nor riches to plunder, as if worldly wealth was the only justification for fighting there.

~Is the Holy Land not enough of itself? Is the relic of the Holy Cross not worth fighting to regain for its own sake, or the place of Christ's death?~ Robin demanded, as if he could not believe what he was hearing.

You know by now why he would say that, Brother, and not just for the beliefs that you and I hold. Too many of his friends had given their *lives in that cause for it not to weigh heavily on his mind. So you may imagine what a blow to the heart it was to him when Mellitus, supposedly a man of the Church, replied, ~No!~ in response, as if there was no possible other answer.*

Robin went white, they told me. White with anger, though. And none of them were close enough to him to stay his hand as he drew back his sword hand and ran Mellitus through with his blade, screaming, ~Then you are no priest! Die you heathen cur!~

You are shocked, Brother, and so was I when I heard – and I must tell you that I first heard of these events when we were summoned back to the castle by a distraught Sir Hugh as the first back on the scene. Can you imagine my horror as we were told these things by Durand and a couple of servants, all shaking with shock? My cousin had killed a cleric from Canterbury, and while he may have been a poor apology for a priest, nonetheless I felt sick to the depths of my being at what my cousin had done. I had told him via Allan to act against the clerks rather than Sheriff Briwere, but I had never in my wildest nightmares imagined that Robin would <u>kill</u> one in cold blood. Such a thing was unthinkable to me!

It was only later that I realised that my genuine shock had been perceived as being the same as the others of the castle had displayed. I did not have to explain myself in any way, and for that at least I was grateful, for I am not sure what I would have said in those first days – I may even have given Robin up, for I certainly feared that he was totally insane at that point. He was not, it seems, and apparently he calmed down surprisingly swiftly as they fled Nottingham, possibly more than the others did.

Certainly several of them spoke alone with Tuck later that night, I was told, worried about what had happened, but what bothered me most when I finally caught up with Allan and Roger was that Tuck apparently never once remonstrated with Robin. Nor did he take him on one side once they reached the safety of the camp, and that, Brother, spoke volumes to me of how far Tuck's feelings had shifted. He was staying for the sake of the others, now, not Robin's.

As for Briwere, he declared that since someone would have to explain to Archbishop Walter what had happened to the money and his clerk, then the archbishop's knight could damned-well do it, since he had been the one to let Robin Hood walk out of the castle. I did not like Durand, but even he did not deserve that, and he left us to ride to court looking extremely deflated from the puffed-up young knight who had arrived. He would return, though, and bearing a terrible grudge towards Robin Hood because of how he was treated by the archbishop, and for his humiliation in the castle's hall – although for that I had less sympathy.

Briwere's discovery of the wine flagons had done nothing to lessen his ire, since he believed that Durand and Mellitus had been too far in their cups to resist Robin Hood; and Briwere's wrath concerning that matter, Durand brought upon himself. And to give Briwere some credit, he did refuse outright to try and collect the carucage a second time from those who had already paid. The archbishop's envoys had lost it, he declared, therefore they could make up the shortfall. That was something to be grateful for. I would not have wanted to go in search of those funds from the poor souls who had been stripped bare already.

So are you hearing me becoming more of the sheriff's man and against Robin Hood, like the legends tell, you ask? For truth, Gervase, no! But Robin was in the wrong that time, so very wrong, while Briwere surprised me with a glimpse of what kind of sheriff he might have been under a king like King Henry. He would always have been a tough man to be around, but King Richard's blind and unreasoned demands for money brought out the worst in men like our sheriff who depended so heavily on the king for their positions.

As for myself, I felt a terrible guilt settling upon me for ever having suggested that Robin look to the clerks. I never told him to maim or kill any of them, and my head kept telling me that, given that all I had requested was that their overweening pride be dented somewhat, what had happened was not my fault. But I always had more conscience than Robin over such things, and my heart remained heavy for a long time after that day, all of which loomed between us when we next met and did little to make our relationship any better.

And what of the monks who came to inspect the sheriff? Ah, that we shall come to next, Brother.

Chapter 16

So what of the brothers from Caen? Well the bishop of Caen might have been in charge of collecting the monies overall, but he was certainly not sending his own clerics to tramp the length and breadth of England. To do so would have been to have left his abbey very depleted of brothers, and he was not going to do that, not even for King Richard. However, what you might not know was that the foolish man had brought this upon himself. Like an idiot, he had opened his mouth to King Richard to deride the small amounts of money coming out of England, without having the first notion of how hard our people had already been taxed.

The king's response was therefore to send him to accompany one Philip of Poitiers, who was coming to England to take up the vacancy at Durham left by Bishop Hugh's death. I will never forget hearing that this Bishop Robert of Caen had arrived and had dinner with Archbishop Walter on Palm Sunday, was taken ill at the table, and died five days later. Yes, Brother, died! Tuck said it was a sign of God's displeasure at these churchmen's avarice, and I did not feel inclined to argue, then or now.

What was more revealing was Hubert Walter's own fury at the implications of this inspection, for do not forget that this rebounded on him too, as the ultimate power left in our land. I am told that he made his indignation fully known to the king, and that even Richard realised that he might have overstepped the mark – not least because if Hubert Walter threw his resignation as king's representative back at him, who then would have governed England in Richard's absence? But it went even further than that, Gervase. For the first time the archbishop truly stood up for the people of England, and that gladdened my heart even if Robin made many a sarcastic comment about it.

Now I have not made much of this as yet, Brother, for I knew you wanted the adventures and the excitement, but you now have to come to the realities of life for a moment to appreciate what came next. You are far too young to have any memory of this, but the 1193 harvest had not been good, and our harvests had just carried on getting worse with each year. As a result, by the time we got to 1196, with folk trying to eke out the pitiful crop of the 1195 harvest, many of the ordinary people in the land were actually at the point of starvation. We were lucky living in Nottinghamshire – much of our farmland was on soil enriched by the various rivers' winter floods, and as a result, although our people were hit hard by the dreadful forest laws, at least there were great swathes of our shire where you could grow just about anything reasonably well, even in a bad year. Our friends on the higher lands in Derbyshire had been suffering badly, but they too had a reserve in the form of money from the mines. Now our plans for hoarding part of the mined ore were vital, for they allowed the miners to start selling bits of it as extra to what they had just produced, and were therefore able to afford both the taxes and the grain from the Nottinghamshire farms in order to stay alive. Other shires had not been so fortunate.

However, even we could not wholly escape the consequences of so many failed harvests and, what was worse for me, I found myself caught up in the deaths in my role as coroner. Under different circumstances things might have worked out differently, but as he travelled north, the dreadful Philip of Poitiers made a point of visiting those sheriffdoms which were on his way, and so once again we found ourselves with one of the archbishop's spies in our midst just when we least needed him to be there.

On the day when things all started to spiral downwards and out of control, I had for once been out to villages south of Nottingham and across the Trent. Keyworth and Stanton-on-the-Wolds were on relatively high ground compared to most of the rest of the shire, and their fields were not so fertile, but worse, they had borne the brunt of a couple of vicious storms in the spring which had either flattened or wholly washed away their winter grain, so that when their stores ran out there was nothing to harvest to replace them. As a result two men had died out in the fields, too exhausted and hungry to work, yet desperately trying to drive on an equally thin ox to plough the land, in the hope that their villages would be able to hold on until the summer grain and vegetables could be picked. Until that point, Gervase, I never seen a man who had starved to death and it was a horrifying sight. They were just bones covered with shrivelled skin – and the rest of the villages were just the walking dead.

I was shocked, my friend, shocked and appalled. How had we come to this in England? We had been the richest land from here to Jerusalem in the days of King Edward, before the Conquest, yet now Englishmen whose families had been on these farms since time immemorial were dropping down dead behind their ploughs for want of basic food. It was *wrong, and I was sickened – which was no doubt why I did not guard my tongue enough with the new bishop of Durham when I walked in and found him stuffing his face on succulent lamb beside Briwere, whose face was also smeared with the grease from the meat.*

Nottinghamshire
April – May, the Year of Our Lord 1196

"Ah, Gisborne," Briwere drawled. "All sorted, I hope?"

Guy gritted his teeth, and forced himself to some sort of calm in his voice at least, even if he couldn't manage that inside.

"Sorted ...yes. The poor souls starved to death. There was no foul play."

"'Oo is zis man?" the person who had to be Philip of Poitiers demanded.

Briwere gave an airy wave of his hand and dismissed Guy with, "Oh, just one of my knights. He's very useful in his own way. Not much of a knight, but good for some of the dirtier jobs." Bishop Philip quirked a cynical eyebrow, forcing Briwere to explain further, "Gisborne is one of my coroners. Not my first choice, I admit, but others here said he was a man who knew a deal about hunting and bodies, and so he seemed a ...practical ...choice. He certainly does an effective job."

Philip's lip curled. "*Non*, sheriff, you are mistaken. Zis man has missed something vital."

Briwere was sly enough to realise that Philip was about to drop a heavy hint and merely raised his eyebrows back with, "Missed? Really?"

"Oui! What 'appens when a man is murdered?"

"We raise a hue and cry for the murderer," Briwere said tentatively. "It's one of our archbishop's latest edicts – all men of adult age must swear to take part in it on pain of a fine... Oh!"

Briwere saw what Philip was driving at, but so did Guy. If a man was killed then there had always been a murder-fine to pay (which in theory went to the bereaved, but which sometimes got to them considerably lighter after its passage through the sheriff's hands), but if the villagers in the vicinity of where the crime had taken place had failed to raise, or join in with, the hunt for the murderer, then they also got fined. The new bishop of Durham had just given Briwere a heavy hint that extracting these fines, regardless of whether murder had been committed or not, would have a blind eye turned to them if they brought more of the demanded more into the Exchequer.

"So," Bishop Philip said, turning to Guy with a supercilious smile, "you were mistaken, *non*? A murder 'ad been committed and you failed to collect ze correct fine."

Guy felt his blood starting to boil, and the haunting image of the hollow-faced villagers would not let him submit to this without a fight.

"No, I was not mistaken!" he snapped back.

"*Non*, you were!" Bishop Philip insisted. "'Oo are you to argue wiz me on zis matter?"

"A man who's seen far more dead bodies than you apparently have!" Guy riposted.

He saw Philip go white with anger. "'ow dare you challenge me!" he spluttered. "You ...you 'edge knight born of a cur!"

"I'd rather be born of an English bitch than a Norman whore!" Guy snarled back, for once losing his temper and rising to his feet with clenched fists.

The next thing he knew, several of his friends had piled on top of him and were hustling him out of the hall at speed.

"God's wounds, Guy!" Sir Hugh gasped when they all reached the relative safety of the outer bailey. "Get a grip on yourself! I know he insulted your mother and he was beyond wrong to do that, but have a care! The man is dangerous!"

Sir Richard, still holding Guy who was quivering with anger, said with some awe, "I don't know about that. I thought you were going to kill him with your bare hands, Guy! Christ in Heaven, what's got you so riled?"

"The people," Guy said through clenched teeth. "You ask Sir Hugo when you next see him. He went home shaking with shock, and Sewel fitz Henry took one look at the skeletons staggering towards him, clapped his spurs to his horse, and bolted from the village. We found him heaving his guts up a mile down the road, and nothing we said would persuade him to come back and help us ...or rather me. Sir Hugo couldn't take his eyes off the children, much less look at the corpses. Even the fucking ox dropped down dead a day later!"

His fist clenched again. "Murder? Those poor bastards couldn't wring a chicken's neck – if they'd even had one – much less kill a man! I had to cut the ox up for them, because none of them had the strength to take a knife through its hide."

He stood straighter and shook Richard's hand off. "I'd better make myself scarce, I suppose, for all your sakes, but I will *not* act as coroner in this matter! If Briwere wants to make the accusation of murder, he can bloody-well go and do it himself!"

Sir Martin had come out to them, and now said, "I'll tell the sheriff that we've had a report of poaching up in the Peak, and I've sent you to investigate in readiness for the woodmote. Go on, Guy, get a horse and those two monstrous dogs, and get out of here before Briwere loses his temper." He said it kindly, though, and Guy knew he and Sir Walter would cover his back in his absence.

Looking at all of his friends, Guy said in warning, "If you go with him, brace yourselves for some shocking sights. I've had my dreams haunted every night since then. You won't be sleeping easy, that I can assure you!"

Fetching Máel and Domnell, and taking his favourite gelding from the stables, Guy rode out into the night and made for the hideout by Hucknall. That would suffice for the night and he'd be safe there, which would give him time to think. As he lit a small fire to ward off the still-chilly night air, Guy recognised that Briwere would have to act. Philip of Poitier had his episcopal nose wedged so far up the king's arse it was a wonder he wasn't brown from head to foot, but that made the man horribly dangerous to men like Briwere, because they knew who the king would believe if it came to an argument. No, if Briwere wanted to hold on to his sheriffdom he would have to seem to be dancing to Poitier's tune, however much he might dread doing so. Yet Guy also reckoned that once Briwere saw the people of Keyworth and Stanton-on-the-Wolds, he was not so daft as to not realise who had told him the truth.

So from his own point of view, as long as he stayed out of the way while Poitier was still at the castle, the chances were that Briwere would accept him back into the fold – especially if Guy could slip the hint as to what the archbishop might say if the full details were to reach him. Already rumours were leaking out of the court that Hubert Walter was for once arguing back at the king that he had taken all England could give, and might even have tendered his resignation at least once, or possibly twice, and that this was just the sort of thing the archbishop was railing against. As long as Briwere therefore saw Guy's actions as being on the same side as the powerful archbishop, his position ought to be secure if not comfortable.

The bigger problem was what to do about Robin? Philip of Poitier could not be killed, that was utterly beyond doubt. If he was, then the king would descend once more on the shire he would see as a hotbed of rebellion, filled with choler and blood, and would burn all in his path to cinders as a punishment, of that Guy was sure. But this had to be stopped, nipped in the bud before any real charges of murder could be brought, and for that Guy knew he would need the outlaws' help. Equally he knew that he must have a specific target in mind this time – he had learned the hard way that sending Robin flying like an arrow at a general target without an end result firmly in mind would end in disaster.

With a heavy heart he mounted his horse when dawn lit the eastern sky, and tried to think where the outlaws might be. A woodmote was due on the feast of St James the Less, which this year fell on the coming Friday, giving him just three days to find them. He knew that Robin would strike at one court or another, and that at the ones held back at the end of March on the feast of St Mark, they had hit the Edwinstowe court. That had been on the twenty-ninth, and as a result, had left weeks for Robin to kick his heels and stoke his frustrations without a clear target.

Guy guessed the saner heads had suggested Edwinstowe. It always had the greatest number of fines, and therefore the largest amount of money, but it was also the one it was easiest to vanish from afterwards. But if Guy had any inkling left of how his cousin thought these days, this next time around they would go for the court at Calverton – the one right on the sheriff's doorstep. So with that in mind he made for the hideout by Epperstone, and was relieved beyond measure to find them there.

Having had no sleep at all since he'd been to the villages, except for those times when he'd fallen into an exhausted slumber only to be woken soon after by scream-torn nightmares, his compassion for his cousin had increased considerably, and so when he saw Robin, Guy's first reaction had been to go and hug him, saying,

"I am so sorry if I've been less than patient with you! I had no idea what it was like to be so haunted by nightmares that you would be frightened to close your eyes."

What rocked him to the core was the way Robin stiffened and pulled away from him.

"If you aren't man enough to face what you've brought on people, Guy, then that's your problem," Robin declared haughtily. "I have no such problems! Don't presume to foist your own weaknesses off on me!" and turning on his heels, Robin stomped away to the other side of the camp, leaving Guy with his face wet with tears and shaking, but utterly bemused as to what he could have said wrong.

Somewhere after that, and probably barely heartbeats away, Guy became aware of Tuck's big arms wrapping around him and pulling him away, softly saying, "My dear friend, whatever has happened? Come. Tell me what has you so distressed?"

Later Guy would hear from the others how Robin had looked back and been shocked to see Will and the other crusaders starting to follow Guy and Tuck. Worse, Marianne was also turning to follow, prompting Robin to demand,

"You would waste your sympathy on him?"

"Yes," Guy was told Marianne replied, and when asked why, answered, "Because he still remembers what it is to be human. He can still be hurt by seeing other people's misery. You don't even notice! You've turned inwards so much that you think what you feel is normal and spit on anyone who tries to help you, because you can't even see that you *do* need help anymore." She shook her head. "I can't help you, Robin, because you don't care when you hurt me when I do. At least Guy's never done that to me, so yes, I will go and try to find out what's wrong."

All Guy knew was that he looked up from sobbing his heart out on Tuck's shoulder to find himself within a circle of sympathetic faces.

"Can you tell me what's wrong, *brawd*?" Tuck asked him gently, and Guy found himself tripping over his own tongue to tell them of the famished villagers on the other side of the Trent.

"God forgive me for not looking their way," he sobbed to Tuck. "I was so obsessed with the villages who fall within the royal forest that I never gave those on the other side of the Trent a second thought. It never occurred to me to think about how they were coping with the bad harvests. By *Dewi Sant*, I've been there a few years ago, I know how poor their soil is. I should have remembered! I should have come and asked you to check on them. Their souls are on my conscience!"

"Not a chance!" Will growled, giving him an affectionate punch on the arm to wake him up. "Don't you dare take this all on yourself! You're not the only one who knew that. We've all of us been that way and we didn't think of it either. This doesn't fall on you alone, Guy!"

His words were some comfort to Guy, but he couldn't hold back now from adding his fears over how they might act and blurted them out. "Fucking Philip is untouchable!" he finished with a hiccup. "Harm a bloody hair of his tonsure and it will only rebound on the villages ten times over!"

There was a moment's pause and then Mariota's Scottish lilt declared, "Then I think we do what you wanted to be done originally – I say we tar and feather the monks who've come with this bloody man from Poitier who's so ingratiated with the king. Surely that's a start?"

Guy gave her look of deep gratitude. "Thank you, yes, that would be a good start." Then he hung his head and wept again as he added, "But I fear it's all too late for the villagers. If there's anyone left alive for Briwere to make his accusations to it would be a miracle. It's been a week already, and although I asked at every village on my way back, they each confessed that they only have enough to keep themselves going. None of them had anything to spare to send to any others even worse off. I pray that the ox I butchered and got cooking to make a nourishing broth will have helped, but they needed more than that, far more."

"We've got stores here," Marianne declared immediately. "We can strip this place bare! There's more up at Loxley we can bring down here later on, and if we need to use this while it's empty none of us are so starved that we can't go a day or so without until we get to our next hideout. That's far better than those poor souls!"

"We're only one long day's march away from them," Hugh agreed with her, giving her a look of deep affection. "I'll come and help you pack."

"Agreed. We're doing this," Will said, looking to the others and getting nods of agreement.

As they hurried off to start packing supplies into sacks which could be slung over their shoulders, Guy was left sitting with Tuck.

"They didn't ask Robin," he said softly to Tuck in surprise.

"No, my friend, they didn't," Tuck answered with a sigh. "I haven't wanted to burden you with this, but I fear the group is splitting. Robin just hasn't accepted that he can't demand and always get, and it rankles with the experienced fighters. They feel he's dismissing their expertise ...that he's not listening to them. The newer lads still see him as Robin Hood – the man and the symbol in one. But the others see 'Robin Hood' as something they use. ...An image which serves a purpose. None of them expect your cousin to be that ...thing. ...That more-than-human creature who cannot fail."

Tuck gave a deep sigh. "Even I have lost patience with him over that. There is something deep in his soul which craves that adulation, something very unhealthy, and no amount of reasoning affects the way he ultimately behaves when he believes that the persona of Robin Hood ought to take action. As you heard, he's even stopped thinking that he was damaged in any way by the crusades. In his head *he* sees everything in the right light, and if we don't agree then we are the ones who are misguided. I fear for your cousin's soul, Guy, I truly do, but I've recognised that there's nothing more I can do to save him from himself. All I can do is make sure that he drags none of the others down into the pits of Hell with him."

"Blessed St Issui!" Guy gulped, shaken out of his own misery by the thought of his once much-loved cousin rotting in Hell for eternity. "Do you think he's so lost? Truly, Tuck?"

The big Welsh monk shook his head sadly. "I hope not, because I wouldn't wish that on anyone. And if my prayers are worth an iota of God's compassion, then I've prayed with all my heart that what he did in the Holy Land will weigh in his favour when his time comes, but I would not presume to anticipate the Almighty on this matter. Robin has made his bed and will have to lie on it in that respect, Guy. We mere mortals have done all we can.

"On the other hand, I would like to give you what comfort I can in your time of great need. Would it help you if I heard your confession? I don't believe you have anything to be guilty of, but it does you credit that you feel the weight of those poor souls, and I will relieve you of that burden if I can?"

Guy found himself smiling for the first time in what felt like an eternity. "It would give me great comfort, Tuck. You're the only one I can speak to in that way with total honesty and not betray my friends, and it's been so long."

As Guy blurted out his confession to Tuck over in a far corner of the camp, the others continued with their packing. Only as he sat back, drained, but for the first time in ages feeling lighter in spirit, did he realise that Siward and Gilbert were sitting not far behind him flanking Domnall and Máel, two human watchdogs matching his canine ones. They had to have heard some of what he was saying, and that was confirmed by the way Siward came and hugged him, but clearly they had been determined that Robin would not barge in on the sacred moment, and for that Guy was deeply grateful.

"What you said about Robin," Siward said softly in his ear, "I've been feeling like that too," and he gave Guy a tighter squeeze.

"How long?" Guy asked him back as quietly. This was between just the two of them.

"Since I had to bring him back," Siward admitted. "Many's the night I've wished I'd just up and left that night when he got thrown out of the king's tent. Nothing we've done since then has required him and him alone."

"Not even those arrows into Bolsover Castle, or parting the rope around Ernwine's neck?" Guy wondered.

"Malik could have done as well if he'd had to," Siward said with a sniff of despair, "he just never got asked. And to be honest so could Thomas. Robin practices daily now, but those two have been archers since they were at their fathers' knees. It all balances out. It's just that as they don't make such a song and dance about being able to do such things, that they get a bit overlooked when Robin's pride comes into play."

Gilbert linked a friendly arm through Guy's as they turned towards the camp fire where a meal was bubbling in the big cauldron over the fire. "We're with you on this one," the flame-haired Irishman declared. "We don't need Robin's approval for it. He can come or stay, but we're going."

"You don't need all of us to take that stuff," Robin announced after everyone had eaten, and were preparing to get an early night's rest with the intention of starting out before dawn. "Who wants to come with me to take the Calverton woodmote?"

The experienced men immediately looked dismayed.

"The sheriff will have soldiers present, Robin," Will warned, as the same naive six who had joined him in the Christmas attacks immediately shouted their willingness to join him. Clearly taking supplies to villagers was nothing compared to the excitement of a full raid, but the others knew the real dangers.

"Think carefully," Tuck warned, as Gilbert added,

"Those of us with the most experience won't be with you, you know."

That made Robin scowl. Clearly he had anticipated that the thought of the novices volunteering would make some of the others come with him and leaving Guy's party all the smaller for that. It chaffed at Guy that the villagers were, in Robin's eyes, just counters on a game board when it came to the popularity contest between the two of them – or at least how it must be playing out in Robin's mind.

"I don't mind if only a few of you come," he felt prodded into saying. "As long as we have enough to carry everything that's all, and we can load my horse up – I'll happily walk not just there but back again."

"We're with you, Guy," Marianne immediately responded, with Mariota and Tuck nodding their assent too.

What surprised Guy was the way Piers, of all people, also spoke up for himself and his brothers, saying that they would come and hunt along the way to try and give the villagers some game to hang and cook up later. Malik also added,

"We have seen great need in our homeland," gesturing to Khalīl and Janah. "We will come and give what help we can. One court going by without some sort of attack will not make much difference to how the sheriff sees us. This is more important."

Then John nearly undid Guy's thin layer of calm all over again by saying, "Your mother taught us that living in the manor came at a price, Guy, and that was that we had to look after the small folk. I've never forgotten going with her to take food to the poorest families when we had that bad harvest and winter when we were lads. We all complained about cold feet and hands until we saw those serfs. You were there, and if this is so much worse, then it has to be bad."

"It is worse," Guy admitted thickly, his voice almost failing him. "Ten times worse!"

"Then we're coming," Allan agreed, and that seemed to settle that.

However, having had a successful hunt as they passed through Sherwood, and with several geese, a brace of large hares, and a couple of roe deer now slung over Guy's horse as they reached the point where they would have to leave to cover of the trees and cross the Trent, Guy now turned to his friends.

"I'm beyond grateful that you've come with me," he began, "but those six who've gone with Robin haven't a clue what they're heading into. Briwere is going to have the courts guarded like never before with that Devil's bishop at his heels." He looked at the Coshams. "Would you go and watch for them? Please? I'd never forgive myself if one of them died because Robin was too stiff-necked to back down because of me."

Will ambled over and patted his arm. "I'll go too. The four of us should be able to put down enough covering arrows to let them make a good escape." Then he grasped Guy by both arms and made him look him in the eye. "We're not going to go in with them though, do you understand? Robin chose to do this. He has to take the consequences."

"But the lads…!" Guy began to protest.

"…Have been warned enough times!" Bilan chipped in with. "I've lost count of the number of times I've reminded Much of how careless Robin was with his life after the siege, and Martin and

Simon have been there more often than not. You can only warn them so many times, Guy. They need to have the experience if they won't listen. It's not just you who's been wasting your breath."

It made Guy realize how much Bilan had grown up into a man over these last years while Much, who was of a similar age, was resolutely stuck in his boyhood and always looking to others to make decisions for him."

"If it makes you feel better, I'll go too," Gilbert declared, "but I'm with Will – we'll only act if they get into serious trouble. A fright will be no bad thing where those six are concerned."

And so it was that Guy crossed the Trent with his cousins and Tuck, Marianne and Mariota, Hugh, Roger and Siward, and the three former turcopoles, none of them expecting any sort of trouble on their mission.

And now, Gervase, we are about to come to something you will not want to hear, for I was about to steal Robin's crown for a while. But before you judge me too harshly, think on what I said of those villagers. I have not embellished the truth, indeed I have somewhat understated it. You have never seen people starving to death from here in your protected cloisters, whereas I know that tonight, despite your best ministrations, I will once again be haunted in my dreams by the remembrance of those poor people. How they were so gaunt that every bone stood out, and how the children were too small for their ages. It is their eyes that linger with me, Brother – huge eyes staring at me, yet with so little life left in them that you knew they already had one foot in their graves. It was a terrible time and one I pray never comes upon us again, but the salt which was rubbed into those spiritual wounds was made up of my cousin's arrogance. To this day I cannot forgive him for believing that it was more important for him as ~Robin Hood~ to strike one more blow against the sheriff, than to help all those souls in dire need. I believe that was the day when he stopped being my cousin Baldwin in my heart forever.

Chapter 17

However, you must know that when we set off across the Trent, my friends and I, we were wholly convinced that we had nothing more to do than deliver those emergency supplies, and try to get the two villages back on their feet again. To us, it was Robin's party who were heading into danger. They were the ones who would have to fight, not us. What happened, therefore, was never planned for or remotely anticipated, although after what I had heard in the castle, had I been less distraught, I might have guessed at it.

South Nottinghamshire, May, the Year of Our Lord, 1196

"Here, put this on," John said to Guy, untying a bundle of cloth which had been strapped to the top of the mighty sack he was carrying on his back. It shook out into one of the dark-green wool jerkins the other wore, with a hood to match. "Just in case anyone sees us, you need to be one of the gang, not recognisable as Sir Guy from the castle."

"God bless you, John," Guy said gratefully, pulling them on. "I'm such a mess I never thought of that. No, it wouldn't do for someone to say they'd seen me in your company, would it?"

Tuck gave him a pat on the shoulder with, "That's what friends are for, *brawd*," while Mariota added in surprise,

"You're a good deal more gracious about accepting help than your cousin," making Guy wonder just how many times these good folk had had their heads snapped off of late by Robin.

However, this wasn't the time or place to be debating Robin's sanity. They had crossed the Trent on the last of the old Roman fords before Nottingham (even now still paved with the Romans' heavy stone blocks which the Trent had yet to dislodge), but even so, that put them far north of where they wanted to be. And so they kept as close to the river bank as they could, so that the plentiful small stands of trees along it hid them from view as they marched. In the distance they saw many folk out in the fields, but as the afternoon drew on and they began to move away from the Trent, they began to see the first signs of the famine. Fields which should have been full of sprouting shoots were patchy here, speaking of poor seed grain planted thinly.

"*Dewi Sant*," Tuck breathed, "this is by far the worst I've seen!"

"It gets worse," Guy said darkly, making all of the others look at him in despair.

As they began to climb the low rise up onto the wolds, it became noticeable that there were fewer folk about. Cropwell Bishop seemed, at least from a distance, to be functioning, and Guy voiced the hope that with the whole place being owned by the bishop, that he had sent some much needed help from Newark. Two miles further on, Cotgrave was a different story. Painfully thin men were slowly weeding the fields, desperately trying to give what straggling wheat seedlings they had a chance of producing something, and Guy heard Marianne and Mariota making stifled sobs.

"We have to give them something," Hugh declared, and nobody argued.

The villagers gratefully took a large bag of grain and one of the roe deer, but the headman impressed them all by refusing more, saying,

"Take some to our neighbours up at Clipstone. They're as badly off as us."

A little over a mile onwards and the truth of that was confirmed. Clipstone was only a small hamlet, but they too were beyond grateful for the bag of wheat and one of the large and plump hares that Thomas had brought down in the forest.

"Has anyone heard of Normanton or Stanton?" Guy dared to ask of the next two nearest villages when they got to Warborough and found the same, hoping that his voice wasn't too distinctive.

What had seemed like ample supplies for one village were dwindling fast at this rate.

"Normanton's alright, but I fear at Stanton they're all dead," the leading man of Clipstone said. "Mary married a man over there and she came back to us two days ago with her daughter, saying her man and son were both gone. Now she's followed them."

"How many were in the village?" Tuck asked.

"About twenty, plus children."

"All gone? God in Heaven! So many!" and Tuck bowed his head in prayer.

In Stanton itself the sight was shocking. Several bodies lay where they had dropped, with nobody there to bury them. Several of the party wanted to stop and bury them now, but others pointed out that the living – if there were any – in Keyworth would need their help more urgently. The burying could be done on the way back.

Yet as they trudged up the slopes towards Keyworth in the lowering light Allan's keen eyes spotted something and he called softly,

"Horses! In the village!"

Instinctively they all stopped and dropped down, Guy being the slowest by far as the one least used to being furtive. For a moment nobody could see anything, then between two houses a beautiful dappled grey horse appeared.

"That's that bastard Poitier's horse!" Guy hissed, appalled. "What in God's name is he doing here?"

Without a word being spoken, Siward was already signalling Roger and Allan to scout the one way, while Malik, Janah and Khalīl scooted low the other way around the top of the high patch of land on which the village lay. Hugh and Siward wormed their way forwards on their bellies to see what they could make out, everyone having shrugged off their packs which Marianne and Mariota were now carefully dragging back to a small depression they had not long passed, where they could be hidden until needed. Realising the problem, Guy rose into a crouch and led his horse into the shadows of a couple of big old oaks down in the same hollow before it could start whinnying to its stable mates. It was a good tempered dark bay, which normally caused no trouble and wasn't particularly visible in the forest, but it wasn't to know that it shouldn't welcome its friends. So Guy was grateful that there was a lush patch of weeds which it happily began cropping, for there had been little time for it to feed and no oats to spare at the camp.

"The sheriff's there," Allan reported back as he slid in, "and what looks like half a dozen of the castle men-at-arms. That big brute who's always getting drunk at *The Trip* is one of them – I'd know his ugly mug anywhere!"

Guy grunted in disgust. "That probably means his mate, Pod, is with him. They're never far apart. Scruffy wretch with straggly black hair?" Allan nodded. "Well, watch him!" Guy warned. "He's too handy with a knife for my liking, and nobody but Big Gerth – the brute you recognised – knows where he came from, but it wouldn't surprise me if he hadn't ended up here on the run from a murder in some other shire."

"He's the first for an arrow, then," Siward decided.

Malik's threesome came back reporting that Philip of Poitier was sitting on his white dappled palfrey at the end of the village, accompanied by two other clerics, also mounted.

"Not monks like Tuck, though," Malik was quick to add. "Men like Poitier. Rich men's sons sent to the church. They sit too well on those horses to not have been riding for years."

"So they could be fighters," Guy warned, "just like Mellitus! Don't let those tonsures and cowls fool you. They may have spent their youth training in arms alongside older brothers."

However it was Siward and Hugh who brought the most troubling news.

"They're scouring the village!" Hugh whispered in disbelief. "They're taking everything of value they can find – the smith's tools, some woven wool and fleeces, everything!"

"And there's what looks worryingly like a noose being strung from the branch of that big oak on the westward side of the village," Siward added bitterly. "I can hardly believe it, but I think they might be about to hang someone!"

Marianne and Mariota were already kneeling up and stringing their bows, and the others weren't slow to follow suit. Suddenly Guy felt a savage glee. For once he would be able to join in! He'd had his bow slung along his saddle, and he'd thought to bring it and his quiver up from where he'd left his horse, so now he too strung his big Welsh bow, then saw the others grinning at him.

"Good to have you along," John said with a huge smile and playful punch at Guy's arm, while Allan added,

"About time you had a chance at some vengeance!" and it felt like that to Guy, too – a chance to finally act according to his heart, not his head.

"You come with us," Malik said, also looking pleased, "you're a good enough archer to take these shots."

The four of them skirmished around to the north, while the others went south to get to the other end of the main street, although it was little more than a trampled-earth lane. It positioned Guy and his group close to the men-at-arms, with the others creeping in behind the three priests, and Guy felt a bubbling delight welling up at the thought of what Tuck would be saying to them shortly.

Now that he could see who the men-at-arms were, he had no compunction in saying softly, "Don't mess about – kill them. These six are the scum of the earth. I've never been able to get through to them. They've no conscience or Christian kindness in them."

An owl hooted not far away and Malik nodded to them all – that had been the signal that the others were in position. Then Siward's voice rang out boldly,

"Halt in the name of Robin Hood!"

The soldiers all jumped as if stung at that, but three of them fell to Guy, Maik and Khalīl's arrows, Janah muttering darkly as his target ducked behind his falling mate just fast enough to only get an arrow caught in his jerkin. Typically it had been Big Gurth and Pod who had moved fastest and were still on their feet, but Guy was shocked to see that Durand fitz Sewel was with them as well, along with the two sergeants who had accompanied Bishop Philip. They were on their feet besides their horses and that hampered the archers'.

"Kill him!" they heard Briwere screaming, and Guy was glad he'd left the two wolfhounds tethered back at the camp, because they would have picked up on Briwere's aggression and would have torn him to shreds. "Kill Robin Hood!"

Siward stepped forward and went to clash swords with Briwere, but Tuck and John had their hands full with the priests, and so Guy plunged into the fray, his blood boiling at the sight of Philip of

Poitiers running an emaciated villager through just to get him out of his way.

"Here I am!" Guy snarled in what he hoped was a good imitation of Baldwin. "You want Robin Hood? Come and get me!" and he drew the beautiful Damascus-forged blade Will had made for him which he'd never dared use openly at the castle.

"Can you use that, cur?" Philip demanded, giving his own fine blade a twirl in his hands and then heeling his horse at Guy.

Guy fooled him, though, flipping his sword backwards out of the way and ducking under Philip's slashing cut, but getting close enough to be able to get both of his fists under the stirrup on this side and shove upwards. The unexpected move threw Philip up out of the saddle to topple off his horse on the other side to Guy.

The terrified palfrey took advantage of Philip loosing its reins and bolted, leaving Philip to scramble to his feet, snatching his sword out of the dirt as Guy strode towards him. The exchange of blades that followed had Philip backing up all the while, his face getting whiter and whiter as the reality sank in that he was losing his fight against this outlaw who was no mere peasant. When he finally fetched up against the village smithy's forge it was a good thing for him that it was cold, for Guy bent him backwards over it, his blade at Philip's throat and the fine edge already drawing a trickle of blood where it touched.

"You pitiful excuse for a churchman!" Guy snarled. "How dare you treat these people like this! Where's your compassion? Where's your pity?"

Luckily Malik came up to Guy's side to say,

"We did not fight in the Holy Land for Jerusalem just for you to get rich."

Malik's accented English was the final straw for Philip, and Guy heard the priest's bladder give way, but it also brought him back to earth. Had he himself not said that Philip must not be killed? And yet he had just been a breath away from doing just that!

"Take him!" he growled to Malik and turned away, hearing Malik cuff the priest hard, and Janah come up on the other side as they each grabbed one of Philip's arms to drag him away. It was a nice touch that they conversed in their own tongue as they did it, and suddenly Guy felt more like laughing than killing. Philip's pleas were those of a weak bully, not a truly dangerous man, and his rising terror at the presence of what he no doubt thought of as Saracens here in England would be a lingering torment.

Looking around him, Guy saw that the two trouble makers from the castle were lying in puddles of their own blood on the ground, and that Khalīl was cleaning his and his friends' blades on their clothing. So, the castle bullies had met their match in real fighters from the Holy Land, had they? That felt right. They wouldn't be terrorising the town's girls anymore, praise be. And Tuck had the two priests on their knees in the dirt and was giving them a piece of his mind, although how much they understood was debatable due to his lapses back into Welsh when he ran out of English words in his passion. Philip, now limp in a faint, was joining them, and Durand was out cold and being trussed up by Allan and Roger; but Guy's biggest problem was Briwere, currently forced to his knees by Hugh and Siward, yet still glowering furiously at them.

"Which one of you is Robin Hood?" he was snarling, so furious that he was actually frothing at the mouth and sending flecks of white spittle at them with every word. And now Guy saw his chance, for both Hugh and Siward had their hoods pulled well forwards so that their faces were totally hidden in the shadows, something helped by the growing dusk. Three men all of similar height and build and dressed similarly – what was there that Briwere could take away that was specific to him? Grabbing Durand's gloves to cover his hands, Guy tugged his own hood forwards, ducked his head a little, and swaggered up to Briwere to lean threateningly on his sword, positioning it so that it was right in front of the sheriff's nose, but with it blocking his view too.

"You called?" he drawled. Now what would Robin say in these circumstances? Because it wouldn't do for it to be too clear that there was more than one man playing the part as yet. One day, maybe, they might need to use that to devastating effect, so best to keep that in reserve. "I warned you at the tourney," Guy continued, remembering Robin's words and trying to pitch his voice to the same level, although his own voice was noticeably deeper than Robin's these days. "I told you I would not stand by and allow you to harm my people."

Luckily Briwere was in such a state he was far beyond noticing details. This affront to his dignity and office was beyond anything he could tolerate.

"Your people?" he screamed. "What authority do you think you have, crusader?"

"The earned right to act as God's people's defender," Siward answered for him in a flash, "which is a good deal more than those pathetic excuses for churchmen you brought with you have. You think God looks down kindly on *them*?"

Tuck was still giving them a good tongue lashing, which now included a wide-eyed Philip of Poitier, who probably hadn't been spoken to like that since he was a very young novice, and it was proving to be a far more harrowing experience than he could ever have dreamt. All three were regularly flinching as Tuck's words hit home like daggers, and Guy couldn't resist saying to Briwere,

"It looks like your tame priests are having a harsh lesson in humility."

"My priests?" Briwere shrieked. "They're not *my* priests! They're the king's!"

"Then King Richard ought to know better," Hugh riposted from Guy's other side. "What true knight of the Cross would commend his priest to murder?"

"And that's what it is, sheriff," Guy continued, realising that this was his chance to strike his message home. "These people have committed no murder. Look at them!" and he waved his gloved hand at the shivering wrecks standing and staring in mute awe at what had just happened in their humble village, too exhausted to react any more strongly. "You are the murderers here, not them. What do you think Archbishop Walter will say to that, eh? Do you think he would *not* notice a sudden rash of unsolved murders on your records, *none* of which raised a hue and cry to search for the perpetrators? You take him for a fool if you think you can pull the wool over his eyes like that, and from all I have heard of the man, he's not that!"

The mention of Hubert Walter doused Briwere's anger like nothing else. He might be many things, but Briwere was no fool, and now he saw what Guy wanted him to – that he had been swayed too far by Poitier. Blinking as the sun in the west hit his eyes, Briwere squinted at the villagers and Guy saw the realisation sinking in that if he had carried on, then Keyworth would have become a deserted village, and deserted villages paid no taxes. That definitely would get noticed come the returns at Michaelmas!

All Guy had to do now was get Briwere out of here in some way that would dent his pride, but not wind him up to vengeance again.

"Strip him!" he ordered Siward and Hugh. "Down to his braes! It's not that cold at this time of year, and he has enough fat on him to cope. Tie him to his saddle. The horses will find their own way home." Because he was standing looking away from the sunset, Guy could see the mischievous grins on both of his friends' faces. They were enjoying this as much as him.

And so as Marianne and Mariota began distributing the food (although they kept the produce of the illegal hunt out of sight until Briwere was out of sight), the others stripped the three clerics, Durand and Briwere down to their underclothes, and then John and Tuck hoisted them up onto their horses, tying their feet into the stirrups, and their hands behind them to the saddles. Their fine clothes Guy had folded and tied to the backs of the saddles too.

"We have to be careful with these representatives of the king," he told the others in a hurried discussion. "We humiliate them much more effectively if they return with nothing stolen. What can they complain of to the king then? Dented pride? I don't see King Richard of all men being very sympathetic to that! Their robes may be worth a fortune, but where could you sell them anyway? And Briwere's had enough of a punishment without pushing him over the edge."

However, Guy did put Briwere's fancy bonnet back on his head at a jaunty angle, just to make sure that everyone knew who he was. He knew Briwere was ridiculously fond of this daft confection of velvet and feathers and wouldn't dream of shaking it off into the mud, even if that would have saved his pride a little, for without it Briwere wasn't such a recognised face by the common folk to have been instantly identified.

They were all grinning and Mariota gave Guy's hand a squeeze as she passed him to return to the food.

"I like your way of doing things," she said with an approving smile. "Robin wants blood too often these days."

What Guy also knew was which horses would make straight back to their stables, and so he put those as the leading pair with Briwere and Durand on, and the others linked to them in a line by re-jigging the reins with some additional rope. The bodies of the eight guards they piled onto the village's lone large wagon, and harnessed the two castle horses the visiting clerics had borrowed to it, then sat the two of them on the front seat, but still carefully tied down so that they couldn't make a run for it or grab the reins.

"You caused these men's death," Tuck told them with a stern wag of his finger. "So on the way back, you make sure you say prayers for their souls. Remember! God...is...watching!"

By the way the two men's eyes shot Heaven-wards in fear indicated that Tuck's lecture had hit home, and that they feared being struck down at any moment. Poitier was less awestruck, but this ritual humiliation was certainly getting to him going by the expressions flitting across his aristocratic features, and Guy knew he wouldn't forget this in a long time. Allan and Roger led the wagon's horses, and Malik, Khalīl and Janah the riders', and together they took them down to the West Bridgeford road to set them on their way. The horses would take their time but would make progress through the night, and Guy had no doubts that they would actually be found well before they had to negotiate the bridge over the Trent.

In the meantime, what were left of the villagers had clustered in the centre, and were eagerly awaiting a nourishing broth being cooked up over the fire John had got going.

"Little and often," Marianne and Mariota kept telling folk, as they handed out flatbreads as soon as they came off the pan. "Eat too much in one go and you'll be sick."

At first it was hard to persuade the villagers not to bolt the food, but as it sank in that they were full up on only a fraction of what they had once ate, they began to listen more to what the two former Hospitaller sisters were saying.

By dawn the outlaws felt they had done all they could. They now knew that a couple of other villages were really struggling too, but they would need to go back for more supplies before they could do anything for them, and it was a relief to find that Keyworth had been the worst affected simply because it had been hit hardest by the bad autumn storm, which had ripped away their winter grain.

"Let's get out of here before the sheriff sends anyone to hunt us," Guy suggested.

"Aye, and let's go and see what Robin's been up to," John added. "Dear God, I hope he hasn't done anything rash."

They left Keyworth and headed for West Bridgeford themselves. In part this was because they had to cross the Trent somewhere and there weren't that many bridges, fords or ferries to choose from, and partly because Guy wanted to make sure that their captives had actually been found. Having them left for dead by the side of the road wasn't part of the plan, but Guy feared Durand or Briwere might try something foolish, and end up half in and half out of the saddle where their heads could get bashed against a tree.

Happily they got the bridge without finding any bodies by the roadside, and to find everyone too excited by the earlier sight of the sheriff in his braes to be worried by any strangers. But Guy realised that it was also now very close to the time when the woodmote courts would start their proceedings.

"We should swing east straight away," he said to the others, "not just for me to avoid being seen in Nottingham, but to get to Calverton as fast as possible."

"What's the hurry, Guy?" Allan asked, bemused. "Will and the others will make sure nothing bad happens."

Guy felt his insides knot up all over again. "Look, I don't want you to think that I'm getting as bad as Robin over us finding fault in one another, alright? But the sheriff would have been found hours ago. That also means that potentially someone could have been in Nottingham making an early start for the woodmote to witness that. Do you think Briwere or Durand would have been quiet about the whole Robin Hood thing? If they were overheard, someone might be very alert to Robin going on the rampage. Too alert!"

"Aww, bollocks!" Roger groaned. "And the sheriff'll get his braes in a right knot if 'e 'ears of 'Robin Hood' doin' sommat after this, won't 'e?"

As the others all looked aghast, Guy apologised, "I'm sorry. I hope I'm wrong, I really do, but I'd feel a whole lot better if we were on hand to sort any trouble out, not least because I don't want Will, Gilbert and the Coshams risking their necks to haul Robin's chestnuts out of the fire. Will might say that he wouldn't go in, but we all know Will, don't we? He's as honourable as they come, and I don't see him leaving Much or one of the other lads to swing without lifting a hand."

"We'd better get a move on, then," Tuck sighed, flexing an ankle already sore from the long walk.

"The only consolation is that I think he'll wait until into the afternoon to strike," Siward rationalised, "because even if his pride is dented, he'll want there to be as much coin there as possible. We still have a few hours."

"Then everyone rides in turn," Guy declared. "This horse is big enough to carry even you, John, so up you get, Tuck!"

They made it to Calverton by the early afternoon, but not before one of Guy's fears had manifested into reality, as they had to get off the road as the sound of galloping hooves came on the road behind them. With Guy's horse masked by a lumbering wagon, they watched as half a dozen riders streamed by, all of them knights or sergeants.

"Who are they, Guy?" Mariota asked in dismay.

"Knights who've come to do their service at the castle," he replied miserably. "Briwere's not daft, and he must be in a fair rage at the moment, so he's making sure that those courts he can protect *are* protected."

"Does he think Robin Hood can fly?" wondered a confused Marianne. "Surely he doesn't think Robin could have got from Keyworth to Calverton in that time? Or at least not in time to make mischief."

"We will," Hugh pointed out, "albeit a bit late in the day, and I think what Guy's saying is that the sheriff won't have thought that Robin would have stopped to serve the villagers dinner as we did. He'll assume that the proud outlaw would have taken his applause, bowed and left, and moved on to his next target."

"Saint Issui watch over our friends!" Tuck intoned and crossed himself, then hissed at another thought. "If Robin had come with us then the sheriff would have been chasing his tail for nothing, wouldn't he?"

"Robin's become predictable," Guy sighed. "You rarely hit the Mansfield courts because they're held in the town, and you did Edwinstowe last time, so the chances were always that Robin would strike at Calverton or Linby this time, and they're the ones Briwere can most easily send men to. Briwere could have had this planned already, you know. That might even be why he thought he could go to Keyworth with Poitier..."

"...because he knew his courts would be protected," Siwards sighed. "Shit! What a mess! You've been trying to warn us about this for some time, haven't you, Guy? That Robin's been taking it for granted that he can just turn up and raid a court with impunity?"

Guy tried to muster a smile for his friends but couldn't. "I'm afraid so. You've succeeded so far because you've always turned up *en masse*, and with your greater experience as fighters you've had the upper hand. But Briwere's crafty – he's no Wendenal to be easily hoodwinked. You've only got away with it this long because he had so much distracting him when he first arrived, what with the eyre and then the carucage, but sooner or later he was going to get time to turn his attention fully on you – I just never knew for certain when it would be."

"We'd better hurry, then," Hugh said, "because I don't see Robin halting his plans just because more knights have turned up."

Noon came and went, but they got to Calverton while the court was still in session as Guy knew it would be, for Griffin Presbiter took every opportunity to play on his authority. This was Presbiter's only real claim to any power except over his modest manor, and he milked it for all it was worth. So they could hear his voice droning on from within the wooden hall, whose doors stood open to allow air in – with so many people crammed inside it tended to get stifling after a while, and a gentle drizzle was making the air very humid even outside, let alone in a hall with only the one window at the far end.

"This way," Hugh said softly, leading Guy with the others following, around the edge of the village making sure the houses hid them. "Tie your horse up here, Guy," he gestured. "Nobody comes to this rickety old barn except during harvest time."

"We normally take up position here on this bit of high land," Malik told him. "Mostly it means we have the sun at our backs, which makes for easier aiming and any soldiers are looking into the sun – if there is any!" and he gave a wry smile and rolled his eyes to the slate grey English sky, so very different to his homeland.

An unseasonably early swift trilled to their right, and immediately all the outlaws changed direction towards it, Will and the others melting out of a tiny coppice of silver birches to meet them.

"Sorted?" Will asked as he gave Guy a friendly grasp of the hand in welcome.

"Definitely! You have a couple of other villages who need some help, but Keyworth might just survive now."

"Well I don't know what Robin is planning, but we can't find hide nor hair of him here," Will said with a worried frown. "We've searched all our usual spots for ambushes, and God knows there aren't that many here for us to have lost him."

"The lads could be down in the crowd," Thomas said with a sigh, "but Robin himself...? You couldn't hide someone that tall. We were just wondering whether he's up in the hall roof somewhere."

"We hung back a bit, you see," Piers explained, "not wanting to tip Robin off that we were here, so we've only come up close to the village when the ordinary people had all gone in."

Siward, Malik and Hugh immediately looked worried while Marianne and Mariota's faces creased in perplexed frowns.

"How can he not be here?" Mariota asked, and in that moment Guy knew why.

"Fuck!" he exploded.

"Guy?" several of them questioned in unison.

"The bastard! The stupid, daft bastard!" Guy ranted, just about managing to keep his voice down so that only they could hear. "He guessed! He bloody guessed that some of you would have second thoughts and come after him, and he's punishing you for siding with me – he's not here, he's gone on to Linby!"

"Sweet Jesu! The fool!" Tuck gasped as the others swore according to their own inclinations.

"Guy," Siward gasped, "are there enough knights come to do their duty that Briwere could have sent the same number to Linby too?"

One look at Guy's face was enough to answer that.

"*Dewi Sant!*" Bilan intoned. "They have no chance, not up against trained knights! Not without any archers to cover their retreat, none at all!"

We were in shock, Gervase, total shock, none of us able to believe that Robin had done something so mindlessly cruel and careless. And we knew we could never get there in time now. Even as the crow flew it was six miles westwards to Linby, and those miles had no direct road, with the twisting and boggy course of the River Leen to cross as well.

You may think me foolish, but I had had a bad feeling about all of this right from the moment when I had left the castle, and not only because of the starving villagers. Something deep inside of me had known that this time Robin would try to do something which would end in disaster, and now it had materialised. Yet we could do nothing until we knew for certain what had happened, and with that in mind, I instantly declared that I should cut across country and pick up the Mansfield road, for that would be the easiest way I would have used to come back from the Peak and the one I would be expected to be on. Allan and Roger volunteered to go straight to Nottingham. That way they would be on hand if I had discovered anything that needed reporting back. With that thought in mind, Hugh and Siward said that they would go with them too, just in case someone needed to remain in the town to keep a watch, although at that stage we could only speculate on what, but if there were prisoners brought in before I got back, it would be good to know who they were.

The only remotely good thing any of us could think at that point was that Robin had not had time to make for the Mansfield woodmote. In the streets of that bustling town it would have been suicide to make an attack with such an inexperienced company, whereas Linby was more important for the manors around it than for any imposing village; and it had the virtue of having an awful lot of woodland around the village's fields, which were close enough that some hope remained that some of the party might have eluded capture.

The matter of which hideout they might make for afterwards was harder to decide. I recall us all thinking that while the Inkersall hideaway might be tempting, that Robin would more likely make for one of the smaller ones as long as he was still in some semblance of his right mind. A camp that if it got compromised could be written off and deserted, whereas Inkersall was far too important to abandon it unless absolutely necessary. Everyone agreed that hopefully he would head for the River Erewash and try to put that between him and any pursuit, especially if he feared they might set dogs onto him, and at that point I remembered that I had the wolfhounds with me. I would have to go to *the Epperstone camp and fetch them, for I could not go back without them without raising some vigorous questions about where I had left them. I had forgotten them because I normally never brought them out when I was going to meet my friends for this kind of venture, but I could not leave them tethered any longer.*

I remember cursing vigorously at that point, for it meant that it would take me that much longer to get back to the castle. It was only three or so miles away, but those miles were in the wrong direction to the one I needed to take and worse, I could hardly gallop my horse after he had been on the go for two days and a night already. Indeed, we were all weary to the bone, and finally sense in the form of Marianne and Mariot got the upper hand. We would all go to the small camp just south of Hucknall village which was snuggled in a small wood between two low knolls, and protected to the west by a loop of the Leen which was blessedly on the same side of that river as we were now – all that was except Bilan and Gilbert, who volunteered to go to the other camp and bring Domnall and Máel to me, they having done less of a trek than I and those with me had done. And so, dog-tired, we stumbled into the small hideout and cooked up the supplies hidden there, more grateful than normal that we had enough food and could eat our fill.

Chapter 18

You are shocked at Robin, Brother? So were we all. It was Robin's oblivion to the inexperience of those he had taken with him that shook us the most, I think. We sadly recognised that sooner or later he would feel the need to act to prove me wrong, but to do it in such a way and at such a time was a worrying sign of his mental decline.

However, you want to know what happened, and I will not delay. I got back to Nottingham not the next day but the day after, for after a restoring night's sleep we all agreed that I should not seem to be stumbling into Nottingham right on the sheriff's heels. Whatever had happened, there was nothing I could do in that day which would make any difference. If Briwere was in a hanging mood, then I was already too late, and if he had retained an iota of calm and sense, and was waiting for the eyre, then that was not due until later in the year and our friends would endure some days of deep discomfort in the dungeon, but not necessarily anything any worse. And so I trotted in through the bailey gate with Máel and Domnall on leashes on either side of me, my guts churning in anticipation, and breathed a massive sigh of relief when I saw no makeshift gibbets, nor anyone hanging from the battlements echoing what the king had done.

You grin and say, so Robin did pull it off after all! No, Gervase, he did not, and I take no pleasure in telling you the next part of this tale for it is a sorry affair, and even at the time I would have happily settled for being wrong if it had avoid the final outcome. You are intrigued? Good! I shall continue.

Nottingham Castle
Early Summer, the Year of Our Lord, 1196

Guy handed his horse over to Harry personally, whispering to him, "I've had to use him hard these last few days. Don't ask why. I can't tell you. But make sure he has a good rest, will you?"

Harry pursed his lips and gave Guy a knowing look. "You sail very close to the wind sometimes, you know. Just make sure you don't get caught!"

"I'm doing my very best," Guy assured him, but then hurried off into the castle. How he was received by Briwere was going to determine very much what he would be able to do for a while, and he entered the great hall with his heart pounding.

"Ah, Gisborne!" Briwere called almost cheerfully, spotting him instantly. "Found the poacher, did you?"

"No poaching, my lord sheriff," Guy replied with considerably more calm than he felt. "The hind had fallen and broken a leg. Her foot was still in the hole dug by a hare so there was no doubt about it, it just took a little time to find her."

Briwere simply tutted and looked away to continue the conversation he had been having with Sir Hugh and Sir Walter. That was positively benign compared to most of Briwere's responses, and Guy dared to hope that he was no longer in the sheriff's bad graces. He scanned the hall and met Sir Martin's eye, getting the signal to make his way over to him.

"What's happened?" Guy asked, hoping he was showing just the right level of curiosity. "Where's Bishop Philip?"

Sir Martin snorted. "Well you missed a treat there, to be sure." He turned away from the sheriff and then grinned broadly at Guy. "Our much unloved sheriff appeared in his braes and bonnet at the bridge yesterday morning, tied to his horse and spitting feathers. Piotier was the same!"

"God's hooks!" Guy gasped. "Where had they been to get into that state?" *Oh please, God, let me not give myself away*, he added in silent supplication.

"They went to Keyworth on Poitier's instruction," Sir Martin informed him, his eyes glittering with suppressed amusement. "It seems Robin Hood was there offering help to the villagers and took exception to Poitier wanting to hang a few of them."

"Sweet Jesu! What happened next?"

"*Hmph*! They won't say! But the two priests have been wearing their knees out in the chapel ever since, until Briwere sent them all off under armed guard to Durham this morning. Something, or some*one*, has put the fear of God into them like never before!"

Guy's snort of mirth escaped before he could contain himself, but was astonished to find Sir Martin chuckling too and saying, "That was pretty much everyone's reaction here. Between Mellitus and this lot, I think we've all had our fill of pompous Norman clerics."

"But why is Briwere in..." and Guy cast a quick confirming look over his shoulder to double check, "...what looks very much like a good mood?"

"Ah! That would be because we have two of Robin Hood's men in the dungeon."

Guy knew his jaw dropped and hoped it would be misread from what he was thinking. "How?"

"*Ach*, the bastard's been getting cocky and careless. We'd worked out he'd hit Linby or Calverton woodmote this time. Our three castle knights had a quick chat with Sir Walter and me, and we thought it worth sending the knights who've come to do their service to each of them." He gave another grin and shook his head. "Would you believe Robin Hood sent some mouthy double in his stead while he was at Keyworth?"

"Lookalike?" Oh God in Heaven, if this got back to Robin he would be in an even greater temper. Bad enough to fail, but to be thought a mere substitute while Guy's mission was read as the more important one would have him in an apoplexy!

"Oh, we don't who he was – the lookalike, I mean. He escaped. It was two of his cronies who got caught." Sir Martin suddenly sobered a little, gave a quick glance around to make sure he wasn't about to be overheard, then confessed, "Actually, I feel a bit sorry for them. I doubt they're any of the hardcore gang. The one's just a poor Irish peasant – probably signed up with the outlaws thinking it was going to be some great romantic rebellion. You know what these Celts can be like."

Bloody hell, that had to be Colm! But who else? "How did they catch him?" Guy asked, not having to fake hanging on to Sir Martin's every word.

Sir Martin shrugged. "He just didn't run fast enough. According to Walter fitz Robert the poor sod was already lagging, and then he caught his foot in a branch and went flying. His mate was the only one who turned back for him. Northern lad by the sounds of him."

Oh no, that had to be Ed! Guy really liked the young carpenter from Durham, and he'd just gone up in Guy's estimation for being the one to go back and try to help Colm. Yet he could feel his blood starting to boil too. Where had Robin been in all of this? Why had the master of archery not laid down a few arrows to slow the knights' approach? These men who came to do their duty at the castle for a few months were no heroes. They turned up, did their forty days' service and felt like they were the dog's bollocks for doing it, and then went back to helping run the family manor, quite happy that nothing more stressful had happened. The likelihood of any of them facing down a volley of arrows from Robin was nil.

"What's the sheriff going to do with them?" he managed to ask Sir Martin without his voice betraying his inner turmoil.

"The eyre comes in August. We don't know who's coming on the circuit yet, but you can bet that Briwere will know at least two of the three judges well enough to ask them to hand out the heaviest sentence. Those two are going to swing, and if Briwere has his way they might get a flogging beforehand. Of course, what he's really hoping is that Robin Hood is arrogant enough to try and launch a rescue mission sooner rather than later, and that he has the whole gang hanging from the battlements before he goes to the Michaelmas courts."

Guy swallowed hard. "That would really make his day, wouldn't it?" And horribly all too likely unless the others could sit on Robin for a few weeks, and for that length of time it just wasn't going to be possible.

"It would, but the good news from your point of view is that you've come out of this on the right side of the sheriff."

"Me?"

"Yes. It seems it was dinned into Briwere's thick skull somewhere on that chilly ride back to the castle that you had been right all along, that there were no murderers in Keyworth, and therefore had he listened to you instead of Poitier, he might have stayed safe in his bedchamber on that night. None of us have dared to ask what he would have said to a man with as much influence as Poitier to avoid that wild goose chase, mind you. Best to let that sleeping dog lie!

"But you, my friend, are – if not a hero – at least totally vindicated. Briwere's even gone as far as to call you useful and someone with sound opinions. I wouldn't presume on that too much, though. You know how fickle the man can be. But you can certainly walk around here without watching your every step for a while."

Guy managed to wring out a wry smile. "That has to be an improvement, I suppose, but I won't be celebrating at *The Trip* any time soon."

"Good man," Sir Martin said, clapping him on the shoulder. "Now go and let him crow over you for a moment, and then keep your head down like you always do."

It took until that night before Guy could slip out to *The Trip* to meet his friends, and when he told them what he had discovered they were as appalled as he was. By the descriptions people in the crowds had given of the prisoners they had already worked out who the two were, but the news that Robin had left them behind shocked all of them. It went against everything they believed in as soldiers.

"Now I know it's grim," Guy told them, as they took their ales outside, and round to the nook formed by the rock wall beneath the castle and the brewhouse, "but you're going to have to be patient. Briwere wants this to be a visible humiliation. He's not going to string them up from the nearest hook without a very public trial beforehand, so we have time."

"'Ave you gotta plan?" Roger asked. "You 'ave, ain't yer! You're vhe clever one, you knows vhat castle like vhe back o' yer hand!"

Guy was touched by Roger's faith in him, but had to say, "Not exactly a plan, I'm afraid, but the Assizes will come around before long. That always means some movement of prisoners between the town gaol and the dungeon, now that Briwere's got the local legal system running more as it ought to have been. Under Ralph Murdac the Assizes were minor things, just sorting out local misdemeanours such as the odd drunken brawl. Briwere sees them as another means of raking in fines, and he makes quite the song and dance about them, sitting in judgement in his finery, and because of that he likes to hold them here in the castle. He feels it overawes the locals to be dragged into that big hall, past the inner gate with its murder holes and portcullis, and I suspect he's not wrong there.

"But that means that the night before, we have to bring those who were being held in the town gaol up here, and also bring in the ones who have posted bail and been at large in the town. Briwere doesn't want them suddenly getting twitchy on the morning of the hearing and making a run for it, you see. And in that chaos – because it's always something of a muddle with that many temporary prisoners – I should be able to get Ed and Colm away. If nothing else that also means that I have a few weeks to iron out the details of how I'm going to do it."

"Weeks?" Allan gasped. "Blessed St Thomas, Guy, we'll never be able to sit on Robin for that long!"

"Well you're going to have to!" Guy snapped. "I'm not a bloody miracle worker, Allan! I'll smuggle as many loaves of dog bread as necessary to them, so they won't starve, and they may come out filthy and smelly, but they'll come out alive. That's the best guarantee I can give you."

His younger cousin leaned in and gave him a hug. "Sorry, Guy! I know you'll do all you can. It was just a bit of a shock hearing you say weeks."

Hugh patted Allan on the back in sympathy. "We all feel like that. And I suppose the one good thing is that it's those two who are steady lads. Blessed St Thomas, who knows what might have happened already if it had been Martin and Simon? I don't see either of them keeping quiet in their panic at being thrown down into the dark," reminding Guy of how he had first met Hugh in that same dungeon as prisoner of a previous sheriff.

"When is the Assize?" Siward asked.

Guy kneaded his tired eyes as he tried to recall, then suddenly brightened. "It's on the twenty-seventh of May, a Monday – the

Feast of St Augustine, but also of one of Tuck's and my favourite saints, St Melangell! Oh, that's auspicious! That gives me hope."

"Not so bad," Siward ventured, "as long as we can keep Robin on a short leash."

"Maybe a few of you should point out to him that they wouldn't even be here if it wasn't for him," Guy said darkly.

"Oh, we will," Siward assured him. "And I imagine that Gilbert will already have turned the air above the camp blue once he found out that Colm was one of the ones lost. Those two have become very close. I don't imagine Robin's been cut any slack by him. Go back and get some rest, Guy. One of us will come again next week to meet you, and in the meantime we'll do all we can to keep Robin from doing anything else stupid."

However, a week further on and it was Will and Gilbert breaking their news to Guy.

"We came because if I didn't get out of there I was going to punch Robin," Gilbert confessed, "and that would probably addle what little wits he's got left. He's not accepting any responsibility at all. He says he was making sure that Simon and Martin got away and that the other two were old enough to watch out for themselves. *Grrrr!* Like Colm or Ed have any experience of proper fighting? He should have checked. He should have looked back!"

Will gave a sympathetic growl, hinting that he too had been running out of patience. "I'm afraid he might make a move whatever we do," he said with a heavy sigh. "We actually tied him up at one point, but that puts a strain on everybody else because it means somebody has to take him to the latrines, and someone else has to watch them in turn in case he tries to jump the one helping him. ...And there's always the danger that he'll hoodwink someone into cutting him free, anyway." Will tactfully didn't say who, but Guy guessed he meant Much or one of the two Walesby boys. "It was easier to have him loose and just watch him. We've moved camp, and by now the others should have got him back up to Loxley, and up there he can scream and call us all the names he likes – there's only sheep to hear him."

"I'm afraid he's playing on everyone's liking for Ed and Colm," Gilbert said in disgust. "He keeps bringing up how easy it was getting into the castle back when we grabbed the carucage money, and to those who don't know any better it sounds plausible."

"Who?" Guy asked in despair.

"The three you might expect," Will answered resignedly, "but the two lasses don't have the tactical knowhow to see the flaws, and your John and Allan are being swayed too, I fear, but out of the kindness of their hearts towards the two prisoners. Your most vocal advocates aside from us two are Tuck, Siward and Roger. The Coshams are reluctant to go against your advice, but they've got faith in those big bows of theirs, and they're starting to think that if they can get close enough, that they'd be able to cover an escape if only someone can get in. Malik's trying to explain it all to Janah and Khalīl, but I think he's having trouble getting through to them the problems of entering the castle. Compared to the Templar fortresses in the Holy Land, from the outside Nottingham looks a relatively easy nut to crack, but they're forgetting that they don't have a whole troop of fellow well-trained turcopoles running alongside them but a misfit bunch, some with very limited fighting skills. If the others decide to go then I think those three will go too, if only to try and save some lives."

"Oh Christ on the Cross," Guy groaned and slid down the wall of *The Trip* to crouch with his head buried in his hands.

"Everythin' alright over there?" one of a group of visiting merchants called across, hearing Guy.

"Yeah, our mate's just had a bit more of the strong ale than he can hold," Will said with a dismissive wave, and the air of one who's hauled many a man home drunk as a lord. Then he bent down and put a comforting hand on Guy's shoulder. "Robin's too bloody good at playing on everyone's feelings, Guy. If he decides to try to break in, don't endanger yourself trying to protect him. You've put your neck on the block more than he deserves already."

"It's not Robin," Guy sighed, hauling himself wearily back to his feet, "it's the others! By the time the Assizes come around, the knights and their sergeants would be getting ready to go back home. The shine of being here will have worn off. They'll be bored and they'll be careless. But I need those extra few weeks for them to get into that state! Briwere's already bawled a couple of them out in public, and he'll do it to others as sure as night is day, and all of that discourages them from being any too enthusiastic in whatever he demands they do – do you see what I'm getting at? By the end of May I can do what I said I would, but I need *time*." He broke off and drew in a ragged breath. "But if Robin comes sooner, what happens if others get taken prisoner? I can't organise a mass break out from the dungeons! I can't rescue them all!"

Only later would Guy hear of the massive row within the outlaw camp which split them in two – firstly with Robin vastly outnumbered, and then gradually getting more and more to his way of thinking. Quite how Robin could be so obnoxious one moment and so able to twist people's emotions the next, Guy never could understand, but somewhere in the shouting and blame-throwing Robin got his way – they would try to affect a rescue from the castle.

The first he knew of it, though, was seeing a familiarly fletched arrow coming winging over the castle's palisade as he sought some solace up on the battlements of the older tower in which his room lay. At first he thought he'd imagined it, because he still hadn't been sleeping well, but when he saw a shadowy figure swarming over the outer bailey palisade he knew all of his nightmares had arrived in the flesh. Momentarily paralyzed in horror, he was just about to run for the stairs when it occurred to him that he might save some lives if he left a rope there. It was in a totally different section of the sprawling castle to the one anyone would expect men to try make an escape via because of the escarpment below, and that meant that if some of the outlaws could get here and run upwards, they could shin down the rope to the rocks beneath and get free.

Blessing the fact that he nowadays kept a rope hidden under an old sack ever since he'd had to meet Roger up here, he tied it off around one of the great blocks of battlement stone, but resisted throwing the rest over. If they didn't come this way it wouldn't do for someone on the outside to see the rope dangling, and report back that there was another way prepared to escape from the castle. Then he was off and running down the tight spiral of the tower's stair, across the inner ward and through to the inner bailey.

He had to slide to a halt and walk as softly as he could when he got to the buildings around the inner bailey, though, for the men-at-arms who had come with the knights to do service, and also their sergeants, were all bedded down on straw mattresses or on the benches in the main hall, and he couldn't afford to risk waking them. Halting behind the doorway into the hall, he frantically wondered how far the outlaws might have got? Could he intercept them? They had come over where the cliff was lowest by the stables into the outer bailey. That gave them a short run past the small barns where the supplies were kept, and where they would be unlikely to have run into anyone at this point in the small hours of the night, but they still had to get through the massively fortified inner barbican into the castle proper.

Had Briwere dropped the portcullis tonight? No, Guy thought not, if only because he knew he wanted to lure Robin Hood into the killing ground of the inner bailey where there was no easy wall to escape over. And if anybody was daft enough to try escaping down into the dry moat, the chances were that they'd still be there come the morning with broken ankles, given the ragged rocks down there. This was bad! Very bad!

And then he heard it, the first call of alarm from a guard, followed by the clanging of the bell Briwere had had installed in the guardroom of the main keep for just this eventuality. Immediately Guy heard the men in the hall start to cough, hawk and swear, as they were roused from their slumbers, and then the clumsy stumbling to their feet and grabbing of weapons. No chance to intercept his friends now, all he could do was limit the damage, but how?

Frantically casting about him and thinking furiously, Guy realised that he couldn't afford to get trapped behind the other men. There'd be no way any of the others would see his signals that way. He had to be above them, and that meant the castle walls. Turning off leftwards and hammering up a spiral stair as tight as the one he'd just careered down, he arrived up on the western wall of the castle above the great hall King Henry had built. That was good because nobody in the courtyard of the inner bailey could see him yet.

It took him until he was halfway along the wall to the main keep before he could see much, either, but then his blood ran cold as he saw the outlaws being backed up to the keep. They must have fought off the guards of the keep itself, but the extra men swarming into the bailey were more than they could hope to handle. And Mary, Mother of God! Was that Marianne and Mariota he could see at the back of their group and closest to the keep door? What had possessed Robin to bring *them* along? Had he no grasp of what their fate would be if caught? They wouldn't get a hanging, or at least not straight away. They'd be handed round the guards to be taught a lesson, and it was all Guy could do to not heave up his dinner at that prospect.

Worse, there was already such a racket going on down there that anything like their usual swift's-call warning would go unheard. In desperation he got a bit further along and then gave his sharpest whistle – the one he used when he wanted the dogs to come back from a distance. *Please hear that*, he prayed, then almost sobbed in relief as he saw Will's head whip round and upwards.

Nobody from the castle looked up and Guy was able to wave at Will to come up, gesturing frantically towards the two women. Blessedly, Will caught on straight away, and turned to yell something to Hugh, who took several steps back out of the line and began shoving the two women back to the keep door. The laughter from some of the guards said that they thought the trio were just going into the trap faster than the others, but Guy knew otherwise. He had scurried crab-like, low and fast, under the battlement shadows to the small door which gave out to the wall from the keep, and called down the stairwell, "Up here!"

Pounding feet told him that his friends had heard, but as soon as Hugh saw Guy he made as if to turn back.

"No, Hugh!" Guy cried urgently. "You have to make sure these two get out! They'll be raped until they die otherwise! Keep low! Go along this wall into the old keep. There's a rope you can get down by there. *Go!*"

To his relief, Hugh instantly grasped what Guy was trying to tell him, and hustled Marianne and Mariota past him, the three going almost on all fours to stay on the shadows, and Guy blessed the fact that the two women were wearing trews, not skirts which would have tripped them in no time.

He was about to try and signal again when he heard more feet and Janah and Khalīl appeared at the doorway, followed moments later by Malik. The three of them emerged onto the battlements, each going down on one knee, and then beginning to lay down a lethal rain of arrows. Yet that meant Guy couldn't risk staying there when eyes were now turned upwards.

Hissing the escape route to them, he ducked into the darkness of the keep and ran up to the top room of the keep, hoping like mad that he'd not imagined it that there was some rope abandoned up there, too, from when the workmen had been in. The room was never used by Briwere for anything on a daily basis, and it existed more in case the entire castle garrison ever had to withdraw into the keep in an emergency than for any everyday use, so it tended to accumulate junk and only get cleared once a year. Yes, there it was, a good length of stout rope! And Guy grabbed it and hared up to the battlement to make another hitch around the stone work. This rope didn't quite reach the ground, and whoever came this way would have to drop the best part of ten feet on to the shallow-sloping rocks, but beggars couldn't be choosers.

Pounding back down the stairs he almost collided with Allan and Roger coming up, and sent them upwards with a warning of the drop at the other end. Those two were light and nimble enough to cope, though.

At the last moment he thought to call after them, "Tuck and John?" and to his relief got a shake of Roger's head as he vanished. Thank God for that! How he would have got those two out was beyond him, for the ropes would never have taken their weight without the knots giving way. So who else was there? Will, for sure, and he was pretty sure he'd seen Gilbert's red hair as a hood had got shoved back. Siward would undoubtedly be in the fray somewhere, but what of the Coshams?

Then he heard a scream and then another, and a voice which he was sure must be Robin's howling in dismay. *Dewi Sant*, had someone died? "No, no, no," he found himself muttering in despair as he headed downwards to see Much cowering inside the doorway, paralysed by fear.

Reaching down, he grabbed Much by the scruff and hauled him upwards, snatching the bow and arrows off him as he did so.

"Upstairs! Go!" he snapped, and the sound of a familiar voice seemed to bring Much around a little, although he went up the stairs on all fours like a beaten dog, unable to pull himself upright.

Crouching in the stairwell, Guy drew the bow, realising that his own hands were shaking with the stress, if not as badly as Much's.

The call of, "Coming up!" in Will's voice saved him from skewering his friend, and when he appeared Guy flattened himself out of the way, calling softly, "Much is up there. One rope off here, but it's short. Another off the old tower."

Will gave a terse nod and pounded on.

Guy moved back up a couple of steps and heard more feet, but also Will's above him, then saw Will's shadow with Much over his shoulder heading out across the wall doubled up like some deformed, bulky dwarf.

"Who else?" Guy demanded as Gilbert and Siward appeared around the bend.

"Just Robin," Siward said through streaming tears.

"Hit me!" Guy told Gilbert, and the Irish knight knew what he meant and why and clipped Guy smartly on the cheekbone enough to leave a good bruise but without doing serious damage. Then as they took his directions upwards, he slid out onto the wall and dropped several arrows down into the inner bailey tight by the keep's wall, allowing the three turcopoles to slip away to the old tower without it looking too suspicious. He hadn't a good enough angle to hit anyone, but it did stop the castle men from swarming into the keep the moment the clashing of swords stopped and the keep door slammed shut, which Guy was sure meant that his cousin was on the way up.

Sure enough Robin appeared and for a heartbeat he looked at Guy with teeth bared savagely, spoiling for a fight. Then Gilbert's hand shot out of the darkness and pulled Robin upwards, at which point Guy threw Much's bow and the empty quiver over the wall, and did a fast scamper on all fours himself over to the middle of the wall but just above the great hall, at which point he threw himself down in what he hoped was a good imitation of a man who'd been knocked out. All he could do was wait until someone found him now, and he didn't have long to wait.

"Hey up, it's Sir Guy!" he heard Torwald, a knight who barely qualified as such and who came from a tiny manor in the far north of the shire, exclaiming. "He must have tried to stop them all by himself."

"Brave but bloody daft," another of the temporary knights said, at which point Guy felt he could legitimately make a few theatrical groans and start to come around.

By the time he got down to the great hall he was able to protest that he was fine, just a bit groggy, and refuse to go and join the other wounded. Even better, when Briwere demanded why he had tackled the intruders, Guy was able to bristle convincingly and remind the sheriff,

"I owe that bastard one for what he did to me at the tournament! The Devil take him, one of his men hit me as I was turning, then another one tripped me from behind before I could take my dagger to him! But I'll have the bastard yet, I swear I will!"

"Yes, yes," the sheriff smirked, "I'm sure you will, Gisborne, but your protestations would be more convincing if you didn't keep getting knocked out."

Shit! He would have to think of something else for the next time or he was also becoming too predictable, but Guy was able to splutter indignantly, "But I got hit from behind this time! That could happen to anyone!"

"Yes, but it happened to you," smirked Briwere, then adding with a glare to the others, "but at least you did your best, even if it's not much. What were the rest of you arse-kissing milksops doing? Twenty of you and soldiers, and yet all I have are two corpses? Unbelievable! You lot are a fucking disgrace!"

"They had Saracens with them," one of the temporary knights at the back said in awed tones.

"I don't care if they had the pagan lords of Hell and a dozen fallen angels!" Briwere roared. "How did they get away? Fly?"

"They found a rope up in the keep," someone else ventured, and suddenly Guy knew he had to go and untie the one in the old tower before that was discovered. The keep could be blamed on bad luck, because everyone knew there were building supplies up there unattended, but not in the other tower. That would reek of a man on the inside. And so shaking his head, albeit very carefully, Guy backed out of the hall, muttering to Sir Walter as he passed him that he needed the latrines.

Once out of sight, though, Guy took off like a scalded cat to the roof, where he undid the rope and coiled it up, taking it down and shoving it into the shadows behind the sacking which covered the old garderobe up on the top floor of the old tower. Then he ran like a hare down to the latrines in the lower part of the inner ward, convincingly fiddling with the laces on his trews as his old enemy Sir Henry came towards them.

"Loosened the bladder for you, did it?" sneered Henry, never one to miss an opportunity to have a go at Guy.

"I'm not the one who just got a bollocking off the sheriff," Guy pointed out with an evil grin, knowing how it must hurt Henry's pride to have to stand there and take that.

"Oh I didn't!" Henry smirked. "I was one of those who ran one of those little shits through. Two rats less in the nest to set the dogs onto, thanks to me and Sir Mahel! Better than you did, eh?"

Luckily Guy had already passed him and so Sir Henry didn't see his face at that news. Oh God, no! Two dead? He didn't have to fake looking pale now, and he walked through to the inner bailey, steeling himself for who it might be. Piers, Thomas or Bilan lying there might have him running for the garderobe for real, and none would sit easily with him. He feared one might be Balak, the former Templar feeling he had no choice but to come, but losing the will to fight at the worst moment. Blessed St Thomas, what a tragedy that would be for the poor man, having just found some peace.

But then he was into the inner bailey and the two fair-haired headed bodies lying in their own blood told him who they were without going any closer. Martin and Simon, the two lads from Walesby, lay dead on the cobbles. They were the ones who had screamed, and Guy felt a terrible anger building in himself towards Robin. Those lads had hero-worshipped him, would have followed him through the very gates of Hell if he'd asked, and this was how he'd repaid that loyalty.

Feeling sick as a dog, Guy headed back into the great hall to hear his name being called by Briwere.

"Gisborne? Gisborne, where are you?"

"Here, my lord."

"Right, let's see how good those hounds are at hunting! With first light I want you out with my kennelman and the greyhounds, and those two savages of mine you seem to have half-tamed. We're going on a man hunt!"

Blessed Saint Issui, I shall not forget that morning! At the first crack of dawn we took the dogs around to the northern end of the walls, and with all the knights and men-at-arms following us, Hubert the kennelman, his assistant, Godfrey, and I with Máel and Domnall, set to try and track the infamous Robin Hood. I should not by now have to tell you how I felt about that, yet along with all the inevitable feelings, there was a burning anger within me. How many more times would Robin put me in this dreadful position? What, by Our Lady, did he think I could do if we caught up with them?

I can still feel it now, Brother, after all these years – that desperation and outright fury that he would not believe me when I said that I would get Ed and Colm out somehow, and instead had launched his half-baked scheme at the castle which had got two naive and trusting lads killed as a result. In my eyes, nobody else was to blame for their deaths, and as I sit here making this confession to you, Gervase, I must own to a growing desire to catch Robin on that day. Just Robin, mind you, not any of the others, for I was starting to see that ˜Robin Hood˜ could successfully carry on without my insane cousin always being the man under the hood.

You are shocked. At what? Robin's perfidy towards the other outlaws? The pointless loss of two lives? Oh, I see, at my lack of loyalty to someone I professed to love and who was a great man. Now I must argue that point with you, Gervase, for by this time I do not think he was great at all. What was left by then was a shadow of the cousin I had once held so dear, and the stranger he had become was a very sick man, although hale and hearty to look at. But let me finish this part of my tale and you may see why I still become angry at this memory.

I thought about Hugh and those who had gone over the wall at the old tower, and hoped that they had had the sense to stay separate from Robin. And I also prayed that Tuck, John and the Coshams had heard the commotion and had realised that things had gone terribly wrong, and had not hung about too close to where we were heading. The dogs had certainly picked up on somebody's scent, and I belatedly realised that the bundle of cloth that Hubert had stuffed his hounds' noses into were Gilbert's hood, which he had shed somewhere along the way, and one of the smaller men's hoods; but I could not recall who that might have been until I remembered Roger going past me bareheaded on the stairs. Not Roger, I remember praying with every stride as I ran to keep up with the hounds, please Lord, do not let it be Roger that I catch.

North we ran, across the fields leaving the villagers of Radford barely rising from their slumbers to our west, and I began to fear that Robin was running straight for the camp near Hucknall we had been at only days before. That made my blood run cold, Brother, for my wolfhounds had been there with me you recall, and I feared there would still be their large paw marks in the soft mud of the small pool where they had gone to drink. We had had some dry days since then and the mud would have baked hard, so those imprints would still be there, and I had no illusions of Hubert having any loyalty towards me. He would spot them and would instantly know that only my giants could have made them, and then the game would be up, for he would surely call back to Briwere, who was riding behind us, and could I kill Hubert in cold blood to save my own neck? I knew I could not.

Then joy of joys, we reached where the River Leen was joined by the Day Brook, and in the reeds and boggy bits, suddenly the dogs lost the scent. We crossed the brook, but found no trace of anyone there, but Briwere was quick to direct us to get the dogs to the other side of the Leen, and on its far bank we picked up the scent again. However, in the mud of the far river bank I was gladdened to see only the footprints of three large men. Wherever Roger and – because they were inseparable – Allan had got to, at least it was not in front of us now.

I could breathe a bit easier in mind if not in body as I ran, now, for we were also on the other side of the Leen to the hideout, and that meant I was in less danger too. The tracks now swung towards Hempshill and Nuthall, and I recalled Allan telling me that there was a cluster of villages over this way who were very sympathetic to Robin. The ground also fell away more sharply beyond Kimberley, and in the rougher and more wooded ground there, no doubt Robin hoped to lose us, for surely by now he must know we were on his trail? He had had a couple of hours' head start on us to be sure, but had he reckoned on such a pursuit? I thought probably not. Overconfidence was Robin's weakness, and having once got out of the castle and away from its immediate vicinity, I could imagine him slowing those with him down to a steady pace, rather than keeping going as fast as they could.

After what I estimated must have been several hours, we reached the banks of the Erewash and the border between Nottinghamshire and Derbyshire – not that that would halt our hunt, for both shires were under Briwere's authority – but the Erewash was a bigger water course to cross for the dogs, at least, and by now the greyhounds were exhausted. I recall Hubert telling Briwere, ˜They can go no further, my lord, they must rest or you will kill them.˜

Greyhounds are wonders of speed over short distances, but we should have had rougher hounds for this work, of the kind Sheriff de Braose had over on the Welsh border. And so for a short time we stopped to allow men and horses, as well as the dogs, a brief respite from the hunt. But Briwere knew we had to have caught up with Robin Hood, and so while Hubert and Godfrey prepared to lead the greyhounds back, I and my wolfhounds were not so spared. ˜Come, Gisborne, show me what these brutes can do,˜ he demanded, and what could I do but continue?

Yet little over two miles on after we had crossed the Erewash, things came to a head in the stands of oaks around Shipley. The first I knew of it was hearing the distinctive thrum of a big wyche-elm bow and then Domnall screaming in pain as my beautiful big dog was impaled by an arrow. I ...I ran to him. ...Yes, Brother, I still weep over this. My beautiful dog had been transfixed through his noble heart, and before I could even think, my dearest Máel was being thrown back into me with an arrow piercing his side. Somewhere in my mental pain I heard a familiar voice screaming, ˜Robin, no!˜, but then another arrow hit Máel through his stomach and slammed into my leg, pinning me to him. We went down together, me trapped by his weight, for he weighed more than I did, and as I collapsed across Domnall, with Máel's dead weight across my legs, I felt the fletching of another arrow pass so close to me that the clipped, sharp edges of the feathers sliced my cheek.

I remember little else of the immediate aftermath for besides my leg wound I was distraught beyond belief. How could Robin do this? I would rather he had killed me than my dogs! I am told that two more arrows found their mark in two knights, throwing them from their horses with the force of them, but mercifully not killing either of them, although one was crippled for life. Briwere screamed at the men to attack, but fear created chaos, and by the time he had them back in something close enough to order for a proper attack, the woods had fallen silent and Robin Hood had escaped again. Later I was to learn that it was Robin, Gilbert and Siward whom we had been following, and that they had taken to the thick rushes surrounding a shallow pool in the woods and lain low, masked both visibly and by the strong dank smell, until Briwere gave up.

As for me, I was beside myself with grief. After all I had done to bring these two lovely beasts back to life, to have them so cruel cut down right before my eyes was too much for me to bear. I was grateful then for Sir Walter getting Sirs Giles and Thorsten with a couple of the more kindly men-at-arms to help extricate me from the bodies and to bind my leg wound, which was bleeding badly. It was Sir Walter who brusquely commandeered the cart from Shipley village for the bodies of Máel and Domnal to be loaded onto, so that they could be brought back to Nottingham and buried, not left for carrion, and I am told I rode home with them, fading in and out of consciousness.

In a bizarre twist, Briwere was suddenly incensed that someone should kill <u>his</u> dogs, despite his own treatment of them earlier, and was strangely sympathetic to my intense feelings over their loss, which put me in the incredibly strange position of feeling more of a kinship with this sometimes monstrous sheriff than with my cousin who had killed them. And I knew that it would have been Robin's arrows that did that. I knew that even in my grief. The voice of protest had been Siward's, and Gilbert had adored the two prize hounds from his homeland and would never have harmed a hair of them. My cousin did that. My cousin killed my friends. And now I must take a little wine before we continue, for even now the pain of that day cuts my soul like a knife.

Chapter 19

Now, what did you just ask me? What happened to the others? Ah... Well Allan and Roger, I learned, had feigned exhaustion to get away from Robin, for they, Siward and Gilbert realised that nobody had gone to warn Tuck, John and the Coshams to run. Those five had been stationed by Sneinton, a village so close to Nottingham it was almost in it, with the intention of them covering the others' escape, although Tuck and John had been left behind primarily because they were too heavy to be able to climb the wall at speed. And so Allan and Roger had taken to the water by the Day Brook, and washed their scent off for a mile along its course, before climbing out and running like deer for where the others were hiding. Praise be, none of them had been spotted, and indeed, once they saw the hunting party setting out, they guessed that those inside the castle were not coming out as planned, and had begun to move northwards with great caution along hidden ways they all knew anyway.

As for the rest of them, Hugh, Will and Malik had had the good sense to head southwest with their group, and to take to the marshes where the Erewash meets the Trent. They had a couple of cold, wet and hungry days on one of the muddy islets in the river, but they then made it back to Loxley by travelling at night and hiding up by day, and within a week, everyone was safely back there.

What happened once they got there, however, was anything but a happy reunion. Gilbert, Thomas, Will, Siward and Hugh were full of recriminations, reminding Robin that he had been warned about the sheriff, and yet had ignore those warnings solely because they had come from me. And when the others heard from Siward and Gilbert of how Robin had killed Domnall and Máel on top of the death of the two boys, I am told that he was expelled from the camp and told to go away and think about what he had done. The fact that every last one of the others united in this was a shocking awakening for him. Even Much had finally had the veil lifted from his eyes and would not even speak to Robin nor let him anywhere near him, and that must have been quite a blow to Robin's pride, for of everyone, Much had been the one who had been faithful without question. Sadly I think it was the death of my wolfhounds which was the last straw for Much, the thing that opened his eyes to Robin. I wish it had not had to be so.

Did they take Robin back? I am afraid that they did in a way, and in part it was because nobody spoke to me for several weeks, by which time it was too late and decisions had been made. You see, in the immediate aftermath of this terrible event, I took the opportunity to ask Briwere if I could go and visit my Gisborne manor. I had not been there in over two years since before the siege, and even Briwere acknowledged that if he had failed to capture Robin Hood, then at least he had given him a seriously bloody nose. Therefore with the castle about to take on the next influx of knights to take over their forty-day duties, if ever there was a time for me to go it was now, before the closing of the forest for a month on St Edmund's Day.

I just about managed to remember to ask Harry to take some dog bread to the prisoners in the dungeon, for I could not harden my heart towards poor Colm and Ed, who had been let down as badly as I had. In fact, I managed to creep down to them the night before I left and told them of what had happened. Of course their guards had taunted them with the deaths of Martin and Simon, but they had not heard of what Robin had done to me, and their grief over that was genuine.

So I departed for Gisborne knowing that this time round there would now be no chance of me getting Ed and Colm out during the assizes. The whole of the castle was buzzing like a beehive, and in some ways the safest place for those two was where they were. They knew that, too, but I felt no compulsion to let any of the others know. For once they had to see it for themselves, and in my head I was already thinking that if they made another insane rescue attempt when the assizes came around, then I did not want to be anywhere near the castle or be any part of it. Let them see what it was like without my help and cooperation, I thought bitterly, for it would surely be a rude awakening for many of them.

I made my way north and licked my wounds with Maelgwn and Ianto, who by now was a very weak old man, and with Elyas, who had grown into a fine young man and who was becoming an excellent reeve for me on my little manor under Maelgwn's tutelage. It did me good to see that my tenants had prospered too, and to learn that if the carucage money had been hard to find, it nonetheless had not crippled us as it had so many. Even the worst of the bad harvests had passed us by, and so if my folk were not getting fat, neither were they in any danger of starving – and that was something I needed to see as a salve for my *shattered soul, Gervase. I had to know that I, personally, had done some good in this world.*

I therefore only returned to Nottingham at the start of July, and was immediately swept up in the business of closing the royal forest for the deer's fawning season. I did not attempt to visit Loxley on my way back as I had done in the past, and I made no attempt to contact the outlaws, for much as my heart wished to see my friends, in my mind I knew that they had some decisions to make. It had gone on too long, this habit of me handing out warnings which I risked my neck to take to them, only to have them ignored because they did not fit with Robin's vision of how the world should be. Well no longer. Either they took into account my warnings, regardless of how Robin felt about that, or I would take them no longer. Or at least that was how I felt that summer in the depths of my distress.

In reality such detachment was harder to find, and not least because of Colm and Ed's continued presence in the dungeon. I could not fail to admire the fortitude and stoicism with which they bore their imprisonment, and then when the next assizes came around, Briwere had already been sent elsewhere to act as a judge on a different circuit in the impending eyre. This was the opportunity I needed, and as the castle filled up with prisoners for both courts, I was able to switch Colm and Ed for a pair of disreputable rogues who had been caught lifting purses in the market, but who had been too handy with their knives against the men-at-arms who brought them in not to be habitual brawlers at best – personally I believed that they had not been above slitting throats to cut purses, and so they went to the gallows in Colm and Ed's places.

And no, Brother, the sheriff did not spot the difference. Did you honestly think a man like him would recognise two peaseants after months in his dungeons, when he had never once bothered to look at them since the time they had come in? No, the only way that would have happened would have been if one of my substitutes had been missing an arm, or the like, and I was better at deceiving than that!

In the meantime, as prisoners were brought in and out of the dungeons, I managed to get Colm and Ed out of there and hidden away in the stable loft. The castle gates were closed and guarded for the duration of the assizes, for Briwere was not such a fool as to give anyone easy ingress, but it meant I could not let them out until afterwards, and I was in no hurry to use the rope over the wall again. So a day passed after the court ended, the gates reopened, the guards relaxed, and I saw my chance. And so I let my two friends out of the castle on a typically dark and rainy English September night, with directions as to how to get out of the town safely, and was about to go back into the castle when I heard someone softly calling my name.

Nottingham
Autumn, the Year of Our Lord, 1196

"Guy?" A moment later he was almost bowled over as someone launched themselves at him and wrapped their arms around him in a bear hug. "Christ, I thought he might have killed you!" Allan's voice came from his jerkin front. "We've kept coming and looking for you, and the longer we didn't see you the more worried we got!"

"I went to Gisborne," Guy said coldly. "Some of us have responsibilities we take seriously." His cousin's obvious distress touched him, but he was still too wounded to be able to just fall back into their old ways. Every day he had to walk past the empty kennel where his wolfhounds had been, meaning there was no fast moving on for him.

"Is Robin still at the camp?" Colm asked from back in the darkness. "Because if he is, I don't know that I want to go there. If he hadn't left us behind in the first place we'd never have needed rescuing, and given that we'd have starved to death long ago if it hadn't been for Guy, let alone out here, if we've got to choose between Robin or Guy, then we're with Guy every time."

There was a sudden torrent of Gaelic from another direction, signalling Gilbert's presence, and he and Colm could be heard having a vigorous discussion, but clearly they were in agreement, not arguing.

Meanwhile, as Ed added, "I'm with Colm on this,"

Siward's voice announced, "Robin is not at Loxley, if that's what you're asking."

Then as Guy turned to walk back into the castle, Siward emerged from the blackness to catch him by the sleeve. "Please, Guy, wait! You need to hear this."

"I'm not sure that I do or care," Guy said bitterly, but Siward wasn't letting him go, and Guy didn't have the energy to fight him.

"I tried to stop him, truly I did!" Siward's voice was thick with emotion. "Christ! Your hounds! I couldn't believe it! But I was in the next tree to him, and words alone weren't doing anything."

"You could have shot the bastard and saved us all the pain."

Allan's intake of breath came with him letting Guy go. "You don't mean that?"

"Why? He fucking shot me! It was only because I was falling under the weight of Máel that he didn't kill *me*. I've still got the fresh scar on my leg and I'm still limping from the one arrow. They had to cut its head out of me – Brother Hubert says it chipped the bone – and it may always ache in the winter from now on. And the fletching cut my face from the other. That's how close he came! And you expect me to care about him?"

Allan swallowed hard. "Christ on the Cross!"

"We didn't know he did *that*," Will's voice came from a little further back, "but I warned you lot that you shouldn't come here expecting Guy to welcome us with open arms. Robin went way beyond that back in May, and for the second time, too."

Allan's hand touched Guy's shoulder, but ever so lightly. "I'm *so* sorry, Guy, so very sorry. I had no idea."

"Not your fault," Guy muttered, dismayed at how easily his feelings towards his youngest cousin were warming again, despite all of his resolutions.

"No, it *is* our fault," Will said firmly, coming closer. "Several of us protested, but we didn't argue hard enough. Not as hard as we should've, anyway." He gave a grunt of disgust. "Anyway, we can argue about that 'til the cows come home. What you need to know now, Guy, is that we turfed Robin out of the camp when we got back. We sent him off to go and think about what he'd done. And you won't be surprised to hear that it took him well over a week to come back with his tail between his legs asking to be forgiven. But before you get too angry over that, we made a condition."

"We made several, actually," Siward interrupted.

"Yes we did. The first was that he had to accept some kind of punishment for what he'd done. Two people were dead, and he had to accept he was responsible for that – their blood on his hands, and no-one else's. Him, Robin, alone. Because without him pushing so hard, those two would never have gone into such danger. You warned him. You warned all of us – and we should have listened harder."

That was something of a salve for Guy. But Will hadn't finished by far.

"So the first thing we'd decided on before he came back was that if he did return, then he would be sent on a pilgrimage. We needed time away from him, too. Tuck picked it out. He has to go to Lindisfarne to the site of the monastery where Saint Cuthbert preached. It's out on an island you can only get to on a causeway, and it's cut off from the world by the tide twice a day. He's to stay there, or at the nearest monastery, until Christmas.

"If he wants to come back after that, then he has to bring back a pilgrim token to show that he's been there. If not from the island – because Tuck says that they are rebuilding some of the priory, and he's not sure if they accommodate pilgrims fully yet – then Tuck said he must get a token from the monastery at Jarrow, which Tuck believes is the nearest one big enough to give pilgrims tokens, or we won't believe him. If he appears much before Candlemas, he'll have to be very convincing that he's not just gone through the motions and then come haring back as soon as he could, but actually done it in the spirit of our intentions."

Guy had to admit that they had taken Robin's behaviour seriously this time, and it sounded as though, having realised that he could no longer in conscience hear Robin's confessions, that Tuck had sent him to men who could. If Robin chose to lie to them about his guilt, then there was nothing anyone could do about that, it was out of their hands. But there was one other thing gnawing at Guy.

"What of the villagers?" he asked guardedly. Not a single court had been attacked since they had parted company, and while Guy was relieved over that, he was also realistic enough to know that the outlaws didn't have a bottomless fund of money to hand out. "Have they been left to fend for themselves?"

"Ah," Will said with a chuckle.

Guy was taken by surprise by that. "Ah?"

Will's voice was suddenly much more cheery. "Well we've changed our tactics a bit."

"A lot, actually!" Allan interrupted.

"Yes, we knew the courts would be suicide to attempt. You were absolutely right, Guy, we'd become horribly predictable, and with the courts being held in only four places we should have seen that one coming for ourselves." Will's voice got a little gruff. "We all agreed on this: we apologise ...without reservation. We're truly sorry for not valuing what you told us. If *we* had, we might not have been so easily swept along by Robin – we all see that now."

With a deep sigh, Guy knew that he had to be gracious and accept that apology. For men as experienced in war as the likes of Will and Gilbert to eat humble pie over a matter of tactics was a huge concession, and Guy found himself not wanting to throw their friendship away for the sake of his pride.

"Thank you," he said with all the grace he could muster, and was startled to hear the sighs of relief from all round.

"We weren't even sure you'd accept the apology," Siward admitted. "Several of us warned that you'd been hit so hard on account of us that it might take some forgiving." That was a tactful reference to his hounds, of course, but the fact that some of them had realised the depth of his hurt, did a lot to dissipate any anger he was feeling towards anyone other than Robin himself.

"And as for the villagers," Will continued, "we launched a few raids over into Lincolnshire – not for coin but for grain. We talked it through and we realised that if we gave the villagers money, we'd have to give them so much to afford wheat at its current price it would drain our reserve, and there was always the danger of someone asking how half-starved tenant farmers could suddenly come up with so much coin. But in Lincolnshire, on that rich earth, they've had a good harvest – good enough that their lords are due to turn a huge profit this year when what's in the manor and tithe barns gets sold, because of the scarcity of wheat in other parts. So we've done several forays, split into two groups, and raided a different tithe barn each time and kept the pattern scattered."

"And we never took the lot," Gilbert added. "Each time we only took what we thought a particular village would need to sow a good crop, and to keep themselves in just enough bread to get through the winter." He sighed. "It was harsh, on us and them, but we thought long and hard about what you've said to us in the past about how the sheriff looks at things, and it came to us that villagers looking *well*-fed would seem every bit as suspicious as if they suddenly had sacks of money."

Guy could feel himself choking up. At last! At last they had finally woken up to what he had been trying to tell them over and over again, and that made a huge difference to him as to how he felt about them. Yet there was more.

"We've also taken our raids over into Yorkshire," Will said, his voice filled with relish at what they'd done. "There's a cracking good spot just above the little River Went that looks out over the Great North Road after it's crossed the River Aire, and before it gets to Doncaster. You can see people coming from a long way when you're up on the big bank there, and it's covered in trees, so you can't be seen. You'll remember it from when we brought the Jews out of York, because it's where you caught up with us.

"So we've been extracting a tithe for going into Sherwood." He chuckled. "Well not exactly a tithe in the true sense – not a tenth! We've relieved merchants and rich folk of their purses, nothing else, just their purses. What you said in Keyworth stuck with those who were with you, about how on earth you'd ever sell on the rich clothes and stuff."

Siward agreed. "By Our Lady, Guy, you were so right. How in God's name we never saw that before, I don't know – too befuddled by Robin's charm, I suppose. We've got one of the old part-ruined cottages up at Loxley filled with stuff we can't shift – we surely don't need anymore! Robin would have stripped those merchants of everything we could carry, but it's not worth it, is it? It's the coin we need, so why not just take that? And then we realised that if we left them their goods and livelihoods, then we could 'tax' them again the next time they come through with purses fat from one of the fairs at York or wherever."

And before he could stop himself, Guy was adding, "Even better, the sheriff's hardly heard a word of these raids, you know. In the castle we've not heard a thing about Robin Hood all summer." Damn it, he'd been sucked in again! Yet it didn't feel so very bad when it was those he still thought of as friends. And if they were keeping things this quiet, then he wasn't going to be walking on eggshells all the time dreading he'd be called upon to hunt the down.

"Ah, the Robin Hood thing," Gilbert was saying, also with much amusement in his voice. "Well the thing is, we realised that we didn't need 'Robin' to do or say much every bloody time. All we needed was for someone to stand there, all in green with his face covered by his hood, and seem to be directing things. So since we've already set it up that 'Robin Hood' is a tall bloke, but not chunky like John or Tuck, it's been mainly Hugh or Siward here wearing the hood..."

"...Although Gilbert had some fun as him swearing in Irish at some very pompous and un-Christianly wealthy canons who we relieved of their heavy pockets," Allan added with a laugh. "They went off crossing themselves repeatedly and muttering prayers like they hadn't done for what we guessed might be a long time!"

That was it, Guy couldn't help but laugh out loud at the thought of Gilbert putting the fear of God into those too-worldly canons who possibly thought they'd been visited by the Devil, and he knew he was back on their side despite all of his reservations. The logical side of him was still cautious, but for now he was prepared to go along with them and see how things stood until Robin came back – if he did.

As a result, the year rolled by and Guy heard very little of Robin Hood in the castle, but when out on his travels through the forest he heard whispers of food and money being handed out, if not with the same dash and flair as before, then on a more subtle and widespread scale. The woodmotes and swanimotes passed without incident, and so did the assizes, and for the first time in what felt like a very long time, Guy began to relax a little. Reports of wealthy travellers being waylaid in Sherwood filtered through periodically, but again, they presented such a contrast to the dramatic holdups when Robin had been leader that most were just ascribed to random outlaws, not the most famous one.

In fact, Guy's biggest problems came once again from within the castle, for King Richard had announced that another carucage would be levied before 1196 was out to help fund his campaigns in Normandy, and that worried everyone, even Briwere. Knights, they were informed would have to pay scutage to avoid having to go and fight in person in Normandy, and since there were few real fighters left, everyone knew that what the king really wanted was their money to hire mercenaries, not their presence over there.

"God's hooks! Where does the bloody king think we're going to find this money?" Briwere demanded of everyone and no-one as they assembled to hear the demand letter read out by one of the scribes. "There's nothing left to take! We'll all be starving in the gutters at this rate if we have to send what little grain we have to be sold abroad – and it'll have to be in Flanders or France because nobody here can afford the prices!"

It was the beginning of October and Briwere had returned from the Michaelmas court in a foul mood. The Honour of The Peak had been in his hands for a while now, although he only went there sporadically, and the castle was run for him by his beremaster, John Buche. That was the reason why Briwere thought honours were desirable, and that The Peak paid its way just like any other; never for one moment suspecting that the folk up there had been regularly sending less than what they had actually mined to market, in order to keep some back for when times were hard. Consequently, last year Briwere had tried to get his hands on what he perceived as one of the other lucrative honours in the region, and had found out this time at court that he had been outbid by Eustace de Morton for Peveril, and worse, had been completely overlooked by the king who had granted Tickhill to one of his mercenaries from Normandy, one Robert de Veteripont.

"A bloody mercenary captain, I bet!" Briwere had fumed. "Veteripont? Where, by St Thomas, has he come from? That's not a name of a proper manor or castle, is it? Not even in fucking Normandy! What is he, some Flemish hired killer?"

"He could be from somewhere like Savoi or Genoa or Rome?" ventured Sir Mahel unwisely.

"Then he's still a bloody *foreigner*, isn't he?" Briwere shrieked back. "What's he done to warrant such a reward? Scaled the bloody heights of some Normandy castle on his own? Oh, no! He's got rich on plunder, you mark my words! He's filled his grubby pockets with treasures from the Holy Land or somewhere, and now he's carving a patch for himself out of *my* shire!"

By now the sharper knights within the castle knew to keep quiet on the matter, realising that what Briwere had hoped would be a profitable venture into the Midland shires was now barely breaking even, thanks to the king's demands, and Briwere had probably never managed to recoup the money he had forked out for his position here. So no wonder he was bitter at being outbid – hence the constant jibes about wealthy Flemings and Frenchmen.

"Well we'd better hope that the eyre brings some decent fines in," Briwere declared, and Guy felt his blood run cold. This was when it would be a real test of what 'Robin Hood' could still do, because Guy had a nasty feeling that the forest fines were going to be crippling.

Mercifully, Briwere left the next day, still fuming, and when Hugh Bardolf, the sheriff who was about to move from Yorkshire to Westmoreland and Northumberland, rode into the castle to conduct the first court of the eyre in the town, it was Guy who found himself summoned to Bardolf's presence to answer questions about the royal forest crimes and fines.

"Is this right?" Bardolf asked in what sounded very much like disbelief. "Roger de Normanton is charged twenty pence? What for?"

Guy could understand why Bardolf was challenging this. Twenty pence was no small amount, but equally, as normal criminal fines went it wasn't that much either. On paper it looked odd.

"Illegal clearing of the forest, my lord sheriff," Guy answered calmly.

"*Hmph.* ...And Henry fitz Thomas the same amount for presumably the same?"

"Yes, my lord sheriff."

Bardolf looked up at Guy, still standing formally before him and waved him to the other leather chair. "For God's sake, man, sit down," he said kindly. "You're making me feel uncomfortable just watching you!"

Surprised, Guy took a seat and scrutinised this new sheriff. Bardolf was noticeably older than Briwere and reminded Guy a lot of Ralf Murdac, and of course Guy had met him – albeit briefly – several times back in those days of increasingly happier memories. Could they have been lucky enough this time as to get one of the few blessedly competent survivors from King Henry's reign on their eyre? Certainly Bardolf had an eye for detail, and by the time they had moved on from the forest fines to matters such as one William de Bellofago and others being brought before the eyre for selling wine contrary to the assize, Guy was glad he had been able to read the charges for himself – something Bardolf picked up on.

"You're very well informed, young man. How's that?"

"I can read, my lord sheriff."

"Blessed St Thomas, man, you don't have to be so formal with me in private!" Bardolf said with mock exasperation. "As simple 'sire' will suffice, you know," and he peered up from the hand-held lens through which he was scrutinising the parchments. He tapped the lens with a finger. "Had this made by one of the Jews in London, you know. I sorted a matter out for him, and out of gratitude he presented me with this."

He gave Guy a wink. "Very useful when you get to my age, I can tell you. Unlike your sheriff, I too can read, which is why the king made me one of the men to oversee the affairs of the Jews in England. They are too valuable to him for them to be so persecuted that they leave and take their considerable loans with them to elsewhere."

Bardolf leaned back in the chair and gazed thoughtfully at Guy. "It's a rare ability, being able to read. Yet your name was not mentioned to me as one of the leading knights in the castle by Sheriff Briwere. Why is that?"

Guy was warming to this sharp old man with every question.

"I'm afraid he doesn't think me much of a knight, sire. My father was a very lowly knight over on the Welsh borders in King Henry's day, and since then I've had to work to earn my keep. My manor is a very humble place over in Lancashire."

"Lancashire? Then why, by all that's holy, are you serving the sheriff here?"

"Because I did something which pleased King Henry, and he decided that if I came and did service here it would be taken as payment for what Earl Ranulph owed him. I cannot tell you more of the matter, sire. I gave my word to the old king that I'd keep silent, and I've no wish to break that vow."

"How long ago?" Bardolf asked.

"Oh back in …1185," Guy answered, suddenly blinking in shock to realise that he had been here in Nottingham for eleven years now. It threw him off balance enough that he added, "I was working for

Sheriff de Braose in the Marches at the time," before it struck him that perhaps he'd given too much away. He had.

"Oh ...you're *that* knight, are you?" Bardolf said, smiling. "Ah, that makes more sense. But does Briwere know this?"

"No, only that I was knighted at the old king's personal request."

Bardolf chortled. "Oh, I bet that's had him worried a few times, and I'm guessing that you don't play the courtly games and try to ingratiate yourself with him? You don't look like the sort who would."

"No, sire, I don't. I'm quite happy being a forest knight. I'd rather be out in Sherwood than in some court. I was a good huntsman to sheriff de Braose, and now I also fulfil the role of coroner here, alongside Sir Hugo Bassett and Sir Sewel fitz Henry."

"One of the new coroners, eh? As a former huntsman I would bet on you doing a good job at that."

"Sheriff Briwere doesn't always think so."

"No I'm sure he doesn't!" Bardolf laughed. "I don't see you allowing a charge of murder to go through just because it brings in more fines."

"No, sire." *Dewi Sant*, Guy thought, *has he been a fly on the bloody wall, or something? He surely seems to know an awful lot!*

However, Bardolf was moving on, and before he knew it, Guy found himself being requested to shepherd this very different sheriff and judge around the shires, which Sirs Walter and Martin readily agreed to, and that was how he came to be on the scene when things took a turn for the worse at the court in Derby.

Twelve local jurors were standing in the wool merchant's hall where the court was being held, quaking in their boots before Sir Hugh Bardolf, which was something Guy didn't take much notice of having got so used to that whenever Briwere appeared in public. So it was only when Bardolf declared,

"So Sheriff Briwere is intending to take this house into the hands of the crown. Can you confirm that the late Peter of Derby's son wrongly holds this manor and should be disseized of it?" that Guy suddenly sat upright in shock at the answer the leading man made.

"Yes, my lord," the man answered tremulously. "'Tis said that it was his wife's family's, and not his heirs to have after their deaths seeing as they're his first wife's children, not hers."

Guy blinked in shock. He didn't know many of the people in southern Derbyshire, but Peter had been one of the humble knights who came to do their forty-day service at the castle, and Guy knew that his father and grandfather before him had come to do the same, which implied that the manor from which the service was due had always been in Peter's family. Why were the jury lying?

And then it came to him. Briwere had long admired the house the family had in the town. Had he put pressure on these jurors to testify to that effect? As a widow, Rametta would have to ask for permission to marry when there was property like that at stake, and no doubt Briwere had been going to ask for the house as his payment to give his consent as the king's local representative, but had now found a way to both have it and still get paid.

Guy looked at the twelve men, all of them local merchants and farmers whose land was close to Derby and all of them needed access to Derby's markets. Just by refusing them permission to trade, Briwere could ruin every one of them.

"My lord sheriff," Guy said urgently, "may I have a word?"

Hugh Bardolf turned to him quizzically, but beckoned Guy nearer. Whispering in the old man's ear, Guy told him of his suspicions, but Bardolf could only shake his head.

"I can do nothing, Gisborne. Unless these men confess to being coerced and having been subjected to illegal duress, I have to take their word for it. And do you want to risk ruining all twelve just so that one widow can keep the family's second house? She's not going to be homeless, is she? She'll still have the manor house out with the land."

Guy grimaced and then turned and looked back at the twelve, at which point he saw their panic-stricken faces. Pleading eyes were turned on him, and he knew that if he didn't allow this to go ahead then Briwere would not bother asking why, he'd just assume that the twelve had disregarded his orders and punish them accordingly. And Briwere would want to punish somebody if he didn't get his own way, Guy realised, and the sheriff could hardly vent his anger on Bardolf, who was if anything even more highly placed within the hierarchy surrounding Archbishop Walter than he was.

Sighing, Guy sat down and let the travesty go ahead. Afterwards the leading tanner of the town, who had been one of the jurors, sought Guy out.

"I'm sorry, Sir Guy, we had no choice," he began.

"What did Briwere threaten you with?" Guy asked, making the man blink with shock that Guy had worked it out already.

"No access to the Nottingham fairs, refusing permission for my daughter to marry, for Harold's mother to hand the business on to him, everyone except Ralph from Litchurch and Henry from Mackworth had something personal he found he could use, and for them it was simply that Briwere would fine anyone who traded with them if they didn't comply. We were told to present ourselves for this case, we had no option. He said if we didn't, he'd be sending knights and soldiers here regularly to make sure what he'd threatened got carried out."

Guy felt that, knowing who Briwere would send, the chances of them knowing one farmer from another were beyond slim, but of course that could mean that some complete innocent could fall foul of his plots, and those two farmers and the other jurors would know that too. It was ruin for them or their neighbours, maybe both, and in a close community like here that probably meant that everyone was related in some way to each other, so it would be their own or their in-law's family they'd be dragging down, not some stranger's. And in that moment Guy knew that he would be going to his friends to ask for their help in persuading Briwere to undo the damage he was making.

Three more sittings of the court further on and his anger was being stoked into an inferno. In every court there had been one case where the jurors had blatantly been got at to testify falsely, and in all three – as with the Derby case – it involved property which could be acquired by Briwere in the aftermath of the courts. Property which would go some way towards compensating Briwere for what he perceived as his losses. But there had to be a way to reverse all of them if he could only think how.

In all other respects, though, the eyre was a total contrast to the previous one, and at every court Guy became more impressed with Hugh Bardolf. The old man was hard but scrupulously fair, never handing down a sentence more than the crime demanded, and by the time Guy handed him over to Sir Richard who would take him around the Nottingham courts, he was genuinely sorry to see him go. If only Bardolf would come to Nottingham and Briwere be the one to be sent elsewhere, life would actually be tolerable.

Yet with his duties fulfilled, Guy now had chance to head northwards under the pretext of checking the forest for illegal felling and hunting in this closed season, for by now it was into November. And so he heeled his horse on to Loxley, and approached the camp with great trepidation, where, to his immense relief, there was no sign of Robin. Instead, he was greeted with great delight by his friends, and when he told them of what had happened, they were all eager to help.

"What do you want us to do?" Siward asked.

Guy gave a big sigh. "I wish I knew! To be honest I just wanted to come and talk this out with you first. By myself I'm coming up with a few ideas, but they're not stringing together into anything meaningful. Ideally we need one big gesture. Something that will make Briwere realise that he's not going to get away with this, and abandon the whole scheme without us having to go and haul him out of every house and farm he's grabbed. I'm just not sure what that is."

It was Roger who piped up with, "I fink he needs a fright, like what we did wiv vhat prior!"

"That's not a bad idea!" Marianne immediately approved. "If we really frighten him once, it might be enough."

"We can't just duplicate what we did at Felley with Prior Henry Gretwold and sub-prior Galf Furmentin, even if it is four years ago," Guy warned, "and not just in case people remember. Briwere's not a man who will be so struck down by Tuck's fury!"

Tuck agreed. "We need to think of something that will hit him where it hurts – his pockets or his pride. But I think Roger's right. We should strike at night when he's most likely to be alone. Which place do you think he'll go to first, Guy?"

"Oh, without a doubt the Derby house! He's wanted a place of comfort to go to when he's in Derby ever since he got here. As you know, there's no castle anymore at Derby because the old motte might still be there but the timber castle fell down years ago. So there's no place of prestige for Briwere to stay in if he has more than one day's worth of business to deal with there. Yes, I think he'll go to that place first of all of them. The others are just financial gains, but that one's personal."

"And where's the house?" Will queried.

"On the Gayle, by the corn market," Guy told them. "It's right in the middle of the town."

"Does it stand alone?" Gilbert wondered.

"It's in a row of houses," Guy said thoughtfully, "but it's not one propped up by its neighbours either. Unlike the houses on either side, the ground floor is built of stone – that's why Briwere wants it, because it's secure – and then the upper floor is timber and infill, but of course it rises above its neighbours' roofs."

Gilbert gave a wolfish grin. "So if Briwere is up there in his bed, his neighbours won't hear his screams for help through the walls?"

Guy grinned back. "Not unless he shouts very loudly! And if you were to do something like that, I might suggest you do it on a Wednesday when the cattle market is due to take place. People expect to hear a certain amount of commotion as the cattle start coming into the town in the early hours. There's one due in three weeks as they're only held once a month, and Briwere is likely to be back by then and wanting to inspect his new prize."

Marianne was smiling broadly as she asked, "So we know when. Now what are we actually going to do?"

Thomas cleared his throat. "I think we need to frighten him. You publicly humiliated him back at Keyworth, Guy, but taking what you've often said to us into account, how many times can we do that before someone higher up starts to see him as ineffective and replaces him, and with whom?"

Guy's relieved expression signalled that Thomas had hit another nail on the head. "Yes, exactly! You may not have heard this, because the man actually in Tickhill Castle at the moment hasn't changed, but it looks as though King Richard has granted it to one of his mercenary captains, Robert de Veteripont, either as a reward, or the bastard has got hold of enough plundered goods and coin to pay for it – either way it isn't good! He's a complete unknown, but given the circumstances, he could be the very sort of man I was warning you about earlier in the year – someone who will turn up with his hardened soldiers, strip the place and then go, not caring about what he leaves behind. Now if you were in the king's boots, who would you send in if Briwere, the experienced court man, fails?"

Will was nodding in agreement even before Guy had finished. "We could fight him and win, because this Veteripont is unlikely to come with more than a dozen men, but we can't afford to have an all-out war on our hands. Like you said, Guy, the king won't stand for that, and if we hammer Veteripont as well as Briwere, we're just asking for King Richard to put his plans for Normandy to one side for a month or two and come and scour the shires like the Conqueror did."

"And God help the ordinary people then!" Hugh said from the heart. "My family still have memories handed down of what that was like. No, we definitely don't want that!"

Yet it was Aneirin, the master bowyer, who came up with the best idea. "You have enough of us who speak the Celtic tongues," he said with a mischievous glint in his eye. "Now you know the language, Guy, but does Briwere? Would he know that what he's hearing is Welsh?"

"I doubt it. He'd never seen a Welsh bow until I showed him one, and you'd think if he'd been anywhere near Wales he'd have seen one of them."

"So would he think it the Devil's tongue?" Aneirin asked with feigned innocence. "Enough maybe to frighten him out of his skin? Tuck preaching the right path he might ignore, but if he was visited by devils...?"

Suddenly Malik was chuckling too. "And now there are three of us who speak the tongue of the Holy Land, too. Even if he knows what that is, would he not be fearful of it if heard in his bedchamber?"

"Probably enough to soil his fancy silk braes," Guy chortled. "Oh yes! I like this idea!"

Tuck had been staring off into the distance, deep in thought, but now added, "I think it wouldn't hurt if we gave him a bit of help. There are some interesting mushrooms growing in the forest at the moment. Some are poisonous, of course, and we don't want those, but there are others whose effects would make Briwere feel ...hazy. Enough so that he would believe what he was seeing and hearing rather more than if he was fully comprehending, you understand."

Guy looked dubiously at his old friend. "Great idea, Tuck, but how would you get it to him?"

However Tuck was already ahead of him there. "Well I can't imagine Peter of Derby's widow being enamoured of the situation, and her poor servants even less. Would you want the sheriff as her replacement unless she's an absolute harridan?"

"No," Guy conceded, "and if what I've heard is true, she's actually a rather nice lady, which is why she's not short of suitors."

Tuck beamed beatifically. "Then I think that we should slip into Derby and arrange for Allan and Roger to replace a couple of the household servants before Briwere gets there."

"Or better," Will said with a more wicked grin, "let Briwere be introduced to his staff as they are, and then on the night in question swap Allan and Roger in, 'cause they'll never get as far as serving at the table, will they? Some older woman or bloke will do that. All they have to do is get in close enough to dose the wine Briwere's going to drink."

"And it would be enough to steep the mushrooms in some wine," Tuck added. "We don't want him so out of his head that he can't remember anything of the night, just doped enough to be gullible. So yes, we'll use some of that nice rich French red we've got hidden away in the far cottage, dose one lot in a small flask, and then send a larger unadulterated amount for Briwere to have as his first drink so that he doesn't suspect anything."

Guy was grinning too, now. "And Briwere will be drinking to his success. That's one thing he does do! I've never seen him look at a woman with much interest, and he's not a glutton, but good wine, especially, is his downfall."

In fact it had to wait until the cattle market just before Christmas, as Briwere was detained by his duties on eyre, and did not come back until four weeks after he was expected. He was then snowed under with matters requiring his attention in Nottingham, and so it was almost the festive season before he got away and went to relish his new acquisition. That had worked in the outlaws' favour though, as Allan and Roger had frequently visited Nottingham and had been kept up to date by Guy on these matters, and it had given them time for 'Robin Hood' in the form of Hugh to visit Rametta, Peter of Derby's widow, and explain to her how they were going to get her house back to her. Rametta had been only too willing to go along with the plan, and so happily took herself off to the humble country manor which she still owned, and Allan and Roger got introduced to the workings of a modestly wealthy household.

As a result, when Briwere strode in through the front door, everyone was prepared. Sigeberht, Rametta's senior man in the household, ingratiated himself with the sheriff as if he was expecting to have to live with this dreadful man turning up at frequent intervals, and the following day the cook prepared the demanded rich meal to be served to their new lord and master. The duck was soused in the drugged wine, and everyone else warned not to touch it. Meanwhile Sigeberht took in a large silver flask of the French wine, declaring it to be the last of his master's best.

Briwere, of course, promptly drank heartily of it, and when he called for more, Roger slid into the small hall in the shadows behind Briwere's chair, filled the decorated chalice that Sigeberht held out with the drugged wine, and flitted out again before Briwere even knew he was there. The night drew on, Briwere began to feel drowsy, but ascribed it to the heavy meal and wine, and retired to the bedroom which shared the upper floor with the beautifully painted little hall. Meanwhile, the servants retreated downstairs and locked themselves away, blessing the fact that their sleeping quarters were at the other end of the house to the bedroom as well as one floor below it. All, that was, except for Allan and Roger, who tiptoed upstairs and stationed themselves outside of Briwere's door. Once they heard him tossing and turning and starting to mutter in his sleep, Allan slipped downstairs and opened the back door and the outlaws slid in.

The next thing Briwere knew, he was awoken by unholy chanting coming from around his bed, and peeled open drowsy eyes to see nine cloaked and shadowy figures arranged around his bed.

"*Aaaagh!*" he squealed, eyes bulging in terror as the effects of the mushrooms made the figures seem to writhe.

Tuck had managed to get his hands on some incense, and Malik had got small amounts of charcoal burning in a couple of proper little incense dishes hung by chains – which had been liberated from some wealthy monks in Sherwood – held by someone on each side of the bed, to which they then added the incense. These were now smouldering well and adding to the atmosphere, for the only incense

Tuck had been able to get was the one used in churches to mask the scent of rather pungent corpses. Alongside that they had added three tiny candles back against the walls of the room, which gave just enough flickering light for the sheriff to see the figures and cast some strange shadows. The overall effect was quite ghoulish.

Chanting in unison, but in four different languages, the outlaws declared, "William Briwere, you are a sinner! We will come for you! You have wronged these people. You have wronged this widow. God sees all! But the Devil is watching you! You have forced men to break their vows to tell the truth. God hears! God knows! But the Devil will take you! Their sins are on you now. Repent while you can! Give it back. Give it all back. The Devil is everywhere. He is watching. He is waiting. He is waiting for you! We will come again. We will come for you!" They took it slowly, Gilbert and Colm to the sheriff's right chanting in Irish; Malik, Janah and Khalīl on his left chanting in Arabic; and Thomas, Piers and Bilan towards the foot, speaking Welsh; with Tuck in the centre of the footboard speaking in heavily accented English, for they had all agreed that there had to be some English in there so that Briwere would recall what had been said.

As soon as they had finished they all spun round together, blew out the candles, and slipped through the door which Allan closed silently after them. Silent in bare feet, the outlaws hurried downstairs and to the cellar, where they could let their mirth rip, but Allan and Roger remained on duty watching. When they thought the sheriff had finally drifted off into a deep sleep again, they all repeated the performance.

This time Briwere was less sleepy but the drug had got further into his system.

"*Aaaagh!* Who are you? What do you want?" he challenged them, but there was only fear, not aggression, in his voice. "Go away! Be gone! *Noooo!* Don't come closer!"

"*Fucheddoch i mewn arswyda chan 'n dragwyddol damnedigaeth,*" Tuck declared in his powerful voice, "*achos Celi ewyllysia na 'n bellach drugarhau arnat.* May you live in fear of eternal damnation, for God will no longer have mercy upon you!" And then they began all over again, only they had added just the tiniest pinch of sulphur to the incense this time, just enough for Briwere to be able to smell it.

"The fires of Hell are waiting for you!" Tuck pronounced at the end, and again they vanished.

This time, Allan wedged the door shut slightly, for as they expected, Briwere stumbled out of bed and blundered to the door, heaving and tugging at it in his panic. When it finally opened with a lurch, it was enough to send him flying backwards to the bed, thumping against the wooden box of it, and missing his footing to step neatly into the piss-pot he had availed himself of before turning in. Still dizzy and swearing furiously, Briwere finally got himself back into bed, taking a long swig of what he thought was weak beer in the pewter mug beside his bed, but which had also been dosed with water the mushrooms had been steeped in. Nobody was taking any chances of Briwere coming to his full senses.

By now Roger was the only one not so helpless with suppressed laughter as to be incapable of silence, and still able to go up and keep watch.

"*Duw*! His sins will find him out," Tuck giggled happily down in the cellar. "Straight in the piss-pot! There's lovely! There's justice!"

By the time Briwere got off to sleep again the outlaws knew they didn't have long before dawn, and they would have to make a swift retreat from the house to allow the servants to say in all truth that they had seen nothing. Therefore Tuck, as one of the slower runners, now left to join those waiting out in the fields, but the outlaws were determined that Guy should have a piece of the fun.

"Don't worry, he won't see you," Janah said with relish, and as they got upstairs Guy discovered why. Out in the hall they got a couple of pieces of oil-soaked rag smoldering nicely, just enough to make good thick smoke, and as they filed in Janah and Thomas swirled them around so that the bedroom had trails of smoke swirling around it even before Briwere opened his eyes.

Bending over ever so slightly under his cloak so that he was the same height as the others, Guy also pitched his voice as low as it would go and told the quivering sheriff with a growl,

"You must give this back to the widow. You must give it all back! You lied, sheriff! You made other men lie too! Your soul will be forfeit!" and then the others joined in with the main chant again.

Driven to distraction by these apparitions, Briwere hurled himself out of bed at Malik, but he simply side stepped and whisked his cloak out of the way of Briwere's grasping fingers. As Briwere fell to his knees with a thump, those on that side of the bed made their exit first into the blackness of the hall, where not even the moon shone in, as the windows had their shutters up against the winter night's chill. Tottering to his feet, Briwere tried to grab hold of another of the ghostly figures, but it too eluded his grasp and flittered out of the room.

Panicked, Briwere turned around, found himself now alone and made a stumbling run for the door. As his nightshirt sleeve caught on the door latch it spun him around, and as he lost his footing altogether, he head-butted the doorframe, saw stars for a moment and then totally blacked out.

"Turn him on his front," Guy said softly. "I don't want him choking on his own puke when he comes around – that would defeat the whole object of tonight."

Allan nimbly stepped over the sheriff and replaced the mug with the one containing just the normal thin beer, and then all of them slipped out of the house by the back door, across the yard and its vegetable plot and out into the deserted back alley and away.

And did it work? Most definitely it did! We heard that Briwere had been found by the servant going up to start the fire in the brazier in his bedroom not long afterwards, and to Briwere's mortification, the servants summoned the local apothecary who administered a strong emetic, thinking that Briwere had suffered from a surfeit of wine and rich food. So the sheriff suffered the indignity of turning himself inside out in the gaze of the apothecary and several worried servants, who all twittered like so many sparrows, worried about what would happen if the sheriff died on them.

Consequently, Briwere decided that the house had lost its allure for him, and we might have put it down to just the after-effects had it not been for the fact that he was most careful to put the other manors he had been ready to sweep up to be bid upon by others. He could not allow the original owners to simply walk back in, of course, for the reasons for taking them were now a matter of court record. However Briwere was never very good at taking notice of those beneath his station, and so when the outlaws provided more than one son with the means to buy back the family farms in their mother's maiden names, they got them because Briwere never made the connections.

Chapter 20

So that was a rousing success on the part of the outlaws operating without Robin at their helm, and I think ...no, indeed I _know_, that we all felt rather better for it. That period while Robin was away did a lot to give the others the confidence they needed to believe that no matter what happened to Robin himself, his men could still continue, and would still be Robin Hood's men even if there was no Robin.

What was that? You are still surprised by the depths of my feelings for Domnall and Máel, and think it unnatural, and perverse that I should value two hounds above my cousin? No, Gervase it was not, it was not like that at all. We are about to enter into the year of 1197, and I was a man of thirty-six, approaching thirty-seven, and I had never married or had a family because I had never really had the chance to, not because I was disinclined.

No, I was not such a saint that I had not enjoyed a night with a woman from time to time, but those were not the things a true relationship is made of. And I was not such a good catch as to have fathers lining up to wed their daughters to me. That had been the fate of Sir Mahel and a couple of the other knights I shared duties with, married off to young women they had barely laid eyes on and with the expectation that they would produce an heir as fast as possible. Those unfortunate ladies were found accommodation in Nottingham and had to endure regular, if not nightly, visits from their probably loathed husbands.

I, however, was not of their slice of society. And somewhat worse, I had spent so much of my adult life in the company of men that I was quite hopeless at talking to any young women who did pass within my orbit. Were there such women? Oh yes, for Briwere did entertain wealthy merchants and their families at times, usually when he wanted something, I will admit. But I was not of sufficient use to be dangled as inducement by him, and I know I came across as gruff and cold on the times I tried to make conversation with the ones I found attractive.

So you must therefore allow that I was singularly lacking in companionship in those years. I was friends with Harry still, but as a knight I could not be seen to be wandering down into the stables all the time and preferring the company of servants to other knights, however much that might have been true. Máel and Domnall had given me that excuse to spend more time in the outer bailey, but they were also creatures whom I could bring up into the castle too, especially if Briwere was away for the night or longer.

And you should not disregard the feelings I had which came from my rescuing them. You cannot take creatures as lovely as they were, rescue them from near death and not feel something; and even more so when you know that you were the only one around who knew what had to be done and how to do it. That was not arrogance, Brother, but the genuine delight in knowing that I had saved them from a lingering and painful death. So they were not some perverse replacement for my cousin, or a wife I had never had, but I did have some of the feelings towards them that a proud father might have for his children. And they loved me back unconditionally – probably the only ones who did. How could I not be cut to the core by losing them?

Had they died in other circumstances I would still have been devastated and mourned them deeply, but to have had them viciously slain by someone who knew just what they meant to me, that was the keenest cut, Gervase. I know Robin was trying to halt the pursuit, but a man who could loose an arrow with such accuracy at any target could have scared off the men without doing that. So I knew... I knew beyond a shadow of a doubt, that Robin had done that deliberately. None of the others would even have dreamt that I would turn my wolfhounds onto them – ever! And so would never have seen a reason to stop them. Only Robin was so determined to think the worst of me at every turn that he saw fault when there was none, or blame, or treachery.

I do not wish to sound like a whining and petulant child who complains to his mother that his cousin started the trouble, but sadly that was the truth of it. Robin <u>did</u> start the trouble between us, and every time I gave him another chance, all he did was throw it back in my face. But the killing of my dogs killed something inside of me too, I am sad to say. From that point onwards there was no going back for me, and so, as we now come to the point where Robin returned, if you wish to hear more of his exploits then you must be aware that I am only able to repeat what the others told me, for I wanted nothing to do with him. I would discuss anything at length with them, but nothing with him.

Nottinghamshire & Yorkshire
Late Winter, the Year of Our Lord, 1197

"Robin's back!" Allan puffed, as he jogged up to Guy at their arranged meeting at a small hideout they had in north-eastern Derbyshire, not far from Beighton. It was a freezing cold, late January day, and Guy had lit a small fire while waiting, knowing that he was breaking the very rules he was supposed to keep in doing it, for if Beighton wasn't actually forested, it was nonetheless under forest law. Gathering even fallen firewood in the forest while it was closed was still breaking the law.

"Is he," Guy said with a bitter smile. Specifically why his cousin should be back he couldn't summon the enthusiasm to ask after, but Allan told him anyway.

"He went to Lindisfarne as we told him, but the thing is, Guy, he's come back because somebody else needs our help."

"Really?" Guy knew that came out incredibly sarcastically.

Allan's face fell. "There truly is no going back for you, is there?"

"No, I'm sorry, Allan, there isn't. But tell me anyway, because I want to know about what's going to affect the rest of you."

By now Roger had caught Allan up, and the two of them flopped themselves down by Guy's fire and gratefully took the chunks of wholesome dog-bread and hot broth he offered, sharing his pewter mug between them.

"Robin did go to Lindisfarne," Allan began, "and it seemed to do him some good. Enough, anyway, that he thought he would go to Whitby Abbey after the monks at Lindisfarne told him that Whitby was the scene of one of the earliest conversions to Christianity in England. They lost the relics of St Hild to Glastonbury, supposedly for safe keeping when the Vikings were here, but they still have other sacred relics, and Robin decided he'd like to go and see them and pray before them.

"Well so far so good. He got to Whitby and spent several days there. He said the abbey they are building is quite magnificent, and it's perched up on a cliff looking out over the town and the sea. But he was there when a local farmer came in in a terrible state wanting to speak to the abbot. He was brought before the abbot during the evening meal, and so Robin heard what he had to say. Apparently there's a small cell attached to Whitby made up of nuns who are at Hackness, just up on the moors from the coast to the south of Whitby. The farmer said he saw rough men there, and when he and another man crept closer under the cover of darkness they saw that the sisters had been taken prisoner.

"Well the abbot said he would send for the sheriff, and one of the brothers set off the next morning, but then someone remembered that the old sheriff was moving on, and they don't know if the new one has even arrived yet, because it's Geoffrey Plantagenet who's got the post!"

Guy groaned, "And of course he's in Normandy with the king, isn't he. God's wounds! Hugh Bardolf told me that he'd continued acting as sheriff for a while in Yorkshire, despite having been replaced, in the hope that Geoffrey would return, but at the moment I know Bardolf's over in Westmoreland just as you say. He said that was where he was going as soon as the eyre finished, because there were a lot of things he needed to sort out."

"That's pretty much what Robin said he'd found out, too," Allan sighed. "I'm sorry, Guy, but on this one we've decided that despite the fact that it sends out all the wrong signals to Robin, we can hardly turn our backs and just leave those nuns to their fate. It would be different if they were somewhere like Kirklees. There'd be local knights around who could be appealed to. But these sisters chose a remote spot for the contemplative life, and all they have around them are peasant sheep farmers and lay brothers who tend the monastic flocks, and none of them are up to fighting off well-armed ruffians."

"How do you know they're well-armed?" Guy asked.

"Because Robin went and had a quick look. What he saw had him running for Loxley as fast as he could. He reckons that they're former mercenaries – probably men who've had enough of fighting in Normandy, went looking for a softer target, got thrown out of places in Flanders as they worked their way up the coast, and so decided to come across to here. They probably heard that all of our fighting men got taken to Normandy by the king, and are thinking they won't have much competition for the rich pickings."

Guy felt his heart sink. Of course they couldn't leave the sisters to suffer. "I can't think of anyone I could take the message to for you," he sighed. "Briwere won't cross the county boundary, not even for nuns, and Bardolf's too far away. No, I can see that you have to go. I just wish it wasn't like this – you know, with the whole 'Robin's only just set foot in the camp' thing, and already he's giving you missions to go on. It doesn't sit right with me, but you don't have a choice. When do you leave?"

"First 'fing tomorrow," Roger told him. "We come to let you know. We *told* Robin we was doin' it, not asked!"

Allan smiled as his friend's fierce defence of Guy. "Yes we did. We all did! We made it very clear that somebody would come and let you know, while the others got themselves fully armed and packed up. We're going to follow the River Rother from here and meet them where it joins the River Don. Ideally, we'd like to stay fairly well to the west until we've managed to cross the Aire – can't really go traipsing across the bridge at Doncaster and then the ferry over the Aire armed to the teeth, can we?"

And so long before the late winter dawn, Guy waved them off with a heavy heart and a couple of prearranged meetings for subsequent months, and prayed that he would see them again. His faith in Robin keeping any of them safe had been shattered beyond repair.

Allan and Roger had no trouble connecting with the others, and soon the whole gang was heading north through Yorkshire. It was a difficult journey, for none of them were that familiar with the terrain once they got beyond the River Aire. Tuck was the one who could best trace a route, and once they got past York even he was far from sure. All Robin could remember was that he had found a well-used and ancient road which ran along the southern edge of the high moors and passed by a place called Pickering, and so the outlaws marched on, asking for that and were surprised when they actually found it. They didn't go into the busy little market town, though, conscious that they were now close enough that if they missed their way and were delayed, that word might reach the mercenaries of armed men in the area before they got there. Instead, they skirted it and carried on eastwards, surer now of finding the nunnery.

Seven days after Allan and Roger had seen Guy, they were cold, foot-sore, and weary, but lying deep in the dead winter bracken on the moor, watching the small nunnery in the last of the fading winter light.

"Bless me, they're confident!" Tuck whispered. "Not even a guard out on patrol?"

"They have reason to be," Robin replied. "Don't forget, it took me over a week to get back to you, and they'd been here at least that time again before the locals – such as they are – even began to suspect anything. They've probably been here a month already, and as far as they're aware not even an alarm being raised."

Bilan hissed at the others and beckoned, having wriggled a little further to the north. When Robin, Will and Hugh crabbed across to him, he pointed into the gloom and whispered,

"That looks like they're building something outside the nunnery walls. Look, you can see the dark shadow of one whatever it is, but it's the frame of the other one you can see best with what light there is passing through it. What do you think they are?"

Hugh squinted into the twilight. "Not barns. They're not big enough to be of any practical use like that, and I don't see this lot being farmers, anyway. They're more likely to raid for what they want as and when they need it, not store it."

However Will was already sucking through his teeth in disgust. "I know what they are. They're for more men to sleep in. I saw some rough halls like them when I was in France."

Hugh gave a grunt of disgust, "Jesu! Of course they are! I should have remembered them myself."

"Then that probably means they're expecting more," Robin declared. "They're not here temporarily. They've decided to set up a base here!"

When they were back with the others and had moved away a little, it was Much who asked in bemusement,

"Why here, though? It's out in the middle of nowhere."

"But that's the point," Piers said. "Where's *our* main hideout? In the middle of nowhere! That's where it's safest to hide."

Hugh agreed. "True. But the other thing, Much, is that it's only a couple of days away from here to some very wealthy places like York and Durham. And you have to remember that these men probably don't know much about England at all. So they may well think that there are more places like York a bit further west, all ripe for the plunder. Will and I have seen something of the lands across the sea, and Flanders is full of small but wealthy towns that get their riches from trading, so the fact that they don't see a lot of farming, or things like weaving, fulling and dying going on here – which they'd recognise from the wealthy wool industries in Flanders – won't lessen their belief that there's more here to take than there really is."

Gilbert gave a snort of disgust. "And when they do realise it, it's more than likely that they'll be pretty savage in their retribution. They'll just hack to pieces everyone around about here to make sure they don't tell what they've seen, and move on to somewhere where they think there *is* enough to make them rich men. That's why we have to stop them, Much, before they kill the sisters and probably most of the poor bastards who farm in this Godforsaken place. ...God's hooks, it's cold up here!"

Once darkness had fully fallen, they left Marianne and Mariota with Ed, Colm and Much to watch over their baggage, for the two sisters and Tuck had insisted on bringing plenty of medical supplies, believing they would be needed for the sisters, at least. The rest of them sneaked silently through the bracken until they came up against the nunnery walls. From inside there came the sounds of carousing, but infuriatingly there wasn't a single window looking out onto the world beyond the nunnery, and they knew they would have to retreat until nightfall and then take a chance by scaling the walls.

"I never thought I would curse the contemplative life," Tuck muttered to Will, "but this is ridiculous! We can't see a thing. Did they really think the view through a narrow window to a soggy hillside and a few sheep would corrupt the sisters that badly? *Duw*, some of these Norman monastics have a strange view of God if they think it's so awful to look on his works of nature and be corrupted by them."

Thomas tutted his agreement. "Probably worried they'd see a ram tupping a ewe! No wonder their saints always come to such perverted ends. Give me feisty St Brigit any day over some poor lass who gets her tits cut off for her beliefs. Bloody weird, that!" He was thinking of an image of St Agatha they had seen on a dainty portable triptych carried by a merchant they had stopped a few weeks back, which had showed the martyrdom of St Agatha along with those of

St Barbara and St Agnes, all of whom had met grizzly ends. "Why would you want to scare a lass to death at the thought of being with a man, eh? Bloody Romans have a lot to answer for!"

Tuck laughed at Thomas' indignation, but had to agree with him. "Those poor nuns, who've seen and heard of nothing but the Virgin Martyrs, would've been scared witless when those men turned up anyway – *Duw*, but they'd probably have been as scared of us and with no reason to be! I'd pray that saints Hild and Ælfleda of Whitby are watching out their own, but by the look of things they've not had much success. So I'll be praying to the ones I know who listen a bit harder. To St Melangell, whose feast day is about now if I'm right, and St Cadoc – who I think has had his feast day just a day or so back, if I could only work out what day we're on – and to your St Brigit, Thomas, whose day is shortly to come ...and a word in St Michael's ear wouldn't hurt in this situation, either."

Will, Gilbert and Siward found themselves grinning at one another at Tuck's words. It always amused them the way Tuck spoke as if the Celtic saint were old friends he could go and have a chat with, which was very different from the kind of piety they'd encountered elsewhere, and they saw the perplexed frowns on Janah and Khalīl's faces.

"You'd better explain Tuck's personal touch to those two," Will told Malik with a chuckle, "they look a bit confused! Don't want them thinking we've got some weird reinforcements who are going to turn up in person."

However, by the time the night had truly descended and the nunnery had fallen silent, it was as if Tuck's prayers had been heard, for a thick fog began to develop over the moor, neatly masking the outlaws' approach to the walls once more. Tuck and John made cups of their hands and boosted Will and Siward up over the wall – something Robin wanted to be the one do, but he was firmly told that he wasn't going to go in alone or with just one other, because nobody trusted him not to go off on some wild spree on his own. From the top of the wall, lying flat along it Will and Siward whispered back down that the small area within the walls looked quiet, and that they could hear snoring from inside what they guessed was the dormitory area. They also gave the thumbs up that they were on a stretch of wall without any buildings up against it, and could drop directly to the ground.

Dropping down, the two slipped across to the gate and let the others in, but then barred the gate after them. They didn't want any of these men escaping and warning whoever they were expecting. And with that in mind, all of those who had come inside had their swords drawn, or in Tuck and John's cases their quarterstaffs at the ready, while Ed had proven to be handy with a hefty hammer which Will had forged for him once they had found what the young carpenter's fighting forte was. Again Marianne and Mariota were outside with Much, Allan and Roger (the latter two there to stop the two women from rushing fearlessly in, since nobody believed Much would have any success there), for the men were worried that those they faced might target the two as hostages as a means of getting out in the face of superior opposition.

"Where are the nuns?" Tuck whispered to Robin. "Did you ever find out when you were back here?"

However, Robin shook his head, and so Tuck beckoned to John and Ed, and they vanished off through the tendrils of mist that were sliding in over the walls, in search of where prisoners might be kept. Nobody thought the women would be in the dormitory, even if the mercenaries had been taking advantage of them – even a nun might fight back under such circumstance once the men were asleep.

It didn't take long for the three to come across a stoutly built store house which had a new bar affixed to the outside, and John made the soft dove's coo signal to let the others know that they had found it. In response they got an owl signal back to let them know that the others had heard, and so John and Tuck between them lifted the bar off as silently as they could manage, but didn't open the door yet. They knew it would be likely that the traumatised women within would scream when they went in, and so were waiting to hear the fighting begin so that the others would have the element of surprise.

Like so many avenging ghosts, the outlaws crept inside the dormitory, which was little more than a small wooden hall. This was a far cry from the great monasteries elsewhere, where Norman priors and abbots coming across from the great mother abbeys of Normandy had upgraded, or completely rebuilt, simple wooden Anglo-Saxon buildings in stone, and vastly expanded the attached churches in the newer styles. This was a simple cell for sisters, and not worthy of such expense and finery. All these buildings were soundly built, but in wood beams and wattle infill.

Inside they found the snoring forms of at least fourteen men in the darkness. That decided the men's fate, for there were only twelve of the outlaws here, and Colm and the three Cosham brothers weren't expert at hand-to-hand fighting, whereas none of them doubted that those they faced had more than enough experience of that. Such an eventuality had been discussed beforehand, and although nobody liked the idea of killing in cold blood, realistically they knew that if they were outnumbered, then they had no choice unless they wanted to lose any more of their own.

Consequently, Malik, Janah and Khalīl moved to the right and stood over three of the sleeping men, while Will, Siward and Gilbert went to the left to do the same, leaving Robin and Hugh to deal with the two nearest the door which would then be guarded by the Coshams and Colm. Not a soul had stirred as yet, but the air was rank with the smell of wine and ale, and there was no doubt that their quarry slept so soundly because they were all as drunk as lords. Once roused, though, there was no guarantee that they would be so drunk as to be incapable of fighting. As Will had warned them,

"I've seen men so soused they could barely stand up, but the moment they had to fight they burned off what they'd drunk in sheer rage and turned into vicious killers – so watch yourselves!"

At Robin's soft, "Now!" all eight of them struck without hesitation, plunging sharp knives into the throats of the sleeping mercenaries. Even so, one man thrashed in his dying moments, the heels of the boots he'd failed to take off drumming on the wooden floor; while another turned in his sleep just as Gilbert struck and the knife slid across his neck rather than going straight in, and he screamed. He didn't get a second chance, for Gilbert struck a second time, fast as a viper.

Unfortunately, though, it was enough to wake most of the others and now the fighting began in earnest, for these mercenaries were no soft targets and slept with their weapons even when they thought themselves secure. It was dirty fighting, for the mercenaries lashed out with knives, boots and fists, and far from any elegant swordplay, the fight had more in common with a drunken brawl at an inn than even the mêlée at a tournament.

Will found himself slogging it out in a fist-fight with a huge Hollander who seemed to have the skull of an ox.

"Go down ...you brain-dead ...lump of ...beef!" Will puffed, thumping the swearing man with his fists at each word. "Bloody Hell! ...Don't ...you ...know ...when ...you're dead?" Over the winter Will had sewn some strips of metal from the leftovers of his forge onto his heavy leather gloves in anticipation of a fight like this, and was staggered by how long his opponent had continued to stay on his feet and swing blows back when he was taking such punishment. The metal strips had cut his face to ribbons, yet it had only been on the last blow that the man's eyes had finally rolled back in his head through his already almost closed, bloody lids, and had gone down like a felled oak, shaking the floor with the impact.

Will had picked his man deliberately, despite the blackness, being aware of the man's bulk and had him marked as a brawler. Robin had not been so alert, and now was fighting harder than he had done in years with a man who had far more experience of knife fights in enclosed spaces. Blessing the thick, wool-filled gambesons which they all now possessed, Robin felt it absorb another knife cut which would have opened his ribs up had he not been protected, and tried to land another cut of his own. The man leaned back just enough for Robin's knife to nick his cheek but do no real damage.

"St Lazarus aid me!" Robin wheezed under his breath, and dived in low to try and make an upward cut to the man's groin.

He missed, but the sudden spurt of blood in his face told him that he'd still hit a major artery in the man's leg. Now all he had to do was avoid getting a cut like that himself before the man bled out! And that wasn't so easy to do, for the man must have known his time had come and redoubled his attack with animal ferocity, whipping the long knife back and forth in the direction of Robin's face. Instinctively trying to retreat, Robin tripped on a blanket and went down. To his horror, the man cast a blacker shadow over him and seemed about to fall upon him, driving the knife in with his weight in the process as his strength faded, until he suddenly folded up backwards as the horned end of a longbow struck out of the gloom from behind Robin and took the mercenary in the eye, dropping him backwards instantly.

As Robin struggled to his feet, he felt a hand under his arm and Piers' voice said sardonically, "Don't rush to thank me, then, *cyfaill*."

"Thank you," Robin said, annoyed that his voice shook despite his best efforts not to. That had been a very close call! Being an expert archer hadn't been of any use this time, and it shook Robin more than he wanted to admit.

"See? We're better together," Thomas' voice said from his other side and he realized that the fighting had stopped, and that Bilan had just struck a spark to light one of the candles.

As the room flickered into light it took on the appearance of a scene from Hell. Blood was everywhere, on the floor and on the walls, and men lay sprawled in death in unnatural contortions.

"Is everyone alright?" Siward's voice called out, and Piers' voice at Robin's ear hissed,

"That should have been your first call, *brawd*, if you want to consider yourself our leader." Piers, it seemed, had taken it upon himself to be the voice of Robin's conscience and was doing a good job of it.

Finally it began to sink in with Robin what they had been trying to tell him for so long. It wasn't just about being the best fighter, for Siward surely wasn't that, although he was very good.

"Is anyone wounded?" he managed to call out, and felt contrite when Gilbert took his hand off his arm and said,

"My bastard stuck me with his knife. Not deep but it's bleeding like mad." So even wounded, Gilbert had thought to watch his back? And again Robin felt an irrational guilt and then irritation that he should feel that way.

"Keep your hand on it tight," Thomas said, stepping over corpses to get to Gilbert's side. "Come on, let's get Marianne and Mariota to have a look at it," and took Gilbert's other arm to help him negotiate his way out to the door.

"Anyone else?" Siward asked, and Robin was glad to hear the others responding to only minor gashes and scratches.

As he and Siward were the last two to leave the building, Robin turned to his old friend and apologized. "I've been a lousy leader, haven't I? I got too caught up in the whole Robin Hood thing and I didn't think enough about the rest of you."

"No, you didn't!" Siward replied bluntly, feeling that he'd be doing Robin no favours by sweetening the bitter pill of reality. "You're grand at the plans, Robin, but you're piss-poor at looking after those who follow you."

Robin turned and looked balefully at him, but surprised Siward by not arguing or pleading his case.

Siward decided that now might just be the time to add another truth. "We've got along fine without you over the winter, you know. 'Robin Hood' has put in a few appearances, and if those have been less of the grand performances than when you wear the hood, nonetheless the ordinary people feel like they haven't been forgotten. So you need to think carefully, my friend, about how you want to come back to us.

"You *can* come back, but it won't be like before – we're all agreed on that. Losing Simon and Martin was all down to you and your pride, and none of us wants to ever be in that position again. So in the future we'll all discuss plans together, and if the majority of us decide it's just too dangerous, then whatever the mission, it won't happen, do you understand?

"This was a good call. These poor nuns needed rescuing by us, because if not us then who else? But Colm and Ed were never in such danger, Guy made sure of that. And speaking of Guy, I think you killed stone dead any chance of him ever speaking to you again when you killed his dogs. That cousin is completely lost to you now – make sure you don't lose Allan and John the same way!"

Yet before the conversation could continue they realized that they could hear women screaming and crying, and that Tuck, John and Ed had had as tough a time with the nuns. Tuck was dealing with Gilbert's arm some distance away from the building where the nuns were, and the rest of the men were standing well back from it as John spoke to them.

"Don't even try going in there," he was saying. "We had to go and get Marianne and Mariota. They wouldn't let anyone else inside. Luckily those two seem to have got things a bit more under control now, but they told us not to even try looking inside because it only sets the sisters off again."

"Then let's drag those bodies out to the halls they were building and burn them out there," Will suggested. "The sisters don't need to see that, and it won't help if they think we're intending to burn them all alive inside this place as well, because they'll get even more hysterical."

To Robin's amazement, everyone agreed with Will and turned

back to the hall where they'd fought. No-one had actually ordered it – they just did it.

And so the dawn came in in fire and smoke as the rough hall beyond the wall went up in flames, with the bodies and the bracken-filled mattresses they'd used piled on top of them to add to the pyre. In the wreckage of the nunnery kitchen, Bilan had found enough oil to soak the bodies with, and now the smoke rose up in oily coils, stinking of burnt flesh.

"*Phwar*, I don't think I'll be eating roast pig any time soon," Colm muttered to Ed, and got an answering nod from the young carpenter, whose nose was already wrinkled in disgust at the smell. It was another side of fighting that neither of them had experienced as yet, and one they hadn't been prepared for, but as Gilbert had kindly told them,

"Can't leave them just to rot – that'd bring all sorts of diseases and rats – and we don't have time to dig graves. Anyway, those fuckers don't deserve a Christian burial!"

However, as they all sat down to eat the meal Tuck had prepared from what they'd brought with them, after washing the blood off themselves in the icy stream which drained from the nunnery's water course, Mariota came out looking worried.

"We've managed to get some sense out of a couple of them," she said in her lilting Scottish voice. "That scrofulous bunch of butcher's curs were expecting friends, like you all thought. They should be landing any day now at a small cove just south of Whitby." She gave Robin a stern look. "This job isn't over yet. We've got to stop them, because they've got their aim set on the monastery at Whitby. I know there are fewer of them now than there were, but the monks aren't up to fending that number off."

"How many?" Malik asked.

Mariota shrugged. "Canna' be sure, but the most lucid of the women in there, who's one of the lay sisters and a bit more worldly than the rest, said that she thought one of them said something like there'd be twice as many again when the others arrived."

"Shit, that could be as many as another three dozen," John swore. "You're right, Mariota, the monks will never hold off that many mercenaries until help arrives."

"And that monastery is like a fortress," Robin added. "Where it is up on the headland, it would be a swine to try and lead an assault against if those men barricade themselves in against us once they've taken it. We have to stop them at the coast."

"Then that sounds like archers' work!" Thomas declared cheerfully, slapping Robin on the back. "Now there's a *good* time to show us what a smart arse you are with the bow!"

"How do we get there?" Hugh asked, and for once it was Ed who said,

"I know the way! I know just where the nuns are talking about."

With there being very little the men could do to help, they left the two sisters with Much, Allan and Roger again guarding them, largely because those three were the smallest and least threatening of the men, and marched off again as the sun fully rose. They had helped themselves to whatever arrows they could find amongst the mercenaries stuff, and if the arrows weren't as good as those that Rhys was making for them back at Loxley, they would certainly do to cut down the newcomers.

The short, dim days meant that it took until noon of the next day before they were encamped on the cliffs above the small bay and working out where the mercenaries might land.

"I reckon it'll be at that northern end," Colm said. "They won't risk their boat on the rocks further south." He'd had some experience of boats, his father having had a small fishing boat, and given that nobody else knew any better, they had to take his word for it.

They therefore camped a little inland so that they could light a fire to keep warm, but posted watches of two men at a time on the cliff. They didn't have to wait long. Only a day later, Bilan came haring across the heather to say that a sail had appeared on the horizon unlike the local boats, and seemed to be heading their way.

"They'll expect their mates to be here waiting, I would guess," Hugh said. "They can hardly know this coast so I'd think they'd be expecting some sort of beacon to guide them in, so let's give it to them, and we can use it to light fire-arrows too."

A smoky fire was soon started on the cliff top and, to their gratification, the ship turned towards them. It took some while longer for the ship to beat its way close into shore, but eventually it was near enough that men began jumping out and wading ashore, even if the first ones were almost armpit-high in the waves.

"Let them all come out," Gilbert called softly to the rank of archers made up of the three Coshams, the three former turcopoles, Siward, Hugh, Robin and himself. "We don't want any of them getting back on board and helping those sailors to get the mail sail back up."

There was a strong wind coming off the land which would soon pull the ship back out to sea. It was therefore Tuck, John, Colm and Ed's job to start sending fire arrows out to it to start it burning as fast as possible, but accuracy was less important for that than dealing with the best part of three dozen mercenaries who had now congregated on the beach, which was why those four were designated for the job. No-one had the least doubt that once those mercenaries came under a hail of arrows that they would go on the offensive. That was why the best archers were focusing on them, to drop as many as they could before they even got close to the cliff and the rough path up to the top.

As the men scrambled ashore through the foaming waves, they could be heard calling to one another, making Ed ask,

"What tongue is that?" It was none he'd heard before.

Will cocked his head on one side, cupping his hand to his ear to hear better. "Genoese, I'd say, or at least from that part of the world, and that's not good. They've a reputation for being tough fighters, and worse, they're skilled with crossbows."

"We can't let that lot get ashore and to their weapons," Siward agreed, and was glad to see Malik, Janah and Khalīl already staking arrows in front of them in the soft turf so that they could grab the next ones all the faster. They, too, had come across these mercenaries who came from the rocky coastline east of France before it turned southwards towards Rome. Knew them and how dangerous they were.

"Ed, you're not so good with a bow yet," Gilbert said, managing to make it sound like no criticism was intended. "Would you act as a runner for any of us main archers who call for a fire arrow and bring it to us? If we have to move to come and get one, we'll lose our range."

"No problem," Ed replied with a grin, and moved to stand somewhere in the middle behind the line of archers crouched on the cliff.

The three Coshams were at the southerly end of the line, and the three turcopoles at the northern end, but between them were arrayed Will, Gilbert, Robin, Siward and Hugh. And if Robin thought he was in the middle as the leading archer, the men on either side of him knew that they'd discussed it beforehand, and that they were the ones who would have the least conscience about laying him out if he suddenly lost control and looked like doing something daft or dangerous. Robin still had a way to go before he regained their trust, even in a fight situation like this.

"Hold it, lads," Will's deep voice growled softly. "Let the last ones get out of the rowing boats. Don't want any of the bastards escaping back to the ship and sailing off."

"Have you got the range of the ship?" Thomas called back quietly to the three behind them who had the fire arrows meant for the sails ready and waiting.

"Yes," Colm's soft brogue answered, "But it's at the limit of our range. Would you three take the first shots? If ours fall short it gives them too much time to get the sails up again."

Robin turned and blinked in surprise at that, and was even more shocked to see the black look Colm sent his way. Clearly he would never have asked Robin to do it, and it emphasised again to Robin how far he'd somehow eroded the trust of even the new men. Later he would ask Gilbert why Colm hadn't asked him to make the first shot, and would be stunned to be told bluntly, "Because he thinks you're a show-off and untrustworthy."

Now, though, there was no need for a signal. As soon as the last of the mercenaries got a couple of strides away from the boats, the three Coshams sent fire arrows whistling through the dim January light and neatly struck the one small sail still half up, which was helping to keep the ship steady where it was, and not driven on to the rocks of the promontories at either end of the small bay. Three more fire arrows followed from the Coshams as the rest of the archers took aim at those in the water – the ones next most likely to effect an escape.

As the first of the mercenaries fell into the foam-flecked waves, dead, or wounded and likely to drown, the arrows found targets closer to shore. The three turcopoles, being used to using slightly lighter bows than the big wyche-elm Welsh bows the Coshams had grown up using, had slightly lighter ones, and so concentrated on preventing any of the mercenaries from getting close enough to the sea-cliff to be a danger. Once virtually underneath the outlaws it would be dangerous to lean out to try and target them, and that might mean that the mercenaries could climb the cliff unopposed until they reached the top. That, nobody wanted, being under no illusions that these men would have seen a lot of close-quarter fighting, and recently too, which might mean that they were more than a match for even someone like Will, who had always been the best swordsman of them all.

And so as the three men of the East picked off their targets close-to with devastating efficiency, the others wreaked havoc on the rest, while Tuck and his two companions took over and continued to drop fire arrows onto the ship. By the time they all paused, the ship was burning brightly, its entire rigging aflame, and some of what were no doubt the mercenaries' packs up on deck and waiting to be ferried ashore were also well ablaze. The sailors who had rowed the mercenaries ashore had returned in panic to the ship, but found themselves taking on their fellow sailors, desperate to get off the burning ship before it sank, rather than them being able to take refuge from the lethal rain of arrows.

As Robin stood and loosed an arrow right out into the bay to drop amongst the horrified sailors in the nearest boat, Will stood and grabbed his arm.

"No! Leave them! They've done nothing wrong. If anyone it's their captain who took this commission, and even he probably got threatened. If we kill them it's murder."

"Agreed," said Siward, taking the arrow out of Robin's bow. "The big ship had to go. That was too dangerous, because if any of those fighters got back to it, who knows where they might have forced the sailors to take them. But those men? We've got no quarrel with them. Leave them be."

"What shall we do with the bodies?" Bilan asked.

"We should pull them out of the water," Colm suggested. "We don't want them being washed ashore in the next bays and folk fretting that some ship of their own has foundered."

Gilbert agreed, "Good point, but I think that blaze is going to be seen at quite a distance – or at least the smoke is. We should make sure they're all dead down there and then get away from here before anyone else comes."

Therefore they hurried to the beach and dispatched the handful of men who had not been killed outright. All of them were dragged far enough up the beach to be out of the normal tides, although at this time of year a storm might reach them. And then they hurried up the narrow cliff path to head back to the nunnery, only then realising that they were being watched by a handful of wide-eyed little lads.

"It's alright, son," Will said as he marched past one, ruffling the lad's hair, "This is Robin Hood's bay now, nobody's going to hurt you."

And that was how they told it to me, Brother. I saw Allan and Roger soon after they had got back, having taken the distraught nuns to Whitby and leaving the prior there to sort out which establishment might take them in. They were delighted that such a major confrontation had gone off as well as it did, and that despite taking on double their numbers of mercenaries, that they had come out of it with only a few minor cuts and bruises. But more than that, Allan told me that even men like Will were optimistic about keeping Robin under control. They had got through what could have descended into a bloody fight without him making a mess of things for them, and that, they believed boded well for the future.

But now I do confess most sadly, Gervase, that I could not join in their optimism. Truly, I wished I could have, for if I could believe that my cousin could be brought under control, then there was some hope for the salvation of his soul – some way back for him from the brink of self-destruction which he had brought himself to. And I did, and still do, believe that by this stage it <u>was</u> a matter of choices.

Time and again Tuck had explained things to him, and all of the core members of the gang had alternately tried sympathising with him over the horrors he still carried with him from his crusading days, or pointing out more forcefully that he could not go on as he was. Yet from my vantage point of being a little more detached than the others, I could see with dreadful clarity that all of their pleading, cajoling, and remonstrating only ever had a temporary effect. Sooner, rather than later, Robin always reverted to his old habits, his old ways of thinking about things, and because of that he had reached the final reserves of my patience and tolerance.

Yes, I am sure that will count against me when the final reckoning comes, if God takes your stance against me, but you must allow that at the time I was sorely wounded in spirit and mind. A man does not bounce back from such blows unaffected, Brother, and you would understand that more had your own life been less cloistered. As for why I cannot forgive him now, ah me, that you will see all the clearer by the time we get to the end of today, for I know what is to come and you do not. Had that been the last time we would cross swords, so to speak, then in time I might well have found it within me to find some measure of forgiveness, for I would never forget what he had done to me thus far. But the feud Robin was fuelling between us was far from over, and we shall move on to that after I have had another sip or two of wine to fortify myself.

Chapter 21

Now I know you will not like this much, Gervase, but you will have to put up with Robin not being in this confession for a little while, and that is because during that first half of 1197 in particular, I kept my contact with the outlaws under strict control. If I had a warning to send to them it was always done through those of them who came to meet me, either at the Trip to Jerusalem Inn, or whoever came to me when I was working within the forest. I did not go to the outlaws' camps unless I was very sure that Robin would not be there.

You see I thought at the time that it would be good to separate me and Robin for a goodly while, and that was for two reasons. The first, you will not be surprised to hear, was because I honestly did not know how I would face him. I knew myself to be a fallible enough man that I might take one look at him, and if I had been having a rough time of it in the castle, might be raw enough in mind and soul to be the one to start a fight – a very real, fists and knives fight, too. I will allow you your smug look over that Gervase, for I do confess that there I would have been most definitely at fault. But I was also sensible enough to know that seeing Robin and me trying to tear one another to shreds would be deeply distressing for my other two cousins, and also for members of the gang like Tuck and Marianne who had up until now cared deeply for both of us. Therefore, I believed that it would be a good thing if the outlaws did not see Robin and me eternally at one another's throats, and feeling compelled to choose between us there and then.

That decision was also made somewhat in self-defence, Brother, for I knew I could supply the information they needed without perpetually having to sit in camp and listen to Robin ridiculing my warnings, and actually seeing the others be torn as which one they believed. From a blessedly safe distance, if they acted upon my words in the way I hoped they would, I could take it at face value and be pleased. Or if they did not act, then I did not need to know why; I did not have to face that rejection head on. I could continue in my work believing that they had seen some flaw I had not, rather than having to witness my words being set aside due to Robin's tantrums.

My second reason turned out to be rather more flawed looking back upon it, but I did not realise that at the time. You see, the other side of the coin was that I hoped that over time, if Robin did not see me or speak to me, then all his perceived injuries which he had brought forward from our shared childhood would recede once more into the past. A distant cousin would be far easier for him to deal with, I believed, than me standing right in front of him. I hoped ...oh how I hoped, Brother ...that then he would start to see the warnings in their own light and for what they were.

That, for instance, if I said that the sheriff was going to act badly towards a certain village, that instead of filtering that through a net of ire against me, that he would see that the focus of his attention ought to be on how to help those villagers. By now I did not expect absence to make his heart grown any fonder, but I did hope that his peculiar loathing of me might abate to the extent that it would become a matter of indifference to him if lesser members of the gang – which I was sure then and still am now, was the way he thought of Roger, Colm and Ed – came to meet me. John or Allan coming, I recognised, would always ruffle his feathers, being too much of a reminder of our familial connection, but I swear to you most faithfully that I genuinely hoped that by staying away I was creating a space somewhere in his mind. Somewhere where the warnings I sent could be contemplated without all the attendant anger I raised in him.

Why was that a mistake? Oh dear, Gervase, because all I did was give him time – and lots of it – in which he was able to run me down without me ever being there to defend myself. Time in which my apparent sins against him were able to grow and multiply in his head out of all proportion to reality. And as they did, he became ever quicker to blacken my name, or to sow doubts where none should have been. Worst of all, it gave him the opportunity to say that my lengthy absences were because I was being drawn into the sheriff's orbit and away from them, my friends. That I no longer came because I no longer cared, was the insidious poison he kept dripping into people's ears, and shockingly, some of those who knew me well even had doubts, but only because they recognised how much strain I had been under and feared that I was becoming too weary to carry on aiding them.

Colm and Ed would never be taken in by him ever again, and they joined Roger in being very strongly on my side in all things, and for that reason – for the future as far as you need to know it for today – they often elected to stay behind at Loxley with Aneirin and Rhys, and our former Templar, Balak, working on the store of weapons, rather than going into action when Robin was leading a raid under one of his mistaken assumptions. Marianne and Mariota also found themselves sitting back in camp when Robin came up with some ridiculous reason why they should not join in, and so they saw what was happening with regard to me, because it was a more severe variant of what was happening to them. But having learned the hard way that the gang needed to vary what they did, the others would present Robin with a united refusal if he mentioned raiding the woodmotes again, and he was cunning enough in his growing insanity to back down, choosing only to fight those small but increasingly frequent battles of wills where he knew he could either win outright, or at least have some measure of control.

Therefore in that first half of the year, Robin was only ever out in the forest with the experienced members of the gang, and that became deceptive for everyone. Because of that, you see, with his actions being constrained by what those experienced fighters would or would not do, they came to believe that they had the situation with him under control. But there would come a time when new men would join the gang and that was when things began to really fall apart again. Yet we have a way to go before then, and you need to understand why Robin continued to have a seething grudge against me, for I was successful in dealing with the sheriff on my own over a couple of matters without resorting to needing my friends' help, and that did not go down well at all, Brother, not well at all.

Nottinghamshire
Spring, the Year of Our Lord, 1197

The Assizes were due again, for they came around quarterly, unlike the eyres which were biennial at best. Hitherto Guy had had limited contact with these local courts of justice, the forest ones being more of his personal burden, but now that he was acting as one of the coroners he found that he had to get involved with these lesser courts of the mainstream justice system. Mercifully not to do with murders – they were definitely still a matter for the eyres, and once he had established the cause of death, Guy could hand those over to others to deal with. However, accidental deaths or injuries and which were very clearly such, were different, and that was because the matter of compensation – better known as werguild – still applied. King Henry's reforms of the legal system had made it redundant for the truly felonious crimes, but down at this lower level, things had been slower to change, and so at this court held on St Patrick's Day, Guy was sitting at the assize in Mansfield waiting to give his testimony, and struggling to stay awake.

This year was turning into one massive headache because of the way Easter would fall. He'd already had a week of running around like a headless chicken, and that was because the verderers' attachment courts would come right on the heels of this one, and he'd had to prepare his cases for his appearance at Edwinstowe woodmote before he came here, so that he could go straight to there. Normally it wasn't quite such a rush, and there was time to have the assize after the start of the fiscal new year, which fell on the Feast of the Annunciation on the twenty-fifth of March. But this year Palm Sunday would come just five days after that, and then they would be into the preparations for Easter, at which point there would be no chance of getting a monk, or any other cleric, to come and take the notes. And so the assizes had had to be brought forward to before the woodmotes, which wouldn't have been so bad had Guy been able to attend the various courts in the same locations.

He yawned mightily, smothering it behind his gloved hand, for the wooden merchant's hall in Mansfield was inhospitably chilly at this time of year, and Guy had kept both his heavy cloak and gloves on, knowing how the cold and damp would seep into his bones the longer he sat there. Now, though, his body was trying to tell him it was time to hibernate, and he was drowsy with the stifling atmosphere as all doors and windows were kept shut tight against the bitter winds and cold. Sanson de Strelley, as one of the leading men of the area, sat in both of the Mansfield courts, forest and justice, and at least he tended to get on with things, not drag them out as Griffin Presbiter would be doing soon over at the Calverton woodmote.

"Next case," he heard Strelley call and breathed a sigh of relief, this was the one he was needed for, and after that he would be able to make his excuses and go and sit in the warm of the local alehouse where he had a room for tonight.

"Alfred the Carter," Stelley summoned forward, and gestured to the clerk to read out the charge.

The monk, suffering badly with a streaming cold, blew his nose, coughed thickly and then managed to hoarsely whisper, "You are charged that...*aaashew!*"

As another massive sneeze shook the poor monk, Guy reached over and took the parchment from him before it got showered, reading out, "You are charged that on the twenty-second of January, you blinded the horse belonging to your master, Jordan of Mansfield, a wool merchant, and that in the process the horse then crushed your fellow servant, Oswine, to death against the side of this merchant's hall."

Strelley shot Guy a grateful glance. He would never admit that he couldn't read and was wholly dependent upon the cleric, and it would never have dawned on him to ask Guy if he could, but when such help was offered he was at least gracious enough to appreciate it.

"How do you plead?" Strelley demanded, as Guy gestured two burly farmers forward and quietly asked them to carry Brother John to the inn.

Shifting across to the brother's leather stool, Guy picked up the quill, dipped it in the ink pot and prepared to write down Alfred's plea. Strelley's eyebrows nearly vanished up into his velvet bonnet at the sight, but Guy duly wrote "Not guilty," following Alfred's response.

"And how do you justify such a claim?" Strelley demanded. "We shall be calling jurors to attest that you were using your whip harshly on the beast."

"I was not, my lord!" Alfred protested. "I crack the whip over the horses' heads. I'd never use it directly on them!"

"Then how do you account for how the horse became blinded by your whip catching it in the eye?"

Alfred looked genuinely upset. "It was Oswine, my lord. He'd been in the master's house, which was where I had the cart pulled up to. I kept telling him not to come up alongside Blanche from behind but when he was taken with drink...."

"...Blanche?"

"The horse," Guy supplied.

"Ah, the horse, right. And why would Oswine coming up behind her cause *you* to blind her?"

"Because she was startled, my lord! All of a sudden she was throwing her head up and trying to rear up in the traces of the wagon. I hadn't seen him. I didn't even know he was there! It was a stupid thing to do – come up on the inside of a wagon and behind the horse when it was right close to the wall, let alone as I was about to pull away and had the brake off."

"And then what happened?" Strelley demanded. "Why should I not put you to the eyre for manslaughter?"

Alfred went white. "No, my lord! Please, no!"

Strelley looked across to Guy, who was writing with more speed than the monk had been able to and now looked up. "Can you give your evidence, Sir Guy, and still write it down?"

"Absolutely," Guy said with confidence. "I examined the body of Oswine, and he was most definitely crushed by the wagon. The hub of the big front wheel had been driven into him with some force as Blanche reared up and shoved the wagon backwards. However, I would like to add that I examined not only the corpse but the horse. If Alfred was in the habit of using his whip as harshly on her as has been claimed, there would be marks on her. Instead, I would say that Blanche had been exceptionally well cared for.

"And if you would allow me to make an observation, it is that the men who are prepared to testify that he was whipping her are all Jordan le Grand's fellow merchant's men, but the physical evidence does not back that up. Moreover, I came here within a day of Oswine's death, and I can attest that even after that time he absolutely reeked of strong wine. It's not my place to speculate where he got hold of the wine, although his master's wine cellar would be the obvious guess.

"What I can say is that, in my experience, the wagon had to be hard by the hall before any of this started. If it had been further out, then Blanche would have had to move it much further in order to trap Oswine, and in his state of drunkenness he would have been much more likely to have fallen over and be crushed underneath one of the wheels – not be pinned hard against the wall. And that that happened is borne out by the quantity of his blood still on the wheel; so much so that the wheel has had to be replaced on the wagon because Blanche's replacement cannot abide the smell of it.

"Therefore everything points to things happening the way Alfred says – that Oswine, in his drunken state, foolishly came up behind Blanche on the inside and spooked her. She reared up and by a fluke of fate got caught in the eye by Alfred's whip, at which point, being in pain, she reared and flailed about in the wagon's traces, driving it backwards, and thereby accidentally killing Oswine who had started the whole chain of events. My testimony is therefore that Oswine's death was a tragic accident which he brought about himself."

"What about my wagon?" Jordan le Grand spluttered, rising to his feet. "What about my horse? I've had to buy a new horse, a new wheel, and take on two new men! Why should I have to bear the expense of all that?"

Strelley shot Guy a grateful glance before turning on Jordan the wool merchant. "You, sir, do very well for yourself, as your fine robes and bonnet attest. I would not protest too hard if I was you. Were you the owner of Blanche?"

Timorously, Alfred raised his hand. "No, my lord, I am."

"And have you been able to work since?" Strelley demanded and got a shake of the head in response. "And what of Blanche? Have you had to have her slaughtered?"

"No, my lord!" Alfred gulped. "She's a fine fit horse except for the eye. We could have kept working once she recovered, if Master le Grand had given us the chance."

"Then this is my judgement: Jordan le Grand, for Oswine to have got into that state, you must have been aware of his partaking of your wine, given that he was at your house, in which case you bear some responsibility for Oswine's state on that day. Furthermore you've attempted to profit through this court by the accident and at Alfred the Carter's expense. I therefore rule that the amount of ten shillings be paid to this court by yourself, which will be paid to Alfred the Carter for the damage done to his horse indirectly by your servant – and you should consider yourself having got off lightly for wasting this court's time! ...We will take a break!"

As Jordan the wool merchant stomped out of the hall muttering darkly, and a servant scurried forward with some mulled cider for Strelley and Guy, Strelley turned to Guy and said,

"Tight as a salt cod's arse, that one! You mark my words, he'll be back before us at the next assize for non-payment."

Yet to both of their amazement, the wool merchant appeared again before the court had resumed, slapping down the ten shillings on the table.

"And I hope that fucking horse chokes on it!" he snarled as he turned on his heels to leave.

"I'll take that to Alfred tonight," Guy volunteered. "I know where he lives, having gone there to look at Blanche."

Strelley looked shocked. "That's not really how it's done, Sir Guy," he protested. "The money should go to the sheriff first and be accounted for. Briwere gets nasty if it doesn't all go to Nottingham first."

And in that instant Guy knew what would happen. The sheriff would hold such payments and use them to make up any shortfall in the monies he would be setting off with, in a week or two's time, for the Easter court. In Briwere's eyes it would be better for the small men of the shire to go without than him go to London short of the allotted amount.

"I see you understand," Strelley said calmly. "Good."

"But Alfred and his family will starve!" Guy protested quietly. "With Jordan le Grand against him he'll never work in Mansfield again. That means he needs to move on to somewhere else, and if nothing else he'll need a cart of his own if he can't find another master."

"Not our problem," Strelley said with a dismissive wave of his hand. "We've done our duty."

And this was the point when Guy always found himself at odds with those of the same station as himself. As long as they were alright and their fields got ploughed and harvested, they cared little for the people who actually did the work. Of all those he came into contact with via the two lots of courts, Strelley was definitely one of the better ones. He wasn't deliberately brutal, he just had no idea of what it was like to live as his tenants did, but there was still no point in arguing with him, especially with the clerk prostrate at the inn and too ill to come back and finish the court, which meant that Guy and Strelley would have to work together finish it between them.

By the end of the day, though, by Guy's reckoning the sheriff had a nice little sum of money going back to the castle. And if by itself it wasn't that much, multiply that out across the courts, and then maybe double it if the monies from the last court hadn't been paid out, and Guy could see how Briwere might think that they would save his skin when he had to present less money than the king might like from the two shires.

As he lay in his truckle bed in the small curtained off area of the small inn that night, Guy's thoughts wouldn't let him sleep. There had to be some way that he could get that money to Alfred if only he could think of it. Then, as another massive sneeze shook the place from Brother John, it occurred to Guy to go and look at what had been written down.

Creeping out from behind his private area, candle in hand, Guy managed to negotiate the slumbering figures of the others who hadn't had time to return home before the early fall of night, and get to Brother John's satchel. Rather than try and read it there, and risk being discovered by someone waking to go and find the jakes, Guy slipped silently back to his bed and sat hunched over the candle to read. Yet what he saw there deprived him of what little inclination he had left to sleep. Right up until he had taken over from Brother John, in every instance the timorous clerk had recorded precisely half of the amount set as the fine as was actually required.

Sitting back and rubbing his watering eyes, Guy was aghast at the level of duplicity going on here. How long had this been going on for, for a start off? Was this something new which had come in with Briwere? Or was it so well established that Brother John hadn't had to think twice about what he was being asked to do? The harder he thought, the more Guy reckoned that this defrauding of the court was half the reason why the brothers who came to act as clerks were always in such a state of nervous twitchiness. They must be permanently worried that they were damning their eternal souls by such lies!

But what could he do about it? And then Guy gulped as he realised that in his ignorance he had faithfully recorded the exact amounts due. By Our Lady, the sheriff would be expecting there to be double that amount in the small chest that would be transported back to Nottingham! And what would he do when it wasn't there?

With a groan, Guy pulled on his boots and his heavier, outer clothes. There was only one way out of this. He would have to go out to somewhere like one of the barns and rewrite his own records. It was the only way around it.

Ferreting in Brother John's satchel, Guy was hugely relieved to see that there were more sheets of parchment, and a tentative shake of the portable, sealed inkwell confirmed that there was enough ink in there for his purposes. To his relief there were also the means to sand down the surface of the parchment which had already been written on – a common enough practice with something as valuable as parchment, for if it could be reused it was. The first two sheets of the records were such palimpsests, for Guy could see the faint traces of previous words on them when he held them up in front of the candle's flames, and when he investigated the other supposedly blank sheets, he found that they were all the same. That was good! He could erase the records of today and put the sanded sheets back into the satchel, thereby not causing Brother John any grief for having to account for any lost sheets. The same number would go back with him, just not in the same order.

And so he set to, never so glad that his mother had made him practise his letters than now, for he could write confidently and with some speed, and if he missed some of the more pedantic details out of the court records in his haste this time, then that was no bad thing. Moreover, he was able to reduce the supposedly due amounts by a little more than half in many cases, so that by the time he sat back, with gritty eyes and an aching back, he was fairly sure that he had 'found' enough spare odd pennies and shillings out of those fines that he could give Alfred his dues even before he left for the woodmote. If the sheriff was only expecting double what was now recorded, he would still be satisfied, Guy hoped, as he slipped the satchel back to Brother John's side.

It was only as he was about to head for his own bed that he stopped and listened harder to the brother. Something wasn't right there at all! There was a wetness to the brother's breathing that Guy didn't like one bit, and he risked making a dash for the curtain to throw his heavy cloak behind it, along with his heavy jerkin. Hurrying to the monk's side in what he now hoped would be believable attire, given how cold it was, Guy put his hand to the brother's neck and was appalled to feel how badly the man's pulse was racing, and how he was burning up.

"Ho! Wake up!" he called out, and was relieved to see men struggling into wakefulness as he held the candle aloft.

"What's wrong?" the innkeeper grumbled from his place beside the fireplace.

"The monk – he's seriously ill!" Guy told him firmly. "We need to get him into a cart and taken back to his brothers with all speed. If he stays here others may catch what he's got."

That was enough for the innkeeper. The last thing he wanted was a hall full of sick men.

"Get a small cart and line it with plenty of hay," Guy advised. "That will help to keep him warm for the journey," and then joined with three others in carrying Brother John's shaking body to it. "Where's he from?" he thought to ask, as a scrawny nag was brought over and hitched to the traces.

"Rufford," someone answered.

"Ah, then he's on my way to Edwinstowe," Guy declared. "Nobody needs to come with me. I can lead the horse that far and then ask them to send a lay brother back with it for you."

None of the villagers looked upset about that. With everyone still desperately short of food until the next harvest could be got in, they were only too aware that if a sickness took hold in the village, then many of them might even die, given the way things were.

It was something Guy was quick to take advantage of. With nobody keen to get anywhere close to the cart, he was able to throw the satchel in onto the hay, and then go and fetch the fines box and put that in too. Of course, he knew that both the records and the fines should go with Strelley to Nottingham, but since this was his first time acting in such a position at an assize, Guy was pretty sure that he could get away with taking them under the cover of saying that he thought he could take both these fines and those from the woodmote to Nottingham in one go. This was something he would only ever be able to do once – Briwere was too astute to have the wool pulled over his eyes repeatedly – and even so, as soon as they were clear of the village, Guy reached down into the cart and pulled the fines box up onto his saddle. Having only just written all the numbers down, he knew exactly how much he could extract from the box, and counted the amount out, carefully mixing the denominations so that the box wasn't left with an odd-looking array of coins.

It was a good thing that he did. He'd set out with the first glimmer of dawn, and the morning was scarcely halfway through when he heard hooves hammering up behind him. Sanson de Strelley appeared on his fine horse from around the previous bend, and there was no mistaking his relief at seeing Guy.

"I must have the fines and the records!" he practically begged Guy. "Briwere gets in the most frightful temper if we don't individually account for our courts."

"By Our Lady!" Guy gasped in feigned innocence. "Why ever does he do that? It's not as though the amounts aren't written down plain for all to see. A day or two either way for him to getting them surely makes little difference?" But then he shrugged and handed both over to Strelley, saying sympathetically, "But I understand your concern. Our sheriff is terribly prone to fits of anger. It's a wonder he doesn't sicken with his humour so out of balance."

He got the sickliest of smiles from Strelley as the implication sank in that Guy might have been wholly honest in his recording, and that confirmed to Guy that Strelley was no innocent in all of this. Was he, maybe, getting his own cut of the proceedings? All these minor courts took up a lot of time, time which took Strelley away from his manors and for next to no legitimate reward. A minor knight in an English shire could get squeezed very hard under King Richard's rule, and not just for money but for time and services too.

It might well be that Briwere had come to some arrangement with such men in the shires, because God alone knew that the number of knights eligible to hold such posts just at the moment were few and far between, and the sheriff might well be alert to the fact that he was hardly flush with choices for such essential men. Better to have a semi-honest man like Strelley, who would be content with a small recompense, than be reduced to employing the out-and-out rogues, who might well fleece the sheriff to a far greater extent. Keeping tracks and control on such men would entail more time than even Briwere possessed, let alone the amount of effort that it would require – and Briwere wasn't someone who liked to overexert himself unless left with no other choice.

However in Strelley's case, Guy knew that he had been desperate to inherit his father's lands and title, but had been held up in that process by being fined heavily for having been at the siege of Nottingham, so it was no wonder that he felt he had to dance to whatever tune the sheriff chose to play. A bad word from Briwere to someone like the archbishop, and Strelley might find his family lands being auctioned off to the highest bidder. Men like him had to walk a very fine and precarious line if their families weren't to suddenly become destitute – and given what rode on him retaining his own manor at Gisborne, Guy was all sympathy for that predicament. And so he kept the half-smile on his lips and waved Strelley farewell, as if never a doubt had crossed his mind.

What was rather more of a puzzle was how he was going to get the money to Alfred now. He'd half hoped, that having copied the records out, he would be able to leave Mansfield via Alfred's small holding on the outskirts. But Brother John's state had overridden that, and in all conscience Guy knew he had to get the monk to Rufford with all the speed the poor nag could manage. Indeed, as Strelley disappeared down the road, Guy realised that he needed to hitch his own stronger horse to the wagon and just lead the nag, or he'd be taking a corpse into the abbey.

It was no problem to make the adjustments for an expert horseman like Guy, and he kept his horse at a sharp clip all the way, reaching Rufford Abbey after dark but with the monk still alive, albeit only hanging on by a thread. Explaining the problem to the gate keepers, Guy was horrified to learn that half of the monastic precinct was prostrate with the same feverish complaint.

"We've lost three brothers already," a burly lay brother told him as Guy unhitched his horse. "I hate to be inhospitable when you've brought dear brother John back to us, but if you can find somewhere else to stay for the night, I would! This contagion is no respecter of persons – both the prior and sub-prior are sick as dogs, and they eat a lot better than most of us and have braziers in their rooms through the cold nights."

"Don't worry," Guy reassured him, "I've camped out in the forest before now. I know plenty of spots." And he did. The outlaw camp north-west of Inkersall was only two miles away, and even walking his now tired horse, Guy knew he could be there within the hour, for he knew the route there like the back of his hand by now.

What he wasn't expecting was to smell wood smoke as he got close to the camp. Someone was there! Only a few going by the fact that it had to be a small fire by its faint scent, but he really didn't want to walk in on Robin. So he tethered his horse a little way back and crept in as softly as he could.

To his amazement, Marianne and Mariota sat around a small fire, seemingly on their own, and so he retrieved the horse and then made rather more noise about going in, announcing, "It's only, me, Guy," before he emerged into the open space hidden behind cleverly hedged hawthorns. He didn't want them skewering him with arrows in their fright, and Guy had enough respect for both of their capabilities to know that they could do that.

"Guy!" there was no mistaking the warmth in both the women's voices as they chorused his name and hurried to meet him.

"Whatever brings you here?" Mariota asked, and so over some of the hearty stew they had brewed up, he told them.

"How on earth I'm going to get the money to Alfred, though, I don't know. I have to be in Edwinstowe by mid-morning tomorrow, and I have the nastiest suspicion that Jordan le Grand will do his best to force Alfred to move on before too long. In his eyes he's been made a fool of, and men like him never take well to that."

"We could take it," Marianne offered.

"Really? Aren't you waiting to join the others for something?"

Both women looked awkward and shook their heads, Mariota then saying,

"*Ach*, it's about time somebody told you this anyway, Guy. ...We think Robin is up to his old tricks."

Guy felt his heart sink into his boots. "Tricks? What sort of tricks?"

Marianne snorted. "The kind where he ends up leading his own small army! Blessed St Thomas, I don't know him anymore, I really don't. I can't work out why he's doing what he is, but...!" she threw her hands up in frustration, unable to carry on.

"I think you'd better go back a stage or two and tell me what's going on," Guy said gently to Mariota, and got a grateful smile in return.

"I think it started with us going up to Whitby," she said, obviously measuring her words to gauge what Guy's reaction would be, and he knew that if he broke into a rant about Robin, that they wouldn't tell him even half of what he now desperately wanted to discover. When he stayed silent she seemed relieved and continued, "Oh he was crafty, I'll give him that. He stayed quiet on the subject for three or four weeks. But then gradually he's started dropping in these little hints. We need more men, he said. If things are so bad over in Normandy that mercenaries are starting to look elsewhere for easy targets, then we have to be able to defend the villages, he kept saying."

She sighed. "That was so cunning, Guy. He's learned where he made his mistakes in the past, and he always talks in terms of looking after the people now. ...He doesn't think Marianne or I are worth winning over, if he ever did before, and so he ignores us when he's in one of his moods to try and wheedle around the others, and because of that we end up sitting back and not part of the discussions."

"And so you see things the others don't," Guy caught on.

"Just like you've done," and he got another of Mariota's sympathetic smiles. "Was he always so charming, or is it something he's cultivated?"

That made Guy pause before he answered. "A bit of both, I suppose," he ventured. "Baldwin the boy was always an engaging lad, but I never thought of it as a deliberate attempt at manipulation. I think it was just that with his half-brothers being so much older than him, he grew up knowing that going head to head with them was never going to work. And unless I've got it horribly wrong, I don't think this craftiness you talk about was even there when he first came back from the crusades. If I had to pinpoint a time when that changed, it would be him getting that near-killing blow on the head in King Richard's camp. To me he's been markedly different since then ...but before that? No."

"That's what Tuck said," Marianne agreed. "But I'm glad you think so, because I was starting to wonder how many kinds of fool I'd have to be, to have fallen so in love with him if he'd had this nasty undercurrent inside of him right from when I met him."

"You're no fool, Marianne," Guy declared, immediately wrapping an arm around her shoulders and giving her a hug. "He's changed. I can't see anything of the Baldwin I grew up with in the man this Robin's become. He might as well be a total stranger to me

– and that's not just wounded pride or hurt feelings talking, either. He's not the same at all."

Mariota was giving firms nods of her head at his words. "See? Guy sees it that way, too! Stop berating yourself, Marianne." She turned to Guy. "But what's got us worried is the way Robin is going about all of this. Oh he's realised that just sweeping lads up out of the villages is a bad idea. Whether that has anything to do with him actually caring about their fate is something I wouldn't care to speculate on, though. Tuck gave me one of his disapproving looks when I said this to him, but I for one think that it stems from his bruised pride over how things went wrong in the castle when you had to rescue us. That has left a scar deep inside him, I'm afraid, and us saying how damned glad we were that you were there and acted as you did only seems to have made things worse.

"I fear he's so far gone that Martin and Simon's actual deaths – the fact that they died in such a tragic way, unnecessarily, and wholly because of himself – are barely part of Robin's reasoning. Marianne and I actually heard him saying to Aneirin that they died because they weren't proper fighters!" She turned to Marianne. "I still wish you'd let me slap him that time!"

Marianne smiled for the first time that evening. "I think him hearing you swear at him was shock enough."

Mariota rolled her eyes. "*Tsk*, what did he think we heard out in the Holy Land? In the throes of childbirth we've both heard highborn ladies swearing like fishwives, let alone the wounded soldiers who got brought in to our care. But that, Guy, is part and parcel of why we're here. We wanted some time away from the men. Just the two of us. Because we felt we needed to have a frank discussion about what we're going to do if Robin brings the kind of men he wants into the camp."

Guy's heart found a new depth to plunge to as he asked, "What sort of men?"

"Other outlaws," Marianne sighed. "He's taken to vanishing off into the forest for days on end, and when he comes back he often says that he's found other outlaws who'd be glad to join with 'Robin Hood'."

"What in Jesu's name do Will and Siward and Gilbert say about that?" Guy asked, aghast. "And Hugh and the Coshams? Surely they've protested?"

But Marianne was shaking her head. "The first three you mentioned have said 'no' outright, but the others ...I'm afraid they don't think that there *are* other outlaws. Oh, they know that there are others living rough in the forest. They're not that naive. I mean that they don't think that Robin's even found them, much less been talking them into coming into our band and sharing our hideouts and stuff. They think it's all in his head."

"Oh God in Heaven!" Guy gulped. "So of course they're not taking it seriously."

"No," Marianne said sadly, "but Mariota and I have to think it might happen, and it's because of where that would leave us."

"Jesu! You'd be the two lone women with all of those men!" Guy gasped, and got relieved smiles from both of them.

"And you're the first of the men who's fully grasped that," Mariota said approvingly. "What, by Our Lady, are we supposed to do if three or four of these strangers are left in the camp with us, and they take it into their heads to help themselves to what they think is on offer? Anierin and Rhys couldn't help us fight them off. And because Robin – who rightly or wrongly is likely to be seen as the outright leader by such men – treats us with scant respect these days, there's a very real danger that we'd be seen as nothing more than camp followers, there for any man to enjoy as the mood takes him."

"That's awful!" Guy exclaimed, and immediately put his arms around both of their shoulders and pulled them tight to him. How had such a thing come to pass? "You should leave now, before these men turn up. By the time they're streaming into the camp it'll be too late. Better to leave now, and be able to go back, then for something to happen and you have to leave for good."

"Well that's why we're here," Mariota said tentatively. "You see, we were coming to see you."

"Me?"

"Yes. We wondered if you knew whether your mother would be prepared for us to spend some time at Kirklees? Not to take holy orders, you understand, although we effectively did that when we took our vows to the Hospitaller order. We were thinking of spending some time as lay sisters. We're hardly afraid of hard work, and we have skills we could teach the sisters in exchange for refuge."

"I think she'd be more than happy to take you in," Guy replied. "When do you want to go?"

Marianne sighed. "Well I think we need to let Tuck and some of the others know where we're going. We don't want a repeat of the hunt like the last time we left. And the other thing is, Robin made that sound like we caused the problems after a while – you know, women getting all emotional and going off in a huff. Well we're not going to give him that opening again! They're going to know where we're going and why."

"But we wanted to be sure we had somewhere to go before we said those things," Mariota added hurriedly. "There'd be nothing worse, we thought, than giving all these reasons and then not going for weeks. That would make it seem like there was no real problem as well." She took a deep breath. "And there was something else we wanted to ask you. You can say no if you want to."

Guy quirked an eyebrow at her and smiled. "I think I can guess."

"Really?"

"Well you've just said that you wouldn't want to say permanent vows. So that means that if you felt that you couldn't go back, and several months had passed, you'd be looking for another place to live."

Mariota's jaw fell, making Marianne laugh and say, "I told you Guy was sharp!"

Guy grinned. "Not Gisborne, though! Not because I wouldn't want you there, but because it's too close to Robin under those circumstances. But there is my little manor up in Scotland. I've had letters via a local monk sent from the lads who went up there to make a new life and look after the place for me, and they say the land is good. Even better, you wouldn't be the only women up there because their wives have joined them. You'd be sharing the place with families."

"Bless you!" Mariota breathed. "Oh, that's such a relief!"

"The only condition would be that I take you up there," Guy added, "and you can call me an old fusspot if you want, but it would be because I wouldn't want two women travelling alone on such a long journey. As a knight I have a certain status. It wouldn't help us with any marauding bands, but it does mean that I get rooms at inns and the like without anyone looking sideways at me."

"How would you get away from the sheriff, though?" Marianne fretted.

"Well I am allowed to go up to Gisborne, you know. If I said I needed to go for a couple of weeks, and I got you horses to ride, we should be able to do it in that time. I might be late back, but then given how the other knights stretch their absences out, I wouldn't be abnormal in that."

"Then we'll gladly take your money to this Alfred," Marianne said after she'd hugged him and kissed him on the cheek. "It'll be nice to be able to be the ones doing the giving for a change. That's something else Robin keeps to himself as much as possible."

"There's just one other thing," Guy said tentatively, and got questioning looks back. "...I wouldn't have said anything except for you talking about leaving altogether, you understand. ...But do you realise how much Hugh loves you, Marianne? He'll want to go with you, you know."

The expression on her face said that she hadn't realised, but Mariota was smiling knowingly.

"I'd spotted that too," she added. "And with Hugh you'd have a proper husband – because he wouldn't use you the way Robin was intending to do!"

You weren't expecting that? But I have told you of how I caught Hugh looking at Marianne already. And now you are downcast because you think Robin has been abandoned by his lady – my, you are fickle, Brother! If anything it was the other way around. Marianne had been faithful to the hope that Robin would one day wake up and see her virtues – and Marianne was a virtuous woman, as was Mariota.

Ah, if it stops your pouts so that I can continue with this, then yes, I will tell you what happened between them. The two women did leave the gang for a while and go to my mother, and yes, they repaid the sisters' hospitality by teaching them as many of their nursing skills as those there had the time and talent to learn. Many travellers would benefit over the following years from what the sisters at Kirklees learned during the summer months of 1197. And I know that my dear cousin

Allan made several visits there, under the pretext of visiting my mother – who was not fooled for one moment, I might add – so that Hugh could go to visit Marianne without seeming too much the ardent suitor for the sisters' sensibilities to cope with. But, no, neither woman left permanently, and that was because of what unfolded towards the end of the year, and no, I will not make a shortcut to those events until I have told you the rest of what happened to me in that half year.

You see, I actually managed to subvert the sheriff twice more on my own during those months. Small victories, to be sure, but they were mine and they made me feel so much better about myself and what I was trying to do. And what were they? Well the first was a case of Briwere hanging onto fines again.

A farmer at South Muskham had had his winter grain trampled by two of the bishop's tenants and their men, who had been entertained by his lordship at the castle at Newark, and had gone home rather the worse for wear on his wine. There was no question of their guilt, for half of the village saw them do it. But at the next assize at Newark, which I had to attend because of a man getting gored to death by his own farrowing sow, I heard the stiff fine being handed out to them myself. Forewarned by now, I knew that the money would have to make its circuit via Nottingham Castle, but I was horrified to encounter the farmer in the outer bailey of the castle some four weeks later, begging for his recompense. The poor fellow had great need of that money in order to be able to buy the seeds for his next crop, for he had been able to salvage next to nothing from his trampled fields.

Now I knew that the money should have gone out to him already, and so I managed to divert him to the stables where my friends could keep an eye on him, and went in search of the records. To my shock I found that <u>none</u> of the payments which should have been made from that assize had been made, and that was bad, Brother, very bad. Some were due to men who, while legitimately deserving recompense, would survive without them. But there were three, including the farmer, whom I knew were in a terrible state for not getting justice for the damages done to them, and I resolved to act.

These were not the largest sums due by any means, and therefore they were ones which I could hopeful remove from the funds without too much effort – or rather, I knew I could remove them from the sheriff's secret hoard of coin, kept by him in case of emergency. To take more than a pound's worth from the monies already set aside as coming from that particular assize would have been to immediately signal that someone within the castle had done this deed, for the coins had all been most carefully counted upon arrival, and the whole issue was still recent enough for a man like Briwere to have the final amount fixed in his mind. But the reserve, I knew, had not been counted recently.

How did I know? For truth because, Brother, I had made it my business to visit the two hard-pressed clerics who were currently acting as Briwere's clerks, and to watch what was going on following my encounter with Strelley. I was not going to get caught out like that again! And I was always popular with the brothers who came to serve the sheriff – usually from Lenton Priory – because I knew the forest laws by heart by now, and what fines they should incur, and I had frequently been furtively summoned by them to try and sort out some muddle which had taken place at a woodmote or swanimote. So my turning up in the cramped little room within the main keep which Briwere used as his counting room and strong-room was not going to cause comment, and for once I used it solely to further my own ends and discover the full depths of Briwere's creative accounting system. Now may I continue?

Very well. So I took the money owed to those men, and for once had the great pleasure in taking it to them in person. I took great care, mind you, to impress upon them that I could not do this regularly, and that it was only because a great miscarriage of justice was taking place that I could risk acting at all. The farmer who had come to the castle actually wept with relief, you know, because the market where he needed to buy his grain was taking place the very next day. He could have waited a week until the next one, but by then all that would have been left would have been the poorest scrapings. Not that he would ever have been able to buy the best seed grains, and not only through insufficient funds. Those always got sold on to outside of the shire, and although I do not know for certain to where, I am sure that they got sold across the sea where they would fetch a good price. As I said before, our fertile soil in Nottinghamshire meant that we could grow decent grain in years when others struggled to produce anything but tatters and tares, yet that rarely benefited our own farmers and folk.

The other two poor souls were not being compensated for loss of crops so directly, for one had lost an ox after it had been frightened into bolting into the mud of a swollen river and drowned, and I surmised that he may well have had to use at least a goodly chunk of his money to replace it, leaving him little to buy the seed with. Yet seed without the means to put it in the ground would have been of little use to him, for *preparing a field by hand was not a viable alternative. And the third was a dyer whose business had been burned by a jealous rival, which you might not think of as in quite the same category as the other two, but he needed to buy the seasonally available plant materials to make his dyes from; and again, some of those would not wait for weeks to remain on sale in a state worth having.*

So if he was to rebuild his business he needed to make those purchases now. And he had my sympathy, Gervase, because I knew that the competitor who had acted so viciously towards him was a man whom the sheriff favoured for his own commissions of cloth. Therefore it hardly took a divine revelation to work out that the sheriff was making sure that the man lost his competition, and that in return the guilty dyer would then be dying the wool the sheriff had his eye on for his new attire at a substantially reduced rate.

You are shocked, Gervase? Bless me, such things are the way of the world out beyond these cloisters. It is just that you live so far away from it as to not know that it goes on. But have we finished with my good deeds? Do not sound so wearied of them, Brother! They may not have the dash and excitement of my cousin – no, I did not fight off armed raiders, for truth! – but these happenings were important at the time because they affected how I saw and reacted to Robin soon after.

Oh, very well, then. I will refrain from telling you about my successful disentangling of the events concerning the death of a miller's boy, and how in doing so I prevented the sheriff from seizing the mill into his own hands and a hefty fine from the miller himself. Ha! Now it concerns a death you are all ears, are you? Well I am prickled! This is my <u>confession</u>, Brother, and I do not feel you are taking this in the right spirit at all. And since I was righting a wrong, that incident was hardly something I need to confess to, and so we shall move on and maybe you will be less judgemental over what I am now going to tell you until you have all of the facts.

Chapter 22

By Our Lady, Brother, close your mouth before you start trapping flies!

Oh, you did not expect an old man like me to have such a bite? Well I was no bumbling fool in my youth nor now, and you should have gathered *that* from all I have said. I have stood up in courts and given my testimonies; I have spoken directly with great lords; and I have had the authority to act as the sheriff's – and therefore the king's – forester and to uphold those forest laws, sometimes in the face of very strong opposition. Therefore I am not, and never was, some mewling squire creeping in his master's shadow like a beaten cur. So do not mess with me! There is a saying up across the border where I now live, and it goes, ~Touch not a cat but a targe~, and it means, to put it bluntly, you do not poke a wild cat unless you have a damned good shield, for its claws are sharp when unsheathed and its reactions lightning fast. So do not poke me, Brother, for you do not possess sufficient a shield against my worldly experience, and like the wild cats, I grow crabbit in my old age!

No, I will not be mollified, Gervase. We shall move on to when I next saw Robin, and that is that. And if I continue waspish now, it is at the recollection of the very personal attack which was to come against me from him. An attack which came very close to doing all manner of harm, and for which Robin would never actually apologise to me for, much less make amends.

You are looking at me sideways, Brother... What was the problem this time? Guard your tone, confessor mine! This was not some petty squabble; some childish falling out. It concerned a lady who had already been most badly used by other men, and for her part I was able to forgive her for her accusations, since she was scarcely in her right mind by the time I actually met her. But you must have the full story to grasp how I was maligned, and it began with me arriving back at the castle from Derbyshire, which turned out to be horribly condemning in the short term.

Nottingham & Derbyshire
August, the Year of Our Lord, 1197

Guy was met as he rode in by Harry, his friend's face creased in a worried frown.

"Blessed St Thomas! Thanks be that I've caught you before anyone else has seen you," and there was no mistaking the relief in his voice.

"God's wounds, Harry! Whatever's wrong?" Guy asked. "Nobody's died have they?"

"Come! Into the stables with you, quick, before anyone sees you," was all Harry would say until they were safely within his own domain within the outer bailey.

"For the love of God," Guy said turning to him, "what is it, Harry?"

Instead, Harry gestured him over to a couple of stools at the back of the stable. "You'd better sit down for this, Guy. You're not going to like it. But before I say anymore I have to ask you this: do you know Juetta, the widow of Simon fitz Ranulph, and her daughter Avice?"

Guy's blank look all by itself told Harry what he'd suspected, and that was that Guy had probably never even clapped eyes on either of them. Then as Guy shook his head, said in a voice heavy with dismay, "Then I'm afraid you need to brace yourself, my friend, because you're being accused of raping Avice."

"*What?*" Of all the things Guy had been thinking, this was something he hadn't remotely expected.

"Just listen to me!" Harry said urgently. "We don't have much time before someone comes looking for you – because trust me, my friend, they have been watching for you for the past day, and the sheriff is practically frothing at the mouth over this." Guy swallowed hard, but nodded and let Harry continue. "Right, well if what I've had off the hall servants is right – and you have more friends there than you realise – Hubert fitz Ranulph rode in fair spitting feathers and demanding to see the sheriff the evening before last. You're lucky in that, because the sheriff was at his table, and so there were plenty of servants around to hear him. If he'd come mid afternoon, we might not have had such a warning.

"Now you would know better than me, but apparently fitz Ranulph is struggling to pay a fine for being another one caught in the castle when the siege came..."

"...Yes he was. He was there..."

"...Hmmm, well I don't know whether he's seeing this as a way to get hold of his late brother's lands, but from what was overheard, his late brother, Simon's, main manor lies at Tansley, while his own is closer to Bolsover at Walton."

"Oh, that's right. I know where you mean now."

"Have you ever been there?"

"No. I've ridden in the area around Tansley quite a bit because I'm friends with Sir Richard at The Lea, which is not far away, but I don't know either of the fitz Ranulph brothers except for when Sir Hubert has come here."

Harry sucked through his teeth. "Would Sir Richard vouch for you?"

"I would think so, if needs be."

"You need! I'm telling you – you really need him to! They're saying that back in the spring you rode through, and on a dark and foul night you came knocking at the manor's door. In a fit of Christian charity, and because you are a knight, Juetta is saying that she let you in. Then at some time during the night, you forced your way into her daughter's chamber and raped her."

"Why ever didn't they bring this accusation then?" Guy wondered. "I could have proved my innocence beyond doubt then!"

Harry shook his head. "I think that's the problem, Guy. They don't want you to be able to do that. But it gets worse."

"*Dewi Sant*! Worse? How could it get worse?"

Putting a consoling hand on Guy's shoulder, Harry said, "They're saying you came by three nights ago and tried to take her again, and when she screamed, you beat her. Or the other version – and I have to say that Sir Robert is far from clear on this – is that when you found her with child and she told you it was yours, you beat her for that."

Guy was stunned. As a man who had always treated women with the utmost respect, this was an accusation which totally rocked his world to the very foundations.

"I would never...!"

"I know you wouldn't. ...*We* know you wouldn't!" and Guy became aware that Harry's lads had drifted in and were making sympathetic murmurings. "But what's really put the cat in the dovecote is that three villagers have come forward to say that they recognised you riding away from the manor in the early hours."

"Jesu!" Guy was lost for any other words. How could they have witnessed him when he hadn't even been there?

One of the youngest lads came tearing into the stable. "They know!" he panted. "Sheriff's calling for Sir Guy to be brought before him!"

"You'd better go," in his dazed state Guy heard someone say. "It'll only look worse if they seem to find you hiding in here."

Walking out into the cold evening air, Guy was surprised to see many of the servants stop what they were doing to watch him striding across to the barbican gates and into the inner bailey, although with none of the malice he was half expecting now. But what woke him up was hearing one of the bakers say,

"Poor bastard! Bloody Briwere's always had it in for him. Looks like he's finally found a stick to beat him with – even if it is all bloody lies."

In that moment Guy's shock turned to anger. He would not lie down and let them do this to him, even though as yet he didn't know quite where Briwere was going to take this.

He strode into the main hall, head held high and marched up to where the sheriff sat at the top table, the evening meal being in progress. By Briwere's side was the knight Guy belatedly recognised as Hubert fitz Ranulph, and who rose to his feet with a belligerent expression on his face. But feeling eternally grateful for Harry's loyalty and the warning, Guy was alert to the fact that there was also uncertainty in fitz Ranulph's eyes. Was he worried that Guy might want to defend his honour in a very physical way? After all, he had seen Guy use the huge Welsh bow at the siege, and fighting for real, and maybe he was just that bit scared of going nose to nose in combat with someone whose experience went beyond just coming and posturing at the castle for so many days a year?

"You wanted to see me?" Guy demanded with scant courtesy.

Him going on the offensive instantly put Briwere on the back foot. He'd lost the initiative, and that wasn't how he'd seen this going.

"Yes," Briwere said, tugging his robes' sleeves down in a gesture Guy by now knew meant that he was trying to give himself time to think. "You have been accused of a most grievous matter, Sir Guy."

"By whom?" *Don't let on that you know*, all of Guy's instincts were screaming. *Make them spell it out!*

Fitz Ranulph cleared his throat noisily. "By me."

"And what am I accused of?" Guy cut in with, deliberately not letting fitz Ranulph take control.

As the knight blinked, taken off guard by Guy's challenge, it was Briwere who came in with,

"Of not only raping a lady of quality, but of beating her too. I always knew you were a savage brute, Gisborne, but this goes beyond anything a knight should do!"

"Good job I didn't do it, then!" Guy riposted back.

"My, my, you're very sure of that," Briwere sneered. "You didn't even think about your answer."

"Of course I'm bloody sure! And that's because I've *never* raped any woman, regardless of rank or station!"

Guy could see he'd got Briwere discomforted, but the sheriff was nothing if not dogged in his accusations.

"Oh come now, Gisborne! A man like yourself ...not married. You must have taken your comforts somewhere. Are you saying that you were never tempted by a pretty milkmaid, regardless of how willing she was?"

"I have enjoyed the company of many women," Guy admitted calmly. "But I will swear on the bible itself that every one of them lay with me willingly, and that any woman who turned me down left my company untouched." And now he went further on the attack, leaning in over the table to glare right into Briwere's face. "Who am I supposed to have so mistreated? Are you ever going to give me a name, or are you just going to go and randomly drag one of fitz Ranulph's tenants here to make this ridiculous accusation stand?"

Even those knights who didn't like Guy, and who had been relishing this rather too much up until now, began to develop worried frowns. Guy had been swift to grab the straw the sheriff had unwittingly handed him in that reference to milkmaids, and him assuming – as the other knights saw it – that the accusing woman was just one of the farmers' wives, suddenly had them wondering what was going on.

"You know who!" fitz Ranulph roared, coming to his feet. "My niece, Avice! Do not play with me, sir! You know very well who she is! You met her when she came here with me when the first eyre came around."

Guy felt his heart give a skip. The first provable mistake had just been made, and thank *Dewi Sant* that he wasn't too shocked to jump on it. "Forgive me, Sir Hubert, but you are wrong," he said firmly.

Fitz Ranulph spluttered in his ire. "I am not wrong!" he fumed. "You danced with her! You danced with her right here in this hall. You flattered her and even then you showed an interest in her, even though the poor girl was only recently widowed and on her way back to her mother's home."

Guy kept calm. "No, Sir Hubert, I cannot possibly have met her here, much less danced with her. Everyone here knows that during *that* eyre I was working with Hugo Bassett, and others taking the judges around Derbyshire. I know that I was close by your own manor then, at Bolsover, but I went on north to the Peak. I did not come back here until the eyre was long over. Anyway, if she'd dance with me she would have complained long and hard about getting trampled on, because everyone here knows that I have two left feet when it comes to such courtly dalliances – I'd make a mess of a village May dance, let alone what goes on here. I feel deeply sorry for your niece's plight, sir, but I am not the one who has caused it."

Sir Walter's voice carried over the murmur of voices Guy's response incited, saying, "That's right, Guy wasn't here then."

His words earned Walter a filthy look from Briwere, but Walter simply out-stared him back, and that was another good thing Guy realised. He would be listened to by many. This was not going to be the simple job Briwere had hoped. Emboldened, Guy raised his voice and demanded,

"Now would someone kindly tell me what *exactly* is supposed to have happened?"

"You came to my late brother's house!" fitz Ranulph ranted. "Demanded to be let in to spend the night, and then when the household had gone to bed, you went to my niece's chamber and availed yourself of her..."

"...And when was this?"

"By Our Lady, Gisborne! Long enough ago for her belly to be swelling with your runt!"

"Easter? Before Easter? When?" Guy wasn't going to let them get away with being vague. Not when his very honour was at stake. And he'd done some very rapid calculations over this, because he was betting that Avice hadn't revealed her pregnancy until relatively recently, perhaps because she'd dallied with someone her family wouldn't approve of, or just out of shame if she really had been raped. Therefore even allowing for the looseness of gowns that she might wear, the chances were that she wasn't more than five months gone, and that in turn had to mean that she had conceived in April or possibly late March.

He glanced around the room and could see that the mature married men like Walter, Martin, and the three castle knights, were also doing some rapid calculations and were starting to see the point, even as fitz Ranulph paused, then spluttered,

"Before Easter, you rogue! You came for the witnesses for the assize. Juetta herself says that you came, claiming that you needed to take the men to Derby to bear witness to the affray at Chesterfield."

"That was not me," Guy said firmly. "I attended the Mansfield sitting of the assize, then went on north to the woodmote at Edwinstowe. You have the court records to prove that. Before that I was preparing for the woodmote by collecting evidence up by Cuckney and Clowne – and I can prove that because I stayed at Cuckney Castle, whose lord is no friend of mine, by the way. There is no way that I could have gone from there, done what you claim, and been back at Mansfield in time for the court."

He turned to Briwere and said forcefully, "And *you* know that, sheriff, because I had to take over as scribe when the ague struck down the brother from Rufford. Do you not recall? That terrible ailment that started like a cold and within days had claimed the lives of so many? Sanson de Strelley can vouch for me there, and the king's own Keeper, Sir Ralph fitz Stephen, can vouch for me at the woodmote."

Briwere was starting to look distinctly sickly. He knew he was being made to look a fool by all of this, and a better man than him would have taken fitz Ranulph on one side and made the point that maybe Juetta and Avice were mistaken, but Briwere never did know when to let something go.

"Then why did you return, Gisborne?"

"Return? Return where? Here?"

"No, you conniving dolt, to the fitz Ranulph manor at Tansley!"

"Return there? Sheriff, I've never even *been* there, much less gone back!"

Briwere's expression soured even further. "Don't play games with me, Gisborne! Three nights ago you went back to the manor house, forced your way in, and then – when you found out about Lady Avice's condition – you laid into her with your fists. She's lucky to be alive. Argue your way out of that one if you can!"

Now for the first time Guy told an outright lie, praying as he did so that both his friend would back him up, if the need arose, and that he wouldn't be struck down by the saints he had recently appealed to for doing so. *If I'm to not only save myself, but get to the bottom of who did actually hurt this poor soul*, he offered up to the heavens, *I have to do this*.

"I stayed that night with Sir Richard of The Lea," he said with all the confidence he could muster, and because it came on the back of so many reasoned rebuttals of these accusations, he was relieved to see that his word was accepted.

Only Briwere queried it, demanding, "And why did you do that?"

Guy didn't have to fake rolling his eyes in exasperation. "Because I've known Sir Richard for a good many years, not least because we've both at times had the care of the castle at The Peak. And that, by the way, is also why I would never have asked to stay at the widow's house – I have a friend nearby. I often call in to see him if I'm in the area, if for no other reason than because he has his eye on matters in that area with considerably more astuteness than most of his neighbours. He usually knows when a tree has just come down in a gale or been felled, for instance, so I am doing my duty when I go there, sheriff, not just dallying on the way. So there was nothing abnormal about my visit, and no, I wasn't deliberately setting myself an alibi, should you think that I was anticipating these accusations. His household will confirm this, too, not just Sir Richard himself."

Yet that made Briwere even tetchier. "Then how do you account for three men of the village all saying that they saw you at the fitz Ranulph manor at Tansley?"

That did worry Guy. What possible incentive did they have for blackening his name? "Did they see me? Me specifically? Or did they just see a knight, and with the two ladies supplying a name, you've put the two together?"

"They named you, Gisborne!" Briwere crowed triumphantly. "They named you!"

Guy tried to remain calm. "Then maybe they saw me riding back from The Lea, but on the following day."

This was all too much for Hubert fitz Ranulph. "You absolute scoundrel!" he screamed. "You defile the ladies of my household, and then you have the gall to call them liars, too? Shame upon you! May you rot in Hell for this, Gisborne! Because to add to your shame, you're a liar!"

"I do not lie," Guy snapped back frostily, "and I will prove to you that I don't! And before you shout too loudly, maybe you should stop to think why people must be wondering why you have taken so long to point the finger of blame at me. If I am such a blight on your family's name, surely you should have come to see the sheriff the moment he returned here from the Easter court?" At which he turned on his heels and stormed out of the hall, followed by the sound of Briwere screaming his name, and for him to return. The rising hum of other voices, though, told him that even the dimmest had suddenly caught on that this didn't make any sense except in fitz Ranulph and Briwere's heads.

Yet wanting no company and time to think, he retreated up to the top of the old keep. Those village men bothered him. He was sure that Tansley was one of the villages which had been helped by Robin, and that it was one of the outlaws' safe places. The very fact that they had one of their lesser hideouts barely a mile outside of the village, and yet had never been betrayed, said that that was still probably the case. Was that even the reason why? Did they think that he, Guy, was an enemy of Robin Hood's, and with a little prodding from their lord, had thought to aid their hero in some strange way? Yet why had none of the gang put the villagers right in that case? Guy was mystified and not a little scared. He could clear – and indeed he hoped probably already had – his name of the initial rape, but this beating of Avice was going to be harder to dismiss if there were witnesses who would appear before a court.

He hadn't realised how long he'd been up there, resting his aching head on the cool stones, when a voice came behind him,

"Ah, there you are!"

He started and turned around, only to be even more surprised to see the three castle knights with Walter and Martin.

"Well this is a right mess," Sir Hugh said amiably, coming to lean on the parapet beside Guy. "You do get yourself into the most incredibly scrapes, Guy."

"You believe me?" Guy asked worriedly.

"Of course we do, you nitwit," Sir Richard of Burscot tutted fondly. "We didn't believe it when bloody fitz Ranulph turned up – it all sounded too vague by half – but we hadn't heard the details, so we couldn't put our fingers on what was wrong."

"We know you," Sir Martin said with a sad smile. "Of all the knights in the castle you're probably the last one any of us would think such a thing of."

Sir Walter was nodding in accompaniment to his friend, adding, "But you kept your head in there. Well done! I'm not sure I would have been so calm if I'd had that dropped on me."

"I was warned by the stable lads," Guy confessed. "It wasn't much, but at least it wasn't quite the bolt from the blue Briwere no doubt wanted it to be."

"Well they certainly did you a good turn there," Martin agreed.

Guy rolled his shoulders in an attempt to ease the tension in them, then asked. "Can any of you tell me why this is happening? I mean, aside from Briwere's perennial dislike of me. There must be something they hope to gain for all of this?"

Sir Robert of Packringham gave a grunt of disgust. "I believe that Sir Hubert would rather like to get his hands on his brother's lands. Unfortunately, his first attempt went wrong before he could do anything."

"Oh?"

"Yes, you see Avice's first husband was one of Sir Hubert's liege men." He gave a sardonic laugh. "Hubert must be spitting feathers, because he got greedy and pretty much forced the lad to go to Normandy with King Richard, firstly to save Hubert the scutage money in lieu of service, and also to gain him some advancement which Hubert, as part of his family now, could take advantage of. But the poor sod got skewered on some French knight's lance and died, and with not even an heir on the way that Hubert could claim the wardship of."

"Why did he never claim Avice as his ward? Surely that would have been the simpler option?" Guy wondered, at which Sir Robert gave a wry smile.

"Oh, I think his brother was wise to Hubert's avarice. Simon might have been the younger of the two, but he got his mother's lands, you see, so he was able to gift them where he would, given that Hubert got all of the father's lands and could hardly say he'd been overlooked. So when Simon died, Hubert found out that he'd made Juetta the gift of the manor and lands for as long as she lives. Of course Simon believed that Avice was married and therefore taken care of, but he was canny enough to make the condition that should she be widowed – knowing the lad was with the king – then she was to be returned, along with her dowry, to Juetta's care – thereby depriving Hubert of the ability to claim Avice's husband's goods and chattels, even though he owns the house they lived in."

"Good grief!" Guy gasped, "There really wasn't any love lost there, was there?"

"Not a scrap," Robert agreed. "Now I can't say for definite, you understand, but my guess – knowing Sir Hubert as I do from the number of times he's been here – is that he has some idea of you marrying the now very plump Avice, and taking her and her mother off to your manor to live at your expense. ...He'll probably come up with some shit about them not feeling safe at the Tansley manor anymore, if pressed."

And suddenly Guy saw the light. "But then somebody has to look after the manor if they're gone, and who else would the sheriff appoint but Hubert?"

Robert patted him on the back. "You've got it! And the extra income would mean that Hubert could pay his fine to the sheriff..."

"...And Briwere looks good in the royal court's eyes for getting more of the fines in!" Guy snorted in derision. "No wonder Briwere doesn't want me defending myself! He really is a conniving shit, isn't he!"

His friends all agreed, but there was still the matter of the three witnesses bothering Guy.

"Who are these men?" he asked them. "I can't think of any of the villagers who might deliberately lie over something like this. I've always played fair with them over the forest laws. They know I'm not like some of the others here, who'll trump up false charges just to make themselves look good in Briwere's eyes. And there was that case of the dead stag a couple of years ago that I sorted out, don't forget – that could have turned ugly for them if not for me." Well he could hardly say the additional truth: that they possibly knew that he was working hand-in-glove with Robin Hood.

"Now they are a mystery," Sir Hugh confessed, but then had a moment of inspiration. "If we could get their names off fitz Ranulph, though, we must have some records here in the castle of who lives there, if only because of the additional taxes we've been bleeding them for for the last few years. We ought to be able to identify them that way."

"Hugh, you're a bloody miracle!" Guy gasped gratefully. "Yes, we ought to be able to tell if they're really villagers from Tansley, or if they're men Hubert's paid off to swear to my guilt."

His friends faces broke into smiles, and Martin added, "And if they don't even live in Tansley, then that turns everything upside down, because fitz Ranulph will have to have some very plausible reason for them being there in the first place."

"I'll go press him now," Sir Hugh said with a wink. "He's in his cups already, and too drunk to think straight enough to lie with any conviction."

"And the rest of you can come with me to the scribes' room," said Guy, feeling suddenly lighter in spirit. "If I can find the right piece of parchment, I'll hand it to you and you can be the ones to ask a scribe to read it out in Briwere's presence tomorrow morning."

Although it was getting late, Martin, Walter and Richard sat up with Guy as he ransacked the scribes' pigeonholes of their scrolls, while Robert went with Hugh to quiz fitz Ranulph. Despite his racing pulse, Guy made himself be methodical in his search. The monks who came here stored like with like, and so he only had to undo a rolled bundle and look at the first sheet to know what the rest were about, and before too long he had narrowed his search down to the pigeonholes where the lists of taxes due were. It then took a little longer to retrieve the right bundle, but as a distant bell was heard over the fields calling the monks of Lenton from their beds to Matins, he suddenly exclaimed, "Got it!"

His friends had been sat on stools leant against the wall, and Martin had almost dropped off, Guy's cry of triumph making him start and nearly fall off the stool, but all three came to their feet.

"That's it?" Walter asked.

Guy nodded. "See here? That's where the list of the men of Tansley and their worth is recorded. And that bit under the line there is the total amount of what Simon fitz Ranulph had to pay at the last carucage, and what his widow will need to collect for any future ones. Hugh was right, they have to be named, because that was one of the things Archbishop Walter was most insistent of this time – that men should not be charged twice. So everyone has to be assigned to somewhere, to one place only, and the only way to do that is by having every man who ought to make payment recorded at his lord's manor. If fitz Ranulph hopes to make this stick, he has no choice. He has to use men who are at least the heads of their households, because somebody's serf, or the boy who guards the sheep, wouldn't be admissible in any court to provide testimony – not the forest courts nor the judicial ones, not even the local hundredal courts."

"Blessed St Thomas!" Richard gasped. "Not having so much to do with the courts as you three, I'd totally forgotten that! But you're right, these men have to be of a minimum standing within the village if fitz Ranulph wants to bring them before a court as jurors."

Walter gave a dry laugh. "And with charges this serious, why wouldn't he want to press them further? He's going to make a right fool of himself if he then stands up in the hall and says he hadn't thought of doing that."

Guy thrust the piece of parchment at Sir Richard. "You take this. The mood Briwere's in, and with Walter having spoken up for me back in the hall, he might just try to dismiss this evidence as my friends trying to muddy the waters. But he doesn't know how closely we work together with you three, so you'll be believed more."

When morning came, Guy kept himself occupied within the outer bailey. He had to trust to his friends to prove his innocence now, but he'd barely got to work on mending the leather grip on one of his knives when he was summoned to the hall again. Even walking in he was surprised to see others quietly filtering in, even though they could have had no business which took them there in the normal run of things. For a moment he felt a rush of irritation at what he took to be ghoulish delight at his misfortune, but then heard someone in the shadows saying to another,

"If he can do this to Guy, none of us are safe. Who's he going to trump charges up against next?"

And it belatedly sank in with Guy that there must be quite a few of the knights here in the castle – both forest and those here doing service – for whom this was of far greater symbolic importance than he'd taken into consideration.

He looked to Briwere, and now that he was further into the hall and could see the sheriff's face through the gloom, for nobody wasted candles during the day, he could see that his face was as sour as a salted cod's. To one side stood fitz Ranulph, and he looked as sick as a dog, while to the other stood the three castle knights, their faces determinedly set solemn, but there was no mistaking the glint of triumph in their eyes.

"Well, Gisborne," Briwere drawled as Guy came to stand with a couple of feet of the sheriff's chair, "it seems that you have friends."

"We just wanted justice done," Sir Richard said firmly. "Every knight here could see that something wasn't right in all of this. And if such weak charges were allowed to stick to Sir Guy, then what might others of us be accused of in the future?"

Guy admired Richard for being so forthright, but then he saw Briwere's reaction, and realised that actually Richard had been right to say such a thing out loud, because Briwere's face was a picture. He'd obviously not thought this through that far, and the realisation that all these men, on whom he was reliant in order to keep the two shires under some semblance of order, were vicariously feeling threatened was a nasty shock.

"I'm going to repeat the names you told Sir Robert and me last night," Sir Hugh said icily to fitz Ranulph. "You said they were Godwin the carter, Harold Bellfield, and Martin son of Ansculf. Do you still stand by those names?"

Fitz Ranulph's cheeks wobbled as he puffed in indignation. "Yes... Yes! I mean ...those are the names Juetta gave me. ...And she brought them into the manor's hall for me to speak to. They were as real as any man here!"

Sir Robert stabbed an accusing finger in the direction of the parchment, which a worried looking monk was holding in quivering hands close by a lone candle so that he could read it. "Then how do you account for the fact that *none* of these men are actually tenants of your late brother's manor? Not one!"

"But ...but ...they must be!" fitz Ranulph spluttered. "Juetta wouldn't lie!"

Feeling that he ought to intervene before this became a matter of saving himself but defaming the widow, Guy interrupted with,

"But did she find these men, or did they come to her? Do you see the difference, Sir Hubert? If your brother's widow went out and enquired amongst the men of the village and actually *found* these men who were prepared to swear falsely that they had seen me, that's one thing. But if they came to her, saying they had heard what had happened at the manor, and offered to swear to you who they'd seen, then Widow Juetta has been duped in her distress. She is not at fault at all."

Seeing a way out of this without making a further fool of himself, Briwere seized on Guy's words. "I think you should return to your manor, fitz Ranulph, and try to find these so-called witnesses again, don't you?"

As fitz Ranulph went pale, suddenly realising that the sheriff had done an about face and was now accusing him by implication, if not in so many words, Guy threw another stone into this pool full of ripples.

"No, I think *several* of us should go and find these witnesses!" he declared firmly. "And that's not just to clear my name. These rogues, whoever they are, have very deliberately set out to give false evidence, and we need to know why – not least because it might be to cover up the trail of the person who *did* harm Lady Avice. If justice for her is to be done, we're only doing half the job if we prove that it wasn't me."

Even his friends turned to him wide-eyed at that, and as they filed out of the hall, with Hugh, two of the knights there to do service, and two of the forest knights, who were all to accompany Guy and fitz Ranulph back to Tansley, Sir Richard said,

"That's uncommonly gracious of you, Guy. I'm not so sure I would be so kindly disposed towards a woman who'd made such accusations against me."

Guy stopped and turned to him, forcing the others around them to stop in the confines of the narrow passageway.

"But she didn't, did she? I was thinking about this last night after you left. Not once in all of this mess has fitz Ranulph come out and said, "My niece Avice accuses you of being her assailant." Not once! And if she had, why wouldn't he have said so? Because then it becomes my word against that of a lady of higher station than me."

"God's hooks!" Hugh breathed. "By Our Lady, Guy, you're right! I didn't think of that, but of course he would have, wouldn't he?"

Guy nodded firmly. "And that probably means that this poor lass is in too much of a state to say much of anything, and *that* makes me angry. To me, she's now become as much a victim in all of this as me, and I want justice for her too. She shouldn't have to live with this brutal act, with no-one being made to account for her injuries, just because I didn't roll over and play dead. So we need to find out if it was these strange witnesses who first mentioned my name, because from where I'm standing, it's looking like I was never mentioned by name by either woman."

He took a few more steps, then stopped again, nearly causing another collision. "And there's one more thing. I want to see Avice face to face. If I really was her assailant, she should run from the room screaming just at the sight of me. But when she doesn't – and I'm convinced she won't – then you'll all be there to bear witness to the fact."

Sir Robert snorted. "God's wounds! I never want to get on the wrong side of you, Guy! You're sharper than the rest of us put together!"

"But he's right ...again," Sir Hugh said respectfully. "Someone's played Guy for a fool and lost."

At Tansley, Guy's prediction came true. Avice was brought into the hall before the men, shaking like a leaf and crying, but her eyes passed over Guy blankly without even a flicker of recognition. Admittedly she was in a shocking state, with one eye blackened and fully closed, but if she looked with fear on anyone, it was her uncle, and that made Guy very suspicious. He'd come prepared with a bag full of his salves and rubs, fearing that she might be in a bad way, and now he used that.

"We should let Lady Avice retreat to her chambers," he said to the rest of the assembled men, "but if you can try and find those rogues who hoodwinked Lady Juetta, I have something with me that might help Lady Avice." He turned to Juetta. "I've had some experience with injuries, madam. Would you let me come with you and apply some salve to Lady Avice's bruises?" He turned to Avice, who was sitting shaking badly on the hall's only chair, and dropping to one knee, began to talk to her as he had his frightened wolfhounds.

"It's alright," he said softly, very gently reaching out and just placing a hand over hers. "I won't hurt you. ...You're safe with me. ...I want to help you, if you'll let me. I have some salve in this bag that will ease that eye for you. May I come with you and put some on? If you want me to leave I'll go, and your mother can put the salve on; or she can sit with you the whole time. Would you like me to take some of the pain away?" He got a shaky nod. "Alright, then, let's go to somewhere quieter, eh?" and he put a gently hand under her arm to help her to her feet.

However, he also saw the glare that fitz Ranulp sent Juetta's way, and it was all he could do to keep breathing calmly and not let his anger show. More and more he was convinced that it might have been fitz Ranulph himself who had given Avice this beating, probably out of spite at the prospect of her having an heir who would inherit this estate, and cut her uncle out of it forever.

In the quiet of her tiny chamber, Avice became a little calmer. At first Guy got the pot of salve out and knelt before her as she sat on her bed, gently applying the salve to her face.

"That actually smells rather nice," Juetta said in surprise.

"It's got roses in it," Guy told her, "and mallows, but the two main things are willow bark and honey. They're what do the deep healing."

"How does a knight like you know such things?" wondered the older lady. "I wouldn't expect someone like you to be versed in such matters?"

Guy smiled at her, "Ah, well it's all to do with dogs," he began, and told her of his life over on the borders as he began to work some of the salve into Avice's badly bruised fingers too.

"Well, you are a rare one!" Juetta said as he finished. "Who are you?"

Guy gently held on to Avice's hand as he said, "I'm Guy of Gisborne ...the real Guy of Gisborne!"

The two women gasped in unison.

"But you're not him!" Avice whimpered. "You're not the man who came here!"

"No, I'm not," Guy agreed, "And I would never have done such a thing to you. But I promise you this: I will find who did, and they will be brought to justice!" Then as they continued to stare at him in surprise, decided he had nothing to lose by asking the questions he most desperately wanted the answers to. The first was,

"Who gave you my name, Avice?"

Yet it was Juetta who answered instantly with, "Why, the men who said they'd seen you riding away! They said they knew you."

Well that cleared that up! Someone hated his guts, but it wasn't these two.

"Is he the father of this child?" Guy then dared to ask, and got a shake of Avice's head as reply.

Not wanting to be a churl and pressure this frightened woman in front of him, Guy refrained from asking further whose it was, but he desperately wanted to know the answer to the next question,

"Was it Sir Robert who actually beat you, Avice?"

Her bursting into tears and nodding was something he was expecting by now, but he hadn't anticipated Juetta grasping his sleeve urgently and saying,

"You mustn't let him know that you know! Please! If you do, he'll think we told you, and then ...and then..." Her eyes travelled back to Avice and Guy knew what she was trying to tell him. She and Avice would be on the receiving end of fitz Ranulph's anger again.

Guy's mind was working frantically. Juetta didn't seem to be the kind of woman who was overly bothered by status. This was a nice enough manor house to be sure, but there were no signs that she had tried to fill it with whatever fancies and trimmings her husband had been able to afford. And so Guy dared to make a suggestion.

"Would you like to be away from here? Or at least until Avice's child is born?"

"We have nowhere to go," Juetta said with tears rising in her eyes. "If we had, we'd have gone by now. The baby's father ...he's not free to follow his heart. He can't help us. This place doesn't mean as much to me as it did to Simon. For him it was his mother's house and special, but I hardly knew her."

Guy grinned. "Then I think I have a plan. Would you like me to take you to Kirklees Abbey? My mother is prioress there, and if I explain the situation to her, I'm sure she'd allow you to stay with them. Then once Avice's child is born, you can make some decisions about what you want to do. I know it's probably unfair, but Sir Hubert can have the proceeds of the harvest to get the sheriff off his back – and that all by itself will ease things for you, because he shouldn't be in such a foul mood all the time. But if you decide you'd like to stay at Kirklees and in safety, then as the mistress of this manor, you'd be quite entitled to gift it to Kirklees in exchange for being able to live there." He didn't add, 'if you want to truly revenge yourself on Sir Hubert', but the expression of deep satisfaction which lit up Juetta's face said that she had understood the implication without him having to say more.

"I think that sounds like an ideal solution," she said gratefully. "I have been a widow for three years, and have been dreading Hubert parading suitors before me from amongst his men, even before this happened. It's been my nightmare that he would find some widowed older man for me who has a son whom Hubert, in his callous way, would think would also do for Avice. This would save both of us from marriages we do not want."

Guy grinned back at her. "Then I'll go and ask a couple of the knights with us if they'll come with me to take you there. Three heavily armed men should guarantee your safe arrival."

And so we took the two ladies to Kirklees, Brother. As you have no doubt gathered, the three supposed witnesses were nowhere to be found. Nobody in Tansley village had ever seen them until the day they came

out of the forest and walked up to the manor. Yes, Gervase, out of the forest. You are beginning to see where this leads, and once I heard that, so did I. While we rode with those two misused ladies I did not dare allow myself to dwell on the matter, for I have often been told that when I am angry it shows on my face as clear as day, and I had no wish to alarm either of them.

But once we were back at Nottingham, I made a point of having a quiet word with Briwere, with the castle knights present, and informed him that it had been fitz Ranulph himself who had beaten his niece when he had found out that she was with child, and could effectively cut him off from the Tansley estate forever if she had a boy, because of the terms of his brother's will. I got no apology from the sheriff, of course. I did not expect one. But he was crafty enough to realise that actually he had been saved from making a massive fool of himself by backing the wrong man, and how that would have looked if, God forbid, it had ever come before another sheriff at the next eyre. Therefore the usual armed truce between the two of us resumed, with me not trusting him, and him loathing my guts but recognising that he could not do without me.

Yet this story needs a further conclusion, and that begins with me meeting Allan and Roger at the Trip to Jerusalem only the day after I got back to Nottingham. The gossip had spread that Sir Guy was in trouble, and they had loitered, worried sick that I might be in mortal danger. Their relief at hearing all was well once more was heartening to me, but they agreed that the matter of the three men was most perplexing. None of the gang as it stood had been anywhere near that part of Sherwood at either time, and so they could shed no light on things for me. However, they decided that they would go home via the Tansley hideout, and take a day or so to look around in the forest thereabouts. Three men must have had to make camp, we reasoned, but of course I had not had chance to look around when over there, and as I said to them, I had not wanted to offer to try tracking in case I took the other knights too close to the hideout in the process. I had had to walk a fine line over that.

Therefore I went back to the normal forest business, but was shocked to have Ed sneak into the castle outer bailey a week later, and into the stables, from where I was summoned by Harry. I arrived to find Ed in quite a state, and he told me that Allan and Roger had indeed gone to the Tansley hideout, but only to find a gang of ruffians using it for their own. When challenged, the gang of half a dozen told them that they were there by invitation of Robin Hood himself. Of course, Allan and Roger had protested, and Allan had said that as Robin's cousin he would know if such a thing were true. What had Ed in such a state of anxiety was that the gang had then set upon our two, saying that they must be more of Robin's traitorous family in that case. The only thing that had saved our friends had been that they knew the forest thereabouts like the backs of their hands, and they had been able to go to ground while the gang stamped around searching for them, after which they had fled the camp before they were beaten to death.

That reference to traitorous family had stuck with both of them, though, and they had limped into the larger camp further north up the Derwent valley, battered and heavily bruised, and told the others who were waiting there what had been said. All eyes had turned to Robin, at which point he said that he had already told them, had he not, that he was recruiting others who lived in the forest? Ed said that there had been a major row following that, which had concluded with Robin storming off, saying that he would go to those who followed him more willingly. What Ed said they had not been able to get out of him before he went, was whether he had told these other men about me. Clearly the rest of my friends were in turmoil over the possibility that Robin had been stupid enough to tell virtual strangers that he had an inside man within Nottingham Castle itself, and worse who that person might be.

I will confess that for a moment I felt quite sick at that thought, but then I was able to reassure Ed that my identity was probably safe. That was not because I had any faith in Robin, by the way. Rather, as I told Ed, it was that I felt that Robin would not admit to anyone that part of his success was down to me passing information to him regularly. He would want to play the infallible and all-knowing hero to these men who did not know otherwise, I thought, and with much relief, Ed agreed. I also said that I felt that if Robin wanted to use that against me directly, then it would have been far more effective to simply disclose me for the traitor I was. Moreover, the fact that I was not yet swinging from the battlements was probably a good indicator that no such accusations had been made. The more I thought about it, the more it seemed to me that Robin had taken an existing situation – the rape of Avice – and just used the outcome for his own ends.

As Ed calmed down, and we worked dates out backwards, we realised that these men Robin had been so taken with had probably been in the area for a while, and certainly since the spring. We could both believe that Robin was cunning enough that if these men had said that fitz Ranulph had been combing the area for a tall, dark-haired knight –

who in reality was no doubt Avice's lover – then Robin had seen a way to spite me by telling his so-called friends to go and supply my name to Widow Juetta. His haughty cousin would be cut down to size, he had no doubt thought. And Ed and I agreed that there had probably been no small degree of relish on Robin's part over that, but sadly that also there were only so many members of our own gang whom we could say it outright to. It required a conviction regarding the depth of Robin's malice towards me that not all of the outlaws possessed as yet. There were still some, like the Coshams, who would see it as thoughtlessness, or even recklessness, on Robin's part, but who would still believe that he had had some belief that I would be untouchable up here in the castle, that I would be scathed in reputation but with no thought of a trial. But Ed and I reckoned that in reality Robin's motives had run much deeper and darker than that.

And I was deeply touched by Ed coming to me, by the way. You must not forget that it had not been so long ago that he and Colm had been prisoners in the castle, and there was a real danger that he would be recognised. But he came because Allan and Roger could not, and he was one of the few of our number who could pass as just another servant. However Siward and our Hugh – not my other friend, Sir Hugh – were apparently waiting for him out in the town, along with John and Tuck, ready to whisk him away if things got too dangerous. Indeed, I walked him out of the castle myself, seemingly separate from him, and with me just going for some unspecified item from the market in the town, but never more than an arm's span from him. I felt I owed Ed that, and I was deeply touched by the relief of my four other friends too. Whatever my lunatic cousin's feelings might be towards me, they cared very much whether I lived or died.

And what of Robin himself? Well a few days later he came back into the camp with his tail between his legs, it seems, although I did not hear of that for another few weeks. His so-called followers had made a right mess of the Tansley camp, but had gone before Robin got there. Their tracks went westwards, Robin said, and indeed when the others went to try and repair the camp in case they needed it themselves, what they found seemed to confirm this.

Robin tried to bluster his way through this by saying that they must have known how angry he would be with them for attacking Allan, but everyone else thought that it was more likely that the pickings had not been rich enough for them, and they had gone elsewhere to ply their wicked trade. I might even have chased them off *myself by turning up at the manor with five other heavily armed knights – after all, they were not to know that I was the only useful fighter amongst them, and if this gang had seen any fighting in Normandy as foot soldiers, they would have had a healthy fear of knights on horseback.*

Therefore, we returned more or less to the way we were, but with the exception that half of the gang and I were convinced that Robin had deliberately tried to blacken my name, or worse, to have me put on trial for the rape and assault of Avice fitz Ranulph. Only my quick wits had saved me this time, and it made me all the more wary of Robin.

...And did the two ladies stay at Kirklees? Yes, Brother, they did, and in the process would meet Mariota and Marianne, who had retreated there for a while. My mother welcomed me with open arms, going so far as to praise me for thinking to bring the two ladies to her, and they did indeed gift the manor's produce to the nuns during the rest of Juetta's lifetime. What happened after that I do not know, for it did not concern me; but I was glad to have saved both of them from further distress, and they would greet me as their saviour on those times after then when I visited my mother.

Chapter 23

Yet as we come towards the end of the year, that incident was to have further repercussions. For a start the rest of the gang put their collective foot down with Robin, and demanded to know just who it was who he had been recruiting. They were most careful not to mention me, but Robin had given them good reason to ask on their own account with the disclosure of the Tansley hideout. He had been beyond careless, they told him. Had he not thought to test these men further before giving them the means to get everyone else hanged?

I am told that Robin protested vigorously, but that it was also clear that he was more than a little shaken at having had Allan so hurt on his account, for it was more than a week before Allan and Roger felt that they could make the journey up to Loxley and greater safety. Moreover, it emphasised that Marianne and Mariota, who had already left for Kirklees, had not been being foolish to worry about their fate at the hands of random men – the state of Allan and Roger was proof of that.

And the matter of Loxley itself was rammed home to Robin most forcefully, because the others repeatedly pointed out to him that such a spot would not be easy to find again. Nestled in its quiet, steep-sided valley on the way to nowhere in particular, the old deserted village was as good as it was possible to get as a secure base; and the fact that Aneirin had managed to make a good bowyer's workshop out of another deserted cottage's stone relics, alongside Will's forge, emphasised that these were resources they might never be able to recreate again.

Now I am not telling you this without reason, Brother, because it leads directly into my next tale. You see they all had a great debate about how to handle future new additions to the gang in the light of what had just gone on, and some decisions were made which had nothing to do with Robin's likes or desires – indeed he was not party to these decisions at all. The first was that the camp they had up on Kinder, beyond Castleton and High Peak Castle, had rarely been used to date, but they realised now that if ever Loxley became compromised it was the obvious one to make into a new main base. It was isolated and well away from passing travellers, and the miners up there were our friends, therefore no new men would <u>ever</u> be taken there; and the camp would be used as little as possible, except to provision it with things like *firewood*, so that it would remain hidden and in a crisis everyone could evacuate to there at speed.

Along the course of the Derwent's valley in all there were five more camps, starting in the north with one just outside of Hathersage, then the one south and east of Chatsworth, which was the one Allan and Roger had crawled back to. Both of these had great value if anyone was being hunted, not least because it was not too far to get across the river and therefore out of the designated royal forest. Tansley, the middle one, was the next south, and might or might not already be compromised, and for that reason it was thought unfair to expose men who might be genuine recruits to the dangers of being caught before they had even been brought into the gang.

Beyond that there was a camp near to Codnor, and then there was a small camp down by Sandiacre and Bramcote, right on the border of our two shires, which was also a useful place to run to if anyone had to make an escape from Nottingham in an unexpected direction. Therefore these five were discounted as places to hide new men. However, there was another camp on the two shires' borders further north between Teversall and Hardstoft, and after much discussion it was decided that if pressed, this one could be considered expendable, and therefore this would be the camp that new men were brought into first.

What say you, Brother? You had no idea that they had so many hideouts? Oh indeed, yes, and there was another in the north of Derbyshire and eight others within Nottinghamshire, including our most valuable one after Loxley at Inkersall, and another key one up by Worksop. The reason none of those were considered, though, was because my friends felt that they needed to have a camp that was reasonably swiftly accessible from Loxley. The danger was, they felt, that if these new men were too far away, then in the winter months it would mean that the two sides of the band – the old and the new – would become quite separated, and everyone wanted to keep an eye on who Robin was talking to by now.

The small camp up by Beighton in north Derbyshire was actually <u>too</u> close to Loxley, though – they did not want some enterprising soul tracking them over such a short distance back to Loxley! But the Hardstoft camp was close enough without being on Loxley's doorstep. And it had the advantage of having clusters of villages not far away, so if any men went rogue and started attacking people on their own account, they knew they would hear about it fast.

Yes, I am getting to the point, Gervase. Patience! All this is relevant. Now having made the decision that Hardstoft would be the base for the new men, they also made another decision, and it was also one which Robin was not party to. They collectively agreed that yet again I had had too close a brush with danger, and that I was worryingly vulnerable to accusations, especially if they were made by men who knew just enough to be able to drop sufficiently pertinent facts out to be convincing. Therefore they all agreed that these new recruits would never hear my name. Not at all, and under no circumstances.

And of course they hoped that if they never spoke of me in front of Robin, that he was hardly of a mind to bring me up in conversation. I was the relative he would dearly have loved to forget he had. In these new men's presence, therefore, Allan and John would never mention that there was a fourth cousin called Guy, much less that I was someone who was feeding them information.

Was I still doing that? Of course I was, Gervase! I knew of things like heavily guarded merchant trains passing up the Great North Road headed for York, for York was an important centre of commerce even if it was no rival to London. So I would pass on warnings of how heavily guarded such merchants might be, ensuring that the outlaws either left them well alone, or if they did levy their tax for passing through Sherwood, that they went in prepared and forewarned that they might need to fight, and fight hard. And I passed on information about certain soft targets, where they might get the kind of mixture of coins that they could easily hand out again.

Later on I was to learn how hard it was sometimes to stop Robin from taking all manner of items off those they stopped. He really could be most impractical at times. But the others by now had become far more sensible about what they could and could not use. Therefore, just because I have not sung my own praises of what I was doing does not mean that I was not involved anymore, and I meant what I said a while back, Brother, that it was Robin I was avoiding but that I met with the others where I could.

But this all led to another close encounter for me, and it began with Robin taking the others to meet some men who were, as best they could see, genuinely on the run from injustices. Already clustered in a small hollow near the Rainworth Water were four men who said they were on the run from their masters. One was little more than a boy who had been beaten so often that he was permanently hunchbacked, while two were men who had been dragged off from their homes to accompany *their local knight to Normandy, and who had managed to break free just before being loaded onto a ship.*

They had no idea where they were. Sherwood might have been on the other side of the world for all they knew, and it transpired that they were natives of Dorset, and so a very long way from home. The last one said he, too, had been a soldier who had fled Normandy, and right from the start Will took a dislike to him. When he next saw me – and in fact Will made a particular effort to be one of the ones to come the next time I met them – he gave me a detailed description of the man, saying he could not put his finger on exactly why he thought the man was a bad apple, but that all of his instincts were screaming it at him.

Was Will right? You shall have to wait and see, Brother, but he was right to give me that description, because it turned out that the man was wanted for murder over the border in Leicestershire. But how he fitted into the story is not as predictable as you no doubt think.

Nottingham and Sherwood
Winter, the Year of Our Lord 1197

"We've got ten new men sitting in the Hardstoft camp," Allan said gloomily as he, Roger and Guy huddled in the farthest corner of the *Trip to Jerusalem* on a gloomy November Monday, with a biting wind whistling in from the north which sought out every nook and cranny of the brewhouse, despite the doors being shut and the chimneys all in use with fires. The *Trip* had next to no windows, being cut into the very rock the castle sat upon, and for which it acted as its own brewhouse, but still the wind was cutting them around the ankles. He took a grateful gulp of the mulled ale Guy handed him as Roger added forcefully,

"An' we don't trust any o' them!"

Guy raised an eyebrow. "Oh? That doesn't sound good."

Allan took another slurp of the beer, cradled the mug in his hands to warm them, and with a deep sigh said, "No, Guy, it isn't. Robin's convinced that all they need is more training and then they'll make valuable additions to our number, but to most of us the real problem is that they just don't have the right approach. I think the beaten lad and the two ordinary men we found up at Rainworth Water are bloody dangerous, if for no other reason than them being so embittered towards pretty much anyone who isn't a serf that they feed Robin's wilder views. They're so soured by life that they'd happily slaughter every Norman in England in their beds if they could."

"Ouch," Guy breathed. "Oh dear, I can see why you'd be worried by that. The more extreme Robin's ideas become, the more they'll applaud him at every turn."

"Vhey already bleedin' are!" Roger grumbled, disgusted. "Not a brain between 'em to see that nuffin' vhey do 'appens in its own little soap-bubble." He shook his head resignedly, which would have been comical if what he was talking about hadn't been so serious.

Even now, after all these years of Tuck's wholesome cooking, Roger was still painfully thin and in poor light would pass for some teenage urchin, not the grown man he was. Consequently, some of his more dour pronouncements and expressions seemed comical coming from his thin little face, as if a child had unwittingly spoken the weighty words of an old man. It was something which made Robin underestimate Roger time and time again, but Guy felt that sometimes Roger had one of the keenest eyes when it came to relationships within the gang, and so now he encouraged Roger to continue.

Taking a deep breath, Roger began, "I finks Robin ain't seein' anythin' clearly anymore. 'Cause all he can fink about is gettin' a bigger gang. It's like he finks of it as a bigger stick to beat vhe sheriff wiv'. But we all sez to him back in L…" he just stopped himself from saying the name out loud, but Guy nodded his acknowledgement of where Roger had meant.

"Up vhere," Roger continued cautiously, "we sez vhat if he wants t' use vhese new men, vhen it ought'a be just for raids on big merchant trains goin' frough vhe forest. Vhem what's got lots'a men-at-arms wiv' 'em!"

"We did," Allan confirmed, "primarily because if any of them get out of control, I'm afraid we decided that we would melt away into the forest and let them take their chances. We can't afford to have men amongst us who are like wild dogs, we told Robin." Allan sighed. "He heard the words, but he didn't listen, if you know what I mean. And then we found out that Robin had six more men cached away in, of all places, the bloody hideout by Hucknall."

"Hucknall!" Guy spluttered through his beer, glad that he'd been taking a mouthful at the time because it had muffled his shocked exclamation. "But that's on our bloody doorstep! God's hooks, it's practically on top of the Linby court, and that's only a handful of miles from here! Has he totally lost his mind? That was at best a refuge." He shuddered. "An uncontrolled gang of thugs there is just asking for the sheriff to hunt them."

Roger looked pleadingly at Guy. "You gets to ride around here more vhan we do. Do you know any o'ver place what we could use if we has to run from here? 'Cause we an' a few o'vers ain't sure we ever want to trust to vhat place bein' secure again."

"No, I can see why you wouldn't," Guy agreed, "and I'm glad you told me this. I'll make sure that until you tell me otherwise, that I never go there – not that Hucknall was a place I frequented, you understand. But if I ever wanted to vanish it might have been useful for me, too." He stopped and thought carefully. "You know I'm glad you decided to keep the Sandiacre hideout secret, because at least that's going southwest from here, and that's not a direction the sheriff will ever think of you running in. ...Or at least not unless someone actually tells him that you're there."

"But we can't trust Robin to have kept his mouth shut," Allan sighed. "These extra six are apparently men who've fallen foul of Briwere in one way or another. So there's always the danger that, if Robin thinks they need moving on to safety against our wishes, that he'd use that camp for them. Our northern hideouts are safe, so far, because the new men aren't anywhere near them, but for all we know the ones down here could all be compromised. What Roger is asking for is for a brand new site that Robin won't know at all."

Guy sighed and thoughtfully swirled the dregs of his beer. It took him until he'd gone and got a refill for all of them before he'd come to a conclusion, because the more he thought about it, the more worried he became.

"I have to say that I'm dismayed at Robin betraying possibly both of those camps," he admitted, "because every time I think of a new place, the moment I think of you making a run for them in an emergency, I keep hitting the same obstacle – and that's the number of decent sized rivers around here. I think I'd say to you that if you're in Nottingham itself, or right close by, then your best bet would be to cross the river. And that's because the sheriff nowadays instantly thinks of you making for the forest. By crossing the Trent, even going out over the main bridge, you'd both be going in the wrong direction as he sees things, *and* be out of the actual royal forest too – and if necessary you wouldn't be too far away to make a run for the shire border. Being in another sheriff's jurisdiction would give you some temporary respite, especially if one of you was injured in some way."

He puffed his cheeks out in a sigh of dismay. "But within the forest?" He shook his head. "I know you would've always had to cross the Leen and the Erewash to get to the Sandiacre camp, and in summer neither river is particularly deep or dangerous. But it's also the reason you didn't use that camp very often, especially once they got fuller with winter rains, and that's the same reason why I can't think of somewhere west of Nottingham that's really useful for you." He gave a groan. "Why in God's name could Robin have not taken those men to Sandiacre in the first place? Granted it was potentially useful, but nothing like as useful as the camp he's betrayed by Hucknall.

"As for going east, the problem that way is that I know most of the knights who hold manors around there, and they're given to riding around their lands pretty frequently. These are manors on rich land that used to be outside of the royal forest, and that's why there are so many holdings around there – they're potentially wealthy. And there's another problem: the Trent wanders and meanders so much around there that anywhere close to the river is beset with marshes, and therefore the secure higher ground is where it's heavily inhabited. What's worse, since all of that land got sucked into the royal forest, and because there are two or three times the numbers of villages around there than in the old forest, the folk there depend heavily on the river for extra food.

"I should have thought to warn you of this earlier, but be very careful if you ever end up in the shallow waters anywhere between

Nottingham and Newark. The locals set traps for eels, and while eel isn't pleasant eating in my opinion, given that people have been desperately short of food, if it's starve or eat eel, they eat the eels. And there are some monsters in those mazes of channels. I've seen ones as long as I am tall, and as fat as my arm!"

He gave a shudder. "And the teeth on them! Blessed Saints Cadoc and Melengell preserve me from ever getting bitten by one of those! And they can be damned aggressive as well. But traps big enough to catch the large eels are big enough to trap a man by the leg, so if the eels don't get you, the traps might!

"The only safe way for you to use the shallows would be to build a raft for yourselves, but even if that were possible, there's just too great a danger of it being discovered by local fishermen, or those out hunting water birds. And again, there's a huge incentive to get out in a boat and go after fish, ducks and geese, because the forest law ends at the river bank, so when the forest is officially closed, and they daren't go after hare or roe deer, the river is their larder."

"Bloody Robin," Allan swore softly. "He's become a damned menace!"

Guy sighed. "I have to agree, because the only other wisp of a hope I can give you is to say that if you are in Nottingham, to take refuge in one of the churches. The one advantage of us being just down the river from Newark and the Great North Road, is that there are always some poor souls who end up taking shelter in the church porches. It's not like Mansfield, where you'd stand out like sore thumbs, or even Derby. We get a lot of travellers through here, and that's to your benefit."

He sighed heavily again. "But that only works for you two, and probably Colm and Ed and Much. None of the others could mingle into the crowd as well – not even the Coshams, because although they're not overly tall aside from Bilan, the moment they open their mouths they betray themselves as Welsh. I'm so sorry. I truly don't know where to suggest."

"It's alright," Allan consoled him. "It's not your problem to solve. We just hoped that you'd have a spot in mind, that's all."

Yet long after they had left, the problem plagued Guy. Robin's increasing recklessness was becoming an escalating danger to all of his friends, but for the life of him he couldn't think of a way around it. What they had done was give Guy a detailed description of each of the ten men, and that night he risked going down to the scribes' room and purloining a small piece of parchment, on which he wrote the salient points for each one down. One man or two he could have trusted to his memory for, but he knew that if one of these turned up in four months' time, that he wouldn't necessarily make the connection without a reminder. He hoped he would never have to use the parchment, which he rolled up tightly and slid into the small inner pocket he had in his working jerkin which he sometimes used to sheath a knife in. One thing he dared not do was leave it amongst his few possessions in the shared room where he slept, for if it got found how could he explain away the need to know who ten felons were whom the sheriff knew nothing of?

Yet before such problems materialised Guy's way, something else happened of far greater personal importance. Briwere returned home having been away at court for longer than usual, and when he arrived he had worrying news for Guy.

"It has been decided," Briwere declared pompously to the assembled men of the castle, "that Ralph fitz Stephen is no longer fit enough to act as hereditary Keeper of the Forest of Nottingham. Since that role is obsolete, given that the Old Forest has long been part of the greater forest of Sherwood, the king's head forester, Geoffrey fitz Peter, had decided that with immediate effect, all of the forest laws will be administered from here by me." He sat back with a self-satisfied smirk on his face.

"I wonder how much he's had to pay out to get that," Sir Mahel muttered gloomily from behind Guy. And well might Mahel be dismayed. He was one of the eight knights who had the care of what was called the Forest of Le Clay, but which was actually the eastern half of Nottinghamshire between the Trent and what had been the boundary of the Old Forest, formed for the most part by the River Idle in the north, and the River Maun in the centre of the shire. If anyone was going to have to work harder now, it was these eight, for if Briwere chose, they could end up with double the territory to cover.

However, Guy had a different question for Briwere. "Will Sir Ralph and Lady Maud be staying at Laxton Castle?" he wondered. It was a reasonable question, because Laxton wasn't just the fitz

Stephens' home, it was the administrative hub of the Old Forest, even though it didn't lie within its boundaries.

"They will be departing for one of their other manors, not in these shires," Briwere said with another nasty smirk. "We shall be using Laxton for more of the forest courts from now on, given that the Edwinstowe courts are overwhelmed. From now on, everything north of Laxton in the Le Clay section of the forest will have its hearings at Laxton, thereby leaving Edwinstowe free to deal with the Old Forest cases. The Calverton court will continue to hear the southern half of Le Clay's cases."

That might have seemed unfair on Calverton, but in reality Guy knew that once you got from Laxton down to Southwell, from there on the le Clay forest border tapered southwards to a point where it hit the Trent. And most of that land was a mixture of marsh and cultivated fields with hardly a wood in sight, meaning that there weren't many cases arising around there. North of Laxton, however, was a different matter, and if not exactly heavily forested, it was certainly well wooded enough to have been a running sore in the sides of the forester knights. The new Laxton courts were unlikely to be lacking in things to administer!

"Will there be a keeper at Laxton?" Sir Martin asked, realising why Guy was looking increasingly worried. Sir Ralph had had eight foresters of his own who had helped patrol the forest, albeit not mounted men of the calibre of Guy and the other knights who had been serving the sheriff directly for many years now. Someone ought to be overseeing those men.

"I shall be visiting Laxton regularly," Briwere said haughtily, and nobody needed it spelling out that he thought he had risen in the world by having yet another castle under his lordship. "In the meantime I shall be making some changes amongst you forest knights. We cannot have these mere walking foresters of fitz Stephen's making decisions by themselves. Therefore I have decided that I shall be taking four knights from our existing areas, and making *them* responsible for overseeing the Old Forest. To compensate, I shall be appointing new riding foresters to work under Sirs Martin and Walter. I have not decided yet whether they will come from local knights' families, or will be taken from the ranks of the sergeants."

He had nothing more to say on the matter, but the moment they were out of the hall, Martin and Walter cornered Guy.

"You'll be one of the four," Martin said gloomily. "He wants you under his thumb, Guy, so watch yourself!"

"I'll be sorry to lose you," Walter told him mournfully. "You're the best by a long way. Nobody else can find their way around those tangled woods up by the Derwent like you. But I fear Martin's right, Briwere will grab you to do his dirty work for him. I'm going to really struggle when three of mine are Fredegis, Walkelin and Henry. None of them could find their own arses in the dark with both hands. Osmaer and Thorsten have learned a thing or two from you over the years, but Durand and Humphrey are dead weights too."

Guy grimaced. "I have a nasty feeling that Briwere might well want one of the first three you mentioned, if not all of them. If nothing else, they're good at extorting fines out of people by fear alone – none of your knights, Martin, are like them. If I were you, I'd be prepared for you to have to send a couple of your knights across to patrol the Derwent to Erewash section of the forest to help Walter."

And in that Guy proved to be horribly correct.

No sooner did word come that the fitz Stephens had left than Briwere was summoning Guy and the three knights whom Guy probably loathed the most, and announced that they would be riding over to Laxton. It was a miserable journey, with Sirs Henry, Walkelin and Fredegis all trying to out-brag one another to Briwere, as they rode, about how they would make sure things would be different in this part of the forest now. All Guy could do was hang back a little and remain silent.

However he was quietly amused to realise that these three had probably never been any deeper into the dense woodland of the Old Forest than what they saw from the major roads which ran through it, and he began to visualise the panic they might feel if caught outside at night amongst the mighty oaks, rambling hawthorns and wispy birches. A full moon could cast terrifyingly eerie shadows through the undergrowth, and if accompanied by night birds' calls and the odd bat, might scare the unprepared out of what little wits they possessed. And with some relish he began to plot as to how to give these three a rough and revelatory introduction to their new territory.

At Laxton, Briwere fell into a temper, for the fitz Stephens had obviously decided that while they might not be allowed to live in their ancestral home anymore, that didn't mean that they had to leave their belongings behind. Three large and heavily carved beds remained in the private chambers, which had probably been assembled in there and couldn't be moved, but there wasn't a mattress worth having anywhere, and Briwere had to resign himself to having two bracken-filled sacks commandeered from the servants for his bed that night. The three other knights had also clearly had high expectations of being able to lord it in what would become their own castle, they believed, and were angry at finding that they would be sleeping in poorer conditions than they'd had back at Nottingham until the castle could be replenished with furniture.

Laxton was a considerable fortification compared to motte and wooden-palisade castles like Bolsover or Tickhill, and the de Caux family had done much to enhance it over the generations. However, although the motte was ringed with a stout stone wall, within that wall there was no great stone keep, much less two of them as Nottingham had. Instead there were three well-made wooden halls, comfortably appointed enough for a family home, but not remotely in the same class as some of the great stone castles in Normandy that the king was currently trying to retake from his rebellious lords. If the three knights had been dreaming of setting themselves up in competition with Briwere, they'd had a rude awakening.

Henry, Walkelin and Fredegis weren't so naive as to think that they would be getting such a great stone edifice as Nottingham, of course, but they had clearly hoped that they would have a substantial keep for their own, presuming that all within the stone walls on top of the motte's mound was one solid building. That in turn made Guy realise that they had probably never got further into Laxton than the inner bailey, if they had ever been here before. Sir Ralph had obviously known how to keep such men who would spy for the sheriffs at a distance.

The inner bailey was also ringed with stone and shared part of the motte's deep ditch, but had within it the assortment of wooden buildings commonly associated with castles less grand than Nottingham. Two substantial gatehouses provided access to it – one giving on to the flight of steps which ascended the motte on the bailey's north side; and the other gatehouse was on the eastern side of its square walls which led into the outer bailey, but nothing on the scale of Nottingham's towered barbican. Meanwhile, the outer bailey had a ditch of sorts surrounding its tall wooden palisade, and what had no doubt misled the three knights was the size of this outer bailey, which was twice the size of Nottingham's. But then this was a rural defence, and had room within it to bring cattle and sheep in, and had spaces to cultivate crops to feed the castle's inhabitants. It wasn't surrounded by a town which provided for it.

Yet all this played nicely into Guy's hands. By the time morning came around, while he had slept comfortably enough in a small chamber in what the few remaining servants said had been Lady Maud's father's guest hall, the others had frozen in the main building, stoking one another's ire with grumbles throughout the night. And so when the three riding foresters, the four walking foresters, plus the woodward and forester who were supposed to keep an eye on Carburton and Budby parks in the north of the Old Forest, all turned up to present themselves to the sheriff as summoned, only Guy was in a fit state to take any notice of them.

The woodward and his forester seemed like decent enough men. Certainly they made sure that they stayed well back, and exchanged nervous glances with one another as Briwere snapped and snarled his way through the introductions, and then his expectation of how things would change. Given some of the things Briwere said, Guy could understand their dismay, for they were simply not practicable. A full head-count of deer, for instance, was just never going to happen in such dense woodland, let alone identification of where the wild boar all were, so that those close to the farmlands of Le Clay's new royal forest could be eradicated to better protect crops from their damages.

However, the evil gleam in two of the riding foresters' eyes told Guy that this pair would be trouble. The fact that they were already assuring Briwere that his wild schemes would be carried out could only mean one of two things. Either they thought Briwere was a fool to be pacified – in which case they were in for a nasty shock – or they had never been particularly ardent in their work before, and had no idea of how unrealistic Briwere's demands were. And Guy thought it was probably a bit of both.

As the morning wore on, with Briwere continuing to ramble on at length, Guy decided that the walking foresters were probably just men trying to do their jobs. They weren't enthusiastically endorsing Briwere's every word, but equally they'd possibly never been that ardent about doing the work, either. This was just a means of hanging on to the cottages which went with the jobs, and which their families had had for generations. It might even be that a son was the one actually doing the work, Guy thought, given that two of them were distinctly on the old side to be covering that much ground regularly on foot.

The final forester was as different again. He already had a visible paunch on him, and Guy decided that he was both idle and corrupt. As long as he got a good cut from a poached deer, he wouldn't say a word unless he could avoid it. He could be trouble, Guy feared.

The forester from the north, though, was doing a very good job of disguising his feelings, but as the morning drew on, Guy was sure the man's dismay was rising, and he decided that he would try and find a way to get him alone to speak to. And by the time Briwere dismissed everyone, the man was casting furtive glances Guy's way, as if wondering who this silent knight was, and how much of a problem he was going to be if the garrulous trio and the sheriff were the stuff of his nightmares.

Therefore Guy let him escape to the sanctity of the servant's hall and then slid onto the bench beside him, making him jump.

"What's your name?" Guy asked civilly.

"Hereward, Godric's son," was the cautious reply.

"I'm Sir Guy of Gisborne. What you might not have gathered from what the sheriff said, is that I'm also one of these new coroners that Archbishop Walter has decreed we must have to decide whether deaths are natural or not." Hereward's eyebrows went up at that, and he looked at Guy with renewed interest. They went up even further as Guy added, "I got appointed not because I'm so very highly born, but because having served as Sheriff de Braose's huntsman, I know how carcases can be butchered." He left it at that and waited for Hereward's response, which came swiftly enough.

"Oh! *You're* that knight!" It was said more with respect than dread or derision, making Guy think that it might be possible to forge a working relationship with this man. When he added, "I've heard that you're a first-class tracker too?" Guy dared to ask another question.

"You looked worried in the hall there, would you mind telling me why?"

Hereward was startled, but Guy thought it was probably because he was being asked rather than commanded, not that he was worried about speaking the truth. The forester leaned a little closer to Guy.

"Does the sheriff not understand that we've *never* patrolled the whole forest? There's just me and Bertwald the woodward, and we oversee the two hunting parks at Budby and Carburton. Even in King Henry's reign we were never expected to do more than that."

Now it was Guy's turn to be a bit surprised. His own common sense had always told him that these men couldn't have covered the whole forest all of the time, because he'd long known how many men fitz Stephen had working for him. Yet strangely he'd never thought to ask the royal keeper just what land his men *did* cover, and finding out how small a proportion of the forest was actually monitored was quite the revelation. No wonder they had been able to bring so many small cases to the courts – they'd had a fraction of the territory to patrol as Guy had covered.

"You're surprised too," Hereward sighed mournfully.

"I knew you had to focus your efforts," Guy admitted. "Anyone who's been out into Sherwood has to realise that you couldn't possibly cover it all regularly. I just hadn't realised your territories were so defined." That was better than saying 'so tiny', which was what he felt. "So what do the others do?"

Hereward looked at him balefully. "Well there are three keepings in the Old Forest. Mine is the most northerly one. Then there's what was known as High Forest, and that includes Birkland Hay and Billahaugh Hay plus Clipstone Park – the royal hunting lodge that's had so much work done on it over the years. But that still only means the actual hunting parks, however thick the woodland might be, not the whole forest thereabouts." He gave Guy an appraising look. "If you betray me over what I'm going to say next, I shall deny it, you know."

Guy nodded. "I understand. I just want to know what on earth I've been let in for."

Hereward gave a flicker of a smile. "As do I. Sir Ralph was always a fair master. A bit uninterested in the last few years, I'll grant you, especially after he had that nasty fall."

"He was in a lot of pain with that," Guy agreed. "My liniment gave him relief, but I don't think the pain ever fully went away."

"God's wounds! That was you! Of course, I remember you now. Sir Ralph always spoke kindly of you."

The recollection seemed to break down Hereward's reserve. "Watch yourself with the two foresters in High Forest. They're cousins – Jonas and Bertin of Clipstone. They fancy themselves as a cut above the rest of us because they have the royal lodge in their keeping. Godric and Torwald, the two walking foresters who have to work with them, aren't bad men really. They've just had to find ways of coping. So they're not exactly conscientious over their work. They do as little as they can, and then just go along with whatever harebrained scheme the cousins come up with. And believe me, Jonas and Bertin will already be thinking up ways to ingratiate themselves with you knights. You'll notice they haven't come down here with us yet, and it's probably because they're licking the sheriff's boots for all they're worth."

"Much good it will do them," Guy confided. "Briwere's fickle. He changes loyalties with the wind. I consider myself lucky that he loathes my guts every day of the year. At least I know where I stand with that."

"Jesu!" Hereward gulped. "That bad?"

"Oh yes. I'd give just about anything to go back to the days of Ralph Murdac. He was hard but fair. Everyone knew where they stood with him. Some days you have to throw your hat into the hall at Nottingham and see if it gets chucked back at you before you dare even go in." Then Guy grinned at Hereward. "But if you want those two to get their comeuppance, then just leave them in ignorance of what the sheriff is like. They'll soon find out – the hard way!"

"Thanks for the warning. So you'll take this in kind when I say, watch yourself with Cuthbert Lane, too. He's the riding forester for the southernmost of the three keepings – Leen to Dover-beck. It's the one the woodmotes at Linby were originally meant to see to, because it covers the parks of Beskwood Hay, Lindeby Hay and Welley Hay, and being on Nottingham's doorstep, he's already met the sheriff. In fact, I wouldn't be surprised if he's not been the sheriff's spy in Sir Ralph's household on the times when he's been up here. Cuthbert's bone idle, but he's crafty too."

Now Hereward leaned in even further to Guy and dropped his voice to a whisper. "His walking men, Bram and Egfrith are alright, and Bram was saying to my woodward, Bertwald, that Cuthbert was bragging when he was drunk yesterday on Sir Ralph's wine that he'll be the sheriff's favourite soon. And not just through creeping around him, either. Cuthbert said that he's got a man inside Robin Hood's gang, and he'll betray them to the sheriff."

Guy felt his blood run cold. Please God it wasn't somebody he knew. He would be distraught if he'd been so mistaken in his affections. Then common sense took over. No, of course it wouldn't be, it would be one of these new men Robin had brought in. This was a new scheme, therefore it had to be someone new.

"I know," Hereward was continuing, mercifully unaware of Guy's distress, and assuming his shock was at the boldness of the plan. "Nobody gets near to the Hooded Man for years, and then suddenly Cuthbert's found a way. Apparently he – Robin Hood, that is – is recruiting more men because they've got a big raid coming." He sighed. "It's always the way with that sort, isn't it? They start off doing good, but then their greed gets the better of them."

Guy thought that was almost an admission of admiration for Robin Hood as the people's champion. Maybe if Allan and Roger still wanted that hideaway that Robin didn't know about, the far north might just be the place for it if Hereward and Bertwald turned out to be trustworthy? For now, though, Guy just said,

"I know what you mean." That was neutral enough for a first meeting.

Their confidential conversation was cut short by all but the two foresters from Clipstone coming to join them, and as soon as they realised he was approachable, Guy found himself being quizzed urgently by them all, every last one of them desperate to know what impossible tasks the sheriff was going to expect of them. By the time Guy had finished telling them of how he was endlessly out and about patrolling the forest, everyone was looking glum.

"God's hooks," Cuthbert groaned. "You mean he actually expects you to go out beyond a day's ride from home in the winter? Seriously?"

Guy concealed his growing mirth, but did wink at Hereward, who then struggled to hide his own amusement at Cuthbert's expression as Guy elaborated, "I've often had to camp out for three or four nights at a time at this time of year. It's different for the knights who cover the Le Clay section of the forest. They're close enough to villages all the time to at least find an alehouse for the night. But over in the Derwent-to-Erewash section, the villages are a bit thinner on the ground, but nothing like as thin as in the Old Forest. Highborn knights like Sir Henry tend to claim a night at whichever manor is closest, but I only know a couple of places I feel I can presume upon. The villagers tend to be a better bet. They've usually got a warm hay barn you can take shelter in."

"But the villagers hate us!" wailed Egfrith.

As one of Cuthbert's pair of men, that wasn't so surprising. If Cuthbert was endlessly trying to worm his way into Briwere's favour, they'd probably had their orders to come down pretty hard on those villages bordering or within the parks, even for the slightest misdemeanours.

"Then brace yourselves for a cold start to the coming year," Guy warned them, "because Briwere will make it very clear just how far afield he wants you to travel. Given that the whole of Nottinghamshire and a goodly chunk of Derbyshire are under royal forest law these days, he'll expect every foot of it to be inspected and accounted for – however unreasonable that might be."

The chill conditions at the castle easily dissuaded Briwere from spending more than another night at Laxton, and so to Guy's delight they were on their way back to Nottingham the next morning. However, although he had already planned to ride out the very next day under whatever pretext he could find, and carry the warning to the outlaws, he was already too late.

They had barely had chance to warm their boots by the fire in the small hall the forest knights used, when a servant came rushing in.

"The sheriff wants you all in his chambers," she panted anxiously. "There's a man come. He says he can lead you to Robin Hood!"

For once Guy was as eager as the others to get to Briwere, and they all piled into the small chamber that lay off the great hall which

Briwere used as his own. When they got there it was to see a scruffy looking individual standing before Briwere, woolly hat in hand, and wearing the kind of bright-eyed, eager expression Guy was used to seeing on the terriers they used for ratting – the ones always spoiling for a fight, but too daft to know how dangerous some of the huge rats down in the granaries were.

Briwere was positively beaming. "We've got him!" he declared triumphantly. "We've bloody got him, the arrogant bastard!"

"How, my lord?" Sir Giles asked, as ever too dense to know when he should just keep quiet.

And of course Briwere rounded on him with, "Because *some* men know how to do their duty, that's how!"

Giles looked like a kicked puppy, but Guy had given up on trying to tell him to be more circumspect when around the sheriff; Giles was too amiable but dim to begin to grasp when to just keep quiet, and too useless at his job to ever earn Briwere's respect, much less his approval. Luckily, this time Briwere was too eager to tell his news to be bothered with reducing Giles to a crumbling wreck, as so often happened.

"This man belongs to Cuthbert the forester," Briwere said with vulpine delight. "He has infiltrated Robin Hood's gang as a new recruit. ...Go on, tell them what you've told me!"

His pointed nose almost quivering with delight, the man spoke, wringing his hat in his hands as if it was Robin Hood's neck. "I weren't supposed to come so soon, see? But I found sommat out I thought couldn't wait." Even his quick lick of his lips reminded Guy of the stable terrier with the prospect of a good bone. "They'm worse than we thought. They gotta murderer with them! I seen his face and I knowed him from the description what got read out by the priest at Michaelmas." Another lick. "So I gets talkin' to him, see? And he even admits he's from Leicester, so I knowed he was the same man."

He heard Briwere's impatient sigh, glanced at the sheriff and hurried on. "Seems Robin Hood's gotta plan. He wants to kill the sheriff! Robin Hood told us that, he did, with his own mouth. I saw him. I was there! And he sez what we gotta do is lure the sheriff to us, and the murderer – his name is Wilfrid – asks him how we gonna do that, then? And Robin Hood sez that one of us gotta pretend to betray them. One of us gotta come here and say we'll lead the sheriff to their hideout. But really it'll be to a trap. None of the others'd do it, see? So I pretends to be a bit reluctant, then sez that if nobody else'll do it, I will."

"Very cunning," Briwere approved, but decided he'd better continue or the man would be milking his moment of fame for the rest of the night. "Osric, here, is supposed to lead us out not tomorrow, but the day after. That fool Robin Hood thinks Osric is going to linger and not come to us until after tomorrow midday, you see."

Unable to contain himself any longer, Guy asked, "And where was the original ambush supposed to take place?"

"Why does that matter?" Sir Mahel demanded, getting an approving nod from Briwere.

Thinking fast, Guy responded, "Because if it *is* Robin Hood, then he'll have thought it through. We've only got this man's word for all of this so far, but he could still be leading us into a trap."

"Don't be ridiculous, Gisborne," Briwere sniffed. "Cuthbert himself gave me this man's description, right down to the mole on his cheek. He is who he says he is."

Guy silently called on all of his favourite saints to aid and preserve him in this, and persevered with, "Nonetheless, I would still like to know both locations. Where *should* we be going, and where *are* we going? Because it might be no bad thing to make a show of sending a few men towards the original ambush site, just in case someone is watching us."

Even Briwere had to admit that that might be a good thing to do, and he gestured the man to answer Guy.

"I'm supposed to take you out as if we was goin' north. Where the road forks, we take the Mansfield road, not the Doncaster one. Just past there the road dips a bit and there's a lot of thick wood close to the road. That's where they think they're going to catch you."

"Makes sense," Guy conceded. "Not an ideal ambush spot, but then if there are enough of them...?"

"Sixteen men and Robin Hood!" the man answered without even thinking about it. "And there's more going to come from the north, or so Robin sez."

Feeling sicker by the moment, Guy still had to ask, "And where *are* we going?"

"We goes north through Bulwell, but carries on instead of heading for Linby," the man declared with a beaming grin. "That's where their camp is! You'll catch them all there!"

And suddenly Guy knew that the worst had come to pass. One of the new men had just betrayed the Hucknall camp.

Oh Gervase, how I kept hold of the meal I had just eaten I do not know. All I wanted to do was to get away from everyone else and look at that list of men I had. What the man's name was in reality I did not need to know, for he surely would not have been known as Osric by the outlaws. He would be going by some other name, and that would be the one Allan or Roger or one of the others might recognise.

Worse, I could see how Robin was going to manipulate the situation. He was going to send these new men into the lion's maw, as it were, but he was not so far gone as to be expecting them to be able to handle the armed men the sheriff would surely bring with him. No, he would send a message to the real gang, and it would be something which would bring them running to the Hucknall camp just in time to get involved in the fight.

Oh how I remember that night in the sheriff's chamber, and how often I clasped my hands together, or crossed my arms, just so that nobody would see how I was shaking. Only when I was able to get away, and retreat to somewhere where I could think without distraction, did I realise that Robin would not risk my friends getting to Hucknall too soon. That was the real reason for the delay. He had probably got them to come as far as the Hardstoft camp under some excuse of training the new men, or bring the new six into the gang, I thought. And of course, then having got them that far, it would be a simple matter for Robin to make a dash for them when he left the new men at the ambush point just beyond Hucknall. Indeed, I did not think he would have to go all of the way. He would probably have the gang watching for a fire arrow or a smoke signal – something he would have prearranged with them as being a call for help, not a summons to battle.

I went to bed cursing my cousin's name, I do confess, Gervase, and now that saddens me – not only for the damage I did to my immortal soul by it, but for the way Robin repeatedly crushed and crippled my love for a cousin into the hatred a man has for an implacable enemy. I would give so much now for that to not have been so, but the decisions which set us on that path were never made by me. All I could do was try over and over to limit the damage to others, but on this occasion I had to make a decision which still haunts me, Brother. It haunts me most grievously.

Chapter 24

W hat was this decision, you ask? Ah, that comes with the fight itself, but you must allow me to tell you of how I wrestled mentally all of that night, for I was desperate to work out some way that I could detach myself from the main party in order to be able to carry the warning to my friends. Yet when we got up and assembled in the outer bailey, things only got worse. Having been handed this opportunity to grab the pestilent outlaw who had caused him so much grief, Briwere was not leaving anything to chance.

Now, we were fortunate that this happened so late in the year, and so there were no additional knights at the castle with their men to do their forty days' service. But we still had our regular compliment of thirty men-at-arms and sergeants, as well as our three permanent knights, and on that grey and cold dawn, with the sun not yet fully up, I went to get my horse only to be confronted with the sight of Sirs Hugh and Robert mounted up, alongside six of our ten sergeants, and with fourteen of the twenty men-at-arms all lining up to march behind them. It was a hammer intended to crack an irritating nut, and my blood ran cold at the sight.

Yes, Gervase, that many men! And that was far from all, because also mounting up were all eight of the Le Clay knights, along with the three who, alongside me, would soon be taking over the Old Forest. Thirty-four men and the sheriff set out that morning to trap seventeen, carrying torches to light their way; and with it only being five or so miles to the Hucknall camp, I knew that we would be there early enough to catch the men and Robin unawares. Heavy though their mail and gambesons were for those men who had to go on foot, we would be travelling on decent roads for most of our journey, and I knew we would be there long before noon – a whole day ahead of when Robin was expecting us, and with two against one in our favour.

Yet I could not think of any reason why I might divert from the column. I managed to position myself at the back with Hugh and Robert and Sir Joscelin – he being the one I told you about before, Brother, who had taken one blow too many to the head, and therefore was not always either sharp or alert, and so the sheriff had decided he was better in the rear. We others were there, though, to make sure that the men-at-arms *kept up, and that we did not get too spread out as a force. However even back there, I would still need an excuse of some kind to explain me diving off into the forest as soon as I could, and even declaring that I would go and scout for the other outlaws who were supposed to be coming would most definitely not do, since only I had the vaguest inkling of where they would be coming from.*

And so I prayed, Gervase, oh how I prayed! I called upon Dewi Sant to protect his loyal servant, Tuck, and for him and saints Issui, Melangell and Cadoc to watch over all of those whom I called my friends and cared about dearly. Then in the first shaft of watery sunlight they answered me.

I had been worrying so much I had not been thinking straight. This man Osric, whom I now know my friends knew as Sighard, had never said, as far as I was aware, just how many additional men were coming from the north, nor who they were. And I realised that Briwere thought these sixteen men we were off to trap were actually the core members of the gang – he thought he was capturing Little John, Allan of the Dales, Will Scarlet and the other famous men, not some rag-tag bunch of recruits. He was wholly unaware of just how many recruits Robin had, and no doubt thought that only a handful of men would be coming round to attack them from the other side – maybe a couple of key men with a few of the new ones to give them some experience. And in part, Brother, that was because even Briwere was not so by-Our-Lady stupid as to think anyone would attack heavily armed men with raw soldiers who had never been tested in a fight before!

Yes, Gervase, Robin was being stupid – that and cruel – and I repeat that I thought, and still do think, that his head-on collision with the cart in King Richard's camp addled his brains. For although I now realised that my friends would still be securely up at the Hardstoft camp, since there would now be no time for Robin to summon them, what would be their lucky escape really was that – a matter of luck. Robin had not known that ~Sighard~ was a fake, nor that he would not follow his instructions, and I was now very glad that our spy was traipsing miserably at the rear of the column with me – having thought that he would be on his way back to Cuthbert by now – and could not give the sheriff any more pearls of his dubious wisdom along the way. But had ~Sighard~ been real, if he had been one of the other genuine recruits who had been unlucky enough to be captured, for instance, or who would have followed Robin's instructions to the letter and waited until the morrow, then things might have been very different that morning.

As we got close to the camp, Briwere did call Osric up to the front and get him to give directions, but by now Briwere was fully focused on taking the camp by force, not by any twitterings of a man of little consequence, as he thought of Osric. And now I was able to take advantage of Briwere's perception of me as a cold and heartless man, for as we were sent left and right to surround the camp, I rode to the front and declared that I would take care of this man and make sure that he did not have a change of heart and try to warn Robin, saying as an aside to the sheriff that the loyalty of lesser men was likely to be fickle and less steady than our own – something I knew he already believed to be true. I did not want Osric to start babbling and to tell Briwere that the main gang members were coming later, although in truth it might have been that Osric genuinely had no idea of how many were in our original gang – but now was not the time to find out.

However brace yourself, Gervase, because you are not going to be happy about what I have to tell you of what came next. It does not give me any joy, either, and I beg you to keep that in mind as you listen, and not to be affronted on your hero's behalf. Remember, I have a painful confession to make.

Sherwood
Winter, the Year of Our Lord 1197

Guy was less than gentle with Osric as he reached down from his saddle and hauled the man along to the left, as directed by the sheriff.

"No sneaking off to warn your hero," Guy snarled in his ear, and was rewarded with Osric bleating,

"He's not my hero! He's a mad man!"

Guy's sigh of exasperation was misinterpreted by Osric, but in reality Guy was wondering why, by all that was holy, this man – who had known Robin only a few weeks – could see that, when those who supposedly knew him well could not.

It was all Guy could do to hang back and let others find their way around the perimeter of the Hucknall camp. Part of him wanted to forge ahead to double check that his friends hadn't come early and were about to be caught in the trap. But his inner voice kept telling him that if he got near to the front then he would betray himself by being too familiar with the terrain. And if the others did get caught, he forcefully reminded himself, then he would need to be in a position to get them out – something he wouldn't be able to do if he, too, was in the dungeon.

A steady drizzle had set in, enough to discourage inexperienced men from keeping much of a watch, but not so heavy that it made it hard for the attackers to see one another along the line. However, as they manoeuvred into position, Guy managed to ensure that he was at the far left beyond any of the other knights or men-at-arms. If he could allow someone to escape into the rain-grey woods then he would, since there was nobody beyond him to stop them, and there was a tiny gully made by a trickle of a stream which someone, if they had their wits about them, could use, since it was overhung with heavy ferns even at this time of year.

"You can't mistake Little John," Osric whined. "They say he's a giant!"

"Who says?" Guy hissed. "Haven't you seen him yourself?"

"Not yet," Osric replied with that mad-terrier look in his eyes again, "but he's coming! Two of the other lads have met him, him and Tuck and Will Scarlet. They say Scarlet is a fierce fighter."

Yes he is, Guy thought miserably, *and I'm not having him risking his neck for a traitorous wretch like you!*

"How...*many*?" he demanded in exasperated tones, and was stunned to see the confusion in Osric's eyes. "How many are coming?"

"Only a few," the smaller man babbled, finding this forester knight whom the sheriff seemed to dismiss far more terrifying than he'd expected. "We're Robin's main gang now. He said so! He said the others who were with him years ago have left him ...they weren't loyal to him anymore." There was another nervous lick of the lips. "I told the sheriff, I did. 'That's why you ain't heard much of Robin o' late,' I sez. He sez his old gang turned coward after the sheriff nearly caught 'em, but that with us he could hit the sheriff where it hurt again, at the courts."

Guy didn't know whether to laugh with relief or weep with anger. So this man had never seen the Cosham brothers or the three former turcopoles from the east – and they of anyone would stick in his mind, Guy was sure. Hearing Malik, Janah and Khalīl calling to one another in Arabic would seem wildly outlandish to a man who'd never gone beyond the shire borders. And yet his heart ached for them at the same time. They had loyally stuck with Robin through thick and thin, and yet this was going to be their reward, to be cast aside for a bunch of mindless thugs who weren't fit to lick their boots, much less take their places.

That stoked Guy's anger as nothing else had so far, and he swore to himself that Osric would not live beyond today to sneak back to Robin, if his cousin got away. And Robin was daft enough to accept some idiot excuse of the kind that Osric had been left at the castle and had not been at the camp when the blow fell, Guy realised. He would accept it because it was easier than admitting that he had been wrong. Horribly and disastrously wrong, and that what had been obvious to the others had come to pass despite all of their warnings.

As the signal came to advance and close in on the camp, Guy loosened the knife he kept in his boot. If an arrow didn't get Osric, then he would cut the traitor's throat in the confusion. Then as they crushed down the hurdles covered with branches and foliage which had hidden the paths into the camp, and the knights led the charge in, Guy got into the circular enclosure in time to see Robin diving for his bow and arrows, while the others just milled in confusion. None of his other friends were there, thanks be to God, and he offered up a prayer of relief.

Like lambs to the slaughter, the new men were cut down. Half of them never even got as far as getting a weapon in their hands, but those that did showed themselves to be brawlers, not soldiers. They fought individually, never covering one another's backs, inflicting cuts and bruises but never anything worse. The only one who had much impact was the man who turned out to be the murderer from Leicester, and he went straight for the sheriff, diving under Sir Mahel's horse to get to him, and giving Briwere a nasty, slicing cut to his leg before being impaled on Mahel's sword.

Yet that scuffle around the sheriff was what saved Briwere's life, for the one person who did cause mayhem was Robin himself, and much as he wanted to target the sheriff, he never got a clear view of him around Mahel, another mounted man, and the attacker. Leaping up onto the makeshift roof of the shelter, Robin loosed arrow after arrow into the affray, every one finding a mark, although sometimes men hid behind their already wounded comrades to get closer to him. And that was his limitation, sooner or later men got too close for the big bow to be an effective weapon, and he did not have his sword to hand.

As the soldiers got closer and closer to him, Guy saw him glancing over his shoulder in the hope of getting out at the rear, but men-at-arms were waiting for him there too. Then just as five of the men-at-arms were about to hedge him about with spears, Robin spotted Guy. His face creased in an angry roar, and he aimed straight at Guy, clearly thinking him the traitor. As the long barbed arrow flew straight at Guy, what saved him was that he had already dismounted.

Had he been on the horse he would never have been able to move in time. As it was, he instinctively spun to one side, but without letting go of Osric who was dragged into the arrow's path. The arrow penetrated Osric's shoulder with such power that it came out the other side, to lodge with its flights sticking out of the front of his jerkin. With a howl of pain, Osric staggered into Guy and they both went down, but Guy regained his feet in time to see Robin being hauled down off the roof and be marched towards the sheriff.

Yet as Robin struggled in his captors' arms, he caught sight of Guy again. The way he suddenly focused on him made Guy certain that he was about to betray him, and so he hauled Osric to his feet and in front of him.

As Robin screamed, "Traitor!" and men followed his glare, what they all saw was Guy holding up Osric, the one they all knew was the informant anyway, and so they took no notice. But Robin did. Somewhere in his mental chaos it registered that he knew this man with the arrow sticking out of his shoulder. And then one of the four surviving other men of the gang screamed,

"I'll bloody kill you, Sighard, you bastard!" and realisation hit Robin.

He'd been betrayed not by the cousin he hated, but by one of the new men he'd put so much faith into. And now Guy knew that Osric must not live to go back to the castle. The terrified faces of the four ordinary captives were sufficient indication that all Briwere would get out of them was wild panicking and nothing of substance. And with luck, anything Robin said about other members of the gang would be taken as bragging to try and make people at the castle believe that they were in danger, and thereby drop their guard enough for Robin to make his escape.

But Osric, he knew too much of the truth, even if it was far from all of it, and he knew that here and now they had not captured Little John, Will Scarlet or Brother Tuck. And even though Briwere's face was creased in agony as a sergeant bound his leg wound, Guy knew that that knowledge would only make him more vicious and thirsty for revenge. Maybe even to the extent of leaving the hapless men-at-arms with a sergeant and knight, to wait in ambush for the others to come tomorrow.

No, that must not happen. Briwere had to go back to the castle with all of the men to give Guy time to warn the outlaws. Oh, Briwere would want to hunt them down, there was no doubt about that, but not here, not now.

With all of his strength Guy flung Osric in the direction of one of the paths out, and at the same time bellowed, "Come back here, you wretch!" and launching himself after the hapless spy.

As Guy brought Osric down by throwing his full weight onto him, the smaller man's head cracked on one of the large stones which had propped the hurdles up, and went limp. One look at his eyes told Guy that he was dead even before he reached for his neck to find a pulse. *Blessed St Issui, thank you for saving me from having to commit murder*, Guy silently offered up, for his insides had been twisting up at the prospect, even though his choices were that or do nothing and risk others suffering a far worse fate.

"*Pffah*! The Devil takes care of his own!" Guy exclaimed in disgust, as he got to his feet and was joined by two of the sergeants.

"Bad luck," one of them sympathised. "It would have been interesting to see how his story compared with Robin Hood's," making Guy's responding snort one of relief, rather than the disgust the two sergeants thought it was. That was precisely what he'd been trying to avoid.

All the way back, Guy lurked at the rear of the column, making very sure that he was never in Robin's line of sight, and at the castle he allowed others to be the ones to manhandle his cousin into the dungeon under the main keep. Nor did he go there after night had fallen. His great fear was that if he did, then Robin would start bawling and shouting and wake others up, expending energy on accusing Guy, rather than accepting whatever help Guy could give him. And with ever growing dismay, Guy realised that there was very little he could do for Robin without ending down in the dungeon himself. The sheriff would want an early trial, that was certain, maybe even to the extent of asking for a neighbouring sheriff to come in and do the honours, and at that point Guy's stomach did an almighty lurch as a realisation hit him, sending him running for the jakes.

Who else would Briwere call upon but the new sheriff of Yorkshire, Geoffrey fitz Peter, the royal head forester? The king had presumably come to his senses and realised that his errant and permanently absent half-brother, the archbishop of York, was not a wise choice as sheriff for such a vast shire as York's, but to choose the royal forester was an equally terrible choice. And fitz Peter was a cruel bastard. Robin wouldn't die as cleanly as even those poor sergeants and knights who had been hung after the siege. No, his fate would be to be hung, drawn and quartered – probably in some ghastly public spectacle in the outer bailey. And that was a grisly fate, for a man so condemned was cut down from the noose before he'd actually died, although not before his neck had been stretched; then had to endure his guts being cut out while still alive. And if he lived after that, then he would surely die as his body was chopped into quarters and his head cut off, the various pieces being displayed on castle walls and town gates as a warning. Guy might have known what such a thing was, but he had never actually seen it done, and he didn't want the first time to be someone he knew, however bad their relationship had gone.

Yet try as he might, in the next couple of days, Guy couldn't find a convincing reason for him to leave the castle to be able to go and warn the others. And with Robin safely in the dungeon, Briwere was lying in his robes, milking his wound for all it was worth, and hadn't even bothered questioning Robin yet. That had at least saved Guy from any accusations so far, and he wasn't sure whether it would be better to be in the hall when the time came, and therefore know if he was betrayed, or stay away in the hope that if Robin didn't see him, he wouldn't be provoked into some act of defiance. Therefore the only thing Guy dared do to help his cousin was to tell the guards and servants to make sure that Robin was kept well-fed and with enough water.

"The sheriff will want this to be an impressive trial," he warned them, "and that means having a villain worth making a song and dance about, not some half-starved skeleton who's too dazed for want of water to even know his name. So for your own sakes, feed him!"

And this was when Guy's reputation with the servants worked in his favour, for they genuinely believed that he was trying to save them from at least another tongue-lashing by Briwere, if not an actual whipping, which Briwere was also known to hand out. Moreover, Briwere was so confident that he had his prisoner secure that he was quite happy to leave the outer bailey gates open during daylight hours, as was the custom, and so for the next two days the outer bailey seethed with local folk, all hoping to catch a glimpse of the infamous outlaw. That in turn gave Guy a good excuse to be down there to keep an eye on things, and as one of the few knights who were remotely comfortable being on foot in a sea of peasants, Guy hardly had much competition for the job.

Consequently, he was on hand on the third morning when instead of him finding them, the outlaws found him.

"Guy!" Will's familiar voice hissed at his shoulder. "Don't turn! Walk towards the bread ovens."

Aware of Will following close behind him, Guy sauntered with as much calm as he could to the baker's area of the outer bailey, and then wandered around the back of the two big brick-built ovens, as if he'd heard something. Round there he found Hugh, Siward, Allan and Roger, and then Will slid in from one side and Ed from the other.

"*Dewi Sant* be blessed, I've found you!" Guy gulped, shocked at how close to tears of relief he was.

"What the Hell happened?" Will demanded, and almost stumbling over his words, Guy told them, and by the time he had finished they were all groaning in despair.

"The stupid, stupid, bastard," Will growled, turning to lean his head against the still-warm bricks of the oven in despair. "What in God's name was he thinking?"

"Heaven alone knows," Siward sighed, but thought of something Guy hadn't. "Is there any chance this Geoffrey fitz Peter might bring an experienced torturer with him?"

That was just the last straw for Guy and he sank to his knees, retching into the winter mud. He became aware of Will and Ed hoisting him to his feet and holding him upright as he was then enfolded in a hug by Allan, their corner of the bailey being too far back to see the main part, and so mercifully free of stares from the curious.

There was nothing but sympathy in his cousin's voice as he asked worriedly, "Will you be able to get out alright if he does?"

Nobody doubted now that Robin would betray Guy, even if he held out over the names of the others in the gang. And while men like Gilbert, Malik and the Coshams had nothing to fear aside from the obvious, Hugh, Siward and Much still had relatives in the area who might feel the sheriff's wrath, even if their immediate families were long gone, so Robin's silence on their behalves was no small matter, either.

"Probably," Guy answered shakily. "I suppose it depends on whether he's so far gone that he genuinely thinks you lot did betray him, in spirit if not in deed. If he can really think that of you, then there's no chance he'll keep quiet about me. But I can't just vanish, either. I have to come up with some legitimate reason for leaving the castle so that I have several days head start on any who come hunting me."

"I'm so sorry," Siward said mournfully. "We probably set him off on that tack. You see he came back and said that these new men were asking when they were going to meet us, and we pretty much refused outright. We said that we'd come to their aid if they were in trouble, but that we'd need a whole lot more reassurance that they were committed to our cause than them just turning up in the forest and asking to join us."

"Oh God," Guy gulped, "and he took it that one step further and said that you were no longer part of his gang. But whether that was just the excuse that bloody Osric heard, or whether that's what he believes, is anyone's guess."

"Have you seen him?" Will asked cautiously, prompting Guy's honest reply of,

"I haven't dared! ...What would I have done if he'd started screaming my name, Will? No way should he know that! There are guards all over the place at the moment. I'd never get clear of the dungeons before they came looking, wondering why this famous outlaw would be calling my name. Harry's been and taken him bread each night, but he says all he can hear is Robin praying over and over. He didn't respond when Harry called down to ask if he needed any clean water ...and Harry didn't dare ask more with a guard at his side. I'm just grateful he took the risk and went at all."

"At least we know he's alive," Allan sighed, and hugged Guy that bit tighter.

However it was Hugh who asked, "Do you think we can get him out?" As Guy looked up at him in surprise, Hugh shrugged and explained, "He could betray us all, Guy. For that reason if none other, we need to try and avoid him being tortured to give up his secrets. ...Thank God Marianne and Mariota are at Kirklees and out of harm's way."

Guy sighed deeply. "You'll have to hang around in Nottingham if you want my help. I'm just going to have to take things day by day. If this was Ralph Murdac in command he'd be taking no chances, the gates would all have been shut and barred, and you'd never have got in this far, but Briwere wants to make a show of it."

Roger sidled a little closer to Guy. "If we was already in the castle, would it be easier?"

Guy gulped again. It was a clever idea. Briwere only thought on men fighting their way *into* the castle at the time of any trial, and would be alert for that. But if the outlaws could be inside well before then, all they would have to do would be to fight their way out, and for that they would have a greater element of surprise.

"Is there somewhere we could hide?" Allan asked.

"As long as you had food and water with you, so that you didn't need to appear in amongst the servants, err, yes. I could hide you on the top floor of the old keep. It's where the knights who come to do service sleep if there's no room in the main keep or the hall, so it's deserted at this time of year." He thought hard. "I think it would have to be just you two, though, Allan and Roger, because you could always walk out in the guise of servants. But if you were up there, and armed with plenty of rope, then you could drop it down for the others to climb up closer to the time of the escape."

"That'd be good for you, too," Will said with an affectionate punch at Guy's arm. "If you're asleep with the other knights in your room, you'd have witnesses to prove you weren't involved. I think in this case you need to be seen as spotlessly clean by the sheriff."

"Thank you!" Guy's heartfelt response was not lost on the others. If they got Robin out, but he was implicated, there might not be a second chance for them to get in and rescue him.

"Is there any way we could slip some of Tuck's poppy juice into food or drinks?" Siward wondered. "I don't mean to knock them out totally, just make them a bit more sluggish and slower to respond."

"I'll see what I can find out," Guy agreed. "Can you meet me tomorrow if I make an excuse to get out just into the town?"

The next day there was no opportunity to do anything more than smuggle Allan and Roger up to the top of the keep under the pretence of servants carting something up there to store. However the heavy sacks they laboured twice up the stairs with contained not only rope but supplies, and then in the dead of night, weapons were hoisted up into the castle.

However, the day after, Guy was able to get up to them and announce,

"It's salt cod stew tonight! You could put anything in that and nobody would notice – especially the way our cook makes it! Do you want me to go to the kitchens?"

However, they said no, and it was Roger who skulked down, and with the ease of the practised cut-purse that he used to be, slipped the contents of the bottle Tuck gave him into the stew. Guy came late to the table, and finding that there was no stew left, made do with bread, complaining, but not too hard since everyone else was muttering about how bad the stew had been. It filled empty stomachs, but that was about all that could be said for it, and mostly the men were grateful for the fact that there was so much barley and vegetables that they took away the worst of the fish taste.

Watching everyone like a hawk, Guy noticed that even the ones who normally stayed up drinking if there were no duties outside of the castle the next day, were wilting considerably earlier than usual, and heading for their beds. As he joined the majority of the forest knights in returning to the old keep, and their cramped, shared rooms there, Guy's sharp eyes caught a glimpse of Roger. The small outlaw was making much of trying to remove something from one of the steps of the flight leading up from the first floor with a stiff hand-brush, and doing a good job of instinctively shrinking against the wall as various knights stamped past him, taking no more notice of him than if he was a beetle. But Guy could tell he was counting the knights going to bed.

In his room, Guy prepared for bed as usual, but lay awake listening for Sir Osmaer's snores to start. Being up on the second floor of the old keep, they were wedged into a tiny chamber built into the thickness of the wall, since there was only one decent sized room up here, and that was shared by Thorsten, Giles, Simon and Hermer, which at least meant that Guy only had one companion to watch. However the four next door on the other side of the stairwell were not men to lie awake worrying about anything, and when he tiptoed out and stuck his head around their door, they were all snoring like pigs, dead to the world.

It was only a short while later that Guy faintly heard feet on the stairs outside. The outlaws were being very careful to move silently, and it was only because he was sitting up listening for them that Guy heard them at all. He thought about sticking his head out around the door to them, but then decided that if he didn't, when questioned he could be absolutely honest and say he had seen nothing.

Forcing himself to lie down, Guy found the night dragging on interminably. At any moment he expected the alarm to be sounded, and his every sense was at full stretch waiting for it. Yet it didn't come, and eventually sheer exhaustion took over, and without meaning to, he fell asleep.

When the alarm came it was already just about light. The clanging of the alarm bell and people shouting below woke Guy at the same time as Osmaer, and they both stumbled, bleary-eyed, out to the stairs, shrugging on warm jerkins at the same time as the four others were also emerging.

Down in the inner court of the old castle, they were met by Sir Hugh, telling them in dismay,

"Robin Hood's escaped!"

"What?" Guy was able to exclaim along with the others. "I never heard a thing!"

And he hadn't! What a contrast to Robin's foray into the castle over a year ago! Part of Guy had always been waiting for the moment when things went bad, and he'd have to leap out of bed, try and play his part for his fellow knights, and yet at the same time come up with some way, some near impossible way, to get as many of his friends out of harm's way as he could. And how often could he do the rope over the wall thing before someone asked how on earth the outlaws kept finding said rope?

Yet this time his friends had come and gone like ghosts, and suddenly Guy felt like a weight had been lifted. If Robin himself wasn't ordering the attacks there was clearly way less danger of them being seen, let alone caught. At which point Guy also felt sadness at wishing so fervently that his cousin wouldn't be part of the gang anymore. But it was true, and last night was the proof, that if Robin was no longer in charge, then Guy and the others could work together to great effect, and with himself in a far less precarious position too.

However, by now they were all in the hall, all the men there in various stages of undress, although Guy noted that they'd all had the presence of mind to grab their swords. And it was the three castle knights standing before them grim-faced. Briwere could be heard ranting and raving in his quarters, and the first words out of Sir Robert's mouth were,

"Sheriff Briwere's wound has turned infected. He cannot rise from his bed, so it's us coordinating the search for this villain."

Sir Richard grimaced as something else hit the wall of the sheriff's room with a crunch, then began, "I know what you're all wondering – how, in God's name, did that by-Our-Lady rogue do it? How did he escape? Well somehow others got in to him. We found out when the guard was changed at the sound of the Laud's bell – or rather after it, when the servants roused the next watch after they realised that nobody from the keep had come to wake their replacements."

Guy knew that four men had been on guard above Robin ever since they had brought him in, and that one of them should have gone to wake those taking the Lauds to Nones shift, which covered the morning and early afternoon. Lenton Priory was close enough for the bells to be easily heard across the fields at night and early morning. Others would then take over until four turns of the hourglass after the Compline bell; and so the outlaws had been clever in waiting until they had been relieved, for then they had a clear eight hours until the morning before anyone would notice something was wrong.

"They found the guards trussed up and drugged," Sir Richard announced with a sigh. "Seems that they all had something which we think was poppy juice poured down their throats, but what's got us all foxed is that in other ways they're unharmed ...well aside from a few nasty bruises and a couple of minor cuts where they put up an initial fight. We've questioned them, and they say that these men came silently and fast, and that they were outnumbered at least two to one."

"But who were they?" dim Giles asked. "We caught all of his gang!"

And now Guy felt safe to speak. "No we didn't," he said stepping forward from the group with a rueful shake of his head. "I've been waiting for the sheriff to stop being such a bear with a sore head ...well, leg," and he got a titter of amusement from all there, who knew exactly what he meant.

"But honestly, did those pathetic creatures we rounded up in the forest feel anything like the gang we fought here in the castle back last summer? They didn't to me. That's why I was so suspicious of Osric. As soon as we broke into that compound, and they all started fumbling around for weapons, they looked nothing like the tough fighters we've gone up against before. I think the core of the gang is still at large."

There was a sudden explosion of voices at that, giving Guy chance to breathe and think. He'd not betrayed anyone by this, because sooner rather than later one of the others was going to come to the same conclusion, and that was borne out by Sir Hugh's next words.

"I'm glad Sir Guy has said that," he declared after the room had been called to order. "Sir Richard, Sir Robert and I had been discussing that, and though the sheriff hasn't been able to see the four men who came in with the outlaw, we have. They know nothing. Truly, they don't know where other hideouts are – and because they had no real supplies in that place to see them through the winter, there has to be somewhere else, at least, and probably more. And we asked who were Little John and Will Scarlet of those we caught, and finally one of them said they weren't there."

Again there was another burst of chatter.

"So if they weren't there, then there's a good chance that others weren't either. And the final thing which convinced us was that we told the men-at-arms to gather up all of the weapons. Well there were a lot of spears and some rough but serviceable swords, but the only bows we found were light hunting bows of the kind any halfway competent village bowyer could make. We didn't find a single big Welsh bow aside from the one Robin Hood himself was using. So Sir Guy's right, we don't think the real gang was there. We think that this was a trap for us, and our only advantage was that Osric got us there a day early."

Guy wasn't going to argue with that. If the knights wanted to think of it that way, let them, because he certainly wasn't about to divulge the rifts within the gang.

"What is new," Sir Robert added, "is that a cooler head was clearly in charge of this attack. Someone really thought it through. Now it may be that we really did have Robin Hood himself in the dungeon. But it could equally be that the man who was down there was one of the hotheads of the gang, who was deliberately left to wind up the new men to make a good show of attacking us while the others lay in wait – because none of it feels right for a cunning outlaw who has evaded capture for years."

It was all Guy could do not to punch the air with joy at these words. This was proof, had he ever needed it, that the gang would survive if Robin went, because 'Robin Hood' was more than just one man.

"Are we going to hunt for him?" Sir Henry was asking with his usual belligerence. Robin Hood was a sore point with him after he had barely escaped with his life from an ambush, and he still had the scars to prove it which ached something shocking in this cold winter weather.

"We've already sent the rest of the men out to scour the town," Sir Richard said with a placatory wave of his hand, "But to be honest, we don't have much hope of finding anything. They've had hours in which to escape, and during the dead of night, too. It would be little short of a miracle if some worthy in the town woke in the night and just happened to see them."

Guy cleared his throat. "And it's been soaking it down all night, Sir Henry." He always gave the touchy knight his title, whether in public or private, even though they were equals. "Even if we get the hounds out now, the scent will long have washed away, and as we found the last time we chased them, they're crafty enough woodsmen to take to the streams for a while to lose us. ...And I don't have my wolfhounds anymore who might just have found them." He didn't have to fake the bitterness in his voice at that, and again that meant he was believed, but he was touched by Sir Hugh's response of,

"We know you'd be the first to hunt him down, Guy, after what he did to your beloved beasts. Even Briwere must rue their loss just now, but for you it must be a keen reminder that their killer's at large still."

Yes, Brother, it was a sad fact that my friends within the castle were more considerate of me than my cousin at this time. However, as you are my confessor, I must say to you that when the crisis had passed, I felt very badly about Osric. He was not in so very different a position to myself, I realised. His master, the dreadful Cuthbert, had the power to mislead Sir Ralph, and of course by the end of the mission the sheriff also, into thinking that Osric would not do his required duties, had he declined to act as ordered. Therefore if he wished to keep both his job and his home, Osric had had no choice. And Osric had a family, I found out. A family who upon his death were turned out of their humble cottage with nowhere to go, because he had only daughters, and there was nobody to take Osric's job over to keep it. Cuthbert did nothing to help them, and I became aware of them when they came to beg in Nottingham and they were brought before the sheriff for vagrancy.

For truth, Gervase! No, I am not merely regretful now because I am making what might turn out to be my last confession! At the time I was genuinely remorseful at Osric's death. He had only been doing what he believed was right, just as I did. That we were on opposing sides did not mean that he acted out of malice or bad faith. And this was where I had always clashed with my cousin, for I could always see the other side when it came to men like Osric. Yes, I was forced into a dreadful situation back at that camp, and I truly believed with all my heart that if Osric had lived then my friends would have been in mortal danger. I had to weigh one life against many. Do not forget, Brother, that all the sheriff had to do was to wait at that camp and they would have been caught. But that did not mean that once away from the crisis I could not see how Osric had been cruelly used, however, objectionable he was to me at the time.

And now I must tell you how it went from my friends' point of view, for it proves that what I had surmised was not so far from the truth. Robin had told them that he had these other recruits at the Hucknall camp, and to their credit, my friends decided that despite not wanting these men within their ranks, that nevertheless, Hucknall was far too close to the sheriff to have anyone living there for any length of time. Also, Tuck's kind heart feared for their health living there, because it had never been intended to be anything other than somewhere to stop overnight, and we were coming into the time of year when the weather would be cruellest.

Therefore Tuck told Robin that if he wanted to have these men follow him, then he had to wake up to the responsibility. They would not be like his fellow crusaders and experienced soldiers, Tuck reminded him. They would not know how to make a camp secure, nor would they know how to survive in the forest, since all of them were used to village life, or being within a large army which was provisioned.

˜You wish to be their leader,˜ I am told Tuck said to him in front of everyone else, ˜so you <u>must</u> lead. You have craved unquestioning followers, but this is what goes with that,˜ he told Robin most forcefully. ˜God has answered your prayers, and if this is not what you expected, then nonetheless you must still honour His gift and do what is right by these men.˜

I am told that Robin assured everyone that he would, and the plan – as far as my friends had known – was that they would come in force down to the Hucknall camp, and escort these new men to the camp down by Sandiacre. Allan and Roger had relayed my thoughts back to the others, you see, and upon reflection they had agreed with me that this was the least useful of the camps on account of the rivers which had to be crossed to get to it if they were coming from Nottingham. Therefore that would be the one they would make good for these men to see out the winter in. But they were coming with no notion of getting *involved in a fight! That, it turned out, had been Robin's cockeyed plan to show them how much more effective they could be with double the men, and he genuinely had hoped to kill Briwere in that attack, blindly disregarding the vengeance which the king would bring down on the shire as a result.*

Oh yes, Brother, your hero was planning cold-blooded murder too. This insane trap had no other purpose, aside from demonstrating that Robin had been right and all the others wrong, but to kill William Briwere. And I am glad that I did not know that at the time. Moreover, I repented deeply of my decision to kill, whereas I fear my cousin never did of any of his. And my repentance was not just in prayer, either. When Osric's widow was taken, it was me who stood up in front of the sheriff and begged for her to be taken in as one of the servants at the castle, and got backed in that by the castle knights, I might add. I found her a place amongst the washer women, where she would be kindly treated, and while I know that does not absolve my sin, it does prove that I was not without a conscience.

But you wish to hear about the escape, I know. So this time Allan and Roger had played things very cleverly. They lowered ropes down into the rough, rocky gully which formed the boundary between the inner and outer baileys. In a different castle this would have been a moat and filled with water, but with Nottingham Castle sitting up on its knoll, the rocky gulch served the same purpose. No man in mail would ever get up there, but my light-footed friends could, especially with the aid of the ropes.

Therefore they scaled the inner wall without ever having to get over the outer one, clambering up into the castle between the old keep and the barbican. And who came? You will not be surprised to hear that it was Siward, Will and Gilbert, and with them came Malik and his two turcopole friends, who were very adept at such silent movements. Also, Hugh and the Coshams came, so in all twelve outlaws managed to sneak through the castle without so much as disturbing a mouse. And Allan and Roger had put their day hidden within the castle to good use, spying out the land and the times when the guards seemed to be changed. It was amazing, they said, how many people never noticed a scruffy man walking about with a broom and a bucket! All of which meant that they had got the others up and inside the castle before the change of the guard, and then all they had to do was to let those going off duty settle down and go to sleep, which at that time of night did not take long.

Then with Allan confidently leading the way, they slunk through the shadows of the night and crossed the inner bailey, into the keep, and on down to the dungeons. There they found the drowsy guards half-heartedly playing at dice in a vague attempt to remain awake. It was the easiest thing to wait until they actually began to nod off and flit in, and though the men soon woke up when they felt hands going across their mouths, they were no match for my alert friends. And so as Malik, Khalīl and Janah trussed the four up like chickens awaiting the spit, and the Coshams kept watch with drawn bows, the others found a ladder and went and got Robin. I am told that he was in such a state that it took a couple of hefty slaps from Will to wake him up and get him moving.

No, Gervase, that was not the friendliest of acts, and I am sure that some of Will's frustration crept in there, because I know that he was furious over the way Robin had behaved. But he did have reason. Robin was no small man, and if he would not climb the narrow ladder on his own, then getting him out was going to take way too long, if it did not actually endanger someone else.

You do not understand? Brother, that ladder was only wide enough for one man and it was not that solid, either! Therefore nobody could climb up alongside Robin since there was no room, and it was doubtful whether any of the rungs would have withstood the combined weight if one of them had slung Robin over his shoulder. And even if they had, the angle that the ladder had to go at to reach both the top of the dungeon and its base was very sharp, and there would always be the danger that whoever was carrying him would overbalance backwards and fall back down again. So, no, I do not blame Will for those slaps, quite aside from whether Robin deserved them. And even so, they told me that he tottered a few times on the way up.

Yet they did get him out of the dungeon, but then came the harsh choice of whether they dared take the other men, and I am afraid that what I had told Allan and Roger came into play now. They had told the others of my belief that the sheriff and his men would realise sooner rather than later that these poor souls whom they had slaughtered were not the core of the gang. Therefore there was no reason to try and free the four survivors in terms of them betraying anything more, and the harsh truth was that they were more likely to jeopardise the whole mission if they began making a noise, or got halfway out and then froze in terror. So with great guilt my friends left them where they were and hustled Robin out, but it was some consolation that the four left behind never even cried out at being left – they were too sunk in their despair to even take notice. However, for my part in that decision which led to those four's hangings I ask forgiveness – mea culpa, mea culpa, mea maxima culpa.

So with Will on one side of Robin, and Gilbert on the other, they got back across the inner bailey, and I have to tell you that that was no mean feat. You see, if they went left from the main keep, then they had to go past the chambers built against and into the wall, which were empty unless someone very important came to stay. That would seem the obvious way except that they would soon come to the barbican and then have to get past it, and within it there were guards posted. Now those guards were unlikely to see much of anything across to the far side of the inner bailey, but for so many men to get past its opening right by them was far more of a risk. In the still of the night, and that close to, they could have been heard as much as seen.

Yet going to the right also had its dangers, and that was because there was a stretch where there was nothing below or in front of the castle walls. It was just a blank stretch of stone, and against that, movement would stand out far more than against the broken outlines of doors and the different angles where there were buildings projecting from the wall. Moreover, they still had to get past the barbican, because beyond it was the only place where they could get to the outer wall without climbing up to where they would be silhouetted against the night sky.

Yes, if they had got into the chambers and up to the wall top, they could have got down to the dry moat, it is true, but the drop was far longer from there just as it would be from the old keep, and they would then have to get under the stone bridge which ran out from the barbican to the outer bailey. Indeed you could get under it, Brother, but again, that was right beneath the guards inside that great gatehouse. It was also very dark down there because it was narrow and towered over on both sides, and there was the increased danger of a man turning an ankle or even breaking a leg. It would only take someone crying out in pain and all would be for nought. My friends had thought it out, Gervase, and the route they took was the best of a bunch of poor choices, but it worked. They got Robin to the wall, several of them went down first, and they told me that they had two ropes going now so that someone could go down alongside Robin, while the archers and Will as the strongest, lowered him down.

Once down it was easy to vanish off into the woods, and I was glad that they seemed to vanish off the face of the earth for the next few months to everyone but me, and even then they did not come into Nottingham, not even Allan and Roger. They thought it best to give any other servants who had seen them the chance to forget their faces. And so it was at the Inkersall camp when we next met, and I was able to tell them that it would be harder for us to meet up now, because I was going to be more in the heart of the Old Forest. Yet if anything they were cheered by this. With the woodland far denser, and with fewer villages to avoid, they could simply catch up with me when needed.

We therefore decided on some places where messages could be left – hollow, lightning-blasted oaks or old charcoal-burners' huts and the like – for do not forget that while John struggled with his letters, Allan was as literate as me. We would not have great sheets of parchment at our disposal, but we could get hold of scraps which, if wrapped well in oiled cloth, would survive a week or two in a dry place outside. And consequently as Christmas passed and the year moved towards spring once more, I was actually feeling close to optimistic.

Robin had finally come to the end of everyone's patience, I believed, and I would no longer have to endure the torment of never knowing when he was going to launch some crackpot scheme. I was also going to be virtually on my own in my work except for some lesser men, for I was under no illusion that Sirs Henry, Walkelin or Fredegis would be riding out into the depths of the forest, and the walking foresters were limited to their specific parks by the practical matter of how far they could get on foot in one day. The wider forest, as a result, was mine to play in as I wished, I believed.

Play? Oh yes, Gervase! For once I had some fun, and you will hear of this after so much doom and gloom, if only to show that I was not such a morose and miserable wretch that I always saw the worst possible outcome in things, and therefore that I am not now looking back and endlessly putting the darkest interpretations on how things turned out with Robin and me.

Chapter 25

Now then, Brother, for you to understand what happens next I must bore you with a small detail concerning the forest. Do you know what the parks were? No, I thought not. You should not presume them to be in any way like a pleasure garden. They were not the places to walk a lady whilst whispering sweet nothings in her ear, and playing with her fingers, beneath bowers of sweet smelling roses and honeysuckles. However, they were areas of carefully managed woodland, deliberately kept in order to provide the best conditions for the deer, so that they thrived and provided their lord with good hunting. The foresters therein were primarily woodsmen, who did things like ensuring that fodder was available for the deer in the depths of a harsh winter, that there was plenty of cover for the does to hide their tiny fawns in, and that things like ivy did not strangle the trees. Or at least that had been the theory when the Conqueror had first created parks and hunting preserves in England.

However, the reality was sometimes less than the idea. For a start, our Norman lords were thinking of the spotted fallow deer they introduced from places like Cyprus when they first created these spaces, but as I have said previously, those were used to warmer climes than chilly England, and did not adapt as swiftly as the kings who wished to hunt them no doubt hoped. And our native red deer were very different in size and temperament. The fences which kept the fallow deer within the park close by Nottingham Castle, for instance, were elsewhere simply shoved out of the way or trampled by the bigger red deer when they prevented them from going in a direction they had always done, for they roamed a large territory. Nor did they take kindly to men trying to inspect their young, either. And they were in far less need of assistance with fodder in the depths of winter, being native to our land.

Yet that had not stopped King Henry from setting up specific parks within the greater Sherwood when he created that vast royal forest back in 1177, with the intention of providing his beloved youngest son with a palace suitable for him to live in as an adult, and with sufficient parks to provide the meat for him to entertain on a princely scale. You remember? Good, for young prince John, and later on King John, is so integral to the creation of Sherwood that he cannot be unravelled from its history. If King Henry had not lacked a kingdom to leave John, he would never have upgraded Nottingham Castle to the extent that he did, there would have been no role of forester for me to fill, and no need for a man like Robin Hood.

But to return to the tale at hand, all of this meant that within what had been the traditional ˜keepings˜ in the Old Forest of Nottingham, there were eleven parks in all, aside from the one right by the castle. And if they were not quite so perfectly managed as some of the parks in the south of England closer to the royal courts, they were nevertheless considerably tamer than the surrounding tracts of the Old Forest. Some parts of the old woodland were truly ancient, Brother, and I loved them dearly. They had a spirit, a real feeling of a living, breathing entity, which had been there since time immemorial.

...Oh do not sniff, Gervase, I am not being a pagan by saying that! Here in your cloisters, you think that the only way to see God is in a stone-vaulted church with monks singing, but I tell you for truth that he sometimes wears a very different face out in the wilder parts of the world – you just have to stop and look and listen. There is great beauty out there. I have seen drifts of snowdrops lit by a shaft of sunlight as if sent straight from heaven in groves which few men ever trod; smelt the scent of newly blooming bluebells through the greenery; and heard music in the choirs of birds and the soughing of the wind in the branches.

And that is all part of His world, too, Brother, so hold onto those ideas and do not judge me harshly before you have fully heard how I introduced the three arrogant knights to a side of God they had never seen before. A side which also put the fear of God into them in a way that no priest with his contemplations of spending eternity in Hell had ever done, and that was because up until then they had never encountered something not made by man which they could not control. Of course they had seen lightning and storms, and yes, those are acts of God, too, but you must allow, dear Brother, that you have a very different perspective on that lightning bolt if you are in the forest and standing next to a mighty tree which gets blasted, rather than watching from the safety of a stone castle.

And what of Robin? Oh you will hear of him again soon enough. For now though, be content with this tale, for it is setting our stage for what is to come, and explains why sometimes those three knights would tell the sheriff that they had fully scoured Sherwood for the elusive *outlaws when they had only really ridden through the somewhat tamer parks.*

Sherwood – the Old Forest
Spring, the Year of Our Lord 1198

With Briwere still barely hobbling on his slow-to-heal leg, and with his attendant bad mood, Guy was glad to get out into the forest and be alone. Although it was still only the start of February, a spell of mild and fairly fine weather had set in, and Guy had decided that it would be a good time to take a ride up to the more northern parts of the Old Forest. It was a blessing to get out into the peace and quiet, and to breathe the fresh spring air, and the only regret was that he didn't have any of his dogs to trot beside him. Maybe it was his fancy, being in this slightly fey stretch of forest, where the woods were densest and where the trees overhung the narrow tracks, but he could have sworn that he half saw, half felt, the ghostly shades of Domnall and Máel beside him at times, and he welcomed their presence.

For weeks now, the four knights had been going back and forth between Nottingham and Laxton castles, and it had been a considerable relief to Guy that Briwere had finally made a pronouncement on the situation. Calling Guy into his presence he declared with asperity,

"As of Ash Wednesday next week, Fredegis, Walkelin and Henry will be living permanently at Laxton. However, you are too useful a coroner, Gisborne, damn you, and I cannot have you half a shire away all the time. Therefore you will divide your time equally between both castles. I am assured by Sir Walter that being you, you will cope with riding through the forest to do your forester duties on those journeys between. He said something about you making a larger circuit from Laxton. To be frank, I don't care how you do it as long as you do keep an eye on the forest."

Briwere leaned back in his chair, wincing as his propped up leg twinged sharply.

"I don't trust you, Gisborne, never have, and I've made no secret of that. You're too bloody clever by far! Why some of the others seem to like you I do not know. But you're competent, I'll give you that, and Sir Walter tells me that you're the best woodsman of all this scrofulous bunch of wretched hedge-knights. I can trust Henry, Fredegis and Walkelin to chivvy fitz Stephen's foresters into doing their jobs properly now, but you, I'm told, will be the one to actually know if they are.

"So I want you to ride out and make as full an inspection of the Old Forest as you can, but get yourself back to Laxton by the end of the month so that you can take the other three and show them anything you think is suspicious or wants watching. But I want you back here in the castle in the first week of March to check to see if anything warrants your investigation. You may then return to Laxton for the woodmote on the feast of St Joseph of Arimathea on the seventeenth and after."

Briwere shifted his position and winced again. "Damn that bloody peasant to the depths of Hell! This leg throbs like the Devil himself had made the cut!"

Guy found himself sighing and saying, "For pity's sake, sheriff, allow me to take a look at it. I know what I'm doing." Not that he cared that Briwere was in pain, but watching the entire castle's population going around as if walking on eggshells was starting to wear.

There was some mumbling and grumbling, but Briwere must have been in such agony that he finally agreed to let Guy tend to him. When he saw the wound, Guy half wished that he'd not offered, because if he hadn't there was a real danger the sheriff would lose his leg and he would be gone from here. But then if he died or was crippled, the king might think it convenient to make fitz Peter the sheriff of a neighbouring shire to Yorkshire too, and that Guy didn't want. So with an even deeper sigh, he looked at the massively swollen leg and its array of livid colours, and went for his kit, but also for four of the other knights to hold Briwere down while he cut him back open again.

There was real shock at how much pus Guy drained out of the leg, although mercifully Briwere passed out at the first incision. Retrieving maggots from the kitchen cellar, which would eat away the dead and septic flesh, Guy packed them into the wound, and then plastered the leg and wound with every healing herb he possessed and plenty of honey, both to heal and to keep it sealed up. By the time he'd done, the leg was huge again, but this time with bandages.

"Don't let that damned butcher from the town near him while I'm gone!" Guy instructed his friends. "On his orders, I'm to ride out, but instead of going straight to Laxton, I'll come back here and check on him. Can you tell that to whichever of the three devils I have to work with now who you see before Wednesday? Otherwise they'll be expecting me sooner."

With Briwere in an exhausted sleep, Guy made his getaway. The sheriff might always walk with a limp, but with luck he wouldn't now die, and Guy thought it one of the more bizarre twists in his life that he should be praying that Briwere remained as sheriff. The man was a bloody nightmare, but at least they'd got the measure of him by now, and with that in mind, Guy resolved to make as thorough inspection of the Old Forest as it was possible for one man to do. And in the process, if he could find another couple of useful hideaways for his friends, then that would be wonderful.

So now he was north of Edwinstowe, which lay about six miles directly west of Laxton as the crow flew, and he decided to explore a part of the Old Forest he was not familiar with. The outlaws had a small camp not far from the little village of Walesby, in a cave by the River Maun, but that was just outside of the Old Forest on the Le Clay side of the river. Within the Old Forest, though, this eastern side was one he'd never had to deal with. And so he decided to follow the River Maun's western bank from Rufford Abbey and see where it led him.

He began after spending the night at Bothamsall Castle, which sat on a small shelf above the River Meden, and was there to guard the crossing of the main road between Retford and Otherton at one of the few places where the river was fordable. Already past its prime when it had been owned by the Viking lord Tostig, it was now held by a knight of little consequence simply to ensure that the crossing remained watched and safe. But Guy had another reason for being curious about the place. Its little Saxon-built chapel was these days part of Elkesley's parish, but the priest who tended to the hamlet came from Welbeck Abbey, and that made them part of Abbot Michael's flock. Guy had been to see the radical-thinking abbot on more than one occasion since his stay there, and now he was wondering whether this might be another village and environs which would be sympathetic to the outlaws if their abbot sent the right kind of priest here. But that would all depend on whether the location would make a good refuge in the first place.

So once over the Meden's ford, instead of continuing the quarter mile or so to cross the Maun, too, Guy turned left and began to negotiate the web of trickling streams and watercourses. Yet there was a good reason why the two rivers had not joined to form a lake, and that was a solid bank of land in between them which was virtually an island. It was land which would no doubt flood heavily in a wet spell, and that was probably why his friends hadn't made more use of it, but it would be an excellent place to lead pursuers to and get them bogged down. There wasn't the dense foliage of the oak woods here, but alders and willows thrived along with birches, and someone was clearly coppicing them for their valuable supple branches. That meant that the trunks of those trees were shorter but much fatter than their naturally growing counterparts – plenty fat enough for even a big man like John to hide behind, and that gave Guy an idea. One day he would bring his three terrible fellow foresters back this way at dusk, and if he could persuade maybe Allan and Roger to help him, he would give the three a real fright.

Much cheered by the thought, Guy rode on and found that he could get off the virtual island where the road from West Drayton forded the rivers to Elkesley. Again this was an important route, for it came up from Newark in the south-east and connected with the Great North Road, so the fords were always kept in good repair and he could guarantee being able to lead the knights across in all but the worst weather. That was good, because it meant he could plan well ahead.

And so coming back onto the western bank of what at this stretch was now called the River Idle, Guy continued to explore. By the end of the day he had made his way to Retford and its surrounding villages, and now he could see why there were fewer parks up here. He was still in this maze of small waterways, and if it was fertile farmland when it was dry enough, it wasn't ideal either for the deer or for hunting over.

He spent an uncomfortable night in the cold and sparse guest cell at Mattersey Priory, and by now knew where he was again. If he went west he was not that many miles from Blyth and the site of the infamous tournament, and should he turn south from there he would soon be at Worksop. But he decided to stay in the centre of the Old Forest and at Ranskill picked up the Great North Road southwards. The old Roman road ran straight as an arrow for miles, passing through Barnby, Hugh's old home, and Guy was able to appease his conscience that he was in fact working by being able to report that the undergrowth was indeed being kept well cut back from this most important of roads.

There was limited opportunity for outlaws to hold anyone up here. Yet once he was down as far as Ranby things began to change. There were fewer small farms and manors around here now, and so fewer people to keep the wilderness of the forest at bay. Guy loved this part of Sherwood, but coming to it at nightfall, it was freshly apparent to him how forbidding that mass of dense greenery could be.

He therefore made a speedy return to Nottingham and was pleased to discover that, if not actively up and about yet, the sheriff was now showing definite signs of healing. And so Guy left after only one night and made for Laxton. The following morning, though, he decided that he wouldn't wait for help; he would give the boorish trio an early introduction to the perils of the forest!

"I know the sheriff has said that the Le Clay woodmotes will be held here from now on," he said casually, as they broke their fast together the next morning, "but we'll still have to go to Edwinstowe and account for the Old Forest. On the sheriff's orders I rode through the forest and there's something I think you should see."

A collective groan went up, confirming Guy's suspicions that without Briwere cracking the whip over them, these three would do as little as possible, and when Sir Walkelin declared, "Well it can wait another day. It's raining," Guy knew he was right.

Deciding to play on their already held belief that he was eccentric, Guy left them toasting themselves by the fire and went out again. It would be no bad thing, he thought, if they developed a fear of the area between Barnby and Ranby. They were nicely away from any courts there, and so with the limited brain power of the three in question, they were unlikely to make any connection with outlaws unless it was bludgeoned into them, and what Guy wanted was for them to become afraid of the forest itself. And with that in mind, he went equipped to spend a night outside, and headed north once more.

He spent a happy day exploring the coverts and groves in his chosen area, and then set to making a few subtle changes. A couple of branches trained just a little more sideways, and held in place by rope disguised with ivy, made a useful screen; while an old boar wallow now cut by a rivulet – once suitably disguised – would make a handy pit for someone to be brought off their horse in without harming the horse. An old lightning-blasted oak needed only a little work with his heaviest knife and small axe to resemble a face with eyes in poor light, and Guy knew that in this winter weather it wouldn't be long before the paler cuts went as dark as the rest of the old tree. Better still, it was on a neat loop where he could pretend to lead, seem to vanish behind a screen, and cut across while being able to taunt the knights with ghostly calls, yet still emerge out on the track to appear to have been ahead of them all the time. So by the time he'd finished, Guy knew that he had a nice rat-run which he could lead the knights through. All he needed now was the right time.

It didn't come quite as fast as he would have liked, but at the woodmote it was so clear that only he had done anything to bring any cases forward, and with the attendant drop in fines, that the three were summoned to Nottingham and given the verbal roasting of the year by Briwere. Arriving back at Laxton with their tails between their legs, they were just ripe for Guy's plans, and so as the rest of the shire went into the preparations for Easter that Palm Sunday in late March, Guy again suggested a ride out into the forest. All three were good at going through the motions regarding the proper observations, but Guy knew that they believed in God and the saints only in as far as anyone of their era did – devout they were not – so they wouldn't be bothered by not spending the whole week in prayer. If he did this right, though, that would change.

He took them on an easy day's ride up to Retford, and allowed them an evening of carousing in the inn there. The more relaxed and complacent they were for the following day the better. He didn't even rouse them particularly early the next morning – all must seem to be very much what they *thought* he did on his rides out. But St Melangell and St Cadoc had surely heard his prayers, because they were not two miles down the winding tracks into old Sherwood when a fine drizzle set in, which played straight into Guy's hands.

As the three stopped their horses to fiddle around wrapping oiled cloaks around themselves, he rode on as if unaware that they had stopped. And then, when they went to set out and couldn't see him anymore, and began calling his name, he rode back from just around the next bend where he'd been watching them through the empty winter branches as if he'd barley noticed they'd not been there. With the water dripping from his longer than fashionable dark hair, and his vague disdain for their fussing over a bit of rain, he suddenly looked a little wild himself, and he knew he made the three feel uncomfortable. But just as they would never look about them, in which case they would have spotted Guy without having to call for him, they would also never admit that he was the better man out here, and that would be their undoing.

By now Guy was making a meal of pointing out this chopped down tree, or that dubiously legal enclosure for sheep, or a grove of coppicing that might or might not be allowed, all safe in the knowledge that they would remember none of it by tonight. He also got them used to the fact that he would often get well ahead of them, and that he would be waiting for them at the next spot where there was some other boring piece of forest law minutia to be pointed out. Therefore he knew they wouldn't panic the moment he vanished at his proposed ambush site.

They got there as the early afternoon turned dark and dreary, but the drizzle eased, and Guy offered up another prayer of thanks. There was one point where he needed to light a couple of candles in the 'eyes' of the dead oak, and that would be a lot easier if he could strike the spark in the dry. The flint and small pieces of dried fungus and lichen to take that spark had stayed dry and snug within his shirt, and so as soon as he turned the bend, he vaulted off his horse, led her through the narrow gap to one side of the track, and drew the prepared branch across it to ensure the trio went onwards. Mounting up he trotted her as fast as he dared without making too much noise, and got to the old oak. The candles he'd left there were still dry in their wrapping, and he quickly unfolded them and set them in their places, then struck the sparks.

Soon the old oak had two nicely glowing and flickering eyes in place, and Guy had picked this one because it was just the other side of a tiny stream from the track. Too far for anyone to reach out to from on horseback, and not quite accessible by foot either from the way the three were coming. They could not get close enough to investigate should, against the odds, their dubious courage hold. Then he ran back on foot, and got to where he had tied a long, supple branch back just in time to see the knights coming around the next twist in the track.

With one cut of his knife, Guy sliced the restraining thin rope, and it whipped back to its original form, over compensating with the pent up force, and nicely coming close to whipping Sir Henry and his horse in the face. The horse reared and as well as getting a face-full of water, Sir Henry found himself on his arse in the mud and in danger of getting trampled on by the other two spooked horses. For an awful second, Guy thought the horse might bolt, in which case he would have to catch it or they'd all wonder why he hadn't if he'd been where they expected him to be. But the other two blocked its path, and since the only thing that was hurt was Henry's pride, he was soon on his feet and grabbing the reins.

It had nicely disconcerted them, though, and so when they came around the next turn and could see for a short stretch that nobody was ahead, they were doubly shocked when Guy loosed another branch their way. Again they got a soaking, and again the horses got spooked, but the great thing about Guy's plan was that these branches had never fully overhung the path in their natural state, and so once they settled back, it was impossible to tell which branch had actually been the one to move.

"Who's there?" he heard one of the two Flemish knights call out in his still heavily-accented English. "Show yourself, you coward!"

In reply Guy made an owl call, and it was all he could do not to laugh when a pair of irate crows immediately took off squawking just above the knights' head. They must have been nesting and fearing the owl's predations on their young, although it was still a little early for most birds to have begun breeding. Either that or the

Welsh saints were having as much fun as Guy over this, and sending the odd bird to help, and that Guy found an encouraging thought.

Then Walkelin in the lead found the lightly covered wallow and water runnel, his horse stumbled, and he too found himself down in the mud. With the scattered old bracken fronds Guy had covered the runnel with blending in to all the rest of the dead bracken around there, in the dim light there seemed to be no reason why Walkelin's horse should have tripped, and again the knights looked around bemused. This was nothing like anywhere they'd been before.

So when they made another turn on the twisting path, and suddenly found themselves looking into the 'face' of a old oak, whose 'eyes' flickered eerily, suddenly all restraint collapsed. As Fredegis squealed like a girl in shock, Guy was glad that he'd already mounted up, because all three clapped their heels to their horses' sides, and he only just managed to get back out on the track in time.

"Charcoal burners mound…" Guy began to say before he was nearly ridden down, "…Whoa! Have a care! *Dewi Sant*, what's got into you?"

"Back there!" Walkelin blurted out. "Eyes in the forest!"

It said everything about how rattled he was that he didn't stop to think how ridiculous what he was saying sounded.

Assuming a worldly weariness, Guy said, "Probably a fox or a stag watching you. Sometimes their eyes do just catch the light."

"They glowed!" Fredegis protested.

With a long-suffering sigh, Guy turned his horse and rode back down the track, stopping at where he knew his lights had been, and calling out, "There's nothing here." And indeed there wasn't, because the wind had blown the candles out by now. As he got back to the three thoroughly unsettled knights, Guy couldn't resist adding, "It's all perfectly normal for the forest. You just have to get used to the fact that it has a life of its own."

They looked at him as though he was mad. The kind of madness that had men volunteering to be first over the castle wall in a siege, or running into a burning building to save a damsel in distress – not the kinds of things any of them would ever dream of doing.

They weren't much better by the time they rode into Barnby and demanded that room be made for them at the inn there. It seemed there was some sort of celebration going on in the village and the place was packed. That suited Guy. Forced to rub shoulders with the peasantry, the three had no space in which to discuss what had happened that day, and they certainly wouldn't be voicing their fears in front of their inferiors. That meant each one of them would be multiplying their own version of what they had seen into something which hopefully would haunt their dreams that night. But what really made Guy's day complete was to see Hugh and Marianne in amongst the crowd.

The two of them were hardly distinguishable from any other person there, but as soon as the three knights had grumbled their way off to the scant privacy of three sacking mattresses behind a tatty curtain, they were quick to catch Guy's eye and to head outside.

"What on earth are you doing here?" Guy asked in delight as soon as they met up several houses away from the inn.

"My youngest cousin got married today," Hugh admitted. "It's been planned for some time, but I thought it would be a rare occasion for Marianne to meet my family when they're all here."

Guy felt his grin growing even wider. "And will this be the only wedding in your family this year?"

Marianne's blush said it all, but she was smiling happily all the same. Hugh was positively glowing with pride and Guy impulsively hugged them both.

"I'm so pleased for you both," then to Marianne, "And it's long overdue that you had somebody who valued you!"

He got an even wider smile from her for that, but then Hugh asked,

"What are you doing here? Is this part of your new territory, and why are there four of you?"

By the time Guy had finished telling them of what he'd done, Hugh and Marianne were helpless with laughter, but both agreed that it was a marvelous idea.

"If we can get them terrified of the forest itself, then that means we have the densest parts to ourselves again," Hugh agreed. "What did you have in mind for Allan and Roger to do, then?"

"Well they've got the lightest voices of all of you, except for you and Mariota, Marianne. I had the idea that someone smallish and light on their feet could scurry through the undergrowth without it hardly seeming to be disturbed, and while those three wouldn't be dismayed by what they think of as men's voices, something lighter and able to sound a bit more fey might really start to play on their fears."

"Oooh! Wood-sprites!" Marianne said with relish. "Oh yes, you can count Mariota and me in on that! And don't forget that while Malik has a deep bass voice, Janah and Khalīl have much lighter voices too. Get them calling in their own tongue and pitched high, and you really might give those three nightmares! They haven't served in the crusades, have they?"

"Not that I'm aware of," Guy admitted. "I think their main fighting was always around Normandy as mercenaries. I've never once heard them mention the east, and in fact, I think that I've heard them talking as though they thought the crusade was like that, because they couldn't understand why King Richard couldn't bring the Saracens to battle and defeat them. So no, I don't think they'll have ever heard our friends' native tongue."

"Oh good!" Marianne said with a grin. "Because Mariota and I have been keeping our knowledge of it fresh by trying to talk to them – in fact we've learned some more of it – so all we need to do is get Allan and Roger clued up and we can sound truly alien to them."

With the promise of meeting his friends with a view to planning this greater ambush, Guy left them and the following morning took the trio on a relatively sedate ride back down through Ranby, Ollerton and home to Laxton. His mood was downright buoyant by the time they got back, though, and in stark contrast to the twitching of the other three, because Marianne and Hugh had obviously thought to make a start on things.

As Guy had led his foursome into another dense tract of forest beyond the crossroad to Worksop, they began making calls. Hugh was doing a great job of making slightly strange bird calls, but Marianne excelled herself in fragments of songs in Arabic, in a high, ethereal voice. They never overdid it, and they didn't keep it up for too long. Guy knew that it was also because they were having to run between points where they knew they had good cover, and so he slowed the pace just a little – enough that the three knights didn't notice, but it gave Hugh and Marianne that bit more time. At the River Poulter, Marianne gave one final performance from deep within the rushes there, and Guy was delighted to see that the normally boorish Walkelin's hands were shaking just a little on the reins. Henry was distinctly paler than normal, and while Fredegis might have been scowling ferociously, there was a tell-tale tic in his one eye that said he was covering fear with anger.

At the castle Guy never said a thing, acting as though nothing out of the ordinary had happened, and if the three made great play of going and organising the unfortunate walking foresters at the parks while ignoring the greater forest over the next week, Guy nonetheless pretended he hadn't noticed. But as soon as Easter was over, the meeting he had thought would be with just a few of his friends turned out to be with all of them, and over a cheerful meal at the camp near Worksop they expressed their enthusiasm for the project. Only Will, Ed, John and Robin were missing, and that was because Robin was still too brittle to be let loose outside of the camp, and the three with the worst singing voices had volunteered to stay behind and keep an eye on him with Aneirin and Rhys. What was even more cheering to Guy was the fact that they'd clearly been giving this a lot of thought.

"We really like the idea of making the knights frightened of the forest itself," Siward enthused. "The more we thought about it the better it got. As you said to Hugh and Marianne, the sheriff hasn't exactly got a great choice of knights to pick from when it comes to leaving them alone at Laxton, and so even if these three seem to be doing no better than old Sir Ralph, they won't be replaced because there's nobody to take their place. So if we can make them actively frightened of Sherwood, then that's great!"

"And look at this!" Gilbert chortled, having disappeared inside the shelter and come out lugging a huge sack, which when he upended it produced the pelt, head and antlers of a magnificent red stag. "We found this old boy trailing an injured leg back just after Christmas. It was a kindness to bring him down – saved him from a lingering death by starvation. But then funnily enough we all thought that it might be an idea to have something one of us could put on to make us look like a stag in human form, if you know what I mean. So he's been properly cured to make a sort of cloak with the head as a hat."

"It has to be one of the taller ones of us," Tuck added, "And John's the man to wear it if we might need to run, because he's got the strength as well as the size to carry it. But if we're just thinking of a few appearances..."

"...Back-lit under some trees! Lovely!" Piers added, becoming very Welsh in his eagerness. "Make him a bit more ghostly, see?"

"...then it doesn't matter so much who does the wearing." Even Tuck was grinning now. "The Hooded Man has indeed come to the forest to pass judgement on these knights!"

"And you should hear Malik singing some deep notes," Marianne told Guy with an affectionate glance Malik's way. "He can hum right down at this deep level. We stood him in an old hollow oak and it was the creepiest thing you've ever heard! It was almost as though the tree was vibrating."

"And Colm and I have experimented with an old Gaelic lament," continued Gilbert, "and if we can't sing it particularly high, we can whistle it. Blessed St Brigit, we nearly scared the crap out of ourselves, so God knows what it'll do to those three of yours!"

"You'd be amazed," Siward laughed, "at what we came up with once you'd got us onto this idea. After Gilbert and Colm came up with their lament, Thomas, Piers and Bilan said they might have something, vanished off to just outside of the camp, and came back with an old Celtic death song that would put the willies up St Thomas himself. Thomas and Peirs whistle the tune softly, and Bilan's voice is high enough that he can sing the words over them. I tell you, we all had goose bumps after they'd given that one a go. And we think we know just the area to try all this out too. When's your next woodmote due?"

"Right at the beginning of May, but we'd normally inspect the forest just before it reopens on the twenty-third of April." Guy could already feel a sense of relish growing at the prospect of this. "It would be an ideal time to get the terrible trio out and about. It's not too long to wait and I think, actually, that giving them a break between what they experienced with me and a whole new set of terrors will heighten the effect, not diminish it. Do them too close together, and we have nothing to play with later without putting an awful lot of regular effort into just frightening three knights. We've only got three weeks to go until then, and that's time for them to start thinking they imagined it all, but not to forget it."

Gilbert chuckled, "Oh dear, and then we'll go and give them a nasty reminder."

Guy laughed with him. "Yes, but this will be a bigger step up in fear, so all the worse."

With Guy able to control his own comings and goings now, the outlaws were able to take him to the part of Sherwood they thought would be best and show him the various sites where they could ambush the knights. And by the time they had got down to not far from Edwinstowe, Guy had revised his intentions again.

"This is marvellous," he congratulated the others, "but I actually think that you've too many spots to use all in one go. We've got enough material here to scare them silly in April and do it again in late May before we close the forest for the fawning from early June. I think we definitely save that magnificent stag's head for then – that's just the cream on top of everything else. I suggest we use..." and he went through the spots he thought would be nicely spread out for the next outing.

It took a little refinement, for the others were more familiar with the qualities of each place, and some were better suited to certain effects than others, but by the time they split up they had everything worked out, and the only thing left to chance was when Guy could get all three to ride out with him.

You think I am building myself up at Robin's expense? Oh Gervase, you have no idea how prophetic your words are, but for the wrong reason. No, I never set out to do this thing with the intention of diminishing my cousin. I really did only want to get Henry, Fredegis and Walkelin so damned scared of the forest that my friends would be in less danger when the sheriff began to badger those three to do more.

I knew them of old. All three were bullies of the worst sort. They would think nothing of putting pressure on those unfortunate folk who scraped a living within the forest to betray Robin Hood and his men. And I was conscious of the sad reality that if the villages had the dire choice no longer daring to do a spot of illegal poaching during the winter to keep body and soul together, because the three knights were ever present, or betraying Robin Hood, then I knew that sooner or later somebody would weaken. And my friends could not hope to supply food to every village in Sherwood all of the time.

Therefore the better solution was to ensure that the three dreadful knights at Laxton would do their worst only in the more civilised parks, and leave the wilder forest to the lesser foresters and me. And you must realise that I could hardly take charge and tell those three where they would or would not patrol. That would have roused all sorts of suspicions, not that they would have taken a blind bit of notice of me, anyway. And if you want any more confirmation that we did the right thing in this, then I tell you that back then I believed that the Welsh saints I called upon approved of my plan, and I still do.

No, do not sniff at me, Brother! You cannot have it all ways. One moment you as good as call me a pagan for planting ideas of a living forest with a mind of its own, and then when I attribute that to local saints whom you happen not heard of until from me, you sniff again. I do not deride great saints like St Peter, or Our Lady. I have great reverence for them.

But I had also been infected – as you would no doubt think – by Tuck's view that the great saints had enough on their plate dealing with the greater ills of the world, over which they were being called on by far more people than just me. If you wanted someone to take notice at a local level, he always believed, then you needed to call upon the local saints, or at least the lesser ones with an affinity with the cause at hand. And as I told you yesterday, both St Cadoc and St Melangell had an affinity with the animals of the forests and the wild moors, which was why I was sure that they would approve of a solution which involved no killing in their sacred spaces.

Yes, Gervase, you had forgotten that side of it, had you not? My plan got nobody wounded or killed, just frightened to the same level of fear that they habitually inflicted on others. May I now continue? Good.

Chapter 26

However, I will placate you by telling you that however innocent our intentions, the effect on Robin himself would turn out to be disastrous. This, he believed, was me showing my true colours at last. It was me doing what he – and he alone, I might add – thought had been my long-held desire, to become the leader in absentia of the gang.

It was a ridiculous notion, for I had not been in the camp when my friends seized on what I had intended to be quite a simple thing, and had embroidered it substantially. They were the ones who chose to expand it to include virtually the whole gang, not me. I had no inkling of that until I was presented with the already near complete plan at the Worksop camp. But Robin would never believe that, and there was something else, too, which you have not picked up.

In his own warped way I belatedly realised that Robin actually did love Marianne. That was something I still find tragic, Brother, because he tied himself in so many knots over what he thought were vows made in the Holy Land, that he could not express his feelings for her. God knows that I was no great romantic – I could become tongue-tied and trip over my words like a village idiot with the best of them. But I was not so by-Our-Lady foolish or blind as to expect a woman to be content with the kind of distant relationship Robin tried to force upon Marianne.

And that does not make her the one at fault, either, Gervase. Had she remained within the Hospitaller order – and you must allow that, knowing now as you do, that she came back to England with that intention, and was only prevented from so doing by King Henry's high-handed actions towards all of her sisters – then she would have remained true to her vows. But those vows had been to be useful within a community. She had never promised to abide by the kind of segregation a nun would, and even then, having had limited choices for where to go, once within the forest with my friends it was inevitable that more earthly feelings would come into play. Marianne was a virtuous woman, but she was not a saint and made no claim to be.

But having shoved her so callously aside, Robin then had the cheek to be insulted when she turned away from him – and here I am simply referring to her no longer supporting him unconditionally, Brother. So you can imagine how he reacted when he realised that Hugh was playing court to what he thought was <u>his</u> lady. Too blind to see how he had driven Marianne away all by himself, Robin then became insanely jealous of Hugh, but even more bizarrely, decided that in some way I had encouraged Hugh, or even set this whole thing up just to spite him. Quite how he thought that I could force Hugh's affections, I do not know, and he was hardly the only one of the outlaws with whom I was now a close friend, but then this is why I keep telling you that I think that by now Robin was scarcely sane.

And in that vein we must move on, for you have yet to hear more of our ˜haunting˜ of the forest, and even more poignantly, the results of it.

Laxton & Sherwood
Late Spring, the Year of Our Lord 1198

When the day came it was easier than Guy had expected.

"We really need to ride through the rest of the Old Forest, you know," he prompted the three as they ate supper together at Laxton, and was heartened to have Sir Henry immediately reply,

"Well I'm not going through there alone!"

In a clear attempt to justify himself not riding alone, either, Fredegis declared with false conscientiousness, "None of us is familiar enough with those parts of the forest yet to do a good job alone. We will do a better job for the sheriff if we ride together." The fact that he very obviously didn't look at Guy, who could easily have done the job alone, while he said it, amused Guy, but he nearly guffawed out loud when Fredegis added, "Maybe next year we will do it alone."

Not if I have anything to do with it, you won't! Guy thought merrily. 1198 was turning out to be a lot better year than he could ever have expected. He was keeping his time in Nottingham down to the minimum, he was bringing in more cases to the woodmotes than the other three knights put together, which put him in a good light and kept Briwere happy with him, and yet he was spending a lot more time out in the forest on his own or with his friends. The only things which would have made his life complete, he thought as he went to bed with cheerful thoughts of the coming day, would be if he could have a dog of his own again. With Robin not likely to ever lead the gang again, if what Tuck said turned out to be right, then he might just risk trying to get the kennels here at Laxton occupied once more, fitz Stephen having taken his own hounds with him.

The morning dawned fair, but with wisps of mist hanging about over the streams and rivers, and Guy felt that yet again his much-loved Welsh saints were doing their part in the coming day by making the forest eerie. The wisps swirled and folded, sometimes vanishing altogether only to then come upon them again as they crossed the water of some tiny stream or rivulet. He had insisted on an early start and for once the three had complied, no doubt in the hope that the sooner this was started, the sooner they could retreat to the sanctuary of Laxton Castle again.

They made the five mile ride from Laxton to Ollerton in time to make a late morning break there, but Guy wasn't about to let them linger and try the local excellent ale the innkeeper brewed. Instead he made them ride on, with comments of how far they had yet to go once the horses had had a rest and a drink from the village trough; and turning north now, a couple of miles further on and near to Budby, the ancient forest really began to close in around them. Guy had hung an old red woollen undershirt over the wall at Laxton late the previous night, and had seen a distant fire-arrow go up to let him know that whoever was keeping watch had seen it, so he was expecting things to get lively any time from now onwards.

He didn't have long to wait. As they came close to a small low-lying mere, ringed with the old husks of last year's bulrushes, an eerie whistling began. Guy had to admire his friends' artistry. It was perfectly done – not too loud or obvious, but equally impossible to ignore – and he guessed this was the Coshams giving the Welsh lament their all. And they were right, had he not known what was going on he would have had the shivers himself, for the tune was mournful and haunting; but what took even him by surprise was what he saw as the reeds thinned for a few yards and they could see the whole of the mere clearly. Out on the water floated tiny flames.

As he instinctively gasped, "By Our Lady," Guy suddenly realised that he could take the lead here. The oath had been in admiration, but he swiftly made much play of crossing himself in such a way that the other three would see him doing it. It certainly made the three behind him look to the mere and swear oaths of their own, and then a faint laugh carried across the water. No doubt it was one of the outlaws who had been unable to hold it back any longer, but its slightly strangled, muffled quality only added to the unearthly air of the place.

"God's hooks! Let's get away from this place!" Fredegis swore and clapped his heels to his horse's flanks.

They cantered for a short way, but the track Guy had them on was just too narrow and twisting to keep it up for long, and soon they were back down to the slower pace. However, just as they were about to pass into the park at Budby, three shrill buzzards' screeches came from within the trees, and immediately there was an almighty commotion from the rest of the nesting birds, all thinking that somehow buzzards had come down within the wood to raid their nests. As blackbirds, thrushes, two jackdaws and even a woodpecker shot across the path in different directions, and thoroughly spooking the horses when they flew right under their noses, Guy could see the other three looking about them anxiously as they tried to see the cause of the commotion. They weren't good enough woodsmen themselves to recognise a buzzard's call, and so it all seemed scarily random. Guy, on the other hand, guessed that this was Tuck and Hugh adding to the fun.

They managed to meet with Hereward the forester and his woodward, Bertwald, both of whom caught on to Guy's barely smothered smile when Walkelin demanded to know if they had trouble of an unearthly kind hereabouts.

"Oh the forest can be a dangerous place," Hereward said straight-faced, then had to struggle to keep it in place as Guy mimed fluttering birds with his hands under his horse's nose, back out of the line of sight of the others. Guy liked Hereward and Bertwald. Of all the men from Sir Ralph's time, they were the ones he thought of as real woodsmen. They cared about the forest in its entirety, not just for the sake of the deer, and they were prepared to turn a blind eye to things like the locals collecting firewood in the closed season as long as they didn't actually fetch whole trees down. Simple gathering actually helped, because it allowed the new greenery to come through thicker, and that meant the fawns which would arrive soon had more cover to hide in. That kind of common sense approach was how the forest should be run, in Guy's opinion, and therefore he was prepared to drop heavy hints to them that his fellow forester knights wouldn't know the difference one way or the other if some dead wood got taken.

With a wink, Guy told Hereward, "We'll ride on to Carburton Park. No need for you two to come with us unless there's something you want us to see?"

"No, nothing we haven't already reported," Hereward said gratefully, with a suppressed sigh of relief at not having to go and get his shaggy work horse and put up with the three grumpy knights for hours.

Guy was glad he took the hint, because as they headed westwards and he led the others down to the River Poulter, with the intention of crossing to get to Welbeck Abbey for the night, the outlaws struck again. This time it was Gilbert and Colm, Guy thought, because it was another eerie whistling of a different tune. What made the hairs stand up on the back of his neck, even though he knew what was going on, was hearing a distant woman's wailing in accompaniment. Either Marianne or Mariota was doing a splendid job of keeping in time with the two men, and the unearthly 'music' faded away as if on the breeze as the others once again clapped their heels to their horses.

There was no way Guy was going to let them gallop all the way to Welbeck when the horses had been ridden all day already. And he pulled them up after a mile. Nonetheless, Abbot Michael probably hadn't had such an enthusiastic greeting off men like these three in a long time – to say that they were glad to be within the monastic enclosure was an understatement.

"Brother Tuck paid me a visit," the abbot confided to Guy with a smile, as they were ushered into the refectory to eat with everyone else. "I gather the greenwood has developed sudden and new perils?"

"Only for the ungodly, Father," Guy reassured him with a wink, and was rewarded by a knowing, "Ah!" which came with a definite twinkle in Abbot Michael's eyes.

Later that evening, Hugh and Will slipped into the monastic compound with a surly Robin in tow.

"Which way are you heading tomorrow?" Will asked with a grin.

"We'll cross the Poulter here," Guy told them, "and then up the long valley to Hardwick, where we'll pick up the lane up to the Worksop road crossroads. Then it'll be up to Ranby and then back across to Retford."

"Great news," Hugh chuckled. "We can hit them in the morning in the densest woodland."

Guy suddenly realised how Robin was glowering at Hugh's back, but there was no time to get Will on his own and ask about why. He could make a good guess that more than a little was to do with Marianne, yet he got the strange feeling that Robin might have some cockeyed notion that because of that, Hugh was making a bid to lead the gang, too. Sighing, Guy took himself off to bed, but offered up some heartfelt prayers that Robin might decide to enter the contemplative life out in some isolated monastery. It would probably be the safest place for him.

As they rode out in the morning Guy was pleased that it was a pleasantly bright day, for that would mean that once back at Laxton the three would not be able to say that what they thought they saw or heard was because their imaginations were running riot in the prevailing conditions. Today was not the day for wisps of mist, or covering drizzle. Whatever his friends had planned would be all the more effective if it managed to terrify the knights in the clear light of a sunny day. The seeds had been sown in their minds, now they had to take root.

He didn't have long to wait. They had no sooner crossed the Poulter than they were in amongst thick, ancient forest again, and suddenly they heard laughter.

"Who's there?" Walkelin demanded, reining in his horse and looking about them belligerently. "Come out and show yourselves now!"

Yet all they heard was more soft laughter, and then a rustling of bushes just off the track.

"Oh leave it," Guy told Walkelin in bored tones. "It's probably just some urchins."

"Then I will teach them respect!" Walkelin snapped, and urged his horse off the narrow track to force its way through the sprouting bracken and ferns and other undergrowth.

Yet when he got to where the bushes had rustled, it was clear that Walkelin could find nothing. "Where are you, you little bastards?" he snarled.

But all that happened was that the bushes rustled again a little further on. As Walkelin urge his horse on deeper into the undergrowth, Guy called,

"I wouldn't if I were you," but Walkelin took no notice.

Another rustling and more laughter drew the belligerent knight deeper in, and Guy could feel Fredegis and Henry getting restive beside him. Walkelin only had to go a little further and he would be out of sight behind some big old oaks and their attendant hawthorns.

Then another rustling and laughing came, and just as Walkelin went to make the fateful move deeper in past a huge old hawthorn, one of its large branches came thrashing out of nowhere at him and smacked him hard in the upper chest. With a shriek that was a mix of fear and pain, Walkelin was shot backwards off his horse into the undergrowth, his vanishing from sight accompanied by a painful thud as he hit the ground.

Guy's explosive "Ha!" of amusement was mercifully smothered by Fredegis and Henry's simultaneous cries of shock and disbelief, and he managed to straighten his face in time for when they turned to him. Together they forged into the undergrowth and found Walkelin swearing profusely in his native Flemish, and quite literally spitting feathers.

Guy just about managed to choke out, "I'll go and get the horse," and urged his own further on before he cracked up. Some wit amongst the outlaws had stuck downy feathers to the branch with what looked like fairly fresh goose shit, and it had held on for long enough on the hawthorn's spines to liberally splatter Walkelin with the revolting down and shit mixture.

He made sure he got out of line of sight of the knights before letting his mirth loose, knowing that his shaking shoulders would cause comment should Fredegis or Henry have looked up. Happily he didn't have to go far for the horse, which was held just beyond the next oak by John.

"Whose idea was the shit?" Guy asked, wiping the tears of merriment from his eyes.

John chuckled. "Who do you think? Roger and Allan, of course."

"Bloody rascals," Guy said affectionately, "but tell them to hold back a bit. Me falling out of my saddle laughing won't help our cause! I have to at least try and make out that this is all normal for the old forest."

It didn't help his composure to return to find Fredegis and Henry trying to help Walkelin walk out of the undergrowth, but at the same time keeping him at arms' length, and when Guy got closer he could tell why. Walkelin stank! No shit was pleasant, but water birds' was downright rank because of the fish, molluscs or water plants they ate, and it was also distinctly green in places, giving Walkelin a strange jester's motley of colours across the front of the expensive leather jerkin he would insist on wearing for every day to highlight his status. That was never going to be the same again, Guy knew, because by the time they got to somewhere where he could clean it properly, the stains would be permanent even if the physical remains came off.

Literally biting his lip to stop himself from smirking like an idiot, Guy went and gave Walkelin a leg up onto his horse, then led the way onwards as if nothing much had happened. Being out in front, Guy could at least allow himself a grin which felt as though it went from ear to ear, and there was a blessed lack of conversation from the others so that he didn't need to speak.

The outlaws' timing was immaculate, and they didn't strike again until after Guy and the knights had crossed the small road which came up from Budby to Worksop. But then nicely up out of reach, even from on horseback, they saw fluttering collections of feathers high in the branches, seeming to hang in thin air, just as another faint singing began. Guy knew the basis of this was the Saracen's call to prayer, because Malik and James long ago had told him of it, and given him an example when they were explaining the difference between that and the eastern Christianity they followed, but the other three had never heard the like. And Guy had to admit that it sounded eerie deep in the forest.

It had to be some combination like Janah and Marianne on one side, and Khalīl and Mariota on the other, Guy guessed, but they were joined by a couple of people on each side also faintly whistling the tune in an almost breathy manner. A feather fluttered down in front of Guy, and he thought for an instant that one of the strands of feathers had come loose, and that wouldn't do because then it would be clear that they'd been tied by human hand. But as he looked up he saw more feathers fluttering down, and realised that at least two of the outlaws had to be up in the oaks and throwing them.

The forest was just really starting to green up by now. Not the thick canopy of summertime, but enough to blur the outlines of the branches, and in the briefest of flashes, Guy saw someone who he thought was probably Much, and who was wearing one of the leaf-green woollen jerkins which blended so well with the foliage. Certainly the knights would never spot them, of that Guy was sure.

"I hate bloody feathers!" Walkelin screamed, as a couple more stuck to him, and Fredegis and Henry looked around in fear, wondering if they would be next for some ghastly shock.

"Go faster, Gisborne!" Henry barked. "You're blocking the path!"

But as Guy urged his horse to a brisk trot a new peril struck. From out of nowhere they began to be struck by flying acorns. With his sharper eyes, Guy saw Roger pop up from behind a huge tangle of brambles and loose one off with a catapult, and then duck down even as he heard Henry yelp, "Ouch!"

He turned in his saddle to see the redheaded knight rubbing his nose and his eyes starting to stream. Roger really was a demon shot with the sling! He would never be a good archer, he hadn't the muscle, but he was hitting his mark every time with the springy catapult.

As they clipped along at a brisk rate and passed beyond the outlaws, Guy was very glad that he was having to rise in the saddle, because he was losing the battle not to laugh. At least while trotting it wasn't so obvious. Yet there was a final coup de grace. With Hardwick village just coming into sight – or at least the smoke from its fires was – they turned on the track and there was a lightning-blasted oak just up above the worn hollow of their path. And as they got closer they began to hear a deep and resonating hum. It wasn't a tune, just a deep sustained note which seemed to echo from within the tree.

The oak wasn't big. In fact it had clearly suffered such a strike as to crack it off only six or seven feet from the ground, and what was left of the top of it had crumbled into shards. So because it wasn't tall enough for a man to stand in anymore, the three knights clearly never suspected that a human voice was behind this. And the effect was enhanced by the way that the outlaws had given the tree a crown of mistletoe and ivy, delicately woven around the top of the shattered fingers of wood which still pointed skywards.

And now the outlaws were very clever. They had covered over a hollow just as Guy had done, except that this time it was him whose horse stumbled and threw him. As he suddenly found himself sailing through the air, Guy instinctive rolled as he landed, and so didn't get winded as Walkelin had done, but as he got to his feet he recognised that he couldn't seem to be the one who got off without anything happening to him. And so, having kept hold of his horse's reins, he simply calmed her with a few reassuring words and pats, and remounted.

"God's hooks, Gisborne!" Henry spluttered. "You act as if nothing had happened!" thereby confirming that the outlaws had been right to not pre-warn Guy.

And so Guy shrugged and replied, "It's happened before. The forest doesn't like it when you don't show it proper respect. After a while you get a feel for where the sacred groves are and treat them a bit more carefully. I was foolish there. I should have remembered that old oak is a tricky one."

The last of the three knight's restraint broke, and they tore past Guy into Hardwick village, demanding strong beer, and warm water to wash Walkelin down with, when they got there. As Guy arrived rather more sedately behind them, he caught the astonished stares of the villagers at the knights, and knew that word of this would soon spread.

Matthew, the headman, wandered over to Guy with a mug of beer and asked softly, "What, by St Thomas, happened out there?"

Guy manfully restrained himself to a tight smile. "They got a taste of how scary the forest can be, courtesy, I suspect, of Robin Hood and his men. They were in mischievous mood today as you can tell by the state of Sir Walkelin."

Matthew also managed to restrain himself, but his sparkling eyes revealed his amusement. "Well I don't envy you your ride back, Sir

Guy. Your fellow knight is going to be no sweeter smelling by the time you reach Laxton."

"No," Guy sighed, "I don't suppose he is. ...Do you have anything to report to me?"

It was an empty question. Guy knew full well that they wouldn't be telling the likes of him about any illegal felling or hunting, but he always went through the motions of asking. Then he often ended up telling them to make a certain tree stump look a bit older than the fresh cut which was showing, or to make sure that the village dogs gnawed on big bones off where no-one could see them. For such leniency he was generally respected, even if none of the villagers round here had got as far as trusting or liking him yet. But they did take the hint that there was nothing for them to worry about in the forest which surrounded them, and for that Guy was glad, because the last thing he wanted was for the simple folk to become fearful of the spirits and shades of the forest. They might be Christian on Sundays, but there was still a thread of the old ways lingering, even if the sacred wells and revered old trees were now dedicated to minor local saints, not pagan gods and goddesses.

They returned to Laxton by nightfall, and for the next few days Guy left the knights to lick their wounds, but stayed near to the castle so that he could gauge their reactions. And he realised that they'd been right to think of not doing anything more until closer to the forest's summer closure. At the moment the three were shaken badly, and the worst thing the outlaws could do now was overdo things so that the fear lost its edge.

However, Guy could never have guessed how that third outing would play out in reality, and it began with an urgent message from of all people the abbot at Rufford.

"We had travellers come in," the lay brother sent to Laxton told the four knights. "Nothing odd about that – we'd been expecting them because they'd stopped with us on the way up to York, and had said they would come again on their way back to Warwick. But on their way through the forest they came upon two young lads sobbing about three dead men. The Abbot was going to send for the sheriff, but then the sub-prior remembered that you were closer to hand here, Sir Guy, and that you're one of these new coroners. Please will you come?"

And so, with Henry, Fredegis and Walkelin deciding that this might be something a bit more to their bloodthirsty tastes than tramping after deer, all four of them rode out that same afternoon to make the five mile ride to Rufford.

When they got to the abbey it was to find the leading men of the tiny village of Perlethorpe there as well, and things became a little clearer.

"They'd been mending hedges, my lord," Guy heard Simon of Perlethorpe saying to the abbot as he came in. "That was why they needed their tools mending. They were trying to *keep* the law by keeping the pigs in."

"And who is 'they'?" Guy asked calmly, making heads turn as he walked up to the group clustered around the abbot. "Were they all from your village?"

"Aye!" Simon answered. "It's Eric and his brother, Torwald, and their nearest neighbour, Cedric. They're the ones who live on the edge of the village, see? So they have responsibility for making sure nothing strays into the forest from that side."

"And yet you say they're now dead," Henry drawled with knightly disdain for the death of mere peasants, having flopped onto one of the few leather chairs in the guesthouse, and taking a mug of ale from a servant, clearly not taking this too seriously as yet, but he sat bolt upright at Simon's next words.

"Ah, my lord, killed by poachers!"

"Poachers?" Fredegis spluttered indignantly. "But the forest is about to close! How dare they! Who dares to flout the law so blatantly?"

"Wealthy young men, my lord," Simon said with a sad shake of his head. "They thought they'd got away with it. They didn't know that Eric's son had gone off the lane to pee. Poor lad, he saw his dad and uncle getting butchered like hogs – hasn't stopped shaking since. And Cedric's son was just lucky. They didn't spot him when he dived under the handcart out of the way."

Guy stepped forward. "You're very specific. 'Butchered' you say? What makes you say that?"

There was no mistaking the relief on Simon's face at seeing Guy. The villagers in that area only knew Guy as one of the coroners, but already he had a reputation for being hard but fair, not fickle like the sheriff.

Abbot Adam smiled faintly at Guy's arrival, although Guy could tell he was less happy about having the other three boorish knights in his hall. "Thank you for coming so promptly, Sir Guy. We weren't expecting you until tomorrow, and one of our lay brothers said he thought he recognised one of the lads as coming from Perlethorpe. So he went there to enquire and came back with Simon and his four companions. With someone they knew around them the lads have just calmed down enough to be able to tell us what's happened."

"I say 'butchered', Sir Guy, because young Wilfred – that's Eric's son – just told me that he recognised one of the three men. He's from Worksop." Simon took over. "Like I was just saying to the abbot, they'd been to Worksop to get their tools mended. But you have to turn off the proper road onto the lane to get to our village, and that's through the forest, but they had a lawful reason to be travelling it, my lord."

Guy patted him on the arm consolingly. "Their actions aren't what I need to investigate, Simon. But again I ask you, why do you say 'butchered'?"

"Because the one is the son of the tanner in Worksop," Simon said bitterly. "The Good Lord knows he's carved up enough cows, sheep and pigs in his time to know what he's about with a knife. He's taken to hanging around with the son of that big brute who's Sir Robert Veteripont's constable at Tickhill. Since Sir Robert took over we've seen more of that lad and his pal from the castle than we'd like, especially since they're over the border into Yorkshire really."

Veteripont had yet to make his appearance in the shire, but Guy knew who the constable was and he was obviously another former mercenary, hard and cold, and so it was no wonder his son was cut from the same cloth.

"So why do they come to Worksop, then?" demanded Henry, clearly losing patience already, but he wasn't prepared for Simon's blunt retort of,

"Because they've already been kicked out of every alehouse in Doncaster, and the town watch won't let them stay in the town after dark."

"And this tanner's son...?" Guy prompted.

Simon gave a sniff of disgust. "His father's richer than his neighbours, I'll grant you that, but the fool boy has started to give himself airs and graces. Thinks that by sucking up to a couple of knights' sons, that he'll be able to work his way into their society, too. But what he does know, Sir Guy, is where it's possible to hunt without getting caught. His father never seems to be short of skins to work on, but 'cause he finds some nice leather for the sheriff and others, it gets a blind eye turned," and his gaze drifted towards Fredegis and Walkelin, who suddenly became very self-conscious of their rather fine leather gloves.

A well-dressed man stepped forwards and now added his part of the story. "We were on the road when the two boys came tearing out of the forest screaming and covered in blood." He shook his head. "Poor souls, I have a son that age myself, and I know when a child is terrified, and they were. We had no idea where they'd come from, and they were in too much of a state to tell us anything, so we thought the best thing to do was to bring them here where they could be cared for."

"Very sensible of you," Guy praised him. "I presume that you never saw the bodies?"

"Heavens, no!" the man exclaimed. "I think the boys had been running for some way, because they were stumbling with exhaustion and could hardly draw breath."

Guy gave a terse nod, then turned to the assembled men about him. Addressing Fredegis, Walkelin and Henry first, he said, "We should all go tomorrow to find the bodies, just in case these fools are still around and drunk enough to fancy trying the same thing twice." The way the three promptly sat up that bit straighter with belligerent expressions on their faces told Guy that in this, at least, they would do their duty.

To the abbot he said, "If we could possibly have four lay-brothers and a couple of hand carts to put the bodies on, Father, that would be most helpful," and got a nod of agreement. And finally to the men of the village he added, "You should come with us to help us find them. You know which paths they would have taken, but I'm sorry, the bodies will have to come back here first so that I can examine them. Where do your folk go to to be buried?"

"Welbeck provides the priest who comes to our village chapel," Simon replied, "but for burials we have to take the bodies to Edwinstowe to St Mary's."

That was a mercy. Not every village was quite so close to the Church's officially designated burial ground for it, especially here in the Old Forest, where villages were sometimes quite spread out. And better, Guy knew the priest at St Mary's to be a reasonable man who would allow the villagers to pay him just part of the burial fee, and the remainder when they could scrape it together. Just at the moment everyone was broke again, because in March there had been yet another carucage announced, and this time even Archbishop Walter had had enough and was reported to have resigned his post over it. Even Briwere had given up making any pretence of being able to collect this one.

With no body to inspect and the boys unable to say more than they had already given up, there was nothing Guy could do but go to bed and wait for the morning. However he was glad that the monastic bell for Lauds got them all up at dawn, because for once he was able to chivvy the other three knights out at a sensible hour. He didn't want those bodies left any longer than possible, and there was already the danger that they might have been found by boar or foxes and partly eaten.

The man in charge of the monastery's carts and animals helpfully let Guy have a small cart and pony, and two mules for Simon and his friend, Walter, so that they could ride. The other villagers would take the boys back to their mothers and break the bad news to the families, but Guy set out at the front of a strange cavalcade with Simon and Walter, followed by the three knights who were all trying to look fierce, and a lay brother bringing up the rear with the cart.

It wasn't lost on Guy that they were heading back into the same part of the forest where the four of them had been waylaid, and had the occasion not been so sad, he would have found a savage glee in the way that the three knights kept fingering their sword's hilts nervously. Then he suddenly hoped that his friends would be alert to the fact that something more serious was afoot, because they were expecting Guy and the others any day now. Yet even Guy was surprised when they came upon the three bodies and found them laid out reverently on the roadside, their arms crossed over their chests and their eyes closed.

"God bless you, Tuck," he breathed as he knelt down beside them, having been faster off his horse than the other knights, but not realising how quickly Simon and Walter had joined him. It earned him a sideways glance from Simon, and there was no way he was going to try and explain here. As it was, someone had obviously kept watch over the bodies throughout the night, because there was no sign of any animal activity, and that said to Guy that his friends had camped nearby and watched over the bodies.

Carefully lifting the blood-stiff garments aside, Guy couldn't help but gasp. Butchered was right! Someone had treated these poor souls as if they were a cow to be gutted for the spit. Bruising on their faces and hands told of them trying to defend themselves in a fight just before they'd died, but whoever had cut them had done it in a calculated way. It was just too cleanly done to have been done in the heat of the moment, and that made Guy angry.

"They've been murdered in cold blood," he declared, standing up again. "No doubt about it. Sir Henry, come closer please and witness these wounds ...and you two, please." His fellow knights weren't pleased at having to come and look at the bloody wreckage of the three men, but did so once Guy had added, "If you witness this, then the brother and their friends can take them and get them properly buried. Their families don't need to see this. Four knights swearing to the sheriff that foul murder has been done will surely be enough even if one of these wretches turns out to be something like Veteripont's nephew."

"And what else are we to do?" Fredegis asked warily.

"We – or rather, I, with you three with me – are going to track these bastards," Guy said savagely. "We're going to hunt them down and bring them to justice."

For a moment he was puzzled by the way Henry, Fredegis and Walkelin were regarding him warily, then remembered that they had rarely seen him angry. Unlike them, he wasn't constantly blowing up in a storm of a temper at every slight insult, imagined or real. Well it wouldn't hurt them to have the reminder that Guy was not just some fey woodsman who rode around hugging trees, but a dangerous opponent. Their eyes opened that bit wider when he took his Welsh bow from its wrapping where it had been slung along his saddle, and put his quiver of arrows across his shoulder.

"Found it at Laxton," Guy lied smoothly, because the only longbow they'd been aware of at Nottingham was the one still locked up in the keep there, and not used since the siege. "I've been having a bit of a practise with it. If they have hunting bows it'll be good to have the advantage of range over them."

"It's hardly a knight's weapon, Guy," Henry declared with an air of distaste.

"Maybe not," Guy riposted, "But it might well stop you from getting skewered from a distance like a boar, so don't complain!"

The thought that someone less than a knight, or at the very least a man-at-arms, might do him some harm sobered Henry up fast, and when they rode off he kept a respectful distance back from Guy.

Leaning low in his saddle, Guy rode at a stead walk, carefully following the hoof imprints, which turned from the murder site back into the depths of the forest.

"*Hmph* ...not making for Budby, more's the pity," he observed. "Shame. It would have been good to drag them out of the inn there and give them a humiliating beating in front of those they so look down on."

"Guy?" he heard Fredegis gulp faintly from behind him, but didn't deign that with an answer. Let him and the others think what they would, but they equally were too fond of trampling on those they saw as beneath them. It would do no harm to remind them that the law also protected the ordinary folk of England.

They were heading for Carburton, Guy realised after a while, but that made sense if the one lad wanted to get back to Worksop, and the others to beyond there and across the shire border. Even allowing for the twists and turns in the forest, the chances were that they would catch the lads in Worksop not long after noon, for they couldn't have more than about five miles to go. Yet it was after they had passed Carburton, and come to the crossing of the Poulter, that the first surprise came.

There, swinging by his heels from a branch, and dangling perilously close to the water was a thickset lad who'd clearly taken a serious beating.

"Help me!" he blubbered through swollen and split lips. "Help me!"

They cut him down, and sat him on the river bank so that Guy could wash some of the stiff, dried blood off.

"Don't let him get me!" the lad pleaded, constantly twitching and trying to look around, even though he was obviously stiffening up from the beating.

"Who?" Fredegis demanded, giving him an unsympathetic cuff. "Stupid boy. There's nobody here but us."

"Him!" the tanner's son whimpered. "The Horned Hunter!"

"Who?" scoffed Walkelin.

"Him!" the lad actually screamed, throwing a terrified arm out to point across the water, and there, just as the small river slightly turned and on the opposite bank, stood something which was upright like a man, but which had the head of a stag and its rack of antlers. In his one 'hand' he had a tall staff which was topped by another antler, making it look for all the world like Death's scythe as seen on so many paintings in the churches.

The figure solemnly brought the staff down until it was pointing directly at the lad, then made a dignified turn and vanished into the greenwood. At that point Guy realised that the tanner's son had fainted.

"Let's throw him over my horse," he sighed. "At this speed it'll cope with two of us, although he's a great lump of a young man. He hasn't been going short of food, so I reckon Simon's right – his father's probably hunted illegally, or at least turned a blind eye to his son doing it, because you can't imagine the lad's sat at the table stuffing his face while the rest of the family's gone hungry."

Yet Guy's horse didn't have to carry the lad far. His own horse was found placidly cropping the fresh grass not far away, and they shifted him across on to it, with Guy leading it. It was also clear that the three knights were also distinctly skittish now. That sight of the Horned Man had brought all of their fears rushing back in, and so when they all heard voices, Guy could tell that they were torn between fight and flight. Halting the horses so that he could listen more intently, Guy realised that these were voices crying out in fear. They had found the other two.

"This way," Guy declared confidently, but no sooner had he turned onto the small side path than he saw signs clearly put there for him by the outlaws, and taking him in the right direction. And if the knights wondered at him picking up the pace, they hardly had time to express it, because they suddenly emerged into a small clearing to find two young men darting hither and thither in their underwear.

Someone had stripped them of their finery, which now hung high above their heads in the branches of the trees, but as they went to dart one way they would get a bird call from right in front of them. Then as they spun and tried to run another way, a new bird call would come from right in front of them there too. And there were several long arrows embedded in the soft turf of the clearing proclaiming the more physical discouragements which had been made.

As the pair turned and saw Guy and the other knights, they ran to them, begging,

"Help us, please! Get us out of here!"

And then the taller of the two made his worst error. "My father will make it worth your while if you do," he proclaimed.

"Will he, now," Guy said coldly, leaning back in his saddle and folding his arms to look down his nose at the young man. "And why should he have to do that? What have you been doing?"

The youth with his fashionable Norman haircut blinked owlishly, his fear-addled brain slowly realising that maybe he hadn't said the right thing.

"Tell me what you've done," Guy repeated sternly. "Or shall I tell you? You two and this lump of meat here were hunting illegally."

"The forest's not closed yet!" his friend protested.

"No it isn't," Guy agreed, "but nevertheless you should have got permission off the sheriff to hunt, or at least come to us at Laxton for permission." Guy knew that he was on sound ground here, because the only time Briwere allowed anyone to hunt was when they personally could do something to help him in some way, and these two callow youths were not in that league. "So even though the forest does not close for another five days, you should still not have been hunting."

"We might not have been hunting..." the lad who was no doubt the constable's son said slyly, then leapt in the air with a shriek as an arrow thumped into the ground right between his feet with a hare tied to it.

Guy knew that whoever had done it had to have been right behind him, because the arrow would have been unwieldy in the extreme with the large animal tied to it, even though it was one of the yard-long barbed arrows the outlaws specialised in. That had come from over a handful of yards at best, but he never twitched a muscle or looked back, and where he was sitting on his horse prevented any of the other knights from plunging into the undergrowth behind him.

Yet before they could even react, much less shove Guy aside to find the bowman, their attention was taken by something far more unnerving. A hollow triple thumping came from across the clearing, and from out of the shadows came the Horned Man. Not fully out, just out of the deepest shadows, and with that Reaper's staff of his, he pointed first to the hare on the arrow, and then at the constable's son.

"It seems somebody disagrees with you," Guy said calmly, even though he had heard the collective gasps from everyone else.

Then to the shock of everyone, the bushes suddenly parted and a roe deer's carcass flew through the air and landed with a thump in the clearing, making the horses rear and snort in shock too. As a result it was only once the beasts were back under control that Walkelin suddenly called out,

"Look! What's that? ...And there!"

On the turf lay two hunting bows and quivers with just a few arrows left in each.

"Yours?" Guy asked the constable's son, and though he tried to brazen it out by demanding,

"Who are you to ask?" his friend blurted out,

"Yes!"

"We," Guy said with an expansive wave to include Henry, Fredegis and Walkelin, "are the sheriff's forest knights. And we four in particular are the ones who have taken over from Sir Ralph fitz Stephen at Laxton, so I think we have every authority to ask, don't you?"

He saw his words sink in and the two youths go pale. Technically, as sheriff, Briwere was Veteripont's superior, and that meant that he was most definitely above the constable; and with the sheriff of Yorkshire now being the royal head forester, there wasn't much doubt that fitz Peter would back Briwere on a forest matter like this. The young men were going to be in for a stiff fine if nothing else, and that depended on the answer to Guy's next question.

"So who killed the three villagers?"

"He did!" they chorused, pointing to the tanner's son, still unconscious across his own saddle.

"Really?" Guy was sceptical. "All by himself he waylaid three grown men and gutted them like the beasts at the slaughterhouse? Oh, I don't doubt that his was the hand that wielded the knife. The cuts on those bodies were too well-practiced for it to have been either of you who did it. But do you seriously expect us to believe that they just stood there and let him fillet them? ...No, I think that you two 'heroes' held them, after you'd beaten them bloody. You held them while this stupid sod did your dirty work for you. So you're coming back with us to Nottingham, and you're going into the dungeons until the eyre comes around, at which point you will be tried for murder."

Three hollow knocks came from across the clearing, the Horned Man inclined his head to Guy just fractionally, and then he stepped backwards until he disappeared into the greenery. Too stunned to argue, the three other knights did as Guy instructed and tied the two youths up, past being surprised when their horses suddenly emerged into the clearing of their own accord.

It was only as they were on the road back towards Nottingham, for Guy was insistent that they make all speed to the castle, that Fredegis tentatively asked,

"Will the judge on eyre believe this? Will he believe you?"

"He will after we've stopped at Edwinstowe for the night and you've witnessed me making an exact match between the arrows in these quivers with the one in this roe deer," Guy said, patting the small deer's carcass which was slung across his knees. "They're fancy arrowheads – not the sort most folk have – and that'll be their undoing. And under some bright light, I have high hopes of finding some strands of cloth from the men's clothing still in the blade of that idiot's knife," and he gestured to the tanner's lad, who had come to, but was swaying wretchedly in his saddle. "It's a serrated blade – great for cutting through bone and the like, but you really have to keep on top of cleaning it, which I don't think this bonehead will have done."

Did I make that comparison? Oh yes, Brother, and all three suffered the full weight of the law for their crimes. But of equal importance for me was that it embedded in my fellow knights' minds that the Old Forest was a dangerous place to venture into. Under other circumstances the appearance of the Horned Man might not have made quite such a lasting impression, and while I would have given anything to have saved the lives of those three poor villagers, nevertheless I was glad that something fruitful came out of their deaths.

And who was under the stag's hood? Ah! In the first place it was John, although with my more fleet-footed other cousin, Allan, and Roger, with him. As soon as John had vanished from our view, those two had run, Allan carrying the antlered head, and Roger the bundled cloak, making sure to get to the clearing as fast as they could. They already knew, you see, that the youths' tracks would take me in something of a loop. And I must confess that they had appropriated the two horses and tethered them not far off, so they got to ride most of the way, and that was how they outpaced us. However, at the clearing it was Gilbert who assumed the mask, because my friends needed Tuck's strength to help throw that roe deer and John had not caught up yet. So it was never just one of them who assumed the mantle.

But what of Robin, you ask? Ah me, Brother, sadly it was him who had lost control with the tanner's lad and given him such a beating. Being in the area, my friends had heard the screams of the two small boys, you see, and although they had been hot on their heels, had seen the travellers take them and knew that they would be cared for. Yet it had only been Allan, Roger, Much and Bilan who had chased after the boys. The rest of my friends had gone to the site of the murder, and as I had guessed, dear Tuck had done his best for the fallen men.

What none of them had fully appreciated was how upset Robin became at the sight. He seemed to take it very personally, talking about how dare someone attack his people? Even so, none of the others were prepared for the explosion of violence which came when they caught up with the trio, who were riding along as if having come from the fair, and bragging to one another about who had done what. Whatever Robin's mental state, he was still a big, well-built man, and he could move at surprising speed when he chose to, which was how he came to pounce on the tanner's boy and near beat him to death before Will, Tuck and John managed to haul him off.

Unfortunately that distraction had allowed the other two to run off, and the gang had to split up to find them, with the result that overnight just four of my friends got them pinned down in a small hollow, but did not get to dig them out of their refuge until the others were able to catch up with them in the morning, and not that long before I arrived. The four who had gone after the little boys decided to follow the travellers and had been hanging around close to Rufford Abbey, so that was how everyone knew that I was already on my way. They saw me go in and knew that come the morning I would set out on the hunt. And so they had gone ahead and managed to track the others down nicely in time to allow the performance I witnessed.

Yes, Brother, there were a lot of coincidences there, and that's why I felt the hands of my sympathetic saints in all of it. We had done our taunting of my fellow knights without bloodshed or harm to any others, and because of that I truly believe that we were used as the instruments of some divine justice for those fallen villagers.

As for Robin, that was to have some serious repercussions as I shall tell you after more restorative wine for what is to come.

Chapter 27

With the month-long closure of the forest upon us, I did not have much time to spend with my friends for a while, although as I was out and about they did catch up with me. Of course at first it was to ask about what happened to the three youths, and I was glad to report that Briwere had thrown a blue fit over the matter. Constable's son or not, the leading lad suffered the full weight of the sheriff's wrath, and so did his friends. The tanner's son was hanged, but even the other two paid hefty fines and had the lash, constable's son or not.

And bizarrely it even cemented a strange kind of union between me and the three knights. Briwere actually commended us for our speedy reactions to the situation, and having been on the receiving end of several beratings from him up until now, the three suddenly saw me as a very useful ally, even though we would never be friends. Given that they would never have set much store on three peasants' deaths, they were wily enough to realise that, had they followed their own inclinations and only done a cursory inspection for the bodies, then they would have been in even hotter water with Briwere. Therefore they dimly comprehended that I had saved them from that, and it put me in a new light with them.

That was good, Brother, because it meant that they now tolerated what they saw as my strange affinity with the forest, and at times even called upon me for my opinion in the following weeks. When that brought benefits in the form of Briwere saying that at last they were getting to grips with their posts, and he had begun to leave us alone a little more, they finally saw the point of having me around. Then Briwere went off on eyre for a couple of months, and you may think that the forest descended into a brief time of peace.

However, I must now highlight a different legal matter for you, because it impacts directly on our story soon. Now I have talked to you of Geoffrey fitz Peter, the royal forester, and how much of a blight he was, but there was one thing he could not do alone – he could not call a forest eyre. That was something only the king could do because the forests were directly under the king's jurisdiction, not the normal courts in the preserve of judiciaries like Hubert Walter and fitz Peter himself. And because King Richard was uninterested in hunting, his *only concern for the forests was how much revenue they brought in. That in turn was informed by the bail monies relatively well-off individuals would pay to keep themselves out of their nearest town gaols, and of course it was better to have them keep on paying those every six months than let them pay the one-off fine and be done with the matter. And the king did not think of the consequences to the lesser folk trapped in this system – they were so far beneath him as to be invisible, and their fines were never going to amount to much.*

So I must now tell you the shocking truth that there had not been a single forest eyre in the whole of King Richard's reign. Not one! Nine long years in which some poor souls had languished in gaols if they were too poor to scrape together the fines, which many were. And of course that was getting worse with every one of those damned carucages the king inflicted on us, which had become an annual burden, despite being supposed to be extraordinary taxes to be used in a major emergency. By now most people were so drained of resources they were struggling to even pay the regular rents and tithes, much less any extra burdens like fines for poaching.

Therefore our goal in Nottingham was stuffed to the brim, and I was now grateful that we had at least emptied it once, for we were the worst off in all of England because of virtually the whole of Nottinghamshire being under forest law. Not even the unfortunates within the limits of the New Forest down in the south were as badly off as us. For while their forest was large, the legal perimeter was still confined to the forest itself, whereas ours took in vast swathes of open farmland thanks to King Henry's generosity to his son John.

However, by now we had had to start finding room for prisoners within the castle itself, for want of anywhere else, and I am sure that it was situations like our own which prompted fitz Peter to his next move. He was a hard man by anyone's reckoning, but my own opinion on the matter is that he must have become frustrated beyond measure with the king over this. After all, we had reached a stage where we were praying for the regular eyre to come around again just to make some room, and we were far from afflicted with murderers and rogues – this was Nottingham, not London! Yet because of those rotting in confinement for forest offences, we were stuffed to bursting point.

And if fitz Peter was ever the one to tell King Richard that the forest fines would be useful in the first place, he must by now have been wishing he had never opened his mouth on the subject. Given the king's almost permanent absence from his realm, it might have been better if he had officially handed over the calling of forest eyres to fitz Peter in a fit of boredom, and let him get on with it. But he did not, and now fitz Peter was forced into doing something extreme.

Good King Henry had long ago stopped the vile punishment of blinding and castration for the killing of the king's deer, but that was now brought back accompanied by an expansion of the existing fines in a new Assize of the Forest. You are shocked, Brother, and well might you be, yet you wonder why I partly excuse fitz Peter? Well it is because although he did bring this in, he also resigned as royal head forester within weeks, choosing to focus instead on being a co-justiciar of England with Archbishop Walter. Now I did not like fitz Peter on the rare occasions I had contact with him, but knowing now how he would serve as justiciar in a harsh but fair way for many years after this, I have to conclude that this was not his idea, or at least not his alone. Moreover, you must remember that this happened at the same time as when Archbishop Walter had resigned as chief justiciar in protest over King Richard's excessive demands with the carucages, and Walter and fitz Peter had a very close working relationship. What was more, though Walter would be reinstated by the king – after the king being made to see some sense, we heard – and fitz Peter did not resign wholesale in protest, he did resign as head forester at that time never to return, and I think that says much about his views on the king's avarice.

However, we were hardly jubilant at the announcement of his successor when it was brought back to us by the sheriff. It was to be Hugh de Neville, and if we did not know Hugh, we certainly recalled his infamous uncle, Alan de Neville, who had been royal head forester early in King Henry's reign. Hugh de Neville came to the post with a bloody pedigree! I had never worked under Alan de Neville's overlordship for he had died the year I came to Nottingham, but I recalled well how Ralph Murdac had never had a good word to say about the man, and I had the dreadful premonition that we would be doing the same with his nephew. Mark Hugh de Neville well, Brother, for he remained royal head forester throughout most of King John's reign, too – we will encounter him again.

But of course, I now had to tell my friends of this, and I see that you are already ahead of me with your wide-eyed stare as to the effect it had on Robin.

Sherwood,
Summer, the Year of Our Lord 1198

"That's immoral!" Robin exploded. "Now will you see sense and see that we have to get rid of this sheriff?"

It was the first time Guy had been in the same camp as Robin in many months, and he wouldn't have come now had the news not been so urgent, but Robin's wild proclamation immediately opened up all the old wounds.

Mercifully it was Will who responded first with, "Christ on the Cross, Robin! Haven't you heard what Guy just said? This comes from the *king*, not just the sheriff! If we kill Briwere, then bloody King Richard will just appoint someone else who'll do the job, and if we kill him, then another and another!"

"Then why come and tell us at all?" Robin demanded with childish petulance.

Gilbert gave a snort. "To warn us, you daft English bastard!" He turned to Guy rolling his eyes in exasperation at Robin's blinkered view of the world. "You clearly have something in mind, Guy. What is it?"

"Oh, Guy has a plan!" muttered Robin sarcastically, making all of the others chorus,

"Shut up!"

Taking a deep breath, Guy began, "I'm worried about those deer that just die a natural death. I might just be able to keep some semblance of sanity in the Old Forest, but the Derwent-to-Erewash section of the forest has some very inept knights working it now. They won't have a clue as to what's a natural death and what's poaching, and I have a dread of some poor innocent suffering this terrible punishment for something that was just a natural occurrence. Fines you could help people out with, but you can't give a man back his sight and his balls. So I'm going to ask you to keep a thorough watch on the forest, and if you come across a dead deer, burn it, bury it, do whatever you can with it, but for pity's sake hide it as best you can."

"It's a fair point," Tuck said with a stern glance Robin's way. "There's more than one way to help the people than just with money, and this is definitely something we can do."

"And I'm going to ask you to do something else," Guy said apologetically. "The main places like Worksop and Mansfield will have heard the proclamation by now, and so anyone who goes to those markets will also know. But can you get to some of the outlying villages up in the Peak and northern Sherwood and tell them, please? And if you can spread the word to those folk just over the border in Yorkshire who might think to come this way, too?"

Siward put a reassuring hand on Guy's shoulder. "We'll do our best, my friend."

"*Hmph!*" muttered Robin, glowering at Siward. "And what about this new carucage, eh? Every carucate or hide has to come up with two shillings now and three later – that's every family having to find that, you realise? *Shillings*, Guy, not pence! And if they can't give that, then a peasant working someone else's land has to give their best plough beast. Best? Most of them are lucky to have one! You know most villages share plough oxen. ...And freemen have to give their goods? What goods? What goods do they think they have left these days? We need to be out getting more money from the rich *now*, not running your errands, Guy, because everybody is going to need Robin Hood's help this year!"

"Oh, Robin," John sighed, "why do you always take it out on Guy? And yes, we'll need to help as many people as we can, but am I right, Guy, in thinking that the sheriff is going to see the insanity of that demand?"

"*Dewi Sant*, yes!" Guy agreed. "The first thing he said when he'd told us the news was, 'and how the king thinks we're going to collect this, I do not know.' He knows he's been given an impossible task. In fact when Sir Hugh said 'the shire will riot,' Briwere just winced and said, 'That's what Archbishop Walter said when he told us.' From the highest in the land, they know this is just not going to happen."

He turned and gave Robin an icy stare. "Did you not hear me saying that the two chief justiciars resigned positions over this, Robin? What kind of message do you think that sends out to all sheriffs, *huh*? Not one of them is going to push too hard to collect this until they find out who King Richard is going to put in

Archbishop Walter's place, and therefore who they will have to deal with. So we have time over the carucage. But this forest law ...that comes into effect immediately!"

Robin just turned and stalked off, throwing black looks back over his shoulder at Guy.

"The best place for him would be a monastery," Guy said bitterly. "He's got no grasp on reality anymore, and he's a bloody danger to you all. ...*Ach*, listen to me! I'd better get going. Anyway, you don't need me inciting him to mayhem just by being here."

Tuck plonked a hefty paw on Guy's shoulder, forcing him to sit again. "You are not being driven out by Robin," he said firmly. "And for what it's worth, I've been thinking the very same thing. The best place for Robin would be a monastery, but not around here! He needs to be somewhere where he hears nothing of what's happening in Sherwood. Nothing that would disturb his thoughts and his soul, because he should spend a very long time in contemplation over some of the things he's done. Maybe somewhere like Melrose over the border into Scotland. I hear they have an ancient connection with Whithorn out in the west of Scotland, and that's even more isolated from us."

Guy breathed a sigh of relief. Thank God his friends were starting to see that this situation couldn't carry on. That episode with the tanner's lad had proven it in Guy's mind, at least. Even when he wasn't leading, Robin was too unstable now to be out and about with the rest of the gang. Just at the moment every move needed to be weighed up, not have someone charging in like an enraged bull at every turn.

"It might be no bad idea if you could think of a way to fake Robin's death," he said cautiously to all of them. "If the sheriff thinks that Robin Hood himself is dead – and don't forget that these days Briwere associates Robin's face directly with Robin Hood – that gives you time to get him away to somewhere, and for him to be left in peace there. The rest of you can carry on as you have been these last few months, and maybe next year you could resurrect Robin Hood again once it's clear that it must be a different man under the hood. If you need to massage Robin's pride for a bit, tell him that 'Robin Hood' has to die and let him think that nobody else will be taking over the mantle."

"But what reason could we give him?" Much asked worriedly. "He'd want a reason."

Guy had no hesitation in saying, "Tell him that Briwere has such a bee in his bonnet about Robin Hood that he's talking about launching a scouring of Sherwood to find him and bring him to justice. This new forest law might just play into your hands. If you say that the sheriff wants to publicly blind and castrate him to prove to this new royal head forester that he's doing his job ...indeed emphasise that Briwere knows that if he does that to any *ordinary* person that there'll be a riot.

"That's not far from the truth, you know. So to just stretching it a bit, and saying that Briwere needs one good public demonstration – and what better than the famous outlaw – isn't that much of a mental leap. That way you're telling Robin that you're bumping off his alter ego to save lots of people. And just maybe, if there's going to be no Robin Hood for him to play, then you might get the real Robin to take those vows rather more willingly."

"My word, Couz'," Allan said admiringly, "that's a crafty plan and a half, and it might just work!"

Tuck was nodding too. "And if we don't push him too hard for a few weeks, but just make the odd comment now and then about how we can't use Robin Hood to do this or that, then he might well swallow the bait. I confess that I would be much happier if we could meet you at Christmas and say that he's safely housed away from the world, and all its temptations and dangers."

However, Guy had to deflect the sheriff's ire towards the outlaws far sooner than he anticipated. Whether one of the other three had said something to Briwere about the forester Cuthbert's idleness, or he was feeling the need to prove he had a solid grip on the Old Forest to de Neville now that fitz Stephen had gone, was something which was never shared with Guy; but suddenly Briwere announced that he would visit the three parks closest to the castle – Linby, Welley and Beskwood Hays – and observe the foresters at work. This didn't bother Guy one bit on his own account. He knew exactly how much hadn't been done there, but had made it very clear to Briwere that he alone was the one riding through the northern half of the forest. Never enough to make Briwere think that he thought the others idle – having put all that work into making them scared stiff of the forest, Guy didn't want to have to go through it all again if they got replaced. But he had dropped hints that he covered the largely uninhabited tracts in the north, while the other three focused on the villages in the southern half.

Unfortunately, though, it also meant that on this inspection the sheriff had to travel right by the ruins of the outlaws' Hucknall camp, and Guy knew that it would dredge up memories of how Robin Hood had escaped justice. For himself it wasn't a pleasant reminder either, and he'd hoped to avoid being there at all, but Briwere had other ideas.

"You'll come, too, Gisborne," he announced. "I want someone with me who knows how tell if a deer has fallen prey to wolves or poachers."

Guy didn't like to tell him that no healthy wolf had been seen in such a densely populated area for decades. They were few and far between in these shires nowadays, hunted to the brink of extinction already in the name of preserving deer for a king who never came hunting. Guy would have liked to see more of them about – they would have kept the increasing numbers of rabbits which escaped from warrens under control.

Up here the winters were too harsh for the cosseted rabbits to survive in numbers in the wild year upon year, but Guy had the feeling that the warren keepers on the manors where they had been introduced for food (just like the trout in many a manor pond), and where they were fed and fattened with provided grain and hay, had no idea just how far they had tunnelled beyond the original enclosures. And at this time of year, after they had bred prolifically in the spring, they were becoming a pest in the fields, especially when in theory nobody could hunt them if all hunting was banned for months at a time, and apart from then only by licence. So Guy would have gladly seen a few packs of wolves in Sherwood, but he knew he was one of the few who grasped how beneficial they could be.

And so Guy rode out with Briwere and the rest of the entourage, his long Welsh bow slung across his back, and a quiver of the yard-long arrows to go with it also resting between his shoulder blades. The sheriff was far from pleased at the state of first Beskwood Hay, and then Welley Hay, and Guy began to get the nagging twinges of worry in his gut as Briwere's face grew grimmer, and his questions of Cuthbert and the three knights more acerbic. As Guy had anticipated, Briwere insisted on turning aside to look at the outlaws' camp, and it was here that Briwere's mood began to turn really black. Across the clearing had been dug a neat row of graves, and at the head of each was a small wooden cross.

"Who did this?" Briwere spluttered, outraged. "I specifically gave orders that the bodies were to be left here to rot as a warning!"

"I doubt any villagers came here," Guy said soothingly. "It was probably those who broke Robin Hood out of the castle who did this. Nobody who heard your order defied it, sheriff." He knew full well that it had been them. Tuck wouldn't have left them to be chewed up by birds and beasts unless he'd had absolutely no other choice.

"Break those crosses down!" Briwere screamed. "I will not have these murdering thieves granted Christian burials!"

Typically it was Henry, Fredegis and Walkelin who were fastest to obey, riding over the low mounds of the graves and reaching down to pull the humble crosses out as they went. It was something over which Guy repeatedly crossed himself, and was grateful that they had done the wretched deed before he could have got his own horse past Briwere's to comply, even if he'd wanted to. He knew that part of his reaction was due to his own knowledge of just how sanctified those graves were, for Tuck would have given them his full attention, regardless of his opinion of those men in life. These three knights were building up trouble for their immortal souls at a rate that would worry him stiff.

What he wasn't expecting was to hear a muffled sob off to one side. He was sure he was the only one who heard it, for he was hanging back as Briwere chivvied everyone else onwards for Linby Hay. Scouring the bushes and trees, he suddenly saw Robin pinned against the trunk high in the branches of a particularly old and sprawling oak by Tuck and John. They must have come to tend the graves, for there had been old, dead flowers on the mounds, and Guy guessed that Tuck had meant it as reinforcement to Robin that he had to atone for having led those men into such danger.

"I'm sorry," he mouthed silently to Tuck and was glad his old friend nodded sympathetically. But what could he have done? He was one man, and Briwere had brought six men-at-arms out with them, thinking that they might have to escort prisoners back into custody if they could not pay up whatever bail he set for them when caught. With Briwere and the three knights that would have made it one against ten, and with that sort of odds, Guy couldn't hope to have won had he been foolish enough to fight. Had it been over a living person he might still have tried, but the dead had mightier defenders in Tuck's saints than him, and he urged his horse into a trot to catch up with the others. He couldn't hope to speak to Tuck now, and he didn't want to with Robin there twisting everything he said.

However he could have kicked himself for letting Robin distract him when they got as far as Papplewick village, having found that Linby Hay wasn't any better kept than the other two, and with Briwere now stoked up into a right temper. He should have known that others of the gang wouldn't be too far away. There was no way that Tuck and John would have gone any distance alone with Robin in the state he was in.

His first inkling that something was afoot was seeing a small boy from the village spotting them from up ahead on the narrow lane from Linby, and turn to run like mad for the village.

"They're in awe of you, sheriff," Henry declared, valiantly trying to ingratiate himself with Briwere – a foolish move when the sheriff was in such a temper, he'd have been better keeping quiet.

"Of course they are, you lack-witted lump of toads' spawn!" Briwere snapped, "I'm the bloody sheriff! They ought to be scared – I'd be bloody worried if they weren't!"

Henry subsided, red-faced and sullen, but Guy instinctively knew that there was more to it than that. As they rode into the village he saw a figure that could only be Much, over by some robust fencing which proclaimed that that was where one of the village pigs was kept. Although the domestic pigs weren't as big as some of the wild boars in the area, they were still powerful beasts, and when the mood took them they were capable of barging through fences which would have kept a whole flock of sheep in order. And depending on whether they had bred back into the wild, some of these pigs were exceedingly bad-tempered as well. A sow in heat out in the forest, during the times when such things were allowed, might draw a male wild boar just as much as a domestic one, and Guy knew that the villagers saw the value in such interbreeding because it kept the domestic stock vigorous.

However, it also meant that you had to be careful of the pigs in certain villages. A sow with piglets could be a vicious opponent, especially if she thought that her little ones were in danger, and of course Guy knew of one sub-prior who had vanished without trace after being consumed by wild boar. It was why he instantly realised that Much was probably disposing of some bones. If the outlaws knew that the Papplewick pigs had been bred a bit too close to their wild cousins, it was an ideal way of getting rid of evidence. After all, pigs like humans would eat both meat and vegetables, and with their powerful jaws they would crunch up deer bones without any trouble.

Struck by guilt that Much might be caught on his account, Guy did his best to move his horse in between the younger outlaw and Briwere. Had he not been the one to tell them to dispose of evidence? *I'll never forgive myself if Much comes to harm because of me*, Guy thought desperately, but then a cry of alarm went up from the other side of the village.

Out of the forest came a huge young male boar, and like an arrow he made straight for the pen where Much was. As the big beast came barrelling towards him, it was all Guy could do to yank his horse out of the way and call the warning,

"Boar! Get out of its way!"

Much dived out of the way of the charging beast just in time. The boar went through the reinforced hurdles like they were so much parchment. For a moment Guy was too taken up with trying to control his panicked horse, but when he'd got her under control he guffawed out loud. There in the wreckage of the pen, the boar was humping the sow for all he was worth, far too busy attending to his needs to worry about the men around him who might skewer him to death.

Briwere did not have the same sense of humour on the matter. As the boar had shot beneath his horse's nose it had reared, depositing him straight into the village manure heap, and now he was screaming blue murder.

"Kill that fucking pig!" he bellowed over and over.

Given that the pig was quite definitely fucking, that only reduced Guy to further helpless laughter, but a sergeant known for his belligerence made the fatal mistake of trying to attack the boar with his spear just as it dismounted the sow. The boar did not appreciate the interruption, and it turned on the sergeant with all of its ferocity.

He'd been stupid to even think of doing such a thing, but Guy would not let a man die like that without at least trying to help. Sobering up fast he vaulted off his horse in order to string his long bow, plucked an arrow from his quiver, and aimed at the boar. His problem was that the brute had got the sergeant in its jaws and was shaking him like a child in a temper shaking a rag doll. Just when Guy thought he had a clear shot the sergeant would be thrown back into his line of sight.

Crabbing sideways, but never taking his eyes off the boar, Guy finally got a clear shot at the creature, and loosed. The yard-long barbed arrow hammered into it, and at such close range actually penetrated the boar's thick hide to embed itself deep in its side.

With a scream that was half pain and half rage, the boar dropped the sergeant and turned towards what had cause it such agony. Its head came down, and Guy knew it was going to charge him even as he loosed another arrow into it. This arrow slide beneath the shoulder flesh but didn't sink in any deeper, and Guy found himself frantically nocking another arrow and trying to get a line on one of the beady eyes. They were the only weak spot in the heavy-boned skull that was coming straight towards him at high speed now.

He loosed at the last moment and saw the arrow slide into the cheek, even as he dived to one side out of its path. His last-moment movement saved him because the boar was going too fast, and was too close, to be able to turn with him. Instead it saw its chance of escape from this painful place and thundered on into the woods which surrounded the village.

"Well what are you waiting for?" he heard Briwere scream. "Is bloody Gisborne the only one of you with the balls to hunt a fucking pig? Get after it! I want its head on my table! ...Tonight!"

"But, my lord, we haven't got the weapons..."protested Walkelin.

"You're fucking foresters!" Briwere snarled, storming over to Walkelin, having extracted himself from the manure heap and shedding rotting vegetation and droppings with every stride from his fancy cloak, which would never be the same again. "*Why* don't you have the weapons? You're supposed to be ready to deal with the forest! Why aren't you? By St Thomas' balls, I'll have *yours* if you don't do as I say *now!*"

Walkelin blanched, backing away from the apoplectic sheriff as fast as he could, and gratefully accepting the reins of his horse which were thrust into his hand by Fredegis.

Guy decided that the best way to avoid any further disasters was to mount up and pursue the boar with them, but he'd only got a few hundred yards into the woodland when he found the boar lying twitching in its last throes, another long barbed arrow sticking out of its eye. For the briefest instant he saw Will melt out of the shadows, give a swift wave, and then vanish again, and Guy knew that he must position himself so that it looked as though he had made the killing because he could hear the others coming up behind him.

He'd just got himself to its head, having put another arrow into its side to make it look more plausible, when the three other knights came into view. They had no doubt exited the village at speed for the sheriff's benefit, but they weren't so daft as to come chasing a boar without weapons, and they were proceeding with great caution.

"It's alright," Guy called softly to them, "It's dead."

It said a lot for the fear the boar had incited in the three bullies that they all crossed themselves in thanks – something Guy almost never saw them do. He went and began yanking his arrows out, having to put a boot on the beast's carcass and haul with all of his might, ensuring that Will's arrow vanished into his quiver with his own. When all were free he looked up at the others, still sitting on their horses looking worried and realised he had to do something to aid them, but also that if he did, then that put them in his debt – and that could be useful one day.

He went to his horse and pulled out a rope from a saddlebag, looping it around the boar's forefeet and then the rear, then turned to the three. "You take it back," he said, holding out the one end of the rope. "Go on, you need to placate Briwere more than I do at the moment."

Their jaws fell in astonishment.

"Why?" Henry managed to choke out. "Why help us?"

Guy sniffed. "Well you know as well as me, now, that we can't hope to patrol the whole forest. So we've all got to work together on this one to keep Briwere happy. It does me no favours if he's crowing over me and berating you, because he'll then expect you to do the impossible, and me to help you do it. Go on ...get out of here with that thing. Just tell Briwere that I'm making sure it doesn't have a pal hiding in the woods out here. I'll be back well before you leave the village, but you let him have a moment to calm down."

Still scarcely able to believe their luck, Fredegis and Walkelin leaned down and grabbed the ropes at either end of the giant hog and lugged it back to the village with Henry as escort.

Once they were out of earshot, Guy called softly, "Will? Are you still there?"

The burly smith melted silently out of the shadows. "Of course I am," he said with a chuckle.

"That was Much I saw, wasn't it? Feeding the sow deer bones, by any chance?"

Will nodded as Guy handed him arrow back. "But we came here because of that nasty brute you've just stuck with arrows. We got a message that it's been terrorising the village ever since the sow came into season. If it's the one we think it is, it killed its older rival at the start of the breeding season and took over his territory. A couple of other villages have had a close call with it, so we thought we'd tempt it with some deer remains we found, and the village sow was an ideal place to get rid of the head and other obvious bits in case we killed him before he'd eaten enough. ...Never expected you to show up, though."

"*Ach*, bloody Briwere feeling his oats again! Felt he had to come out and make sure the foresters are at least keeping the parks in order. He's in a foul temper because Cuthbert's an idle sod and has let things go, and my three idiot companions have been taken in by his craftiness and done nothing about it."

Guy heard someone in the distance yell, "Gisborne!"

"Look, Will, I have to go, but you should know that Briwere visited the old Hucknall camp and went mad when he saw the graves. He had those three destroy the crosses."

"Oh crap."

"But what's worse ...Robin saw them do it and me do nothing to stop them. But I couldn't, Will! Not alone against that many!"

Will slapped Guy on the back. "Don't be daft, of course you couldn't. Don't worry, I'll make sure all the others know the full story. Now go on, get back before you get into any more trouble."

However, trouble was waiting for Guy when he got back to the village. Briwere was sitting on his horse, puce-coloured, and ranting.

"Who did it?" he screamed, and clearly not for the first time. "Who loosed that boar at me? By Judas' balls I'll have the eyes and balls of every man in this village if you don't tell me!"

Henry sidled up to Guy and said softly, "The sergeant's dead. Gored to death, poor bastard. Even I don't need your skills to tell that."

Guy groaned. He had to stop this before it went any further, because he knew that his friends in the forest would not stand by and let the villagers suffer for an accident.

"My lord sheriff," he said firmly, riding his horse across in front of Briwere's. "Nobody released the boar. I've just met a swineherd in the forest who tells me this wild boar has been menacing the village for weeks now. It was already here. You were just unlucky enough to cross its path. ...Seems it was crazed even for one of its kind. The sergeant was unlucky."

The sergeant had been bloody stupid, Guy thought, but saying so wouldn't have the desired effect. Yet this was when Briwere's unpredictability made things worse. In an instant he had flipped and was off on another mental track.

"Menaced you say?"

"Err, yes." Guy struggled to see where Briwere was heading, but he was soon told.

Turning on Cuthbert, Briwere vented all of his rage onto him. "You are supposed to keep this place in order!" he ranted. "We're not a mile from Linby Hay, and yet there's a mad boar terrorising villages here? What part of your feeble brain thought this wasn't your concern? Answer me you scrotum-faced spawn of a worm-raddled bitch!"

Cuthbert had gone white with fear. He'd never seen Briwere in one of his tempers, and unlike his two assistants, he'd only been in the job a few years, and all of them protected by Ralph fitz Stephen. "M..m..my lord!" he bleated. "D..d..don't have the means to k..k..kill boar."

"D..d..don't you?" mimicked Briwere savagely. "Then what fucking use are you to me as a forester, then? You should have had that pig's balls! Well I shall have yours!"

With castration suddenly high in everyone's minds, Cuthbert clearly thought the sheriff meant it literally and fainted.

But Briwere hadn't satiated his anger yet and turned on Guy. "And what do you mean, swineherd in the forest? God's balls, Gisborne, you should know better! Am I surrounded by incompetents? What is the matter with you all?"

He was in such a state that Briwere had begun to froth at the mouth, but Guy kept calm.

"Sheriff, the man was retrieving an escaped piglet," he said firmly. "The sow's previous piglets are still only four months old and small enough to get through gaps their mother can't. This one got out through a gap the boar made on his last visit, and the man's been searching for it. Nobody broke the law, sheriff. He has the piglet. It'll be in its pen by nightfall."

It was a total fiction, of course, but the villagers were all giving him grateful glances and nobody was contradicting him. Better still, Briwere had worked himself up into such a state that he had exhausted himself, and now he suddenly came down from the peak of his fury to slump in his saddle.

"Everyone! Back to the castle!" Guy bellowed, grabbing the chance while it lasted, and all of the men and knights gratefully mounted up, the dead sergeant draped across his own horse and being led by another.

Briwere's horse turned with its stable-mates and began walking with them without any control by the sheriff, and it gave Guy the chance to speak briefly to the head man of the village.

"Don't worry," he reassured the frightened man. "If anyone's going to suffer it's going to be Cuthbert – the sheriff won't come after you."

The man nodded. "Good. Cuthbert's no loss. He's a bully and a brute, and he's cunning. He steals off us, Sir Guy. Demands his cut of everything, if you know what I mean."

So Cuthbert had turned a blind eye to poaching, officially never reporting anything, but blackmailing the villagers to give him probably more than they could afford of what they caught. And Guy was under no illusions as to what that would be – a few roe deer and the odd hare would be the best these folk would manage, never the red deer the king was supposed to want to hunt, and suddenly he knew what he would do.

"Harold. Cedric. Hold on a moment," he called to the two men who had drawn the short straw for lugging the boar back to Nottingham. "We can't possibly drag that thing all the way to the castle without a cart. Hold on. I'll cut it up. Briwere will never know the difference once it's on his plate."

He dismounted and took his knife to the boar, gutting it with professional ease.

"Have you got a couple of sacks?" he asked the villagers, and two appeared with speed. Into the one he put the two haunches, and the body from the waist to the neck in another. The head he managed to separate and would carry himself, but all the forequarters and the innards he left for the villagers, who were gratefully slopping them into whatever receptacles they had to hand, and Guy knew that they would be eating well on sausages for a while, quite aside from the actual meat.

"Here you go, lads," Guy said, handing a sack up to each of the soldiers, who gratefully took the much lighter burdens and hurried after the others.

"God bless you, Sir Guy," one of the women said, and there was a murmur of agreement from the others.

"I'll sort Cuthbert out, don't you worry," Guy said firmly. "He won't trouble you again."

But he had hardly mounted up, and was riding off with the boar's head perched upside down in front of him so that it didn't bleed all over him and his horse, when a familiar voice came from the trees.

"Bless you, Sir Guy!" it mimicked sarcastically, and for a heartbeat Guy thought it was the sheriff.

Then Robin stepped out onto the track in front of him, and Guy's heart sank.

"What a hero you are," Robin snarled bitterly. "You'll take care of the forester, will you? So you *can* do it when you want to. Why haven't you wanted to before, eh? I've always told the others you're the sheriff's man at heart, and this proves it. You just wait 'til I tell them!"

As Guy sat there, too stunned by Robin's twisted interpretations of his every move to speak, he heard a crashing through the undergrowth and then John, Tuck, Will and Malik came stumbling out onto the track to pounce on Robin.

"Don't you ever thump Much like that again!" Will said angrily as he grabbed one of Robin's arms tightly.

Guy eased his horse around them, but halted just beside Robin. "You are wrong," he said with as much calm as he could muster. "I can't control the foresters and I certainly can't control Briwere. All I've even been able to do is try to limit the damage they do. I can only deal with Cuthbert because Briwere is already furious with him, and he's broken his own laws. I don't know why you hate me so much, Robin. All I've ever done is try to help you."

He heeled his horse onwards, but was dismayed to hear Robin screaming after him, "You know why!"

Back at the castle Guy knew he had to make good on his promise to cut Cuthbert's claws, if only for the villagers' sake.

"Sheriff, Cuthbert has to go," Guy ventured as he brought in some juicy slices of the best cuts from the boar for the sheriff's own platter. The two haunches would be roasted for tomorrow, but Guy had gone to the kitchens and helped cut off some rib steaks which could be served up that night to appease their querulous lord.

Briwere gave him a baleful glare, but was too busy at first spearing the tender slices and gorging himself on them. The food satiated him the way Guy had hoped it would, even though it was a shame to drench good pork in as much wine sauce as Briwere demanded. With the sheriff feeling that he had dined appropriately to his station for once – since everyone, including him, was suffering from shortages just at the moment – he was prepared to listen a little more closely to what Guy had to say.

"Go on, Gisborne."

Guy thought a little flattery was worth it, and though he normally refused to 'my lord' Briwere, he did so now. "My lord, after you'd left, the villagers confessed to me that Cuthbert has been forcing them to set traps for hares by threatening them with you. He told them that he'd tell you they'd been illegally hunting, even when they hadn't, if they didn't do as he said. But then he took the hares for himself, telling them that they could still say nothing because now they really had hunted illegally. He's been using your name in vain, my lord, to get what he wants." Guy paused and looked over to where Cuthbert had been made to sit, quivering, in the corner of the main hall but within sight of the sheriff. "He's not been going without his meat, has he?"

It was all the prompting Briwere needed. Having finally got his teeth around meat that hadn't been cut up finely to make it stretch as far as possible, and usually almost invisible in stews that were more root vegetables and barley than anything, the thought that portly Cuthbert, with his big round belly, had been stuffing his face on what he'd been denied was just too much to bear.

"You," he snarled, jabbing an accusing finger at Cuthbert, "are a disgrace! Take my name in vain, would you? Well you won't again! Guards! ...Take him to the dungeons! Let's see what forty days on those rations do for him. And when you come out, you miserable wretch, you are banned from these shires, do you hear me? You will leave and never come back!"

As Cuthbert was dragged away screaming, Briwere turned to Guy. "We shall need another riding forester. See to it."

And did I? Yes I did, by promoting Egfrith, the more reasonable one of Cuthbert's two walking foresters, and who was a man I knew would apply a lot more sense to his role. Bran, the other walking forester was not a bad man, but he was under the influence of his father, Angold, who had been the forester before him, and Angold I did not trust. It was a satisfactory arrangement, but I confess that after that I left the other three knights to find themselves a new man. I was too cut to the quick by Robin's words, and needed to go off on my own to lick my wounds.

It troubled me mighty, Gervase, that Robin seemed to be able to keep on getting away from the others like that, and I feared that sooner or later, he would appear at a time when his wild accusation would do some real damage, either to me or some unfortunate whom he thought was a friend or confidant of mine. And so I resolved that I must put some pressure on my friends now to find that safe place to send Robin to. Yet when I finally could face seeing them again some weeks closer to autumn, it was to find that they had been thinking the very same thing.

Chapter 28

Yes, Brother, I am aware that night draws on and we must stop soon, but I want to get to the end of this phase of my life before then, and you will see why that is so pressing very soon. This situation between Robin and myself was to be the source of all the tales of Guy of Gisborne being Robin Hood's enemy, and by now it was not so far from the truth if you mean Robin Hood as my cousin, for already I was separating the Hooded Man who acted for the people, from him as the man. The Hooded Man as a means of justice I still believed in, Robin I could not. Whatever love we had once shared had been torn to shreds by Robin's actions and words, and in that autumn of 1198 I think I truly did hate him. Nowadays I am filled with sorrow that things had become so bad, and I can look back on my cousin and see a very sick man. He had paid a terrible price for fighting in the Holy Land, and then at the hands of a king he thought he could admire and trust in the way he had King Baldwin in Jerusalem – a price more than he could withstand – and for that I am deeply saddened.

But this is my confession, and I confess to you now, Brother, that as a mere mortal, I was not filled with saintly goodness and found myself unable to turn the other cheek by this stage. Too much had happened, and I could not forgive and I could not forget. All I could think about was finding a way to get Robin off to some isolated monastery somewhere, to a place where he could indulge his religious obsessions day and night, and we would never have to face one another ever again. And I swear to you that that much is true. I did not wish him any greater harm, even after all the grief he had brought me, but I could not bear to even look at him anymore.

What do I mean by all that? Let me eat this stew your fellow brother has brought us and I will continue. Sharpen your quill and have more ink and parchment ready, for once I start to tell you of what came next I dare not stop until it is done.

Sherwood & Creswell Crags, Autumn, the Year of Our Lord 1198

"He's getting worse," Will said to Guy, who'd managed to meet up with them at the camp near Worksop. "We asked you to come because we've had more incidents, and we all agreed you needed to be in our decisions."

Robin himself was sleeping heavily thanks to a strong dose of poppy that Tuck had given him before they'd let Guy into the camp. With luck he would never know that his cousin had even been there, and for once Guy hadn't had to ask for that to be the case, the others had already decided this was how it would be.

"I heard," Guy said, shaking his head in despair. "I'm not even going to ask how he got away from you. I think he's getting cunning in his madness. But to attack Walkelin and Fredegis as they were coming out of Cuckney Castle? Is there any explanation? Can he tell you why he did it?"

Fredegis and Walkelin had been to speak to Richard de Cuckney at the castle, and had been just coming out of its gate when they found themselves confronted by a lone archer with a very large Welsh bow. By now considerably more wary of such weapons having seen Guy use one, they began reversing their horses back under the gateway, and it had been that which saved their lives. Robin had loosed one arrow which had only averted skewering Fredegis through the heart because his horse had danced in protest at the very last. Even so, he was now in Nottingham Castle nursing a shoulder which might never be fully functional again. The big bow had punched the arrow straight through, shattering much of his shoulder blade in the process.

Walkelin had made to dive off his horse, and for his effort at least only got pierced in the side through his flesh as he fell, but he too would not be riding anywhere for a while. Luckily, de Cuckney's servants had reacted swiftly, hauling the knights back inside and slamming the gate shut. At that point nobody knew if this demon archer would try to force his way inside, and Guy now told the others that it had only been fear of Fredegis dying that had made Sir Richard (for their old adversary from York had now inherited the constable's post from his father), send to Nottingham, and even so he had only opened the gate far enough to let one terrified servant on a horse out and then barricaded himself in again.

"They'll both live, may Our Lady be blessed," Guy concluded, "because had they died I dread to think what Briwere's reaction would have been. He has to be seen to be strong at the moment with de Neville taking over. *Dewi Sant* preserve me, I know Briwere can be an evil swine, and he can be as unpredictable as a rat with the bellyache, but we could have worse. I never thought I'd say such a thing a couple of years ago, but the way King Richard is settling posts and land on former mercenaries in the place of our own lords, who can't afford to pay up in order to inherit their own family's lands, there's a very real danger that we could have some absolute murdering butcher come here. Someone who the king thinks would control a rebellious shire with an iron hand."

He looked around at the others and saw them all looking glum. It was Siward who first spoke after a moment's pause.

"Well we're at our wits' end with Robin. That time he sneaked out in the depths of night, and I was one of the ones on watch and I still don't know how he got past us. We'd tried taking him to Abbot Michael, you see, and asked him if he would let Robin stay with the brothers for a while. Not that we intended it to be anything like permanent! We're with you even more than ever that Robin will have to go a long way away from here if he's to ever find any peace and sanity. But Tuck hoped – well we all did – that some time spent where he could do nothing but pray would be a good thing, a salve for his soul that would get him into a state fit to travel. That was just after the boar incident."

Siward shook his head in despair. "He lasted two days. Luckily we'd told Abbot Michael that we'd hang on here to make sure he settled, and one of the lay brothers came out and found us."

Tuck tutted. "We feel awful about this, because we've had to let on to the brothers where this hideout is, and that means we've put them in a position where they might have to lie for us. We never wanted that." He shook his head regretfully, "But it's a good thing we did. We caught up with Robin that time not far from Worksop Manor. Jesu alone knows what he was going to do there – I don't think even he did. So we took him back to Abbot Michael, and I spent hours there with him explaining why he needed to stay put. I'm afraid I gave up on trying to get through any message to him other than that he was imperilling his immortal soul with the way he's behaved. I thought I got through to him – I didn't."

"It wasn't your fault, Tuck," Mariota said firmly. "No-one could have tried harder than you." She met Guy's worried gaze. "You've already guessed, haven't you, that he did the same? Four days later the brother was back again, and this time we lost him for three days! God bless the good souls of Beighton, because they sent a young man to come and tell us that they'd seen a man who looked like Robin wandering alone through the woods, but talking as if he could see people beside him. It was a week before we got him back, filthy and half-starved, and then all he could talk about was how it was ten years since Hattin, and how the heroes from there should have been remembered."

"It isn't," Gilbert added. "The anniversary was back at the start of July, and it was eleven years ago this year, not ten. He was a year and two months adrift, so I've no idea why it suddenly became so urgent for him."

John took over now. "Since then we've been trying to keep him in the camp. We haven't dared take him back up to Loxley, because from there we won't get the warning from villagers like we do here. He could vanish into the moors from there and die up there, not to mention how long we might waste time searching for him. And to be honest we don't know what he might do with all the weaponry we've got secreted up there. You're not seeing Ed and Colm because we sent them back up to Loxley with Much – we were scared that Robin might forget who they were, being relative newcomers to him, and might attack them. Much went because he was distraught at the way Robin turned on him at the village when you were there. Robin's never stopped being his hero, and to have him call him names and punch him about was more than the lad could stand."

"But we've got to decide what to do," Will said firmly. "This can't go on. If nothing else, winter is coming soon and we need to be able to go back up to Loxley if it looks like the weather's going to turn nasty. Even here we haven't the supplies to see us through a bad spell. But we thought you needed to be in on the decision."

Guy could see what Will meant. They were running out of time in all sorts of ways. Heaving a deep sigh, he said,

"I think 'Robin Hood' has got to die, then. That way we separate our Robin from the outlaw legend, but we also give Briwere what he needs to placate de Neville. I must confess I've been giving this a lot of thought, and the best I can come up with so far is Creswell Crags."

Thomas was the first to ask, "Why the Crags?" although several others said the same.

"Because I think we need to put on a show for the sheriff," Guy explained. "He needs to see it for himself, yet at the same time he mustn't be close enough for him, or any others who are with him, to easily intervene. And the more I've thought about it, the more I think you're going to have to play 'Robin Hood', Siward. It's got to be someone who can throw the hood back, and for the sheriff to see a tall man with thick dark hair who bears a passing resemblance to the man he had in the dungeons. Nothing less will do, and even before you told me all of this, I'd already come to the conclusion that Robin's too far gone to ask him to pretend anything. So someone else has to be Robin Hood in his place."

"Makes perfect sense," Will agreed for the others, who had all been nodding at each of Guy's points. "So what's your plan?"

"Well that's the tricky bit," Guy admitted. "This has to be me acting the forester, you see, because I think I need to 'capture' one of Robin Hood's key men. It has to be plausible, if you follow me, that Robin Hood would expose himself to danger to rescue someone." He gave another sigh. "And I'm afraid it has to come down to you, Allan, or Will. The sheriff knows about Little John, but you aren't handy enough with a sword to look good from a distance, John."

He didn't want to add that John was awful at dissembling, too. There was no way that John would convince anyone that he was lashing out in real anger at Guy.

"And he knows about you, Tuck, but I'm loathed to use you for this for two reasons. God forbid but someone gets hurt for real, we may need your skills, and that's not a chance I'm prepared to take. And the other is that I want to make this fast and furious. I want to be chasing someone at speed up onto that ledge at the top of the crags. Too fast for anyone else to follow."

"Enough said," Tuck laughed, and patted his waistline, which had expanded over the years.

"So that leaves 'Will Scarlet' or 'Allan of the Dales'," Guy concluded. "I don't mind which one of you does it, but you're the ones we can have the others calling your legend names out and be believable – and I don't want someone like you, Bilan, in case in the heat of the moment someone forgets and calls your real name. This has got to be flawless for it to work."

"I'll do it," Will immediately volunteered. "I can work out some sword moves with you to make it look good. And it ought to be someone who can take a beating, just in case something goes wrong and I end up in the dungeon. No offence, Allan, but you're not a big chap, and this ought to be someone who looks like he can menace someone of Guy's size, too."

Guy was glad that Will had said that, because Will was his ideal choice for all of those reasons. "There's one other thing," he added, "and again it's really just in case anything goes horribly wrong. At Creswell we're only a couple of miles west of Welbeck and Abbot Michael's infirmary."

"You are being pessimistic!" Gilbert teased. "Have some faith in us!"

"It's not faith in *you* that's lacking," Guy replied. "It's knowing how bloody unpredictable Briwere can be when he's got his temper up. I can set him up to a point where he can only seem to go one way, but I've learned the hard way that he can suddenly veer off at the most unexpected tangents. This is supposed to be to save lives, not lose them."

"So when do you want to do it?" Piers asked.

"As soon as the leaves fall," Guy responded. "Three or four weeks' time? We need the trees to be well on the way to being bare so that there's a clear view of the rocky edge. Can you keep Robin cooped up for that long?"

"If we have to bloody hog-tie him, we will," John said firmly. "So what can we do in the meantime?"

They mulled it over and eventually decided that if the outlaws kept moving it would help in two ways. Firstly, if they were marching with Robin all day, then he would be tired at night, and also he was unlikely to endanger one of the useful camps by escaping and then leading pursuers back there. But also, Guy wanted 'Robin Hood' to be seen in lots of different parts of the shire.

"I don't want Briwere drawn down on one part of Sherwood because of what he might do," Guy confided. "The folk of Whitwell, Clowne and Elmton near to the Crags don't deserve to be raided by Briwere in a temper because he thinks this is where Robin Hood's gang have been hiding all this time. And if you're here one day and there the next, then we're winding Briwere up like a windlass in the right way. It'll mean that when I come in and say – or maybe send a message from Loxley – that I've heard of where I can waylay Will Scarlet, he'll come running without thinking about it.

"Ideally I want him to have already come galloping out of the castle at least a couple of times before the real event. When he's frustrated he makes mistakes – that's one thing I do know about him. Could you start from the Sandiacre camp? If you can make it look as though you're all gradually heading northwards, then that also will make a confrontation up at the Crags believable even in retrospect. He can never know he's been hoodwinked and that Siward will be 'killed' as Robin Hood."

It was therefore a week later when Guy heard via one of the sergeants who had come up to Loxley from Nottingham, that Robin Hood had been spotted.

"There he was, bold as you like, with a deer across his shoulders, wading through the river!" the man told Guy excitedly. "The villagers at Bramcote sent a message saying they thought they'd seen him in the area, and by St Thomas he was!"

"Did they catch him?" Guy asked enthusiastically. This was ideal. The villagers at Bramcote had been sympathetic to the outlaws for years, so they had obviously been helping, not hindering.

The man's enthusiasm dimmed. "No, not quite. Sir Hermer and Sir Hamon gave chase with two of the mounted sergeants, but he lost them in the bulrushes of the Erewash. The sheriff's happy, though. He thinks we've made the shire uncomfortable for the rogue. He's confident we'll catch him soon."

Guy didn't have to fake saying, "Excellent news!" and meaning it, although for totally different reasons – Briwere was taking the bait.

Three more weeks went by, with four more sightings, and all the while moving crabwise back and forth across the shire, but generally heading northwards. And then, as if all of Guy's prayers were being answered, the leaves started to fall earlier than normal, and within the week a storm came tearing in from the southwest, battering the forest, and ripping leaves down before the full autumn show of colours was done.

Riding out with the excuse that with two knights down he had to do more until they recovered, or replacements were found, Guy made it to the Worksop camp again and was glad to see just Hugh, Allan and Roger there.

"We've got Robin up at the camp by Beighton, ready to move him on," Hugh told Guy. "He's worn out with all of the travelling we've been doing, and he's been quieter this last week or so. So when do you want to do this?"

"The sooner the better," Guy said with feeling. "We can't string Briwere along much longer. Let's go up to the Crags tomorrow and have a look."

To his delight, those trees actually scattered up the cliff of the short run of rough limestone gorge had taken a real beating with the wind, and were nearly bare already. But better still, the river which had carved the gorge out had acted like a funnel for the wind, and the opposite side of it, where Guy wanted the sheriff to be to witness the fake fight, had also lost most of its tree canopy.

"This is ideal!" Guy enthused. "He'll be able to see well, but not perfectly. Can Will and Siward meet me at the abbey the day after tomorrow to plan our fight? I'll send word to the sheriff after then as soon as I can – Richard de Cuckney can make himself useful to us for that!"

And so it was that Sheriff Briwere rode into Cuckney Castle to meet Guy, who was full of how he'd heard that the infamous Will Scarlet was very taken with one of the women in the nearby village of Whitwell – a part admirably played by Mariota. She and Will had twice given the unsuspecting villagers the treat of seeing him pursue her across open ground, and her stand her ground to box his ears the first time, and to seemingly knee him in the groin the second time. They would only need to tell the truth if questioned later, and that was all to the good in Guy's mind. The fewer people they had to lean on to dissemble or outright lie for them, the better.

With the autumn dawn, they got up and began riding up the road which would continue on to Clowne and eventually across into Yorkshire, confident that they would catch this man who seemed to like to try and catch his quarry on her way out to the fields in the morning. Guy could have wished it a little clearer, for as they got up to the minute hamlet of Creswell – little more than a couple of farms and peasant's cotts – there were wisps of mists hanging about. But then half the time the river which lead into the gorge vanished into the limestone, only to reappear again a short way on, so there was water in the air even when there didn't seem to be any pools or streams nearby.

"You know best," he offered up softly to Saints Issui, Cadoc and Melangell, whom he'd been on his knees to for half of the night. If this didn't work, he didn't know what they were going to do for Robin, for the umpteenth time adding, "But please let this work. Let him go to where he can serve you and be healed."

They got to the end of the gorge where a trickle of a stream came out, and there, lobbing stones moodily into the end of the long pool which sat in the bottom of the gorge, was Will. He'd made himself unmistakable, dressed up in the outlaws' green wool and with a sword at his hip and a longbow at his back. And at Briwere's screech of, "There he is! Get him!" Will took off like a scalded cat.

At first Will ran along the wider side of the river, neatly drawing Briwere and all the attendant riders after him along the planned route. But of course they were soon gaining on him, and in a great show of suddenly realising this, Will veered left to wade across the pooled river to the cliff's side. He reached the lowest trees, and Guy, who was at the front of the chase, saw a flicker of red there. They'd left Will a marker, and it was immediately clear why – this was a good climbing route.

As Will began going up the limestone like a mountain goat, one or two of the men-at-arms managed to get their crossbows wound up, and a few bolts were released. Luckily they were all lousy shots and the bolts never got anywhere near Will, but then Guy was off his horse and climbing fast behind him, and he heard someone call for the archers to stop to avoid hitting him.

Then across the crisp morning air Guy heard Briwere calling, "I want that man alive! He's the bait for Robin Hood!" and knew that he was in no danger of getting skewered, too.

At one point Will and Guy had to make use of a tangle of mistletoe on a stunted oak to pull themselves up, and it was as Guy got his foot up onto the next secure hold and pushed off with his other that he heard the creak. Looking over his shoulder worriedly, he saw the big lump of rock he thought he'd skirted, suddenly toppling over to go crashing down the cliff into the path of the four soldiers who'd thought to follow him. They were knocked down to the river once more, and as Guy turned back to focus on climbing he saw Allan's face in the bush rooted in a hollow, and winking as he held up a stout metal bar for Guy to see. They had deliberately planted the rock to be levered down to ensure only Will and he got to the top, and suddenly Guy was enjoying himself again.

Now he climbed with enthusiasm, and getting to the top found Will with drawn sword waiting for him. As Guy rolled out of his way, Will made a nice show of trying to stab at him. Then Guy was on his feet, and he and Will began the intricate dance they had worked out a few days ago. From down below it must have looked good, because there were vigorous shouts of encouragement for Guy coming from those down there, and no-one was trying to come too close to the cliff because they lost their view of this gripping fight when they did.

Back and forth they went, sometimes Guy getting the upper hand, sometimes Will forcing him backwards. At the arranged point, Guy lunged, and Will faked getting stabbed on the side away from the audience, but came back with screams and seeming renewed ferocity. They battered away at one another for a few moments longer, but Will was convincingly faking flagging with his 'wound', and then Guy made the coup de grace. Sliding his sword under Will's arm, he stabbed the bladder of blood Will had concealed there, and his sword appeared on the other side in a spurt of blood. Will had been half turned towards the river to give the best possible view, and now with a wink at Guy, he folded up at the knees and fell to the floor where he lay laughing.

"Stop it, you daft sod," Guy hissed, struggling not to laugh himself, as from within the woodland at the back of the cliffs Siward was heard to scream, "Will!" and then 'Robin Hood' came charging out of the trees, sword drawn.

"You do not kill one of my men!" Siward screamed with all of his might, and was rewarded with cries from down by the river of,

"It's Robin Hood!"

"He's up there!"

"Kill him!"

"Kill him, Gisborne!" and more.

As they began another rehearsed dance, Siward was grinning at Guy, saying,

"Fuck me, it's working!"

"Keep going!" Guy panted. "Dance around me a bit while I catch my breath!"

Siward dutifully circled Guy, making lunges at him which Guy deflected, and then when Guy was ready and gave him the nod, they began to move again. The important thing was to get as far along the cliff as possible, because while the sheriff could send men around to ride up to the cliff tops from the back, he'd been too caught off balance to make that order until now; and even so, if Guy and Siward were in the middle of the cliff, then it would take a goodly time for those men to get to them. And as they crabbed along the cliff top, they were drawing the majority of their audience after them, along to where the pool was that much wider and deeper.

The two fighters had reached a point where there was a good view from below, but also where others of the gang were concealed for the next part of the plot, for the sheriff had to have good reason for there to be no body to retrieve, and that meant the other outlaws turning up to carry their fallen leader away. Another small red tag of cloth stuck in the turf too low to be seen from below signalled that Guy and Siward were in the right spot, and glancing to his left, Guy saw Gilbert, Malik and the Coshams all waiting.

Siward had long since thrown his hood back, and the wind was whipping his long, dark hair around his face, and as he used his free hand to push it back, Guy said, "Ready?"

"Let's do it!"

Siward spun and struck at Guy with his fist, a blow which connected with him, but which Guy rode out having known it was coming. As he fell backwards to choruses of dismay from below,

Siward pretended to advance with sword held high as if to plunge into Guy. And as Siward loomed over Guy, Guy in his turn reared up from the grass with his sword and seemed to run 'Robin Hood' through. Siward staggered back theatrically, clutching Guy's sword so that it appeared stuck through his middle, although in truth it was clamped to his side with his elbow. Dropping to his knees, he toppled over, and a great cheer went up from down by the pool.

And in that moment of complete success it all went horribly wrong.

Out of the trees came the outlaws as planned, bows drawn on Guy who was still prostrate on the grass, while John and Tuck emerged behind him to scoop up Will, Tuck calling out as if in warning,

"No! Robin's dead! Killing the sheriff's man won't bring him back! Leave him or we'll all be hunted down!" and his powerful voice carried clearly to all beneath.

But someone else came thundering out of the trees, screaming like a madman, and jumped onto Guy to begin belabouring him with his fists. As he frantically fought his cousin off, Guy heard Marianne scream,

"Robin, no!"

Later he would hear that it was just good timing that Malik and Gilbert had just lifted up Siward, who was hanging limply in their arms, and so the facade held that Robin Hood had died, but Thomas, Piers and Bilan were behind those three, and with little room to move up on the cliff, couldn't get past them to Guy and Robin. The plan had been that Hugh would stay out of view so that it never occurred to the sheriff that there was more than one tall, well-built, dark-haired man in the gang aside from 'Robin Hood', but he had no choice but to come running now. And even so he was too late, his fingers repeatedly slipping as he tried to grab handful after handful of jerkin as Robin flailed around erratically.

Stumbling to his feet, Guy managed to get free of Robin's fists for a moment, horrified to hear his cousin screaming at him,

"You murdering bastard! You're evil, Gisborne! Evil!"

"Baldwin, for God's sake! It's me!" Guy hissed frantically, but to no effect, the childhood memories were lost for good, and then Robin drew back his fist and hit Guy hard, even as Hugh tried to grab him.

The next thing Guy knew he was falling out into the air. "I'm going to die," he thought, then the world went black as he struck the trunk of one of the cliff-side trees.

Yes, obviously I survived, Brother, but you need not be so superior about it. There were tragic consequences to that day.

I fell, and the tree broke my fall so that I did not drop the full height of the cliff, but I then crashed down through the branches to lie unconscious at the roots, the only things stopping me from falling further. It would take five men to haul me up again, and I knew nothing of it, but I had broken ribs and was lucky not to have suffered worse. Up above me, my friends wrestled Robin back from the cliff and into the trees, and once out of sight, Siward and Will joined the others in running at speed from the scene. Allan and Roger, though, had always been intended to play the part of local villagers who stumbled on the scene, so that we had some inkling of how the ordinary men had seen things. Now Roger played the willing peasant, and was the one who climbed up to me and made sure I fell no further until help came. And they waited until someone came with a cart to carry me away, before slinking off to report back to our friends that I was mercifully still in the land of the living.

I would never speak to my cousin again, so it was from the others that I learned that when they dared stop running they tried to get some sense out of Robin, but he seemed to not understand what they were saying. May God forgive me, Brother, but my clever plan to save Robin's life had had the terrible effect of robbing him of what little sanity he had left. He thought Will was dead, even when Will stood in front of him and shouted at him. And I had ceased to be his cousin at all. I was the sheriff's man, nothing more.

Yes, I am weeping. I am weeping for the soul of a man I loved as a brother. A man who no longer knew what he did. And yet our torment was not over, for I was taken to the very place we had planned on for our own emergencies, Welbeck Abbey.

Chapter 29

Having had to take the long way round, the outlaws did not know that the sheriff had sent me under escort to Welbeck, and when they arrived there with Robin, the soldiers had left to march back to Cuckney and I was in the infirmary being bandaged up. I knew nothing of it, having been given some poppy for the pain and was fuzzy-headed, but apparently Tuck led the way in, saw me, and immediately stopped the others before Robin could see me. Abbot Michael proved himself a good friend to us both then, saying that I should stay in the infirmary since I was no danger to anyone, but that they had a monk's cell where the door could be locked. It had been intended for any brother who needed punishment for being persistently disobedient, but it now ensured that Robin harmed neither himself nor anyone else. It would have been understandable if Abbot Michael had refused to have Robin back again, but my friends said that they would stay to watch him, and would be taking him away within days. All they were waiting for was for Robin to be able to walk unaided, or to find a cart they could take him in.

By the following morning I was awake but in a lot of pain; Robin was still raving; and so while I gratefully attended mass with considerable help, it was thought too dangerous to let Robin out. That situation continued for five more days, during which I came out in the most spectacular bruises which stiffened and made it nigh on impossible for me to attend to the simplest of my needs without assistance. And that was how Sir Henry found me when he rode into the abbey to see how I was doing.

Creswell Crags & Sherwood
Late Autumn, the Year of Our Lord 1198

"By Our Lady, Gisborne, you're a sight!" Sir Henry gulped, as Guy managed to view him balefully from the cushioned seat in a wall recess outside the infirmary, where he was trying to make the most of a sunny morning. By some fluke of fate, the one thing he had managed to avoid was getting black eyes. The rest of his face was a mess, and his jaw was so puffed up and swollen all he could eat was soup, and now he could only grunt in response. "The sheriff said I was to come and escort you back to the castle – Nottingham, that is. You're getting quite the hero's welcome, but I shall have to tell Briwere it will be at least another week before you can return."

The infirmarer coughed discreetly at Sir Henry's elbow and said, "At the very least. We do not know for sure if he bleeds inside. Even the jolting in a cart might do damage – he's only allowed to move a little just to stop him from stiffening up altogether. We know he has at least three broken ribs, but the bruising means we can't tell if one or more of them is in danger of puncturing a lung. So we have to wait for the bruising to go down. I'm sorry, but he cannot possibly travel."

Abbot Michael had told the infirmarer to extend Guy's stay for as long as possible, believing that Guy needed some time in peace after Robin had been led away. It was something Guy had accepted gratefully, and so now he nodded as best he could at the infirmarer's words. Mercifully, Henry decided to return to Cuckney Castle for the night and its more convivial atmosphere – he seemed deeply uncomfortable in the presence of so many monks – and so the outlaws were able to slip back out of the barn, where they had hurriedly hidden when Henry had so unexpectedly arrived.

"We'll take Robin away tomorrow," Tuck announced as he, Hugh, Will and Malik joined Guy in the infirmary to help him eat his soup, his hands being painfully swollen and he found it hard to grasp even the spoon. As Tuck eased another spoonful past Guy's thickened and stiff lips he added. "I think it would be a good thing if he never saw you again. I dread to think what he might do, and while you'll hold back from doing your worst, he won't anymore."

Malik sighed. "It is most tragic," he said regretfully. "He has never had reason to hate you like this, but Tuck is right, he is a danger to you now."

"Who's going to take him?" Guy managed to mumble.

"Me," Will announced, "and Gilbert, John, Allan and Tuck and the Coshams. Ed's coming, too, so that there are nine of us and we can sit watch over him in threes through the nights. Siward's staying in the area in case 'Robin Hood' is suddenly needed, because if he is, then it will be a real emergency – we won't risk it otherwise – but nonetheless we felt we couldn't in all conscience leave the villagers completely defenceless."

"It's going to take quite awhile to get up to one of the Scottish monasteries," Tuck said regretfully, "and more than ever I think it has to be one of them and in a desolate spot too. It won't be the first one we come to, sadly."

"I'm staying as well," Hugh told Guy. "He's become more irrational around me and Marianne for obvious reasons, and those taking him need him to be as quiet as possible on the journey. Roger won't go, not for anything, and neither will Much."

"I would go," Malik declared, "but it is not fair to leave Janah and Khalīl behind, and they have said that they are wary of how they would be received at places of Christian devotion deeper into England, let alone Scotland. They have already had bad experiences of being called Saracens and infidels – oddly more than I did when I first came here. Indeed, I think they may decide to leave. They think that Andalucia may be a safer place for them to live, and Khalīl in particular is wondering whether he might not be able to get some of his family to come and join him there, if it turns out to be a tolerant place."

"We'll miss them both," Will said regretfully. "They're useful lads with a bow and arrow and they're steady. No rushing off in the heat of the moment with them, but this whole business with Robin has badly unsettled them."

"Unsettled everyone," Guy managed to mumble. "Worried m'self what's going to happen." He paused to ease the twinging of his facial bruises. "Can't see Fredegis coming back to Laxton. Not with that shoulder. ...Bet Walkelin won't come without him, even if he's fit enough." He winced again. "Bollocks! All that effort to make 'em 'fraid of the forest gone to waste!"

Will gently patted the bit of Guy's arm where he couldn't see bruises. "*Naah*, not gone to waste, mate. We'd never thought of turning the forest itself on men like him until then. It was a bloody marvellous idea of yours, that! And now we know what works, we can always use it again. Let's face it, Briwere won't risk sending you some totally new blokes. He still loathes the sight of you, even though you're a hero at the moment, so he won't risk you 'infecting' some virgin knight with your strange ideas and rebellious attitudes. He'll send some of the existing knights over, and you've long said they aren't the sharpest knives in the armoury!"

"*Ouch*! *Owww*! Oh, don't m'ke me laugh!" Guy pleaded, but giving Will a grateful glance. He was right about how Briwere would react, and that was one worry less for Guy. What worked on Fredegis and Walkelin would also work on the likes of Mahel. This was a setback, not a disaster.

Come the morning, Guy determinedly got up from his sick bed to go and see Robin off. He made sure he stayed out of his cousin's line of sight, but he, John and Allan shared a gently cousinly hug in their misery, and he knew he had to make a show of support with them for what they had to do.

Allan in particular was deeply affected, grasping both Guy and John's hands and saying, "I don't think until now I fully understood the pain you suffered on my account all those years ago when you took me up to York and made me leave. If I've never said it before, I'm saying it now: I'm sorry. I'm so sorry I put you two through all that."

"At least you came back to us," John said through tears. "The Baldwin we knew and loved is gone forever. I know this sounds dreadful, but I almost wish he'd died out in the east. Wish he'd died with that king he loved so much. I'd have given anything to save him from all this pain."

Forcing himself to speak, though his bruising had eased somewhat this morning, Guy pulled John to him as best he could, saying, "I know what you mean, John, but I think you're wrong. The crusade took a terrible toll on him, that's true. But look at Siward. Remember what a mess he was when he got here? I know he still has nightmares, and at times it's tough for him, but he made choices, choices Robin could have made too. And this crazy way he's behaved towards me – that was a choice. He resisted growing up just like you did, Allan, but when the world showed you how things had changed, you chose to change. Robin chose to stay frozen in that time.

"He could have had Marianne. He could have been friends with me as man to man – different to when we were boys, yes, but then at our ages it ought to have been." He stopped, panting a little with the pain from the effort, but was glad to see that John's tears had dried and he was just nodding sadly now.

"You're right," John said mournfully. "Robin's resisted every effort to help him. Some men seem to do that, don't they? Change out of all recognition? You look back at the boy and wonder where on earth he went to in the man? The you I knew, I can still see, and you, Allan, but Baldwin? No, nothing remains."

Gilbert and Piers came out of the cloisters with Robin between them, and Guy was appalled to see how pale and haggard he looked. It was because of that, he realised later on, that his friends' grip on Robin wasn't as firm as it should have been. As his head came up and he blinked to look about him, Robin suddenly spied Hugh with his arms around a sobbing Marianne.

With a scream of rage, Robin wrenched himself free, snatching the knife from Piers' belt at the same time, and launched himself at Hugh screaming, "Take my wife, would you, you bastard?" And as he lifted his arm to strike at Hugh as he covered the distance between them, he shocked everyone with the cry of, "You take everything from me, Gisborne! Everything!"

Hugh spun Marianne out of the way of the wildly slashing knife, then cried out in pain as one of Robin's more energetic swings connected with his arm.

"Robin! No!" Marianne screamed, battering at him with her fists to no avail.

As the next closest, Janah and Khalīl tried to grapple with Robin, but his madness leant him strength, and he repeatedly threw them off, but then wheeled and with a mighty slash opened up Khalīl's throat. As Janah howled in distress and caught his brother-in-law in his arms as he fell, Malik struggled to reach over them and grab Robin, but he was just too far away, and Malik's fingers slipped off his now blood-soaked tunic.

And then Robin's mind flipped direction and he was off sprinting across the abbey's outer precinct to where a couple of journeymen were about to mount up after a night spent in the guest house. Snatching the reins of a horse from one of them, Robin was up on its back before anyone could stop him, and digging his heels into its side, thundered out through the gateway.

Somewhere deep inside Guy, he of anyone had half been expecting something to happen, and so he recovered the fastest. It helped that he, John and Allan had been standing close to the horses, and so he didn't have to run more than a couple of steps. With a howl of pain as his ribs and bruises protested, nonetheless Guy hauled himself onto the second horse, and reaching out to snatch the bow and quiver Allan had left resting on a nearby cart, heeled his horse into pursuit. The cries of his friends resonated from behind him, but all Guy could think was that he must not let Robin get away. All plans to aid his cousin were gone now. This lunatic was a danger to everyone who crossed his path, and Guy clenched his teeth against the pain and rode on.

Why Robin made for Creswell Crags again nobody ever really knew. If there was a reason other than being close by, it was in his head alone, but Guy was grateful that it wasn't further.

Beyond the abbey, Robin took the north side of the Milwood Brook which ran out of the gorge and which, after making a northerly loop, would come to run past the abbey itself. In no time, he was beginning the ascent which would take him to the top of the limestone cliff of the Crags, today shining whitely in the late autumn sunshine with a light dusting of frost, and Guy wondered what on earth his cousin's purpose could be going back there.

Was it him returning to the place where he thought Will and Siward had died? If that was so, then Guy was struck with guilt. He had never intended to wound his fragile cousin that deeply, and he eased his horse's pace a little in order to hang back. If Robin dismounted and fell on the spot of the faked deaths weeping, then Guy would not approach him. He'd wait for the others to come and help. Only if Robin rode on would he pursue him, although what he would do then he didn't know.

Robin did dismount, but he then walked towards the cliff edge, and Guy risked getting closer to hear what he was crying out.

"Leave me alone!" he heard Robin sob. "All of you, go away!" He batted at thin air, as if striking at someone only he could see. "Stop it! No, get away from me Martin ...and you Simon! And you ...and you ...and you! Why do you haunt me? ...You chose to come with me. I'm not to blame. ...No, I'm not!"

A cold shiver ran down Guy's spine as he almost lay across the saddle to try and ease the agony in his ribs. Martin and Simon? Blessed St Issui, were the shades of those whose deaths he had caused haunting him?

"God forgive you, Robin," Guy hissed painfully, as the realisation came upon him that his cousin had yet to repent for those he had led to ruin. And now it might be too late. Could Robin make a last confession in his current state? Guy feared not. Not only could he not recollect anything clearly enough, but who was there to hear him?

Frantically forcing himself to twist and look over his shoulder, despite the pain it caused, Guy saw some of his friends galloping on a motley collection of hurriedly seized mounts up the valley towards him, but Tuck wasn't amongst them. And then turning back to Robin, Guy was horrified to see his cousin staggering towards the cliff edge, sobbing, "I can't take this anymore. ...It's too much. ...It's too much."

"Baldwin?" Guy screamed, as he realised his cousin meant to throw himself over the edge. "Noooo!"

Suicide was a mortal sin, punished by an eternity in Hell. He would not let that happen.

No, it must not happen. Not to Baldwin.

Not that on top of all his other sins.

He had to all intents and purposes murdered others through his sin of excessive pride, but to condemn his own soul for eternity? No, not even now did Robin deserve that – or was it Baldwin? Had his cousin returned at this last?

As he saw Robin pick up his pace for the last couple of strides and then launch himself off and out into space, Guy didn't think. Instinctively he seized an arrow and had it nocked in the bow, in his panic oblivious to the agony it caused him. And with the flight brushing his cheek, Guy had aimed and let fly before Robin had vanished from view.

Then his own wounds took over and the blackness came. Yet even as he fainted from the searing pain, he was sure he heard a twin tortured scream to his own and knew he had succeeded. He had saved Baldwin's soul even if he had condemned his own for the murder.

When he came to yet again he was back in the familiar surroundings of Welbeck Abbey, and for a moment he thought – indeed prayed – that Robin's death had all been a terrible nightmare. Then he blinked and saw Tuck's familiar figure sitting beside him. He blinked again, and as his vision cleared he realised that Tuck's eyes were red from crying, and he knew that it had been no dream.

Tuck was looking up at the wooden cross above Guy's bed, and Guy realised that he wasn't aware that he'd woken, because Tuck's lips were moving silently in prayer.

"I had to do it," Guy managed to croak. "Couldn't let it happen. ...Couldn't let him be damned as a suicide ...not even after everything."

"Oh my dear *brawd*," Tuck sniffed, immediately focusing on Guy. "Your heart is too big sometimes." He gently took Guy's nearest hand in both of his, his lips quivering with emotion, too overcome for a moment to speak. With a big sniff he managed to compose himself enough to say, "Will thought it might have been that."

"Ah, I was right, then," Will's gruff voice came from the door, and the big smith eased his way in clutching a bowl and spoon. "More soup for you, I'm afraid, Guy, at least until the infirmarer and this one here decide you're safe to eat solids. Me, I'd give you the best cut of meat we could find in this place, but I suppose you wouldn't be able to chew it anyway."

"No," Guy agreed with the closest thing he could manage in the way of a smile. "Is he...?" He couldn't force himself to ask outright, 'Is Robin dead?' especially when it would now be at his own hand.

Will came around to Guy's other side and pulled up a stool. "Yes. ...Oh don't look at me like that, Tuck. He deserves the truth. Yes, Guy, he was definitely dead when we pulled his body out of the pool, but your arrow took him through the throat. His head was crushed by the impact, 'cause that pool's not deep enough for the water to cushion anything falling that far and fast. But he was dead when he hit the rocky bottom. You saved him from that agony and ...well, you know, ...the other thing."

"At the risk of your own soul," Tuck said with a huge sigh.

"You need one of your own sermons," Will said affectionately, reaching over Guy to grab Tuck's arm and give it a squeeze. "Robin had already stepped into the void. I saw that beyond doubt. His death wasn't preventable by then, not in any way. In my mind that means that his death was inevitable and that what Guy did wasn't murder. Morally, surely you can't murder a man who an instant later was going to be dead anyway? Dead beyond any shadow of a doubt ...and with that death only a heartbeat or two away?

"And what have you always said to us? God sees not just the deed, but the intention behind it? Well now you need to believe that He will have seen Guy's intentions. He will see it as the act of love it was, and if he doesn't, then those saints you keep having cosy chats with will surely intercede for Guy in this instance."

"I prayed to them," Guy croaked hoarsely, realising his throat must be so sore from screaming in pain. "Time and again, Tuck, I prayed to them that Baldwin could go to somewhere quiet and live out his days in service of them. I don't know why they didn't answer me this time."

Will patted his hand. "Maybe because they knew Robin had gone far beyond that point. If they see all things, even into someone's heart, then wouldn't they know if Robin was beyond men to save? And think of what he might have done if we'd have left him with some unsuspecting brothers, eh?

"How would we all feel if in a few weeks' time, we'd heard of all the monks in some little monastery being killed by a madman? We'd never have forgiven ourselves, would we? No, Tuck, in some strange way maybe things have worked out the only halfway good way they could. Your saints may have answered our prayers after all. It's just our pain that stops us from seeing it that way."

Tuck gave another big sigh, then shook himself like a huge dog coming up out of water. "*Duw*, but you're right, Will! I should have more faith myself. I should trust in God and the saints over this. But it's shaken me as a man more than I cared to admit. I feel so guilty that I couldn't reach him in this last year or two." Then as Will started to say,

"Give it a rest, T..." added,

"But They must have seen that he was beyond mortal man to cure. Yes, you're right, They would know what we couldn't. ...may *Dewi Sant* intercede for him. *Dduw drugarhau arnom* ...God have mercy upon us ...on all of us. Robin was in danger of dragging us all to perdition."

"And surely He saw it," Will said reassuringly, with another pat on the big Welsh monk's arm. "Maybe it was Him who guided Guy's aim in those last breaths – because I for one don't know how he managed to make that last shot with his ribs in the state he's in. He shouldn't have been able to draw that bow, not even with it being Allan's, much less loose that arrow with such accuracy. To me he was half in a faint from the pain as the arrow left the bow.

"I couldn't believe it when we finally got down to the pool and it was red with blood, and we realized there was an arrow straight through that big blood vessel in Robin's neck. I honestly thought we'd find it had just nicked his shoulder, or something, not killed him. That arrow was divinely guided or my name's not William Scathlock. And I won't apologize for going to Guy first, because I was worried sick that he'd damaged his ribs even further when he slid from the saddle. Robin, I knew, couldn't have survived that fall, and I chose to see to the living first."

"Thank you," Guy said gratefully.

"No," Will said with a shake of his head. "You deserved my help. Robin didn't. Have you told him, Tuck?" The monk shook his head mournfully, making Will groan, "*Awww*, sod it. ...I'm sorry, Guy, but Khalīl's dead too. He died here in the abbey."

"*Nooo!*"

"Yes. I'm afraid that Robin sliced his wind pipe open. Poor Janah's distraught. That's why Malik isn't here. He wanted to come, but he's been helping Abbot Michael to arrange for a funeral in the eastern tradition for Khalīl. Gilbert and Siward have been helping him, although they've all been sticking their heads around the door every so often to see if you were awake yet."

"Hugh?" Guy asked with sinking heart, as the memories came back.

"Oh he's fine," Will said, but with obvious relief. "It's a nasty slash, and it's going to take time to heal, but Marianne's taken a very personal interest in his care, as you'd imagine, and he'll make a full recovery."

"Good!" Guy couldn't imagine how the gang would have recovered from losing a third person they'd cared about, even if one of those had been the cause of the others' deaths.

Over the course of that evening, all of Guy's friends came in to see him, and he learned that they would be burying Khalīl in the monk's graveyard the next day. Yet when the morning came, Guy could not get out of bed. His body had decided enough was enough, no matter what his head and heart wanted. And so he lay in bed and wept as he listened to the strains of the monks' chanting drifting across the cloister from the funeral going on in the church.

Later on Janah and Malik came to sit with Guy for a while.

"I shall stay now," Janah told Guy. "Khalīl was the one who wanted to bring his wife and my sister and her husband – his brother – to join us somewhere. I miss them deeply, but I can see that without us there, they are probably just as safe staying at home. I never did like this idea that we would be safe amongst the Moors in Andalucia. Khalīl had heard they were more tolerant, but I always had my doubts about how they would view Christian Arabs."

Malik smiled, although Guy could see how his eyes were still sad. "I am glad you're staying," he said. "I had not realized how much it meant to me to have someone I could talk to about home. ...And without R... without *him* here, things will be simpler. Quieter. At least in camp, anyway. And Marianne and Hugh can stay now."

"Stay?" Guy was horrified. "I didn't know they were leaving!"

Malik gave one of his half-shrugs. "How could they stay? Hugh said to me – well, to us, actually – that he and Marianne couldn't live with Ro... *him* constantly looking daggers at them. It was robbing them of their joy at being together, and Marianne had had a premonition that one day he would lash out at Hugh."

"Well I'm very glad you're all staying," Guy said as firmly as he could. "I think you're all going to need one another for a while."

It was only the next day that it occurred to him that no-one had spoken of Robin's funeral.

"Where is he?" he asked Will when he next came. Of everyone, Will seemed to be taking the most pragmatic view of things, and while he was sad, he was the one who already looked as though a heavy burden had been lifted off him.

Will shook his head in wonder. "Of all people, you ought to be the one least involved in such decisions. But I'm very glad to have someone to talk it over with sensibly. I've tried to work round to it with Tuck, but for once he's too badly affected as yet to think straight. ...As to where the body is, we wrapped him in his cloak and piled stones over him to keep the animals off. Thank Heaven it's got bitterly cold these last few days, but we can't leave him there indefinitely."

"I don't think we can ask Abbot Michael to let him rest here."

"No, not after what he did to Khalīl. A murderer in the abbey graveyard wouldn't go down well."

Guy grimaced. "We really owe Abbot Michael several favours over this. I can't imagine how his brothers have coped with so much chaos and violence. Some of them must have taken to this life to get away from such things, not have them stuffed in their faces again."

He thought a moment longer. "I hate to ask this of her, but the only place where I can think we'd stand even a chance of getting Robin buried on sanctified ground, is up with my mother at Kirklees. Half of me doesn't want to ask her, not least because of how much it will distress her to tell her the truth. And we will have to tell her the truth, because otherwise she'll wonder why he can't be buried here. But the other half is saying there's no other choice left to us."

As he stopped and looked Will in the face again, he thought for a moment he must be oozing blood or something, because there was an expression of such intense pity on Will's face.

"Will? What's wrong?"

His voice thick with emotion, Will answered, "He didn't deserve you for a cousin. Not that I think he deserved all the second chances Allan and John gave him. But you? You took the brunt of all of his accusations and bitterness, and yet after all of that, here you are, still worrying about whether he'll be buried on sanctified ground or not. I'm not sure I'd be as charitable to any cousin of mine who'd put me through all of that. You're a better man than you give yourself credit for, Guy."

Guy gave a wry smile. "I'm not sure 'good' is the right word – 'daft' is probably closer to it – but thank you anyway. However, much as I feel I ought to be the one to take on the burden of telling my mother, having volunteered her for this, there's no way I can ride up to Kirklees, and anyway, I ought to be here in case someone from the sheriff comes to see how I am. So could you go and ask Allan to come and see me?"

Will squeezed his hand. "I'll do better than that – I'll go and get Allan and Roger. The lads from the camp rolled in last night. Rumours had reached them of Robin Hood's death, and they thought it sounded as though our plan had gone badly astray and were worried."

By the time Guy had explained things to Allan and Roger, and they had agreed to go to Kirkless, Will had evidently told the others of what Guy was proposing and soon several of the others were crammed into his tiny cell, and the rest were in the corridor outside listening in. Marianne and Mariota offered to go with Allan, saying that they now had a firm friendship with Prioress Marion, which of course meant that Hugh would go, too. Tuck said he would go as well, but for once all the others put their foot down and said no.

"You need some time for yourself here with Abbot Michael," Siward said firmly. "You act as confessor for all of us, so you're long due some time to soothe your soul."

"He's right," came Gilbert's voice from outside, his flame-red hair a bright patch in the dark of the corridor. "Let the lasses and Allan do the news breaking. They know this lady the best, so it will come better from them than anyone other than Guy – although how there's a 'better' in any of this, I don't know."

What Guy hadn't dared say to any of them was that there was little chance of him being able to attend Robin's funeral, even if his mother said yes. The same problem over the sheriff applied, and Guy had been very careful to keep any suggestion of who his mother was from the sheriff. Briwere was too volatile, too unpredictable and too prone to exacting revenge against Guy for misdemeanours only he saw, to risk that. He would never forgive himself if a future wrong move by himself rebounded onto her and the nuns with her. But that meant that he had no excuse for going north either.

With that in mind, as soon as he was able to rise from his bed and walk by himself, he went to find Abbot Michael.

Having explained what he'd been thinking, he said, "I'm sorry, but because of that, I need to ask your help. Please will you persuade my friends not to delay Robin's funeral for me? I intend to be gone from here and back at the castle by the time Allan gets back, and they go to retrieve Robin's body. I know that they'll try to pressure me into going with them, and my heart would say yes. But lying in bed I've had a lot of time to think, and I reckon that there is still much good we can do for the folk of the forest, because I think you and I know that life is not going to get any easier for any of us in the near future.

"Whether we revive 'Robin Hood' as the Hooded Man is a whole different matter. But people like Will and Gilbert and Malik have nowhere else to go but back up to Loxley. Had Robin effectively forced Hugh out, and therefore Marianne and with her Mariota; and if Janah and Khalīl had left as planned – maybe even taking Malik with them – then I don't think the gang could have survived in its existing form. But in a strange way, everything has turned out in a way that they will all still want to be together."

They were standing in front of the high altar in the abbey church, and as Guy was finishing speaking, a shaft of sunlight came through one of the high clerestory windows and shone straight onto the altar.

"I think you have your blessing for that," Michael said with a smile. "It's rare we ever have sunshine do that, and it always seems portentous. And before you go, come and see me and we will partake of mass together. I feel compelled to offer you that, and when I get such a strong sense of what would be the right thing to do, I've come to realise that it's because I'm being guided by a higher authority to do it."

"And I'll gratefully accept," Guy thanked him.

Four days later he heaved himself into the saddle of his horse and set off back to Nottingham, lighter in spirit if still sore and stiff. Not by himself, though. Will, Siward, Gilbert and Malik wouldn't hear of him going alone, and said that they would come and walk alongside him until he was right at the town. At first Guy thought that Malik was coming to have a little breathing space from Janah's grief, but as they made camp at Inkersall it turned out to be for something completely different.

"We need a new leader," Malik broached the subject after they'd eaten. "We've not said anything to the others yet. We'll wait until we have Robin properly buried for that."

"Aye," Gilbert said firmly, "and you should know that we have a wee deserted chapel up on the moors in mind if your mother says no. Looks like it was some hermit's cell, once upon a time, but it has stout flagstones for a floor, and if we lift them and put him beneath, he won't be dug up by foxes or whatever. But Malik's right – we need to start thinking how we're going to carry on in the future. Someone has to have the last word."

"And we'd like that person to be you," Siward said cautiously.

Without hesitation Guy said, "No. No, I'm sorry, I can't." He saw the disappointment on all of their faces and felt rotten. "Look, if this had happened some other way, then I'd probably have said yes, alright? But if I take Robin's place now, then I shall always feel that he'll be looking down on me and saying, 'so you did want to lead, after all! You did want my place!' And I can't live with that. If, in a couple of years' time, whoever you choose decides that they've had enough and wants to step down, then if you want to ask me again the answer might be very different. But not now. Not after what's just happened."

"I told you he'd say that," Will said sadly.

"But we had to try," Malik countered.

"Yes we did," Will agreed, but now turned back to Guy. "But having said 'no', have you any idea of how we can do this thing where some of the quieter members of the gang, like Ed and Much, will feel that they can have their say?"

Guy could see what he meant. The younger ones like Bilan, Ed and Much had every bit as much of a right to choose, but would find it hard to go against what someone like Will or Gilbert said, and John would probably feel it disloyal to say he wanted anyone at all so close to Robin's death. Yet these four were right. Time would not stand still while they made up their minds, and who knew when the next crisis might happen?

It took until halfway through the next day for Guy to come up with what he thought was the right answer. "While I don't like to ask Abbot Michael for any more favours," he began, "I think that in this case he might see why you are asking for his help. If you go to him and tell him that under the seal of the confessional, you would like each of the gang to come to him and tell him who they would like as the leader, and also as the second-in-command, then there's no comeback on anyone.

"And that's the reason why I wouldn't want Tuck to do this. If something goes wrong in the future, I don't want him to be confronted by any group within the gang saying that if he hadn't thrown the vote one way or the other, then things would be different. Tuck needs to be able to have his say just like the rest of you without carrying any additional burden.

"When everyone's had their say, the abbot can reveal who had the most votes for each. With luck it will be conclusive, but if not, then work out who had the most votes overall. So for instance, if you, Malik, get as many votes to be leader as second-in-command, you might have more votes overall than say Thomas might have to just be leader; or maybe Hugh might have to be second, if neither of them have many votes for the other's position. It might get tricky if you have three or four of you with very close numbers, and at worst you may need to go for another vote between just the closest contenders, but at least this way it's fair."

"I think that's a great idea," Siward immediately agreed. "Absolutely no way we can know who voted which way, so there'll be no hard feelings to take back to Loxley with us. And I think we need to do it before we leave for Kirkless or the chapel. Everyone will be at Welbeck by that time," for the Coshams had gone north to fetch Aneirin and Rhys, "and we can have it all sorted out fairly."

Riding back into the castle at Nottingham alone was the loneliest feeling Guy had ever had, but if he thought his return would go unnoticed he was mistaken. No sooner had he passed through the gate of the outer bailey than he heard someone calling to others that he had returned, and Harry and the grooms came running to greet him before he'd got near to the stables.

"Guy? Are you alright?" Harry asked anxiously, for he alone knew of the connection between Robin and Guy.

"No, not really," Guy confessed, "but it all went out of my control, Harry. He went mad. He just went completely mad."

Everyone else had by now heard of the attack on Guy by the madman, and thought he was just referring to that. Only Harry grasped the full import of what Guy was saying and looked suitably horrified.

Then as Guy hobbled painfully into the great hall, he was taken aback to find the other knights coming streaming into it to greet him, and a spontaneous clapping and cheering start up.

Blinking in amazement, he made his way up to where Briwere was sat in his normal place behind his heavy carved oak table.

"You took your time getting back," Briwere said, but for once the words contained no malice, and he was as near to smiling at him as Guy had ever seen. "I knew you had your uses, Gisborne, but in killing Robin Hood you truly excelled yourself."

How did I feel about being so congratulated? Sick, Brother. Sick as a dog, but I could not show it. All I wanted to do was sink to my knees and mourn my lost cousin, but had I done that, then all of our efforts to convince the sheriff that the legend had died would have been for nothing. And I felt deep in my heart that we all needed some breathing space by now. With the famous outlaw dead, Briwere would focus his venom elsewhere for a while, and that took pressure off me to be forever listening out for some scheme of his to trap the Hooded Man, but also off my friends from being hunted.

What I had not begun to appreciate was that Briwere had called upon all of those knights who had been with us on that day, to add their names to a report sent to the new chief royal forester, witnessing the fact that the notorious outlaw had been killed by one of his own men. I confess I thought it a little heavy-handed, Briwere maybe crowing just a little too hard, when I first heard of this. But then Martin and Walter had me come to their room, and told me that our dreaded new chief forester had written to Briwere saying that he had heard of this Robin Hood, and that if Briwere could not deal with him, then fitz Neville would bring a force of his own down to Sherwood to deal with him.

Later on fitz Neville would learn the folly of such a boast, but having barely got his hands on the office, he did not know better yet. That letter had been waiting for Briwere when he had returned without me, and so my standing had trebled or quadrupled for saving Briwere from such ignominy. I never had any illusions that such favour would last – I knew Briwere too well by now to ever think that – but again, it was a respite which I was grateful to have.

And what of my fellow knights, you ask? Did Fredegis and Walkelin ever come back to Laxton with me? No, Gervase, they did not. Fredegis was crippled for life by that arrow of Robin's, and he would suffer pain with it every time it turned really wet – which in our part of the world is an awful lot of the time!

At times I would feel very sorry for him, and think that, pain in the neck though he had been, he had not deserved that. Other times, though, I would remember the dozens of people he had terrorised and caused pain and anguish to, and his punishment seemed to fit his crimes. As for Walkelin, he did make a recovery if not much more so, but I admit that it was now that I realised just how much older than me they were, and both men were reaching a point where they would have had to retire in a few years anyway. So it was no surprise to have them announce that they would be leaving the sheriff's service.

I had often wondered whether, when this time came, they would return to their native Flanders, but when Sir Martin expressed the same thought, they both said that things had changed too much over there for them to be able to return. I did wonder, maybe uncharitably, if they had made too many enemies over there before coming to England, and now feared being there as weak, old men. Fear of retribution might have played a large part in their decision, and that was emphasised to me by them deciding to purchase a house in a small town down on the Kentish coast well away from Sherwood, too, although the name they said meant nothing to me, and so I have not remembered it. All you need to know, though, Brother, is that they were gone by Christmas and I never saw them again, although word would sometimes come back to the castle.

As for Sir Henry, some of his fire went out when those two went, and he actually asked Briwere if he could maybe exchange roles with one of the castle knights so that he could remain in Nottingham more often. He pleaded that his old wounds were starting to play him up, but I felt that he had become genuinely too frightened to go out into the forest. Well Briwere would not break up the successful team he had in Sirs Robert, Richard and Hugh, and so he decided that Sir Henry would be put in charge of the Nottingham town goal. It certainly needed someone with a strong hand there, because the congestion was not improving, nor likely to, but Henry was not the man for that job as you will hear tomorrow when we begin again.

But you want to hear of Robin's funeral at this late hour, and I shall not deny you, for I shall sleep a little better if I have come fully to the end of this part of my life story. My dear, beloved mother could not turn Robin away in death any more than she would have done in life, and so a week after I returned to Nottingham, the rest of my friends set off with a borrowed cart from Abbot Michael and reclaimed the ruined body of my cousin. They told me later of what a trial that journey was, and I fear I gave thanks for not having had to undertake it. Time had not done much for the state of Robin's corpse, and they had to exchange drivers frequently as each of them became queasy from the stench of him, but God bless them, they stuck at it and got him up to Kirklees.

Out of consideration for the nuns, I am told that Will, Siward, Malik and Gilbert kept watch over him out in the woods on the night they arrived, while the others dug like moles to have a grave deep and ready for him for the first crack of dawn. With the late dawn of winter coming as the sisters rose to celebrate Prime, Tuck found himself conducting Robin's funeral while they could hear the sisters singing behind them in the church, and they all said that it was strangely comforting to know that he would lie where he would hear nothing but the religious life he had so craved.

My mother came out and joined them, and wept for her sister's son who had come to such ruin, and my friends were kind enough not to tell her that it was my arrow which had ended his life, instead telling her that a soldier's arrow had done for him. Yes, it was a lie, Gervase, but one done only out of a desire to save her the suffering I had gone through. And yes, he lies there still. That is the Robin Hood who is buried at Kirkless which the rumours speak of, though only I know where exactly.

Just before Christmas I would manage to make the journey up to Kirklees alone, and my mother and I went out to that grave and said prayers of our own there, and I planted a small sapling over him, for we dared give him no other marker. But I confess to you that I felt a strange relief at knowing that he was now past all of his earthly torments. He could do nothing more to imperil his immortal soul now, and if he was having to atone for what he had done, at least the list would now not grow longer.

Now I must away to my bed, Gervase, for I am exhausted by these memories, but I know you want the answer to just one last question before we part for the night – who replaced Robin?

My friends did make use of my suggestion, but before they went to the cloister one by one to tell Abbot Michael who they wanted, the four former crusaders and Tuck sat everyone down and told them that whoever they chose, whoever led would not necessarily be the one who wore the Hood. ˜We have seen the burden being the leader and the legend brings,˜ Tuck told them solemnly, ˜and we will never ask that of just one man again.˜

Therefore John and Tuck would share wearing the stag's mantle and hood when an appearance was needed, with Gilbert in reserve, for with age Gilbert had begun to bulk up, too, and like Tuck and John, had both the height and the width of shoulders for the job. On the other hand, if ˜Robin Hood˜ needed to appear and actually speak, then that role would be taken up by Siward and Hugh, since both of them had local accents. It was that more than their physical resemblance to Robin which prompted that choice, but it played no small part in resurrecting Robin's name amongst the ordinary folk – if Sheriff Briwere believed he had killed his nemesis, the people did not. However, it was lost on none of us that those two were the ones, along with Robin and myself, who had first played the part all those years ago back at Cuckney Castle. How fate toys with us, Gervase, given that ˜Robin Hood˜ had his conception and death so close to that same place!

Yet now it was time to elect a leader for the outlaws, and that was a different matter altogether. Tuck said that they must think about who would make wise decisions in hard times, who had the sense to take advice when needed, but whom they would trust to lead them into a fight. It was no small request to make of anyone, and for that reason Tuck also asked if anyone felt strongly enough about the matter to refuse either role if elected, they should say so now. It was therefore no surprise when Hugh spoke up and said that while he would happily support someone else as leader in the role of second, should he be asked, for the same reasons I had declined, he too felt he could not step into Robin's shoes just at this time. He and Marianne would wed at Yule up at Loxley, with all agreeing that they need wait no longer, but there was still that sadness lingering over how Robin had taken the news, and that coloured how Hugh felt about leading.

So my friends all trooped through to Abbot Michael, and when the bell came for the evening meal, the outlaws had a new leader. It had been close, Abbot Michael said, but Siward was definitely the overall top choice, and I for one was delighted when the news reached me. Siward was intelligent and an experienced fighter, but was very good at seeing where everyone's strengths were. Hugh, Will and Malik had all come very close to being voted in as second, Abbot Michael told them truthfully, but what had tipped the balance Hugh's way was two things. Malik was thought, perhaps, to not have quite the local knowledge needed in some people's view, even though they thought him the best man for the job; and Will was thought to be just that bit to impulsive and fiery – a criticism I know he did not take kindly to at the time, but did come to accept. Therefore when the outlaws would emerge from their winter hideout, it would be with Siward at their head, and Hugh at his side.

I think we all thought that as the year turned past Yule they would be in demand again, for we all believed that in his folly, King Richard would demand yet another carucage at his Easter court, despite anything the reinstated Hubert Walter said. None of us remotely foresaw that by the time ˜Robin Hood˜ reappeared, that the king would have died in Normandy, and that his pestilent younger brother would have ascended the throne. We have come to the close of Robin Hood's time as the people's champion during King Richard's trying reign, but the legend would have his work cut out during King John's!

THE END

Thank you for taking the time to read this book. Before you move on to the notes which give you a bit of background to the story, I would like to invite to to join my mailing list. I promise I won't bombard you with endless emails, but I would like to be able to let you know when any new books come out, or of any special offers I have on the existing ones.

Simply go to my website www.ljhutton.com and follow the links. You will be offered two free eBooks as well.

Also, if you've enjoyed this book you personally (yes, *you*) can make a big difference to what happens next.

Reviews are one of the best ways to get other people to discover my books. I'm an independent author, so I don't have a publisher paying big bucks to spread the word or arrange huge promos in bookstore chains, there's just me and my computer.

But I have something that's actually better than all that corporate money – it's you, my enthusiastic readers. Honest reviews help bring them to the attention of other readers better than anything else (although if you think something needs fixing I would really like you to tell me first). So if you've enjoyed this book, it would mean a great deal to me if you would spend a couple of minutes posting a review on the site where you purchased it.

Thank you so much.

Historical Notes

I debated long and hard over whether to try and use the place names as they would originally have been in this era, as Bernard Cornwell has done so well with Utred's story in the Anglo-Saxon era. However, he had fewer to contend with than I have, and when writing about villages within the confines of just two shires, I felt it was better for people to have a real sense of where things were happening. There was also the problem of evolving names, and while we have Domesday to refer to, by now Guy is more than a century on from there, and things have changed, some places being beyond their first Anglo-Saxon names, but not yet at their modern ones. So for everyone's sanity, I deliberately chose to stick with the modern names, and you can find most of them on any decent map of the area. As I said back at the start: all the locations are real, and though Sherwood Forest is now only a tiny fraction of the size it once was, you can still visit these places. The creation of the Shire Wood was dealt with back at the start of this series, but to briefly recap, it really was created with the intention of providing a home and revenue from lands for the youngest of King Henry and Queen Eleanor's brood – the future King John.

There is no consensus on how to spell William Briwere's name, and in contemporary documents the spellings vary even within such documents as the Pipe Rolls. Some have translated his name as straightforward 'Brewer'. However I did not want to use this variant as it seemed bound to cause confusion with lower ranking Englishmen whose craft-based surname was Brewer. Other variations on William's surname are Brewere, Briwerre, and the one I have chosen to consistently use, Briwere. It's impossible to say which of these variants could be regarded as the 'correct' one, especially from an age when spelling was rarely regularised, so it's rather a case of 'take your pick'.

It's actually true that he never again held onto a shire for as long as he did Notts & Derby, and beyond his time there, you see him acting as sheriff of various shires, but none of those offices lasting into years. The men of the West Country really did pay the king to have him removed, and he was gone within the year of his appointment, so he was clearly an unpleasant character even to men used to the brutality of the normal Norman lords. He also shows up briefly in places such as Hampshire and Oxfordshire again, but never for long, almost seeming to be taking a caretaking role rather than being the new appointee to the sheriffdom. You have to wonder what happened that such a useful sheriff would not be used by King John to the same extent as he had been by King Richard, and this was ripe for picking for Robin Hood. However, his downfall will come in the next book!

As for the king's brother, John, he had fled England at the time of the siege at Nottingham, and he was not to set foot in England again until he came back as king. That does not mean that he didn't play any part in English politics, because he certainly had control over certain lands and rights of appointment. However, his actions were all from the safe distance of Normandy during the time-span of this book, where he was working hard to ingratiate himself with his brother to ensure that he became his heir. As the king's brother, he was in a strong position, but so, too, was their late brother Geoffrey's son, Arthur of Brittany. Arthur's death in 1202 would provoke much speculation, but for the course of this book he was alive and well, and John remains quite firmly in the background, no longer causing mayhem in Guy's two shires.

It is from this era that we have the start of the commercial new year in April, although back in the medieval era it was tied to the feast of the Annunciation (when, according to doctrine, the Virgin Mary was told she was expecting God's son). This day is also known as Lady Day, and is one of the four religious quarter days, the others being Midsummer (June 24th), Michaelmas (Sept 29th) and Christmas Day, when all debts and rents had to be settled by. As I've mentioned before, back then religion ruled ordinary people's lives to an extent that we find hard to believe nowadays, but why the Norman Church (who were the medieval bureaucrats who kept the records for kings and lords) chose Christ's conception as the new year instead of his birth is less obvious.

The Anglo-Saxons seem to have celebrated the turn of the year at the solstice, which is why I have had Guy and the ordinary people still thinking of it as such in the previous books, because this change can only have come about late in the previous century, and William the Conqueror is said to also have observed astronomical turning point because he used it as his coronation day. So whenever the shift came, it was not that long ago to people like Guy, possibly only four or five generations past in an era when people primarily passed information down by word of mouth – and what your grandfather told you would surely carry more weight than what must have seemed like some lord's passing fancy. It wasn't until the Gregorian Reforms of the calendars in 1582 that 1st January was reinstated as the official new year, having been rejected by the church back in 567 by the Council of Tours, because the remnants of the Roman celebrations of the god Janus (he who has two faces to look both backwards and forwards) on that day were considered to be too pagan!

Where this change of year really had significance was in accounting for money. While Michaelmas remained the point in the year when annual rents were due to be paid, although the sheriffs ideally went to the court at Westminster or Winchester around this time to pay whatever monies were due then, the real accounting took place on March 25th (the Feast of the Assumption). The Pipe Rolls give a clear picture of this happening, but also that when a sheriff changed, as happens at the start of this book, if he had served less than half the year before one of the two major courts, he was not expected to account for his shires for the full term at that court. Hence the fact that the Pipe Roll for the year 1194-1195 states that Ralph Murdac had to account for the first half of the year up to Michaelmas, and then Briwere for the rest of the year.

But given that 1194 had been a year of such turmoil in the two shires, and that Murdac was effectively in disgrace and would have been unlikely to be at court, I felt it would have been unlikely that the newly appointed Briwere would have gone either. Briwere had got his hands on the lucrative town of Chesterfield, and he is called up on in that Roll to account for his *ferm* of that *manor* (not just a house or farm in this case, but a much larger allocation of land) but little is said about the shires, which I interpret as him being given time to get the shire under control after the 'rebellion' of the previous spring.

And just for those who like these interesting bits of information: Britain remained the odd man out in Europe when it came to the rest of the Julian calendar reforms, and so when the Gregorian Reforms to the calendars were made in 1752 it was discovered that Britain was by now 11 days adrift from the rest of Europe! In a spectacularly mercenary act, the Church of England (by now the official religion) knocked the 11 days off September to bring the celebrations of Christmas back into line with Europe; but so that the Church did not lose revenue for that year, shifted the accounting date 11 days *forward* from 25th March to 5th April, which is where the modern UK tax year remains. Who says medieval history has no relevance to us now, eh?

St George didn't become the patron saint of England until 1348, well after Guy's time, but the 23rd of April wasn't officially made his feast day in England until 1222, either. This makes the choice of the twenty-third for the official reopening of the forest more than a little unusual in medieval terms, because it wasn't the feast of any particularly noteworthy saint in an era when most official days related to something within the Church. It was the feast of St Felix, but he would hardly have been as well known as many other saints. I have found no explanation for this, but have assumed that St George would have been known of from Continental sources. The previous patron saint of England was the Anglo-Saxon martyred king, Edmund, but his feast day is in November.

Although we know who the justices were who went on the eyres during Richard I's reign, exactly who went on which circuit is not so easily determined. Despite much digging, I have therefore had to make a decision about who I put on the eyres that went to the East Midlands, and putting William Briwere on this circuit helps explain some of the conflicting information about when he took up office as sheriff. The Earl of Derby is listed as the sheriff between Ralph Murdac and Briwere, but some historians say he was only sheriff for a few weeks. That would seem to match the Pipe Rolls, given that the earl is not called to account for the shires.

My problem then came with why, if the earl had already been replaced by the early summer of 1194, did Briwere not get called upon to account for the two shires for the full year? And the only practical solution I could come up with was that it allowed him to go on the eyre to his new shires which technically, as their sheriff, he ought not to have done, given that sheriffs were not supposed to sit in judgement in their own territories. My choice of the other two, I'm afraid, came down to them being good candidates for furthering the story. If further information comes to light which puts them elsewhere at the time this will simply have to be written off as artistic licence, but to the best of my knowledge and with reference to the standard works on the legal practices of the day, which judge went on which eyre remains unknown.

What is connected to that first eyre of King Richard's reign in 1194 is the creation of the role of coroner, and the duties were precisely as I've stated in the book. Where it differs markedly from modern practices is that these were men without any specialist knowledge – they had to do the best they could with what they knew! Heaven only knows what three knights (who at best could only have seen the odd battle wound), and a monastic clerk, made of messy deaths with their lack of medical knowledge! There must have been some shocking miscarriages of justice. So with this historic legal landmark cropping up, it was too good an opportunity to miss not to make Guy one of these new coroners, thereby giving him a reason to get involved in things beyond his forester remit.

Who the coroners were in reality is not possible to say any more than whom the judges were who then heard these cases. However, what is correct is that this was not a paid job, and in fact was viewed as an onerous imposition alongside other unpaid bureaucratic jobs like some of the royal forest roles. That, in a shire like Nottingham, such an election could be viewed as a punishment is not too big a leap, and therefore I have made Guy's fellow knights men like himself, who would end up paying heavily for getting caught up in the siege of Nottingham, even if they had had no political leanings one way or the other. Certainly the fines such men paid seem to have been heavy, King Richard never being one to miss a chance to wring more money out of England to finance his fights in Normandy and further afield.

The castle at Bolsover which stands today is wholly seventeenth century or later, and bears no resemblance to the castle which would have stood in Robin and Guy's time. Even when John Leland was making his survey for Henry VIII, the old castle was completely in ruins, and so we don't even have his description to go on. The most that can be said is that it was a wooden castle – so very different to its grand neighbour at Nottingham. When seen in plan, the Fountain garden at Bolsover has every appearance of being the shape of an old bailey, and given that the still-standing Little Castle occupies the same sort of site as Nottingham Castle (i.e. with an escarpment on one side), I have assumed that the original castle would have stood here.

The earthworks at Laxton remain, and the village is the last left in England which still uses the medieval field system, so it's well worth a visit. As you'll see, it truly was a huge castle, but of a very different construction to Nottingham's.

The real abbot of Welbeck at this time was Abbot Richard. However, with so many Richard's already in the plot by this stage, I have, for the sake of everyone's sanity in trying to keep track of characters, changed his name to Abbot Michael – a far more unusual medieval name despite its link to the archangel. I chose Welbeck to use as the rebellious monastery because it was under the Premonstratensian Order, dedicated to St James the Great, and founded by the Cuckney family – which gives Robin and Guy a reason to be involved in the first place, given their previous encounters with the Cuckneys.

The Premonstratensians were founded in 1120 by Saint Norbert at Prémontré near Leon, which is why they are sometimes known as the Norbertines. In England they were more commonly known as the White Canons because of their clothing, which distinguished them from the Black Canons (the Augustinian Order), the Black Monks (the Benedictine Order), and the White Monks (the Cistercian Order). As a relatively new order, they came to England first in 1143 to a house at Newburgh, Lincoln, and it was this local element which drew me to use them in the episodes in this book. Dryburgh Abbey on the Scottish Borders, and Whithorn Priory in Dumfries & Galloway were other early houses established by them, so they clearly looked northwards to where there were gaps in the authority of the more established orders, and it is this northern viewpoint which allows Abbot Michael a measure of cynicism towards Winchester and London.

Blyth was indeed one of the four tournament grounds licensed by King Richard, and was most likely on the area known nowadays as Whitewater Common.

Two Scottish clans have references to wildcats as their motto. The MacBeans have "touch not the catt bot a targe," which is the saying I have Guy using; while Clan MacPherson more famously have, "touch not the cat but a glove," which, aside from the obvious interpretation, is sometimes read as the pad of the cat being the glove, and that when angered the cat's claws are not sheathed (or 'gloved'). For two major clans across the north of Scotland to have this motto only a few centuries later on, I have presumed that the saying was probably well known a good deal earlier. I hope clan members will forgive me for stealing their motto for Guy's use!

There is no definitive answer as to when the fitz Stephens left Laxton Castle. It had been Sir Ralph's father-in-law's estate, which he gained by marrying Maud de Caux, her father's only heir. With it had come the keepership of the old Forest of Nottingham, but as I mentioned in the first book in this series, unravelling how and with what legal set-ups this got subsumed into King Henry's new Forest of Sherwood, which encompassed all of Nottinghamshire north of the River Trent, is harder to tell, as is what the keeper's role was in this larger administrative area.

As far as recorded history goes, we know that King John would seize Laxton for his own in 1204. By this time Sir Ralph had been dead for almost two years, having died in 1202, but it is from Maud's later efforts to reclaim her father's holdings and titles for her family that we learn that Sir Ralph had ceased to be the hereditary keeper well before that in 1197. Unfortunately, though, records like the Pipe Rolls give no clue as to exactly when or why this happened. Certainly by 1197 Sir Ralph would have been an elderly man (for the times) of fifty-eight or -nine, and it may be that it was felt that he could no longer fulfil the role. Yet that doesn't explain why the sons who would finally regain their home decades later were not allowed to inherit their father's position back then.

So I'm afraid I have had to make some decisions over this, but which are founded in what we know of the times. Given that King Richard was by this time wringing out every penny he could from anyone who hoped to inherit their family lands (including people as senior as William Ferrers, heir to the earldom of Derbyshire), it would not be out of character for some demand for payment to have been made of the fitz Stephens if they wanted to stay on at Laxton, and for a son to take on Sir Ralph's role. And given that everyone had been taxed to breaking point by then, it is also reasonable to think that the fitz Stephens simply didn't have enough money to appease King Richard's two main administrators in England – Archbishop Hubert Walter, and the chief forester of all England, Geoffrey fitz Peter.

Clearly fitz Peter had his eye on the north of England, because he worked his way into the sheriffdom of Yorkshire only a year at most after the fitz Stephens lost out – if, as I've presumed, both decisions were made at the respective Michaelmas courts. Certainly by the time of the Pipe Roll which runs from Michaelmas 1197 to 1198, Geoffrey fitz Peter is suddenly much more prominent in the Nottinghamshire records, so if he wasn't actually in the shire, there's good reason to think that William Briwere was by now feeling the pressure of having the royal forester breathing down his neck from just over the shire border! As for the fitz Stephens, like most ennobled families of the time, they would have had more than one manor, and so it was reasonable to think that they would have been told to evacuate Laxton Castle since it went with the keepership, and would have moved to another of their manors, albeit considerably less grand.

Later on we hear of someone actually being appointed to Laxton as keeper, but that would come during King John's reign. So at this tail end of King Richard's reign, I believe it is reasonable to think that since the sheriff was overseeing the keeping of all the rest of Sherwood's forest laws, and that fitz Peter decided to hand him the keeping of the old forest too – not out of any altruism, but because it would allow more of the fines to be handed directly to the king's funds without the fitz Stephen family having whatever their dues had been from this lucrative pot. And as for the sheriffdom of Yorkshire, while the king's illegitimate half-brother, Geoffrey Plantagenet was indeed sheriff from 1194 (the time of the siege), by 1198 it must have become apparent that having a sheriff who was absent most of the time was not a good thing.

Quite what the exact circumstances were are again lost to us, but Geoffrey fitz Peter is the recorded sheriff of the shire when the accounts are required at the end of 1198. He would serve in this capacity until 1201, and then again briefly from 1203-4. He became Earl of Essex at the time of King John's coronation having married Beatrice de Say, the daughter and heiress of the previous earl. From July 1198 until King Richard's death in the following April, fitz Peter would act as the second chief justiciar of England, and so for these eight months fitz Peter was one of the two most powerful men in England.

Hubert Walter resigned that July after many rows with the king over the money which could be extracted from England. Already Hubert Walter had protested over the king's demand for another 300 knights to come from England to fight with him in Normandy, but the last straw seems to have been the king's displeasure at the limited money which came from yet another carucage in early 1198. Quite what Richard thought could be extracted from an England already bled white is a mystery, and it's to Archbishop Walter's credit that he said so – he was nothing if not a practical man. And there was clearly no bad feeling between him and fitz Peter, because they would work closely with one another again in the early years of King John's reign.

In more modern times we have come to think of King Richard as 'good' and his brother John as 'bad', but while Richard was still alive he could hardly have been thought so by his ordinary subjects, especially in comparison to the good governance of their father. It says a lot about King John that in retrospect Richard should gain such a reputation as a good king. However, Richard was at least absent, and he never alienated the Church in the way his brother would come to do – the spectacular fallout from which would hit every family in England. By the time the whole of England had been excommunicated by the pope for several years, people must have looked back to his crusader brother and prayed that he had gained sufficient 'credit' with heaven to avoid them all being consigned to Hell when they died. However, that is in the future for our heroes.

Few readers will have heard of the saints Guy and Tuck call upon, but they are not my creations. St Cadoc founded the monastery of Llancarfan in South Wales in the fifth or sixth century in a valley revealed to him by pigs – hence his appearance in the various wild boar incidents. St Melangell is associated with the ancient Welsh kingdom of Powys and hares, and her church is the oldest Romanesque shrine in northern Europe. St Issui is a very local saint in the Black Mountains of southern Powys near to Crickhowell. And being Welsh, of course Tuck calls upon St David – *Dewi Sant*. Without the benefits of modern science to explain things, people of this era had faith to an extent we now find alien, and even the most hardened of criminals and soldiers would have believed in *something* approximating to Christianity, despite railing against the hold the Church corporeal had on their material lives – it was a time when atheism was an alien concept.

All locations are real places and can be visited.

In the next book we shall move on to the early years of King John's reign, but for now, thank you for taking the time to read this book. I have tried to make it as historically accurate as possible, with the obvious exceptions of Guy, Robin and the outlaws, for whom the historical record is at best sketchy and mostly nonexistent. However, if there was ever a time when Sherwood needed a Robin Hood, this is it!

About the Author

L. J. Hutton lives in Worcestershire and writes history, mystery and fantasy novels. If you would like to know more about any of these books you are very welcome to come and visit my online home at www.ljhutton.com

Alternatively, you can connect with me at Facebook https://www.facebook.com/L-J-Hutton-Author-305490860248605/

Printed in Great Britain
by Amazon